Born in 1802, the son of a high officer in Napoleon's army, Victor Hugo spent his childhood against a background of military life in Elba, Corsica, Naples, and Madrid. After the Napoleonic defeat, the Hugo family settled in straitened circumstances in Paris, where at the age of fifteen, Victor Hugo commenced his literary career with a poem submitted to a contest sponsored by the Académie Française. Twenty-four years later, Hugo was elected to the Académie, having helped revolutionize French literature with his poems, plays, and novels. Entering politics, he won a seat in the National Assembly in 1848; but in 1851, he was forced to flee the country because of his opposition to Louis Napoleon. In exile on the Isle of Guernsey, he became a symbol of French resistance to tyranny; upon his return to Paris after the Revolution of 1870, he was greeted as a national hero. He continued to serve in public life and to write with unabated vigor until his death in 1885. He was buried in the Pantheon with every honor the French nation could bestow.

The Hunchback
of
Notre-Dame

Victor Hugo

Translated by Walter J. Cobb
With an Afterword by Graham Robb

SIGNET CLASSICS
the Chamberlain Bros. edition
a member of Penguin Group (USA) Inc.

CHAMBERLAIN BROS.
Published by the Penguin Group
Penguin Group (USA) Inc., 375 Hudson Street, New York, New York 10014, USA
Penguin Group (Canada), 90 Eglinton Avenue East, Suite 700, Toronto, Ontario
M4P 2Y3, Canada (a division of Pearson Penguin Canada Inc.)
Penguin Books Ltd, 80 Strand, London WC2R 0RL, England
Penguin Ireland, 25 St Stephen's Green, Dublin 2, Ireland (a division of Penguin
Books Ltd)
Penguin Group (Australia), 250 Camberwell Road, Camberwell, Victoria 3124,
Australia (a division of Pearson Australia Group Pty Ltd)
Penguin Books India Pvt Ltd, 11 Community Centre, Panchsheel Park, New
Delhi–110 017, India
Penguin Books (NZ), Cnr Airborne and Rosedale Roads, Albany, Auckland
1310, New Zealand (a division of Pearson New Zealand Ltd)
Penguin Books (South Africa) (Pty) Ltd, 24 Sturdee Avenue, Rosebank,
Johannesburg 2196, South Africa

Penguin Books Ltd, Registered Offices: 80 Strand, London WC2R 0RL, England

Published by Signet Classics, an imprint of New American Library, and Chamberlain Bros., members of Penguin Group (USA) Inc.

First Signet Classics Printing (Cobb translation), October 1964
First Signet Classics Printing (Robb Afterword), April 2001
First Chamberlain Bros. edition, 2005

An application has been submitted to register this book with the Library of
Congress.

ISBN 1-59609-171-1

Printed in the United States of America
10 9 8 7 6 5 4 3 2 1

While the author has made every effort to provide accurate telephone numbers
and Internet addresses at the time of publication, neither the publisher nor the
author assumes any responsibility for errors, or for changes that occur after publication. Further, the publisher does not have any control over and does not assume
any responsibility for author or third-party websites or their content.

Contents

BOOK IX

BOOK X

BOOK XI

Preface

A few years ago, while visiting or, rather, rummaging about Notre-Dame, the author of this book found, in an obscure nook of one of the towers, the following word, engraved by hand upon the wall:—

'ΑΝΆΓΚΗ (fate)

These Greek capitals, black with age, and quite deeply graven in the stone, with I know not what signs peculiar to Gothic calligraphy imprinted upon their forms and upon their attitudes, as though with the purpose of revealing that it had been a hand of the Middle Ages which had inscribed them there, and especially the fatal and melancholy meaning contained in them, struck the author deeply.

He questioned himself; he sought to divine who could have been that soul in torment which had not been willing to quit this world without leaving this stigma of crime or unhappiness upon the brow of the ancient church.

Afterward, the wall was whitewashed or scraped down, I know not which, and the inscription disappeared. For it is thus that people have been in the habit of proceeding with the marvelous churches of the Middle Ages for the last two hundred years. Mutilations come to them from every quarter, from within as well as from without. The priest whitewashes them, the archdeacon scrapes them down; then the populace arrives and demolishes them.

Thus, with the exception of the fragile memory which the author of this book here consecrates to it, there remains today nothing whatever of the mysterious word engraved within the gloomy tower of Notre-Dame—nothing of the destiny which it so sadly summed up. The man who wrote that word upon the wall disappeared from the midst of the generations of man many centuries ago; the word, in its turn, has been effaced from the wall of the church; the church will, perhaps, itself soon disappear from the face of the earth.

It is upon this word that this book is founded.

March, 1831
(translated by Isabel F. Hapgood)

BOOK I

1

The Great Hall

It is three hundred forty-eight years, six months, and nineteen days ago today that the citizens of Paris were awakened by the pealing of all the bells in the triple precincts of the City, the University, and the Town.

Yet the sixth of January, 1482, is not a day preserved in history. There was nothing remarkable about the event which, so early in the morning, thus set in motion the bells and the good people of Paris. It was neither a Picardian nor a Burgundian assault, nor a reliquary carried in procession, nor a students' revolt, nor an entry of "our most honored lord, Monsieur the King," nor even a good hanging of thieves, male or female, in front of the Palace of Justice. Neither was it the sudden arrival, so frequent in the fifteenth century, of some bedizened and befeathered ambassador. Scarcely two days had elapsed since the last cavalcade of this sort, that of the Flemish envoys commissioned to conclude the marriage treaty between the dauphin and Margaret of Flanders, had entered Paris, to the great annoyance of the Cardinal of Bourbon, who, in order to please the king, had been obliged to give a gracious reception to those rude Flemish burgomasters, and to entertain them, at his Hotel de

9

Bourbon, with "a very fine morality play, comedy and farce," while a driving rain drenched the magnificent tapestry at his door.

But on the sixth of January, what had bestirred the whole population of Paris, as Jean de Troyes phrases it, was the joint observance, as from time immemorial, of the Day of the Kings and the Feast of Fools.

On that day there would be bonfires in the Place de Grève, a maypole would be planted at the chapel of Braque, and a mystery play would be performed at the Palace of Justice. These events had been proclaimed the day before by trumpets blown at all street corners by the provost's men, dressed in fine actons of purple camlet, with large white crosses on the breast.

Crowds of people accordingly wended their way in the morning from all parts of the town, leaving their houses and shops closed, toward one of the three above-mentioned places. Each had made his choice. It must be noted, however, in appreciation of the usual good sense of the lower class of Paris that most of these people directed their steps toward the bonfire, which was perfectly seasonable, or toward the mystery play, which was to be performed in the Great Hall of the Palace, well-covered and sheltered, and that all wisely agreed to let the poor ill-dressed maypole shiver all alone, under the January sky, in the cemetery of the chapel of Braque.

People swarmed especially in the avenues of the Palace of Justice, because it was known that the Flemish ambassadors, who had arrived two days before, planned to attend the mystery play and to assist at the election of the Pope of Fools, which was likewise to take place in the Great Hall.

On this day it was no easy matter for one to get into this Great Hall, although it was then reputed to be the largest single enclosure in the world. (It is true that Sauval had not measured the great hall of the castle of Montargis.) The square in front of the Palace, thronged with people, presented to the gazers from the windows the appearance of a sea, into which five or six streets, like the mouths of so many rivers, were emptying at every moment new waves of human heads. The waves, ever swelling, broke against the corners of the houses, which projected here and there, like so many promontories, into the irregularly shaped basin of the square. In the center of the high Gothic facade of the Palace, the long flight of stone steps was incessantly ascended and descended by a double stream of people, which, after being broken by a landing, spread its broad waves over two lateral declivities, and continuously poured a stream into the square like a cascade into a lake. The shouts, the loud laughter, the scuffing of those thousands of feet, made altogether a great noise and clamor. From time to time this racket redoubled; the stream which carried all this crowd toward the stone steps was turned back, became disturbed, and was thrown into an eddy. This was caused by some lancer's thrust, or by the horse of one of the provost's sergeants, prancing about to establish order. This admirable maneuver the provosts bequeathed to the constables, the constables to the marshals, and the marshals to our gendarmes of Paris.

Doors, windows, and roofs swarmed with thousands of happy bourgeois looking calmly yet soberly at the Palace or at the crowd, and desiring to do nothing more; for most of the good people of Paris are quite content with the spectacle of spectators—indeed, even a wall behind which something is happening is to us an object of interest.

If it could be given to us mortals of 1830 to mingle in imagination with those Parisians of the fifteenth century and, jostled, elbowed, and squeezed by them, to enter that immense hall of the Palace, which was really too small on that sixth of January, 1482, the spectacle would not be without interest or charm, for we should find around us things so ancient that they would appear completely new.

With the reader's kind permission, we shall endeavor to create in his mind's eye the impression he would have had when crossing with us the threshold of that Great Hall, among that motley throng in surcoat, acton, and *cottehardie*.

First of all, our ears are ringing with the din! Our eyes are dazzled by what we see. Above us is a double ribbed vault, paneled with carved wood, painted azure, and sprinkled with golden fleurs-de-lis; under our feet is a marble pavement of black and white squares; a few paces from us rises an enormous pillar—then another—then another—in all, seven down the length of the hall, supporting, in a central line, the springing of the double vault. Around the first four pillars are shops or stalls, all glittering with glass and jewelry; around the last three are oaken benches, worn and polished by the pleaders' breeches and the attorneys' robes. Around the hall, along its lofty walls, between the doors, between the windows, between the pillars we see innumerable statues of all the kings of France since Pharamond: the do-nothing kings, with downcast eyes and arms hanging limply; the valiant and warlike kings, with heads and hands raised boldly toward heaven. We see glowing in the long pointed windows stained glass of a thousand colors. At the high entrances to the hall are rich doors, finely carved; and the whole interior—vaults, pillars, walls, cornices, paneling, doors, and statues—is splendidly painted with blue and gold, which, already a little tarnished at the period in which we see it, had almost entirely disappeared under dust and cobwebs, in the year of grace 1549, when Du Breul still admired it through written accounts.

Now just imagine that immense, oblong hall, poorly lit by the dim light of a January day, stormed by a motley and noisy throng of people pouring in along the walls and circling the seven pillars, and you will have immediately the whole picture, of which we will endeavor to point out more precisely the curious details.

It is certain that if Ravaillac had not assassinated Henry IV, there would have been no documents about the trial of Ravaillac recorded in the registry of the Palace of Justice, no accomplices interested in causing the disappearance of said documents, consequently no incendiaries obliged, for want of any better expedient, to burn the registry in order to burn the documents, and to burn the Palace of Justice in order to burn the registry—in short, no fire of 1618. The old palace would still be standing with its Great Hall, and I could say to the reader, "Go see it," and thus we would both be spared trouble—myself the trouble of writing, and him that of perusing, such a description. All of which proves this very novel truth—that great events have incalculable consequences.

It is quite possible that Ravaillac's accomplices had nothing at all to do with the fire of 1618. We have two other very plausible explanations. The first is the great fiery star, a foot wide and a foot and a half high, which fell, as everyone

knows, from the sky right upon the Palace, just after midnight, on the seventh of March. Second is this quatrain of
Theophile's:

> Indeed, it was a sorry sport
> When in Paris Dame Justice,
> For having eaten too much spice,
> Set fire to the palace.

Whatever you may think of these three explanations—
political, physical, and poetical—concerning the conflagra-
tion of the Palace of Justice in 1618, it is unfortunately a
certain fact that there was a fire. Because of that catastrophe,
and moreover because of the many successive restorations,
there now remains very little of the original residence of the
kings of France, of that palace which was the elder sister of
the Louvre, and so ancient, even in the time of Philippe le
Bel, that it was difficult to discover any traces of the magnificent building erected there by King Robert and described
by Helgaldus. Nearly all has disappeared. What has become
of the chancery chamber where St. Louis "consummated his
marriage"? What of the garden where he administered justice "clad in a tunic of camlet, a sleeveless surcoat of linsey-
woolsey, and over that a mantle of black sendal, lying upon
carpets reading his Joinville"? Where is the chamber of the
Emperor Sigismund? that of Charles IV? that of Jean sans
Terre? Where is the staircase from which Charles IV read
his "Edict of Pardon"? Where is the flagstone on which
Marcel, in the presence of the dauphin, cut the throats of
Robert de Clermont and the Maréchal de Champagne?
Where is the wicket at which the papal bulls of the antipope
Benedict were torn, and through which those who had
brought them there were led, coped and mitered in derision,
thus doing public penance through all of Paris? And where
is the Great Hall itself, with its gilding, its azure, its pointed
arches, its statuary, its pillars, its immense vaults all decorated with carving? Where is the gilded chamber? and the
stone lion which stood at its doorway, with its head bowed
and its tail between its legs, like the lions about King Solomon's throne, in a posture of humiliation appropriate to
Strength in the presence of Justice? Where are the beautiful

doors, and the stained-glass windows, and the wrought-iron work, the perfection of which discouraged Biscornette, and the delicate cabinetwork of Du Hancy?... What has time, what has man done with all those wonders? What has been given to us in exchange for all that Gaulish history, for all that Gothic art? In art we now have the heavy, lowering arches of Monsieur de Brosse, the awkward architect for the porch of Saint-Gervais, and for history, we have the prattling reminiscences of the great pillar, still resounding with the gossip of the Patruses.

That isn't much to boast about.—But let us go back to the real Great Hall of the real Palace of Justice.

At one end of this huge parallelogram was the famous marble table, so long, so wide, so thick, that, say the old territorial records in a style which might have whet even Gargantua's appetite, "never was there seen such a slab of marble in the world." At the other end was the chapel in which Louis XI posed for a statue, in which he was kneeling in front of the Virgin. Also, to this place, he had transferred—indifferent to the fact that thereby two niches were left empty in the line of royal statues—those of Charlemagne and St. Louis, two saints whom, having been kings of France, he supposed to be very influential in heaven. This chapel, only six years old, had been built in that charming style of delicate architecture, with its marvelous stonework, its bold yet exquisite tracery, which in France marked the end of the Gothic period, and which prevailed until about the middle of the sixteenth century in the fairy fantasies of the Renaissance. The little rose-shaped window above the door was in particular a masterpiece of grace and lightness; its frame and sash had almost the airiness of lace.

In the middle of the hall, opposite the big door, there had been erected for the convenience of the Flemish envoys and the other great personages invited to the performance of the mystery play a gallery, canopied with gold brocade. This raised surface was fixed against the wall; a private entrance to it had been contrived by means of a window from the gilded chamber.

It was upon the marble table, according to custom, that the mystery was to take place. Preparations for this had been readying since early morning. On the rich marble floor, marred by the heels of law clerks, stood a high wooden structure, the upper floor of which, visible from every part of the hall, was to serve as a stage, while its interior, hung round with draperies, was to serve as the actors' dressing room. A ladder, placed outside in full view of the audience, formed the connecting link between stage and dressing room, serving also for entrances and exits. There was no character however unexpected, no change of scene, no stage effect which was not obliged to mount this ladder. O innocent and venerable infancy of art and machinery!

Four sergeants of the bailiff of the Palace—the appointed guardians of all popular amusements, whether festivals or executions—stood on duty at the four corners of the marble table.

It was not till the stroke of twelve noon, sounded by the great clock of the Palace, that the play was to begin. This was undoubtedly very late for a theatrical performance, but it was necessary to suit the convenience of the ambassadors.

Now, all the multitude had been waiting since morning. A goodly number of these honest, curious people had stood shivering since daybreak before the great steps of the Palace; some even affirmed that they had spent the night in front of the great door to make sure of getting in first. The crowd was increasing every moment, and like water rising above its usual level, began to creep up the walls, to swell around the pillars, to overflow the entablatures, the cornices, the windowsills, every architectural or sculptural projection. Also, the discomfort, the general impatience, the boredom, the freedom allowed by a licentious holiday, the quarrels incessantly occasioned by a sharp elbow or a hobnailed boot, the fatigue of long waiting—all produced, long before the hour when the ambassadors were to arrive, a bitter sharp tone to the clamor of this imprisoned, squeezed, jostled, jammed crowd. Nothing could be heard but complaints and imprecations against the Flemings, the provost of the merchants, the Cardinal of Bourbon, the bailiff of the Palace, Lady Margaret of Austria, the beadles, the cold, the heat, the bad weather, the Bishop of Paris, the Fools' Pope, the pillars, the statues, this closed door, that open window—all to the great amusement of bands of students and lackeys scat-

tered through the crowd, who added to the discontent by
their mischievous tricks and jests, pricking with pins, so to
speak, the general ill-humor of the crowd.

There was, among these merry devils, a group who, after
knocking out the glass of a window, had boldly seated themselves in the frame, and thence cast their glances and their
railleries by turns at the crowd inside the hall and at those
outside in the square. By their buffoonery, boisterous laughter, and the jeers which they exchanged with their comrades
from one end of the hall to the other, it was easy to see that
these young clerks suffered none of the boredom or the fatigue of the rest of the assemblage, and that they very well
knew how, for their own particular enjoyment, to extract
from the scene actually before them sufficient entertainment
to enable them to wait patiently for the next.

"Why, upon my soul, it's you, *Joannes Frollo de
Molendino*!" shouted one of them to a little blond rascal
with a handsome mischievous face, who had perched himself on the foliage of one of the pillar's capitals. "You are
rightly named Jehan of the Mill, for your two arms and legs
look like the sails of a windmill! How long have you been
here?"

"By the devil's mercy," answered Joannes Frollo, "for
more than four hours, and I sincerely hope that they'll be
credited to my time in purgatory. I heard the King of Sicily's
eight chanters intone the first verse of high Mass at seven in
the Sainte-Chapelle."

"Fine chanters!" returned the other, "with voices sharper
than the points of their caps! The king, before he founded a
Mass to Monsieur Saint Jean, should have inquired if Saint
Jean was fond of Latin chanted with a Provençal accent."

"It was all for the sake of employing those cursed chanters of the King of Sicily that he did it!" bitterly screamed an
old woman in the crowd beneath the window. "I ask you—a
thousand livres parisis for a Mass, and that is what is
charged for the license to sell salt-water fish in the fish market of Paris!"

"Be quiet, old woman!" replied a portly gentleman who
was holding his nose as he stood beside the fishwife. "A
Mass had to be founded. Would you have the king sick
again?"

"Bravely spoken, Sir Gilles Lecornu, master-furrier of the king's wardrobe!" cried the little scholar clinging to the capital.

A burst of laughter from the whole band of scholars greeted the unlucky name of the poor furrier to the king's robes.

"Lecornu! Gilles Lecornu!" shouted some.

"Cornutus et hirsutus!"[1] answered another.

"Oh, to be sure," continued the little imp at the top of the pillar. "But what do they have to laugh about? Is not the worthy Gilles Lecornu brother to Master Jehan Lecornu, provost of the royal household, son of Master Mahiet Lecornu, first gate-keeper of the Forest of Vincennes, all citizens of Paris, all married, from father to son?"

Their mirth redoubled. The fat furrier, without uttering a word, tried to escape the stares fixed upon him from all sides, but perspiring, he puffed and struggled in vain. Like a wedge driven into wood, his efforts only served to fix his broad apoplectic face, purple with rage and vexation, more firmly between the shoulders of his neighbors.

One of these neighbors, fat, short, and dignified, who resembled Lecornu, came to his aid.

"Fie on you! How dare you students talk thus to a townsman! In my time you would have been beaten with rods and then burned."

At this the whole group shouted, "Hear, hear! What's he saying? Who's that old bird of ill omen?"

"Hey, I know him," said one. "That's Master Andry Musnier."

"One of the four booksellers appointed by the University," said another.

"Everything's by fours in that shop," cried a third, "four nations, four faculties, four holidays, four proctors, four electors, and four booksellers!"

"Well," returned Jehan Frollo, "we'll quadruple the devil for them."

"Musnier, we'll burn your books."

"Musnier, we'll beat your lackey."

"Musnier, we'll tickle your wife, the good fat Madam

[1] "Horned and hairy."

Oudarde, who is as fresh and buxom as if she were a widow."

"The devil take you!" growled Master Andry Musnier.

"Master Andry," said Jehan, still hanging to the capital, "hold your tongue, or I'll drop on your head!"

Master Andry looked up, and appeared to calculate for a moment the height of the pillar and the weight of this rogue, multiplied in his mind the weight by the square of the velocity, and held his peace.

Jehan, thus master of the field, continued triumphantly. "And I would do it too, even though I am the brother of an archdeacon!"

"Fine lads, those from the University, not even on a day like this do they see that rights are respected! There's a maypole and a bonfire in the town, a Fools' Pope and Flemish ambassadors in the City, but at the University, nothing."

"And yet the Place Maubert is large enough!" observed one of the young clerks ensconced in a corner of the windowsill.

"Down with the rector, the electors, and the procurators!" yelled Jehan.

"We'll make a bonfire tonight in the Champ Gaillard with Master Andry's books," added another.

"And the desks of the scribes!" cried his neighbor.

"And the rods of the beadles!"

"And the spitting boxes of the deans!"

"And the buffets of the procurators!"

"And the tubs of the electors!"

"And the rector's stools!"

"Down!" yelled little Jehan with a roaring voice, "down with Master Andry, the beadles, the scribes; down with the theologians, the doctors, and the priests; down with the procurators, the electors, and the rector!"

"It's the end of the world!" muttered Master Andry, his hands to his ears.

"Well, here's the rector himself! Here he comes through the square," cried one of those sitting in the window. And they all turned toward the square.

"Is it really our venerable rector, Master Thibault?" asked Jehan Frollo du Moulin, who, from his pillar inside, could not see what was going on outside.

"Yes, yes," they all chorused; "it's him, indeed it is! Master Thibault, the rector."

It was, in fact, the rector, accompanied by all the dignitaries of the University going in procession to welcome the ambassadors, who were just now crossing the square in front of the Palace. The students, crowded in the window, greeted them as they passed with jeers and sarcasm. The rector, who headed the procession, received the first broadside, and it was indeed a rude one.

"Good day, Monsieur the Rector! Hollo! Good day to you!"

"How comes it the old gambler is here? Has he really left his dice?"

"Look at him jogging along on his mule. Its ears are not so long as his!"

"Hollo, good day, Monsieur the Rector Thibault! *Tybalde aleator!*[2] You old nitwit! You old gambler!"

"God save you! Did you throw double sixes last night?"

"Oh, what a scarecrow face—gray and drawn and lined by his love of dice and gaming."

"Where are you going now, Thibault, *Tybalde ad dados*[3]—turning your back on the University, and trotting toward town?"

"No doubt, he's going to seek lodging in the rue Thibautodé," cried Jehan du Moulin.

The whole band repeated the pun with booming voices and furious clapping of hands.

"You're going to seek lodgings in the rue Thibautodé, aren't you, Monsieur the Rector, the devil's own partner?"

Then, as the other dignitaries appeared, they became the students' targets.

"Down with the beadles! down with the mace-bearers!"

"Say, Robin Poussepain, who's that over there?"

"It's Gilbert de Suilly, *Gilbertus de Soliaco*, Chancellor of the College of Autun."

"Here, take my shoe, you're in a better position than me—throw it at his face!"

[2] "O Thibault, you dice player!"
[3] "O Thibault, to the dice."

"Saturnalitias mittimus ecce nuces!"[4]

"Down with the six theologians in their white surplices!"

"Are they the theologians? I thought they were the six white geese that Sainte-Geneviève gave to the city for the fief of Roogny."

"Down with the doctors!"

"Down with all important and nonsensical disputations!"

"Here goes my hat at you, Chancellor of Sainte-Geneviève! You did me wrong! That's true! You gave my place in Normandy to that little Ascanio Falzaspada, who was from Bourges, because he's Italian."

"That was wrong!" chanted all the students. "Down with the Chancellor of Sainte-Geneviève!"

"Hey, there, Master Joachin de Ladehors! Hey, there! Louis Dahuille!"

"Hey, Lambert Hoctement!"

"May the devil strangle the German proctor!"

"And the chaplains of the Sainte-Chapelle too, with their gray amices; *cum tunicis grisis!*"

"Seu de pellibus grisis fourratis!"[5]

"There go the Masters of Art! See all their beautiful black copes!"

"They all make a fine tail for the Rector."

"One would say he looks like the Doge of Venice going to marry the sea."

"Look, Jehan! the canons of Sainte-Geneviève!"

"The devil take them all!"

"Abbé Claude Choart! Doctor Claude Choart! Are you looking for Marie la Giffarde?"

"She's in the rue Glatigny."

"She's making a bed for the king of the ribalds."

"She pays her four deniers, *quattuor denarios.*"

"Aut unum bombum."[6]

"Would you have her pay you with one in the nose?"

"Comrades! Behold Master Simon Sanguin, the elector from Picardy, with his wife riding behind him."

---

[4] "See, we send you nuts of Saturnalia."
[5] "With their gray tunics!" "Or stuffed with gray skins!"
[6] "Or a bomb."

"Post equitem sedet atra cura."[7]

"Be brave, Master Simon."

"Good day to you, Monsieur the Elector! Good night, Madame the Electrice."

"Now, aren't they in the window lucky to be able to see all that?" said Joannes de Molendino with a sigh, from his perch on the capital.

Meanwhile, Master Andry Musnier, appointed bookseller in the University, leaned over and whispered to the king's furrier, Master Gilles Lecornu, "I tell you, sir, it's the end of the world. Never has there been loose such an unruly mob of students! It's the accursed inventions of the age that are ruining everything—the artillery, the muskets, the cannons, and above all the printing press, that scourge brought from Germany. No more manuscripts, no more books. Printing is ruining bookselling. The end of the world is upon us."

"I see it is, marked especially by velvet's coming so much into fashion!" sighed the furrier.

At that moment it struck twelve.

"Ha!" exclaimed the whole crowd with one voice.

The students held their peace. There was a general detonation of coughing and blowing of noses, and a great shuffling about, a universal movement of feet and heads, each trying to place himself to the best advantage for the spectacle. Then there was silence; every neck was outstretched, every mouth opened, every eye fixed on the marble table. But nothing appeared. The bailiff's four sergeants just stood there, stiff and motionless, like four painted statues. All eyes then turned toward the platform reserved for the Flemish envoys. The door remained shut and the gallery empty. The crowd had been awaiting three things since early morning; namely noon, the Flemish ambassadors, and the mystery play. But only noon had arrived, and on time. This was too bad.

They waited one, two, three, five minutes, a quarter of an hour; nothing else came. The platform remained deserted, the stage, silent. Meanwhile impatience gave way to anger. Indignant words circulated, though as yet only in whispers. "The play! the play!" they murmured. The temper of the crowd began to rise. A storm, which was yet only a rumble,

7 "Behind the rider sits dark care."

was ruffling the surface of that human sea. It was Jehan du Moulin who threw the first bolt.

"The mystery, and to the devil with these Flemings!" he shouted at the top of his voice, writhing around his pillar like a serpent.

The multitude clapped their hands. "The mystery!" they all shouted, "and let all of Flanders go to the devil."

"Let us have the mystery now," resumed the student, "or, for my part, I would have us hang the bailiff of the Palace by way of a morality play."

"Well said," shouted the crowd, "and let's begin with hanging the sergeants."

A great roar of approval followed. Those four poor devils instantly turned pale and looked apprehensively at one another. The multitude surged toward them. They saw the frail wooden barricade between them and the crowd bulge and bend inward under the pressure of the surging crowd.

The moment was critical.

"Hang them! hang them!" shouted everyone from all sides.

At that instant, the drapery of the dressing room, which we have described above, was raised to make way for a personage, the mere sight of whom arrested the crowd, and, as if by magic, changed their anger into curiosity.

"Silence! Silence!"

This personage, but slightly reassured, and trembling from head to foot, came forward to the edge of the marble table, making a series of bows, which, the nearer he approached, resembled more and more genuflections.

Calm, however, was gradually restored. There remained only that faint hum which is always noticeable in an expectant crowd.

"Messieurs the bourgeois," he said, "and mesdemoiselles, we shall have the honor of declaiming and performing before His Eminence, Monsieur the Cardinal, a very fine morality play, entitled *The Good Judgment of Our Lady the Virgin Mary.* I play Jupiter. His Eminence at this very moment is accompanying the most honorable ambassadors from Monsieur the Duke of Austria, who are just now detained to listen to the harangue of Monsieur the Rector of the University at the Porte Baudets. As soon as the most eminent cardinal arrives, we shall begin."

It is certain that nothing less than the intervention of Jupiter would have saved the bailiff's unhappy sergeants. If we had the pleasure of inventing this true story, and were consequently responsible for it to Our Lady of Criticism, the classical rule could not be cited against us, *Nec Deus intersit.*[8] Besides, the costume of Lord Jupiter was most exquisite, and had contributed not a little in calming the crowd by attracting all their attention. Jupiter was clad in a brigandine fastened with gilt nails and covered with black velvet. His headdress was a helmet decorated with silver-plated buttons. But for the rouge and the great beard which covered his whole face, but for the gilt scroll of pasteboard pierced with iron spikes and stuck all over with jagged strips of tinsel, which experienced eyes easily could imagine to be thunderbolts, and but for his feet, bare except for sandals bound with ribbons *à la grecque*—he might have been compared, on account of the severity of his aspect, with a Breton archer of that day in Monsieur de Berry's corps.

2

Pierre Gringoire

However, while Jupiter was delivering his speech, the pleasure and admiration so universally excited by his costume were dispelled by his words; and when he arrived at that unfortunate conclusion: "As soon as the most eminent cardinal arrives, we shall begin," his voice was drowned out by a roar of hoots.

"Begin immediately! The mystery! The play at once!" screamed the people. Above all the other voices, piercing through the general uproar, like the sound of a fife in a charivari at Nimes, was that of Joannes de Molendino.

"Begin at once!" piped the student.

"Down with Jupiter and the Cardinal of Bourbon!" yelled

[8] "Let no god intercede."

Robin Poussepain and the other clerks perched on the window ledge.

"The morality play now!" roared the crowd. "At once! Immediately! The sack and the rope for the players and the cardinal!"

Poor Jupiter, haggard, frightened, and pale beneath his rouge, let fall his thunderbolts, took his helmet in his hand; then, bowing and trembling, he stammered, "His Eminence ... the ambassadors ... Lady Margaret of Flanders ..." He did not know what to say next. In truth he was afraid of being hanged by the populace for waiting this long, or of being hanged by the cardinal for not waiting. In either case he saw only an abyss, that is to say, a gibbet.

Fortunately someone came forward to extricate him from his plight and to assume responsibility.

An individual who stood inside the barricade in the space left clear around the marble table, and whom up till now no one had noticed, so completely was his long and slender figure concealed from every eye by the size of the pillar against which he had leaned—this person, we say, tall, thin, pale, light complexioned, still young, though wrinkles were already visible in his forehead and cheeks, with sparkling eyes and smiling mouth, clad in a garment of black serge, tattered and shiny with age—approached the marble table and made a sign to the wretched victim. But Jupiter, in his perturbation, did not notice.

The newcomer advanced another step farther.

"Jupiter," he said, "my dear Jupiter!"

Still the other did not hear him.

At last the tall fair man, losing all his patience, shouted almost in his face: "Michel Giborne!"

"Who calls me?" said Jupiter, as if awakened from a trance.

"I," replied the personage all in black.

"Ah!" said Jupiter.

"Begin at once," returned the other. "Satisfy the people, and I will appease the bailiff, who will in turn appease the cardinal."

Jupiter now sighed with relief.

"Messeigneurs the bourgeois," he shouted as loudly as he

could to the crowd, who continued to hoot at him, "we are going to begin now."

"*Evoe, Jupiter! Plaudite, cives!*"[1] cried the scholars.

"Noël! Noël!" cried the people.

There was deafening applause; even after Jupiter had withdrawn behind his tapestry, the hall still rang with acclamations.

Meanwhile the unknown, who had so magically changed the tempest into a calm, had modestly retired into the shadow of his pillar, and no doubt would have remained there, unobtrusive, motionless, and silent as before, had he not been drawn out by two young women who, being in the first row of spectators, had heard his colloquy with Michel Giborne Jupiter.

"Master," said one, beckoning him to approach . . .

"Hush, my dear Liénarde," said her neighbor, pretty, rosy-cheeked, and quite unself-conscious on account of her elegant holiday attire. "He is not a clerk, he's a layman. You should not say 'Master' to him, but 'Messire.' "

"Messire!" then said Liénarde.

The unknown approached the barrier.

"And what do you want with me, mesdemoiselles?" he asked with an air of complaisance.

"Oh! nothing!" said Liénarde, all confused. "It's my neighbor here, Gisquette la Gencienne, who would speak with you."

"No, no!" said Gisquette, blushing; "it was Liénarde who said 'Master' to you; I only told her that she ought to say 'Messire'!"

The two girls demurely lowered their eyes.

The gentleman, who was eager to talk with them, smiled and answered, "You have nothing to say to me then, mesdemoiselles?"

"Nothing at all," answered Gisquette.

"Nothing," repeated Liénarde.

The young man made a step to retire, but the two curious damsels had no mind to let him go so easily.

"Messire," said Gisquette, with the impetuosity of a sluice that is suddenly opened or a woman making a resolution,

[1] "*Evoe* (shout of the Bacchantes), Jupiter! Applaud, citizens!"

"then you know this soldier that's going to play the part of Our Lady the Virgin in the mystery?"

"You mean the part of Jupiter?" returned the unknown.

"O my! Yes!" said Liénarde. "Is she stupid! So, you know Jupiter then?"

"Michel Giborne? Yes, madame."

"He has a splendid beard!" answered Liénarde.

"Will what they are going to play be very fine?" asked Gisquette timidly.

"Very fine indeed, mademoiselle," answered their informant without the least hesitation.

"What will it be?" said Liénarde.

The Good Judgment of Our Lady the Virgin, a morality play, if it please you, mademoiselle."

"Ah, that's different!" returned Liénarde.

A short sentence was begun, but it was interrupted by the young man. "It is an entirely new morality play," he said, "which has never been performed before."

"Then it's not the same," said Gisquette, "as the one played two years ago, on the day of the entry of Monsieur the Legate, in which there were three beautiful girls who performed . . ."

"As sirens," finished Liénarde.

"And all naked," added the young man.

Liénarde modestly cast down her eyes. Gisquette looked at her, and did likewise. The gentleman continued, smiling, "It was a very pretty thing to see. But today it is a play expressly written for Madame the Lady of Flanders."

"Will they sing love songs?" asked Gisquette.

"Oh, fie!" said he. "What! in a morality play? You must not confound one kind of play with another. Now, if it were a *sotie,* well and good."

"That's a pity," replied Gisquette. "That day at the Ponceau fountain there were wild men and women who fought with one another and formed themselves into different groups, singing little motets and love songs."

"What is suitable for a legate," said the stranger dryly, "is not suitable for a princess."

"And close by," continued Liénarde, "were playing a number of bass instruments that carried wonderful melodies."

"And to refresh the passersby," resumed Gisquette, "the fountain gushed forth wine, milk, and hippocras from three mouths, and everyone drank what he wanted."

"And a little below the Ponceau fountain," continued Liénarde, "at the Trinity fountain, there was a passion play acted without words."

"Oh yes, how I remember it!" exclaimed Gisquette. "God on the cross, and the two thieves on each side of Him!"

Here the two friends, warming to the recollection of the legate's entry, began speaking both at once.

"And farther on, at the Porte-aux-Peintres, there were other characters, very richly dressed."

"And at the fountain of the Holy Innocents, do you remember that huntsman following a hind, with a great noise of dogs and hunting trumpets?"

"And then at the Boucherie de Paris, those scaffolds representing the fortress of Dieppe!"

"And when the legate passed, remember, Gisquette? They sounded the assault, and the English all had their throats slit."

"And what fine characters there were against the Châtelet Gate!"

"And on the Pont-au-Change, which was all covered with draperies!"

"And when the legate went over it they let fly from the bridge over two hundred dozen birds of all kinds. Wasn't that a fine sight, Liénarde?"

"There will be a finer performance today," at length interrupted the stranger, who seemed to listen to them impatiently.

"You promise us that this mystery shall be a fine one?" asked Gisquette.

"Without a doubt," he answered. And then he added with peculiar emphasis, "Mesdemoiselles, I wrote it."

"Really?" said the young ladies, in amazement.

"Really!" answered the poet, bridling a little. "That is, there were two of us: Jehan Marchand, who sawed the planks and put together the wooden structure of the stage; and myself who wrote the play. My name is Pierre Gringoire." The author of *The Cid* could not have said with greater pride: *Pierre Corneille*.

Our readers may have observed that some time must have elapsed since Jupiter retired behind the drapery and the author of this new morality play revealed himself thus abruptly to the naive admiration of Gisquette and Liénarde. Strange to say, all that multitude, who a few minutes before had been so tumultuous, now waited patiently with implicit faith in the player's word—an evidence of that everlasting truth, still demonstrated daily in our theaters, that the best means of making the audience wait patiently is to assure them that the performance will commence immediately.

However, the student Joannes did not fall asleep. "Hollo!" he suddenly shouted, amid the peaceful expectation which had succeeded the disturbance, "Jupiter! Madame the Virgin, ye rowers of the devil's boat! Are you making sport of us? The play! The play! Begin, or we'll begin again!"

That was enough. Music from high- and low-keyed instruments was heard coming from beneath the structure; the curtain was raised; and four characters in motley attire and with painted faces came out, clambered up the steep ladder onto the upper platform, ranged themselves in a row facing the audience, whom they greeted, each bowing low; then the overture ended. The play was about to begin.

After receiving abundant payment for their bows by the plaudits of the multitude, the four characters, now honored by a profound silence, proceeded to deliver their prologue, which we will graciously spare the reader. However, as still happens in our own time, the audience paid more attention to the costuming of the performers than to the roles they enacted; and in truth they did rightly. All four were dressed in gowns half yellow and half white, different from each other only in the nature of the material—the first being of gold and silver brocade, the second of silk, the third of wool, and the fourth of linen. The first of these characters carried in his right hand a sword, the second two gold keys, the third a scale, and the fourth a spade. And in order to assist the sluggish wits who might not have clearly understood these properties, on the hem of the brocade robe was embroidered in huge black letters, "I AM NOBILITY"; on the silk one, "I AM CLERGY"; on the woolen one, "I AM TRADE"; and on the linen one, "I AM LABOR." The sex of the two male characters was plainly indicated by the comparative shortness of their garments, and by their Phrygian caps; while the two female ones wore longer robes and hoods.

It would indeed have indicated perversity if one could not have seen through the poetic drapery of the prologue that Labor was married to Trade, and Clergy to Nobility, and that these two happy couples possessed in common a magnificent golden dolphin, which they proposed to award to the most beautiful damsel. Accordingly, they were traveling over the whole world in quest of this beauty; and, after successively having rejected the Queen of Golconda, the Princess of Trebizond, the daughter of the Grand Khan of Tartary, etc., etc., Labor and Clergy, Nobility and Trade had come to rest themselves on the marble table of the Palace of Justice, and deliver at the same time to the worthy audience as many moral sentiments and maxims as might in that day be expended upon the members of the faculty of arts at the examinations, sophisms, determinants, figures and acts, when the masters took their degrees.

All this was in truth very fine.

Meanwhile, in all that assemblage upon which the four allegorical characters were pouring out floods of metaphors, there was no ear more attentive, no heart more palpitating, no eye more eager, no neck more outstretched, than the ears, eyes, neck, and heart of the author, the poet, the gallant Pierre Gringoire, who a moment before had been unable to resist the temptation to tell his name to two pretty girls. He had retired again behind his pillar, and there it was that he listened, watched, and enjoyed. The favorable applause which had greeted the opening of his prologue was still resounding in his breast, and he was completely absorbed in that kind of ecstatic contemplation with which a dramatic author follows his ideas as they tumble one by one from the lips of the actor, in the silence of a vast auditorium. O worthy Pierre Gringoire!

It pains us to mention it, but this first ecstasy was very soon disturbed. Scarcely had the lips of Gringoire approached this intoxicating cup of joy and triumph than a drop of bitterness mingled with it.

A tattered beggar, who, lost as he was among the crowd, could receive no contributions, and who, we may suppose, had not found sufficient indemnity in the pockets of his neighbors, had conceived the bright idea of perching himself conspicuously in order that he might attract the attention and the alms of the audience. Accordingly, while the first lines of the prologue were being recited, he had climbed, by means of the pillars that supported the reserved gallery, to the cornice which ran around the bottom of its balustrade; and there he seated himself, soliciting the attention and the pity of the crowd by his rags and a hideous sore that covered his right arm. But he spoke not a word.

The silence which he kept allowed the prologue to proceed without incident; and no perceptible disorder would have occurred, but that, as ill luck would have it, the student Joannes espied, from his own perch upon one of the great pillars, the beggar and his antics. A wild fit of laughter seized the young rascal, and having no regard for his interruption of the performance, and his disturbance of the general attention, he cried out in a tone of gaiety, "Look at that fraud over there begging!"

Anyone who has ever thrown a stone into a pond full of frogs, or fired a gun among a flock of birds, can have some idea of the effect produced by these unseasonable words which interrupted the attention fixed upon the heroes of the mystery. Gringoire jerked as if he had felt an electric shock. The prologue was cut short, and all heads suddenly turned toward the beggar, who, far from being disconcerted, found in this incident a good opportunity to make a harvest, so he began to whine in a piteous voice, with his eyes half closed, "Charity, I beg you!"

"Why, as I live," resumed Joannes, "it's Clopin Trouillefou. Hollo, friend, so your sore wasn't comfortable on your leg, so you have put it on your arm, have you?"

And so saying, he threw, with the dexterity of a monkey, a small white coin into the old greasy felt hat which the beggar held out with his diseased arm. The beggar received both the alms and the sarcasm without flinching, and continued piteously, "Charity, I beg you!"

This episode had considerably distracted the assembly, and a good number of spectators, led by Robin Poussepain and all the clerks, merrily applauded this whimsical duet, spontaneous as it was, performed in the middle of the prologue, by the student with his shrill voice and the beggar with his monotonous drone.

Gringoire was very much displeased. Having recovered from his first astonishment, he yelled to the four characters on the stage, "Go on! What the devil? Go on!" without even glancing at the two interrupters.

At that moment, he felt someone tug the tail of his coat. He turned around, not without some ill-humor, and forced a smile, for it was Gisquette la Gencienne who had thrust a pretty arm through the barricade to get his attention.

"Monsieur," said the young girl, "will they go on?"

"Yes, of course," answered Gringoire, rather offended by her question.

"In that case, messire," she continued, "would you kindly explain to me . . ."

"What they are going to say?" interrupted Gringoire. "Well, listen!"

"No," said Gisquette, "what they have already said."

Gringoire started like a man whose open wound has been touched.

"A plague on the stupid, witless, little wench!" he muttered. And for that moment Gisquette was utterly ruined in his estimation.

Meanwhile the actors had obeyed his injunction. The public, seeing that they were once more trying to speak, settled back to listen, not, however, without having lost much poetic beauty, in trying to solder the two parts into which the play had been so abruptly broken. Gringoire bitterly realized this. However, tranquillity was gradually restored; the student held his tongue, the beggar was busy counting some coins in his hat, and the play resumed.

Really it was a very fine composition, and we truly think that with a few modifications it would well be played even today. The plot, overly drawn and a bit dry, was simple, and Gringoire, in security of his own judgment, admired its clearness. As may well be supposed, the four allegorical personages were a little fatigued by traveling over three parts of the globe without finding anyone suitable to receive their golden dolphin. Hence a long eulogy upon the marvelous fish, with countless delicate allusions to the young prince, betrothed to Margaret of Flanders, but who at this time was in very dismal seclusion at Amboise, not having the slightest idea that Labor and Clergy, Nobility and Trade had just been making a tour of the world on his account. The said dolphin, then, was young, handsome, strong, and above all possessed the greatest of all virtues, being the son of the lion of France. I declare that this bold metaphor is admirable, and that dramatic natural history, in a day of allegory and in a royal epithalamium, finds nothing at all odd in a dolphin's being the son of a lion. On the contrary, it is precisely those rare and Pindaric mixtures that prove the poet's enthusiasm. However, as a just critic, I must declare that the poet could have developed this beautiful idea in less than two hundred lines. It is true that, according to the order of Monsieur the Provost, the play was to last from noon until four o'clock; hence it was necessary to use a lot of words.

Besides, everyone was listening patiently.

All at once, just in the middle of a quarrel between Madame Trade and Madame Nobility, when Master Labor was reciting this wondrous line:

Beast more triumphant never in the woods I've seen,

the door to the reserved gallery, which until then had remained so unseasonably shut, now opened even more unseasonably, and the stentorian voice of the doorkeeper abruptly announced: "His Eminence Monseigneur the Cardinal of Bourbon!"

3

Monsieur the Cardinal

Poor Gringoire! The noise of all the double petards set off on the feast of Saint-Jean, the discharge of twenty harquebuses, the detonation of that famous cannon of the Tower of Billy, which, at the time of the siege of Paris, on Sunday, the twenty-ninth of September, killed seven Burgundians at a shot, the explosion of all the gunpowder stored at the Temple Gate would have split his ears less violently at that solemn and dramatic moment, than those few words from the lips of the usher, "His Eminence Monseigneur the Cardinal of Bourbon!"

Not that Pierre Gringoire either feared the cardinal or despised him. He had neither that weakness nor that arrogance. A true eclectic, as he would nowadays be called, Gringoire had one of those steady and elevated minds, calm and temperate, which can preserve their composure under all circumstances, *stare in dimidio rerum.*[1] It was one of those minds which are full of reason and liberal philosophy, but at the same time, that are respectful to cardinals. An admirable and uninterrupted race of philosophers, to whom Wisdom, like another Ariadne, seems to have given a ball of thread which they have gone on unwinding from the beginning of the world through the whole labyrinth of human affairs. They are to be found in all times, and ever the same—that is to say, ever adapting themselves to the age. And not to mention our Pierre Gringoire, who would be their representative in the fifteenth century, if we could succeed in obtaining for him the distinction which he deserves. It was certainly their spirit which inspired Father du Breul in the sixteenth, when writing these words of sublime simplicity, worthy of any age: "I am a Parisian by my birthplace, and a Parrhisian by my speech, for *parrhisia* in Greek means freedom of speech, which freedom I have used even to messeigneurs the cardinals, uncle and brother to Monseigneur the Prince of Conti, albeit with respect for their greatness, and without offending anyone in their train, and that is saying much."

So there was neither hatred for the cardinal, nor contempt for his presence, in the disagreeable effect which it made upon Pierre Gringoire. On the contrary, our poet had too much good sense and too threadbare a frock not to attach a particular value to the fact that many an allusion in his prologue, and particularly the glorification of the dolphin, son of the lion of France, would fall upon His Eminence's ear. But self-interest is not the ruling motive in the noble nature of poets. Supposing the entity of a poet to be represented by the number ten, it is certain that a chemist, on analyzing and "pharmacopolizing" it, as Rabelais says, would find it to be

[1] "Stay within the mean."

composed of one part self-interest and nine parts vanity. Now, at the moment that the door was opened for the grand entrance of the cardinal, the nine parts vanity of Gringoire, puffed up by the breath of popular admiration, were prodigiously enlarged, thus quite smothering that imperceptible molecule of self-interest which we just now pointed out to be in the constitution of poets; an invaluable ingredient, by the way, a ballast of reality and humanity, without which they could never come down to earth. It was pure enjoyment for Gringoire to see and to feel, to touch, so to speak, an entire assemblage (varlets, it is true, but what matter?) stupefied, petrified, and as if asphyxiated by the immeasurable tirades which burst from every part of his epithalamium. I affirm that he himself shared the general happiness, and that, unlike La Fontaine, who, at the performance of his play, *The Florentine,* asked, "What poor wretch wrote that rhapsody?" Gringoire would have willingly asked his neighbor, "Whose masterpiece is this?" Hence it may be imagined what effect was produced upon him by the sudden and untimely arrival of the cardinal.

All his fears were fully realized. The entrance of the cardinal threw the whole auditory into commotion. All heads turned toward the gallery. One could hear nothing but "The cardinal! The cardinal!" repeated by every tongue. The unfortunate prologue was cut short a second time.

The cardinal paused dramatically on the threshold of the gallery. As he looked over the assembly rather indifferently, the tumult redoubled. Everyone wanted to catch a better glimpse of him, each one stretching his neck over his neighbor's shoulder.

The cardinal was in fact a distinguished personage, the sight of whom was worth more than any other spectacle. Charles, Cardinal of Bourbon, Archbishop and Count of Lyons, Primate of Gaul, was allied both to Louis XI, through his brother, Pierre, Seigneur of Beaujeu, who had married the king's eldest daughter, and at the same time allied to Charles the Bold through his mother, Agnes of Burgundy. Now the dominant trait, the characteristic and distinctive feature of this Primate of Gaul, was his courtierlike spirit and his devotion to those in power. Hence it may be well understood in what numberless perplexities this double relationship had involved him, and among how many temporal shoals his spiritual bark must have tacked about, in order to have escaped foundering either upon Louis or upon Charles, the Charybdis and the Scylla which had swallowed up the Duke of Nemours and the Constable of Saint-Pol. However, Heaven be praised! he had got happily through his voyage, and had reached Rome without mishap. But, although he was now safely in port, and precisely because he was in port, he never remembered without anxiety the diverse fortunes of his political life, which had so long been perilous and laborious. So, also, he used to say that the year 1476 had been for him both black and white; meaning thereby that he had lost in that one year his mother, the Duchess of Bourbonnais, and his cousin, the Duke of Burgundy, and that one mourning had consoled him for the other.

Furthermore, he was a good sort of man; he led a merry life as a cardinal, loved to be gay with wine of the royal vintage of Chaillot, did not hate Richarde la Garmoise and Thomasse la Saillarde, gave alms to pretty girls rather than to old hags, and for all these reasons was in high favor with the people of Paris. Wherever he went, he was always surrounded by a little coterie of bishops and abbots of high lineage, gay, sociable men, fond of good eating. More than once the pious women of Saint-Germain d'Auxerre, as they passed in the evening under the windows of the Hotel de Bourbon, all ablaze with lights, had been scandalized to hear the same voices which had been chanting vespers to them in the daytime, singing, to the sound of clinking glasses, the bacchanalian verses of Benedict XII, the pope who had added a third crown to the tiara, *"Bibamus papaliter."*[2]

It was no doubt this popularity, so justly acquired, which preserved him at his entrance from anything like an ill reception on the part of the crowd, which a few moments before had been so dissatisfied, and so little disposed to accord respect to a cardinal, even on the day when they were going to elect a pope. But Parisians are not malicious. Besides, by making the performance begin by their own authority, the good citizens had had the better of the cardinal, and his triumphant though late arrival satisfied them. Moreover, Mon-

---

[2] "Let us drink like popes."

sieur the Cardinal was a handsome man; he had an elegant scarlet robe, which he wore in excellent style, thus assuring him all the women's favor; and consequently, that of the better half of the hall. Certainly it would be both unjust and in bad taste to hoot at a cardinal for coming late to a play, when he is handsome and wears handsomely his red robe.

He entered, then, saluted the company with that usual smile which the great always reserve for the people, and made his way slowly toward the armchair of scarlet velvet, looking as if some more important matter occupied his mind. His cortege, which today we would call his staff, composed of bishops and abbots, followed him into the gallery, exciting redoubled tumult and curiosity among the spectators. All were busy pointing them out, telling their names, each one striving to show that he knew at least one of them; some pointing to the Bishop of Marseilles, Alaudet, if I remember correctly; some to the Dean of Saint-Denis; others to Robert de Lespinasse, Abbot of Saint-Germain-des-Prés, the libertine brother of a mistress of Louis XI—all their names being repeated with a thousand mistakes and mispronunciations. As for the students, they cursed. It was their day, their feast of fools, their saturnalia, the annual orgy of the Basoche and the University. No turpitude but was a matter of right to be held sacred that day. And then there were the mad hussies down in the crowd—Simone Quatrelivres, Agnes la Gadine, Robine Piédebou. Was it not then the least the students could do to swear as they liked, and to profane God's name a little, on such a day as this, in such good company with churchmen and harlots? Accordingly, they took full advantage of the occasion, and into this general uproar, there poured a frightful din of blasphemies and enormities of every description from these clerks and scholars—tongue-tied all the rest of the year by the fear of Saint Louis's branding-iron. Poor Saint Louis! How they did devil him in his own Palace of Justice! Each one of them had singled out among the newly arrived company some one of the cassocks—black, gray, white, or violet. As for Joannes Frollo de Molendino, as brother to an archdeacon, it was the red robe that he audaciously assailed. Fixing his shameless eyes upon the cardinal, he yelled as loudly as he could bawl, *"Cappa repleta mero!"*[3]

All these details, which we here lay bare for the edification of the reader, were so completely drowned out by the general din of the crowd that they were lost before they reached the reserved gallery. Anyway, the cardinal would have paid little heed to them, so intimately did the license of the day belong to the manners of the age. He had something else to think about—another cause of concern, which followed close behind him, and rose to the platform at the same time as himself. This was the Flemish embassy.

Not that he was a profound politician, or concerned himself too much about the possible consequences of the marriage of madame, his cousin, Margaret of Burgundy, with monsieur, his cousin, Charles, Dauphin of Vienna; nor how long the patched-up reconciliation between the Duke of Austria and the King of France would last; nor how the King of England would receive this slight toward his daughter. These matters troubled him very little; and each night he drank the wine of the royal vineyard of Chaillot, without ever suspecting that a few flasks of that same wine (doctored a little, it is true, by the physician Coictier), and cordially presented to Edward IV by Louis XI, would, some fine morning, rid Louis XI of Edward IV. "The most honorable embassy of Monsieur the Duke of Austria" brought none of these cares to the cardinal's mind, but annoyed him in another way. In truth, it was no small hardship, and we have already said a word or two about it on the second page of this book, that he should be obliged to give reception and entertainment, he, Charles of Bourbon, to a band of obscure burghers; he, a cardinal, to a pack of scurvy sheriffs; he, a Frenchman and a connoisseur of good living, to Flemish beer-drinkers; and in public too! Certainly, it was one of the most irksome parts he had ever had to play to please the king.

However, he had so perfectly studied the part, that when the usher announced in a sonorous voice, "Messieurs, the envoys of Monsieur the Duke of Austria," he turned toward

[3] "Cope full of wine!"

the door with the best grace in the world. Needless to say, the entire hall did the same.

Then arrived, two by two, with a gravity which contrasted with the flippancy of the cardinal's ecclesiastical train, the forty-eight ambassadors of Maximilian of Austria, led by the reverend father in God, Jehan, Abbot of Saint-Bertin, Chancellor of the Golden Fleece, and Jacques de Goy, Sieur Dauby, High Bailiff of Ghent. There was deep silence in the assembly, a general titter being suppressed in order to listen to all the uncouth names and bourgeois qualifications which each one of these personages transmitted with imperturbable seriousness to the usher, who then gave out their names and titles, pell-mell and with all sorts of mutilations, to the crowd below. There were Master Loys Roelof, Sheriff of the city of Louvain, Messire Clays d'Etuelde, Sheriff of Brussels; Messire Paul de Baeust, Sieur of Voirmizelle, President of Flanders; Master Jehan Coleghens, Burgomaster of Antwerp; Master George de la Moere, First Sheriff of the Court of Law of Ghent; Master Gheldolf van der Hage, First Sheriff of the *parchons* of the said city; and the Sieur of Bierbecque, and Jehan Pinnock, and Jehan Dymaerzelle, etc., etc., etc.; bailiffs, sheriffs, burgomasters; burgomasters, sheriffs, bailiffs; all stiff, starched, formal creatures, dressed in velvet and damask, and hooded with black velvet cramignoles with great tassels of the gold thread of Cyprus; after all, good Flemish heads, with severe and dignified sober faces, like those which Rembrandt has made stand out with such clearness and gravity from the dark background of his picture, "The Night Watch," personages on every one of whose foreheads it was written that Maximilian of Austria had done right in "confiding to the full," as his manifesto expressed it, "in their sense, valor, expedience, loyalty, and good endowments."

There was one exception. It was a cunning, intelligent face, a kind of mixture of the monkey and the diplomat, to whom the cardinal advanced three steps and made a low bow, but who, nevertheless, was called simply Guillaume Rym, counselor and pensionary of the city of Ghent.

Few persons at the time knew who this Guillaume Rym was; this rare genius, who, in the time of the revolution, would have appeared on the scene and would have made an

impression, but, who, in the fifteenth century, was confined
to the practice of low intrigue, was "to live in the saps," as
the Duke of Saint-Simon expresses it. However, he was ap-
preciated by the most notorious "sapper" in Europe; he was
familiarly associated with the secret operations of Louis XI,
all of which was entirely unknown to this crowd, who were
amazed at the cardinal's politeness to that sorry-looking
Flemish bailiff.

4

Master Jacques Coppenole

While the pensionary from Ghent and His Eminence were
exchanging very low bows and a few words in a still lower
voice, a tall man, with a large face and broad shoulders,
stepped forward to enter side by side with Guillaume Rym;
he looked like a bulldog beside a fox. His felt cap and his
leather vest were conspicuous amid the velvet and silk of so
many notables. Presuming that he was some out-of-place
groom, the usher stopped him.

'Hey, friend, you can't go in there."

The man in the leather vest shouldered the usher out of
the way.

"What do you mean?" he shouted, with a voice that drew
the attention of the entire hall. "Don't you see that I'm one
of them?"

"Your name?" demanded the usher.

"Jacques Coppenole."

"Your title?"

"Hosier, at the sign of the Three Chains, in Ghent."

The usher drew back. To announce sheriffs and burgomasters was bad enough; but a hosier, that was too much! The
cardinal was on pins and needles. The whole assembly listened and stared. For two days His Eminence had done his
best to cater to these Flemish bears, in order to make them
a little more presentable in public, but this fellow was too
much. Meanwhile Guillaume Rym, with his cunning smile,
went up to the usher, and whispered, "Announce Master
Jacques Coppenole, clerk to the sheriffs of Ghent."

"Usher," said the cardinal in a loud voice, "announce Master Jacques Coppenole, clerk to the sheriffs of the illustrious city of Ghent."

This was an error. Guillaume Rym, by himself, would have circumvented the difficulty; but Coppenole had heard the cardinal.

"No, by God's Cross!" he thundered. "Jacques Coppenole, hosier. Do you hear me, usher? No more, no less. By God's cross! a hosier—that's fine enough. Monsieur the Archduke has more than once looked for his gloves among my hose!"

There was a burst of laughter and applause. A pun is immediately understood in Paris, and consequently always applauded.

We must add that Coppenole was of the bourgeoisie, and that the assembly around him belonged to the same class. Consequently the communication between them and him had been immediate, electric, and, as it were, sympathetic. The bravado of the Flemish hosier, by humbling these courtiers, had stirred in all those plebeian hearts a certain feeling of dignity, which in the fifteenth century was still rather elusive. They beheld an equal in this hosier, who had just stood up to the cardinal! He became a soothing antidote for poor devils accustomed to paying respects and obedience even to the servants of the sergeants of the bailiff of the Abbot of Sainte-Geneviève, the cardinal's train-bearer.

Coppenole bowed haughtily to His Eminence, who returned the salute of this powerful burgher, feared by Louis XI. But Guillaume Rym, "a cunning, spiteful man," as Philippe de Comines writes, observed their civilities with a scornful superior smile, as they took their places. The cardinal was mortified and concerned; Coppenole, quite calm and haughty, thinking, no doubt, that, after all, his title of hosier was as good as any other, and that Mary of Burgundy, mother of that Margaret whose marriage Coppenole came to celebrate today, would have feared him less as a cardinal than as the hosier he was. It was not a cardinal who would have stirred up the people of Ghent against the favorites of Charles the Bold's daughter; it was not a cardinal who would have steeled the crowd, by a single word, against her tears and her entreaties, when the Lady of Flanders came to plead with her people on their behalf even to the foot of their scaffold. But it was the hosier who had only to raise his elbow and off came your heads, you most illustrious seigneurs, Guy d'Hymbercourt and Chancellor Guillaume Hugonet!

But the poor cardinal's torture was not yet over; he was to drink to the bitter dregs the cup of humiliation for being in such evil company.

The reader has probably not forgotten the audacious beggar, who at the beginning of the prologue had climbed up to the frieze of the gallery reserved for the cardinal. The arrival of the illustrious guests had not in the least disturbed him, and while the prelates and ambassadors were packing themselves like real Flemish herrings into the stalls of the gallery, he was very comfortable and at ease, with his legs securely crossed on the architrave. At first, no one had noticed this extraordinary bit of insolence, everybody's attention being fixed elsewhere. He, for his part, took notice of nothing that was going on in the hall; he just kept moving his head back and forth, with the unconcern of a Neapolitan, repeating mechanically, amid the general hum, "Charity, I beg you!" And indeed, among all those present, he was probably the only one who had not deigned to notice the altercation between Coppenole and the usher. Now, as luck would have it, his hosiership of Ghent, with whom the people already so warmly sympathized and upon whom all eyes were fixed, found a seat in the front row of the gallery, directly above the beggar. It caused no small astonishment when this Flemish ambassador, after scrutinizing the beggar below him, gave him a friendly slap on his ragged shoulder. The poor fellow turned around; surprise, recognition, and pleasure were expressed on both faces. Then, without the least concern for the spectators, the hosier and the beggar fell into a low-voiced conversation, holding each other's hands, while the rags of Clopin Trouillefou, against the cloth of gold draperies of the balustrade, looked like a caterpillar on an orange.

The novelty of this unusual scene excited such noisy mirth in the hall that the cardinal's attention was aroused. He leaned slightly forward; and as, from the point where he was seated, he caught only an imperfect glimpse of Trouillefou in his shabby clothing, he very naturally imagined that the beggar was asking alms. Indignant at such audacity, he exclaimed, "Monsieur the Bailiff of the Palace, throw that fellow into the river!"

"By the Cross! Monseigneur the Cardinal!" said Coppenole, still holding Clopin's hand, "this is one of my friends."

"Noël! Noël!" shouted the mob.

From that moment Master Coppenole was just as popular in Paris as he was in Ghent; "in great favor with the people, for men of great stature are so," says Philippe de Comines, "when they are disorderly."

The cardinal bit his lip. He leaned over to the Abbot of Sainte-Geneviève and said to him half in a whisper, "Very pleasant ambassadors these Monsieur the Archduke sends to announce Lady Margaret!"

"Your Eminence's politeness," returned the abbot, "is lost upon these Flemish pigs. *Margaritas ante porcos!*"[1]

"Say, rather," rejoined the cardinal, smiling: *"Porcos ante Margaritam."*[2]

The whole petty cassocked court was in ecstasy over this play on words. The cardinal felt a little relieved. He was now even with Coppenole, for he too had won applause for a pun.

And now, let those of our readers who have the capacity of generalizing an image or an idea, as we say nowadays, permit us to ask them if they have a clear conception of the spectacle presented at that moment in the Great Hall of the Palace.

In the middle of the hall, on the western side, there is a spacious and magnificent gallery, with drapery of gold brocade, into which enters, by means of a small Gothic doorway, a procession of sober personages, announced successively by the shrill voice of an usher. On the front benches, already seated in dignified silence, are a number of venerable figures, wrapped in ermine, velvet, and scarlet cloth. Below and all about this gallery, the crowd is making

[1] "Pearls before the swine."
[2] "Swine before Marguerite." (*Margarita* means both pearl and Marguerite.)

plenty of noise. A thousand stares cover every face in the gallery; a thousand whispers arise at the mention of each name. This show is indeed an interesting one and well merits the attention of the spectators. But, at the same time, what is that down there on that sort of mountebank stage, with four motley puppets upon it, and four others below? And to the side of the stage, who is that pale-faced man attired in a dingy black coat? Alas! dear reader, it is an unfinished prologue and its author, Pierre Gringoire. We had all completely forgotten him. And that was precisely what Gringoire was afraid might happen.

From the moment the cardinal had entered, Gringoire had never ceased his efforts to save his prologue. First he had enjoined the actors, who had discontinued, to proceed, and to speak louder; then, perceiving that no one was listening, he had stopped them; and for nearly a quarter of an hour— the interruption had lasted that long—he had been constantly stamping his foot, fuming, calling to Gisquette and Liénarde, and urging those near him to go on with the prologue. But all was in vain. No one could take his eyes off the cardinal, the embassy, and the gallery, the center of attention in this vast circle. We regret, also, that, when His Eminence's arrival made such a momentous distraction, the prologue was beginning to bore the audience. After all, in the gallery itself, and on the marble table, the play was the same: the conflict was between Labor and Clergy, Nobility and Trade. Many of the bourgeois preferred to see these classes alive, breathing, acting, elbowing one another in actual flesh and blood on the platform, in the Flemish embassy, in that episcopal court, under the cardinal's robe or Coppenole's leather vest, than speaking in verse, as painted, tricked-out, mere stuffed puppets, performing in yellow and white robes, as Gringoire had dressed them.

Nevertheless, seeing order somewhat restored, our poet concocted a stratagem which might have saved the entire performance.

"Monsieur," he said, turning to one of the persons nearest him, a stout man with a long-suffering countenance, "suppose we begin again."

"Begin what?" said the man.

"Why, the mystery play," said Gringoire.

"As you please," returned the other.

This half-approbation was enough for Gringoire and, taking the whole affair into his own hands, he began to call out, while mingling as much as possible with the crowd: "Begin the play again! Begin again!"

"What the devil is all that noise about down there?" said Joannes de Molendino. (For Gringoire was making enough noise for four.) "Tell me, comrades, isn't that mystery play finished? They want to begin again. That's not fair!"

"No! No!" shouted all the students. "Down with the play! Down with it!"

But Gringoire only multiplied his efforts and shouted all the louder, "Begin again! Begin again!"

These cries attracted the cardinal's attention.

"Monsieur the Bailiff of the Palace," he said to a tall dark man standing a few paces from him, "are those rogues in the holy water font, that they are making such an infernal noise?"

The bailiff of the Palace was a kind of amphibious magistrate, a sort of bat of the judicial order, a mixture of rat and bird, judge and soldier.

He approached His Eminence, and with no small apprehension of his displeasure, he stammered an explanation of the crowd's unseemly behavior: how noon had arrived before His Eminence, and how the players had been forced to begin without waiting for His Eminence.

The cardinal burst out laughing.

"By my faith, Monsieur the Rector of the University should have done likewise. What say you, Master Guillaume Rym?"

"Monseigneur," answered Rym, "let us be thankful that we have missed half the play. 'Tis so much gained."

"May those rogues continue with their farce?" inquired the bailiff.

"Go on! Go on!" said the cardinal. "It makes no difference to me. I am going to be reading my breviary anyway."

The bailiff advanced to the edge of the platform, motioned for silence, and called out, "Burghers, townsmen, citizens! To satisfy those who desire that the play should begin again, and those who desire it should finish, His Eminence orders it to be continued."

Thus both factions were obliged to yield, although as consequence both the author and the auditory long bore a grudge against the cardinal.

The characters onstage accordingly resumed the dialogue, and Gringoire hoped that at least the rest of his piece would be heard. This hope, however, like his other illusions, was soon shattered. Silence had indeed been restored in the hall; but Gringoire had not noticed that, at the moment when the cardinal had given the order to continue with the play, the gallery was far from being full, and that after the arrival of the Flemish envoys there were other personages forming part of the cardinal's train whose names and titles were still being thrown out in the midst of his dialogue by the intermittent bawling of the usher. Naturally this spoiled the dialogue. Imagine, indeed, the yelping of the doorkeeper thrown into the middle of a dramatic sequence, breaking in between two lines of a couplet, or between the first half of a line and the last.

Listen to him:

"Master Jacques Charmolue, Procurator of the King in the Ecclesiastical Court!

"Jehan de Harlay, Esquire, Keeper of the Office of Horseman of the Night-watch of the city of Paris!

"Messire Galiot de Genoilhac, Knight, Seigneur of Brussac, Master of the King's Artillery!

"Master Dreux-Raguier, Inspector of our Lord the King's Waters and Forests, in the dominions of France, Champagne, and Brie!

"Messire Louis de Graville, Knight, Councillor and Champberlain of the King, Admiral of France, Keeper of the Bois de Vincennes!

"Master Denis le Mercier, Keeper of the House for the Blind in Paris!"

It was becoming unbearable.

All this strange accompaniment, which made the play impossible to follow, was most annoying to Gringoire, because he felt the interest would increase as the play advanced, and that his composition lacked nothing but an attentive audience. It was, indeed, difficult to imagine a plot more ingeniously or dramatically woven. While the four characters of the prologue were bewailing their hopeless perplexity, Venus in person—*vera incessu patuit dea*³—appeared before them, clad in a beautiful robe emblazoned with the arms of the city of Paris. She had come to claim for herself the dolphin promised to the most beautiful. She had the support of Jupiter, whose thunder was heard rumbling in the dressing room; and the goddess was about to bear away the prize; that is, in plain words, to marry Monsieur the Dauphin, when a little girl, dressed in white damask, and holding in her hand a marguerite (an obvious personification of the Lady of Flanders), came to contest with Venus for the prize. Here was a dramatic moment and a change.

After some proper dialogue, Venus, Margaret, and the supporting players agreed to refer the matter to the Virgin Mary's judgment. Then entered another fine character, Don Pedro, King of Mesopotamia, but with so many interruptions, it was difficult to figure out his connection with the plot. All these characters had gotten onstage by means of the ladder.

But the play was done for. Its beauty was neither observed nor understood. At the cardinal's entrance it seemed as if some invisible magic thread had suddenly drawn all eyes from the marble table to the gallery, from the southern extremity of the hall to its western side. Nothing could break the spell of the audience. All eyes were fixed in that direction, and the newcomers, with their cursed names, and their faces, and their dresses, were one long distraction. It was distressing. Excepting Gisquette and Liénarde, who turned aside from time to time when Gringoire pulled them by the sleeve, excepting their big long-suffering neighbor, no one was listening, no one was watching the poor, forsaken morality play. Gringoire could see nothing but profiles.

With what bitterness did he watch his edifice of glorious poetry crumble to pieces! And to think that this multitude had been on the point of rebelling against Monsieur the Bailiff, out of impatience to hear his work! And now that they had it, they cared nothing about it. This same performance, too, that had begun with such unanimous acclamation! Oh, the eternal tides of popular favor! To think that they had al-

³ "Her bearing itself revealed the goddess."

most hung the bailiff's sergeants! What he would not have given to recall that glorious moment!

The usher's brutal monologue ceased at last. Everyone had arrived; Gringoire breathed easily once more. The actors continued courageously. But all at once what should Master Coppenole, the hosier, do but stand up, and Gringoire heard him interrupt once more the universal attention to his play by delivering this harangue:

"Messires the burghers and squires of Paris, by the rood, pray tell, what are we doing here? I do indeed see, down there in that corner, on a kind of stage, some people who look as if they want to fight. I do not know whether that is what you call a mystery; but I do know it isn't very funny. They are fighting only with their tongues. For the past quarter of an hour, I have been waiting for the first blow. But nothing happens. They're all cowards, who insult one another only with their foul words. It would have been better to have brought here boxers from London or Rotterdam; then you would have had some thumps that could have been heard from here to the square! But these characters are pitiful. They might have at least given us a morris dance, or some other bit of mummery. No one told me it was going to be like this. I was promised a Feast of Fools and an election of a pope. We at Ghent, too, have our Fools' Pope, and, by God, in that we're behind nobody. This is how we do it. A mob assembles, like here. Then each in his turn puts his head through a hole and makes faces at the others. He who makes the ugliest face, by universal consent, is elected pope. It's all very amusing. Shall we elect your pope as we do in my country? At any rate, it will not be so tiring as listening to these babblers! If they want to come and make faces through the hole, each can have his turn. What say you, master burghers? We have here a sufficient number of grotesque specimens of both sexes to have a good hearty Flemish laugh, and enough ugly faces so that we can hope for a fine grinning-match."

Gringoire wanted to reply, but amazement, resentment, indignation robbed him of words. Besides, the suggestion of the popular hosier was received so enthusiastically by these townsfolk, flattered at being called "squires," that further resistance was futile. All that could be done now was to go along with the crowd. Gringoire buried his face in his hands, not being so fortunate as to possess a cloak with which to hide his head like the Agamemnon of Timanthes.

5

Quasimodo

In the wink of an eye everything was ready to carry out Coppenole's suggestion. Burghers, students, Basochians had set to work. The small chapel opposite the marble table was chosen for the scene of the face-making contest. A pane of glass broken out of the beautiful rose-window above the door left an empty ring of stone through which it was agreed that the contestants would pass their heads. To reach it, they had only to stand on two barrels, which had been procured from somewhere or other, and set one upon the other rather precariously. It was decided that each candidate, male or female (for you could have a female pope), in order to leave a vivid impression of his grin, should cover his face and remain unseen in the chapel until the moment of making an appearance at the hole.

In an instant the chapel was filled with contestants, and the door was closed behind them.

Coppenole from his seat in the gallery ordered, directed, arranged everything. During all this confusion, the cardinal, no less disconcerted than Gringoire, on pretext of business and the hour of vespers, had retired with his entire train; and the crowd, which had been so noisily aroused by his arrival, seemed not the least interested in his departure. Guillaume Rym was the only one who noticed the discomfiture of His Eminence. Popular attention, like the sun, pursued its revolution; after rising at one end of the hall, it had stayed for a while in the middle of it, and was now setting at the other end. The marble table, the draped gallery, each had its moment, now it was the turn of Louis XI's chapel. The field was henceforward open for every sort of folly. The Flemings and the rabble had the whole hall to themselves.

The making of faces began. The first to appear in the hole, with eyelids turned inside out, with mouth wide open,

with forehead wrinkled like the hussar boots of the Empire
period, excited such a burst of inextinguishable laughter that
Homer would have taken all these boors for gods. Nevertheless, the Great Hall was anything but an Olympus, as
Gringoire's poor Jupiter, better than anyone, could well attest. A second face and a third followed, then another, then
another; and with each face the rollicking laughter redoubled
and the stamping of feet grew louder. This spectacle produced in everyone a certain twirling in the brain, a certain
intoxication and fascination almost impossible to describe to
the reader of our day, or to the habitué of our modern drawing rooms. Just imagine a series of faces, presenting successively every geometric figure, from the triangle to the
trapezium, from the cone to the polyhedron; every human
expression, from anger to lust; every age, from the wrinkles
of a newborn babe to the wrinkles of an old lady on the
verge of death; every religious phantasm, from Faunus to
Beelzebub; every animal profile, from the jowl to the beak,
from the snout to the muzzle. Picture to yourself all the grotesque heads sculptured on the Pont-Neuf, those nightmares
carved by the hand of Germain Pilon, taking life and breath,
and coming one after the other to sear your face with their
flaming eyes; all the masks of a Venetian carnival passing in
succession before you—in short, a human kaleidoscope.

The orgy became more and more Flemish. Teniers himself
would have given but a very imperfect idea of it. Imagine,
if you can, a "battle" of Salvator Rosa bacchanalized. There
was no longer any distinction between people—students,
ambassadors, burghers, men, women—all were the same;
there was now neither a Clopin Trouillefou, nor a Gilles
Lecornu, nor a Marie Quatrelivres, nor a Robin Poussepain.
All identity was lost in common license. The Great Hall was
nothing more than one vast furnace of audacity and joviality,
in which every mouth was a shout, every eye a flash, every
face a grin, every individual a gesticulation—all was shouting and roaring. The strange faces that followed one after
another, gnashing their teeth in the window, were like so
many brands cast into the fire; and from all that effervescent
mob there escaped, like vapor from a furnace, a sharp, shrill,
hissing noise, like the buzzing wings of ten thousand gnats.

"Curses!"

"Look at that face!"

"That's nothing."

"Let's have another."

"Guillemette Maugerepius, look at that bull's head; it has everything but horns. Isn't that your husband?"

"There's another."

"For God's sake, what's that?"

"Hey, that's cheating. You're only allowed to show your face."

"That devil Perrette Callebotte! Just like her!"

"Noël! Noël!"

"This is too much!"

"Here's one whose ears can't get through!" etc., etc.

We must, however, do justice to our friend Jehan. In the midst of all this commotion you could still see him on the top of his pillar like a sailor on the topsail, carrying on like a wild man. His mouth was wide open, as from it came a cry that no one could hear; not that it was drowned by the general din, intense as that was, but because, no doubt, it had reached the limit of audible high notes, the twelve thousand vibrations of Sauveur, or the eight thousand of Biot.

As for Gringoire, as soon as the first moment of depression was over, he had regained his composure. He had hardened himself in the face of adversity. "Go on!" he had said for the third time to his actors, his speaking machines. Then pacing with long strides in front of the marble table, he was seized with a wild notion to go and take his turn at the hole in the chapel window, if only to have the pleasure of making a face at this ungrateful mob. "But no," he said to himself, "that would be unworthy of us; no vengeance! We will fight to the end. The power of poetry over the people is great. I shall bring them back. We shall see which of the two shall overcome—funny faces or belles-lettres."

Alas, he was the only spectator of his play!

It was even worse than before, for now he saw nothing but backs.

No, I am wrong. The big, long-suffering man whom he had consulted at a critical moment still faced the stage. As for Gisquette and Liénarde, they had left long since.

Gringoire was moved to the bottom of his heart by the fidelity of this audience of one. He went over to him, tugged him gently by the arm, for the good man was leaning against the barricade, dozing a little.

"Monsieur," said Gringoire, "thank you."

"Sir," answered the man with a yawn, "what for?"

"I see what annoys you," replied our poet. "All this noise and confusion prevent you from hearing comfortably. But never mind; your name shall pass on to posterity. What is your name, please?"

"Renault Château, Keeper of the Seal of the Châtelet of Paris, at your service."

"Monsieur," said Gringoire, "you are the sole representative of the Muses among this vast audience."

"You are too kind, sir," replied the Keeper of the Seal of the Châtelet.

"You are the only one," continued Gringoire, "kind enough to pay any attention to my play. How do you like it?"

"Hmm, hmm," replied the big magistrate but half awake, "quite funny indeed."

Gringoire had to be content with this bit of eulogy, for a thunder of applause, mingled with a prodigious acclamation, cut short their conversation. The Fools' Pope was at last chosen.

"Noël! Noël!" shouted the people on all sides.

It was indeed a marvelous face that now beamed through the circular window. After all the faces, pentagonal, hexagonal, and heteroclite, that had followed each other at this window without fully appreciating the idea of the grotesque which the crowd had fabricated in their imaginations so excited by the orgy, it required nothing less, to win all the votes, than the sublime face which had just now dazzled the assemblage. Even Master Coppenole roundly applauded; and Clopin Trouillefou, who had been in the running (and God knows the degree of ugliness his face could assume), acknowledged himself defeated. We shall do likewise. We shall not try to describe for the reader that tetrahedron nose, that horseshoe mouth, that small left eye obscured by red bushy eyebrows; the right eye which disappeared completely under an enormous wart; those jagged teeth, with gaps here and there, like the battlements of a fortress; that horny lip, over which one of those teeth protruded like the tusk of an elephant; that forked chin, and, above all, the expression on the whole face, a mixture of malice, astonishment, and sadness. Let the reader, if he can, imagine the whole of it.

The applause was unanimous, spontaneous, and overwhelming. All rushed toward the chapel. In triumph the lucky Pope of Fools was led out. But it was then the admiration and the surprise of the crowd reached its height. The grimace they had applauded was his natural face.

Rather his whole person was a grimace. His enormous head bristled with red hair; between his shoulders was an enormous hump, counterbalanced by a protuberance in front; he had a framework of thighs and legs so strangely askew that they could touch only at the knees, and, seen from the front, resembled two sickles joined together at the handles. The feet were huge; the hands monstrous. Yet with all that deformity was a certain fearsome appearance of vigor, agility, and courage; a strange exception to the eternal rule prescribing that strength, like beauty, shall result from harmony. Such was the pope whom the fools had chosen.

He looked like a giant that had been broken and badly repaired.

When this sort of Cyclops appeared on the threshold of the chapel, motionless, chunky, and almost as broad as he was high, "the square of his base," as one great man puts it, the populace immediately recognized him by his coat, half red and half purple, sprinkled with little silver bells, and especially by the perfection of his ugliness—the populace recognized him, I say, and cried out with one voice:

"It's Quasimodo, the bellringer. It's Quasimodo, the hunchback of Notre-Dame! Quasimodo the one-eyed! Quasimodo the bowlegged! Noël! Noël!" The poor wretch, it seems, had a number of nicknames.

"Let all pregnant women beware!" cried the students.

"Or those who want to be," added Joannes.

The women in fact hid their faces.

"Oh that hideous ape!" said one.

"As wicked as he is ugly," replied another.

"It's the devil," added a third.

"Unfortunately I live near Notre-Dame, and at night I often hear him roaming about in the gutters."

"With the cats."

"He's always on our rooftops."

"He casts spells at us down our chimneys."

"The other night he came and made faces at me through my window. I thought it was a man. How afraid I was!"

"I am sure he goes to meet with witches. Once he left a broomstick on my leads."

"Oh that ugly hunchback!"

"That vile creature!"

On the contrary, the men were delighted and applauded loudly.

Quasimodo, the object of the tumult, stood in the doorway of the chapel, weird and grave, letting himself be admired.

One of the students, Robin Poussepain, I do believe, came up close and laughed in his face. Quasimodo, without a word, simply grabbed him by the belt and hurled him a full ten paces into the crowd.

Master Coppenole, amazed, went over to him. "God's Cross! Holy Saint Peter! you are the ugliest creature I have ever seen! You deserve to be Pope of Rome as well as of Paris."

So saying, he good-naturedly rested his hand on the monster's shoulder. Quasimodo did not move.

Coppenole continued, "You're a fellow with whom I have a longing to carouse though it should cost me a new *douzain* of twelve *tournois*. What do you say?"

Quasimodo made no reply.

"By God! are you deaf!" cried the hosier.

In fact Quasimodo was.

However, he was beginning to lose patience with Coppenole's manner. Suddenly he turned on him with such a snarl that the Flemish giant recoiled like a bulldog before a cat.

A circle of terror and respect then formed around the strange personage, the radius of which was at least fifteen geometrical paces. An old lady explained to Master Coppenole that Quasimodo was deaf.

"Deaf!" cried the hosier with his boisterous Flemish laugh. "By God, then he is a pope!"

"Ha! I know him," shouted Jehan, who now was coming down the pillar to catch a closer look at Quasimodo. "He's my brother's bellringer. Good day to you, Quasimodo!"

"A devil of a man," said Robin Poussepain, bruised from

his fall. "He shows himself; he's a hunchback. He walks; he's bowlegged. He looks at you; and he has only one eye. You speak to him; but he is deaf. Why, what does this Polyphemus do with his tongue?"

"He speaks when he wishes," said the old woman. "The ringing of the bells has made him deaf. But he's not dumb."

"So that is lacking to him?" observed Jehan.

"And he has one eye too many," added Robin Poussepain.

"Not so," said Jehan judiciously. "A one-eyed man is much more incomplete than a blind man, for he knows what it is that's lacking."

Meanwhile all the beggars, all the lackeys, all the pickpockets, together with the students, had gone in procession to fetch from the wardrobe of the Basoche the pasteboard tiara and the mock robe worn in derision by the Fools' Pope. Quasimodo allowed himself to be clothed in them with a kind of proud docility. They then seated him on a motley colored chair. Twelve officers of the brotherhood of fools hoisted him to their shoulders; and a kind of bitter and disdainful joy seemed to spread over the morose face of the Cyclops when he beheld under his deformed feet all those heads of good-looking and well-shaped men. Then the whole roaring ragged procession set out, to make, according to custom, the internal circuit of the galleries of the Palace before parading in the streets and public squares of the city.

6

La Esmeralda

We are delighted to inform our readers that during the whole of this scene Gringoire and his play held out. His actors, spurred on by him, had not discontinued their enactment of the play nor had he ceased to give it his full attention. Gringoire had contributed his share to the general uproar, and was determined to proceed to the end, confident that the public's attention would again be captured. This spark of hope became brighter when he saw Quasimodo, Coppenole, and the whole noisy cortege of the Pope of Fools clamorously leave the hall. The mob rushed out after them.

"Good," he said to himself. "We are rid of all those rabble rousers." Unfortunately the rabble rousers were the whole assembly. In a twinkling of an eye the Great Hall was empty.

It is true there still remained a few spectators, some scattered about, and others grouped around the pillars—women, old men, and children who had had enough of the noise and confusion. A few of the students, too, still remained, straddling the entablature of the windows, and looking out onto the square.

"Well," thought Gringoire, "here are still some to hear the end of my mystery. They are few, but a select audience—a literate audience."

But a moment afterward, a symphony which was to have emphasized the arrival of the Holy Virgin was missing. Gringoire noticed that his music had been swept away in the procession of the Fools' Pope.

"Skip that," he said stoically.

He approached a group of townspeople who seemed to him to be talking about his play. He caught only scraps of their conversation:

"Master Cheneteau, you recall the Hotel de Navarre, which belonged to Monsieur de Nemours?"

"Yes, opposite the chapel of Braque."

"Well, the Minister of Finance has just leased it to Guillaume Alixandre, that writer of historical subjects, for six livres eight sol parisis a year."

"How rents are rising!"

"So!" said Gringoire with a sigh. "Well, those others are listening."

"Comrades!" suddenly cried one of the young fellows in the window, "La Esmeralda! It's La Esmeralda down in the square!"

The word had a magical effect. All who were left in the hall rushed toward the windows, climbing up the walls to see, repeating, "La Esmeralda! La Esmeralda!" At the same time a thunder of applause rose from the square.

"What do they mean by 'La Esmeralda'?" said Gringoire, wringing his hands in despair. "Oh! my God! it appears that the windows are the attraction now!"

He turned toward the marble table and saw that the performance had stopped. It was precisely the moment when

Jupiter was to appear with his thunder. But Jupiter was standing motionless below the edge of the stage.

"Michel Giborne!" cried the irritated poet. "What are you doing? Is that your role? Go up!"

"Alas!" exclaimed Jupiter, "one of the students has just taken the ladder away."

Gringoire looked. It was but too true. All communication between his plot and its dénouement was cut off.

"Rogue!" he muttered. "But why did he take the ladder?"

"To go see Esmeralda," cried Jupiter in a piteous tone. " 'Say,' he said, 'here's a ladder no one is using,' and off he went with it."

This was the last blow. Gringoire received it with resignation.

"May the devil take you all!" he said to the players, "and if they pay me, I'll pay you."

Then he made his retreat, hanging his head, but still the last on the field, like a general who has fought well.

And as he descended the winding stairs of the Palace, "What a fine mob of asses and boobies these Parisians are!" he grumbled. "They come to a mystery, but hear none of it! They paid attention to everyone else—to Clopin Trouillefou, the cardinal, Coppenole, Quasimodo, the devil!—but to Our Lady the Virgin, not at all. If I'd known it, I'd have given you Virgin Marys, you wretched fools! Me! to come here to see faces, and to see nothing but backs! to be a poet, and to have the success of an apothecary! True, Homer begged his way through the Greek towns, and Naso died in exile among the Muscovites. But may the devil strangle me if I understand what they mean by this Esmeralda! What kind of a word is that? It must be Egyptian!"

BOOK II

1

From Charybdis to Scylla

Night comes early in January. The streets were already dark when Gringoire left the Palace. He welcomed this darkness, for he longed to reach some obscure, deserted alley where he might meditate in peace, and where philosophy might first apply its dressing to his wounds. Besides, philosophy was his only refuge, for he did not know where to go to find lodging for the night. After the conspicuous miscarriage of his first dramatic attempt, he dared not return to that apartment which he had occupied in the rue Grenier-sur-l'Eau, opposite the Port-au-Foin, having counted upon what the provost would give him for his opus to pay Master Guillaume Doulx-Sire, collector of the cattle taxes in Paris, the six months' rent he owed him; that is, twelve sols parisis, twelve times the value of all he possessed in the world, including his breeches, his shirt, and his cap. Temporarily sheltered under the little gateway to the prison belonging to the treasurer of the Sainte-Chapelle, he considered for a moment the lodging he should select for the night, having all the pavements of Paris from which to choose. He remembered noticing the week before, in the Rue de la Savaterie, at the door of a councillor to parliament, a footstone for mounting a mule. At that time he had said to himself that this stone might serve upon occasion as an excellent pillow for a beggar or a poet. He thanked Providence for having sent him this happy idea. But as he was preparing to cross the square of the Palace in order to reach the tortuous labyrinth of the City, where all those ancient sisters, the streets of la Barillerie, Vieille-Draperie, la Savaterie, la Juiverie, etc., wend their twisting way, and whose nine-story houses are still standing today, he saw the procession of the Fools' Pope, which was also pouring out of the Palace and across the square, still shouting, now illumined by the torches, and, moreover, accompanied by Gringoire's own music. The sight hurt his vanity, and he fled. In the bitterness of his dramatic misadventure, everything which called to mind the festivities of the day accentuated his sorrow—reopened his wounds and caused them to bleed afresh.

He would have crossed the Pont Saint-Michel but children were running up and down with fireworks and firecrackers.

"Curses on those fireworks!" muttered Gringoire, and he turned back to the Pont-au-Change. On the front of the houses near the entrance of the bridge they had attached banners. On three of them were paintings to represent the king, the dauphin, and Margaret of Flanders, and on six smaller banners were portrayed the Duke of Austria, the Cardinal of Bourbon, and Monsieur de Beaujeu, and Madame Jeanne of France, and Monsieur the Bastard of Bourbon, and I don't know who else besides—all lighted by torches. The crowd stood admiring them.

"Happy artist, Jehan Fourbault!" sighed Gringoire, as he turned his back on this exhibition. Before him ran a street so dark and empty that he hoped there to forget all his mental suffering by escaping every glimmer of the festivities. He hurried into it. A few minutes later, he struck his foot against some obstacle; he tripped and fell. It was the bundle of hawthorn branches which the clerks of the Basoche had placed that morning at the door of the president of parliament, in honor of the solemnity of the day. Gringoire bore this new accident heroically. He got up and reached the river's edge, leaving behind him the Civil Court and the Criminal Court, and, passing along the high walls of the royal gardens, on that unpaved strand where he was up to his ankles in mud, he arrived at the western part of the city. For some time he gazed at the small island of the Passeur-aux-Vaches, which has since given way to the Pont-Neuf with its bronze horse. In the semidarkness, the islet appeared to him like a black mass across a narrow stream of glistening water. By the glimmer of a faint light one could make out a beehive-shaped hut where the ferryman sheltered himself during the night.

"O happy ferryman!" thought Gringoire, "you have no dreams of glory nor do you write epithalamiums! What is it to you if the kings and duchesses of Burgundy marry! You know no Marguerites but the daisies which your April meadow gives your cows to crop! While I, a poet, am hooted; I shiver with cold; I owe twelve sous, and the soles of my shoes are so thin that you could use them to glaze your lantern! Thank you, ferryman! Your hut gives rest to my eyes and makes me forget Paris!"

He was awakened from his almost lyric reverie by the explosion of a double petard which suddenly came from that peaceful cabin. It was the ferryman himself who was sharing in the festivities of the day, and setting off his fireworks.

The explosion made Gringoire's hair stand on end.

"O cursed holiday!" he cried. "Will you follow me everywhere? O my God, even to the ferryman's hut!"

Then he gazed at the Seine at his feet, and he was seized with a terrible temptation.

"Oh," said he, "how gladly I would drown myself if the water weren't so cold!"

Then it was that he made a desperate resolution. To wit, since he could not escape the Fools' Pope, Jehan Fourbault's paintings, the bundles of hawthorn, and the firecrackers, he would go to the Place de Grève and plunge himself wholeheartedly and merrily into all these festivities.

"At least," he thought, "I shall be able to warm myself by the bonfire, and to sup on some crumbs from the three great chests of sugarplums that will have been set out there on the public buffets of the city."

2

The Place de Grève

There remains today but a very small vestige of the Place de Grève as it existed formerly, and that is the once-charming turret which occupies the northern corner of the square. It is now covered by unsightly whitewash that encrusts the delicate lines of its sculpture. Likely the whole turret will soon disappear, submerged by that flood of new houses which is so rapidly obliterating all the old facades in Paris.

Those who, like ourselves, never pass over the Place de Grève without looking piteously and sympathetically at this poor turret, squeezed as it is between two paltry houses of the period of Louis XV, can easily reconstruct in imagination the assemblage of edifices to which it belonged, and thus imagine themselves in that fifteenth-century Gothic square.

It was then, as now, an irregular trapezium, bounded on one side by the quay, and on the other three by a series of high, narrow, gloomy houses. During the daytime, one could admire the variety of these buildings, all sculptured in stone or wood, and offering perfect examples of the various kinds of domestic architecture of the Middle Ages, going back from the fifteenth to the eleventh century, from the square window which then was beginning to supersede the pointed arch, back to the semi-circular Roman arch, which had been supplanted by the pointed arch and which still occupied the first story of that ancient house of the Tower of Roland, at the corner of the square next to the Seine, on the same side as the Rue de la Tannerie. By night, nothing was distinguishable of that mass of buildings except the black jagged outline of the roofs encircling the square with their chain of pointed gables. One of the essential differences between the town as it was then and as it is today is that now the fronts of the houses face the squares and streets, but then it was the backs. For two centuries past, the houses have been turned around.

In the center, but toward the eastern side of the square, rose a heavy hybrid pile formed by three masses of houses in juxtaposition. It was called by three names which explain its history, its purpose, and its architecture: the Dauphin's House, because Charles V, when dauphin, had lived in it; the Marchandise, because it served as the Hotel de Ville; and the Pillar House, on account of a series of heavy pillars which supported its three stories. The town had there all that a good town like Paris needs: a chapel to pray in, a courtroom for holding magisterial sittings and on occasion for reprimanding the king's officers, and in the lofts, an arsenal stocked with artillery. For the good people of Paris, well knowing that it is not sufficient in every emergency, to plead and pray for the franchises of the City, have always in reserve, in the attics of the Hotel de Ville, a few good rusty harquebuses.

The Place de Grève then had that sinister aspect which it retains today, owing to the unpleasant ideas which it excites, and owing to the gloomy Hotel de Ville of Dominique Bocador which has replaced the Pillar House. It must be observed that a permanent gibbet and pillory—a *justice* and a *ladder*, as they were then called—erected side by side in the middle of the pavement, contributed not a little to make the passerby avert his eyes from this fatal spot, where so many human beings full of life and health suffered their last agony. It was this gibbet that fifty years later was to give birth to that St. Vallier fever, as it was called, that terror of the scaffold, the most monstrous of all sicknesses, because it is inflicted not by the hand of God, but by man.

It is a consolation, let it be said in passing, to reflect that the death penalty, which, three hundred years ago, then encumbered with its iron wheels, with its stone gibbets, with all its apparatus for execution permanently fixed in the ground, the Place de Grève, Les Halles, the Place Dauphine, the Croix-du-Trahoir, the Marché-aux-Pourceaux, the hideous Montfaucon, the Barrière des Sergents, the Place-aux-Chats, the Porte Saint-Denis, Champeaux, the Porte Baudets, the Porte Saint-Jacques, not to mention the innumerable "ladders" of the provosts, the bishop, the chapters, the abbots, the priors, not to mention the judicial drownings in the river Seine; I repeat it is consoling to reflect that now, after

losing, one by one, all those pieces of her panoply—her profusion of executions, her refined and fanciful torments, her
torture, for applying which she made afresh every five years
a bed of leather, in the Grand-Châtelet—this old queen of
feudal society had nearly been thrust out of our laws and our
towns, tracked from code to code, driven from place to
place, so that she now possesses, in our vast metropolis of
Paris, but one dishonored corner of the Place de Grève, only
one miserable guillotine, stealthy, anxious, ashamed, which
seems always afraid of being taken red-handed, so quickly
does it vanish after dealing its fatal blow!

3

Besos Para Golpes[1]

When Pierre Gringoire arrived at the Place de Grève he
was freezing cold. He had gone by way of the Pont-aux-
Meuniers, to avoid the crowds on the Pont-au-Change and
Jehan Fourbault's banners; but the wheels of all the bishop's
mills had splashed him as he passed by, so that his coat was
soaking wet. Furthermore, it seemed to him that the failure
of his play made him feel the cold even more. Accordingly
he hastened toward the bonfire which was burning magnificently in the middle of the square and joined the good-sized
group already there.

"These damned Parisians!" said he to himself, for
Gringoire, like many dramatic poets, was given to soliloquy.
"Now they block me from the fire! And yet I need the
warmth of some chimney corner. My shoes are full of holes,
and all these cursed mills have been raining on me! The
devil take the Bishop of Paris and his mills! I'd like to know
what a bishop wants with a mill! Does he expect someday to
become a miller-bishop? If he only needs my curses to do
so, I heartily give them to him, and to his cathedral, and to
his mills! Let's see now, if any of these varlets will make
room for me. I'd like to know what they are doing here.

[1] Kisses for blows.

Warming themselves—fine pleasure! Staring into the fire—fine spectacle!"

But, when he looked more closely, he saw that the circle was much larger than was necessary for these people merely to warm themselves. Then he observed that the burning logs were not the only attraction.

In a wide space left clear between the crowd and the fire, a young girl was dancing.

But was it a young girl, or a fairy, or an angel? Gringoire, skeptical philosopher and ironical poet that he was, could not at first decide, so deeply was he fascinated by this dazzling vision.

She was not tall, but her slender lightsomeness made her appear so. Her complexion was dark, but one guessed that by daylight it would have the beautiful golden tint of Andalusian and Roman women. Her small feet, too, were Andalasian, for they seemed at once tight yet comfortable in her dainty shoes. She pirouetted on an old Persian carpet, spread carelessly under her feet. Each time she twirled, her radiant face and her large black eyes seemed to glow for you alone. In the circle all mouths were agape and all eyes staring.

She danced to a Basque tambourine which she tinkled above her head, thus displaying her lovely arms. She wore a golden bodice tightly laced about her delicate body, exposing her beautiful shoulders. Below her wasp waist billowed a multicolored skirt, which, in the whirling dance, gave momentary glimpses of her finely shaped legs. With all this, and her black hair and sparkling eyes, she seemed like something more than human.

"In truth," thought Gringoire, "it is a salamander—a nymph—a goddess—a bacchante of Mount Maenalus!"

At that moment one of the braids of this "salamander's" hair loosened, and the thong of yellow leather that had bound it fell to the ground.

"Oh no!" said he. "It's a gypsy!" All the illusion faded.

As she resumed her dance, she picked up from the ground two swords, the points of which she balanced on her forehead, making them turn in one direction while she spun in another. Indeed, she was a gypsy. Yet, disenchanted as Gringoire might be, the whole scene was not without its charm and magic. The bonfire threw upon her a weird red light which itself danced over the circle of faces as well as over the brown forehead of the girl; and, at the far end of the square, it cast a pale light that mingled on one side with the shimmering shadows of the old, dark, wrinkled facade of the Pillar House, while on the other side, it slid over the stone arms of the gibbet.

Among the many faces which the glow of the fire dyed a crimson red, there was one which seémed to be more than all the rest absorbed in watching the dancer. It was the face of a man, austere, calm, and somber. This man, whose dress was hidden by the crowd, did not appear to be more than thirty-five years of age; yet he was bald, having at his temples only a few clumps of thin gray hair. His broad, high forehead was beginning to show wrinkles, but in his deepset eyes there shone an extraordinary gleam, portending a youthful spirit, an ardent vitality, and a depth of passion. He kept them fixed on the gypsy. But, as the young girl of sixteen continued her frenzied dance to the utter delight of the crowd, his demeanor seemed to grow more and more gloomy. Occasionally a smile and a sigh would meet on his lips, but the smile was the sadder of the two.

Finally the girl, out of breath, stopped dancing, and the people applauded enthusiastically.

"Djali!" cried the gypsy.

Then Gringoire saw a pretty little white goat appear, a lively, nimble, glossy animal with gilt horns, gilt hoofs, and a gilt collar, which he had not noticed before, and which until then had remained crouching on a corner of the carpet watching her mistress dance.

"Djali," said the dancer, "now it's your turn."

Sitting down beside the goat, she gracefully offered the Basque tambourine to her.

"Djali," she continued, "what month of the year is it?"

The goat lifted her forefoot and struck one stroke upon the tambourine. It was in fact the first month. The crowd applauded.

"Djali," resumed the girl, turning her tambourine over, "what day of the month is it?"

Djali lifted her small gilt hoof and struck the tambourine six times.

"Djali," continued the Egyptian, again changing the side of the tambourine, "what time is it?"

Djali struck seven times. And just then the tower clock of the Pillar House struck seven.

The people were amazed.

"There is witchcraft here," yelled one sinister voice in the crowd. This came from the bald man whose eyes had never left the gypsy.

She trembled, and turned away; but the applause burst out again, smothering the morose exclamation.

Apparently her apprehension was thus dispelled. At any rate she continued to interrogate the goat.

"Djali, show us how Master Guichard Grand-Remy, captain of the town pistoleers, walks in the Candlemas procession."

Djali stood up on her hind legs and began bleating, at the same time walking with such a genteel gravity that the entire crowd burst out laughing at this miming of the pompous captain's manner.

"Djali!" resumed the girl, emboldened by her increasing success, "show how Master Jacques Charmolue, the king's attorney in the ecclesiastical court, preaches."

The goat sat down on her rump and began to bleat, shaking her front feet in such a strange fashion that, except for the bad French and bad Latin, as to gestures, accent, and the very posture, it was Jacques Charmolue in the flesh.

The crowd applauded more wildly than before.

"Sacrilege! Profanation!" cried the same voice from the bald-headed man.

Once more the gypsy turned away.

Aside, she said, "Oh, it's that wicked man!" Then, protruding her lower lip beyond her upper, she made a little pout which seemed to be characteristic of her. She arose and, spinning on her heel, began to pass her tambourine for the people's contributions.

Silver and copper coins, large and small, clattered into the receptacle. Presently she paused in front of Gringoire, who absentmindedly put his hand into his pocket. "The devil," muttered the poet as he found at the bottom of his pocket only reality; that is to say, nothing. The pretty girl just waited, holding out her tambourine, and stared at him with her huge eyes. Perspiration beaded Gringoire's forehead.

If he had had all Peru in his pocket, he would certainly have given it to this dancer; but Gringoire had not Peru in his pocket; and besides, America was not yet discovered.

Fortunately he was saved by an unexpected incident.

"Will you be gone, you Egyptian grasshopper?" cried a hoarse voice from the darkest corner of the square. The girl turned away frightened. This wasn't the voice of the bald-headed man; it was a woman's voice, an intense, spiteful voice.

Furthermore, this cry, which had frightened the gypsy, delighted a band of children who were running about.

"It's the recluse from the Tour-Roland," they shouted with excessive bursts of laughter. "It's the *sachette* who's scolding her! Hasn't she eaten yet? Let's carry her something from the town buffet!"

And away they ran to the Pillar House.

Meanwhile, Gringoire took advantage of the girl's trouble to lose himself in the crowd. The shouting of the children reminded him that he, too, had not supped. He therefore also hurried to the public buffet. But the little brats had better legs than he; when he arrived, they had stripped the table clean. There wasn't even a wretched morsel of bread left. There was nothing now against the wall but the light fleurs-de-lis intermingled with rose bushes, painted there in 1434 by Mathieu Biterne, a meager meal indeed.

It is not pleasant to go to bed without supper; it is still less pleasant to go without supper and not to know where one is going to bed. Yet this was Gringoire's plight. No bread, no lodging. He saw himself pressed on all sides by harsh necessity. He had long since discovered this truth: that Jupiter had created men in a fit of misanthropy, and that, throughout the life of a philosopher, his destiny holds his philosophy in a state of siege. As for him, he had never seen the blockade so complete; he heard his empty stomach rumbling, and he thought it very ill-ordained that evil destiny should take his philosophy by famine.

He was sinking deeper and deeper into melancholy, when a strange singing, but remarkably sweet, suddenly aroused him. It was the young Egyptian.

Her voice had the same quality as her beauty and her dance. It was indefinably charming; there was about it something pure, rich, aerial—winged, as it were. It encompassed a succession of variations, of melodies, of unexpected cadences, then simple strains, interspersed with sharp, even whistling notes, running into sounds that would have confused a nightingale, but in which harmony was ever preserved, followed by soft octave undulations which rose and fell even as the bosom of the young singer. Her beautiful face followed with singular expressiveness every capricious variation of the music, from its wildest inspiration to its almost chaste dignity. You would have imagined her at one moment a maniac, at another a queen.

The words she sang were of a language unknown to Gringoire; apparently they were even unknown to her, so little did the expression which she gave in singing correspond with the meaning of the words. Thus, in her voice, these four verses were full of sparkling gaiety:

> *Un confre de gran riqueza*
> *Hallaron dentro un pilar,*
> *Dentro del, nuevas banderas*
> *Con figuras de espantar.*

And, again, a moment afterward, she applied the same tone to this stanza:

> *Alarabes de cavallo*
> *Sin poderse menear,*
> *Con espadas, y los cuellos*
> *Ballestas de buen echar.*

Gringoire felt the tears filling his eyes. Yet her song was a breath of joy, as she sang like a bird, from pure serenity and lightness of heart.

The gypsy's song had troubled Gringoire's thoughts, but gently, as a swan ripples the water. He listened with a kind of rapture and forgetfulness of everything else. In several hours, this was the first interval during which he did not suffer.

The moment was brief.

The same female voice which had interrupted the gypsy's dance rang out again to interrupt her song.

"Will you be quiet, you cricket from hell?" It sounded from the same dark corner of the square.

The poor cricket did stop short. And Gringoire stopped his ears.

"Oh!" he screamed, "you cursed, jagged-toothed saw who come to break the lyre!"

The rest of the spectators murmured like him. "The devil take the old hag!" cried some of them. And the old invisible spoil-sport might have had reason to repent her attacks on the gypsy, had the attention of the crowd not been distracted by the procession of the Pope of Fools, which, having paraded through many streets and neighborhoods, was now, with all its torches and clamor, pouring into the Place de Grève.

This procession, which our readers saw leaving the Palace, had organized itself en route. It had recruited all the ruffians, all the idle thieves, all the unoccupied vagabonds of Paris, so that when it reached the Grève it presented a most disreputable aspect.

First came the Egyptians, led by the Duke of Egypt, followed by his counts on foot, holding his bridle and stirrup. Behind them, pell-mell, came Egyptian men and women, with screaming little children on their backs, all of them— duke, counts, and people—in rags and tinsel. Then came the kingdom of Argot; that is, all the thieves of France, arranged in groups according to their dignity; the lowest coming first. Thus they paraded four by four, with the different insignia proclaiming their degrees in this strange faculty. Most of them were crippled in one way or another; some limped, others lacked an arm. Their ranks included shoplifters, pilgrims, housebreakers, sham epileptics, goldbrickers, drunks, sham cripples, cardsharks, arsonists, hawkers, pickpockets, arch-thieves, master-thieves, dotards, and infirm derelicts—a list long enough to weary Homer himself. In the center of the conclave, surrounded by the arch-thieves and the master-thieves, you could barely make out the king of Argot, the Grand Coësre, squatting in a little wagon pulled by two massive dogs. After the kingdom of Argot came the empire of Galilee. Guillaume Rousseau, Emperor of the Galilean empire, marched majestically in his robe of purple stained with wine, preceded by mummers sham-fighting and dancing war dances. Surrounding this emperor were his mace-bearers, his satellites, and his clerks of finance. Lastly came the Basoche in black robes, with its maypoles, its music worthy of the Sabbath, and its large yellow wax candles. In the center of this mixed parade, the high officers of the brotherhood of fools bore upon their shoulders a litter laden with more candles than the shrine of Sainte-Geneviève at the time of the pestilence. High upon this litter, mitered, coped, resplendent, and carrying a crosier, rode the new Pope of Fools, the bellringer of Notre-Dame, Quasimodo the Hunchback.

Each section of this grotesque procession played its special music: the Egyptians, their balafos, and their African tambourines; the Argotiers, a most unmusical race, had only a viol, a bugle, and a Gothic rebec of the twelfth century; the empire of Galilee, only a little more advanced than the Argotiers, barely could be heard playing re, la, mi, on a rebec. But around the Pope of Fools was executed, in magnificent cacophony, all the musical richness of the age: treble rebecs, tenor rebecs, not to mention flutes and brass instruments. Alas! our readers will recollect that this was Gringoire's orchestra.

It is difficult to give an idea of how much pride and beatific satisfaction was registered on the usually sad and always hideous visage of Quasimodo as he rode in state from the Palace to the Place de Grève. It was the first moment of self-love he had ever enjoyed, indeed, that he had ever experienced. Until now he had known only humiliation, disdain for his condition, and disgust for his person. So, deaf as he was, he savored, like a true pope, the acclamation of those people whom he hated because he had felt himself hated by them. What did it matter if his subjects were a mob of fools, cripples, thieves, beggars! Still they were people and he was their king. He took seriously all the ironical applause, all the mock respect, to which, we hasten to add, there was mixed in the crowd a certain amount of very real fear. Though a hunchback, he was strong; though bowlegged, he was quick; though deaf, he was evil: three attributes that temper ridicule.

Furthermore, it is highly improbable that the new Pope of

Fools himself was fully conscious of the emotions he experienced or of those he inspired. The mind that dwelt in that defective body was necessarily somewhat incomplete and deaf. Also, what he felt at that moment was to him absolutely vague, indistinct, and confused. Only joy filled his heart; pride showed even in his poor bearing. Around that gloomy, unhappy countenance there was a halo of delight.

Therefore, it was not without surprise and dread that, all at once, at the moment when Quasimodo, in this state of half-intoxication, was being borne triumphantly past the Pillar House, a man was seen to dart from the crowd and, with an angry gesture, snatch from the hunchback's hands the crosier of gilt wood, the ensign of his pretended papacy.

This fellow, this rash person, was the same man with the bald head who, a moment ago, half-hidden by the crowd, had frightened the poor gypsy with his threatening words, so full of hatred. Now one could see that he wore a priest's robe. The moment he stepped from the crowd, Gringoire, who had taken no note of him till then, recognized him. "Well!" he cried, with amazement, "it's my master in Hermes, Dom Claude Frollo, the archdeacon! What the devil does he want with that one-eyed monster? He'll get himself eaten!"

Indeed a cry of terror rose from the mob. The formidable Quasimodo had leaped from the litter; women turned away their eyes so as not to see him tear the archdeacon to shreds.

He made one bound to the priest, squinted at him, and fell to his knees.

The priest snatched the tiara from Quasimodo's head, broke the fake crosier, and ripped the tinsel cope.

Quasimodo remained on his knees, with bowed head and joined hands.

Next, these two began a strange dialogue of signs and gesturing; for neither of them spoke a word. The priest, standing there, angry, threatening, imperious; Quasimodo, prostrated, humble, suppliant. Yet it is certain that Quasimodo could have crushed the priest with his thumb.

Directly, the archdeacon, roughly shaking Quasimodo's powerful shoulders, made a sign for him to get up and follow him.

Quasimodo rose.

Then the brotherhood of fools, their first stupor being over, wanted to defend their pope, so rudely dethroned. The Egyptians, the Argotiers, and all the Basoche came yelping around the priest.

Quasimodo stood between the crowd and the priest, clenching his huge fists. He looked at the assailants, gnashing his teeth like an angry tiger.

The priest resumed his somber gravity, made a sign to Quasimodo, and they walked away in silence. Quasimodo preceded him, scattering the crowd as they passed along.

When they had made their way through the multitude and had crossed the square, the mob of curious idlers wanted to follow them. Quasimodo then took up a position behind the archdeacon, but followed him backward, looking as though ready to attack. His monstrous, shaggy body on his awkward bowlegs, his tongue licking his ugly tusks, his growling like a wild beast impressed the crowd. His slightest gesture now caused a tremor of fear to ripple through the mob.

So he and the archdeacon passed into a dark and narrow street, where no one dared to follow, so effectually was its entrance barred by the mere image of Quasimodo, now seeming more beast than man.

"All this is marvelous," said Gringoire, "but where the devil am I to find supper?"

4

The Inconveniences of Following a Pretty Girl in the Streets at Night

Gringoire decided to follow the gypsy girl. He had seen her and her goat turn down the Rue de la Coutellerie.

"Why not?" he said to himself.

Gringoire, a practical philosopher familiar with the streets of Paris, had observed that nothing is more conducive to reverie than following a pretty woman without knowing where she is going. There is in this voluntary abdication of free will, in this submission of one's fantasy to another's, a mixture of fantastic independence and blind obedience, a certain intermediate between slavery and freedom, which appealed to Gringoire, whose mind was essentially mixed, indecisive, and complex, holding the middle between extremes, constantly suspended between all human propensities, and neutralizing one by the other. He compared himself with satisfaction to the tomb of Mohammed, attracted in contrary direction by two lodestones, and hesitating eternally between the top and the bottom, between the roof and the pavement, between the fall and the ascension, between the zenith and the nadir.

If Gringoire had lived in our day, how justly he would have kept to the middle, between the classic and the romantic!

But he was not primitive enough to live three hundred years, and that's a pity. His absence leaves a void which, today, is sorely recognized.

Moreover, there is nothing that better disposes a man to follow pedestrians through the streets (and especially female ones), which Gringoire readily did, than not knowing where to sleep.

Therefore, pensively, he walked along behind the girl, who was quickening her step, causing her cunning little goat to trot along too, as she saw the townspeople reaching home and the taverns closing, the only public places that had been open that day.

"After all," his thoughts ran, "she must have lodging somewhere; the gypsies are warm-hearted. Who knows? . . ."

And there was in the ellipsis which followed his mental reticence certain rather pleasing ideas.

Meanwhile, as he passed groups of belated burghers closing their doors, he caught scraps of their conversation which broke the chain of his pleasing hypotheses.

Now, it was two old men accosting each other.

"Master Thibault Fernicle, do you know it's cold?"

(Gringoire had known that ever since winter had begun.)

"Yes, yes, Master Boniface Disome! Are we going to have a winter like three years ago, in '80, when wood cost eight sols a load?"

"Bah! It was nothing, Master Thibault, compared to the winter of 1407 when there was frost from Saint-Martin's day to Candlemas, and the cold was so bitter that the pen of the registrar of the parliament froze at every third word, even in the Great Chamber. And that interrupted the recording of judgments, I can tell you!"

Farther on, there were two lady neighbors at their windows, holding candles that flickered in the fog:

"Has your husband told you of the accident, Mademoiselle La Boudraque?"

"No, what happened, Mademoiselle Turquant?"

"Master Gilles Godin's horse (Godin was a notary at the Châtelet) was startled by the Flemings and their procession, and knocked down Master Philippot Avrillot, a Celestine lay brother."

"In truth?"

"Yes, really."

"An ordinary horse too! That's rather too bad. If it had been a cavalry horse, what!"

And the windows were shut again. But Gringoire had lost completely the thread of his thoughts. Luckily he picked it up again quickly and pieced his ideas together, assisted by the gypsy and Djali, who still walked on in front of him. These two charming creatures, whose delicate figures, small feet, and pleasing manners he admired, while almost confusing them in his contemplation; regarding them both as young girls, interesting on account of their intelligence and their mutual affection, then, thinking them both goats because of their lightness, agility, and grace.

Meanwhile the streets were rapidly becoming darker and lonelier. Curfew had sounded long ago, and now it was only at long intervals that a person passed on the pavement or a light was to be seen in some window. Following the gypsy, Gringoire had become lost in that inextricable maze of alleys, courts, and dead-end streets which surround the ancient sepulcher of the Holy Innocents, and which resemble a skein of yarn entangled by a kitten. "Illogical streets, I say!" muttered Gringoire, lost in these thousand windings which always kept coming back to their beginnings, but through which the girl, without hesitating and ever increasing her pace, followed a route that seemed familiar to her. For his own part, he would not have had the remotest idea where he was, had he not observed, at a turn in the street, that octagonal mass known as the pillory of Les Halles, the perforated top of which traced its dark outline against a lighted window in the Rue Verdelet.

During the short time that the girl had been aware of his following her, she had several times turned around nervously. Once, too, she had stopped suddenly, had taken advantage of a ray of light that shone through the half-open door of a bakery to scrutinize him attentively from head to foot. Then, before she passed on, Gringoire saw her make that little pouting face which he had already remarked.

This same puckered pretty face gave Gringoire some food for thought. Thereon certainly was registered disdain and mockery. Consequently, he lowered his head, counting the paving stones, and followed the girl at a farther distance. Then, just after she turned into a street which took her for a moment out of his sight, he heard her give a piercing scream.

He quickened his steps.

The street was dark, except for a wick dipped in oil, which was flickering in an iron cage, at the base of a statue of the Virgin, near the corner of the street. This enabled Gringoire to discern the gypsy struggling in the arms of two men, who were trying to muffle her cries. The poor little goat, frightened, lowered its horns and bleated.

"Hither! Hither! gentlemen of the watch," cried Gringoire, as he advanced bravely. One of the men who was holding the girl turned toward him. It was the formidable Quasimodo. Gringoire did not flee, but neither did he advance.

Quasimodo came up to him, and, with a back-handed blow, sent him reeling four or five paces across the pavement. Immediately the hunchback disappeared in the darkness, carrying the young girl, who was folded over his arm like a silken scarf. His companion followed; and, bleating plaintively, the poor goat ran along.

"Murder! Murder!" screamed the unfortunate gypsy.

"Halt! you villains! Let that wench go!" thundered a cavalryman, who suddenly appeared from a neighboring cross street.

It was a captain of the archers with the king's ordnance, armed cap-a-pie, with his saber in his hand.

He snatched the gypsy from the arms of the amazed Quasimodo, laid her across his saddle, and just at the moment when the redoubtable hunchback, having recovered from his surprise, was rushing upon him to seize his prey a second time, fifteen or sixteen archers, who were following close upon their captain, arrived, brandishing their broadswords. This was a detachment making its night rounds, by order of Messire Robert d'Estouteville, keeper of the provosty of Paris.

Quasimodo was surrounded, seized, and bound. He bellowed, he foamed, he bit, and, had it been daylight, no doubt his visage alone, rendered yet more hideous by his rage, would have put to flight the detachment. But night had disarmed him of his most formidable weapon, his ugliness.

The gypsy sat up gracefully in the officer's saddle, placed both her hands on the young man's shoulders, and looked at him intently for a few seconds, as if charmed by his handsome face, and grateful for the timely rescue. Then, speaking first, and using her most dulcet tones, she said to him, "Monsieur le gendarme, what is your name?"

"Captain Phoebus de Châteaupers, at your service, my fair one!" said the officer, saluting.

"Thank you," said she.

And while Captain Phoebus was curling his mustache *à la bourguignonne,* she slid from the saddle like an arrow falling to the ground.

She fled, faster than a bolt of lightning.

"Nombril du Pape!" exclaimed the captain, while he supervised the tightening of Quasimodo's bonds. "I would rather have kept that wench!"

"Why, captain," said one of the gendarmes, "aren't you satisfied? The linnet is flown, but we've made sure of the bat."

5

Sequel of the Inconveniences

Gringoire, quite stunned by his fall, had remained stretched out on the pavement before the good Virgin at the corner of the street. By degrees he regained consciousness. At first, he remained floating in a kind of half-somnolent reverie, which was not altogether disagreeable, because the airy figures of the gypsy and the goat were coupled with the weight of Quasimodo's fist. This state, however, was of short duration. A sensation of something chill against his back shocked him into full consciousness. He thought, "Whence comes this cold?" He then perceived that he was lying deep in a gutter.

"Hang that humpbacked Cyclops!" he grumbled, as he tried to get up. But he was so stunned and bruised that he was forced to stay where he was. Having, however, his hands free, he held his nose and resigned himself to his situation.

"The mud of Paris," he thought (for he now believed fate had decided that the gutter was to be his lodging), "the mud of Paris is especially stinking. It must consist of large quantities of volatile and nitric salts. Such is the opinion of Master Nicolas Flamel and the alchemists."

The word alchemist suddenly reminded him of the Archdeacon Claude Frollo. He recalled the violent scene he had just witnessed—the gypsy struggling with two men, Quasimodo and his companion—then he vaguely remembered seeing the haughty, morose countenance of the archdeacon.

"How strange!" thought he. And upon this basis and with all these data he began to construct a fantastic edifice of hypotheses—a philosopher's house of cards. Then, suddenly, returning once more to reality, "By heavens, I'm freezing!" he cried.

This place was, in fact, becoming less and less tenable. Each drop of water in the gutter carried away more heat from the body of Gringoire, and the equilibrium between the temperature of his body and the temperature of the gutter water was beginning to make itself felt in an unpleasant manner.

All of a sudden he was annoyed in quite a different way. A group of children—little ragamuffin savages, called gamins, that have in all times roamed the streets of Paris, and who, when we were boys, threw stones at us as we were leaving school in the evening, because our trousers were not torn as theirs were—swarmed toward the intersection where Gringoire was lying. They laughed and shouted, in utter disregard for those in the block who might be sleeping. They were dragging after them some sort of shapeless bag; the noise of their wooden shoes alone would have been enough to arouse the dead. Gringoire, who was not quite dead yet, half raised himself.

"Allo! Hennequin Dandèche! Allo, Jehan Pincebourde!" they were crying at the top of their lungs. "Old Eustache Moubon, the ironmonger at the corner, just died. We've got his straw mattress; we're going to make a bonfire with it. Today's *Flamings'* day."

And with that they threw down the mattress right on top of Gringoire, whom they had not seen, while at the same time one of them took a handful of straw, and went to light it at the good Virgin's torch.

"O death of Christ!" muttered Gringoire, "am I now going to be too hot?"

Between fire and water, his plight was critical. He made a superhuman effort, such as a counterfeiter might make in trying to escape being boiled alive. He struggled up, and, pushing the mattress toward the urchins, staggered away.

"Holy Virgin!" cried the boys. "It's the ironmonger's ghost!" And they too scampered off.

The mattress carried the day. Bellefort, Father Le Juge, and Corrozet assure us that the next morning it was taken with great solemnity by the clergy of that part of town, and carried in pomp to the treasury of Saint Opportune's church, where, until the year 1789, the sacristan collected a tidy income from this great miracle worked by the statue of the Virgin at the corner of Rue Mauconseil, which, by its presence alone, on the memorable night between the sixth and seventh of January, 1482, had exorcised the deceased Eustache Moubon, who, to cheat the devil, had, when dying, slyly hidden his soul within his mattress.

6

The Broken Pitcher

After running for some time as fast as his legs would carry him, not knowing whither, after racing around many a corner, jumping over many a gutter, crossing many an alley, or turning into many a blind alley, while seeking flight and passage through all the meanderings of the old streets around Les Halles, exploring in his panic what the elegant Latin of the charters calls *tota via, cheminum, et viaria*,[1] our poet suddenly stopped, first of all because he was out of breath, then because a dilemma had suddenly arisen in his mind.

"It appears to me, Master Pierre Gringoire," said he to himself, putting his finger to his forehead, "that you're running about like a witless blockhead. Those little rogues are just as afraid of you as you are of them. It seems to me, I say, that you heard the clatter of their wooden shoes running away southward while you were running away northward.

"Now one of two things took place: either they ran away, and then the mattress, which they must have forgotten in their terror, is precisely that hospitable bed for which you have been hunting ever since morning, and which the Lady Virgin miraculously sent you as a reward for your having composed in her honor a morality play, accompanied with trumpets and mummeries; or the boys have not run away, and in that case they have set fire to the mattress, and that will be exactly the excellent fire that you need to cheer, warm, and dry you. In either case, warm fire or good bed, the mattress is a gift from heaven. The Blessed Virgin Mary that stands at the corner of the Rue Mauconseil, perhaps caused Eustache Moubon to die for that very purpose; and it is folly for you to run away at such speed, like a Picard from a Frenchman, leaving behind you the very thing you are seeking. You are stupid!"

Then he retraced his steps, and ferreted about to discover where he was. He sniffed the wind and listened. He tried to find his way back to the blessed mattress. But in vain. All he saw was row upon row of houses, blind alleys, a network of streets. At each corner he hesitated, incessantly doubting, and so became more thwarted and entangled in that labyrinth of dark streets than he would have been in the maze of the Hotel de Tournelles itself. At length he lost patience, and he solemnly swore: "Cursed be these intersections! The devil himself has made them after the image of his pitchfork!"

---

[1] "Every way, road, and passage."

This exclamation soothed him somewhat; moreover, a reddish reflection, which at that moment he saw at the end of a long narrow street, helped restore his morale. "God be praised," he said, "there it is—my burning mattress!" And comparing himself to the mariner who is wrecked in the night, he added piously: *"Salve, salve, maris stella!"*[2]

As to whether this fragment of a litany was directed to the Holy Virgin or to the mattress, we truly cannot venture an opinion.

When he had advanced only a few steps down this long, narrow alley, he found its paving ceased so that it became muddier and muddier. Now he observed something rather extraordinary; the street was not deserted. Here and there were to be seen some creatures crawling along in a certain vague, shapeless mass, which moved toward the light flickering at the end of the street. They reminded Gringoire of those heavy insects which drag themselves along at night, from one blade of grass to another, toward a shepherd's fire.

Nothing makes a man more venturesome than an empty stomach, so he continued walking on, and soon came up to one of those larvae which seemed to move itself along slower than the others. Looking more closely, Gringoire perceived that it was really a miserable creature with paralyzed legs, seated in a metal bowl and jumping along on his two hands, something like a mutilated field spider which has only two good legs. When he was about to pass this sort of spider with a human face, it addressed him in a lamentable voice: *"La buona mancia, signor! la buona mancia!"*[3]

"The devil take you and me, too, if I understand you!" And the poet passed on.

He came up to another one of these moving pieces. On examination, it turned out to be a cripple, who was both lame and one-armed and who moved by means of a complicated structure made of crutches and wooden legs which, in supporting him, made him look like a walking scaffold. Gringoire, who was fond of noble and classical similes, compared him in his mind to the living tripod of Vulcan.

This living tripod saluted him as he passed, by lifting his

[2] "Hail, hail, star of the sea."
[3] "Alms, sir! alms!"

hat on one of the crutches to the height of Gringoire's chin, like a shaving bowl. At the same time he shouted, *"Señor caballero, para comprar un pedaso de pan!"*[4]

"It seems," said Gringoire, "that this one speaks too; but it's a barbarous language, and he's luckier than I if he understands it."

Then striking his forehead with a sudden transition of thought, "That reminds me, what the devil did they mean this morning with their *Esmeralda?"*

He wanted to quicken his pace; but for the third time something blocked his way. This something, or rather this someone, was blind, a little blind man with a Jewish face and beard, who, waving a stick in the space about him, and being towed along by a big dog, whined in a nasal Hungarian accent, *"Facitote caritatem!"*[5]

"Good!" said Gringoire, "at last here's one who can speak a Christian language. I must have an almsgiving look that they should ask me for charity, considering the present emaciated state of my purse." Then, turning to the blind man, he said, "My dear friend, last week I sold my last shirt; that is, since you understand only the language of Cicero, *Vendidi hebdomade nuper transita meam ultimam chemisam."*[6]

After that, Gringoire turned his back to the blind man, and went his way. But the blind man quickened his pace too; and now also the cripple and the paralytic came up as fast as they could, with a great clatter of bowl and crutches on the pavement. Then all three, stumbling over each other at poor Gringoire's heels, began to sing out their songs to him:

"Caritatem!" sang the blind man.

"La buona mancia!" sang the paralytic.

And the cripple took up the chant, repeating, *"Un pedaso de pan!"*

Gringoire had to stop his ears. "O Tower of Babel!" he cried.

He began to run. The blind man ran. The cripple ran. The paralytic ran.

And then, as he proceeded farther down the street, more

[4] "Sir Knight, to buy a piece of bread."
[5] "Charity."
[6] "I sold my last shirt a week ago."

paralytics, cripples, and blind men swarmed around him. Also one-armed men, and one-eyed men, and lepers with their open sores. They emerged from the houses, from the little side streets, from the cellars—howling, bellowing, yelping—all hobbling along, making their way toward the light, and wallowing in the mire like so many snails after a rain.

Gringoire, frightened and still pursued by his three persecutors, not knowing well what was going to happen, walked on among the others. He bumped into lepers, stumbled over the paralytics, his feet entangled in that anthill of cripples, like the English captain who found himself beleaguered by a legion of crabs.

The idea occurred to him to try to go back. But it was too late. This whole legion had closed in behind him, and the three beggars were all clutching at him. He went on, therefore, urged simultaneously by that irresistible flood, by fear, and by a dizziness which made it all seem like some kind of a horrible dream.

At last he reached the end of the street. It opened on an immense square where a thousand scattered lights flickered in the thick fog of the night. Gringoire ran into this mist, hoping to escape by his own speed these three diseased specters who had leeched on to him.

"Onde vas, hombre!" [7] cried the cripple, throwing aside his crutches, and running after him with as good a pair of legs as ever measured a geometrical pace upon the pavements of Paris.

Meanwhile the paralytic, standing erect upon his really good feet, bonneted Gringoire with his heavy iron-sheathed bowl, and the blind man stared at him with his large flaming eyes.

"Where am I?" said the terrified poet.

"In the Court of Miracles," answered a fourth specter who had joined them.

"O my soul," rejoined Gringoire, "I see the blind who look and the crippled who run; but where is the Saviour?"

They all answered with a burst of demonic laughter.

The poor poet looked around him. Indeed, he was in that

[7] "Where are you going, man!"

terrible Court of Miracles, which no honest man had ever penetrated at such an hour; a magic circle where the officers of the Châtelet and the sergeants of the provosty who ventured there disappeared like crumbs; the city of thieves, a hideous wart on the face of Paris; a sewer from which there escaped every morning, and to which there returned every night to stagnate that stream of vice, poverty, and vagrancy that ever flows through the streets of capitals; a monstrous hive, to which there came every night all the bees of society with their evil spoils; a sham hospital, where the gypsy, the unfrocked monk, the discredited scholar, the good-for-nothings of every nation—Spaniards, Italians, Germans—of every religion—Jews, Christians, Mohammedans, idolaters— covered with painted sores, beggars in the daytime, transformed themselves at night into robbers; in short, an immense dressing room, where dressed and undressed at that time all the actors of this eternal comedy which robbery, prostitution, and murder enact on the pavements of Paris.

It was a vast square, irregular in shape and badly paved, as all the squares of Paris were then. Fires, around which swarmed strange groups, were blazing here and there. All was commotion, confusion, and shouting. One heard shrieks of laughter, the wailing of children, and the high-pitched voices of women. The hands and heads of this crowd, silhouetted against a luminous background, made a thousand fantastic gestures. Now and then, on the ground, where the light of the fires danced, mixed with large undefined shadows, passed a dog resembling a man, or a man resembling a dog. Racial characteristics seemed to be effaced in this city as in a pandemonium. Men, women, beasts, age, sex, health, sickness—everything seemed to be in common among these people; everything went together, mingled, confused, superimposed; each one took part in everything.

The faint and flickering light of the fires enabled Gringoire to distinguish, in spite of his predicament, all around this immense square, a hideous frame of old houses whose decayed, worm-eaten, and stooping fronts, each pierced by one or two lighted windows, seemed to him, in the dark, like enormous old women's heads, ranged in a circle, monstrous and crabbed, and winking upon the diabolical witchery.

It was to him a new world, incomprehensible, deformed, creeping, crawling, fantastic.

Gringoire, growing more and more frightened, held by the three beggars as if by three vises, deafened by a crowd of other faces that bleated and barked around him—the unfortunate Gringoire tried to regain his presence of mind and to recollect whether this was Saturday or not. But his efforts were vain; the thread of his memory and his thoughts was broken, and doubting everything—floating between what he saw and what he felt—he asked himself this insoluble question: "If I exist, can this be? If this be so, do I exist?"

At that moment, a distinct shout arose from the buzzing mob that surrounded him: "Let's take him to the king! Let's take him to the king!"

"Holy Virgin!" muttered Gringoire, "the king of this place can only be a goat!"

"To the king! To the king!" they all repeated.

They dragged him away, each trying to get his hooks upon him. But the three beggars kept their hold, and snatched him from the others, howling, "He is ours!"

The poet's doublet, already in a piteous condition, gave up the ghost in this struggle.

As he crossed this horrible square, his dizziness was dispelled. He had taken but a few steps when he sensed the reality of his plight, and he began to adjust to the atmosphere of the place.

In these first moments, there had risen from his poetic brain, or perhaps quite simply and prosaically, from his empty stomach, a fume, a vapor, so to speak, which, spreading itself between him and the objects around him, had permitted him to view them only in the incoherent mist of a nightmare, in that darkness of dreams which distorts every outline, and clusters objects together in disproportioned groups, dilating things into chimeras, and men into phantoms. Little by little this hallucination gave way to a less wild and less exaggerated state of mind. Reality was dawning upon him, striking his eyes and his feet, and demolishing piece by piece all the frightful poetic images by which at first he had thought himself surrounded. He could well perceive that he was walking not in the Styx, but in the mud; that he was being elbowed, not by demons, but by thieves;

that his soul was not in danger, but that indeed his life was (since he was without that precious conciliator which places itself so effectually between the robber and the honest man; namely, the purse). In short, on examining the orgy more closely and more calmly, he fell from the witches' Sabbath to the tavern.

The Court of Miracles was, in truth, just a tavern, but a tavern for brigands, as red with blood as with wine.

The sight which presented itself when his bedraggled escort at length deposited him at the end of its march, was not the kind to excite poetry in his soul, were it even poetry from hell. It was more than ever the prosaic and brutal reality of the tavern. If we were not writing of the fifteenth century, we would say that Gringoire had descended from Michelangelo to Callot.

A great fire was burning upon a large round flat stone; its blaze had heated red hot the legs of an iron trivet which was empty for the moment. Some worm-eaten tables were set here and there, without the least attention having been paid to symmetry or order. On these tables gleamed some tankards, brimming over with wine or beer, around which were grouped a number of bacchanalian faces, reddened by both the fire and the wine. There was one man with a jovial face and a huge pot-belly, who noisily embraced a heavy-set, fleshy trollop of the streets. Then there was a make-believe soldier, who whistled cheerfully while he unraveled the bandages from his pretended wound, and then flexed his sound and vigorous knee which had been bound up since morning by a thousand ligatures. Close by, there was a malingerer preparing with celandine sap and ox blood his sore leg, for the following day. Two tables farther on a shyster, in the authentic costume of a pilgrim, was spelling out and practicing a spiritual song, the Complaint of Sainte-Reine, complete with psalmody and nasal twang. Elsewhere, a young rogue was taking a lesson in epilepsy from an old hustler who was teaching him how to foam at the mouth by chewing a piece of soap. Beside them, a dropsical man was removing his swelling, while four or five women thieves were arguing at the same table over a child whom they had kidnaped in the course of the evening. All of these incidents, two centuries later, "appeared so ridiculous to the court," as

Sauval writes, "that they furnished pleasure for the king, in the overture to the royal ballet entitled 'Night,' which was divided into four parts and danced upon the stage of the Petit-Bourbon." "Never," adds a spectator of this performance in 1653, "were the sudden metamorphoses of the Court of Miracles more successfully performed. Benserade prepared us for them with some rather pleasant verses."

From every quarter loud, coarse laughter and obscene songs burst forth. Each did as he pleased, making his own remarks and swearing without regard for his neighbor. Wine jugs gurgled, and quarrels broke out as the cups clinked, and broken mugs led to the tearing of ragged clothing.

A large dog, sitting on his tail, was looking at the fire. Even some young children assisted at this orgy. The kidnaped child was howling. Another, a fat little fellow four years old, seated with his legs dangling from a bench that was too high for him, with his chin just above the table, said not a word; a third was gravely spreading over the table with his finger the melted tallow that oozed from a candle; and a fourth, a little scamp, squatting in the mud, was almost lost headfirst in a great big pot which he was scraping with a piece of tile, thus making sounds that would have made Stradivarius swoon.

A beggar sat on a barrel near the fire. This was the king on his throne.

The three who had laid hold of Gringoire brought him before this barrel, and for a minute the motley mob was silent, except for the urchin at the bottom of the great iron pot.

Gringoire was afraid to breathe or to lift his eyes.

"Hombre, quita tu sombrero,"[8] said one of the three who held him. And before he could understand what that meant, one of the others took his cap—a wretched cap, it is true, but still good for rainy or sunny days. Gringoire heaved a sigh.

Meanwhile the king, from the top of his throne, spoke: "What is this varlet?"

Gringoire trembled. This voice, though menacing, reminded him of another voice which that very morning had given the first blow to his mystery play by whining out in the middle of the auditory:

[8] "Man, take off your hat."

"Charity, I beg you!"

He raised his head. Indeed, it was Clopin Trouillefou. Clopin Trouillefou, arrayed in his regal insignia, wore not a rag more nor a rag less. His sore on the arm had disappeared. He held in his hand one of those whips with lashes of white leather which were used at that time by the vergers to drive back the crowd, and were called *boullayes*. He had on his head a sort of bonnet formed into a circle and closed at the top; but it was difficult to distinguish whether it was a child's cap or a king's crown, so much alike are they.

Gringoire, however, without knowing why, had regained some hope on recognizing the king of the Court of Miracles to be his cursed beggar of the Great Hall.

"Master," he stammered . . . "Monseigneur . . . Sire . . . How should I address you?" he said at last, having arrived at the culminating point of a crescendo, and not knowing how to go higher or how to descend.

"Monseigneur, your majesty, or comrade, call me what you like. But be quick. What do you have to say in your defense?"

"In my defense!" thought Gringoire. "I don't like this." He resumed, stammering, "I am he who this morning . . ."

"By the devil's claws!" interrupted Clopin. "Your name, rogue, and nothing more. Listen. You are before three mighty sovereigns: me, Clopin Trouillefou, King of Thunes, successor to the Grand Coësre, supreme ruler of the kingdom of Argot; Mathias Hungadi Spicali, Duke of Egypt and Bohemia, that sallow old fellow you see there with the turban; Guillaume Rousseau, Emperor of Galilee, that fat fellow who isn't listening to us, the one who's hugging that wench. We are your judges. You entered the kingdom of Argot without being an Argotier, you have violated the privileges of our city. You must be punished, unless you are a *capon*, a *franc-mitou*, or a *rifodé*, that is, in the lingo of honest people, a thief, a beggar, or a vagabond. Are you any of those? Justify yourself. What are your qualifications?"

"Alas!" said Gringoire, "I have not that honor. I am the author . . ."

"That's enough," interrupted Trouillefou without letting him finish. "You will be hanged. A very simple matter, messieurs the honest burghers! Just as you treat our people

among you, so we treat yours among us. The law which you
mete out to the Truands, the Truands mete out to you. If it
is bad, that's your fault. It is quite proper that from time to
time an honest man should be seen grinning through the
hemp collar; that makes the business honorable. Come now,
friend, divide your rags cheerfully among these ladies. I'm
going to hang you for the amusement of the Truands, and
you will give them your purse for a drink or two. If you
have any mummery to do, there is down there, in that corner, a very good stone God the Father that we robbed from
Saint-Pierre-aux-Boeufs. You have four minutes to throw
your soul upon His mercy."

This was a terrible announcement.

"Upon my soul! Well said! Clopin Trouillefou preaches
like Holy Father the Pope!" cried the Emperor of Galilee,
breaking his mug to prop up his table.

"My lords the emperors and kings," said Gringoire calmly
(for somehow or other his courage returned to him and he
spoke quite firmly), "you do not understand. My name is
Pierre Gringoire. I am the poet whose morality play was performed this morning in the Great Hall of the Palace."

"Ah! it's you, master, is it?" said Clopin. "I was there myself, by God! Well, comrade, because you bored us to death
this morning, is there any reason why you shouldn't be
hanged tonight?"

"I'll have trouble getting out of this," thought Gringoire.
However, he made another attempt.

"I don't see why," he began, "poets are not classed as
Truands. Aesop was a vagabond, Homer was a beggar, Mercury was a thief . . ."

Clopin interrupted him, "I think you are trying to bam-
boozle us with your gibberish. Pardieu! Be hanged! and
make no more ado about it."

"Pardon me, Monseigneur the King of Thunes," replied
Gringoire, disputing the ground inch by inch, "it's worth
your while . . . One minute, please! . . . Listen to me . . .
you'll not condemn me without hearing me . . ."

His pleading voice, indeed, was drowned out by the roar
all around him. The little boy was scraping the kettle with
more vigor than ever; and to climax it all, an old woman had
just placed on the red-hot trivet a frying pan full of fat which

crackled over the fire with a noise like the shouts of a band of children who run after a mask at carnival time.

Meanwhile Clopin Trouillefou appeared to be conferring for a moment with the Duke of Egypt and with the Emperor of Galilee, who was completely drunk. Then he yelled sharply, "Silence!" and as the kettle and the frying pan paid no attention to him, but continued their duet, he jumped down from his barrel, gave the kettle a kick, which rolled it and the child ten feet off; gave the frying pan a kick, which upset all the fat into the fire; and then solemnly mounted his throne, caring neither for the smothered cries of the child nor for the grumbling of the old lady whose supper was vanishing into beautiful white 'flames.

Trouillefou made a sign, and the duke and the emperor, and the high officials of the kingdom of Argot came and arranged themselves around him in the form of a horseshoe, of which Gringoire, who was still held fast by his captors, occupied the center. It was a semicircle of rags, tatters, and tinsel, of pitchforks and hatchets, of wobbly legs and fleshy bare arms, of dirty, haggard, and bloated faces. In the middle of this round table of beggary, Clopin Trouillefou, as the doge of this senate, as the king of this peerage, as the pope of this conclave, dominated, in the first place by the height of his barrel; secondly, by a certain haughty, fierce, and formidable air which made his eyes flash and offset in his savage profile the bestial type of the Truand race; he seemed a wild boar among swine.

"Listen," he said to Gringoire, stroking his shapeless chin with his horny hand, "I don't see why you should not be hanged. True, you seem to dislike it, but that is natural. The bourgeois aren't used to it. They think it is all very vulgar. After all, we don't wish you any harm. For the moment, I'd say there's one way of getting out of this mess. Do you want to be one of us?"

You can imagine the effect this proposal made upon Gringoire, who had seen life just about to leave him, and who had felt his grip upon it loosening. He eagerly grasped this proposal.

"Yes, certainly, I do," he said.

"Do you consent," asked Clopin, "to enlist yourself among the purse-snatchers?"

"Among the purse-snatchers—exactly so," replied Gringoire.

"Do you acknowledge yourself a member of the *franche-bourgeoisie?*" continued the King of Thunes.

"Of the *franche-bourgeoisie.*"

"A subject of the kingdom of Argot?"

"Of the kingdom of Argot."

"Truand?"

"Truand."

"With all your soul?"

"With all my soul."

"Take note," said the king, "you will be hanged anyway."

"The devil!" exclaimed our poet.

"Only," continued Clopin, unperturbed, "you'll be hanged later, with more ceremony, at the expense of the good city of Paris, upon a beautiful stone gibbet, and by honest men, and that will be a consolation to you."

"As you say," answered Gringoire.

"There are other advantages. Being a free burgher, you will not have to pay levies on pavements, or lamps, or for the poor, to which the honest burghers of Paris are liable."

"So be it," said the poet. "I agree. I am a Truand, an Argotier, a free burgher, whatever you wish; indeed, I was all these before, Monsieur the King of Thunes, for I am a philosopher, and, as you know, *Et omnia in philosophia, omnes in philosopho continentur.*"[9]

The King of Thunes knit his brows.

"What do you take me for, friend? What kind of Hungarian Jewish gibberish are you speaking now? I don't know any Hebrew. You don't have to be a Jew to be a thief. I don't even rob any more—I'm above that. I kill. A cutthroat, yes, but a cutpurse, no."

Gringoire tried to slip in an excuse between these brief notations, flung with mounting vehemence at him by the angry king. "I beg your pardon, monseigneur. It is not Hebrew, but Latin."

"I tell you," retorted Clopin furiously, "that I am not a Jew, and I'll have you hung, you Jewish pig, as well as that little peddler from Judea beside you, and whom I hope to

[9] "And philosophy contains all things, the philosopher all men."

see, one of these days, nailed to a counter, like the bad piece of coin he is!"

As he spoke, he pointed to a little Hungarian Jew with a long beard who had accosted Gringoire with his *Facitote caritatem!* and who, not understanding the king's language, was surprised at the ill-humor which seemed to be vented upon him.

At length Monseigneur Clopin subsided.

"Knave," he said to our poet, "then you are willing to become a Truand?"

"Undoubtedly," answered Gringoire.

"It is not enough just to will to be so," said Clopin impatiently. "Good intentions don't put one more onion into the soup; they only get you to heaven. But Paradise and Argot are two different places. To be admitted into the kingdom of Argot you must prove that you are good for something, and to do that you must pick a pocket."

"I can do anything you want me to," said Gringoire.

Clopin gave a sign, whereupon several Argotiers left the circle and returned shortly. They brought two poles. Each had at the end a flat piece of wood, which made it stand firmly on the ground. To the upper extremities of these posts they fixed a crossbeam, and the whole formed a very neat portable gallows, which Gringoire had the pleasure to see erected before him in the twinkling of an eye. There was nothing missing, not even the rope which gracefully swung from the crossbeam.

"What do they want with that now?" thought Gringoire to himself, beginning to feel uneasy. But a tinkling of little bells which he heard at that moment put an end to his anxiety. It was a stuffed dummy which the Truands were hanging by the neck to the rope, a sort of scarecrow, dressed in red, and so completely covered with little bells that there would have been enough to harness thirty Castilian donkeys. For a time these thousands of tiny bells jingled by the swinging of the rope, then their sound died away gradually. Finally they became silent when the figure hung motionless by that law of the pendulum which has superseded the use of the water clock and the hourglass.

Then Clopin, pointing to an old rickety stool placed underneath the dummy, said to Gringoire, "Get up on that!"

"Zounds!" protested Gringoire, "I'll break my neck! Your stool wobbles like one of Martial's distichs, one leg is hexameter, and one pentameter."

"Get up!" insisted Clopin. Gringoire got up on the stool, and succeeded, not without some swinging of his head and arms, in recovering his center of gravity.

"Now," continued the King of Thunes, "cross your right leg over your left, and stand on the toes of your left foot."

"Monseigneur," said Gringoire, "then you are determined that I break some of my limbs?"

Clopin shook his head. "Listen, friend, you talk too much. Briefly, this is what you have to do; stand on tiptoe as I told you, and you'll be able to reach the dummy's pocket; put your hand into it and take out the purse that's in it. If you do that without jingling the bells, 'tis well, you will be a Truand. We shall then have nothing more to do but to beat you for a week."

"*Ventre-Dieu!* I shall have to be careful," said Gringoire. "And suppose I make the bells jingle?"

"Then you'll be hanged! Do you understand?"

"No, I don't understand at all," answered Gringoire.

"Listen to me once more. You're to put your hand into the dummy's pocket and take out the purse. If but one bell tinkles, you will be hanged. Understand?"

"Well," said Gringoire, "I understand that. And then?"

"If you manage to lift the purse without ringing the bells, you're a Truand, and will be thrashed every day for a week. Now, you no doubt understand?"

"No, monseigneur, I don't understand. Where is my advantage? To be hanged in one case, or beaten in the other!"

"But you will be a Truand," rejoined Clopin. "To be a Truand! Is that nothing? It is for your own benefit that we shall beat you, to harden you against blows."

"Oh, thank you," replied the poet.

"Let's go, hurry up!" said the king, stamping his foot on the barrel, making it ring. "Pick the dummy's pocket, and be done with it. I warn you for the last time, if I hear one bell, you will swing in the dummy's stead."

The whole band of Argotiers applauded Clopin's words, and ranged themselves around the gallows, laughing so pitilessly that Gringoire saw that he was amusing them so much that he might expect the worst from them. The only hope he had left was the faint chance of succeeding in this delicate test imposed upon him. He decided to risk it, but not without first addressing a fervent prayer to the dummy whom he was going to rob and whose heart he could more easily soften than those of these Truands. The myriad of bells with their little brass tongues seemed to him like so many asps with mouths gaping, ready to hiss and bite.

"Oh!" he whispered to himself, "can it be that my life depends upon the least tintinnabulation of the smallest of those bells? Oh!" he added with his hands joined reverently, "bells, jingle not, tinkle not, I pray you!"

He made one more try with Trouillefou.

"And if there comes a gust of wind?" he asked.

"You will be hanged," answered the other without the slightest hesitation.

Realizing that there was no respite, surcease, or subterfuge possible, he bravely set about the task. He crossed his right leg over his left, stood up on his left foot, and stretched out his arm. But just when he touched the dummy, his body, which was now supported only by one foot, swayed on the three-legged stool; he instinctively grabbed for the dummy, lost his balance, and fell clumsily to the ground, quite deafened by the fatal jangling of the dummy's thousand bells, as, yielding to the impulsion of his hand, it at first spun around, then swung majestically between the two poles.

"Damnation!" he cried as he fell to the ground; and he lay there with his face down as if dead.

However, he heard the awful chiming above him, mixed with the diabolical laughter of the Truands and the voice of Trouillefou, saying, "Pick the fellow up and hang him right away."

He stood up. They had already taken the dummy down to make room for him.

The Argotiers made him get up on the stool again. Clopin came up to him, passed the rope around his neck, and, slapping him on the shoulder, said, "Goodby, friend, you cannot escape now, even if you were the Pope himself!"

The word *mercy* died on Gringoire's lips; he glanced around, but there was no hope. They were all laughing.

"Bellevigne de l'Etoile," said the King of Thunes to an

enormous Truand who stepped forth from the ranks, "climb up on the crossbeam."

Bellevigne de l'Etoile shinnied nimbly up to the crossbeam, and an instant later Gringoire, looking up, terrified, saw him squatting just above his head.

"Now," continued Clopin Trouillefou, "as soon as I clap my hands, Andry le Rouge, with your knee knock the stool from under him; you, François Chante-Prune, hang on to the knave's legs; and you, Bellevigne, jump on his shoulders; and all three at the same time, do you hear?"

Gringoire shuddered.

"Are you ready?" said Clopin Trouillefou to the three Argotiers, who were ready and anxious to fall on Gringoire like three spiders on a fly. The poor sufferer had a moment of horrible suspense, while Clopin quietly pushed into the fire with the toe of his shoe some twigs which the flame had not reached. "Are you ready?" he repeated, holding his hands ready to clap. One more second and it would have been all over.

But he stopped, as if something had suddenly occurred to him. "One moment!" he said. "I forgot something . . . It is customary not to hang a man unless we ask if there is a woman in the crowd who wants him. Comrade, this is your last chance. You must wed either a wench or the rope."

This gypsy law, ridiculous as it may appear to the reader, is to be found set down in detail in old English law. Consult *Burington's Observations.*

Gringoire gave a sigh of relief. It was the second time within a half hour that he had come alive again. He dared not rely too much upon this luck.

"Holà!" shouted Clopin, climbing again on his barrel. "Holà! ye women, ye females, is there any among you, from the witch to her cat, any wench, who wants this varlet? Holà! Colette la Charonne! Elisabeth Trouvain! Simone Jodoudyne! Marie Piédebou! Thonne la Longue! Bérarde Fanouel! Michelle Genaille! Claude Ronge-Oreille! Mathurine Girorou! Holà! Isabeau la Thierrye! Come and look! A man for nothing! Who wants him?"

Gringoire, in this awful predicament, was, assuredly, not very tempting. The Truandesses showed no great enthusiasm for the proposition. The poor unfortunate Gringoire heard them answer, "No! No! hang him! We'll all enjoy it!"

Three of them, however, did step forward to look him over. The first was a large, square-faced girl. She examined closely the philosopher's ragged doublet. His coat was worn and more full of holes than a chestnut roaster. The girl made a face. "Old rags!" she mumbled, and then, addressing Gringoire, "Let's see your cope!"

"I lost it," said Gringoire.

"Your hat?"

"They took it from me."

"Your shoes?"

"They are nearly worn out."

"Your purse?"

"Alas!" stammered Gringoire, "I don't have one denier parisis."

"Let yourself be hanged, and be thankful," replied the Truandess, walking away.

The second woman, old, dark, and wrinkled, so hideous and ugly that she was even conspicuous in the Court of Miracles, walked around Gringoire. He almost trembled lest she should want him. But she muttered, "He's too skinny," and walked away.

The third was a young girl, rosy-cheeked, not too ugly. "Save me!" whispered the poor devil. She looked at him for a moment with an air of pity, then lowered her eyes, fumbled with her skirt, and stood undecided. He watched her every movement; it was his last hope. "No," she said finally. "No, Guillaume Longuejoue would beat me." And she went back into the crowd.

"Comrade," said Clopin, "your luck is bad."

Then, standing up on his barrel, "Doesn't anybody want him?" he cried, mimicking the tone of an auctioneer, to everybody's amusement. "Anyone? . . . Going once . . . going twice . . . thrice!" Then, turning toward the gallows, with a nod of the head, he yelled, "Gone!"

Bellevigne de l'Etoile, Andry le Rouge, and François Chante-Prune again came over to Gringoire.

At that moment, a voice was heard among the Argotiers: "La Esmeralda! La Esmeralda!"

Gringoire shuddered, but turned in the direction of the

shouting. The crowd opened, and made way for a fair and radiant figure. It was the gypsy.

"La Esmeralda!" said Gringoire. Even in his travail, he was amazed by the suddenness with which that magic word linked together all the recollections of the day.

The beauty and charm of this extraordinary creature seemed to move even the Court of Miracles. Argotiers, male and female, gave way gently to let her pass, and their rough faces softened at her look.

She approached the sufferer with a light, graceful step. Her goat, the pretty Djali, followed her. Gringoire felt more dead than alive. She gazed at him in silence for a minute.

"You're going to hang that man?" she asked Clopin gravely.

"Yes, sister," answered the King of Thunes, "unless you will take him for your husband."

Again she showed her characteristic pout.

"I'll take him," she said.

Gringoire was now convinced that he must have been in a dream since morning, and that this was but a continuation. In fact, the turn of events, though gratifying, was an extreme one.

They untied the noose, and let the poet step down from the stool. So emotionally distraught was he that he had to sit for a moment.

The Duke of Egypt, without uttering a word, brought forth a clay pitcher. The gypsy presented it to Gringoire. "Throw it to the ground," she said.

The pitcher broke into four pieces.

"Brother," then said the Duke of Egypt, laying his hands upon their foreheads, "she is your wife; sister, he is your husband—for four years. Now, go!"

7

A Wedding Night

In a few minutes our poet found himself in a little room with a Gothic vaulted ceiling. It was very cozy and warm. Gringoire seated himself at a table which seemed quite ready to receive a few articles from a cupboard suspended nearby. A tête-à-tête with a pretty girl and a good bed were in prospect. The adventure smacked of witchcraft. He began seriously to think himself a character from one of the fairy tales. So, from time to time, he would glance around to see whether the fiery chariot drawn by two winged griffins, which alone could have transported him so rapidly from Tartarus to Paradise, was still there. Now and then, too, he fixed his eyes steadfastly on the holes in his doublet, in order to hold on to reality, so that the earth might not slip away from him altogether. His reason, tossed about by imagination, had only this thread to cling to.

The girl seemed to pay no attention to him, as she moved about, picking up one article, then another, talking to her goat, and making a face now and then. At length she came and sat down near the table. Now Gringoire could study her unhurriedly.

You have been a child, reader, and perhaps luckily you are still one. It is quite certain that more than once (and for my own part I can say that I have spent whole days, the best-spent days of my life) you have followed from bush to bush, beside some babbling brook, one sunshiny day, some pretty dragonfly, greenish blue, darting this way and that, and kissing the ends of many a branch. Surely you recall with what loving curiosity your thoughts and your eyes were fixed upon that little darting, softly humming insect with its purple and azure wings, between which floated a form so slender that your eyes could barely see it, veiled, as it was, by the very rapidity of its flight. The aerial being, confusedly perceptible through the movement of its wings, seemed to you chimerical, imaginary, impossible to touch, impossible to perceive. But when, at last, the dragonfly alighted on the tip of some reed, and you could examine it, holding your breath all the while, the transparent gauzy wings, the long enameled body, the two crystal eyes, what wonder did you not experience, and what fear lest this form should take flight again into the shadows, or into the air! Recall these impressions, and you will readily understand the feelings of Gringoire as he contemplated, in her visible and palpable form, this Esmeralda, of whom, until then, he had caught but a glimpse during her whirling dance, through her song, in the midst of a crowd.

More and more he became immersed in his reveries. "This then," he said to himself, as his eyes scanned her figure, "is Esmeralda—a heavenly creature, a street dancer, so much and yet so little! It was she who gave the finishing blow to my mystery this morning; she it is who saves my life tonight. My evil genius! My good angel! A pretty girl, upon my word! And who must love me madly, to have taken me like this. Which reminds me," he said, suddenly getting up from his seat, with that feeling of reality which formed the substance of his character and his philosophy, "I don't know exactly how all this has happened, but I'm her husband."

With this idea in his head and in his eyes, he approached the young girl in so masterful yet so gallant a fashion that she drew back.

"What do you want with me?" she said.

"How can you ask me such a question, my adorable Esmeralda?" answered Gringoire with such an impassioned tone that he was himself surprised to hear it.

The gypsy opened her large eyes. "I don't know what you mean."

"What!" returned Gringoire, becoming more and more heated, and thinking that, after all, it was only a virtue of the Court of Miracles that he had to deal with. "Am I not yours, my kind friend? Are you not mine?"

And, very gently, he put his arms around her.

Her blouse slipped through his hands like the skin of an eel. She bounded from one end of the room to the other, stooped, and stood straight again with a small poniard in her hand, before Gringoire had time even to observe whence this weapon came. She looked angry and proud, her lips were swollen, her nostrils distended, her cheeks fiery red, and her eyes flashing. At the same time, the little white goat jumped between her and Gringoire, presenting a battle front to him, lowering her two gilded but very sharp horns. All this happened in the twinkling of an eye.

She had turned into a wasp that was ready to sting.

Our philosopher stood there confused, looking stupidly first at the goat, then at Esmeralda.

"Holy Virgin!" he exclaimed at last, as soon as his surprise allowed him to speak, "what a pair of tigers!"

Then the gypsy broke silence. "You must be a very impudent fellow!"

"I beg your pardon, mademoiselle," said Gringoire with a smile. "But why did you take me for your husband?"

"Was I to let you be hanged?"

"So," rejoined the poet, a little disappointed in his amorous hopes, "you had no other intention in marrying me but to save me from the gallows?"

"Should I have had any other reason?"

Gringoire bit his lip.

"Well," he said, "I am not so triumphant in love as I imagined. But then, what was the use of breaking that poor pitcher?"

Meanwhile, Esmeralda's poniard and the goat's horns were still poised defensively.

"Mademoiselle Esmeralda," pursued the poet, "let us make a truce. As I am not a registering clerk at the Châtelet, I shall not quibble with you for carrying a dagger in Paris, against the ordinance and prohibitions of Monsieur the Provost. Certainly you must know that Noël Lescripvain was condemned a week ago to pay a fine of ten sous parisis for carrying a little sword. But that's none of my business; I'll come to the point. I swear to you, by all my hopes of Paradise, that I shall not approach you without your desire and permission. But, pray, give me some supper."

In truth, Gringoire, like Monsieur Depréaux, was "not the lover type." He was not of that chivalrous and swashbuckling class who take young maidens by assault. In love, as in every affair, he was temporizing, and preferred a middle course. A good supper, with a friendly tête-à-tête, seemed to him, especially when he was hungry, to be a very good interlude between the prologue and the finale of an amorous adventure.

The gypsy did not answer. She just puckered her lips disdainfully, raised her head like a bird, then burst out laughing, and the little dagger disappeared as it had come forth, without Gringoire's being able to see where the bee hid its sting.

The next minute, there was on the table a loaf of rye

bread, a slice of bacon, some wrinkled apples, and a jug of beer. Gringoire began to eat ravenously. To hear the furious clanking of his iron fork on his earthenware plate, you would have thought all his love had turned to appetite.

The girl, seated before him, watched him in silence; visibly preoccupied with some other thought, at which she smiled from time to time, while her delicate hand stroked the intelligent head of the goat lying quietly between her knees.

A yellow wax candle lighted this scene of voracity and reflection.

And, now, the first rumblings of his stomach being appeased, Gringoire felt somewhat falsely ashamed when he saw that there was only an apple left. "Aren't you eating, Mademoiselle Esmeralda?"

She shook her head negatively, and stared pensively at the vaulted ceiling of the room.

"What the devil is she thinking about?" thought Gringoire, following with his eyes her upward gaze. "It can't be that grinning dwarf's face sculptured on the cornerstone that absorbs her attention. What the devil! I can certainly withstand that comparison."

He raised his voice: "Mademoiselle!"

She seemed not to hear him.

He spoke louder, "Mademoiselle Esmeralda!"

But in vain. The girl's mind was elsewhere and Gringoire's voice was unable to bring it back. Luckily the goat interfered and gently began to tug her mistress' sleeve.

"What is it, Djali?" said the gypsy sharply, as if wakened suddenly from a dream.

"She's hungry," said Gringoire, pleased with the opportunity to begin a conversation.

Esmeralda began to make crumbs of some bread, which Djali ate gracefully from the palm of her hand.

Gringoire allowed the gypsy no time to resume her dreaming. He ventured a delicate question:

"You won't have me, then, for your husband?"

The girl looked at him fixedly and said, "No."

"For your friend?" asked the poet.

Again she stared at him, and, after a moment's hesitation, said, "Perhaps."

This *perhaps,* so dear to philosophers, encouraged Gringoire.

"Do you know what friendship is?" he asked.

"Yes," she answered. "It is like being brother and sister—two souls meeting without mingling, like two fingers of the same hand."

"And love?" continued the poet.

"Oh, love!" she said, and her voice trembled, and her eyes beamed. "That is to be two, and yet one. A man and a woman joined, as into an angel; that is heaven!"

The street dancer, as she spoke these words, radiated a beauty which singularly touched Gringoire, and seemed to him to be in perfect harmony with the almost Oriental intensity of her words. Her rosy and soft lips were half smiling. Her clear, calm brow, wrinkled now and then by her thoughts, seemed like a mirror clouded by a breath, and between her long, dark, drooping lashes, there emanated a kind of ineffable light which gave to her profile that serenity which Raphael later found at the mystic point of intersection of virginity, maternity, and divinity.

Gringoire nevertheless continued, "What must a man be then to please you?"

"He must be a man."

"And what am I?"

"A man has a helmet on his head, a sword in his hand, and spurs of gold at his heels."

"Good!" said Gringoire, "the horse makes the man. Do you love anyone?"

"As a lover?"

"Yes, as a lover."

She remained pensive for a moment. Then, with a fleeting, inexplicable expression, she answered, "I shall know that soon."

"Why not tonight?" asked the poet tenderly. "Why not me?"

She looked at him gravely.

"I can love only a man who knows how to protect me."

Gringoire blushed, but accepted the remark as being directed at him. It was evident that the girl was alluding to the little aid he had given her in the critical situation in which she had found herself a few hours before. This incident, temporarily erased by his other adventures of the evening, he now remembered. He struck his forehead. "By the way, mademoiselle. I should have mentioned that first. Pardon my mad abstraction. How did you manage to escape Quasimodo's clutches?"

The question made the gypsy shudder.

"Oh that horrible hunchback!" said she, hiding her face in her hands and trembling all over.

"I should say, horrible!" remarked Gringoire, who nevertheless insisted. "But how did you get away from him?"

Esmeralda smiled, sighed, but remained silent.

"Do you know why he followed you?" asked Gringoire, trying to broach the subject in another way.

"I don't know," she answered. And she added brusquely, "But you were following me too. Why were you following me?"

"Really," Gringoire answered. "I don't know."

Neither spoke. Gringoire was digging into the table with his knife. The girl was smiling and seemed to be gazing at something through the wall. Suddenly she began to sing in a voice hardly audible:

> *Quando las pintadas aves*
> *Mudas están, y la tierra* ...[1]

She stopped suddenly, and began to pat Djali.

"You have a pretty animal there," said Gringoire.

"She's my sister," she answered.

"Why do they call you La Esmeralda?" asked the poet.

"I don't know."

"But why?"

She took from her bosom a small oblong bag, suspended from her neck on a chain of berry beads. The bag exuded a strong scent of camphor. It was covered with green silk, and had in the center a large green glass bead like an emerald.

"Perhaps this is why," she answered.

Gringoire wanted to touch the bag, but she drew back.

"Don't touch it. It's a charm. You would break the charm, or the charm would destroy you."

[1] "When the colored birds are still, and the earth ..."

The poet's curiosity was aroused.

"Who gave it to you?"

She put her finger to her lip and hid the amulet again in her bosom. He ventured more questions, but she refused to answer.

"What is the meaning of that word: La Esmeralda?"

"I don't know."

"What language is it?"

"I think it's Egyptian."

"I suspected as much," said Gringoire. "Aren't you French?"

"I don't know."

"Where are your parents?"

She began to sing an old ditty.

> My father is a bird;
> My mother is his mate;
> Over the water I sail without boat.
> Over the water I sail without boat.
> My mother is a bird;
> My father is her mate.

"That's very sweet," remarked Gringoire. "How old were you when you came to France?"

"Very young."

"And to Paris?"

"Last year. When we were entering by the Papal Gate, I saw a red linnet fly into the air. It was the end of August, and I said, 'Winter will be harsh.' "

"It has been," said Gringoire, delighted with the beginning of this conversation. "I have done nothing but blow on my fingers. So you are a prophet?"

Again her answers became laconic.

"No."

"This man whom you call the Duke of Egypt, is he the chief of your tribe?"

"Yes."

"It was, after all, he who married us," observed the poet shyly.

She made her usual pretty face. "I don't even know your name."

"My name? If you want to know, it is Pierre Gringoire."
"I know a finer one," she said.
"You are naughty!" bantered the poet. "Never mind, you
won't make me cross. Who knows, perhaps you will grow to
love me when you know me better. Since you have told me
your story so simply, I feel I must tell you a little about myself. You already know my name is Pierre Gringoire. My father was a notary in Gonesse. Twenty years ago he was
hanged by the Burgundians, and my mother was massacred
by the Picards, during the siege of Paris. When I was six
years old, therefore, I was an orphan, who had nothing but
the pavements of Paris for soles of his shoes. I do not know
how I spent the interval between six and sixteen. A fruit
vender used to give me a plum here, and a baker used to
throw me a crust there. At night the gendarmerie would pick
me up and put me in prison, and there I would find a bundle
of straw for my bed. All that didn't stop me from growing
tall and lean, as you see. In winter I warmed myself in the
sun and under the porch of the Hotel de Sens, and I thought
it very ridiculous that the bonfires for the Feast of Saint-Jean
should be reserved for the dog days. At sixteen I wanted to
choose a profession. I tried everything. I became a soldier,
but I wasn't brave enough. I became a monk, but I wasn't
holy enough; besides, I wasn't a hardy drinker. In despair, I
became an apprentice in the carpenters' guild; but for that I
wasn't strong enough. I had wanted most to be a schoolmaster. True, I didn't know how to read, but that's no obstacle.
I perceived, at the end of a certain time, that I was, for one
reason or another, fit for nothing. So I decided to become a
poet and rhymester. It's a profession one can always take up,
if one's a vagabond; and it's better than stealing, as I was
advised to do by some young brigands of my acquaintance.
Fortunately, one fine day I met Dom Claude Frollo, the reverend archdeacon of Notre-Dame. He took an interest in me,
and I owe it to him that today I am a true man of letters,
knowing Latin, from Cicero's *Offices* to the *Mortuology* of
the Celestine fathers, and not completely ignorant either in
scholastic philosophy or poetics, or rhyming, or even in hermetics, that science of sciences. It is I who wrote the mystery play performed today, with great triumph, before huge
crowds of people, all in the Great Hall of the Palace. I have

also written a book six hundred pages long on the prodigious comet of 1465, about which one man went mad. But I have had other successes too. Being something of an artillery man, I worked upon that great explosion of Jean Maugue, which, you know, destroyed the bridge at Charenton the first time it was tried and killed twenty-four onlookers. You see, I would not be a bad man to marry. Also, I know many clever tricks I could teach your goat. For instance, to mime the Bishop of Paris, that cursed Pharisee whose mills splatter the passersby the whole length of the Pont-aux-Meuniers. And then, my mystery play is going to bring me a lot of money, if they pay me. In short, I am at your service, I, my brain, my knowledge, and my writings—all are ready to live with you, damsel, as it shall please you, chastely or otherwise, as man and wife, if you like, as brother and sister, if you find that better."

Gringoire stopped talking, awaiting the effect of his discourse on the gypsy. She kept her eyes on the floor.

"*Phoebus,*" she said, in a whisper; then turning to the poet, "*Phoebus,* what does that mean?"

Gringoire did not understand very well the connection between his dialogue and this question, but he was pleased to show off his erudition.

"It's a Latin word which means *sun.*"

"The sun?" she repeated.

"It's the name of a very handsome archer, who was a god," added Gringoire.

"A god!" repeated the gypsy. And there was something emphatically pensive and impassioned in her tone.

At that moment, one of her bracelets came unfastened and fell to the floor. Gringoire stooped to pick it up; and when he rose again, the girl and the goat had disappeared. He heard the sound of a bolt. It was on a small door, communicating no doubt with an adjoining room, which someone was closing from the other side.

"Has she left me, at least, a bed?" wondered our philosopher.

He walked around the room. There wasn't a piece of furniture on which he could sleep, except a long wooden chest, and its lid was carved, so that it gave Gringoire, when he stretched himself upon it, a sensation much like Micromegas experienced when he stretched out, full length, to sleep on the Alps.

"Come!" said he, making the best he could of it. "Resignation! But what a strange wedding night. It's a pity. There was something about this marriage, naive and antediluvian, that pleased me."

BOOK III

1

Notre-Dame

Without a doubt the Cathedral of Notre-Dame is, even today, a majestic and sublime edifice. Though it has preserved a noble mien in aging, it is difficult to suppress feelings of sorrow and indignation at the countless injuries and mutilations which time and man have wrought upon this venerable monument between the time of Charlemagne, who laid its first stone, and that of Philip-Augustus, who laid its last.

On the face of this old queen of French cathedrals, beside each wrinkle you always find a scar. *Tempus edox, homo edacior,*[1] which I would translate: Time is blind, but man is stupid.

If we had time to examine with the reader, one by one, the many traces of destruction stamped on this ancient church, the ravages of time would be found to have done the least; the worst destruction has been perpetrated by men, especially by men of art. We must say "men of art," because there have been men in France who, in the last two centuries, have assumed the character of architects.

First of all, to cite only a few outstanding examples, there

[1] "Time gnaws, man gnaws more."

are without any question few finer architectural examples than that facade of the Parisian cathedral, in which, successively and at once, you see three deep Gothic doors; the decorated and indented band of twenty-eight royal niches; the immense central rose-window, flanked by two lateral ones, like the priest flanked by the deacon and subdeacon; the lofty and fragile gallery of trifoliated arcades, supporting a heavy platform upon its delicate columns; finally the two dark and massive towers, with their eaves of slate, harmonious parts of one magnificent whole, rising one above the other in five gigantic stories, unfold themselves to the eye. These towers are grouped, yet unconfused, even with their innumerable details of statuary, sculpture, and carving; they are more powerfully wedded to the tranquil grandeur of the whole. The cathedral is a vast symphony in stone, so to speak, the colossal work of a man and of a nation, a unified complex ensemble, like the Iliads and the Romanceros, to which it is a sister production. Notre-Dame's facade is the prodigious result of the combination of all the resources of an age, in which, upon every stone, is seen displayed in a hundred forms the imagination of the craftsman disciplined by the genius of the artist. Here is a sort of human creation; in short, mighty and fertile like the divine creation, from which this cathedral seems to have borrowed the double character of variety and eternity.

And what we have here said of the facade must be said of the church as a whole; and what we say of the cathedral of Paris must be said of all the churches in Christendom during the Middle Ages. Everything has its place in that self-created, logical, well-proportioned art. By measuring the toe, we estimate the giant.

But let us return to the facade of Notre-Dame as we find it today. We gaze in reverent admiration upon this solemn and mighty cathedral, awesome, as its chroniclers express it: *Quae mole sua terrorem incutit spectantibus.*[2]

Three things of importance are now missing from that facade. First, the flight of eleven steps by which it formerly rose above the level of the ground; secondly, the lower row of statues, which once occupied the niches of the three por-

---

[2] "Which by its mass inspires terror in the spectators."

tals; and finally, the upper series of statues of the twenty-eight or more ancient kings of France, which filled the gallery on the first story, beginning with Childebert and ending with Philip-Augustus, each king holding in his hand "the imperial globe."

Time is responsible for the loss of the eleven steps, since time relentlessly raised the ground level of the city. But while so doing, time added to the cathedral more than it took away. Time spread over her face that dark gray patina which gives to very old monuments their season of beauty.

But who knocked down those two rows of statues? Who left the niches empty? Who chiseled into the very middle of the central portal that new and bastard pointed arch? Who dared to frame it in that heavy, tasteless wooden door carved in the style of Louis XV, beside the arabesque of Biscornette? Men, architects, the artists of our time!

And, if we enter the interior of the edifice, who overturned that colossal Saint Christopher, proverbial among statues for its magnitude as the Great Hall of the Palace was among halls, as the spire of Strasburg was among steeples? And those myriads of statues which thronged all the intercolumniations of the nave and the choir, kneeling, standing on horseback, men, women, children, kings, bishops, warriors, in stone, marble, gold, silver, brass, and even wax; who brutally swept them away? It was not time certainly.

And who substituted for the old Gothic altar, splendidly encumbered with shrines and reliquaries, that clumsy sarcophagus of marble, with angels' heads and clouds, which looks like an unmatched specimen from the Val-de-Grâce or the Invalides? Whose stupidity set that heavy anachronism of stone in the Carolingian pavement of Hercandus? Was it not Louis XIV fulfilling the vow of Louis XIII?

And who put cold white glass in place of those deeply tinted panes which made the wondering eyes of our forefathers hesitate between the rose-window over the grand doorway and the arched ones of the chancel? And what would a subchorister of the sixteenth century say could he see that beautiful yellow washing with which the vandal archbishops besmeared the stone of their cathedral? He would remember that it was the color which the hangman brushed over buildings of ill repute; he would recall the Hotel du Petit-

Bourbon, which had thus been washed all over with yellow because of the constable's treason—"Yellow, after all, so well mixed," writes Sauval, "and so well applied, that the lapse of a century or more has not yet dulled its color." He would think that the holy place had become infamous, and would flee from it.

And then if we ascend the cathedral, without stopping to examine a thousand other barbarisms of every kind, what did they do with that charming miniature steeple which rose from the intersection of the transept and which, no less bold and fragile than its neighbor, the spire (also destroyed) of the Sainte-Chapelle, pierced the sky, yet farther than the towers—slender, sharp, airy, sonorous? An architect of good taste amputated it in 1787, and thought it was enough to hide the wound with that great plaster of lead which resembles the lid of a soup pot.

Thus it is that the magnificent art of the Middle Ages was ill-treated in almost every country, but especially in France. Three distinguishable agents caused Notre-Dame's mutilations. Each made disfigurements of different intensity. First, time, which gradually made inroads here and there, and gnawed over the church's whole surface; then religious and political revolutions, which, blind and angry by nature, rushed tumultuously upon it, and tore its rich garment of sculpture and carving, smashed its rose-shaped windows, broke its necklaces of arabesques and miniature figures, tore down its statues, here for their miter, there for their crown; and lastly, changes of fashion which, growing more and more grotesque and stupid ever since the anarchical yet splendid deviations of the Renaissance, succeeded one another in the necessary decline of architecture. Fashion has done more harm than revolutions. It has cut to the quick; it has attacked the very bone and framework of art. It has mangled, hacked, killed the edifice, in its form as well as in its meaning, in its logic as well as in its beauty. And then, it has remade, which, at least, neither time nor revolutions had pretended to do. In the name of "good taste," fashion has clapped on the wounds of Gothic architecture the wretched gewgaws of the day: marble ribands, metal pompons, a veritable leprosy of ovoli, volutes, scallops, draperies, garlands, fringes, stone flames, brazen clouds, fleshy cupids, and chubby cherubim. All these embellishments began to eat away at art in the oratory of Catherine de Medicis, and made it expire two centuries later, tortured and convulsed, in the boudoir of Madame Du Barry.

Thus to sum up the remarks we have made, three kinds of ravages now disfigure Gothic architecture. Wrinkles and warts have appeared on the surface—these are the work of time. Acts of violence, brutalities, contusions, fractures— these are the work of revolutions, from Luther down to Mirabeau. Mutilations, amputations, dislocation of members, restorations—these are Grecian, Roman, and barbaric labors of the professors according to Vitruvius and Vignola. That magnificent art which the Vandals had produced, the academies murdered. To the work of time and of revolutions, which, at least, devastated with impartiality and magnitude, was added that of a swarm of school-trained architects, licensed, privileged, and patented. They degraded with all the discernment and selection of bad taste, substituting, for instance, the *chicorées* of Louis XV for the Gothic lacework to the greater glory of the Parthenon. This is the kick of the ass at the expiring lion. This is the old oak which, having begun to wither at the top, is stung, gnawed, and cut to pieces by caterpillars.

How vastly different is all this from the time when Robert Cenalis, comparing Notre-Dame in Paris to the famous temple of Diana at Ephesus, 'so much vaunted by the ancient pagans," which immortalized Erostratus, thought the Gaulish cathedral "more excellent in length, breadth, height, and structure."

Notre-Dame, however, as an architectural monument, is not one of those which can be called complete, finished, belonging to a definite class. It is not a Romanesque church, nor is it a Gothic church. It is not typical of any individual style. Notre-Dame has not, like the abbey of Tournus, the massive solemn squareness, the round broad vault, the icy bareness, the majestic simplicity of the edifices which have been based upon the circular arch. Nor is it, like the Cathedral of Bourges, the magnificent, airy, multiform, tufted, pinnacled, florid production of the pointed arch. It cannot be ranked among that antique family of churches—gloomy, mysterious, low, and crushed, as it were, by the weight of the circular arch; almost Egyptian, even to their ceilings; hieroglyphic, sacerdotal, symbolical; more abounding in their ornamentations with lozenges and zigzags than with flowers, with flowers than with animals, with animals than with human figures; these, the work not so much of an architect as of a bishop; the first transformation of the art, all stamped with theocratic and military discipline, which took root in the Lower Empire, and stopped at the time of William the Conqueror. Nor can this cathedral be ranked with that other family of churches—lofty, airy, rich in sculpture and stained-glass windows; with sharp forms and bold outlines; communal and middle-class as political symbols, free, capricious, licentious, as works of art. This is the second transformation of architecture, no longer hieroglyphic, immutable, and sacerdotal, but artistic, progressive, and popular, beginning with the return from the Crusades and ending with Louis XI. Notre-Dame, then, is not of purely Romanesque origin like the first group, nor of purely Arabic origin like the second group.

Notre-Dame is a structure of transition. The Saxon architect was just finishing the first pillars of the nave, when the pointed arch, arriving from the Crusades, came and seated itself like a conqueror upon the broad Romanesque capitals which had been designed to support only circular arches. The pointed arch, thenceforth master of the field, determined the construction of the remainder of the church. However, though inexperienced and timid at its beginnings, we find the pointed arch widening its compass, and, as it were, restraining itself, as though not yet daring to spring up into slender spires and lancets, as it afterward did in so many wonderful cathedrals. This arch might be said to have been affected by the neighboring heavy, Romanesque pillars.

Besides, these edifices, built during the transition from the Romanesque to the Gothic period, are no less valuable for study than the pure examples. They express a nuance of the architectural art which would be lost without them. They illustrate how the pointed style was grafted upon the circular.

Notre-Dame, in particular, is a curious example of this variation. Each face, each stone of this venerable monument is not only a page of the history of the country, but of the history of science and art. Thus, to point out here only some of the principal details: while the small Porte-Rouge attains almost to the limit the Gothic delicacy of the fifteenth century, the pillars of the nave, in their amplitude and solemnity, go back almost as far as the Carolingian abbey of Saint-Germain-des-Prés. One would think there were six centuries between that door and those pillars. Not even the hermetics fail to find, in the emblematical devices of the great portal, a satisfactory compendium of their science, of which the church of Saint-Jacques-de-la-Boucherie was so complete a hieroglyphic. Thus the Romanesque abbey, the philosophical church, Gothic art, Saxon art, the heavy round pillar which reminds us of Gregory VII, the hermetical symbolism by which Nicolas Flamel anticipated Luther, papal unity, the schism, Saint-Germain-des-Prés, and Saint-Jacques-de-la-Boucherie—all are mingled, combined, and amalgamated in Notre-Dame. This central mother-church is a sort of chimera among the other old churches of Paris; it has the head of one, the limbs of another, the back of a third—something from every one.

We repeat: these hybrid structures are none the less interesting to the artist, the antiquarian, and the historian. They make us feel in how great a degree architecture is a primitive art, inasmuch as they also demonstrate the Cyclopean remains, the Egyptian pyramids, and the gigantic Hindu pagodas; and they demonstrate that the greatest productions of architecture are not so much the work of individuals as of society—the offspring rather of national efforts than the outcome of a particular genius; a legacy left by the whole people, the accumulation of ages, the residue of successive evaporations of human society; in short, a species of formations. Each wave of time leaves its alluvium, each race leaves a deposit upon the monument, each individual lays his stone. Such is the process of beavers, such that of bees, such that of men. The great symbol of architecture, Babel, is a hive.

Great edifices, like great mountains, are the work of the ages. Often art undergoes a transformation while they are yet in progress—*pendent opera interrupta*[3]—they go on again quietly, in accordance with the change in art. The new art

[3] "Works, once interrupted, remain suspended."

form takes the structure as it finds it, encrusts itself upon it, assimilates it, develops it after its own fashion, and finishes it if possible. The whole process is accomplished without effort, without reaction, without disturbance, according to a natural and tranquil law. A shoot is grafted on, it grows, the sap circulates; vegetation is in progress. Certainly there is a volume of material, even a history of all human nature, in those successive engraftings of several styles at different heights upon the same structure. The man, the artist, the individual is lost under those great masses without an author's name. Human intelligence can be traced there only in its aggregate. Time is the architect, the nation is the builder.

Let us consider here only the architecture of Christian Europe—that younger sister of the great masonries of the East—which appears as an immense formation, divided into three clearly defined superimposed zones: The Romanesque zone, the Gothic zone, and the zone of the Renaissance, which we would prefer to call Greco-Roman. The Romanesque stratum, the most ancient and the lowest, is occupied by the circular arch, which reappears supported by the Grecian column in the modern and upper stratum of the Renaissance. The pointed arch is somewhere between the two. The edifices which belong to one or the other of these extra strata exclusively are perfectly distinct, uniform, and complete. Such is the Abbey of Jumièges, the Cathedral of Rheims, the Church of Saint-Croix in Orleans. But the three zones mingle, combine, overlap like the colors of a prism. And hence, these complex edifices, these structures of transition: one is Romanesque at the foot, Gothic in the middle, and Greco-Roman in the head. This happened when six hundred years were required to build it. This variety is rare: the dungeon tower of Estampes is an example. But the edifices of two formations are more frequent. Such is Notre-Dame de Paris, an edifice of the pointed arch, the first pillars of which belong to the Romanesque zone like the portal of Saint-Denis and the nave of Saint-Germain-des-Prés. Such is the charming semi-Gothic chapter house of Bocherville, in which the Romanesque layer rises halfway up. Such is the Cathedral of Rouen, which would have been entirely Gothic, had not the extremity of its central spire pierced into the zone of the Renaissance.

However, all these gradations, all these differences affect only the surface of the structures. It is only art that has changed its skin. The constitution of the Christian church itself has remained untouched. It has ever the same internal framework, the same logical disposition of its parts. Whatever may be the sculptured and decorated outside of a cathedral, we constantly find underneath it at least the rudiments of the Roman basilica. It eternally develops itself upon the ground according to the same law. There are invariably two naves crossing each other at right angles, the upper extremity of which cross is rounded into a chancel; there are always two low sides for the internal processions and for the chapels—a sort of lateral ambulatory communicating with the principal nave by the intercolumniations. This being once laid down, the number of chapels, of doorways, of steeples, of spires is variable to infinity, according to the caprice of the age, of the nation, of art. The performance of worship being once provided for and insured, architecture is at liberty to do what it pleases. Statues, stained glass, rose-shaped windows, arabesques, indentations, capitals, and bas-reliefs—all these as best suit it. Hence the prodigious external variety of these edifices; in the main structure of each there dwells much order and uniformity. The trunk of the tree is unchanging, the vegetation is capricious.

2

A Bird's-Eye View of Paris

We have just attempted to reconstruct for the reader this admirable church of Notre-Dame in Paris. We have briefly pointed out the greater part of the beauties which it possessed in the fifteenth century, and which it no longer possesses, but we have omitted the principal one—the view of Paris as it then appeared from the top of its towers.

It was indeed when, after groping your way up the long dark spiral staircase that climbs between the thick walls of the steeple, you at last emerged on one of the two lofty platforms, flooded with light and air, that a breathtaking picture opened before you on every side—a spectacle *sui generis*.

Some idea of this may easily be had by such of our readers as have had the good fortune to see one of the few Gothic towns still left entire, complete, homogeneous; such as Nuremberg in Bavaria, Vittoria in Spain, or even smaller specimens, provided they be in good preservation, as Vitré in Brittany, and Nordhausen in Prussia.

The Paris of three hundred and fifty years ago, the Paris of the fifteenth century, was already a giant city. We Parisians, generally speaking, are mistaken as to the ground which we think it has gained. Paris, since the time of Louis XI, has not grown territorially by much more than a third, and certainly it has lost much more in beauty than it has gained in size.

Paris was born, as everyone knows, on that ancient island of the Cité, or City, which is in the shape of a cradle. The shores of that island were its first walls, the Seine was its first moat. For several centuries Paris remained only on this island. She had two bridges, one on the north, the other on the south. The two bridgeheads, the Grand-Châtelet on the right bank and the Petit-Châtelet on the left, were at once its gates and its fortresses. Then, under the first kings, being too much confined within the limits of its island, and unable to turn itself about, Paris crossed the river. So, on each side, beyond either Châtelet, the first line of walls and towers began to encroach upon the countryside on both sides of the Seine. Of this ancient enclosure, some vestiges still remained as late as the last century; today nothing remains but the memory, and here and there a landmark, such as the Baudets Gate, or Baudoyer—*Porta Bagauda.*

Gradually, the flood of houses, constantly impelled from the heart of the town to the exterior, overflowed, wore away, and erased this enclosure. Philip-Augustus constructed a new wall. He imprisoned Paris within a circular chain of tall, solid, massive towers. For more than a century the houses crowded each other, accumulated, and rose higher in this basin, like water in a reservoir. Story was piled upon story; they climbed, so to speak, one on the other. They shot up like compressed sap, and strove each to lift its head above its neighbors, in order to get a breath of air. The streets became deeper and narrower, as every open space was covered. Finally, the houses leaped over Philip-Augustus' wall, and merrily scattered themselves helter-skelter, like escapees, without plan or order. There they squatted at their ease, and the people carved themselves gardens out of the fields.

By 1367, the suburbs were so extensive that a new enclosure was needed, especially on the right bank, and one was built by Charles V.

But a town like Paris is constantly growing. It is only such towns that become capital cities. They are like funnels into which are poured all the geographical, political, and moral drains of a country, all the natural tendencies of a people; they become the cisterns of civilization, so to speak. Also, they are the sinks, into which commerce, industry, intelligence, population, all the vital juices, all that is life, all that is soul in a nation filters and collects, drop by drop, century by century. The enclosure of Charles V had therefore the same fate as the wall of Philip-Augustus. By the end of the fifteenth century, it too was overtaken and passed, and new suburbs grew. In the sixteenth century, this enclosure seemed visibly to recede and to become buried deeper and deeper in the old town, so dense was the new growth outside of it. Thus, in the fifteenth century—to stop there—Paris had already worn away three concentric circles of walls. At the time of Julian the Apostate Paris was in embryo, so to speak, inside the Grand-Châtelet and the Petit-Châtelet. Then the mighty city successively burst its four wall-belts, like a growing child who can no longer wear the clothing of a year ago. Under Louis XI, one could see rising here and there, in that sea of houses, clusters of ruined towers belonging to the ancient bulwarks, like the tops of hills after an inundation, like archipelagoes of the old Paris submerged by the new.

Since then, Paris has, unfortunately for us, optically undergone yet another change; but it has jumped only one more enclosure; namely, the wall of Louis XV, that miserable wall of mud and rubbish, worthy of the king who constructed it and the man who sang of it:

Le mur murant Paris rend Paris murmurant.[1]

[1] "The wall surrounding Paris makes Paris murmur."

In the fifteenth century, Paris was still divided into three to-
tally distinct and separate cities, each having its own physiognomy, manners, customs, privileges, and history: the City, the
University, and the Town. The City, which occupied the island, was the oldest, the smallest, and the mother of the other
two, squeezed between them like (excuse the comparison) a
little old woman between two tall beautiful daughters. The
University covered the left bank of the Seine, from the
Tournelle to the Tower of Nesle, points corresponding, in
the Paris of today, one to the Halles-aux-Vins, and the other
to the Mint. Its circular wall encroached upon a rather large
plain where Julian had built his baths. It included the Hill of
Sainte-Geneviève. The culminating point of this curve of
walls was the Porte-Papale, that is to say, very nearly, the site
of the present Pantheon. The Town, which was the largest of
the three portions of Paris, occupied the right bank. Its quay,
interrupted at several points, stretched along the Seine, from
the Tower of Billy to the Tower du Bois; that is to say, from
the spot where the Grenier d'Abondance now stands, to the
spot now occupied by the Tuileries. These four points where
the Seine intersected the enclosure of the capital, the
Tournelle, and the Tower of Nesle on the left, the Tower of
Billy and the Tower du Bois on the right, were called "the
four towers of Paris." The Town penetrated still farther into
the country than did the University. The culminating point of
the Town's enclosure (the one constructed by Charles V) was
at the gates of Saint-Denis and Saint-Martin, the sites of
which have not changed to this day.

As we have just remarked, each of these three large divisions of Paris was a town, but each town was too specialized
to be complete in itself. None could do without the other
two. Thus they had three different aspects. In the City,
churches were abundant; in the Town, palaces; in the University, schools. Leaving aside for the moment the secondary
jurisdictions of the old Paris and the capricious intricacies of
the right of way, and noting only the great masses in the
chaos of communal jurisdictions, we may say in general that
the island was controlled by the bishop; the right bank, by
the provost of merchants; the left bank, by the rector of the
University. The provost of Paris, a royal and not a municipal
officer, was in charge of all. The City had Notre-Dame; the

Town had the Louvre and the Hotel de Ville; the University had the Sorbonne. The Town also had Les Halles; the City, the Hotel-Dieu; the University, the Pré-aux-Clercs. For crimes committed by the students on the left bank, in their Pré-aux-Clercs, there were trials at the Palace of Justice on the island, and punishment was meted out on the right bank at Montfaucon, unless the rector, feeling the University to be strong and the king weak, intervened; for it was a privilege of the scholars to be hung in their own district.

Most of these privileges, to note in passing, and some of them were more valuable than the one just mentioned, had been extorted from the kings by revolts and mutinies. It is the time-honored way. The king only yields what the people take. There is an old French charter which defines loyalty quite simply: *Civibus fidelitas in reges, quae tamen aliquoties seditionibus interrupta, multa peperit privilegia.*[2]

In the fifteenth century, five islands of the Seine were embraced within the circuit of Paris: the Ile Louviers, on which there were then trees, though there is now only wood; the Ile-aux-Vaches, the Ile Notre-Dame, both uninhabited (except for one sorry hovel), both fiefs of the bishop. In the seventeenth century these two islands were converted into one, which we call today Ile Saint-Louis. Lastly the City, having at its western extremity the islet of the Passeur-aux-Vaches, now buried under the foundations of the Pont-Neuf, had at that time five bridges: three on the right (the Pont Notre-Dame and the Pont-au-Change, both made of stone, and the Pont-aux-Meuniers, which was made of wood) and two on the left (the Petit-Pont, made of stone, and the Pont Saint-Michel, made of wood). All the bridges were lined with houses.

The University had six gates, all built by Philip-Augustus. Starting from the Tournelle, they were: the Porte Saint-Victor, the Port Bordelle, the Porte-Papale, the Porte Saint-Jacques, the Porte Saint-Michel, and the Porte Saint-Germain.

The Town likewise had six gates, all built by Charles V. Setting from the Tower of Billy, they were: the Porte Saint-

---

[2] "Loyalty to kings, interrupted however by several revolts, has procured many privileges for the citizens."

Antoine, the Porte du Temple, the Porte Saint-Martin, the Porte Saint-Denis, the Porte Montmartre, and the Porte Saint-Honoré. All these gates were strong, and handsome, too, which latter attribute is by no means incompatible with strength. In a wide, deep trench, with a swift current during the winter floods, ran the Seine, washing the base of the walls all around Paris. At night the gates were closed; a heavy iron chain was fastened across the river at each of the two extremities of the town; and Paris slept quietly.

Seen from a bird's-eye view, these three boroughs—the City, the University, the Town—each appeared like an inextricable tangle of weirdly jumbled streets. However, at first glance, you recognized that these three fragments of a city formed a single whole. You immediately distinguished two long parallel streets, running without interruption or deviation, almost in a straight line, through all three sections of Paris, from one extremity to the other, from south to north, at right angles to the Seine. These connecting strands drew the divisions together, and the people ever passing from one precinct to another made the three one. One of these two long streets ran from the Porte Saint-Jacques to the Porte Saint-Martin, and was called in the University, Rue Saint-Jacques; in the City, Rue de la Juiverie; and in the Town, Rue Saint-Martin. It crossed the river twice, under the names of the Petit-Pont and the Pont Notre-Dame. The other street—which was called on the left bank, Rue de la Harpe; on the island, Rue de la Barillerie; on the right bank, Rue Saint-Denis—on one side of the Seine, Pont Saint-Michel, and on the other, Pont-au-Change—ran from the Porte Saint-Michel in the University to the Porte Saint-Denis in the Town. Although there were various names according to the sections they traversed, these still were in fact only two streets, the long mother streets, the two arteries of Paris, which fed all the other veins of the triple city, or into which they flowed.

Independent of these two principal streets, running straight across all Paris, and common to the entire capital, the Town and the University had each its own great street, running parallel to the Seine, and intersecting the two arterial streets at right angles. Thus, in the Town, you descended in a straight line from the Porte Saint-Antoine to the Porte

Saint-Honoré; in the University, from the Porte Saint-Victor to the Porte Saint-Germain. These two large roads, crossing the first two arteries mentioned above, formed with them the framework upon which was laid, knotted, and drawn in every direction the tangled network of the streets of Paris. In this tangle, you might, however, also discover, upon attentive observation, two bunches of wide streets, one in the University and one in the Town, which ran from the bridges to the gates. Something of this same geometrical plan still exists in Paris today.

Now, what else, besides this confusion of streets, could you see from the towers of Notre-Dame in 1482? That is what we shall try to describe.

The spectator, on arriving, out of breath, upon this summit, was at first dazzled by the confusion of roofs, chimneys, streets, bridges, squares, spires, steeples. Everything struck the eye at once: the carved gable, the sharp roofing, the hanging turret at the corner of the walls, the stone pyramid of the eleventh century, the slate obelisk of the fifteenth, the round, naked tower of the castle turret, the square and decorated tower of the church, the large and small, the massive and the light. The gaze for some time was utterly bewildered by this labyrinth, in which everything had its particular originality, its reason, its genius, its beauty, everything had proceeded from art, from the most inconsiderable carved and painted house-front, with external timbers, low doorway, and stories projecting each above the other, to the royal Louvre itself, which, at that time, had a colonnade of towers. But here are the principal masses which were distinguished once the eye became accustomed to this tumult of structures.

First of all, the City. The island of the City, as is observed by Sauval, the most laborious of the old explorers of Parisian antiquity, who among all his incongruities has an occasional good idea; namely, "The island of the City is shaped like a great ship, sunk in the mud, lengthwise in the stream, in about the middle of the Seine." We have already shown that, in the fifteenth century, the ship was moored to the two banks of the river by five bridges. This idea of the hull of a vessel had also struck the heraldic scribes, for, from this circumstance, according to Favyn and Pasquier, and not from the siege by the Normans, came the ship emblazoned upon the old escutcheon of Paris. To him who can decipher it, heraldry is an emblematic language. The whole history of the latter half of the Middle Ages is written in heraldry, as that of the former half is in the symbolism of the Romanesque churches. Thus do the hieroglyphics of feudalism succeed those of theocracy.

The City, then, first presented itself to the viewer with its stern to the east and its prow to the west. Facing the prow, you saw an innumerable congregation of old roofs, with the lead-covered apse of the Sainte-Chapelle rising above them, broad and round, like an elephant's back with a tower upon it. Only, here, that tower was the boldest, airiest, most notched and ornamented spire that ever showed the sky through its lacework cone. Directly in front of Notre-Dame three streets terminated in an open space, a fine square of old houses. The southern side of this square was overhung by the furrowed and rugged front of the Hotel-Dieu, whose roof looks as if it were covered with pimples and warts. And then, right and left, east and west, within that narrow circuit of the City, rose the steeples of its twenty-one churches, of all dates, shapes, and sizes, from the low and decayed Romanesque companile of Saint-Denys-du-Pas, to the delicate spires of Saint-Pierre-aux-Boeufs and Saint-Landry. Behind Notre-Dame extended, northward, the cloister with its Gothic galleries; southward, the semi-Romanesque palace of the bishop; and eastward, the uninhabited point of the island, called the Terrain. Amid that mass of houses, the eye could also distinguish, by the high perforated miters of stone which, at that period, placed aloft upon the roof, crowned even the highest windows of palaces, the mansion given by the Parisians, in the reign of Charles VI, to Juvénal des Ursins; a little farther on, the black, pitch-covered sheds of the market of Palus, and in another direction, the new chancel of Saint-Germain-le-Vieux, lengthened in 1458 by an encroachment upon one end of the Rue-aux-Febves; and also here and there were to be seen some crossways crowded with people; a pillory erected at the corner of a street; some fine pieces of the pavement of Philip-Augustus (magnificent flagstone grooved for horses' hooves in the middle of the street, and so ill-replaced in the sixteenth century by wretched pebbling called *pavé de la Ligue*); a deserted back-yard, with one of those transparent staircase turrets which they used to build in the fifteenth century, one of which is still to be seen in the Rue des Bourdonnais. Lastly, to the right of the Saint-Chapelle, toward the west, the Palace of Justice lifted its group of towers above the water's brink. The groves of the royal gardens, which occupied the western sector of the island, hid from view the islet of the Passeur. As for the river itself, it was hardly visible on either side of the City from the towers of Notre-Dame, because of the Seine's disappearing under the bridges, and the bridges' hiding under the houses.

And when you looked beyond those bridges, whose roofs were tinged with green, having contracted untimely moldiness from the mist which rose from the water, if you cast your eye to the left, toward the University, the first edifice that drew your attention was a large, low cluster of towers, the Petit-Châtelet, the gaping porch of which seemed to devour the extremity of the Petit-Pont. Then, if your view ranged along the shore from east to west, from the Tournelle to the Tower of Nesle, you beheld a long line of houses exhibiting sculptured beams, colored window glass, each story overhanging the one beneath it—an interminable zigzag of ordinary houses, cut off at frequent intervals by the end of some street, and now and then also by the front or the corner of some huge stone mansion, which seemed to stand unconcerned, with its courtyards and gardens, its wings and its compartments, among that rabble of houses crowding and pinching one another, like a great lord among a mob of rustics. There were five or six of these mansions upon the quay, from the Logis de Lorraine, which shared with the house of the Bernardines the great neighboring enclosure of the Tournelle, to the Hotel de Nesle, whose principal tower marked the limits of Paris on that side, and whose pointed roofs cut with their dark triangles, during three months of the year, the scarlet disk of the setting sun.

That side of the Seine was, however, the less mercantile of the two; there was more noise from crowds of scholars than from artisans, and there was not, properly speaking, any quay, except from the Pont Saint-Michel to the Tower of Nesle. The rest of the bank of the Seine was either a bare strand, as was the case beyond the Bernardines, or a close row of houses with water at their foundations, as between the two bridges. There was a great clamor of washerwomen along the waterside, talking, shouting, singing, from morning till night, and beating away at their linens—as they do today, contributing their full share to the gaiety of Paris.

The University brought the eye to a full stop. From one end to the other, it was a compact, homogeneous whole. Those thousand thickset angular roofs, clinging together, nearly all composed of the same geometrical element, when seen from above, looked almost like the crystallization of a single substance. The capricious fissures formed by the streets did not cut this conglomeration of houses into slices too disproportionate. The forty-two colleges were distributed among them very equally, and were to be seen in every quarter. The amusingly varied pinnacles of those beautiful buildings were a product of the same art as the ordinary roofs which they overtopped, being nothing more than the square or the cube of the same geometrical figure. Thus they complicated the whole without confusing it, completed without overloading it. Geometry is a kind of harmony. Several fine mansions, too, lifted their heads proudly here and there above the picturesque attic stories of the left bank; for example, the Logis de Nevers, the Logis de Rome, the Logis de Reims—which have disappeared—and the Hotel de Cluny, which still exists for the artist's consolation, but whose tower was so stupidly uncrowned a few years ago. Near the Hotel de Cluny was that Roman palace, with its fine semi-circular arches, once the Baths of Julian. There were also a number of abbeys, of a beauty more religious, of a grandeur more solemn, than the secular mansions, but neither less handsome nor less spacious. Those which first attracted attention were the abbeys of the Bernardines, with their three steeples; second, that of Sainte-Geneviève, whose square tower, which still exists, makes us so much regret the disappearance of the rest; then the Sorbonne, half college, half monastery, whose admirable nave yet survives; also, the fine quadrilateral Cloister of the Mathurins; and, adjacent to it, the Cloister of Saint-Benedict; the house of the Cordeliers, with its three enormous and contiguous gables; that of the Augustines, whose graceful spire formed, after the Tower of

Nesle, the second indentation on that side of Paris, starting from the west. The colleges, which are, in fact, the intermediate link between the cloister and the world, balanced the architecture between the abbeys and the great mansions, exhibiting a severe elegance, a sculpture less airy than that of the palaces, an architecture less stern than that of the convents. Unfortunately, scarcely anything remains of these structures, in which Gothic art kept so fine a balance between richness and economy. The churches—which were numerous and splendid in the University, and which represented every architectural era, from the round arches of Saint-Julian to the Gothic ones of Saint-Severin—rose above all; and, as one harmony more in that harmonious mass, they accented in close succession the indented outline of the roofs, with their boldly cut spires, with their perforated steeples, and their slender needles, the lines of which were themselves but a magnificent exaggeration of the acute angle of the roofs.

The terrain of the University was hilly. The Hill of Sainte-Geneviève, to the southeast, formed an enormous swelling, and it was curious to see, from the top of Notre-Dame, that multitude of narrow, winding streets, now called the Latin Quarter, those clusters of houses which scattered in every direction from the summit of that eminence, and spread themselves in disorder, almost precipitously, down its sides to the water's edge, some looking as if they were falling, others as if they were climbing up, and all as if clinging to one another, while the continual motion of a thousand dark objects crossing one another upon the pavement gave the whole an appearance of life. These were people on the streets, as beheld thus from on high and at a distance.

Then, in the spaces between those roofs, those spires, those numberless odd buildings, which bent, twisted, and indented the highest outline of the University in so fantastic a manner, were to be seen, here and there, a great patch of moss-covered wall, a solid round tower, an embattled, fortresslike town-gate. This marked the enclosure of Philip-Augustus. Green meadows were spread beyond, across which roads diverged. Along their sides were a few straggling houses, growing fewer as the distance from the protecting wall increased. However, some drew together into

suburbs of considerable size. Leaving the Tournelle, first
was the village of Saint-Victor, with its bridge of one arch
over the Bièvre, its abbey, where the epitaph of King Louis
the Fat could be read, and its church, with an octagonal steeple flanked by four belfries of the eleventh century (such a
one can still be seen at Estampes). Then there was Saint-
Marceau, which already had three churches and a convent.
Next, leaving on the left the mill of Gobelins with its four
white walls, came the village of Saint-Jacques, with its elegant sculptured cross at the crossroads. This place contained
several churches: the church of Saint-Jacques-du-Haut-Pas,
at that time a charming Gothic structure; Saint-Magloire,
with its beautiful nave of the fourteenth century, which Napoleon turned into a hay shed; Notre-Dame-des-Champs,
where were to be seen Byzantine mosaics. Lastly, after leaving the open country where stood the monastery of the Car-
thusians, a rich structure belonging to the same period as the
Palace of Justice, with its little compartmentalized gardens,
and the haunted ruins of Vauvert, the eye fell, to the west,
upon the three Romanesque spires of Saint-Germain-des-
Prés. The village of Saint-Germain, already a large commune, contained fifteen or twenty streets. The sharp steeple
of Saint-Sulpice marked one of the corners of the village.
Close by it was to be distinguished the quadrilateral enclosure of the fair of Saint-Germain, where there is today a
marketplace. Then came the abbey's pillory, a pretty little
round tower, capped by a lead cone; farther on were the tile
factories and the Rue du Four, leading to the manorial bakehouse, and the mill perched upon its mound, and the hospital
for lepers, a small, isolated building, difficult to see.

But what particularly caught the eye, and kept it fixed for
a long time in this direction, was the abbey itself. It is certain that that monastery, which had an air of importance both
as a church and as a lordly residence, that abbatial palace,
where the bishops of Paris deemed themselves fortunate to
sleep a single night, that refectory, to which the architect had
given the air, the beauty, and the splendid rose-window of a
cathedral, that elegant chapel of the Virgin, that monumental
dormitory, those spacious gardens, that portcullis, that drawbridge, that belt of crenelated wall which notched the outline
of the verdure of the surrounding meadow, those courts

where the mail of the men-at-arms gleamed among the golden copes—the whole, grouped around three round-arched spires firmly seated upon a Gothic chancel, made a magnificent outline on the horizon.

When finally, after having contemplated the University at length, you turned toward the right bank, toward the Town, the character of the scene suddenly changed. The Town, in fact, was not only much larger than the University, but also less homogeneous. At first glance it appeared to be divided into several masses, singularly distinct from one another. First of all, to the east, in that sector of the Town which still takes its name from the marsh in which Camulogenes lured Caesar, there was a collection of palaces, which extended to the waterside. Four great, almost contiguous mansions—the hotels of Jouy, Sens, Barbeau, and the Queen's House—cast upon the Seine the reflection of their slated roofs intersected by slender turrets. These four edifices occupied the space from the Rue des Nonaindières to the abbey of the Celestines. The small spire of this abbey formed a graceful relief to the mansions' line of gables and battlements. Some greenish hovels overhanging the water in front of these elaborate buildings did not conceal from view the beautifully ornamented corners of their facades, their large square windows with stone casements, their Gothic porticoes heavy with statuary, the bold, clearcut parapets of their walls, and all those charming oddities of architecture which made Gothic art seem as if it were resorting to new combinations with each new structure. Behind those palaces ran in every direction, sometimes divided, palisaded and embattled like a citadel, sometimes shaded by huge trees like a Carthusian monastery, the immense and multiform enclosure of that miraculous Hotel de Saint-Pol. Here the King of France had room to lodge superbly twenty-two princes equal in rank to the dauphin and the Duke of Burgundy, with their servants and retinues, not to mention the great barons, and the emperor when he came to visit Paris. Even their lions had a hotel to themselves in the royal palace. Let it here be noted that lodgings for a prince then consisted of not less than eleven apartments, from the audience room to the oratory, besides galleries, baths, steam-bath rooms, and other "superfluous places" with which each apartment was provided; not to mention a private garden for each one of the king's guests; not to mention the kitchens, cellars, pantries, and general refectories for the household. Moreover the hotel contained inner courts where there were twenty-two general laboratories from the bakehouse to the royal wine cellar; grounds for every sort of game (mall, tennis, the ring), aviaries, fish ponds, menageries, and stables; libraries, arsenals, and foundries. Such was then the palace of a king, a Louvre, a Hotel de Saint-Pol. It was a city within a city.

From the Notre-Dame tower, the Hotel de Saint-Pol, though almost hidden by the four great mansions of which we have already spoken, was, nevertheless, tremendous and a wonderful sight to see.

The three mansions which Charles V absorbed into his palace, though skillfully connected to the main building by long galleries with windows and small pillars, could be clearly distinguished. These were the Hotel du Petit-Muce, with the lacy balustrade that gracefully bordered its roof; the Hotel of the Abbot of Saint-Maur, having the appearance of a fortress, with its massive tower, its machicolations, shotholes, iron bulwarks, and on its huge Saxon gate, the abbot's escutcheon between the two notches for the drawbridge; and the Hotel of the Count d'Estampes, the turret of which, in ruin at the top, appeared jagged and notched like the comb of a cock. Here and there were three or four old oaks, grouped together in one large bushy clump, like enormous cauliflowers; swans floated in the clear water of the fishponds, all streaked with light and shade. The mansion for the lions, with its low pointed arches supported by short Saxon pillars and its iron bars, roared continuously. Shooting up above this group of buildings, the scaly spire of the Ave-Maria; on the left the residence of the provost of Paris was flanked by four finely wrought turrets. In the middle, in the heart of it all, stood Hotel de Saint-Pol itself, with its multiplicity of facades, its successive embellishments since the time of Charles V, the hybrid excrescences with which the whims of architects had heaped it during two centuries, with all the chancels of its chapels, all the gables of its galleries, its thousand weathercocks, and its two lofty contiguous towers whose conical roofs, surrounded at their base with battlements, looked like pointed hats with the brims turned up.

Let the eye continue to mount the steps of that amphitheater of palaces, and cross a deep fissure in the roofs of the Town, which marks the course of the Rue Saint-Antoine. Soon you would notice the Logis d'Angoulême, an immense structure of several periods, parts of which were quite new and white, harmonizing with the rest hardly better than a red patch on a blue doublet. However, the singularly sharp and elevated roof of the modern palace, bristling with carved spout ends, and covered with sheets of lead, over which ran sparkling encrustations of gilded copper in a thousand fantastic arabesques—that roof so curiously ornamented rose gracefully from the brown ruins of the ancient edifice, whose old massive towers were bellying casklike with age, their height shrunk with decrepitude, and bursting from top to bottom. Behind, rose a forest of needlelike spires on the Palais des Tournelles. There was not a view in the world, not even at Chambord nor at the Alhambra, more magical, more aerial, more captivating, than that grove of spires, belfries, chimneys, weathercocks, spirals, airy lanterns, pavilions, spindle-shaped turrets—all differing in height and position. You could have taken the whole for an immense stone chessboard.

To the right of the Tournelles, that cluster of enormous black towers, black as ink, running one into another, and bound together, as it were, by a circular ditch, that dungeon pierced through with more shot-holes than with windows, that drawbridge always raised, that portcullis always down, that is the Bastille. Those black beaks projecting from the battlements, and which at a distance you mistake for rain spouts, are cannons.

Within their range, at the foot of the formidable structure, is the Porte Saint-Antoine, crouching between its two towers.

Beyond the Tournelles, as far as the wall of Charles V, stretched in rich diversity of verdure and flowers a velvet carpet of gardens and royal parks, in the center of which might be recognized, by its maze of groves and walks, the famous Daedalus garden which Louis XI had given to Coictier. The doctor's observatory rose above the labyrinth like a great isolated column, having a small house for its capital. In that laboratory some terrible astrological crimes were practiced.

Today it is the site of the Palace Royale.

As we have already stated, the palace quarter, of which we have endeavored to give the reader some idea, however sketchily, by detailing only its most important places, filled the corner which Charles V's wall made with the Seine to the east. The center of the Town was occupied by a heap of ordinary houses. In fact it was there that the three bridges of the City on the right bank disgorged their masses of people; and bridges led to houses before palaces. This mass of ordinary dwellings, pressed against each other like the cells in a hive, was not without charm.

And in the waves of the sea, so in the roofs of a great city there is something grand. First of all, the streets, crossing and intertwining, formed a hundred amusing figures. Around Les Halles, it was like a star with a thousand rays. The streets Saint-Denis and Saint-Martin, with their numberless ramifications, ran along beside each other, like two tall trees intertwining their branches. And then there were those tortuous streets, Rue de la Plâtrerie, Rue de la Verrerie, Rue de la Tixeranderie, etc., which snaked through the whole. There were also some handsome edifices which rose above the petrified undulations of this sea of gables. First, at the entrance of the Pont-aux-Changeurs, where the Seine could be seen foaming under the mill wheels at the Pont-aux-Meuniers, was the Châtelet, no longer a Roman tower as under Emperor Julian, but a feudal tower of the thirteenth century, built of stone so hard that three hours' digging with a pick could not remove more than a piece the size of a man's fist. Then there was the rich square belfry tower of Saint-Jacques-de-la-Boucherie, its corners all rounded with statuary, already worthy of admiration, though it was not finished in the fifteenth century. It lacked in particular those four gargoyles which, even to this day, perched at the four corners of its roof, look like so many sphinxes giving to modern Paris an ancient enigma to solve. Rault, the sculptor, placed them there only in 1516, and got twenty francs for his trouble. Also, there was the Maison-aux-Piliers, overlooking that Place de Grève which we have already described. There was the church of Saint-Gervais, that a doorway "in good taste" has since spoiled, the church of Saint-Méry, whose old pointed arches were almost semicircular; and the church of Saint-Jean, whose magnificent spire was proverbial; besides twenty other structures which did not disdain to bury their attractions in that chaos of deep, dark, and narrow streets. Add to these the carved stone crosses, even more frequently seen at crossroads than gibbets themselves; the wall surrounding the cemetery of the Innocents, which could be seen at a distance; the top of Les Halles' pillory, which was visible between the chimneys of the Rue de la Cossonnerie; the gibbet of the Croix-du-Trahoir stood at the corner of a very busy thoroughfare; the circular hovels of the Halle-au-Blé; and broken sections of Philip-Augustus' old wall were distinguishable here and there, buried among houses, ivy-mantled towers, fallen gateways, crumbling and shapeless pieces of wall. Then on the riverbank was the quay with its thousand shops and its bloody skinning yards. Now you come to the Seine itself, covered with boats from the Port-au-Foin to the For-l'Evêque. Thus you have a general idea of the central trapezium of the Town in 1482.

Besides these two quarters—the one of palaces, the other of houses—the Town contributed a third element to the view: that of a long belt of abbeys which bordered almost its whole circumference, from east to west, and, behind the line of fortifications by which Paris was shut in, formed a second internal wall, consisting of convents and chapels. Thus, close to the park of the Tournelles, between the Rue Saint-Antoine and the old Rue du Temple, there was Sainte-Catherine's, with its immense grounds, bounded only by the wall of Paris. Between the old and the new Rue du Temple there was the Temple itself, a frowning bundle of towers, lofty, erect, and isolated in the midst of an extensive embattled enclosure. Between the Rue Neuve-du-Temple and the Rue Saint-Martin, in the midst of its gardens, stood Saint-Martin's, a superb fortified church, whose girdle of towers, whose tiara of steeples, were second in strength and splendor only to Saint-Germain-des-Prés. Between the two streets, Saint-Martin and Saint-Denis, was the enclosure of the Trinity. And, finally, between the Rue Saint-Denis and the Rue Montorgueil was that of the Filles-Dieu. Close by the latter were to be distinguished the decayed roofs and unpaved enclosure of the Court of Miracles, the only profane link that obtruded itself into that chain of religious houses.

Finally, the fourth compartment which rose distinctly in the conglomeration of roofs upon the right bank, occupying the western corner of the great enclosure, down to the river's edge, was another group of palaces and great mansions crowding against the Louvre. The old Louvre of Philip-Augustus, an immense structure, whose great tower mustered around it twenty-three principal towers, besides all the smaller ones, seemed at a distance to be framed, as it were, within the Gothic summits of the Hotel d'Alençon and the Petit-Bourbon. This hydra of towers, this giant guardian of Paris, with its twenty-four upraised heads and with monstrous ridges on its back, sheathed in lead or scaled with slates, and all variegated with glittering metallic streaks, marked in a surprising manner the western boundary of the Town.

Thus, you saw an immense mass, what the Romans called an "island," of ordinary dwellings, flanked on both sides by two great clusters of palaces, topped on one side by the Louvre and on the other by the Tournelles, and bordered on the north by a long belt of abbeys and walled gardens—the whole combined and blended to the sight. Over those thousands of buildings, whose tiled and slated roofs ran in so many fantastic chains, were the engraved, embroidered, and inlaid steeples of the forty-four churches on the right bank. Among them were the myriads of cross streets. The boundary on one side was a line of lofty walls with square towers (that of the University wall being round), and on the other, the Seine, crossed by bridges and crowded with countless boats. Such was Paris in the fifteenth century.

Beyond the walls were the suburbs, huddled against the gates, but less numerous and more scattered than those on the University side. Thus, behind the Bastille, there squatted a score of hovels, clustered around the Cross of Faubin, with its curious sculptures, and the abbey of Saint-Antoine-des-Champs, with its flying buttresses. Also there was then Popincourt, lost amid the cornfields; then La Courtille, a merry village of taverns; the village of Saint-Laurent, with its church, whose belfry from a distance seemed to be a part of the pointed towers of the Porte Saint-Martin; the suburb of Saint-Denis, with the extensive enclosure of Saint-Ladre; outside the Porte Montmartre, the Grange-Batelière encircled with white walls; and behind it the chalky slopes of Montmartre itself. Montmartre then had almost as many churches as windmills, but has retained only the windmills, since society now seeks only bread for the body. And beyond the Louvre, you saw, stretching into the meadows, the suburb of Saint-Honoré, even then of considerable size; green La Petite-Bretagne; and, spreading itself out, the Marché-aux-Pourceaux, in the center of which stood the horrible boiler used for executing those convicted of counterfeiting. Between La Courtille and Saint-Laurent your eye had already remarked, on the summit of a little hill that rose in a lonely plain, a structure which looked from a distance like a ruined colonnade standing over a basement with its foundation exposed. This, however, was neither a Parthenon nor a Temple of the Olympian Jupiter; it was Montfaucon.

Now, if the enumeration of so many edifices, brief as we have tried to be, has not shattered in the reader's mind the general image of old Paris as fast as we have endeavored to construct it, we will recapitulate it in a few words. In the center was the island of the City, resembling in its form an enormous tortoise, extending on either side its bridges all scaly with tiles, like so many feet, from under its gray shell of roofs. On the left, the close, dense, bristling, and homogeneous quadrangle of the University, and on the right the vast semicircle of the Town, much more interspersed with gardens and great edifices. The three masses—City, Town, and University—are veined with innumerable streets. Through the whole runs the Seine, the "life-giving Seine," as Father Du Breul calls it, dotted with islands, crossed by bridges, and boats. All around is an immense plain, checkered with fields, planted with a thousand different sorts of vegetation, and strewn with beautiful villages—on the left, Issy, Vanves, Vaugirard, Montrogue, Gentilly, with its round tower and its square tower, etc.; and on the right twenty others, from Conflans to Ville-l'Evêque. On the horizon a circle of hills formed, as it were, the rim of this vast basin. Finally, in the distance on the east, was Vincennes, with its seven quadrangular towers; on the south, Bicêtre with its pointed turrets; on the north, Saint-Denis and its spire; and on the

west, Saint-Cloud and its castle-keep. Such was the Paris
viewed from the towers of Notre-Dame by the ravens who
lived in 1482.

And yet it is of this city that Voltaire said, "Before the
time of Louis XIV, it possessed only four fine pieces of architecture"; that is to say, the dome of the Sorbonne, the Val-
de-Grâce, the modern Louvre, and I have forgotten the
fourth; perhaps it was the Luxembourg. Fortunately, Voltaire
was nonetheless the author of "Candide"; as such, and for
having made this observation, he proved himself not the
least sardonic of the many men who succeeded him. This
proves, besides, that one may be a genius, and yet understand nothing of an art which he has not yet studied. Didn't
Molière think he was doing a great honor to Raphael and
Michelangelo when he called them "those Mignards of their
age"?

But to return to fifteenth-century Paris.

It was then not only a beautiful city, but a homogeneous
one, an architectural and historical product of the Middle
Ages—a chronicle in stone. It was a city composed of two
architectural strata only, the Romanesque and the Gothic, for
the Roman layer had disappeared long ago except in the
Baths of Julian, where it still pierced through the thick in-
crustation of the Middle Ages. As for the Celtic stratum,
specimens could no longer be found, even when digging a
well.

Fifty years later, when the Renaissance came to blend
with this severe yet diversified unity the dazzling profuse-
ness of its own systems and its fantasies that rioted among
Roman arches, Grecian columns, and Gothic vaults, its delicate and lifelike sculpture, its own peculiar taste for arabesques and foliage, its architectural paganism contemporary
with Luther, Paris was perhaps more beautiful still, though
less harmonious to the eye and to the mind. But that glorious
period was of short duration. The Renaissance was not impartial. Not content with erecting, it thought proper to pull
down; it must be acknowledged, too, that it needed room. So
the Gothic Paris was complete but for a moment. Scarcely
was the tower of Saint-Jacques-de-la-Boucherie completed
before the demolition of the old Louvre was begun.

Since that time, this great city has been daily lapsing into deformity. The Gothic Paris, under which the Romanesque Paris disappeared, passed away in its turn. But what name shall we give to the Paris that has taken its place?

There is the Paris of Catherine de Medicis at the Tuileries, the Paris of Henri II at the Hotel de Ville—two edifices which are still in fine taste; the Paris of Henry IV at the Place Royale—a brick front, faced with stone, and roofed with slate, tri-colored houses; the Paris of Louis XIII at the Val-de-Grâce—a squat, clumsy style, with basket-handle vaults, big-bellied columns, and a hunchbacked dome; the Paris of Louis XIV at the Invalides—great, rich, gilded, and cold; the Paris of Louis XV at Saint-Sulpice—with volutes, knots of ribbons, clouds, vermicelli, and chicory, all in stone; the Paris of Louis XVI at the Pantheon—a wretched copy of St. Peter's in Rome (the building has settled awkwardly, which has by no means rectified its lines); the Paris of the Republic at the School of Medicine, a poor Greek and Roman style, just as much to be compared to the Colosseum or the Parthenon as the constitution of the year III is to the laws of Minos—which style in architecture is called the "Messidor"; the Paris of Napoleon at the Place Vendôme—something sublime, a brazen column composed of melted cannon; the Paris of the Restoration at the Bourse—a very white colonnade, supporting a very smooth frieze; the whole is square and cost twenty million francs.

To each of these characteristic structures is allied, by similarity of style, manner, and arrangement, a certain number of houses scattered over the different quarters of the Town, which the eye of the connoisseur easily distinguishes and assigns to their respective dates. When a man understands the art of seeing, he can trace the spirit of an age and the features of a king even in the knocker on a door.

Contemporary Paris has therefore no general physiognomy. It is a collection of parts from several different ages, and the finest of all have disappeared. This capital is increasing in houses only, and what houses! If it goes on as it is going now, Paris will be rebuilt every fifty years. So also the historical meaning of its architecture is daily wearing away. Its great structures are becoming fewer and fewer, seeming to be swallowed up one after the other by this flood of houses. Our fathers had a Paris of stone, our children will have a Paris of plaster.

As for the modern structures of the new Paris, we shall gladly decline from enlarging upon them. Not, indeed, that we do not pay them all proper admiration. Soufflot's Sainte-Geneviève is certainly the finest Savoy cake that was ever made of stone. The Palace of the Legion of Honor is also a very distinguished piece of pastry. The dome of the Halle-au-Blé is an English jockey-cap on a magnificent scale. The towers of Saint-Sulpice are two great clarinets; now, nobody can deny that a clarinet shape *is* a shape, and then the telegraph, crooked and grinning, makes an admirable diversity upon the roof. The church of Saint-Roch has a doorway with whose magnificence only that of Saint-Thomas Aquinas can compare; it also has a high-relief Calvary down in the cellar, and a sun of gilded wood. These things, it must be owned, are positively marvelous. The lantern of the labyrinth at the Garden of Plants, too, is vastly ingenious. As for the Palais de la Bourse, which is Grecian in its colonnade, Roman in the circular arches of its doors and windows, and of the Renaissance in its great vaulted ceiling, it doubtless is a structure of great correctness and purity of taste, one proof of which is that it is crowned by an attic story such as was never seen in Athens, a fine straight line gracefully intersected here and there by stove pipes. Let us here add that if it be a rule that the architecture of a building should be so adapted to the purpose of the building, that the aspect of the edifice should at once declare that purpose, we cannot too much admire a structure which from its appearance might be either a royal palace, a chamber of deputies, a town hall, a college, a riding house, an academy, a repository, a court of justice, a museum, a barracks, a mausoleum, a temple, or a theater, but which is all the while the Bourse. A building ought moreover to be adapted to the climate. This one has evidently been built expressly for a cold and rainy sky. Its roof is almost flat, as in the East; and consequently in winter, when there is snow, the roof has to be swept. And does anyone doubt that roofs are intended to be swept? As for the purpose of which we have just now been speaking, the building fulfills it admirably. It is the Bourse in France, as it would have been a temple in Greece. True it is that the architect had much ado to conceal the dial of the clock, which would have destroyed the purity of the noble lines of the facade; but to make amends we have that colonnade around the whole structure, under which, on important days of religious solemnity, may be magnificently developed the schemes of money-brokers and stock-jobbers.

These, doubtless, are very superb structures. Add to these many a pretty street, amusing and diversified, like the Rue de Rivoli, and we need not despair that Paris shall one day present, when seen from a balloon, that richness of outline and opulence of detail, that peculiar diversity of aspect, that something surpassingly grand in the simple and striking in the beautiful, which distinguishes a draftboard.

However, admirable as you may think the present Paris, reconstruct in your imagination the Paris of the fifteenth century; look at the sky through that surprising forest of spires, towers, and steeples; pour forth through the midst of the vast city, tear upon the tips of the islands, bend under the arches of the bridges of the Seine with her large patches of green and yellow, more changeable than a serpent's skin; project distinctly upon an azure horizon the Gothic profile of that old Paris; make its outline float in a wintry mist clinging to its innumerable chimneys; plunge it into deep night, and observe the fantastic display of the lights against the darkness of that gloomy labyrinth of buildings; cast upon it a ray of moonlight, showing the city in glimmering vagueness, with its towers lifting their great heads from that foggy sea; or revert again to that dark silhouette, reanimate with shadow the thousand sharp angles of its spires and gables and make it stand out, more jagged than a shark's jaw, against the copper-colored sky of the setting sun.

Now compare.

And if you would receive from the old city an impression which the modern one is quite incapable of giving, ascend, on the morning of some great holiday, at sunrise, on Easter or on Pentecost Sunday, to some elevated point from which your eye can command the whole capital, and attend the awakening of the chimes. Behold, at a signal from heaven—for it is the sun that gives it—those thousand churches starting from their sleep. At first you hear only scattered tinklings from church to church, as when musicians are giving one another notice to begin. Then, all of a sudden, behold—for there are moments when the ear itself seems to see—behold, ascending at the same moment from every steeple a column of sound, as it were, a cloud of harmony. At first, the vibration of each bell mounts direct, clear, and, as it were, isolated from the rest into the splendid morning sky. Then by degrees, as they expand, they mingle, unite, and are lost in one another. All are confounded in one magnificent concert. They become a mass of sonorous vibrations, endlessly sent forth from the innumerable steeples—floating, undulating, bounding, and eddying over the town, and extending far beyond the horizon the deafening circle of its oscillations. Yet that sea of harmony is no chaos. Wide and deep as it is, it has not lost its transparency: you perceive the winding of each group of notes that escapes from the several chimes; you can follow the dialogue by turns grave and clamorous, of the *crescelle* and the *bourdon*; you perceive the octaves leaping from steeple to steeple; you observe them springing aloft, winged, light, and whistling from the silver bell, falling broken and limping from the wooden bell. You admire among them the seven bells of Saint-Eustache, whose peals incessantly descend and ascend. And you see clear and rapid notes running across, as it were, in three or four luminous zigzags, and vanishing like flashes of lightning. Down there in Saint-Martin's Abbey is a shrill and broken-voiced songstress; nearer is the sinister and sullen voice of the Bastille; and farther away is the great tower of the Louvre, with its counter tenor. The royal carillon of the Palace unceasingly casts on every side resplendent trillings, upon which fall at regular intervals the heavy stroke from the great bell of Notre-Dame, making sparkles of sound as a hammer upon an anvil. Frequently, many tones come from the triple peal of Saint-Germain-des-Prés. Then, again, from time to time that mass of sublime noise half opens, and gives passage to the finale of the Ave-Maria, which glitters like a cluster of stars. Below, in the deeps of the concert, you distinguish the confused, internal voices of the churches, exhaled through the vibrating pores of their vaulted roofs. Here, certainly, is an opera worth hearing. Ordinarily, the murmur that escapes from Paris in the daytime is the city talking; in the night, it is the city breathing, but here, it is the city singing. Listen then to this ensemble of the steeples; diffuse over it the murmur of half a million people, the everlasting plaint of the river, the boundless breathings of the wind, the grave and distant quartet of the four forests placed upon the hills in the distance like so many vast organs, immersing in them, as in a demitint, all in the central concert that would otherwise be too raucous or too sharp, and then say whether you know of anything in the world more rich, more joyous, more golden, more dazzling than this tumult of bells and chimes, this furnace of music, these ten thousand voices of brass, all singing together in flutes of stone three hundred feet high—than this city which is no longer anything but an orchestra—than this symphony as loud as a tempest.

BOOK IV

1

Good Souls

Sixteen years before the events here recorded took place, one fine morning, Quasimodo Sunday, a living creature had been deposited after Mass in the church of Notre-Dame in the wooden bed sealed in the pavement on the left hand of the entrance, opposite that great image of St. Christopher, which the kneeling stone figure of Messire Antoine des Essarts, knight, had been contemplating since the year 1413, when it was thought proper to throw down both saint and sinner. Upon this wooden bed it was customary to expose orphans to public charity. Anyone who chose could take them away. In front of this wooden bed there was a copper basin for contributions.

The sort of living creature which was lying upon this plank on the morning of Quasimodo Sunday in the year of Our Lord 1467 seemed to excite, in a high degree, the curiosity of a rather large group which had gathered around it. The group consisted mainly of members of the fair sex. They were nearly all old women.

In the front line, bending low over the bed, were four, who, by their gray habit, most certainly were members of some religious sisterhood. I do not know why history should not hand down to posterity the names of these four discreet and venerable ladies. They were Agnes la Herme, Jehanne de la Tarme, Henriette la Gaultière, and Gauchère la Violette, all four widows, all four good women of the Chapelle Etienne-Haudry, who, with the permission of their Mother Superior and in keeping with the regulations of Pierre d'Ailly, had left their home, and had come to hear the sermon at the cathedral.

However, if these good sisters were observing for the moment the rules of Pierre d'Ailly, they were, undeniably, violating joyfully those of Michel de Brache and the Cardinal of Pisa, which so inhumanly imposed upon them the law of silence.

"Sister, whatever can that be?" said Agnes to Gauchère, as she gazed at the little exposed creature, screaming and twisting in his wooden bed, frightened by so many gaping faces.

"What is the world coming to," said Jehanne, "if that's the way they make children nowadays?"

"I don't know much about children," resumed Agnes, "but it must be a sin to look at this one."

"It's not a child at all, Agnes. It's a deformed ape," observed Gauchère.

"It's a miracle," said Henriette la Gaultière.

"Then," remarked Agnes, "this is the third since Laetare Sunday. For it's not a week since we had the miracle of the mocker of the pilgrims divinely punished by Our Lady of Aubervilliers, and that was the second miracle of the month."

"But, this so-called orphan is an abominable monster," resumed Jehanne.

"He screams loud enough to drown out a chanter," pursued Gauchère. "Be quiet, you little bawler!"

"To say that it's Monsieur of Reims that sends this monstrosity to Monsieur of Paris!" exclaimed la Gaultière, clasping her hands.

"I should guess," said Agnes la Herme, "that it's a beast, an animal—the offspring of a Jew and a sow—something, at any rate, which is not Christian, and which must be thrown into the river or fire."

"I hope no one will claim it," continued la Gaultière.

"My God!" expostulated Agnes, "these poor nurses who live down there in the orphanage at the end of the alley, going down to the river, right next to the bishop's residence! Suppose someone were to take them this little monster to suckle! I'd rather nurse a vampire."

"Poor la Herme! What a simpleton!" rejoined Jehanne. "Don't you see, my sister, that this little monster is at least four years old, and wouldn't have half so much appetite for your breast as for a piece of roast meat."

Indeed, the "little monster" was not a newborn infant. (We ourselves would be much puzzled to give it any other name.) It was a little, angular, twitching mass, imprisoned in a canvas bag, marked with Messire Guillaume Chartier's initials, then Bishop of Paris, with a head peeping out. And that head was so deformed! It was nothing but a forest of red hair, one eye, a mouth, and a few teeth. The eye was weeping; the mouth was crying; and the teeth seemed to want only to bite. The whole lump was struggling violently in the sack, to the great wonderment of the increasing and ever-shifting crowd around it.

Dame Aloise de Gondelaurier, a wealthy and noble lady, who was holding by the hand a pretty little girl about six years old, and trailing after her a long veil attached to the golden horn of her coif, stopped as she passed before the bed, and looked for a moment at the unfortunate creature, while her charming little daughter, Fleur-de-Lys de Gondelaurier, all dressed in silk and velvet, was spelling with her pretty finger, on the permanent sign attached to the bed, the words: "ENFANTS TROUVÉS."

"Really," said the lady, turning away with disgust, "I thought they exposed only children here."

She turned her back, throwing into the basin a silver florin, which jingled among the liards and opened wide the eyes of the poor good sisters of the Chapelle Etienne-Haudry.

A moment later, the grave and learned Robert Mistricolle, king's protonotary, passed by, with an enormous missal under one arm, and his wife under the other (Damoiselle Guillemette la Mairesse), thus having at his side two regulators, the spiritual and the temporal.

"Orphan!" said he, after examining the object. "Yes, probably found on the banks of the Phlegethon!"

"It has only one eye," observed Damoiselle Guillemette, "and over the other there is a wart."

"That's not a wart," exclaimed Master Robert Mistricolle. "It's an egg that contains another demon just like it, with another little egg containing another devil, and so on."

"How do you know?" asked Guillemette la Mairesse.

"I know it for a fact," answered the protonotary.

"Monsieur the Protonotary," asked Gauchère, "what do you prognosticate for this pretended orphan?"

"The greatest calamities," answered Mistricolle.

"Ah! My God!" said an old lady among the bystanders, "and there was already a considerable pestilence last year, and they say the English are going to land in great masses at Harfleur!"

"Perhaps that will prevent the queen from coming to Paris in September," remarked another. "Trade is bad enough as it is!"

"I think," cried Jehanne de la Tarme, "that it would be better for the people of Paris if that little sorcerer there were living upon a faggot than upon a board."

"Yes, on a fine flaming faggot!" added the old lady.

"That would be more prudent," said Mistricolle.

For several minutes a young priest had been listening to the comments of the women and the pronouncements of the protonotary. His face was severe, his forehead broad, and his eyes penetrating. He pushed his way silently through the crowd, examined the "little sorcerer," and stretched his hand over him. It was time, for all the pious ladies were already licking their lips in anticipation of the fine flaming faggot.

"I'll adopt that child," said the priest.

He wrapped it in his cassock and carried it away. The bystanders looked after him with horror. In a minute he had disappeared through the Porte-Rouge which at that time led from the church to the cloister.

When the first surprise was over, Jehanne de la Tarme whispered in the ear of la Gaultière, "Didn't I tell you, sister, that that young cleric, Monsieur Claude Frollo, is a sorcerer?"

2

Claude Frollo

Indeed, Claude Frollo was no ordinary person. He belonged to one of those families, which, in the impertinent language of the last century, were called indifferently the upper middle class or lower aristocracy. His family had inherited from the brothers Paclet the fief of Tirechappe, which was controlled by the Bishop of Paris, and the twenty-one houses of which had been, in the thirteenth century, the object of so many law suits before the official. As owner of this fief, Claude Frollo was one of the one hundred and forty-one seigneurs claiming manorial dues in Paris and its suburbs; and as such his name was long to be seen inscribed between the Hotel de Tancarville, belonging to Master François le Rez, and the College of Tours, in the chartulary deposited in the church of Saint-Martin-des-Champs.

From his childhood Claude Frollo's parents had destined him for the priesthood. He had been taught to read Latin, to cast his eyes down, and to speak softly. While still a child, his father had cloistered him in the College of Torchi, in the University. It was there he had grown up on the missal and the lexicon.

Moreover, he was by nature a melancholy, reserved, serious boy, who studied intently and learned quickly. He never shouted during the recreation hour, he rarely attended the drinking parties on Rue du Fouarre, did not know what it was to *dare alapas et capillos laniare,*[1] and had taken no part in that students' riot in 1463, which the annalists gravely record as "The Sixth Disturbance in the University." It rarely happened that he jibed the poor scholars of Montagu for their short capes, *"cappettes,"* from which they derived their university nickname, or the scholarship students of the College of Dormans for their smooth tonsure and their tri-colored frocks of gray, blue, and purple cloth—

---

[1] "To give blows and pull hair."

azurini coloris et bruni—as reads the charter of the cardinal des Quatres-Couronnes.

On the other hand, he was assiduous at the great and little schools on the Rue Saint-Jean-de-Beauvais. The first student whom the abbot of Saint-Pierre de Val, at the moment he commenced his reading in canon law, always observed was Claude Frollo, firmly seated opposite the abbot's chair, against a pillar of the school of Saint-Vendregesile. The boy came furnished with his inkhorn, his pen, which he chewed, and his notebook, in which he scribbled as it rested on his much-worn knee. In winter, he blew on his fingers. The first auditor whom Messire Miles d'Isliers, doctor of ecclesiastical law, saw arrive every Monday morning, all out of breath, at the opening of the doors of the school of Chef-Saint-Denis, was Claude Frollo. Thus, at sixteen the young cleric was a match for a father of the Church in mystical theology, for a father of the councils in canonical theology, and for a doctor of the Sorbonne in scholastic theology.

When he had finished theology, he rushed into the studies of the decretals. From the "Master of Sentences," he had fallen upon the Capitularies of Charlemagne, and in his thirst for knowledge, he had successively devoured decretal after decretal, those of Theodore, Bishop of Hispalis, those of Bouchard, Bishop of Worms, those of Yves, Bishop of Chartres; then the decretal of Gratian, which followed the Capitularies of Charlemagne, then a collection of Gregory IX's, then Honorius the Third's epistle, "Super Specula." He made himself clearly familiar with the civil and canon law of that vast and tumultuous period when they were in clash and strife with each other in the chaos of the Middle Ages—a period which opens with Bishop Theodore in 618, and closes with Pope Gregory in 1227.

Having thoroughly digested the decretals, he plunged into the study of medicine and the liberal arts. He studied the science of herbs and the science of unguents. He became expert in the cure of fevers and contusions, wounds and abscesses. Jacques d'Espars would have accepted him as a physician and Richard Hellain as a surgeon. Likewise he ran through all the degrees of Licentiate, Master, and Doctor of Arts. He studied languages—Latin, Greek, Hebrew—a triple sanctuary at that time but little frequented. He had a veritable fever for acquiring and hoarding knowledge. At eighteen he had successfully passed four faculties. It seemed to our young man that life had but one purpose: to know.

It was during this period that the excessive heat of the summer of 1466 gave rise to that great pestilence which took the lives of more than forty thousand people in Paris, and among others, says Jean de Troyes, "Master Arnoul, the king's astrologer, a right honest man, wise and pleasant." It was rumored in the University that the Rue Tirechappe was particularly ravaged by the plague. It was there, in the midst of their fief, that the parents of Claude resided. Much alarmed, the young scholar hastened to his paternal residence only to find that both his mother and father had died the day before. A little brother still in swaddling clothes was still alive, and crying, abandoned in his cradle. He was all of Claude's family that remained. The young boy, deep in thought, took the baby under his arm and went away. Hitherto he had existed only in books; now he began to live.

The loss of his parents was a crisis in Claude's life. Now an orphan, the elder boy, head of the family at nineteen, felt himself rudely roused from the reveries of school to the realities of life. Then, moved with pity, he was filled with passionate devotion for this infant brother. How strange and sweet to him was this human affection, to him who had loved only books.

This affection waxed singularly strong. In a soul so unaccustomed to personal feeling, it was like a first love. Separated since childhood from his parents, whom he scarcely knew, cloistered and walled up in his books, eager above everything to study and to learn, exclusively attentive, until then, to his understanding, which expanded itself in science, to his imagination, which grew with literary studies, the poor scholar had not yet had time for emotion. This infant brother, without father or mother, this infant which suddenly dropped from heaven into his arms, made a new person—a man—of him. He discovered that there was something else in the world besides his speculations at the Sorbonne and the poetry of Homer. He found that man needs affection, that life without a warming love is but a dry wheel, creaking and grating as it turns. Only he imagined, for he was still at that age when illusions are as yet replaced only by illusions, that the affections of kith and kin are the only ones necessary, and that a little brother to love would be sufficient to fill up his whole existence.

He threw himself, therefore, into the love of his little Jehan with all the passion of a character which was already deep, ardent, and concentrated. This poor frail creature, pretty, fair, rosy-cheeked, and curly-headed, this orphan with no other support but another orphan, moved him to the very depths of his soul; and like the serious thinker he was, he began to regard Jehan with deep compassion. He bestowed upon him all the attention and care he could, as upon something extremely fragile, and very special. He was more than a brother to the infant, he was its mother.

As little Jehan had lost his mother before he was weaned, Claude put him out to nurse. Besides the fief of Tirechappe, he had inherited from his father the fief of Moulin, wherein stood the square tower of Gentilly, topping a mill standing on a hill near the castle of Winchester, since corrupted into Bicêtre. The miller's wife was nursing a fine boy at the time. If wasn't far from the university, so Claude took his little Jehan to this woman.

Thenceforward, feeling that a great burden rested upon him, he took life very seriously. The thought of his little brother became not only his recreation, but even the object of his studies. He resolved to devote himself entirely to the future of that child for whom he must answer before God, and never to have any other spouse, nor other child than the happiness and welfare of his brother. He plied himself, therefore, more earnestly than ever in his clerical vocation. His merit, his learning, his position as an immediate vassal of the Bishop of Paris, further opened for him the doors of the Church. At twenty, by a special dispensation from the Holy See, he was ordained a priest, and as the youngest of the chaplains of Notre-Dame, he performed the service of the altar called, on account of the late Mass that was said there, *altare pigrorum.*[2]

There, more than ever immersed in his dear books, which he never quitted but to run for an hour to the fief at the mill, this mixture of learning and austerity, so rare at his age,

[2] "At the altar of the lazy."

speedily gained him the respect and admiration of the cloister. From the cloister, his reputation for learning was communicated to the people, by whom, as frequently happened in those days, it was converted into a reputation as a sorcerer.

It was at the moment when he was returning, on Quasimodo Sunday, from saying his Mass at the "altar of the lazy," which was by the door of the choir which opened into the nave, on the right-hand side, near the statue of the Virgin, that his attention had been awakened by the group of old women chattering around the bed for foundlings.

Then it was that he had approached the unfortunate little creature so abhorred and ill-treated. Its distress, its deformity, its abandonment, the remembrance of his little brother, the idea which suddenly crossed his mind that were he himself to die his dear little Jehan, too, might chance to be miserably cast upon those boards—all these ideas crowded into his mind at once, and, moved by a feeling of deep compassion, he had carried away the child.

When he pulled the infant out of the sack, he found it to be deformed indeed. The poor little rascal had a wart over its left eye, the head pushed down between the shoulders, the spine crooked, the breastbone protruding, the legs bowed. Yet it seemed lively enough. And although it was impossible to know what language it was muttering, its yelping indicated a certain degree of health and strength.

Claude's compassion was increased by this ugliness; and he vowed in his heart to rear the child for the love of his brother, in order that, whatever might be the faults, in the future, of little Jehan, there might be placed to his credit this bit of charity performed on his account. It was a sort of putting out of good works at interest, which he transacted in his brother's name—an investment of good actions which he wished to lay up for him in advance—to provide against the chance of the little fellow's one day finding himself short of that sort of coin, the only kind taken at the gate of heaven.

He baptized his adopted child and called him Quasimodo; whether it was that he chose thereby to commemorate the day when he had found him, or that he meant to mark by that name how incomplete and imperfectly molded the poor little creature was. Indeed, Quasimodo, one-eyed, hunchbacked, and bowlegged, could hardly be considered as anything more than an *almost*.

3

Immanis Pecoris Custos Immanior Ipse[1]

Now in 1482, Quasimodo had grown up. He had been for several years ringer of the bells of Notre-Dame, thanks to his foster father, Claude Frollo, who had become archdeacon of Josas, thanks to his liege Messire Louis de Beaumont, who had become Bishop of Paris in 1472, at the death of Guillaume Chartier, thanks to his patron Olivier le Daim, barber to King Louis XI, by the grace of God.

Quasimodo, then, was bellringer of Notre-Dame.

With time, a certain indescribable bond of intimacy had been formed between the bellringer and the church. Separated for always from the world by the double fatality of his unknown parentage and his natural deformity, imprisoned from infancy within that doubly impregnable wall, the poor wretch had been accustomed to see nothing in this world beyond the religious walls which had received him into their shade. Notre-Dame had been to him successively, as he grew up, his egg, his nest, his house, his country, his universe.

And it is certain that, between this creature and this edifice, there was a sort of mysterious and pre-existing harmony. When, while he was still quite young, he used to drag himself along, tortuously and tumblingly, within the gloom of its arches, he seemed, with his human face and his animal-like limbs, a native reptile of that damp, dark stone floor, on which the shadows of the Romanesque capitals projected so many fantastic shapes.

Later, the first time that he hung precariously to the bellrope, suspended himself upon it, and set the bell in motion, the effect upon Claude, his foster father, was like that engendered by a child whose tongue is loosened and who is just beginning to talk.

Thus it was that, gradually, unfolding his being in the

---

[1] "Of a monstrous flock the still more monstrous guardian."

mold of the cathedral, living in it, sleeping in it, hardly ever leaving it, subject every hour to its mysterious impress, he came at length to resemble it, to be encrusted on it, as it were, to become an integral part of it. His salient angles fitted, so to speak, the retreating angles of the edifice, and he seemed to be, not only its inhabitant, but even its natural tenant. One might almost say that he had taken on its shape, as the snail takes on the shape of its shell. It was his dwelling place, his hole, his envelope. Between the old church and himself there was a kind of instinctive, profound empathy; there were so many affinities, mystical as well as material, that he adhered to it in some fashion, like the tortoise to its shell. This hoary cathedral was his carapace.

It is useless to suggest to the reader that he not take literally the figures that we are here obliged to use in order to express that singular assimilation—symmetrical, immediate, almost cosubstantial—of a man to a building. It is needless to say, likewise, to what degree Quasimodo must have familiarized himself with the whole cathedral during so long and so intimate a cohabitation. This dwelling place was his own. It had no depth which he had not penetrated, no height he had not scaled. Many a time he had clambered up its front to various elevations with no help except the rough surface of the sculpture. The towers, over whose external surface he sometimes crept like a lizard gliding upon a perpendicular wall, those twin giants, so tall, so threatening, so formidable, had for him no terror, no threats of vertigo or falls from giddy heights. To see them so gentle under his hand, so easy to scale, one would have thought that he had tamed them. By dint of leaping, climbing, playing over the abysses of the gigantic cathedral, he had become in a way some sort of combined monkey and chamois, like the Calabrian child, who swims before it can run, whose first playmate is the sea.

Moreover, not only did his body seem to have fashioned itself after the cathedral, but likewise his mind. It would be difficult to determine the state of that soul, what folds it had contracted, what form it had taken under that knotty covering, in that savage mode of life. Quasimodo was born one-eyed, hunchbacked, lame. It was with much difficulty and much patience that Claude Frollo had succeeded in teaching him to speak. But an evil fate seemed to stalk the poor orphan. Bellringer of Notre-Dame at fourteen, yet a new infirmity came to complete his apartness. The bells had broken his tympanum, so he had become deaf. The only door that nature had left open wide to the world had suddenly been closed forever.

And its closing cut off the only ray of joy and light that had penetrated to the soul of Quasimodo. That soul was plunged into profound darkness. The wretch's melancholy became incurable and as complete as his deformity. Besides, his deafness rendered him in some way dumb. For, in order that he might not be laughed at, from the moment he knew he was deaf, he resolutely determined to keep silent, which silence he scarcely ever broke except when he was alone. He voluntarily tied that tongue which Claude Frollo had taken so much trouble to untie. And hence it was that, when necessity constrained him to speak, his tongue moved stiffly and awkwardly, like a door whose hinges are rusty.

If now we were to try to fathom the soul of Quasimodo beneath that thick, hard rind; if we could sound the depths of that tormented sea; if it were possible for us to look, with a torch, behind that opaque wall, to explore the dark interior of this creature, to light up its obscure corners, its fantastic culs-de-sac, and all of a sudden to throw a bright light upon the Psyche chained to the bottom of that cave, no doubt, we would find that poor soul in some posture of decrepitude, stunted and rickety, like those prisoners who used to grow old in the dungeons of Venice, doubled over in a stone box, too low to stand up and too short to lie down in.

It is certain that the mind wastes away in a misshapen body. Impressions of objects underwent a considerable refraction before they reached Quasimodo's consciousness. Quasimodo scarcely felt stirring blindly within him a soul made after his own image. His brain was a peculiar medium; ideas which passed through it issued forth all twisted. The reflection which proceeded from that refraction was necessarily divergent and devious.

Hence a thousand optical illusions, hence a thousand aberrations of judgment, hence a thousand wandering ideas, sometimes foolish, sometimes idiotic.

The first effect of this unbalanced organization was to blur the vision of things. He received from them scarcely any immediate perception. The external world seemed to him much farther off than it does to us.

The second effect of his misfortune was that it made him mischievous. He was mischievous, indeed, because he was wild; and he was wild because he was ugly. There was logic in his nature, as there is in ours. His physical strength, also, developed to so extraordinary a degree, was another cause of his mischievousness. *Malus puer robustus,*[2] writes Hobbes.

However, we must do him justice; this mischievousness was perhaps not innate with him. From his earliest experiences with men, he had felt, and later he had seen, himself repulsed, reviled, spat upon. Human speech as directed to him had ever seemed either a jeer or a curse. As he grew up he found around him only hatred. He adopted it. He contracted the general malignancy. He armed himself with the weapons that had wounded him.

After all, he turned toward mankind reluctantly. His cathedral was enough for him. It was peopled with figures in marble, with kings, saints, bishops, who at least did not burst out laughing in his face, but looked upon him with tranquillity and kindness. The other figures, those of the monsters and demons, had no hatred for him, Quasimodo. He was too much like them for that. Rather, they seemed to be scoffing at the rest of mankind. The saints were his friends, and blessed him; the monsters were his friends, and protected him. Consequently he used to commune long with them; he would spend whole hours, squatted in front of one of the statues, chatting alone with it. If anyone happened to approach, he would run off like a lover surprised in a serenade.

And the cathedral was not only his society; it was his universe. It was all of nature to him. He dreamed of no other garden but the stained-glass window ever in flower; of no other shade but that cast by the stone foliage full of birds that spread itself from the leafy capitals of the Roman pillars; of no other mountains but the colossal towers of the cathedral; of no ocean but Paris, which roared against their base.

What he loved above all in this his maternal edifice, what most roused his soul, and made it open wide its poor pinions

[2] "The vigorous child is bad."

which it kept so miserably folded within its cavern, that which sometimes made him happy was the bells. He loved them, caressed them, talked to them, understood them. From the carillon in the steeple of the transept to the great bell over the doorway, they all shared his love. The steeple of the transept and the two towers were to him like three immense cages whose birds, reared by him, sang only for him. It was, however, those same bells that had made him deaf; but a mother often loves best of all the child who has made her suffer most.

It is true that their voices were the only ones that he could still hear. So, the big bell was his best beloved. It was she whom he preferred in this family of noisy daughters that frolicked around him on festival days. This great bell was named Marie. She lived alone in the southern tower while her sister Jacqueline, a bell of smaller dimensions, was shut up in a smaller cage beside hers.

This bell Jacqueline was named after the wife of Jean Montagu, who had donated it to the church—a gift which had not prevented him from ending up without his head at Montfaucon. In the northern tower there were six other bells, and, lastly, six smaller bells inhabited the transept steeple with a wooden bell, which was rung only between noon of Maundy Thursday and the morning of Holy Saturday. Thus Quasimodo had fifteen bells in his seraglio. But big Marie was his favorite.

It would be difficult to appreciate fully his joy on days of the full tolling of the bells. The moment that the archdeacon sent him off with that one word, "Go!" he scrambled up the spiral staircase of the belfry more quickly than another would have descended it. All out of breath, he hurried into the aerial chamber of the great bell, looked at her for a moment intently and lovingly, then talked to her softly, patted her with his hand, like a good horse about to set out on a long journey. He would pity her for the trouble he was going to cause her. After these first caresses, he called out to his assistants, stationed on a lower level of the tower, to begin. They seized the ropes, the capstan creaked, the enormous metal dome began to swing slowly. Quasimodo, panting, followed it with his eye. The first stroke of the clapper against the metal wall shook the wooden scaffolding on which he was standing. Quasimodo vibrated with the bell. "Vah!" he would cry with a burst of mad laughter. Meanwhile the bell swung faster, and as it swung, taking an ever-wider sweep, Quasimodo's eye opened wider and wider, and became more and more phosophorescent and enflamed. At length the full tolling began, and the whole tower trembled—rafters, lead, stone, all groaned at once, from the piles of the foundation to the trifoliations at the summit. Quasimodo was now all wet with perspiration, running to and fro, and shaking with the tower from head to foot. The bell, unleashed and swinging furiously, presented alternately to the two walls of the tower its bronze throat, from whence escaped that tempestuous breath that carried for four leagues around. Quasimodo remained in front of this gaping throat, squatted down, but rose at each return of the bell. He inhaled its boisterous breath, and looked by turns far down at the square swarming with people two hundred feet below him, and at the enormous brazen tongue which came, time after time, to bellow in his ear. It was the only speech he could hear, the only sound that broke the universal silence. He reveled in it like a bird in the sun. All at once, the frenzy of the bell possessed him; his expression became extraordinarily wild. He would wait for the huge bell to pass, as a spider waits for a fly, and then he would fling himself headlong onto it. Then, suspended over the abyss, carried to and fro by the formidable swinging of the bell, he seized the brazen monster by its ears, gripped it between his knees, spurred it with his two heels, and, with the whole force and weight of his body, he would redouble the fury of the pealing. Meanwhile the tower rocked, while he shouted and gnashed his teeth, his red hair bristling, his chest heaving like the blast of a forge, and his eye flaming, while his monstrous steed neighed, panting under him. Then there was no longer either the great bell of Notre-Dame or Quasimodo; it was a dream, a whirlwind, a tempest, vertigo astride a clamor, a spirit clinging to a flying saddle, a strange centaur, half man, half bell—a sort of horrible Astolfo, carried away on a prodigious hippogriff of living bronze.

The presence of this extraordinary being infused the cathedral with a certain breath of life. There seemed to escape from Quasimodo—at least so said the exaggerating superstitions of the crowd—a mysterious emanation which enlivened all the stones of Notre-Dame, and made the ancient church pulsate to its very entrails. When it was known that he was there, it was enough to make you think you saw life and motion in the thousand statues of the galleries and doorways. And indeed, the cathedral did seem like a creature, docile and obedient in his hands. She waited upon his will to lift up her loud voice; she was possessed by him; she was filled with Quasimodo, as with some familiar spirit. You would have said that he made this immense structure breathe. He was everywhere in it; he multiplied himself on every point of the monument. Sometimes, with dread, you saw at the very top of one of the towers, a fantastic dwarf, climbing, twisting, crawling on all fours, descending outside over the abyss, leaping from projection to projection, and worming into the belly of some sculptured gargoyle. It would be Quasimodo unnesting some crows. Sometimes, in a dark corner of the church, you stumbled over some sort of a living chimera, squatting and sullen; it would be Quasimodo in meditation. Sometimes, in one of the steeples, you espied an enormous head and a bundle of deranged limbs swinging wildly at the end of a rope; it would be Quasimodo ringing vespers or the Angelus. Often, at night, a hideous form was seen wandering over the delicate and lacelike balustrade that tops the towers and borders the roof of the chancel; it would again be the hunchback of Notre-Dame. Then, said the good women of the neighborhood, the whole church assumed a fantastic, supernatural, horrible aspect; eyes and mouths opened here and there; the stone dogs, griffins, and dragons who watch day and night, with outstretched necks and gaping jaws, around the monstrous cathedral, were heard to bark. And if it were Christmas night, while the great bell, which seemed to be raging, was calling the faithful to the blazing midnight Mass, there was such an air spread over the somber facade that the great doorway seemed to be devouring hordes of people as the rose-window looked on.

And all this came from Quasimodo. Egypt would have taken him for the god of this temple; the Middle Ages believed him to be its demon. But he was in fact its soul.

So much was this the case that to those who know that

Quasimodo did exist, Notre-Dame today is empty, lifeless, dead. They feel that something has gone out of her. That immense body is empty; it is a skeleton; the spirit has quit it. You see the place of its habitation, but that is all. It is like a skull, where the holes for the eyes remain, but there is no sight.

4

The Dog and His Master

However, there was one human being whom Quasimodo excepted from the malice and the hatred he reserved for others, and whom he loved as much as, perhaps more than, his cathedral. That was Claude Frollo.

It was simple enough to understand. Claude Frollo had accepted him, adopted him, had nourished him, had reared him. While very small it was between the knees of Claude Frollo that he had customarily sought refuge when the dogs and children barked after him. Claude Frollo had taught him to speak, to read, to write. Claude Frollo had made him the bellringer of Notre-Dame, and to give the great bell in marriage to Quasimodo was to give Juliet to Romeo.

Consequently, Quasimodo's gratitude was deep, ardent, boundless, and although the face of his foster father was often gloomy and severe, although his words were habitually brief, harsh, imperious, never had Quasimodo's gratitude waned for a single moment. The archdeacon had in Quasimodo a most submissive slave, a most docile valet, a most vigilant dog. When the poor bellringer lost his hearing, between him and Claude Frollo there was established a language of signs, mysterious and understood by them alone. In this way the archdeacon was the only human being with whom Quasimodo had communication. He was in contact with only two things in the world: Notre-Dame and Claude Frollo.

Nothing is quite comparable to the influence of the archdeacon over the bellringer, nor to the attachment of the bellringer to the archdeacon. A sign from Claude, and the idea of pleasing him would have been enough to cause Qua-

simodo to fling himself from the top of Notre-Dame's towers. It was remarkable how all the physical strength, so extraordinarily developed in Quasimodo, was placed blindly
by him at the disposal of Dom Claude. This undoubtedly
represented filial devotion and domestic attachment, but
there was also indicated a communication between the two
minds. Here was a poor, weak, awkward being who bowed
his head and lowered his one poor eye before an intellect,
lofty, penetrating, sharp, and superior. Finally, and this
above all, there was gratitude—gratitude so deep that we
know not with what to compare it. This virtue is not common among men. Let us say therefore that Quasimodo loved
the archdeacon as no dog, no horse, no elephant ever loved
his master.

5

More About Claude Frollo

In 1482, Quasimodo was about twenty years old, and
Claude Frollo about thirty-six. The one had grown up; the
other had aged.

Claude Frollo was no longer the simple scholar of the
College of Torchi, the tender protector of a small child,
the young dreamy philosopher, so wise and yet so ignorant.
He was an austere, serious, morose priest, in charge of souls;
he was Monsieu the Archdeacon of Josas, the second acolyte
of the bishop, in charge of the two deaneries of Montlhéry
and Châteaufort, and of one hundred and seventy-four rural
parish priests. He was an imposing and somber personage
before whom the choir boys in their albs and surplices trembled, as did also the Brothers of Saint-Augustine, and the
clerics on early morning duty at Notre-Dame, when he
passed slowly under the lofty pointed arches of the choir. He
was pensive, but majestic, with his arms crossed, and his
head so inclined over his chest that nothing of his face could
be seen except his broad high forehead.

Dom Claude Frollo, however, had abandoned neither science, nor the education of his young brother, the two occu-
pations of his life. But in the course of the years some

bitterness had mixed with these two projects which had been so sweet. "With time," says Paul Diacre, "even the best bacon turns rancid." Little Jehan Frollo, surnamed Du Moulin, from the place where he had been nursed, had not grown up in the direction that Claude had desired. The older brother had counted on a pious student, docile, learned, and honorable. But, like those young trees which thwart the efforts of the gardener and turn obstinately toward the side whence come air and sunshine, the younger brother grew and shot forth luxuriant branches only on the side of idleness, ignorance, and debauchery. He was a genuine devil, extremely irresponsible, who made Dom Claude knit his brows; but he was so funny and shrewd, that he just as often made his big brother smile. Claude had matriculated him in that same College of Torchi where he himself had spent his earliest years in study and seclusion. And it pained him that this sanctuary, once honored by the name of Frollo, should now be besmirched by it. He sometimes gave Jehan very long and very severe sermons, which the latter intrepidly endured. After all, the young good-for-nothing had a good heart, as all the comedies declare. But once the sermon was finished, he, not immediately, but soon, resumed his former nefarious activities. Sometimes it was a *béjaune* or "yellow beak," as a newcomer to the university was called, whom he had bullied upon arrival—a precious tradition which has been carefully perpetuated to this day. Sometimes he had been the leader in a band of scholars who had classically fallen upon a cabaret, *quasi classico excitati,*[1] and had beaten the tavern keeper with cudgels, then merrily had pillaged the tavern, had even staved in the wine barrels in the cellar. And then there was a fine report, written in Latin, which the submonitor of Torchi brought sadly to Dom Claude, with this painful annotation: *Rixa: prima causa vinum optimum potatum.*[2] Finally, it was said, a terrible thing for a boy of sixteen, that his excesses frequently took him to houses of ill repute on Rue de Glatigny.

On account of all this, Claude, saddened and discouraged in his human affections, threw himself more ardently than

---

[1] "As if animated by a (war) trumpet."
[2] "Brawl: first cause, drinking excellent wine."

ever into the arms of science, that sister who, at least, doesn't laugh at you, but ever repays you, albeit in coin sometimes rather base, for the attention you have paid her. He became therefore more and more learned, and at the same time, by a natural consequence, more and more severe as a priest, more and more sad as a man. There are, in each of us, certain parallelisms between our intelligence, our manners, and our character which develop in unbroken continuity, and which are broken only by the great crises in life.

As Claude Frollo had from his youth run the full gamut of positive human knowledge, external and lawful, he was forced, unless he was to stop *ubi defuit orbis,*[3] to go further, and to seek other nourishment for the insatiable appetite of his intellect. The ancient symbol of the serpent biting his tail is especially appropriate to knowledge. It seems that Claude Frollo had experienced this. Many serious-minded people affirmed that after exhausting the licit of human knowledge, he dared to penetrate into the illicit. He had, everyone said, successively tasted all the apples of the tree of knowledge, and whether from hunger or disgust, had finished by eating of the forbidden fruit. He had taken his place by turns, as our readers have seen, at the conferences of the theologians at the Sorbonne, at the meetings of the faculty of arts near the image of Saint-Hilary, at the disputes of the decretists near the image of Saint-Martin, at the congregations of physicians at the holy water font of Notre-Dame, *ad cupam Nostrae Dominae.* All the allowed and approved dishes which these four large kitchens, called the four faculties, could prepare and serve the intellect, he had devoured, and satiety had come upon him before his hunger was appeased. Then he had dug further, lower, underneath all that finite, material, limited body of knowledge. He had perhaps risked his soul, and had seated himself in that cavern at the mysterious table of the alchemists, the astrologers, the hermetics, at which Averroes, Guillaume de Paris, and Nicolas Flamel occupy one end in the Middle Ages, and which stretches to the East, under the light of the seven-branched candlestick, to Solomon, Pythagoras, and Zoroaster.

So it was supposed at least, wrongly or rightly.

[3] "Where the circle ended."

It is certain that the archdeacon frequently visited the cemetery of the Holy Innocents, where, to be sure, his father and mother had been buried, with the other victims of the plague of 1466; but he seemed much less devout at the cross at the head of their grave than he was before the strange figures on the tombs of Nicolas Flamel and his wife, Claude Pernelle, which stood by it.

It is certain that he had often been seen stealing along the Rue des Lombards, and furtively entering a small house at the corner of the two streets, Rue des Ecrivains and Rue Marivaulx. This was the house Nicolas Flamel had built, the house where he had died around 1417, and which, uninhabited ever since, was beginning to fall into ruin, so much had the hermetics and the alchemists of all countries worn away its walls by simply carving their names on them. Some of the neighbors even affirmed that they had once seen, through a hole, the archdeacon Claude digging and turning over the earth in the floor of those two cellars, whose door jambs had been scrawled over with innumerable verses and hieroglyphics by Nicolas Flamel himself. It was supposed that Flamel had buried the philosophers' stone in these cellars. Hence the alchemists for two centuries, from Magistri down to Father Pacifique, never ceased to turn the soil over until the house itself, so thoroughly ransacked, had at last crumbled into dust under their feet.

It is certain, too, that the archdeacon had been seized with a most singular passion for the symbolical doorway of Notre-Dame, that page of magic written in stone by Bishop Guillaume de Paris, who has undoubtedly been damned for attaching so infernal a frontispiece to the sacred poem eternally sung by the rest of the structure. Archdeacon Claude was also credited with having delved into the mysteries of the colossal Saint-Christopher and of that long enigmatic statue which then stood at the entrance of the portico, and which the people called in derision "Monsieur Legris." But what everybody might have remarked was the interminable hours which Dom Claude would often spend, seated upon the parapet of the portico, contemplating the sculptured figures of the portal, sometimes examining the foolish virgins with their lamps turned upside down, and the wise virgins with their lamps right end up; at other times, calculating the angle of vision of that crow which clings to the left side of the doorway, casting its eye upon a mysterious point within the church, where the philosophers' stone is surely hidden, if it be not in Nicolas Flamel's cellar.

It was a strange destiny, let us remark in passing, for the church of Notre-Dame, at that period, to be thus loved in two different ways, and with so much devotion, by two beings so unlike as Quasimodo and Claude; loved by the one, a sort of half-human creature, instinctive and savage, for its beauty, for its majesty, for the harmonies dwelling in the magnificent whole; loved by the other, a being of cultivated and fiery imagination, for its significance, its mystic meaning, the symbolic language lurking under the sculpture on its front, like the first text under the second of a palimpsest—in short, for the enigma which Notre-Dame eternally offers to the understanding.

Moreover, it is certain that the archdeacon had furnished for himself in one of the two towers which looks upon the Place de Grève, close by the cage of the bells, a little, secret cell, into which no one entered, not even the bishop, so it was said, without his permission. Long ago this cell had been constructed almost at the top of the tower, among the crows' nests, by Bishop Hugo of Besançon, who had practiced black magic there in his time. What this cell contained no one knew. But to someone on the Terrain at night there often appeared and disappeared, at short and regular intervals, through a small round window at the rear of the tower, a certain red, intermittent, peculiar glow, which seemed to be the result of successive puffings from a bellows. This indicated that the glow came from a flame rather than from a light. In the dark, at that height, it had an eerie appearance; so the good ladies of the neighborhood used to say, "There's the archdeacon blowing! Hell's fire is casting up its sparks!"

Even so, there weren't any great proofs of sorcery in all that. But still there was quite as much smoke as was necessary to suppose a flame, and the archdeacon did have rather a formidable reputation. We are bound to declare, however, that the sciences of Egypt, or necromancy, or magic, even the fairest and most innocent, had no more violent enemy, no more merciless denouncer before the officials of Notre-Dame than Dom Claude Frollo. Whether it was a sincere abhorrence, or merely the trick of a robber who cries, "Stop, thief!" this did not prevent the archdeacon from being accused by the learned heads of the chapter as one who had risked his soul in the vestibule of hell, as one who was lost in the caverns of the Cabala, and who groped in the darkness of the occult sciences. Neither were the people blinded to the real state of affairs. To the mind of everyone possessed of the smallest intelligence Quasimodo was the demon and Claude Frollo the sorcerer. It was evident that the bellringer was to serve the archdeacon for a given time, at the expiration of which he was to carry off Dom Claude's soul by way of payment. So the archdeacon, despite the excessive austerity of his life, was in bad odor with all pious souls; and there was never a nose of a devotee, however inexperienced, but could smell him for a magician.

And if, as he grew older, he had lost himself in scientific depths, still others opened in his heart. So, at least, believed those who watched the priest's face. His soul shone forth only through a murky cloud. Why was his head always bowed? Why did he so often sigh? What secret thought hid behind that bitter smile? Why did his lowering brows approach each other like two angry bulls? Why was his scant hair gray? What caused the fire that occasionally blazed in his eyes, making them look like holes in a burning furnace?

These signs of a violent moral preoccupation had become intense at the same time referred to in our narrative. More than once had a choir boy fled in terror when by chance he came upon Dom Claude alone in the church, so strange and fiery was his glance. More than once in the choir, at service time, the occupant of the stall next to the father's had heard him mingle, in the plain chant *ad omnem tonum*,[4] unintelligible parentheses. More than once, the laundress of the Terrain, whose business it was to "wash the chapter," had observed, not without dread, marks of the nails of clenched fingers in the surplice of Monsieur the Archdeacon of Josas.

However, as his austerity increased, his conduct—if possible—was more exemplary. By disposition as well as by

_____
[4] "On every tone."

his calling, he had always kept at a distance from women. Now he seemed to hate them. The mere rustling of a silken petticoat brought his hood down over his eyes. On this point so jealous were his austerity and his reserve, that when the king's daughter, the Lady of Beaujeu, came in December, 1481, to visit the cloister of Notre-Dame, he solemnly opposed her entrance, reminding the bishop of the statute in the Black Book, dated Saint Bartholomew's Eve, 1334, which forbids access to the cloister "to every woman whatsoever, old or young, mistress or chambermaid." Whereupon the bishop felt constrained to cite to him the ordinance of the legate Odo, which makes an exception in favor of certain ladies of high rank—*aliquae magnates mulieres, quae sine scandalo evitari non possunt.*[5] But the archdeacon still protested, objecting that the legate's ordinance, being dated as far back as the year 1207, was one hundred and twenty-seven years anterior to the Black Book, and was therefore, to all intents and purposes, abrogated by it. Accordingly he refused to make an appearance before the princess.

It was moreover remarked that for some time past his abhorrence of gypsy women and zingari seemed to be redoubled. He had solicited from the bishop an edict expressly forbidding gypsies to dance and play the tambourine in the portico square. Also, he had rummaged among the moldy archives of the official, in order to collect all the cases of wizards and witches condemned to burn or to hang for having been accomplices in sorcery with he-goats, she-goats, or sows.

6

Unpopularity

The archdeacon and the bellringer, as we have said before, were little liked by the people, neither by those of high degree nor by those of low degree, who lived near the cathedral. When Claude and Quasimodo went out together, which happened frequently, they were always seen in the same or-

[5] "Certain great ladies that one cannot keep out without scandal."

der, the servant following the master. As they crossed the chilly, narrow, and gloomy streets in the neighborhood of Notre-Dame, many a snide word, many a derisive laugh, or insulting jibe would harass them on their way, unless Claude Frollo, though this was rare, walked haughtily with his head erect, exhibiting a stern and almost imperial forehead to the startled gaze of his assailants.

Both were known in the neighborhood as "the poets" of whom Régnier says:

> All kinds of people chase after poets,
> Like screech owls after linnets.

Sometimes some ill-natured marmot would risk his hide and bones just to have the ineffable pleasure of sticking a pin in Quasimodo's hump. Sometimes some pretty wench, with more sporting effrontery than was seemly, would brush against the priest's cassock, singing right in his face some naughty song:

> Hide, hide, the devil is taken.

Sometimes a group of squalid old women, crouching in the shadows on the steps of a porch, would heap abuses on the archdeacon and the bellringer as they passed by, or hurl after them with curses the flattering remark: "Hum! There goes one whose soul is like the other's body!" Or some band of schoolboys playing marbles or hopscotch would rise up in mass and salute them in classical manner, with some Latin greeting such as *"Eia! Eia! Claudius cum claudo!"*[1]

---

[1] "Hey, Claude with the cripple."

BOOK V

1

Abbas Beati Martini[1]

Dom Claude Frollo's fame had spread far and wide. Because of it, just about the time he refused to see the Lady Beaujeu, he had visitors whom he remembered for a long time.

It happened one evening, just as he had retired after the evening office to his canonical cell in the cloister of Notre-Dame. Except for a few glass phials that were stacked in a corner full of some powder, which looked very much like an explosive, the cell had nothing special or mysterious about it. Here and there were some inscriptions on the wall, but they were merely learned axioms or pious sayings from good authors. The archdeacon had just seated himself at a huge oak table covered with manuscripts, and had lighted a three-armed brass lamp. He had leaned his elbow on a wide open book by Honorius d'Autun, *De praedestinatione et libero arbitrio*, and, deep in thought, he was leafing through a printed folio, the sole product of a printing press which he had in his cell. While he was thus busy, there came a knock at the door.

[1] "The Abbot of Saint-Martin's."

"Who's there?" called the scholar in the friendly tone of a famished dog disturbed over a bone.

"Your friend Jacques Coictier," answered a voice from outside.

The priest went to open the door.

It was, indeed, the king's physician, a man about fifty years old, whose somber face was somewhat lighted by a look of great cunning. Another man was with him. Both wore long, slate-gray, squirrel-lined robes, fastened from top to bottom and belted around the waist, and hats of the same material. Their hands were hidden in their sleeves, their feet under their robes, and their eyes beneath their caps.

"God help me, messire!" said the archdeacon as he led them in. "I was not expecting such honorable visitors at this hour." And while he spoke thus courteously, he glanced suspiciously and curiously from the physician to his companion.

"The hour is never too late to visit with so distinguished a scholar as Dom Claude Frollo of Tirechappe," replied Doctor Coictier, whose Burgundian accent made all his sentences flow majestically like a trailing robe.

The physician and the archdeacon then began one of those congratulatory prologues which, at that period, customarily introduced every conversation between scholars and which did not prevent them from most cordially hating one another. Moreover, it is the same today; the mouth of every scholar who compliments another is a vessel full of honeyed gall.

The felicitations addressed by Claude Frollo to Jacques Coictier alluded chiefly to the numerous material advantages which the worthy physician had known how to extract, in the course of his much-envied career, from each illness of the king's—a better and more certain kind of alchemy than the pursuit of the philosophers' stone.

"Indeed, Doctor Coictier, I was most happy to learn of the promotion of your nephew, my reverend superior, Pierre Versé, to the bishopric. Isn't he now the Bishop of Amiens?"

"Yes, Monsieur the Archdeacon; it is a gracious and merciful gift of the Lord."

"You know, you looked very well on Christmas day at the head of your company of the Chamber of Accountants, Monsieur the President!"

"Vice-President, Dom Claude. Alas! Nothing more than that."

"And how is your superb mansion in the Rue Saint-André-des-Arts? Really, it's like the Louvre! I greatly admire the apricot tree sculptured on the door with that delightful play on words: *A l'Abri-Cotier.*"

"Alas! Master Claude, all that masonry has cost me dearly. The more I do with the mansion, the more I am being ruined financially."

"Oh, don't you have revenue from the jail, and provost-ship of the Palace of Justice, and rents from all the houses, workshops, booths, and market-stalls all around Paris? That's milking a fine cow!"

"My estate at Poissy has brought me nothing this year."

"But your toll dues at Triel, Saint-James, and Saint-Germain-en-Laye are always sure?"

"Six times twenty pounds, not even parisis."

"But you have your position as counselor to the king. That warrants a fixed income."

"Yes, my confrère Claude, but that cursed manor of Poligny, which they make so much ado about, is not worth more to me than sixty gold crowns, in a good or bad year."

There was in these compliments which Claude addressed to Jacques Coictier a certain veiled, bitter, sardonic raillery, with that sad yet cruel smile of a superior but unfortunate man, who is enjoying a moment's distraction tilting with the gross vulgarity of a prosperous man. The other never even noticed it.

"Upon my soul!" said Claude at last, shaking his hand, "I am pleased to see you in such fine health."

"Thank you, Master Claude."

"Speaking of health," exclaimed Dom Claude, "how is your royal patient?"

"He doesn't pay his physician very well," answered the doctor with a side glance toward his companion.

"Don't you think so, Monsieur Coictier?" said his companion.

These words, uttered in a tone of surprise and reproach, recalled the archdeacon's attention to the stranger's presence, though to tell the truth, he had never, from the moment he crossed the threshold, quite turned away from the unknown guest. Indeed it required the thousand reasons Claude had for humoring the all-powerful physician of Louis XI to make him consent to receive him thus accompanied.

Therefore, his expression was not too friendly when Jacques Coictier said to him, "By the way, Dom Claude, I bring you a colleague, who wanted to meet you, having heard so much about you."

"Monsieur is a scholar?" asked the archdeacon, looking intently at Coictier's companion. From the stranger's eyes Dom Claude met a glance just as piercing and suspicious as his own.

He was, as far as one could make out by the dim lamplight, a man of about sixty, of average height, who seemed to be ill and distraught. His expression, although his features were quite common, indicated power and severity; and under his hat, pulled down almost to his nose, one surmised the broad forehead of a genius. Beneath this, his eyes shone like lights deep in some cave.

He took upon himself to answer the archdeacon's question.

"Reverend master," he said in a serious tone, "I have heard of your fame and I have wanted to consult with you. I am but a poor gentleman from the provinces who should take off his shoes before entering the dwelling of the learned. I must tell you my name. It is Compère Tourangeau."

"An odd name for a gentleman!" thought the archdeacon. However, he felt himself in the presence of someone strong and commanding. His own intelligence made him suspect that here was an intelligence no less gifted beneath the furry cap of Compère Tourangeau. So, as he studied that grave countenance, the ironic sneer that the presence of Jacques Coictier had engendered on his morose face slowly vanished, like the sunset glow of an evening horizon.

Claude Frollo seated himself again, gloomy and silent in his great armchair, his elbow resumed its accustomed place on the table, his head rested on his hand. After a few minutes of reflection, he made a sign to the two visitors to be seated, and then spoke to Compère Tourangeau.

"You come to consult with me, sir, and about what?"

"Reverend," answered Compère Tourangeau, "I am sick,

very sick. They say you are another great Aesculapius, and I have come to you to ask for medical advice."

"Medical advice!" said the archdeacon, shaking his head. He seemed to collect his thoughts a moment, and then he said, "Compère Tourangeau, since that is your name, turn around, and you will find my advice written succinctly on the wall."

Tourangeau obeyed, and read, above his head, an inscription, "Medicine is the daughter of dreams—Jamblichus."

Meanwhile, Doctor Jacques Coictier had listened to his companion's question with a disdain that Dom Claude's answer only served to increase. He leaned over and whispered in Tourangeau's ear, so low that the archdeacon could not hear, "I told you that he was mad! But you wanted to see him!"

"But, Doctor Coictier, it could very well be that he is right, this mad fool!" replied his friend in the same whispered tone and smiling bitterly.

"As you please!" answered Coictier dryly. Then, turning to the archdeacon, he continued, "You are very quick with your answers, Dom Claude, and Hippocrates apparently presents no more difficulties to you than a nut to a monkey. Medicine a dream! I doubt if the apothecaries and doctors, were they here, would refrain from stoning you. So you deny the effect of philters on the blood, of unguents on the skin! You deny that eternal pharmacy of plants and metals which we call the World, created expressly for the eternal patient we call Man!"

"I deny," replied Dom Claude coldly, "neither pharmacy nor the patient. I deny the doctor."

"Therefore it isn't true," went on Coictier heatedly, "that gout is an internal eruption; that a gunshot wound can be cured by the application of a roasted mouse; that young blood, properly injected into the veins, will restore youth to the aged; it is not true then that two and two are four, and that emprosthotonos follows opisthotonos!"

The archdeacon replied calmly, "There are certain subjects about which I think in a certain way."

Coictier flushed with anger.

"Come, come, my good Coictier, let's not be angry," said

Compère Tourangeau. "Monsieur the Archdeacon is our host."

Coictier calmed down, but muttered to himself, "Oh, he's a madman, anyway."

"*Pasquedieu!* Master Claude," resumed Tourangeau, after a moment of silence, "you upset me. I came to consult you on two points: one concerning my health, the other concerning my star."

"Monsieur," replied the archdeacon, "if that is what you want, you would have done better not to have wasted your breath mounting my staircase. I do not believe in medicine, and I don't believe in astrology."

"Is that so?" said Tourangeau, with a hint of surprise.

Coictier forced a laugh. "Can't you see that he's mad?" he whispered again in Tourangeau's ear. "He does not believe in astrology."

"How can anyone believe," continued Dom Claude, "that every ray of a star is a thread attached to a man's head?"

"And what are your beliefs then?" cried Tourangeau.

The archdeacon hesitated a moment, then, with a cold smile which seemed to put the lie to his words, *"Credo in Deum."*

"Dominum nostrum,"[2] added Tourangeau, making the sign of the cross.

"Amen," said Coictier.

"Reverend master," resumed Tourangeau, "I am charmed deeply to see you so devout. But learned man that you are, have you reached the point of no longer believing in science?"

"No!" cried the archdeacon, grabbing Compère Tourangeau's arm, while enthusiasm shone in his eyes. "No, I do not deny science. I have not crawled so long on my belly with my nails dug in the earth through all the innumerable windings of that dark cave of science, without perceiving in the distance, at the end of the dim passage, a light, a flame, a something—the reflection, no doubt, from that dazzling central laboratory where the patient and the wise have encountered God."

[2] "I believe in God, Our lord."

"And now," interrupted Tourangeau, "what do you hold for true and certain?"

"Alchemy!"

Coictier exclaimed, "*Pardieu,* Dom Claude, no doubt there is much truth to be found in alchemy, but why blaspheme medicine and astrology?"

"Your science of man, your science of the heavens is nothing!" said the archdeacon imperiously.

"But that's dealing hardly with Epidaurus and Chaldea," replied the physician with a sneer.

"Listen, Messier Jacques. I say this to you honestly, I am not a king's doctor, and His Majesty did not give me a laboratory in which to observe the heavenly constellations. Now don't get angry; just listen to me. What truth have you extracted—I will not say from medicine—which is really too foolish—but from astrology? Cite for me the virtues of the vertical boustrophedon, or the treasures to be found in the number ziruph, or in the number zephirod."

"Will you deny," queried Coictier, "the sympathetic influence of the clavicle, or that it is the key to all cabalistic science?"

"Errors, Messire Jacques. None of your formulas have proved anything conclusive, but alchemy has. Will you contest these results: ice, buried underground for a thousand years, is converted into rock crystal. Lead is the origin of all metals. (For gold is not a metal; it is light.) Lead requires but four periods of two hundred years each to pass successively from the condition of lead to that of red arsenic, from red arsenic to tin, from tin to silver. Are these facts or not? But to believe in the clavicle, in the mystic significance of the junction of two lines, and in the stars is as ridiculous as to believe, like the inhabitants of Cathay, that the oriole changes into a mole, and grains of wheat into a kind of carp!"

"I have studied hermetics," exclaimed Coictier, "and I affirm . . ."

The archdeacon, raging, would not let him finish. "And I, I have studied medicine, astrology, and hermetics. Here alone is truth!"

And as he spoke, he took up one of those glass phials of which mention has been made, saying, "Here alone is knowledge! Hippocrates, a dream! Urania, a dream; Hermes, a phantasm! Gold is the sun, to make gold is to be God. That's the only science. I have sounded medicine and astrology to their depths! Nothing! Nothing I tell you. The human body, darkness; the stars, darkness!"

Almost regally, he relaxed in his chair. Tourangeau watched him in silence. Coictier forced a sneering grin, shrugged his shoulders slightly, and repeated under his breath, "A madman!"

"Well," expostulated Tourangeau suddenly, "what stupendous results? Have you produced something? Have you made any gold?"

"If I had," answered the archdeacon, articulating slowly as if in deep thought, "the King of France would be named Claude, not Louis."

Tourangeau arched his eyebrows.

"Oh, what am I saying?" resumed Dom Claude with a disdainful smile. "What would the throne of France mean to me since I could reconstruct the Empire of the East."

"Well said!" cried Tourangeau.

"Oh, the poor fool!" murmured Coictier.

"But no," went on the archdeacon, as if he were answering his own thoughts, "I am still crawling, I am still bloodying my face and knees on the stones of the subterranean passage. I can see, but not clearly. I cannot read; I can make out only a few letters!"

"And when you have learned to read," asked Tourangeau, "will you then be able to make gold?"

"Undoubtedly," replied the archdeacon.

"In that case, Our Lady knows that I am in dire need of money, and I would gladly learn to read your book. Tell me, reverend master, isn't your science inimical or displeasing to Our Lady?"

To Tourangeau's question, Dom Claude answered simply, "Whose archdeacon am I?"

"That's true, master. Well, then, would it please you to initiate me? Let me learn to read with you."

Claude assumed a majestic, pontifical attitude like a Samuel, and said, "Old man, it would require more years than yet remain to you to complete the journey into all these mysteries. Your head is already gray. One emerges from the cave with white hair, but one must enter it with black. Science knows well enough how to furrow and shrivel up the face of man; she has no need that age should bring to her faces that are already lined. If, however, you greatly desire to study hard, even at your age, and to decipher the difficult alphabet of the wise men, well and good, come with me, and I will try to help you. I will not command you, poor old man, to visit the sepulchral chamber of the pyramids, of which the ancient Herodotus speaks, nor the brick tower of Babylon, nor the vast white marble sanctuary of the Indian Temple of Eklings. Even I have not seen the Chaldean walls built in accordance with the sacred formula of Sikra, nor the Temple of Solomon, which was destroyed, nor the stone doors of the sepulchers of the Israelite kings, which have crumbled to pieces. We shall content ourselves with the fragments of the Book of Hermes, which we have here. I will explain to you the statue of Saint Christopher, the symbol of the Sower, and that of the two angels sculptured on the door of the Sainte-Chapelle, one of whom has his hand in a vase, and the other in a cloud."

Here, Jacques Coictier, who had been quite overwhelmed by the learned mutterings of the archdeacon, recovered his composure and interrupted him with the triumphant tone of one wise man disputing another, "You err, friend Claude. The symbol is not a number. You mistake Orpheus for Hermes."

"It is you who are in error," retorted the archdeacon. "Daedalus is the foundation; Orpheus is the wall; Hermes is the whole structure. Come when you please," he continued, turning to Tourangeau. "I will show you the particles of gold left in the bottom of Nicolas Flamel's crucible which you can compare with the gold of Guillaume de Paris. I will teach you the strength of the Greek word *peristera*.[3] But above all, I shall have you read, one after another, the marble letters of the alphabet, the granite pages of the book. We shall go from the door of Bishop Guillaume and of Saint-Jean-le-Rond to the Sainte-Chapelle, then to the house of Nicolas Flamel, on Rue Marivaulx, to his tomb in the cemetery of the Holy Innocents, to his two hospices on Rue de

[3] This word has a double meaning: 1) dove or pigeon: 2) verbena.

Montmorency. I shall have you read the hieroglyphics with which the four heavy iron supports in the doorway of the Hospice of Saint-Gervais are covered. Together we shall spell out the facades of Saint-Côme, of Sainte-Geneviève-des-Ardents, of Saint-Martin, of Saint-Jacques-de-la-Boucherie . . ."

For some time past, Tourangeau, who looked so intelligent, did not seem to follow Dom Claude. He interrupted, "*Pasque-Dieu!* What are your books?"

"Here is one," replied the archdeacon, opening the window of his cell; he pointed to the Cathedral of Notre-Dame, whose two black towers, stone walls, and huge roof were silhouetted against the starry vault of heaven, like a monstrous two-headed sphinx in the middle of the City.

For some time the archdeacon contemplated in silence this gigantic structure; then, with a sigh, pointing with his right hand to the printed book opened on the table, and with his left hand to Notre-Dame, and casting a mournful glance from book to church, "Alas!" he said, "this will kill that."

Coictier, who had come over to the book eagerly, exclaimed, "Ha! but what is so remarkable about this: *Glossa in Epistolas D. Pauli, Norimbergae, Antoniue Koburger, 1474.* That is not new. The book is by Pierre Lombard, the Master of Sentences. Is it so powerful because it has been printed?"

"Yes," replied Claude, who seemed absorbed in profound meditation, standing with his finger on the folio which had come from the famous printing press of Nuremberg. Then he added ominous words, "Alas! the small thing shall bring down the great things; a tooth triumphs over a whole carcass. The rat of the Nile destroys the crocodile, the swordfish kills the whale; the book will kill the edifice."

The curfew of the cloister tolled just as Doctor Jacques was repeating in whispered tones to his companion his eternal refrain, "He is mad!" To which Tourangeau this time answered, "I do believe it."

This bell marked the hour when no stranger could longer remain in the cloister.

As the two visitors were leaving, Tourangeau said to the archdeacon, "Master, I like scholars and men of great intel-

lect, and I do respect you. Come tomorrow to the Palace of
Tournelles, and ask for the Abbot of Saint-Martin of Tours."

The archdeacon, dumbfounded, returned to his cell, now
comprehending at last who the person calling himself
Compère Tourangeau really was, for he recalled this passage
from the Charter of Saint-Martin of Tours.: *Abbas beati
Martini*, SCILICET REX FRANCIAE, *est canonicus de con-
seutudine et habet parvam praebendam quam habet sanctus
Venantius et debet sedere in sede thesaurarii.*[4]

It has been said that dating from that visit the archdeacon
had frequent conferences with Louis XI, whenever His Majesty came to Paris, and that the king's regard for Dom
Claude quite overshadowed the renown of Olivier le Daim
and Jacques Coictier; the latter, consequently, as was his
custom, berated the king for it.

2

This Will Kill That

Our readers must excuse us if we stop a moment to investigate the enigmatic words of the archdeacon: "This will kill
that. The book will kill the edifice."

In our opinion, the thought had two meanings. First of all,
it was the view of a priest. It was the fear of an ecclesiastic
before a new force, the printing press. It was the frightened
yet dazzled man of the sanctuary confronting the illuminat-
ing Gutenberg press. It was the pulpit and the manuscript,
the spoken word and the written word, alarmed because of
the printed word; something like a sparrow frozen at the
sight of a legion of angels spreading their six million wings.
It was the cry of the prophet who already hears the rumbling
of emancipated humanity; who sees in the distant future intelligence sapping faith, opinion dethroning belief, the world
shaking the foundations of Rome. It was the prognostication
of a philosopher who sees human thought, volatized by the

---

[4] "The Abbot of Saint-Martin, that is to say the King of France, is
canon according to custom, and has the small benefice which Saint-
Venantius had, and must sit in the seat of the treasurer."

press, evaporating from the theocratic vessel. It was the terror of a soldier who examines the steel battering-ram and says, "The tower will crumble." It signified that one great power was following upon the heels of another great power. It meant: The printing press will destroy the Church.

But besides this first thought, there was, in our opinion, a second, the more obvious of the two, a more modern corollary to the former idea, less easily understood and more likely to be contested. This view is quite as philosophical, but it no longer belongs to the priest alone but to the scholar and to the artist as well. Here was a premonition that human thought had advanced, and, in changing, was about to change its mode of expression, that the important ideas of each new generation would be recorded in a new way, that the book of stone, so solid and so enduring, was about to be supplanted by the paper book, which would become more enduring still. In this respect, the vague formula of the archdeacon had a second meaning: That one art would dethrone another art. It meant: Printing will destroy architecture.

In fact, from the beginning of things to the fifteenth century of the Christian era inclusive, architecture was the great book of the human race, man's principal means of expressing the various stages of his development, physical and mental.

When the legends of primitive races became so numerous, and their reciting was so confused that the stories were about to be lost, people began to transcribe these memories in the most visible, the most lasting, and at the same time the most natural medium. Every tradition was sealed under a monument.

The first records were simply squares of rock "which had not been touched by iron," says Moses. Architecture began like writing. It was first an alphabet. A stone was planted upright to be a letter and each letter became a hieroglyph. And on every hieroglyph there rested a group of ideas, like the capital of a column. Thus primitive races of the same period "wrote" all over the world. One finds the "upright stone" of the Celts in Siberia and on the pampas of America.

Later they made words by superimposing stone upon stone. They coupled those syllables of granite. The verb tried various combinations. The Celtic dolmen and comlech, the Etruscan tumulus, the Hebrew galgal are words. Some, especially the tumulus, are proper nouns. Sometimes, on a vast beach they joined these stone words and wrote a sentence. The immense pile of Karnak is by itself a complete formula.

Lastly, they made books. The traditions had given birth to symbols, under which they disappeared like the trunk of a tree under its foliage. All these symbols, in which humanity believed, grew, multiplied, and became more and more complicated. The first simple stones no longer sufficed to contain them; they overflowed on all sides; scarcely could one decipher the original traditions, which, like the stones, simple and naked, had been planted in the soil. The rock symbols had a need to expand into a structure.

Architecture, therefore, developed concomitantly with human thought; it became a giant with a thousand heads and arms, capable of holding in one visible, tangible, eternal form all this floating symbolism. While Daedalus, who is strength, was measuring; while Orpheus, who is intelligence, was singing; the pillar, which is a letter; the arch, which is a syllable; the pyramid, which is a word, set in motion at once by geometric law and by the law of poetry, began to group themselves together, to combine, to amalgamate, to sink, to rise, to stand side by side on the ground, and to pile themselves up to the sky, until, at the dictation of the prevailing ideas of the era, they had written those marvelous books, which were also marvelous structures; to wit, the Pagoda of Eklinga, the pyramids of Egypt, and the Temple of Solomon.

The germinal idea, the verb, was not only the basis of these edifices, but dictated their form. The Temple of Solomon, for example, was not simply the cover of a sacred book, it was the sacred book itself. On every one of these concentric enclosures, the priests could read the Word translated and manifested visibly; they could thus follow its transformations from sanctuary to sanctuary, until at last they could seize upon it in its final tabernacle, under its most concrete form, which was yet architecture: the Ark. Thus the Word was enclosed in the edifice, but its image was on its outer covering, as the human figure is carved on the coffin of a mummy.

Not only the edifices, but also the location of them revealed the ideas they were to impart. If the thoughts to be expressed were gracious, Greece crowned her mountains with temples harmonious to the eye; if somber, India disemboweled her hills to chisel out those unharmonious, half-subterranean pagodas, which are supported by rows of gigantic granite elephants.

So, during the first six thousand years of the world's history, from the time of the pagoda of Hindustan to that of the cathedral of Cologne, architecture has recorded the great ideas of the human race. Not only every religious symbol, but every human thought has its page in that vast book.

Every civilization begins as a theocracy and ends as a democracy. This law of liberty succeeding unity is recorded in architecture. For, and let us emphasize this point, we must not suppose that architecture is capable only of erecting the temple, only of expressing the sacerdotal myth and symbolism, only of transcribing in hieroglyphics on its stone pages the mysterious tables of the law. If this were so, since there arrives in every human society a moment when the sacred symbol is worn out and is obliterated by free thought, when man divests himself of the priest, when the excrescences of the philosophies and systems eat away the face of religion, architecture would be powerless to reproduce this new phase of the human mind: its pages, written on one side, would be blank on the other side; its work would be cut off; the book would be incomplete. But no, such is not the case.

Let us take, for example, the Middle Ages, which we can understand because this time is nearer to us. During its first period, while theocracy was organizing Europe, while the Vatican was rallying and grouping around itself the elements of a Rome constructed of the Rome which lay in ruin about the capitol, while Christianity was setting out to seek among the ruins of an anterior civilization all the stages of society, and out of its remains rebuilt a new hierarchy of which the priesthood was the keystone, we heard a new architecture stirring faintly in the chaos. Then, gradually, using the breath of Christianity, emerging from the grip of the barbarians, rising out of the rubble of dead architecture, Greek and Roman, there arose that mysterious Romanesque architecture, sister of the theocratic masonry of Egypt and India, that unalterable emblem of pure Catholicism, the immutable hieroglyph of papal unity. All the thought of that time is written in this somber Romanesque style. Everywhere we can sense its authority, its unity, the imperturbable, the absolute, Gregory VII; everywhere the priest, never the man, everywhere the caste, never the people.

Then came the Crusades, a great popular movement, and every great popular movement, whatever its cause and purposes, has as its final precipitate the spirit of liberty. Innovations tried to be born. Here began the stormy period of the Peasant Wars, the Revolt of the Burghers. Authority was topped; unity was split and the divisions went in two directions. Feudalism demanded a share with theocracy. But when "the people" arrived on the scene, they as always took the lion's share. *Quia nominor leo.*[1] Hence we see how feudalism pierced through theocracy, and the people through feudalism. The face of Europe was changed. Well! The face of architecture changed too. Like civilization, it turned a page, and the new spirit of the times found her ready to write its new dictates. She returned from the Crusades bearing the pointed arch, as the nations came home with liberty. Henceforth, as Rome was gradually dismembered, Romanesque architecture began its death throes. The hieroglyph deserted the cathedral and went to assist heraldry in order to heighten the prestige of feudalism. The cathedral itself, that structure once so dogmatic, now invaded by the people, by the spirit of liberty, escaped from the priest and fell into the hands of the artist. The artist designed it as he saw fit. Farewell to mystery, to myth, to law. Now fantasy and caprice became the rule. Provided the priest be left his basilica and his altar, he had nothing to say. The artist now took over the four walls. The architectural book no longer belonged to the priest, to religion, to Rome; it belonged to imagination, to poetry, to the people. Henceforth came the rapid and innumerable transformations of an architecture that would last only three centuries, but which was striking after the six or seven centuries of the stagnant immobility of the Romanesque style.

Meanwhile art marches on with giant strides. Popular ge-

[1] "Because I am called lion."

nius and originality do what formerly the bishops did. Each
passing generation writes its line in the book; it erases the
ancient Romanesque hieroglyphics from the frontispiece of
the cathedral—so thoroughly that one can barely see here
and there some old dogma glimmering faintly through the
new symbol covering it. The religious bone structure is
scarcely visible through this new drapery. One can hardly
grasp the extent of the license taken at that time by the architects, even on the churches. Such are the shamelessly intertwined groups of monks and nuns on the capitals, as in
the Salle des Cheminées of the Palace of Justice in Paris.
Such is the episode from the Book of Noah, sculptured "to
the letter" under the great portal of the Cathedral of
Bourges. Such is the bacchic monk, with ears as large as an
ass's, with a glass in his hand, smiling in the face of the
whole community, on the lavabo of the Abbey of
Bocherville. At that time, for the thought written in stone,
there existed a privilege perfectly comparable to our present
liberty of the press. It was the liberty of architecture.

This liberty went very far. Sometimes a door, a facade, an
entire church presents a symbolical meaning, absolutely un-
connected with the worship, even hostile to the teaching of
the Church. In the thirteenth century Guillaume de Paris, and
Nicolas Flamel in the fifteenth, wrote seditious pages. Saint-
Jacques-de-la-Boucherie was a church full of oppositions.

Because architecture was the only free medium, it therefore found full expression in those books called edifices.
Without them, new ideas would have been burned in the
public square. But a thought written in stone on the door of
a church would have assisted at the torture of a thought written in a book. Thus, having only this one outlet, architecture,
thought rushed toward it at every opportunity. Hence the
countless number of cathedrals spread all over Europe, a
number so prodigious that it is unbelievable, even after you
have counted them. All the material and intellectual forces
of society converged on the same point—architecture. In this
manner, under the pretext of erecting churches to God, art
developed to a high degree.

In those days, he who was born a poet became an architect. Genius spread among the masses, and, crushed down on
all sides under feudalism, as under a *testudo* of brass buck-

lers, and finding no outlet but architecture, escaped by way of that art, and its epics took the form of cathedrals. All the other arts obeyed, and put themselves under the tutelage of architecture. They were the artisans for great work. The architect, the poet, the master, summed up in his own person sculpture, which carved his facade; painting, which colored his stained-glass windows; music, which set his bells in motion and pumped air into his organs. Even poor poetry— properly so called, which still persisted in eking out a scanty existence in manuscripts—was obliged, if she was to be recognized at all, to enroll herself in the service of the edifice, either as a hymn or prosody; it was the same role, after all, played by the tragedies of Aeschylus in the priestly rites of Greece, and by the Book of Genesis in the Temple of Solomon.

Thus, till Gutenberg's time, architecture was the principal, universal form of writing. This gigantic book in stone, begun by the East, continued by ancient Greece and Rome, in the Middle Ages wrote its last page. Moreover, this phenomenon of a people's architecture succeeding an architecture belonging to a caste, which we have just observed in the Middle Ages, occurs in precisely analogous stages in human intelligence during other great epochs of history. Thus, to sum up here a law which would really require volumes: in the Far East, the cradle of primitive history, after Hindu architecture came the Phoenician, that fruitful mother of Arabian architecture; in antiquity, Egyptian architecture, of which the Etruscan style and the Cyclopean monuments are but a variety, was succeeded by the Greek, of which the Roman is merely a prolongation burdened with the Carthaginian dome; then, in modern times, after Romanesque architecture, came the Gothic. If we separate each of these three divisions, we shall find that the three elder sisters— Hindu, Egyptian, and Romanesque architecture—have the same symbol; namely, theocracy, the caste system, unity, dogma, myth, God; and that the three younger sisters— Phoenician, Greek, Gothic architecture—whatever diversity of form is inherent in their nature—have the same significance also: liberty, the people, man.

Let him be called Brahmin, magus, or pope, in Hindu, Egyptian, or Romanesque architecture, we always feel the presence of the priest, and nothing but the priest. It is not the same with an architecture of the people. Their architecture is richer and less saintly. In Phoenician architecture, we feel the impact of the merchant; in the Greek, of the republican; in the Gothic, of the bourgeoisie.

The general characteristics of every theocratic architecture are immutability, horror of progress, preservation of traditional lines, consecration of primitive types, the constant adaptation of every aspect of man and nature to the incomprehensible caprices of the symbol. These are dark, foreboding books which only the initiated can decipher. Furthermore, every form, even every deformity in them has a meaning which renders it inviolable. Don't ask Hindu, Egyptian, or Romanesque architects to reform their designs or to perfect their statuary. Every improvement, to them, is an impiety. Here, it seems that the rigidity of dogma is spread over the stone like a second layer of petrifaction.

On the other hand, the general characteristics of popular architectures are variety, progress, originality, opulence, perpetual movement. They are already sufficiently detached from religion to dream of beauty, to nurture it, to alter without ceasing their ornament of statues and arabesques. They suit the times. They have something human about them which they constantly mix with a divine symbolism, under which they still occur. Hence, structures are accessible to every soul, to every intelligence, to every imagination; though symbolic, they are easily comprehensible, like nature herself. Between theocratic architecture and this style, there is the same difference as between the sacred and vulgar language, as between hieroglyphics and art, as between Solomon and Phidias.

If we summarize what we have here very sketchily pointed out, disregarding a thousand detailed proofs and objections, we are led to conclude: that up to the fifteenth century, architecture was the chief recorder for the human race. During this interval of time every thought, no matter how complicated, was embodied in some structure; every idea that rose from the people, every religious law, had its counterpart in monuments; finally, every important thought of the human race was recorded in stone. And why? Because every thought, be it religious or philosophic, wants to be perpetuated; because an idea which has motivated one generation wants to motivate another, and to leave its trace. But how precarious is the immortality of the manuscript! How far more solid, lasting, and resistant is the edifice, the book in stone! To destroy the written word, you need only a torch and a Turk. To demolish the constructed word, you need a social revolution or an earthquake. Barbarism swept over the Colosseum; a deluge, perhaps, over the pyramids.

In the fifteenth century everything changed.

Human intelligence discovered a way of perpetuating itself, one not only more durable and more resistant than architecture, but also simpler and easier. Architecture was dethroned. The stone letters of Orpheus gave way to the lead letters of Gutenberg.

The book will kill the edifice.

The invention of printing was the greatest event in history. It was the parent revolution; it was the fundamental change in mankind's mode of expression, it was human thought doffing one garment to clothe itself in another; it was the complete and definitive sloughing off of the skin of a serpent, which, since the time of Adam, has symbolized intelligence.

When put into print, thought is more imperishable than ever; it is volatile, intangible, indestructible; it mingles with the air. In the time of architecture, it became a mountain, and made itself master of a century and a region. Now it has been transformed into a flock of birds, scattering to the four winds and filling all air and space.

We repeat: who does not see that in this form thought is more indelible? Instead of being solid it has become long-lived. It has exchanged durability for immortality. We can demolish a substance, but who can extirpate ubiquity? Let a deluge come, birds will still be flying over the mountain long after that mountain has disappeared; and let but a single ark float upon the surface of the cataclysm, and they will seek safety upon it and there await the subsiding of the waters. The new world arising out of this chaos will see, when it awakens, hovering over it, winged and alive, the thought of the world that has been swallowed up.

And when one observes that this mode of expression is not only the most enduring, but also the simplest, the most

convenient, the most practicable, when one considers that it
is not encumbered and does not need an excess of tools;
when one thinks how thought, in order to translate itself into
an edifice, is forced to call to its assistance four or five other
arts and tons of gold, to collect a mountain of stones, a forest of wood, a nation of workmen—when one compares this
with the thought that only needs a little bit of paper, a little
ink, a pen, and a press, in order to become a book, is it any
wonder that human intelligence quitted architecture for
printing? If you abruptly cut off the pristine bed of a river by
means of a canal dug upstream from it, the river will abandon its bed.

Then observe too, how, after the discovery of printing, architecture gradually became dry, withered, naked; how the
spring visibly sank, sap ceased to rise, the thought of the
times and of the people deserted it. This cooling off is
hardly perceptible in the fifteenth century; the press is still
too feeble, and what little it does abstract from all-powerful
architecture is but the superabundance of its strength. But in
the sixteenth century the sickness is quite patent. Already architecture is no longer the essential expression of society; it
miserably degenerates into classic art. From being Gallic,
European, indigenous, it becomes Greek and Roman; from
the genuine and modern, it becomes pseudo-antique. It is
this decadence that we call the Renaissance. A magnificent
decadence, we might add, for the old Gothic genius, that sun
which is now setting behind the gigantic printing press of
Mayence, for a little while still sends its last rays over this
hybrid mass of Latin arches and Corinthian colonnades.

It is to this setting sun that we look for a new dawn.

However, from the moment that architecture is only an art
like any other, it is no longer the master, the sovereign, the
tyrant; it becomes incapable of retaining the services of the
other arts. They emancipate themselves, cast off the yoke of
the architect, and go their separate ways. Each of these other
arts gains by this divorce. Isolation magnifies everything.
Sculpture becomes statuary, imagery becomes painting,
chanting becomes music. One would say that a whole empire crumbles on the death of its Alexander, and that each of
its provinces becomes a kingdom.

Now we are in the time of Raphael, Michelangelo, Jean

Goujon, Palestrina—those splendors of the dazzling sixteenth century.

With the emancipation of the arts, thought, too, is everywhere set free. The freethinkers of the Middle Ages had
already made gaping wounds in the side of Catholicism. The
sixteenth century ripped asunder religious unity. Before the
printing press, the Reformation would have been but a
schism; printing made it a revolution. Take away the press
and heresy is paralyzed. Be it fatal or providential, Gutenberg is the precursor of Luther.

However, when the sun of the Middle Ages has completely set, when the light of the Gothic genius has gone out
forever over the horizon of art, architecture, too, becomes
more and more pale, colorless, and lifeless. The printed
book, that gnawing worm in the structure, sucks its blood
and eventually devours it. It droops, withers, wastes away
before your very eye. It becomes shabby, poor, of no account. It no longer expresses anything, not even the art of
another time. Architecture left to itself, abandoned by the
other arts, because human thought has deserted it, must em-
ploy the artisan in default of the artist. Plain glass replaces
stained glass; the stone mason, the sculptor. Farewell to the
vital juices, to originality, to life, and to intelligence. Like a
lamentable beggar of the studios, it drags itself from copy to
copy. Michelangelo, doubtless aware of its demise in the sixteenth century, made one last despairing attempt to save it.
That titan of the world of art piled the Pantheon on the Parthenon, and so made Saint Peter's of Rome, a gigantic work
that deserved to remain unique, the last expression of architectural originality, the signature of a great artist at the bottom of a colossal register in stone thus closed. But when
Michelangelo was dead, what then did this wretched architecture do, this architecture which only survived as a specter,
as a shadow? It copied Saint Peter's in Rome; it parodied it.
This impulse to imitate became a mania—something to
weep over.

Henceforth each century has its Roman Saint Peter's. In
the seventeenth century, it was the Val-de-Grâce; in the eighteenth, Sainte-Geneviève. Every country has its Saint Peter's. London has hers; St. Petersburg, hers; Paris has two or

three. A paltry legacy, the last drivels of a great but decrepit art, was falling into second childhood before dying.

If, instead of characteristic monuments, such as we have just mentioned, we examine art in general from the sixteenth to the eighteenth century, we would at once observe the same phenomenon of decrepitude and decay. From Francis II the dressing of the edifice is effaced more and more and so lets the geometric design show through, like the bony framework of an emaciated invalid. The graceful lines of art give way to the cold, inexorable lines of geometry. A structure is no longer a structure; it is a polyhedron. Architecture, however, painfully tries to hide this nudity. Hence the Greek pediment set over the Roman pediment, and vice versa. It is forever the Pantheon on the Parthenon, Saint Peter's at Rome. Such are the brick houses with stone corners during the time of Henry IV; to wit, the Place Royale and the Place Dauphine. Such are the churches during the reign of Louis XIII, heavy, squat, top-heavy, laden down with a dome like a hump. Thus, too, the Mazarin architecture, the bad Italian *pasticcio* of the Quatre-Nations, the palaces of Louis XIV, long court barracks, stiff, cold, boring. Such are, lastly, the buildings of Louis XV, with chicory leaves and vermicelli ornaments, and all the warts and fungi which disfigure that aged, toothless, and debased coquette. From Francis II to Louis XV the disease progressed in geometric ratio. Art becomes nothing but skin clothing bones. It dies miserably.

Meanwhile, what of printing? All the life ebbing away from architecture, was being absorbed by printing. As architecture waned, printing waxed.

The store of strength spent hitherto by the human mind on buildings is now spent upon books. By the sixteenth century, the press, grown now to the stature of its fallen rival, wrestles with it and wins. In the seventeenth century, printing is already so dominant, so triumphant, so well-ensconced in the house of victory that it can give to the world the feast of a great literary era. In the eighteenth century, after a long sleep at the court of Louis XIV, it takes up again the old sword of Luther, arms Voltaire with it, and runs headlong to attack that ancient Europe whose architectural expression it has already destroyed. By the end of the eighteenth century, it has completely destroyed the remains. In the nineteenth century it begins to reconstruct.

Now, which of these two arts, we ask, better represents human thought during three centuries? Which of the two expresses, not only its literary and scholastic fancies, but its vast, profound, universal movement as well? Which of the two has superimposed itself, without break or gap, upon the human race, that thousand-footed, lumbering monster? Architecture or printing?

Printing! And make no mistake about it! Architecture is dead, irrevocably dead, killed by the printed book, killed because it is less durable, killed because it is more costly. Every cathedral costs millions. Imagine now the cost necessary to rewrite an architectural book; the cost of rebuilding those countless edifices and spreading them once more over the land; the cost of returning to those eras when their number was such that from the testimony of an eye witness, "You would have thought that the world was casting off its old dress to clothe itself in a white robe of churches." *Erat enim ut si mundus, ipse excutiendo semet, rejecta vetustate, candidam ecclesiarum vestem indueret* (Glaber Radulphus).

A book is so quickly made, costs so little, and can go so far! Is it any wonder that all human thought should use this conveyance? This is not to say that some architect will not make again, here or there, a beautiful monument, some isolated masterpiece. We shall have again, from time to time, during the reign of printing, an obelisk constructed, say, by an entire army out of melted cannons, as, during the reign of architecture, we had the Iliads, the Romanceros, the Mahabharatas, and the Nibelungen, built by whole nations with the welded fragments of a thousand rhapsodies. The great good fortune of having an architect of genius may befall the twentieth century, like a Dante in the thirteenth. But architecture will never be the social, collective, dominant art it was. The great poem, the great structure, the great masterwork of humanity will never again be built; it will be printed.

And, besides, if, by chance, architecture should be revived, it will never again be mistress. It will submit to the laws of literature which once received its laws from architecture. The respective position of the two arts will be reversed. It is certain that during the architectural epoch, the poems, rare, it is true, resemble monuments. The Indian Vyasa is leafy, strange, impenetrable like the pagoda. Egyptian poetry, like its edifices, has great, tranquil lines; in ancient Greece poetry had the beauty, serenity, and calm of its temples; in Christian Europe, writings show the majesty of Catholicism, the popular naïveté, the rich and luxuriant vegetation of an era of rebirth. The Bible resembles the pyramids; the Iliad, the Parthenon; Homer, Phidias. Dante in the thirteenth century is the last Romanesque church; Shakespeare, in the sixteenth, the last Gothic cathedral.

Thus, to recapitulate briefly, the human race has two books, two registers, two testaments: architecture and printing, the stone Bible and the paper Bible. Unquestionably, when one examines these two books, so widely read through the centuries, it is permissible to regret the visible majesty of the granite writing, those gigantic alphabets in colonnades, porches, and obelisks, those kinds of human mountains which cover the world and the past, from the pyramids to the church steeple, from Cheops to Strasbourg. One must read the past in these marble pages. One must admire and leaf through over and over again the book written by architecture; but one must not deny the grandeur of the edifice which printing has raised in its turn.

The edifice is colossal. I cannot name the statistician who calculated that, by piling one upon the other all the volumes issuing from the press since Gutenberg, one would fill the space between the earth and the moon; but it is not that kind of greatness of which we wish to speak. Nevertheless, if we try to form a collective picture of the combined results of printing down to modern times, does not this total picture seem to us like an immense structure, having the whole world for its foundation, a building upon which humanity has worked without cease and whose monstrous head is lost in the impenetrable mist of the future? This printed tower is the swarming ant-hill of intelligences. It is the beehive where all the imaginations, those golden bees, arrive with their honey. The building has a thousand stories. Here and there, opening up on its ramps, can be seen the mysterious caverns of science which intersect in its bowels. Everywhere on its surface art luxuriously exhibits its arabesques, its rose-windows, and its lacework. There every individual work, however capricious or isolated it may seem, has its place and its projection. The result of the ensemble is harmony. From Shakespeare's cathedral to Byron's mosque, a thousand bell-towers throng together pell-mell in this metropolis of universal thought. At its base, there have been recast several ancient titles of humanity which architecture had not registered. To the left of the entrance, there has been attached the old white-marble bas-relief of Homer, to the right the polyglot Bible raises its seven heads. The hydra of the Romancero stands forth further on, as well as several other hybrid forms, the Vedas and the Nibelungen. However, the prodigious building remains forever incomplete. The press, that giant engine, incessantly gorging all the intellectual sap of society, incessantly vomits new material for its work. The entire human race is its scaffolding. Every mind is its mason. Even the humblest may block a hole or lay a stone. Rétif de la Bretonne brings his hod of plaster. Every day a new tier is raised. Besides the original and individual contributions of separate writers, there were collective donations. The eighteenth century contributed the *Encyclopedia;* the Revolution the *Monitor.* Certainly, these too are structures, growing and piling themselves up in endless spirals; here, too, there is a confusion of languages, untiring labor, incessant activity, a furious competition of all humanity, a promised refuge for the intelligence against another deluge, against another submersion by the barbarians.

It is the second Tower of Babel of the human race.

BOOK VI

1

An Impartial Glance at the Ancient Magistracy

A very fortunate personage, in the year of grace 1482, was nobleman Robert d'Estouteville, knight, Sieur of Beyne, Baron of Ivry and Saint-Angry in the Marche, councilor and chamberlain to the king, and keeper of the provostship of Paris. It was already seventeen years since he had received from the king on November 7, 1463, the year of the comet, this fine appointment as provost of Paris, which was reputed to be rather a *seigneurie* than an office: *"Dignitas,"* remarks Joannes Loemnoeus, *"quae cum non exigua potestate, politiam concernente, atque prarogativis multis et juribus conjuncta est."*[1] In 1482, it was considered remarkable that a nobleman, with a king's commission, should have letters of appointment dated as far back as the time of the marriage of a natural daughter of Louis XI with Monsieur the Bastard of Bourbon. The same day that Robert d'Estouteville had replaced Jacques de Villiers as provost of Paris, Master Jean Dauvet replaced Messire Hélye de Thorrettes as first president of the court of parliament, Jean Jouvenel des

---

[1] "A dignity which is associated with considerable police power and with many rights and prerogatives."

Ursins replaced Pierre de Morvilliers as chancellor of France, and Regnault des Dormans relieved Pierre Puy of the post of master of common pleas to the royal household. Now, over how many heads had the presidency, the chancellorship, and the mastership passed since Robert d'Estouteville had been the provost of Paris! The provostship had been "entrusted to his keeping" said the letters patent; and indeed he kept it well. He had clung to it, incorporated himself within it, had identified himself with it so completely that he had survived that mania for change which possessed Louis XI, a distrustful, teasing, industrious king who was anxious to maintain an elasticity in his power, by frequent appointments and dismissals. Moreover, the worthy knight had obtained the succession of his post for his son, and already, for two years, the title of nobleman Jacques d'Estouteville, Esquire, had been entered next to his own at the top of the register of the ordinary of the provosty of Paris—a rare, indeed, and singular favor! It is true that Robert d'Estouteville was a good soldier, that he had loyally lifted his pennon against "the league of the public weal," and that he had presented to the queen, on the day of her grand entry into the city of Paris in 14—, a very marvelous stag made of confectionery. Besides, he was on friendly terms with Messire Tristan l'Hermite, provost-marshal in the king's palace. Therefore, it was a very comfortable and pleasant existence that Messire Robert enjoyed. First of all, he had a good salary, to which were attached and hanging like bunches of grapes on his vine the revenues of the civil and criminal provosty; plus the revenues from the auditory courts of the Châtelet, not to mention some small toll revenue from the bridges of Mantes and Corbeil, and the profits from taxes levied on the grain dealers, owners of sawmills, and salt measurers. Add to this the pleasure of displaying, on his rides through the town, in contrast with the half-red and half-brown gowns of the district officers and sheriffs, his fine military dress, which you may still admire sculptured upon his tomb at the Abbey of Valmont in Normandy, and his richly embossed helmet at Montlhéry. And then, was it nothing to have total supremacy over the keeper, the warden, the jailer, and the two auditors of the Châtelet, the sixteen commissaries of the sixteen quarters of the city, the hundred and twenty horse-patrols, the knight of the watch, with his men of the watch, the under-watch, the counter-watch, and the rear-watch? Was it nothing to dispense high and low justice, to have the right of turning, hanging, and drawing, besides the jurisdiction in minor offenses in the first resort (*in prima instantia*, as the charters say) over the whole viscounty of Paris and the seven noble bailiwicks gloriously thereto appended? Can you imagine anything more gratifying than to pass judgment and sentence, as Messire Robert d'Estouteville did every day in the Grand-Châtelet, under the wide, low-pitched Gothic arches of Philip-Augustus? Can you imagine him returning, as he did every evening, to that charming house situated on the Rue Galilée, within the precincts of the Palais Royal, which he possessed by right of his wife, Madame Ambroise de Loré, to rest from the fatigue of having sent some poor devil to spend his night in "that small lodge on the Rue de l'Escorcherie, in which the provosts and sheriffs were wont to make their prison; and whose dimensions were eleven feet long, seven feet four inches wide, and eleven feet in height?"

And not only had Messire Robert d'Estouteville his own kind of justice as provost and viscount of Paris, but he had, on account of his presence and his abilities, a share in meting out the king's justice. There was no head of any distinction but had passed through his hands before falling to the executioner's. It was he who had gone to take Monsieur de Nemours from the Bastille Saint-Antoine to Les Halles; and to the same place to carry from thence to the Grève Monsieur de Saint-Pol, who sullenly bewailed his fate, to the great joy of Monsieur the Provost, who was no friend of Monsieur the Constable.

Certainly, here was more than enough to make a man's life happy and illustrious, and to earn someday a notable page in that interesting history of the provosts of Paris from which we learn that Oudard de Villeneuve had a house in the Rue des Boucheries, that Guillaume de Hangast bought the great and little Savoie, that Guillaume Thiboust gave his houses on the Rue Clopin to the nuns of Sainte-Geneviève, that Hugues Aubriot lived in the Hotel du Porc-Epic, and other facts of like importance.

And yet, with all these reasons for taking life casually and joyfully, Messire Robert d'Estouteville awoke on the morning of January 7, 1482, in a humor most foul—though for what reason he himself could not have said. Was it because the sky was overcast? because his old Montlhéry swordbelt was too tight, and girded in too military a fashion his provostorial portliness? Or because he had seen a band of ruffians marching along the street, four by four, under his window, jeering at him as they passed? They wore doublets without shirts, hats without crowns, and each a bag and a bottle at his side. Or, was it a vague presentiment of the three hundred and seventy livres sixteen sols eight deniers which the future king, Charles VIII, was to deduct the following year from the revenues of the provostship? Let the reader take his choice. For our part, we should be inclined to believe that he was in a bad humor simply because he was in a bad humor.

Besides, it was the day following a holiday—a day of trouble for everybody, but especially for the magistrate whose business it was to sweep away all the filth—literally and figuratively—that a Paris holiday usually brings, and, then, too, today he had to sit in court at the Grand-Châtelet. The reader will probably have remarked that judges in general contrive matters so that their day of sitting shall also be their day of nasty humor, in order that there shall always be someone upon whom to vent their spleen conveniently, in the name of the king, law, and justice.

Meanwhile, the court proceedings had begun without him. His deputies in civil, criminal, and private causes were acting for him as usual. Even as early as eight o'clock in the morning, some scores of townspeople, men and women, were crowded together in a dark corner of the court of the Châtelet, between a strong oaken door and the wall, and were enjoying the varied and amusing spectacle of civil and criminal justice being administered by Master Florian Barbedienne, auditor at the Châtelet, and deputy of Monsieur the Provost, somewhat pell-mell, and completely haphazardly.

The chamber was small, low, and vaulted. At the far end there was a table, carved with fleurs-de-lis, behind which stood an empty, heavy, carved-oak armchair for the provost. To its left was a stool for the auditor, Master Florian. Further down the table was the clerk, scribbling away. Opposite them were the people. In front of the door, and before the table, were a number of sergeants of the provostship in their violet jerkins with white crosses. Two sergeants of the Parloir-aux-Bourgeois, in jackets half red and half blue, stood sentry before a low closed door, which was visible at the other end behind the table. The only window, a pointed arched one, narrowly framed in the massive wall, allowed a pale January ray of light to rest upon two grotesque countenances—that of the fantastic stone demon carved upon the keystone of the vaulted ceiling, and that of the judge, seated at the other end of the chamber amid the fleurs-de-lis.

Indeed, imagine to yourself a man seated at the provost's table, leaning on his elbows, between two stacks of papers, his foot upon the tail of his plain brown gown, his red harsh-looking face framed by white lambskin, of which his eyebrows seemed a piece, his eyes blinking over cheeks so loaded with flesh that they met under his chin, Master Florian Barbedienne, auditor at the Châtelet.

Now, the auditor was deaf, a slight defect for an auditor. Master Florian nonetheless meted out justice without appeal; and quite competently. It is certain that it is quite sufficient for a judge to appear to listen; and the venerable auditor the better fulfilled this condition, the only one essential to the good administration of justice, as his attention could not possibly be distracted by any noise.

However, there was a merciless censor of his deeds and mannerisms among the audience in the person of our friend Jehan Frollo du Moulin, the little scholar of yesterday's escapades, that stroller who was sure to be met everywhere in Paris except before the professors' chairs.

"Look," said he to his companion Robin Poussepain, who was snickering beside him, while he commented on the scenes that were taking place before them, "there's Jehanneton du Buisson, the pretty girl from the Marché-Neuf! Upon my soul, he's condemning her too, the old buzzard! His eyes are no better than his ears! Fifteen sols, four deniers parisis for wearing two rosary beads! That's a bit exorbitant. Ah, the law is hard! Hey, who's that? Robin Chief-de-Ville, hauberk-maker, who passed the tests and was admitted a master in the said art! Ah! it's his entrance fee. What! two gentlemen among these rascals Aiglet de Soins, Hutin de Mailly, two squires, *Corpus Christi*! Oh! They've been playing dice. When shall I see our rector here! Fined a hundred livres parisis to be paid to the king! Barbedienne hits like a deaf man—which he is! May I be my brother the archdeacon if that would stop me from playing by day, playing by night, living to play, dying to play, and wagering my soul after I've lost my shirt! Holy Virgin, what a bunch of girls! one after another, my lambs! Ambroise Lécuyère! Isabeau la Paynette! Bérarde Gironin! By God, I know them all! Fine them! Fine them! That'll teach you to wear gilt belts! Ten sols parisis apiece, you coquettes! Oh, look at the mug of that judge! Deaf and stupid! Hey! Florian the blockhead! Barbedienne the dolt! Look at him at his table! He devours litigants, he gobbles lawsuits, he eats, he chews, he gorges and stuffs himself. Fines, dues, costs, expenses, wages, damages, torture, jail, and stocks are to him Christmas cakes and midsummer marzipan! Look at him, the pig! Go on. Great! Another street-walker! Thibaud-la-Thibaude in the flesh! For having come out of the Rue Glatigny! Who's that little rascal? Gieffroy Mabonne, one of the bowmen of the guard, for profaning the name of the Father. A fine for La Thibaude! Hey! A fine for Gieffroy! Fine them both! You old deaf stoop! I'll bet ten to one he confounds the two charges and makes the wench pay for the swearing and the soldier for the loving! Hey, Robin Poussepain! Look who they're bringing in now! By Jove! And look at all those sergeants! All the hounds of the pack. There must have been a big catch! A wild boar or something! It is one, Robin—it is one, and a great one, too! By Hercules! It's our prince of yesterday! Our Pope of Fools, the bellringer, the one-eyed, the hunchback! It's Quasimodo!'

It was indeed.

It was Quasimodo, bound, girded, hooped, pinioned, and under heavy guard. The detachment of sergeants surrounding him was accompanied by the knight of the watch himself, bearing the arms of France embroidered on his breast, and those of the town of Paris on his back. However, there was nothing about Quasimodo, except his deformity, to warrant all this display of halberds and harquebuses. He was moody, silent, and tranquil. From time to time, his one eye cast a sullen and resentful glance at the bonds that covered him.

He sometimes threw a long look about him; but he seemed so dull and sleepy that the women pointed him out to each other, but only to laugh at him.

Meanwhile Master Florian, the auditor, attentively scanned the pages of the written charge against Quasimodo, which the clerk had handed to him, and, after taking a sharper glance, seemed to be collecting himself for a minute. Thanks to this precaution, which he was always careful to take before proceeding with his examination, he knew beforehand the name, the titles, and the offense of the accused, and made anticipated replies to anticipated answers, and so succeeded in extricating himself from all the sinuosities of the examination without too much betraying his deafness. The formal written charge was for him like a dog for a blind man. If it so happened that his infirmity disclosed itself here and there by some incoherent apostrophe or unintelligible question, it passed for profundity with some, for stupidity with others. In either case the honor of the magistracy was upheld, for it is better that a judge be considered imbecile or profound, than deaf. So he took great care to hide his deafness from everybody's notice, and he ordinarily succeeded so well that he had come at last even to deceive himself about the matter—a species of deception indeed which is not so difficult as it may be thought. All hunchbacks walk with head erect, all stammerers are given to speechifying, and the deaf always talk in whispers. For his part, the utmost admission that he made to himself on this point was that his hearing was not quite so acute as some people's; it was the only concession in this respect that he could bring himself to make to public opinion, in his moments of candor and examination of conscience.

Therefore, having well turned over in his mind the case of Quasimodo, he threw back his head and half closed his eyes, to look more majestic and impartial, so that at that moment he was in fact blind as well as deaf—a double condition without which no judge is perfect. It was in this magisterial attitude that he commenced the examination.

"Your name?"

Now here was a case which had not been "provided for in

the law," namely, one deaf man interrogating another deaf man.

Quasimodo, receiving no hint that a question had been addressed to him, continued to stare at the judge, without making any answer. The deaf judge, on the other hand, receiving no hint that the accused was deaf, thought that he had answered, as the accused generally did, and continued with his customary stupid aplomb.

"Very good. Your age?"

Quasimodo made no answer to this question either; but the judge, thinking that he had, went on.

"Now, your trade?"

Quasimodo still kept silent. The audience, however, began to whisper and to look at one another.

"That's enough!" replied the imperturbable auditor when he supposed that the accused had finished with his third answer. "You stand accused, before us: *primo,* of a nocturnal disturbance; *secundo,* of an attack upon a lewd woman; *tertio,* of rebellion and disloyalty toward His Majesty's archers. Explain yourself in regard to all these points. Clerk, have you recorded all that the accused has said so far?"

At this untoward question there was a burst of laughter, caught by the audience from the clerk, so violent, so uncontrollable, so contagious, so universal that neither of the deaf men could help noticing it. Quasimodo turned around and shrugged his hump disdainfully; while Master Florian, as surprised as he, and supposing that the laughter of the spectators had been provoked by some irreverent reply from the accused, rendered visible to him by that shrug, addressed him indignantly.

"Fellow, that answer of yours deserves the gallows! Do you know whom you are speaking to?"

This sally was not at all appropriate to check the general uproar. It was to all present so incongruous and so ridiculous that the wild laughter even spread to the sergeants of the Parloir-aux-Bourgeois, a group of servants, carrying pikes, among whom stupidity was part of the uniform. Only Quasimodo maintained a serious air, for the simple reason that he understood nothing that was going on around him. The judge, growing more and more angry, thought himself obliged to continue in the same tone, hoping thereby to instill some terror into the accused which would react on the audience and bring the crowd back to a sense of respect.

"In other words, therefore, perverse and riotous knave that you are, you presume to be impertinent to the auditor of the Châtelet, the magistrate entrusted with the public safety of Paris; the magistrate charged with investigating crimes, offenses, and misdemeanors, to control all trades and forbid monopolies, to repair the pavements; to prevent forestalling and regrating of poultry and wild fowl; to oversee the measuring of firewood and other sorts of wood; to cleanse the town of its mud and the air of contagious diseases; in a word, to slave continually for the public welfare without fee or recompense, or hope for any! Do you know that my name is Florian Barbedienne, Monsieur the Provost's own deputy, and what is more, commissioner, inquisitor, controller, and examiner, with equal power in provostship, bailiwick, conservatorship, and presidial court? . . ."

There is no reason why a deaf person talking to another deaf person should stop. God knows where and when Master Florian would have landed, once launched, full sail, on his ocean of eloquence, had not the low door at the back of the hall suddenly opened to admit Monsieur the Provost in person.

At his entrance, Master Florian did not stop, but spinning around on his heels, and suddenly directing at the provost the harangue which a moment before he had been thundering at Quasimodo, he said, "Monseigneur, I demand such punishment as it shall please you, for the accused here before me, for his serious and flagrant contempt of court."

Then, all out of breath, he sat down again, wiping away rivulets of perspiration which were streaming down his forehead and wetting the parchments spread out before him. Messire Robert d'Estouteville frowned and signaled to Quasimodo with a gesture so imperious and meaningful that the deaf hunchback comprehended a little.

The provost addressed him severely, "What have you done, knave, to be brought here?"

The poor devil, supposing that the provost was asking for his name, now broke his habitual silence, and answered in a hoarse and guttural voice, "Quasimodo."

The answer was so little related to the question that the

mad laughter again began to make the rounds and Messire Robert exclaimed, flushed with anger, "Rogue, do you make sport of me, too?"

"Bellringer at Notre-Dame," answered Quasimodo, thinking this time he had been asked to tell the judge his trade.

"Bellringer!" replied the provost, who, as we have already said, rose that morning in such a vile humor that his fury had no need to be kindled by such impudent responses. "Bellringer! I'll make them ring a peal of rods on your back through every street in Paris! Do you hear me, knave?"

"If it's my age that you want to know," said Quasimodo, "I think I'll be twenty next Martinmas."

This was too much; the provost could take no more.

"So! you mock the provost, you wretch! Messieurs the sergeants of the rod, you will take this miserable rogue to the pillory in the Grève, and flog him for an hour. He shall pay for this impudence, so help me God! And I order that his sentence be proclaimed by the four legally appointed trumpeters in the seven castellanies of the viscounty of Paris."

The clerk of the court duly recorded the sentence.

"*Ventre-Dieu*! That's a good sentence," from his corner cried the little scholar, Jehan Frollo du Moulin.

The provost turned around and again fixed his flashing eyes on Quasimodo. "I believe the fellow said, '*Ventre-Dieu!*' Clerk, add a fine of twelve deniers parisis for swearing; and let one half of it go toward the repairs of Saint-Eustache's church; I have a particular devotion for Saint-Eustache."

In a few minutes the sentence was drawn up. It was simple and brief. The procedure of the provostship and viscounty of Paris had not yet been elaborated by the president, Thibaut Baillet, and Roger Barmne, the king's advocate. It was therefore not yet obscured by that deep forest of chicanery and circumlocution which those two lawyers planted in it at the beginning of the sixteenth century. All was clear, expeditious, and explicit. Each decision went right to the point; right away you saw at the end of every path, unobscured by any thicket or bends in the way, the wheel, the gibbet, or the pillory. At least you knew where you were going.

The clerk presented the sentence to the provost, who af-fixed his seal to it, and then left the chamber to continue his rounds to the several courts of law, in a frame of mind which seemed destined that day to fill every jail in Paris. Jehan Frollo and Robin Poussepain were laughing to themselves. Quasimodo looked upon it all with an air of indifference and astonishment.

However, the clerk, when Master Florian Barbedienne was in his turn reading over the judgment before signing it, felt moved with pity for the poor condemned devil; and, in the hope of obtaining some mitigation of penalty, he ap-proached the auditor's ear as close as he could, and said to him, pointing to Quasimodo, "That man is deaf."

He hoped that a sense of their common infirmity would arouse some sympathy for the condemned man in the breast of Master Florian. But, first of all, as we have already ob-served, Master Florian did not care to have his deafness no-ticed. Secondly, he was so stone deaf that he did not hear one word of what the clerk had said. Nevertheless, wanting to appear that he did understand, he replied, "Ah ha! That's different. I didn't know that. In that case, give him another hour at the pillory."

And with this change, he signed the sentence.

"Well done!" said Robin Poussepain, who still held a grudge against Quasimodo. "That will teach him to handle people roughly."

2

The Rat Hole

With the reader's kind permission let us go back to the Place de Grève, which we left yesterday with Gringoire to follow Esmeralda.

It is ten in the morning. Unmistakably it is the day follow-ing a holiday. Everywhere the streets are strewn with debris, ribbons, rags, feathers, drops of wax from the torches, crumbs from the public banquet. A goodly number of towns-people are "loafing around," as we would say, kicking the charred remains of the bonfire, laughing with glee before the

Maison-aux-Piliers, as they remember the beautiful decorations of the previous day, and today looking at the nails which had held them. The vendors of cider and beer are pushing their carts through several groups of bystanders. Others, intent on their business, are hurrying here and there. The merchants are talking and calling to one another from their shop doors. The holiday, the ambassadors, Coppenole, the Fools' Pope are the subject of every conversation, each person striving to make the wittiest comment or to laugh the loudest. Meanwhile, four sergeants on horseback, who have just posted themselves on four sides of the pillory, have already attracted a large group of the idlers scattered about the square. Many of these people are wearily waiting with hopes of witnessing a small execution.

If the reader, after contemplating this lively and noisy scene in the square, now shifts his glance toward that ancient building, half Gothic, half Romanesque, called the Tower of Roland, which stands on the western corner of the quay, he will notice, at the corner of its facade, a large public breviary. Its richly illuminated pages are protected from the rain by a small penthouse, and from thieves by a grating, which, however, allows the passersby to leaf through it. Next to the breviary and overlooking the square is a narrow, arched window, crossed by two iron bars in the shape of a cross, the only aperture through which a little air and light can pass into a small doorless cell, built on the ground level, in the thick wall of the old mansion. It is filled with a silence made more profound and somber by the noise and gaiety of this public square, the most populous in Paris, swarming and clamoring around it.

This cell had been famous in Paris for nearly three centuries, ever since Madame Rolande, of the Tower of Roland, mourning her father, who died during the Crusades, had it dug out of the wall of her own house to shut herself up in it forever, keeping of her palace only this lodging with a sealed door and an open window, winter and summer, leaving all the rest to the poor and to God. The disconsolate lady awaited death for twenty years in that anticipated tomb, praying day and night for the soul of her father, sleeping upon ashes, without even a stone for a pillow. She wore black sackcloth, and lived only upon the pity of those passersby who felt disposed to leave bread and water upon her window sill. Thus she who had dispensed charity now received. Upon her death, her body was placed in another sepulcher. She had bequeathed this tiny cell in perpetuity to women in affliction—mothers, widows, or maidens, who should have occasion to pray much for themselves or others, and who should wish to bury themselves alive on account of great misfortune or some severe penitence. The poor people in her time had buried her ceremoniously with tears and prayers, but to their great sorrow the pious woman had been unable, for want of patronage, to be canonized a saint. Such of them as were a little given to impiety had hoped that the thing would be done more easily in heaven than in Rome, and had actually presumed to offer up their prayers for the deceased to God himself, in default of the pope. Most of them, however, had contented themselves with holding Rolande's memory sacred, and with converting into relics the rags she left behind. The town of Paris, too, had founded, in pursuance of the lady's intentions, a public breviary, which had been permanently sealed near the window of the cell, in order that passersby might stop before it, now and then, to pray; that prayer might make them think of almsgiving; and thus the poor female recluses inheriting the stony cave of Madame Rolande might not die of starvation and neglect.

In the Middle Ages such tombs for the living were not rare. Frequently, such a one would be found on the busiest street of a town, in the most crowded and noisy marketplace. It might be under the horses' feet and the wagon wheels, as it were—a cellar, a well, a walled and grated cabin—within which there would be praying, day and night, a human being, voluntarily devoted to some everlasting lamentation or some great expiation. And all the reflections that this strange spectacle would arouse in us today—that horrid cell, a sort of intermediate link between the dwelling house and the tomb, between the city and the cemetery; that living being cut off from the communion with mankind, and thenceforth numbered among the dead; that lamp consuming its last drop of oil in the darkness; that remnant of life already wavering in the grave; that breath, that voice, that everlasting prayer encased in stone; that face forever turned toward the other world; that eye already illumined by another sun, that ear pressed against the walls of the sepulcher; that soul a prisoner in that body, that body a prisoner in that dungeon, and under that double covering of flesh and granite, the murmuring of that soul in pain—nothing at all that was perceived by the crowd. The piety of that age, irrational and unrefined, did not see so many facets in an act of religion. It accepted the thing as a whole—honored, venerated, and occasionally sanctified the sacrifice; but did not analyze the suffering attending it, and did not feel any depth of pity. People sometimes gave some pittance to the wretched penitent, peered through the tiny window to see if he was still alive, did not know his name, scarcely knew how many years it was since he had begun to die. To a stranger who questioned the neighbors about the living skeleton rotting in that cave, the answer would simply be, "It's the recluse."

Thus it was that everything was then viewed without metaphysics, without exaggeration, without a magnifying glass—with the naked eye. The microscope had not yet been invented, either for material things, or things of the mind.

However, though they caused little wonder or speculation, examples of this kind of living burial in the heart of towns were in reality quite frequent, as we have already observed. In Paris itself there were several of these cells for penitence and prayer, and nearly all of them were occupied. It is true that the clergy were rather solicitous that they should not be left empty, as that would imply the faithful were lukewarm; so lepers were put into them when penitents were scarce. Besides the cell at the Grève, already described, there was one at Montfaucon, one at the charnel house of the Holy Innocents, another, I don't know just where, at the logis Clichon, I think. Others were scattered about in places where, in default of monuments, their memory is perpetuated by tradition. The University too had its share of them. On the hill of Sainte-Geneviève a sort of Job of the Middle Ages sang repeatedly for thirty years the seven penitential psalms upon a dunghill at the bottom of a cistern. He sang louder in the night time, and today the antiquary still fancies that he hears his voice as he enters the Rue du Puits-qui-parle.[1]

---

[1] "Street of the Talking Well."

But to confine ourselves only to the cell of Roland's Tower, we must say that it had rarely lacked a tenant. Since Madame Rolande's death it had scarcely been vacant even for a year or two. Many women had come there and wept until death over the memory of their parents, their lovers, or their sins. The gossips of Paris, who meddle into everything, even into those things which concern them least, used to maintain that among the number there had been very few widows.

According to the fashion of the age, a Latin legend, inscribed upon the wall, explained to the educated passerby the pious purpose of the cell. This custom of placing a brief explanatory motto above the entrance of a building continued until the middle of the sixteenth century. Thus in France we still read, over the gateway of the prison belonging to the manor house of Tourville, *Sileto et spera*[2]; in Ireland, under the escutcheon placed above the great doorway of Fortescue Castle, *Forte scutum, salus ducum*[3]; and in England, over the main entrance to the hospitable mansion of the earls Cowper, *Tuum est.*[4] For in those days every edifice was a thought.

As there was no door to the walled-up cell of the Tower of Roland, there had been inscribed in great Roman letters over the window these two words:

TU, ORA.[5]

Whence it was that the people, whose straightforward good sense sees few subtleties in things but readily translates *Ludovico Magno*[6] into Porte Saint-Denis, had given to this dark, damp, dismal cavity the name of *Trou aux Rats,* or Rat Hole—a translation less sublime, perhaps, than the other, but, on the other hand, more graphic.

[2] "Be silent and hope."
[3] "Strong shield, well-being of the chiefs."
[4] "(This house) is yours."
[5] "You, pray."
[6] "To Louis-the-Great," a fragment of the Latin inscription on the Porte Saint-Denis.

3

The Story of a Cake

At the time of this story, the cell in the Tower of Roland was occupied. Should the reader desire to know by whom, he has only to listen to three gossips who, at the same moment that we called his attention to the Rat Hole, were headed toward that same spot, going up along the river from the Châtelet toward the Grève.

Two of these women were dressed like very respectable Parisiennes. Their fine white wimples, their woolen skirts, with red and blue stripes, their white knitted stockings, with colors clocked at the ankles, and drawn tight up the leg, their square-toed shoes of brown leather with black soles, and especially their headdresses, each a kind of tinsel-covered horn, topheavy with ribbons and lace which the women of Champagne still wear, as well as the grenadiers of the Russian imperial guard, announced that they belonged to that class of rich tradeswomen who represent the middle caste between what Parisian lackeys call a woman and what they call a lady. They wore neither rings nor golden crosses; but it was easy to perceive that this was owing not to their poverty, but simply to their fear of being fined. Their companion was attired practically in the same fashion, but there was in her dress and manner a certain something that indicated that she was the wife of a provincial attorney. By the way she wore her belt high above her hips, it was evident she had not been long in Paris. Add to that her pleated wimple, bows of ribbons on her shoes, her skirt which was striped crosswise instead of downward; and a hundred other irregularities that flaunted the good taste of Parisians.

The first two walked with an air peculiar to women of Paris who are showing their city to someone from the country. The third held one hand of a big chubby boy, who was clutching a large cake.

We regret to add that with his hands so occupied and owing to the severity of the season, he was using his tongue as a handkerchief.

The boy was being dragged along, *non passibus aequis,*[1] as Virgil says, and stumbling every moment, to the great annoyance of his mother. It is true that his eyes were more often on the cake than on the ground. No doubt, some very serious reason prevented his biting into the cake, for he contented himself with only looking at it longingly. But surely the mother ought to have taken charge of the cake herself; it was cruel thus to make a Tantalus of the chubby youngster.

Meanwhile, the three "damoiselles" (for the title "ladies" at that time was reserved for women of nobility) were all talking at once.

"Let's hurry, Damoiselle Mahiette," said the youngest and the stoutest of the three to the lady from the provinces. "I'm sore afraid we shall arrive too late. They told us at the Châtelet that they were going to take him directly to the pillory."

"Ah, bah! what are you talking about, Damoiselle Oudarde Musnier?" said the other Parisian. "He'll be two hours at the pillory. We have time. Have you ever seen anyone flogged, my dear Mahiette?"

"Yes," said the provincial. "In Rheims."

"Pooh! What's that? Your pillory at Rheims! A paltry cage where they flog no one but peasants!"

"What peasants!" said Mahiette. "Peasants in the Cloth Market at Rheims! We've seen some mighty fine criminals there, people who have killed mothers and fathers! Peasants? What do you take us for, Gervaise?"

It is certain that the lady from the country was about to staunchly defend her pillory. Fortunately, the discreet Oudarde Musnier abruptly changed the subject.

"By the way, Damoiselle Mahiette, what do you say of our Flemish ambassadors? Have you any as handsome in Rheims?"

"I confess," replied Mahiette, "that it's only in Paris you can see Flemings like those."

"Did you see, in the ambassadorial cortège, that tall ambassador who is a hosier?" asked Oudarde.

"Yes," replied Mahiette. "He looks like Saturn!"

[1] "With unequal steps."

"And that fat one with a face like a naked belly? And that little one with beady eyes and red eyelids, with half the lashes pulled out like a withered thistle?"

"Their horses are beautiful," said Oudarde, "all dressed after the fashion of their country."

"Ah, my dear," interrupted the provincial Mahiette, who assumed in her turn an air of superiority, "what would you say, then, if you'd seen, in '61, at the coronation at Rheims, twenty years ago, the horses of the princes and of all the king's retinue? There were housings and trappings of all sorts—some of cloth from Damascus, fine cloth of gold, trimmed with sable; some of velvet, trimmed with ermine; some all loaded with jewels, and gold and silver bells. And the money all that cost! And then the handsome pages who rode them!"

"But," replied Damoiselle Oudarde dryly, "the Flemings, too, have very fine horses, and yesterday they had a splendid supper given to them by Monsieur the Provost-Merchant at the Hotel-de-Ville, where they were served sweetmeats, hippocras, spices, and other tasty dishes."

"What are you talking about, friend?" exclaimed Gervaise. "It was at Monsieur the Cardinal's palace, at the Petit-Bourbon that the Flemings dined."

"No! No! At the Hotel-de-Ville."

"But I say at the Petit-Bourbon."

"I know it was at the Hotel-de-Ville," retorted Oudarde sharply, "because Doctor Scourable made a speech in Latin, and everybody was pleased with it. My husband told me so, and he's one of the official booksellers."

"And I know it was at the Petit-Bourbon," insisted Gervaise, no less emphatically, "and this is what Monsieur the Cardinal presented to them: twelve double quarts of hippocras, white, claret, and vermilion; two dozen cases of gilt double Lyons marzipan; two dozen wax torches, weighing two pounds apiece; and six demihogsheads of Beaune wine, white and claret, the best that could be found; I hope that's proof enough. I have it from my husband, who's in charge of fifty guards at the Parloir-aux-Bourgeois, and who was making a comparison only this morning between the Flemish ambassadors and those of Prester John and the Emperor of Trebizond, both of whom came to Paris from Mesopotamia during the reign of the last king, and wore rings in their ears."

"I am certain they had supper at the Hotel-de-Ville," replied Oudarde, not in the least moved by all this difference of opinion, "and that never before were there so many kinds of meat and sugarplums."

"I tell you, they were served by Le Sec, town sergeant, at the Hotel du Petit-Bourbon, and that's why you're so confused."

"At the Hotel-de-Ville, I tell you!"

"At the Petit-Bourbon, my dear! And what's more, they lighted up with magical glasses the word *Hope* that's written over the doorway."

"I say no!"

"I say yes!"

"I say no!"

The fat Oudarde was readying herself to reply, and the quarrel would perhaps have gone on to the pulling of head-dresses, had not Mahiette suddenly exclaimed, "Hey, look at those people over there, gathered at the end of the bridge! There's something in the middle of the group that they're looking at."

"You're right," said Gervaise. "I hear someone playing the tambourine. Maybe it's little Smeralda doing her tricks with her goat. Hurry, Mahiette! Double your pace and bring your boy! You came here to see all the sights of Paris. Yesterday, you saw the Flemings; today you must see the little gypsy."

"The gypsy!" ejaculated Mahiette, turning suddenly around, and clutching her son's arm with force. "God preserve me from her; she'd steal my child. Come along, Eustache!"

And she began to run along the quay toward the Grève, until she had left the bridge far behind. However, the boy, whom she was dragging along, fell on his knees; and she stopped out of breath. Oudarde and Gervaise caught up with her.

"That gypsy steal your child?" said Gervaise. "What a strange notion!"

Mahiette shook her head thoughtfully.

"What is strange about it," observed Oudarde, "is that the Sachette has the same notion about gypsy women."

"What's the Sachette?" queried Mahiette.

"Why," said Oudarde, "it's Sister Gudule. You must be from Rheims, not to know that! It's the recluse who lives in the Rat Hole."

"What!" exclaimed Mahiette, "that poor woman who is to get this cake we're carrying?"

Oudarde nodded her head affirmatively. "Precisely. You'll see her soon at her window, on the Grève. She thinks the same way you do about those vagabond gypsies that wander around playing their tambourines and telling fortunes. Nobody knows why she has this horror of zingari and gypsies. But you, why do you run away like this, Mahiette, at the sight of them?"

"Oh!" said Mahiette, taking in both her hands the round head of her little boy, "I don't want to happen to me what happened to Pâquette la Chantefleurie!"

"Ah, my good Mahiette, you must tell us that story," said Gervaise, taking her arm.

"I will," replied Mahiette, "but you must be Parisians not to know that one. I will tell you, then, but we need not stop while I tell it to you.

"Pâquette la Chantefleurie was a pretty eighteen-year-old when I was one too, that is to say eighteen years ago, and it's her own fault that she's not, as I am, a good plump, fresh-looking mother at thirty-six, with a husband and a boy. But to get on, from the time she was fourteen years old, it was too late! She was the daughter of Guybertaut, a boat minstrel at Rheims—the same man who played before King Charles VII, at his coronation, when he sailed down our river Vesle from Sillery to Muison, and Madame la Pucelle, even, was on the boat with him. Pâquette's father died while she was still a child, so that she had only her mother left, a sister of Monsieur Mathieu Pradon, a master brazier and tinsmith in Paris, on Rue Parin-Garlin, who died just last year. You see, she came from quite a family. The mother was a good woman, but, unfortunately, she taught Pâquette only a little needlework and toy-making, which didn't hinder the little girl from growing tall and remaining very poor. Both of them lived in Rheims, along the river, on Rue de Folle-

Peine. Note that, for I do think it was there that Pâquette first ran into a lot of bad luck. In '61—the year of our King Louis XI's coronation—may God preserve him—Pâquette was so gay and so pretty that everyone, everywhere, called her La Chantefleurie. Poor girl! She had pretty teeth; she liked to laugh just to show them off. Now, a girl who loves to laugh is on her way to cry; pretty teeth are the ruin of pretty eyes. So it was with La Chantefleurie. She and her mother had a hard time making ends meet. They had sunk very low since the death of the old minstrel. Their needlework hardly brought them more than six deniers a week, which is not quite two liards, only a pittance. How fortune had changed, for there was a time when the father Guybertaut used to earn twelve sols parisis for a single song at a coronation!

"One winter—it was that same year '61—the two women had neither logs nor faggots, and it was very cold, but this gave such beautiful red cheeks to La Chantefleurie, that the men used to call after her, 'Hey, little Pâquette!' Eustache, don't let me see you bite into that cake! We soon realized that she had compromised her virtue because one Sunday she came to church with a gold cross around her neck—and only fourteen too! At first it was the young Viscount de Cormontreuil, whose bell tower is three-quarters of a league from Rheims; then, Messire Henri de Triancourt, the king's master of the horse; then, lower she went, to Chiart de Beaulion, sergeant-at-arms; then, lower still, to Macé de Frépus, Monsieur le Dauphin's barber; next to Thévenin le Moine, one of the king's cooks; then still farther down, always to men less young and less noble, she fell to Guillaume Racine, viol player, and then Thierry de Mer, lampmaker. Poor Chantefleurie, she was all things to all men. She had come to the last sou of her pieces of gold. What shall I say, mesdamoiselles? At the coronation, in the same year '61, it was she who went to bed with the king of the riffraff! In the very same year, mind you!"

Mahiette gave a sigh, and brushed away a tear that trickled down her cheek.

"That's not a very unusual story," commented Gervaise. "And there's not a word about gypsies or children."

"Patience!" resumed Mahiette. "As for a child, I'm coming to that. In '66, it'll be sixteen years ago this month, the feast of St. Paul, Pâquette gave birth to a little girl. Poor unfortunate creature! She was overjoyed. She had wanted a child for so long! Her mother, a good woman who'd never known how to do anything but wink at her daughter's faults, was now dead. Pâquette had no one in the world to love, nor anyone who loved her. For the five years since she had fallen, La Chantefleurie had been a miserable creature. She was alone, all alone in this world, pointed at, screamed at in the streets, beaten by the sergeants, laughed at by little ragamuffins. And then, she turned twenty—and twenty is old for a girl of the streets. Her promiscuity was beginning to bring her no more than her needlework had brought formerly. For every wrinkle that came, she lost a crown. Winter again was very cold. Wood was growing scarcer in her fireplace and bread in her cupboard. She could no longer work, because in becoming licentious, she had become lazy; and she suffered much more than formerly, because while giving way to idleness she gave herself more to pleasure. At least, that's the way Monsieur le Curé of Saint-Rémy explains why women of that kind are colder and hungrier than other poor women, especially as the grow old."

"Yes," observed Gervaise, "but the gypsies?"

"Wait a minute, please, Gervaise!" said Oudarde, who was less impatient. "We'd have nothing at the end of the story if we had everything at the beginning. Pray, Mahiette, go on. That poor Chantefleurie!"

Mahiette continued, "Well, she was very sad, very miserable, and her cheeks were constantly furrowed with her tears. But in her shame, in her promiscuity, in her loneliness, she thought that she would be less ashamed, less infamous, and less lonely, if there were something or someone in the world whom she could love and who would love her. She knew it had to be a child, for only a child would be innocent and uncritical. She had recognized this after she had tried to love a thief, the only man who could have wanted her. But after a short while, she noticed that the thief, too, despised her. These loose women need a lover or a child to fill their hearts. Otherwise they are most unhappy. Since she could keep no lover, she was bent on having a child. And as she had all along gone to church, she prayed God everlastingly to send her one. The Good Lord took pity on her, and sent her a little girl.

"I cannot tell you how overjoyed she was! The baby lived constantly with her mother's happy tears, kisses, and caresses. Pâquette nursed the child herself; she made its swaddling clothes from her coverlet, the only one she had on her bed; but now she felt neither cold nor hunger. She became radiantly beautiful again. An old maid makes a young mother.

"Once more, Chantefleurie took up her old loose ways, and once more she had visitors. And with the money she received she made baby clothes, lace robes, and little satin bonnets—without so much as thinking of buying herself another coverlet.

"Master Eustache, I've told you already not to eat that cake!

"In truth, little Agnès, that was the child's name, its baptismal name, but as to a surname, La Chantefleurie long ago had lost hers—in very truth, little Agnès was more covered with ribbons and embroidery than a dauphin's daughter! Among other things she had a pair of little shoes, the like of which even King Louis XI himself never had! Her mother stitched them and embroidered them herself. She used all her seamstress' art and ornamented them like the robe of our Blessed Lady. They were two of the cutest pink booties you'd ever want to see. They were no longer than my thumb, and you had to see the infant's little feet come out of them; otherwise you would never have believed that they went in. To be sure, these little feet were so tiny, so pretty, so pink—pinker than the satin of the shoes! When you have children, Oudarde, you'll know there's nothing prettier than those little feet and those little hands."

"I ask for nothing better," said Oudarde, with a sigh, "but I must await the good pleasure of Monsieur Andry Musnier."

"However," resumed Mahiette, "Pâquette's infant had more than pretty feet. I saw her when she was only four months old. She was a darling! Her eyes were bigger than her mouth. Her hair was curly, fine and black. What a beautiful brunette she would have been at sixteen! Her mother loved her more wildly day by day. She would hug her, kiss her, tickle her, bathe her, dress her up—nearly devour her.

Pâquette thanked God for the baby. The infant's pretty rosy feet especially were her chief delight and wonder. She was intoxicated with joy. Pâquette often pressed her lips to them, and adored their exquisiteness. She would put them into the little shoes, take them out again, admire them, wonder at them, hold them up to the light, pity them while she pretended to walk Agnès on her bed. This mother would gladly have passed her life on her knees, covering and uncovering those little feet, as if they were the feet of the Infant Jesus!"

"The tale is very good," said Gervaise in a half whisper, "but what is there about gypsies in all that?"

"This," replied Mahiette. "One day there came to Rheims some very odd people. They were beggars and vagabonds, wandering about the country, led by their duke and counts. Their skin was sunburned, their hair curly, and they wore silver rings in their ears. The women were even uglier than the men. Their faces were darker and always uncovered, their hair hung like a horse's tail. Each wore a ragged cloak, made of old woolen cloth, held around the shoulders by cords. The children who scrambled around their mothers' legs would have frightened monkeys. A disinherited people. They all had come directly from lower Egypt to Rheims, by way of Poland. The pope had heard their confessions, it was said, and had given them for penance to travel for seven years through the world without ever sleeping in a bed. So they called themselves penitents and they stank. It seems they had formerly been Saracens, and that is why they believed in Jupiter and demanded, by virtue of a papal bull, ten livres tournois from each archbishop, bishop, or abbot who wore a miter and carried a crosier. They came to Rheims to tell fortunes in the name of the Algerian king and the German emperor. As you can imagine, that was quite enough for them to be forbidden to enter the town. So the whole band camped cheerfully near the Braine Gate, upon that mound where there's a windmill, close by the old chalk pits. All Rheims went to see them. They would look into your palm and read marvelous things. They would have been bold enough to have predicted to Judas that he would be pope. However ugly rumors circulated about them—of child stealing, purse cutting, and eating of human flesh. Wise folk warned the foolish, 'Don't go near them!' and then went themselves by stealth. It was the thing to do.

"The fact is that these strange people said things that would have amazed a cardinal! Mothers made a great fuss over their children after some gypsy woman had read in their palms all sorts of wonders said to be prophesied there in pagan and Turkish signs. One would become an emperor; another, a pope; another, a captain. Poor Chantefleurie became curious. She wanted to know what she had, and whether her pretty little Agnès would some day be Empress of Armenia, or the like. So she took her to the gypsy women.

"The gypsies admired the child, hugged her, kissed her with their black mouths, and marveled over her little hands—all, alas! to the great joy of the mother. They raved especially about the little one's feet and fancy booties. The baby was not yet a year old, but she was already beginning to prattle, and to laugh joyously at her mother. She was chubby and made a thousand little gestures like the angels in Paradise. She was very much frightened by the gypsy women and cried. But her mother kissed her the more and went away delighted at the good fortune which the fortune-tellers had foretold for her Agnès. She would be a beauty, a saint, a queen. So the mother went back to her garret in the Rue Folle-Peine, proud that she carried in her arms a queen.

"The following day, she took advantage of a moment when the child was sleeping on her bed—for the baby always slept with her—left the door slightly ajar, and ran to tell one of her neighbors in the Rue de la Séchesserie that there would come a day when her daughter Agnès would be waited on by the king of England and the archduke of Ethiopia, and would have a hundred other wonderful things befall her.

"When she returned, hearing no cry as she ran up the staircase, she said to herself, 'Good! the little one is still asleep!' The door was more ajar than she had left it. The mother went in and hurried to the bed. The child was not there. The room was empty. There was no sign of the baby except one of her pretty little shoes.

"Pâquette rushed out of the room and down the stairs, and

began beating her head against the wall, screaming, 'My child! My child! Who has taken my child?'

"The street was empty, the house isolated. No one could tell her anything. She ran through the city, looking up and down every street, running everywhere all day long, mad, wild, frantic, peeping in doors and windows like a wild beast that has lost its young. She was panting, disheveled, frightful to behold, and in her eyes burned a fire that dried her tears. She stopped everyone she met, and cried, 'My girl! My little girl! My pretty baby! He who will bring back my girl, I will be his servant, the servant of his dog, and he may eat my heart, if he wishes.' She met Monsieur le Curé of Saint-Rémy and said to him, 'Monsieur le Curé, I'll dig the soil with my nails, but give me back my baby!'

"It would have made your heart bleed, Oudarde. I saw a hard-hearted man, Master Ponce Lacabre, the lawyer, cry bitter tears. Ah! the poor mother!

"In the evening, she went back to her room.

"During her absence one of her neighbors had seen two gypsies sneak in carrying a package under their arms, then come downstairs again, close the door, and flee. After they had gone, someone heard in Pâquette's room a crying, like a child's. On being told this, the mother burst out laughing, flew up the steps, and burst open her door like an explosion of cannon fire. Pâquette entered the room . . . But a frightful thing to tell, Oudarde! Instead of her gentle little Agnès, so soft and rosy, her gift from God, there was a sort of hideous, little, crippled, one-eyed monster with misshapen limbs, crawling and bawling on the floor. She turned away in horror. 'Oh,' she said, 'could the witches have changed my girl into a frightful animal like that?'

"Someone quickly carried away the ugly little thing. He would have driven Pâquette mad. This monstrous child belonged to some gypsy woman who was possessed by the devil. He appeared to be about four years old, and spoke a language that was like no human tongue—impossible words.

"La Chantefleurie snatched up the little shoe, all that was left of everything she had loved. She remained in the room for such a long while, so immobile, so speechless, so breathless that you would have thought her dead. All at once, her whole body trembled, she covered her relic with impassioned kisses, and burst into sobs as if her heart had broken. I assure you we were all crying too. Then she said, 'O my little daughter! my pretty little daughter! Where are you?' It would have torn your soul. I weep still when I think about it. You see, our children are the very marrow of our bones.

"My poor Eustache! You are so handsome! If you only knew how nice he is! Yesterday he said to me, 'I want to be a gendarme.' O my Eustache, if I were to lose you!

"La Chantefleurie rose all of a sudden and began to run through the streets of Rheims crying out, 'To the camp of the gypsies! to the camp of the gypsies! Sergeants, burn the witches!' But the gypsies were gone. The night was pitch-black, so that they couldn't be pursued.

"The next day, two leagues from Rheims, on a heath between Gueux and Tilloy, they found the remains of a great fire, some ribbons which had belonged to Pâquette's little girl, some drops of blood, and some goat's dung. The night just past had been Saturday night. No one doubted but that the gypsies had kept their Sabbath upon that heath, and had devoured the baby in company with Beelzebub, as is done among the Mohammedans.

"When La Chantefleurie learned of these horrible things, she did not weep. She moved her lips as if to speak, but no words came. The next day her hair was gray, and on the next, she had disappeared."

"A dreadful story indeed!" said Oudarde. "It's enough to make a Burgundian weep!"

"No wonder," added Gervaise, "you are so hauntingly afraid of these gypsies!"

"And you did quite right," resumed Oudarde, "to run away just now with your Eustache, seeing that these too are gypsies from Poland."

"No," said Gervaise. "They say they come from Spain and Catalonia."

"Catalonia! Well, that is possible," answered Oudarde. "Polonia, Catalonia, Valonia, I always confound those three provinces. But one thing is sure: they are gypsies."

"And it is also sure," added Gervaise, "that they have teeth long enough to eat children. And I wouldn't be surprised if La Smeralda herself also eats a little, for all she purses up her mouth so small. That white goat of hers has too many mischievous tricks not to have some wickedness also."

Mahiette was walking along in silence. She was absorbed in that kind of reverie which is, as it were, a prolongation of a mournful story, and which does not cease until it has communicated its effect, by vibration after vibration, to the depth of the heart.

Gervaise, however, addressed her, "And no one ever found out what happened to La Chantefleurie?"

Mahiette made no reply.

Gervaise repeated the question, tugging on her sleeve and calling her by name.

Mahiette seemed to awake as from a dream. "What became of La Chantefleurie?" she said, mechanically repeating the words whose impression was fresh in her ear. Then, making an effort to bring her attention to the meaning of the words, "Ah!" she replied, emphatically, "no one ever knew."

After a pause, she added, "Some said they had seen her leave Rheims at eventide by the Fléchembault Gate; others say at daybreak by the Basée Gate. A poor man found her gold cross hung upon the stone cross in the field where the fair is held. It was the very trinket that marked her undoing in '61. It was a gift from the handsome Viscount of Cormontreuil, her first lover. Pâquette had never wanted to part with it. Even in her wretched poverty, she clung to it as to her life. So that, when we found this cross, we all thought she was dead. However, there are some people, in Cabaret-les-Vantes, who said they saw her on the Paris road, walking barefoot over the stones. But, in that case, she must have left by the Vesle Gate, and that doesn't make sense. However, *I* think she went out by the Vesle Gate, quite out of this world."

"I don't understand you," said Gervaise.

"The Vesle," answered Mahiette, with a melancholy smile, "is the river."

"Poor Chantefleurie!" said Oudarde, shuddering. "Drowned!"

"Drowned," replied Mahiette. "And good father Guybertaut never thought when he was passing under the Tinqueux bridge, singing in his boat, that one day his dear little Pâquette would pass under that same bridge too, but with neither boat nor song!"

"And the little shoe?" asked Gervaise.

"Disappeared with the mother," answered Mahiette.

"Poor little shoe!" said Oudarde.

Oudarde, a fat, kind-hearted woman, would have been quite content to sigh with Mahiette. But Gervaise, more curious, was not finished with her questioning.

"And the monster?" she said abruptly to Mahiette.

"What monster?" asked the other.

"The little gypsy monster left by the witches at Pâquette's in exchange for her daughter. What was done with it? I hope it was drowned too."

"Of course not," answered Mahiette.

"What! Burned then? Really, a better fate for a witch's child."

"We did neither, Gervaise. Monsieur the Archbishop took an interest in the child of the gypsies. He exorcised him, blessed him, carefully took the devil from his body, and sent him to Paris to be exposed on the wooden bed at Notre-Dame as a foundling."

"Ah, those bishops!" muttered Gervaise; "because they are learned, they never do anything as we would. Now, I ask you, Oudarde, to put the devil among the foundlings! For surely this little monster was the devil! Well, Mahiette, what did they do with him in Paris? No charitable person wanted him, I trust?"

"I don't know," answered the lady from Rheims. "It was just then that my husband bought a notary's office at Beru, two leagues from the city, and we thought no more about the story, particularly as just in front of Beru are the two little hills of Cernay, which hide the towers of Rheims Cathedral from view."

While talking thus, the three good women arrived at the Place de Grève. They had been so preoccupied that they passed the public breviary in the Tower of Roland without stopping, and were proceeding toward the pillory, around which a crowd was every moment increasing. It is probable that the happenings there which at that moment were drawing every eye would have made them forget the Rat Hole and the perfunctory charity that they had intended to per-

form, had not the chubby six-year-old Eustache suddenly reminded them of it. "Mother," said he, as if some impulse
had apprised him that the Rat Hole was behind him, "now,
may I eat the cake?"

If Eustache had been more clever, that is, less of a pig, he
would have waited a little longer. He would not have asked
until they had returned to the University to Master Andry
Musnier's home on the Rue Madame-la-Valence, where the
two channels of the Seine and the five bridges of the City
would have been between the cake and the Rat Hole.

This same question, however imprudent and inoppor-
tunely posed, aroused Mahiette's attention.

"By the way,"' she exclaimed, "we're forgetting the recluse! Take me to this Rat Hole of yours, that I may give her
the cake."

"Right away!" said Oudarde. "It will be an act of charity."

That was not what Eustache had in mind.

"Say, may I have my cake?" said he, rubbing first one of
his ears upon his shoulder and then the other—a sign in such
cases of supreme dissatisfaction.

The three women turned back, and when they had nearly
reached the cell in the Tower of Roland, Oudarde said to the
other two, "We must not all three look into the hole at once,
lest we should frighten the Sachette. You two, pretend that
you are reading 'Dominus' in the breviary, while I peep in
the window. The Sachette knows me a little. I'll tell you
when you can come."

She went by herself to the window. As she looked inside,
the usually cheerful, carefree face of Oudarde changed abruptly. Pity washed over it, removing all its color, as if she
had suddenly passed from bright sunlight into pale moonlight. Her eyes moistened, and her mouth contracted as if
she was about to cry. A minute later, she put her finger to
her lips, and beckoned to Mahiette to come see.

Alone, Mahiette came, moving silently on tiptoe as one
does when approaching a deathbed.

Indeed, it was a sorrowful sight that the two women saw
as they looked without moving, scarcely breathing, through
the barred window of the Rat Hole.

The cell was small, wider than it was high, with a Gothic
vaulted ceiling, giving it the shape of a bishop's miter. On

the bare flagstone floor, in one corner, a woman sat, hunched over. Her chin rested on her knees, which her two folded arms pressed close against her chest. Thus, clad in brown sackcloth, wrapped loosely around her, with her long gray hair cascading over her face down to her feet, she looked, at first sight, like only a heap, a strange form, against the dark background of the cell—like a sort of dark triangle, which the daylight from the window cut sharply in two halves, one dark, the other light. It resembled one of those specters, half shade, half light, such as are seen in dreams and in the extraordinary paintings of Goya—pale, motionless, sinister, squatting on a tomb, or backed against the grating of a dungeon. It was neither man nor woman, nor living being, nor a definite form; it was a figure, a sort of vision in which the real and the fantastic were intermingled like light and shadow. Through the veil of her hair, you could barely distinguish a severe and emaciated profile. From under the hem of her flowing cloak protruded part of a naked foot, gnarled and twisted, upon the cold floor. What little of the human form was discernible under that envelope of mourning made you shudder.

This figure, which seemed fixed to the floor, appeared to have neither motion, thought, nor breath. Covered only by thin sackcloth, in January, crouching upon a pavement of granite, without fire, in the darkness of a dungeon whose oblique window admitted only the northeast wind and never the sun, she seemed not to shiver, not even to feel. You would have thought she had turned to stone like the dungeon, or to ice like the season. Her hands were clasped, her eyes were staring. At first glance, you mistook her for a specter; at the second, for a statue.

However, at intervals, her blue lips half opened with a sigh and trembled, but their movement was as lifeless and automatic as that of leaves which are scattered by the wind. And from those dull, stony eyes there proceeded a look, ineffable, profound, lugubrious, imperturbable, constantly directed toward one corner of the cell which could not be seen from the outside—a look which seemed to concentrate all the gloomy thoughts of that distressed soul upon some mysterious object.

Such was the creature who because of her abode was

called the *recluse,* and because of her coarse garment, the *Sachette.*

Now, the three women, for Gervaise had joined Mahiette and Oudarde, were looking through the window. Their heads blocked the feeble light into the dungeon, apparently without at all calling the wretched creature's attention in that direction. "Let's not disturb her," whispered Oudarde; "she's in a trance, she's praying."

Meanwhile, Mahiette was gazing with a constantly increasing anxiety upon that wan, withered, disheveled head, and her eyes filled with tears. "That would be very strange!" she muttered.

She pushed her head through the bars of the window, and succeeded in obtaining a glance into that corner of the cell upon which the unfortunate woman's gaze seemed immovably fixed in gloomy absorption.

When she withdrew her head, her face was bathed with tears.

"What is the woman's name?" she asked Oudarde.

"We call her Sister Gudule."

"And I," returned Mahiette, "call her Pâquette la Chantefleurie."

Then, putting her finger to her lips, she made a sign to the amazed Oudarde to put her head through the bars as she had done and to look.

Oudarde looked, and saw in the corner a little shoe of faded pink satin, decorated all over with gold and silver embroidery.

Next Gervaise looked; and then the three women, staring at the unhappy mother, began to weep.

However, neither their peeping nor their weeping had distracted the recluse. Her hands remained clasped, her lips mute, her eyes set, and to anyone who knew her story, that gaze of hers toward the little shoe was heart-rending.

The three women had not uttered a word; they dared not speak, even in a whisper. That silence, that grief, that forgetfulness in which every detail had disappeared save one, had upon them the effect of a high altar at Easter or Christmas. They were silent; they composed themselves, as if about to kneel. They felt as if they had just entered a church during Tenebrae services.

At length, Gervaise, the most curious of the three, and therefore the least sensitive, tried to make the recluse speak, by calling to her, "Sister! Sister Gudule!" She called three times, raising her voice each time. The recluse did not move; there was no word, no glance, no sigh, no sign of life.

Now Oudarde herself, in a softer and kinder tone, spoke. "Sister! Holy Sister Gudule!" But there was the same silence, the same immobility.

"A strange woman!" exclaimed Gervaise. "An explosion wouldn't move her!"

"Perhaps she's deaf," said Oudarde with a sigh.

"Maybe blind!" added Gervaise.

"And maybe dead!" observed Mahiette.

It is certain that if the soul had not yet quitted that inert, torpid, lethargic body, it had at least retired within it, and had hidden itself in such depths that external perception was impossible.

"We shall have to leave the cake on the windowsill," said Oudarde. "But then some lad or other will take it. What can we do to rouse her?"

Eustache, whose attention had until then been diverted by a little wagon drawn by a monstrous dog, which had just passed them, all at once observed that his three conductresses were looking at something through the hole in the wall; and his own curiosity being thus excited, he mounted upon a curbstone, sprang up on his toes, and put his fat rosy face to the opening, crying out, "Mother, let me see too."

At the sound of this child's voice, clear, fresh, and ringing, the recluse gave a start. She turned her head with the dry and sudden motion of a steel spring; her two long, fleshless hands threw aside the hair upon her forehead, and she looked at the child with astonishment, bitterness, and despair. That look was but a flash. "O my God," she exclaimed, hiding her head between her knees, and it seemed as if her hoarse voice was tearing her breast, "at least, let me not see the children of others!"

"Good day, madame," said the boy seriously.

This shock, however, had, as it were, awakened the recluse. A long shiver ran through her body from head to foot; her teeth chattered; she half raised her head, pressed her el-

bows against her hips, and, rubbing her feet as if to restore
their warmth, said, "Oh, the bitter cold!"

"Poor woman!" said Oudarde, deeply touched. "Would
you like a little fire?"

She shook her head negatively.

"Well," resumed Oudarde, offering her a flask, "here is
some hippocras that will warm you. Drink it."

Again she shook her head, looking steadfastly at Oudarde,
and said, "Some water!"

Oudarde insisted. "No, sister, that's no drink for January.
You must take a little hippocras, and eat this leavened wheat
cake that we have baked for you."

She refused the cake, which Mahiette offered her, and
said, "Some black bread!"

"Here!" said Gervaise, seized with charity in her turn,
and, taking off her own woolen robe, "here's a cloak warmer
than yours; put it over your shoulders!"

The recluse refused the cloak, also, and said, "A sack!"

"But at all events," resumed the kindly Oudarde, "you
must know that yesterday was a feast."

"Yes, I know," said the recluse. "For two days now I have
had no water in my pitcher." After a pause, she added, "It's
a feast day, and I'm forgotten. They do well. Why should
anyone think of me? I don't think of them. Cold ashes are
fitting for dead coal!"

And then, as if fatigued with having said so much, she let
her head drop upon her knees again. The simple and charitable Oudarde, thinking that she was to understand from
these last words that the poor woman was still complaining
of the cold, answered her sincerely, "Then will you have a
little fire?"

"Fire!" said the Sachette in an odd tone, "and will you
make one, too, for the little one that has been buried these
fifteen years?"

The Sachette trembled, her voice vibrated, her eyes
flashed. She rose on her knees; she suddenly stretched out
her white emaciated hand toward the child, who was gazing
at her with astonishment.

"Take that child away!" she cried. "The gypsy woman is
coming this way!"

Then she fell with her face to the ground, and her forehead struck the floor with the noise of a stone against a stone. The three women thought she was dead. A minute afterward she moved, and they saw her crawl on her hands and knees to the corner where the little shoe was. They dared not look; they saw her no longer, but they heard a thousand kisses and sighs, intermingled with piercing cries, and dull blows like those of a head knocking against a wall; then, after one of those blows, so violent that it startled all three of them, there was silence.

"Has she killed herself?" said Gervaise, venturing to put her head between the bars. "Sister! Sister Gudule!"

"Sister Gudule!" repeated Oudarde.

"Oh, my God, she isn't moving!" resumed Gervaise. "Do you think she's dead? Gudule! Gudule!"

Mahiette, whose voice had not been heard, now made an effort. "Wait a minute," she said, and then, putting her head in the window, she spoke softly, "Pâquette! Pâquette la Chantefleurie!"

A child having blown upon a supposedly dead firecracker, and having it explode in his face, would not have been more frightened than Mahiette was at the effect of this name thus suddenly whispered into the cell of Sister Gudule.

The recluse was invigorated; every limb came alive. She rose erect upon her naked feet, and flew to the window with eyes so flaming that Oudarde, Gervaise, and their companion, Mahiette, with her boy, all retreated as far as the wall along the quay.

Meanwhile the sinister face of the recluse was pressed close to the window bars. "Oh, oh," she cried with an eerie laugh, "it's the gypsy woman who is calling me."

At that moment a scene which was being enacted at the pillory arrested her haggard eye. Her forehead wrinkled with horror, she stretched out her two skeleton arms and cried out with a voice that rattled in her throat, "So, it's you again, daughter of Egypt, it's you who calls me, stealer of children! Well, curses on you. Be cursed! Cursed! Cursed!"

4
A Tear for a Drop of Water

These words were, so to speak, the cues between two scenes that had thus far been enacted simultaneously, each upon its particular stage; one we have just seen at the Rat Hole; the other, we are about to see at the pillory. The former had been witnessed only by three ladies whom the reader has just met; the latter had for spectators the whole crowd we saw gathering in the Place de Grève around the pillory and the gallows.

This crowd upon seeing four sergeants posted since nine o'clock in the morning at the four corners of the pillory surmised that a penal exhibition of some kind—not certainly a hanging, but a flogging, or a cutting off of the ears, or something of this kind—was about to take place. The crowd had increased so rapidly that the four sergeants, finding themselves too closely pressed, had more than once been obliged to "tighten it," as they used to say, by great lashing of their whips and by urging their horses into the seething mass of humanity.

The populace, however, accustomed to waiting for public executions were not too impatient. They amused themselves by staring at the pillory, a very simple sort of structure. In truth, it consisted only of a cubical mass of masonry some ten feet high, but hollow within; a steep flight of uncut stone steps, the top of which was called the ladder, led to the top, upon which there had been placed a placed a plain, horizontal solid wheel made of oak. The victim was tied to this wheel, on his knees, with his hands bound behind his back. An upright shaft of timber, like an axle, moved by a capstan, concealed within this cubical block, made the wheel turn horizontally and uniformly, thus exposing the culprit's face successively to every side of the city square. This was called "turning" the criminal.

So, you see, the pillory in the Grève was not so fine as the one at the Halles. Here was nothing of architectural or mon-

224

umental beauty. It had no roof at all to be topped with an iron cross; no octagonal lantern, no slender pillars with capitals of foliage and flowers, no carved woodwork, no bold or delicate sculpture. The spectator had to be satisfied with the pillory's four sides of rough stone, and, close by and surmounting it, the two side walls of stone, still rougher, which supported a sorry stone gibbet, meager and bare. All this would be shabby even for an amateur Gothic architect. But it is certain that no one could care less about the architecture of the Middle Ages than the good burghers, especially when considering the construction of a pillory or a gibbet.

Finally, the prisoner arrived, fastened to the back of a cart. As soon as he had been hoisted to the stone platform, so that he could be seen from every part of the square, he was bound with cords and straps to the wheel of the pillory. Then there burst from the crowd loud hoots, mingled with laughter and acclamations. Immediately they recognized Quasimodo.

Indeed it was he. What a strange reversal of fortune too, now to be pilloried in that same square where, the day before, he had been hailed and proclaimed the Pope and Prince of Fools! Here, where he had been carried aloft in the cortège of the Duke of Egypt, the King of Tunis, and the Emperor of Galilee! One thing, however, is certain: there was no person in that crowd—not even himself, who had in turn been an object of triumph and of punishment—who discerned and compared the two situations in his mind. Gringoire and his philosophy were absent from this spectacle.

Presently, Michel Noiret, one of the king's official trumpeters, called for silence, and read the proclamation of the sentence, pursuant to the ordinance and command of Monsieur the Provost. He then retired, with his men in their official liveries, to a place behind the cart.

Quasimodo, quite impassive, did not bat an eye. All resistance was rendered impossible to him by what was then called, in the style of the old criminal law, "the strength and firmness of his bonds." This is to say that the ropes and chains probably cut into his flesh. This is a tradition of jails and convict gangs which is not yet lost, but is carefully preserved among us civilized, mild, humane people (not to mention the penitentiary and the guillotine).

Quasimodo had let them lead him, push him, carry him, hoist him, tie him, and retie him. Nothing was distinguishable in his face but astonishment. He might have been a savage or an idiot. It was known that he was deaf. One would have thought he was blind too.

They forced him to his knees on the wheel, and stripped him to the waist; he made not the least resistance. They tied him with a fresh supply of ropes and thongs; he let them bind and strap him. Only from time to time he breathed heavily, like a calf whose head hangs tossing about over the side of a butcher's cart.

"The stupid idiot!" said Jehan Frollo du Moulin to his friend Robin Poussepain (for the two scholars had followed the victim, as in duty bound); "he understands no more about what is going on than a beetle in a box."

A wild laugh rose from the crowd when they saw the naked, hunched back of Quasimodo, his camel's chest, his scaly and hairy shoulders. During all this merriment, a man, short and robust, dressed in the town livery, mounted the platform, and stood next to the victim. His name was quickly circulated among the crowd; it was Master Pierrat Torterue, official torturer at the Châtelet.

The first thing he did was to set down on one corner of the pillory a black hourglass, the top cup of which was filled with red sand that was filtering through into the lower half. Then he doffed his particolored doublet, and there was seen dangling from his right hand a whip with long slender white lashes, knotted, braided, and shining with metal claws. With his left hand he nonchalantly rolled up his right shirt sleeve as high as the armpit.

Meanwhile Jehan Frollo cried out, lifting his light-haired, curly head above the crowd (for he had climbed for that purpose to the shoulders of Robin Poussepain), "Come see, ladies and gentlemen! They're peremptorily going to flog Master Quasimodo, the bellringer for my brother Monsieur the Archdeacon of Josas, a rare specimen of Oriental architecture, with a back like a dome, and legs like twisted columns!"

And the crowd laughed, especially the boys and girls.

At length, the torturer stamped his foot. The wheel began to turn. Quasimodo staggered under his bonds, and the amazement suddenly depicted on that deformed face drew fresh bursts of laughter all around.

Suddenly, at the moment when the wheel in its rotation presented to Master Pierrat Quasimodo's mountainous back, Master Pierrat raised high his arm, the slender lashes whistled sharply in the air like a handful of vipers, and fell with fury upon the poor wretch's shoulders.

Quasimodo jumped like one startled from sleep. He was now beginning to understand. He twisted in his bonds. A violent contraction of surprise and pain distorted the muscles of his face, but not a sound escaped him. He only moved his head from side to side, back and forward, balancing it like a bull stung by a gadfly.

A second stroke followed the first, then a third, and another, and another, and so on. The wheel continued to turn and the blows to fall. Soon there was blood; you saw it trickling in a thousand streaks over the dark shoulders of the hunchback, and the keen lashes, as they whipped around in the air, scattered drops over the crowd.

Quasimodo had resumed, at least in appearance, his former passiveness. He had tried at first, silently and without any apparent great effort, to burst his bonds. Then his eye flashed, his muscles contracted, his limbs gathered themselves up, and the cords and chains strained. The effort was powerful, prodigious, desperate; but the bonds of the provostship held. They creaked, but that was all. Quasimodo slumped exhausted. The stupefaction on his face was succeeded by an expression of bitter and deep discouragement. He closed his only eye; his head dropped to his chest; and it seemed as if he were dead.

Thenceforth, he did not move. Nothing could make him stir. Neither the blood which flowed freely, nor the strokes of the whip which rained down upon his back with redoubled fury, nor the violence of the torturer who had worked himself up into a sort of intoxication, nor the whistling of those brutal lashes.

At length, an usher of the Châtelet, robed in black, riding a black horse, who had been stationed beside the pillory since the beginning of the flogging, pointed with his ebony riding crop to the hourglass. The torturer stopped. The wheel stopped. Quasimodo's eye slowly opened.

The flagellation was over. Two assistants to the official executioner washed the bleeding shoulders of the victim, rubbed them with some kind of ointment, which immediately closed the wounds, and threw over his shoulders a sort of yellow cloth cut in the form of a chasuble. Meanwhile, Pierrat Torterue held his whip, letting the blood-soaked lashes drain drop by drop upon the ground.

But it was not all over for Quasimodo. He had still to undergo that hour on the pillory which Master Florian Barbedienne had so judiciously added to the sentence of Messire Robert d'Estouteville—to the greater glory of the old physiological and psychological pun of Jean de Cumène—*Surdus absurdus.*[1]

So they turned the hourglass, and left the hunchback tied to the wheel, so that justice might be satisfied completely.

The people, particularly during the Middle Ages, were to society what the children are to the family. As long as they remain in that state of youthful ignorance, or moral and intellectual minority, it may be said of them as of childhood, "It is an age that knows no pity."

We have already shown how Quasimodo was generally hated, for more than one good reason, it is true. There was hardly a spectator in that crowd but either had or thought he had some cause of complaint against the mischievous hunchback of Notre-Dame. All had rejoiced when he made his appearance on the pillory; and the brutal punishment he had just suffered and the piteous condition in which it had left him, far from softening the hearts of the populace, had only made their hatred more malicious by furnishing it with a cause for merriment.

Accordingly, once the "public vengeance" was satisfied, as it is still called in the legal jargon of the day, a thousand private revenges now had their turn. Here, as in the Great Hall, it was the women who were the most spiteful. They all had some grudge against him—some for his mischievousness, others for his ugliness. The last-mentioned were the most vehement.

"Oh! you image of the anti-Christ!" exclaimed one.

"You rider of the broomstick!" cried another.

[1] "Absurd deaf man."

"Look at that fine sad face!" bawled a third, "that would make him Pope of Fools if today were yesterday!"

"Good," said another hag. "That's the pillory face. When will he give us the gallows face?"

"When are you to have your big bell clapped upon your head a hundred feet underground, you cursed bellringer?"

"And to think that this devil rings the Angelus!"

"The one-eyed hunchbacked monster! And deaf too!"

"His is a face to make a woman miscarry, better than any medicine or pharmacies!"

And the two students Jehan Frollo and Robin Poussepain were singing at the top of their lungs the refrain of an old popular song:

> A halter for the gallows rogue,
> A faggot for the maggot.

A thousand other insults, hoots, imprecations, and, from here and there, stones were rained upon him.

Quasimodo was deaf, but his vision was clear; and the public fury was as plainly expressed in their distorted faces as in their words. Besides, the stones that struck him were synchronized with the outbursts of laughter.

At first, he bore up under these additional indignities very well. But by degrees his patience, which had remained inflexible under the whip of the torturer, bent and broke under these insect stings. The Asturian bull that has borne unmoved the attacks of the *picador* is irritated by the dogs and the *banderillas*.

At first, as he slowly spun around, he sent a menacing look at the crowd. But, bound as he was, he was powerless to chase the flies which were stinging his wounds. Then he struggled in his bonds, and his furious efforts made the whole wheel of the pillory creak on its timbers. But all this only increased the shouting and the derision of the mob.

Then the poor wretch, finding himself unable to break the wild beast's chains, became quiet. Only, at intervals, a sigh of rage heaved his great chest. On his face there was neither shame nor blush. He was too far from the state of society and too near the state of nature to know what shame was. Besides, deformed as he was, is infamy a thing that can be felt? But, rage, hatred, and despair were slowly spreading over that hideous face, a cloud that grew more and more black, and more and more charged with an electricity, recognized by a thousand flashes from the eye of the Cyclops.

Nevertheless, for a moment the cloud passed over at the appearance of a mule which passed through the crowd, carrying a priest. The instant he caught a glimpse of this mule and the rider in the distance, the expression on the face of the poor victim changed. The fury which had distorted it gave way to a strange smile, full of sweetness, gentleness, ineffable kindness. As the priest came nearer the smile grew broader, more radiant. It was as if the crucified was hailing a saviour's coming. However, when the mule approached near enough to the pillory for its rider to recognize the culprit, the priest lowered his eyes, turned abruptly around, spurred the mule, as if in haste to escape any humiliating appeals, and as if not at all anxious to be saluted and recognized by a poor devil in such a predicament.

The priest was the archdeacon Dom Claude Frollo.

The cloud returned and fell darker than ever on the face of Quasimodo. The smile, for some time, mingled with the gloom, but it was bitter, discouraged, and profoundly sad.

Time was passing. He had been on the pillory for at least an hour and a half, torn, abused, scoffed at, and almost stoned to death.

Suddenly, he made another desperate effort to loosen his chains. This shook the whole structure; and, breaking the silence which until then he had obstinately kept, he cried out in a raucous and maddened voice, more like a dog's howling than a human cry, loud enough to drown out the noise of the hooting, "Some water!"

This cry of distress, far from moving the crowd to compassion, increased the amusement of the good Parisian mob that was still gathered around the pillory. This mob, it must be admitted, taken as a whole and as a multitude, was in those days no more cruel and brutal than that horrible band of vagabonds, to which we have already introduced the reader. Both encompassed the lowest dregs of society. Not a compassionate voice was raised in behalf of the unfortunate victim. No one spoke but to mock his thirst. True enough, by now he looked more grotesque and repulsive than pitiable, with his face streaming blood, his eye wild, his mouth foaming with rage and suffering, and his tongue lolling. It must be said, too, that, had there been in the crowd any such good charitable soul, male or female, who should have been tempted to bring a glass of water to this miserable creature in pain, there reigned around these ignominious pillory steps such preconceived notions of disgrace and shame, as would have sufficed to repel the Good Samaritan himself.

After a minute or two Quasimodo again looked at the crowd despairingly, and repeated in a tone yet more heartrending, "Some water!"

But again everybody laughed.

"Drink this!" cried Robin Poussepain, throwing in his face a sponge that had been soaked in the gutter. "Here, you deaf scoundrel! I'm your debtor."

A woman threw a stone at Quasimodo's head. "This will teach you to wake us at night with your cursed ringing!"

"Well, lad!" bawled a cripple, trying to reach Quasimodo with his crutch, "will you again cast spells at us from the top of the towers of Notre-Dame?"

"Drink from this!" said one man, hurling a broken pitcher at his chest. "It was you, that only by passing before her, made my wife give birth to a two-headed baby!"

"Some water!" repeated Quasimodo, panting.

Just then, he saw the crowd make way for someone. A young girl, strangely dressed, stepped out of the crowd. She was accompanied by a little white goat with gilded horns, and she carried a Basque tambourine in her hand.

Quasimodo's eye sparkled. It was the gypsy girl whom he had tried to carry off the night before, for which piece of daring he felt in some confused way he was now being punished; but which was by no means the case, since he was being punished for the misfortune of his being deaf, and for having been judged by a deaf judge. He did not doubt that she had come to have her revenge too, and to beat him like the rest of them.

He watched her as she nimbly ascended the stone steps to the pillory. He was choking with rage and disdain. He wished that he could crumble the pillory; and, if the lightning in his eye could have cast a bolt, the gypsy would have been reduced to ashes before she could have reached the top.

Saying nary a word, she approached the victim, who was writhing in vain to escape her. Then unfastening a gourd from her belt, she held it gently to the poor wretch's parched lips.

A big tear rolled from Quasimodo's bloodshot eye, and trickled slowly down his deformed face so long contracted by despair. It was perhaps the first that the poor creature had ever shed.

Meanwhile he forgot to drink. The gypsy impatiently pouted, and then, with a smile, held the neck of the gourd between his jagged teeth. He drank with big gulps, for his thirst was burning.

When he had finished, the poor wretch protruded his black lips, undoubtedly to kiss the fair hand which had just brought him relief. But the girl, who perhaps did not trust him and who perhaps remembered his violent attack on her the night before, drew back her hand with the frightened movement of a child who is afraid of being bitten by some animal.

Then the poor deaf creature stared at her reproachfully and sadly.

Anywhere it would have been a touching scene to watch that beautiful girl, so young, so pure, so charming, and at the same time, so weak, thus piously hastening to the relief of such wretchedness, deformity, and malice. But on the platform of the pillory, it was sublime.

Even the people were struck by it, and began to clap their hands, shouting, "Noël! Noël!"

It was at that moment that the recluse, through the window of her cell, saw the gypsy on the pillory, and launched her sinister imprecation, "Curses on you, daughter of Egypt! Be cursed! Cursed!"

5

The End of the Story of the Cake

Esmeralda turned pale, and staggered down the pillory steps. The voice of the recluse still pursued her. "Come down! Come down! you Egyptian thicf, you will go up again!"

"The Sachette is raging again," muttered the crowd; but that is all they did, for these kinds of women were feared, and that made them sacred. In those days no one was willing to attack even verbally anyone who prayed night and day.

The hour had come to release Quasimodo. He was untied, and the crowd dispersed.

Near the Grand-Pont, Mahiette, who was going away with her two companions, suddenly stopped in her tracks. "By the way, Eustache," she said, "what have you done with the cake?"

"While you were talking to the lady in the hole, there was a big dog that took a bite out of my cake. So, I took a bite too."

"What!" she cried, "have you eaten it all?"

"Mother, it was the dog. I warned him, but he wouldn't listen to me. Then I bit a piece too. And it was all gone!"

"He's a bad one!" said the mother, smiling and scolding at the same time. "See, Oudarde, already he eats by himself all the cherries in our little orchard at Charlerange. Also his grandfather says he'll be a captain. Don't let me catch you again, Master Eustache. Now, come along, you greedy glutton!"

BOOK VII

1

Concerning the Danger of Confiding One's Secret to a Goat

Several weeks had passed.

It was the beginning of March. The sun, which Dubartas, that classic master of the paraphrase, had not yet named "the grandduke of the candles," was nonetheless bright and cheerful. It was one of those days in early spring which are so mild and beautiful that all Paris turns out in the squares and promenades as if it were Sunday. On those bright, warm, serene days, there is one hour especially when you should go to admire the great portal of Notre-Dame. It is then that the sun, declining already in the west, almost looks the cathedral full in the face. Its rays, becoming more and more horizontal, slowly recede from the pavement of the square and mount up the sheer face of the edifice, causing its thousands of figures in relief to stand out from their shadows, while the great central rose-window flames, like a Cyclop's eye lit up by reflections from a forge.

It was now just that hour.

Opposite the lofty cathedral, reddened by the setting sun, upon a stone balcony hanging over the porch of a rich Gothic house, on the corner formed by the square and the Rue du Parvis, some pretty girls were laughing and talking

234

with all the manner of grace and silliness. By the length of
the veils which fell from the top of their pointed pearly
headdresses, down to their heels; by the delicately embroidered neckerchiefs which covered their shoulders, revealing,
according to the engaging fashion of the times, the swell of
their beautiful virgin bosoms; by the richness of their under-
garments, more costly than the outer garments—an admirable refinement; by the gauze, the silk, the velvet with which
their dresses were trimmed; and, above all, by the whiteness
of their hands, proof of their idle, lazy ways, it was easy to
surmise that they were noble, wealthy heiresses. In fact they
were Damoiselle Fleur-de-Lys de Gondelaurier and her companions, Diane de Christeuil, Amelotte de Montmichel,
Colombe de Gaillefontaine, and the diminutive De
Champchevrier, all daughters from good families, gathered
together at that moment at the mansion of the widowed Lady
de Gondelaurier, on account of Monseigneur de Beaujeu and
Madame his wife, who were to come to Paris in April to select the maids-in-waiting for the Dauphiness Marguerite
when they should go to receive her in Picardy whence she
was to be escorted by the Flemings. Now all the gentry for
thirty leagues around were anxious to procure this favor for
their daughters, and a goodly number of them had already
brought or sent them to Paris. The above-mentioned maidens
had been entrusted by their parents into the discreet and venerable keeping of Madame Aloïse de Gondelaurier, widow
of a former officer of the king's crossbowmen, now living in
retirement with her only daughter, in her mansion in the
Place du Parvis Notre-Dame, in Paris.

The balcony, on which these young ladies were chatting,
opened into a room richly tapestried with fawn-colored
Flanders leather printed with gold foliage. The beams that
ran in parallel lines across the ceiling amused the eye by
their thousand unusual carvings, painted and gilded. On the
shelves of a sculptured cupboard, gorgeous enamels glittered; and a china boar's head occupied a prominent place
on a sideboard, whose two steplike sections announced that
the mistress of the house was the wife or widow of a knight-
banneret. At the far end of the room was a high chimney
place, blazoned from top to bottom with coats of arms. Beside it, in a rich velvet chair, was Madame de Gondelaurier,

whose fifty-five years were as distinctly written on her dress as on her face. By her side stood a young man of very haughty mien, vain and brash, one of those handsome fellows whom all women admire, though serious men and physiognomists would shrug their shoulders at such. This young cavalier wore the brilliant uniform of a captain of the king's archers which resembled very closely the costume of Jupiter, which the reader.has already had an opportunity to admire in the first chapter of this history so we will not weary him with a second description.

Some of the young ladies were seated on the balcony, others were seated inside on cushions of Utrecht velvet with gold corner plates. Those outside sat on oak stools carved with flowers and figures. Each of them held on her lap part of a large piece of tapestry on which all were working, while one long end of it lay on the matting which covered the floor.

They were chatting softly among themselves and tittering as is common in an assembly of young girls when there is a young man nearby. The young man, whose presence sparked all this animation, seemed, on his part, little interested in them; and while the pretty ladies were vying with each other in trying to attract his attention, he was especially busy with polishing, with his doeskin glove, the buckle of his sword-belt.

Occasionally the old lady addressed him in a low voice, and he answered as well as he could, with a sort of awkward and strained politeness. From the smiles and significant gestures of Madame Aloïse, as well as from winks she directed toward her daughter, Fleur-de-Lys, as she spoke low to the captain, it was evident that the subject of their conversation was some previous betrothal celebration or some plans regarding the marriage about to take place between the young man and Fleur-de-Lys. From the cold, embarrassed manner of the officer, it was easy to see that, so far as he was concerned at least, love played no part. His whole demeanor betrayed an air of constraint and boredom, which our modern-day barracks officers would admirably express by "What a beastly bore!"

The good lady, infatuated, like any mother, with her daughter's charms, was unaware of the officer's lack of enthusiasm, but exerted herself strenuously to point out in a whisper the infinite grace with which Fleur-de-Lys plied her needle or wound her silk.

"Look, my little cousin," she said, pulling him by the sleeve to whisper in his ear. "Look at her, as she bends over!"

"Yes, indeed," answered the young man, but immediately he fell back into his cold, abstracted silence.

A moment later, as Fleur-de-Lys bent over again, Dame Aloïse remarked, "Have you ever seen a prettier, more charming, more lightsome face than that of your betrothed? Is there anyone more fair or lovely? Look at those fine hands! and that neck—has it not the grace of a swan's? Oh how at times I envy you! and how fortunate you are to be a man, wicked scoundrel that you are! Is not my Fleur-de-Lys adorably beautiful? and are you not madly in love with her?"

"Assuredly," he answered, thinking all the time of something else.

"Go speak to her then," said Madame Aloïse, abruptly pushing him by the shoulder. "Say something to her. You have become quite shy."

We can assure our readers that shyness was neither a virtue nor a fault with the captain. However, he tried to do as he was bid.

"My beautiful cousin," he said, going over to Fleur-de-Lys, "what is the subject of this tapestry you are making?"

"Fair cousin," answered Fleur-de-Lys peevishly, "I have already told you three times. It is Neptune's grotto."

It was evident that Fleur-de-Lys understood better than her mother the cold, unconcerned manner of the captain.

As he felt duty-bound to make conversation, he queried, "And for whom is all this fine Neptune work?"

"It is for the Abbey of Saint-Antoine des Champs," said Fleur-de-Lys, not raising her eyes.

The captain picked up a corner of the tapestry, "And, pray tell, my fair cousin, who is that big gendarme with the puffed-out cheeks, blowing on the trumpet?"

"That is Triton," she answered.

There was still a bit of peevishness in the tone of Fleur-de-Lys' replies, and the young man understood that it was most urgent that he should whisper in her ear some sweet nothing, some gallant compliment or other, no matter what. Accordingly he leaned over, but his imagination could find nothing more tender or more familiar than this, "Why does your mother always wear that gown emblazoned with her coat of arms, like our great-grandmothers did in the time of Charles VII? Do tell her, my fair cousin, that it's no longer the fashion, and that her coat of arms embroidered on her dress makes her look like a walking mantelpiece. Upon my word, no one sits on her banner in that way now, I assure you."

Fleur-de-Lys raised her beautiful round eyes at him reproachfully. "Is that all that you can assure me?" she said softly.

Meanwhile the good Dame Aloïse, delighted to see them leaning toward each other and whispering, exclaimed, fidgeting all the while with the clasps of her book of hours, "What a touching love scene!"

The captain, more embarrassed, turned the conversation again to tapestry. "It is really charming, your tapestry!" he cried.

With this remark, Colombe de Gaillefontaine, another fair-skinned blonde, wearing a high-necked, blue brocade dress, ventured a shy remark to Fleur-de-Lys, and hoped that the handsome captain would answer it, "My dear Gondelaurier, have you ever seen the tapestries in the Hotel de la Roche-Guyon?"

"Is that the hotel which has the garden of Lingère of the Louvre?" asked Diane de Christeuil, who had pretty white teeth, and consequently never spoke without smiling to show them.

"And where there is a big old tower, part of the old wall of Paris?" added Amelotte de Montmichel, a pretty, curly-headed, fresh-looking brunette, who had a habit of sighing, just as the other laughed, without knowing why.

"My dear Colombe," said Dame Aloïse, "are you speaking of the hotel which belonged to Monsieur de Bacqueville during the reign of Charles VI? Indeed there are some superb tapestries."

"Charles VI! King Charles VI!" muttered the young captain, curling his mustache. "My god! What a memory she has for the past!"

"Superb tapestries, indeed!" continued Madame de Gondelaurier; "so superb they are considered unrivaled!"

At that moment, Bérangère de Champchevrier, a winsome little girl of seven, who had been looking down onto the square through the trifoliated balcony, cried out, "Oh, godmother Fleur-de-Lys, look at that pretty girl who is dancing in the street, and playing the tambourine in a circle of people down there!"

In fact, they did hear the rhythmic thumping of the tambourine.

"Some gypsy girl from Bohemia," said Fleur-de-Lys, turning nonchalantly toward the square.

"Let's see! Let's see!" cried her excitable companions, all running to the edge of the balcony, while Fleur-de-Lys, thinking of the coldness of her betrothed, followed them slowly. The young man, relieved by this incident, which cut short an embarrassing conversation, returned to the farther end of the room with the satisfied air of a soldier relieved from duty.

Formerly, service to the lovely and charming Fleur-de-Lys had not been unpleasant. But the captain had by degrees become blasé; and he had become more and more cool to the prospect of marriage. Besides, he was of a fickle disposition, and, if one may say so, of rather vulgar tastes. Although of noble birth, he had contracted, with the help of his officer's uniform, more than one habit of the common soldier. He enjoyed frequenting the tavern and the life he found there. He was never at ease unless surrounded by gross language, military gallantries, easy beauties, and easy conquests. Although he had received from his family some education and polish, he had too early been allowed to run loose. Too early he had tended garrison; each day the polish of the gentleman had become more and more worn away under the friction of the soldier's baldric. Though still continuing to visit his fiancée occasionally, urged by some small remnant of common respect, he felt doubly constrained with Fleur-de-Lys; first, because, by dint of dividing his love among so many different girls, he had very little left for her; and next because, surrounded by a number of fine women of quiet, decorous, and formal manners, he was constantly in fear lest his lips, accustomed to swearing, should inadvertently break through their bounds, and let slip some unfortunate tavern jargon. You could well imagine the effect such would produce!

Moreover, in his character were pretensions to elegance, taste in dress, and noble bearing. Let these things be reconciled as they may. I am only a historian.

He had been standing for some minutes in silence, leaning against the elaborately sculptured fireplace, thinking of something or of nothing, when Fleur-de-Lys, turning suddenly around, addressed him. After all, the poor girl didn't enjoy being cold to him.

"Did you not tell us, cousin, about some little gypsy girl whom you saved, about two months ago, from the hands of a band of thieves, as you were making the counterwatch at night?"

"Yes, I believe I did, fair cousin," said the captain.

"Well," she resumed, "perhaps that's the one who is dancing in the square. Come see if you recognize her, Cousin Phoebus."

In the kind invitation she gave him to draw near her, and in the care she took to call him by his name, there seemed a secret desire for reconciliation. Captain Phoebus de Châteaupers, for it is he about whom we have been speaking in this chapter, slowly went out onto the balcony.

"Look," said Fleur-de-Lys, placing her hand affectionately through Phoebus' arm, "look at that girl dancing in the circle. Is that your gypsy girl?"

Phoebus looked and replied, "Yes, I recognize her by the goat."

"Oh, it is a pretty goat!" exclaimed Amelotte, clasping her hands in delight.

"Are its horns really gold?" asked little Bérangère.

Without moving from her chair, Dame Aloïse inquired, "Is it one of those gypsy girls that arrived last year by the Porte Gibard?"

"My dear mother," said Fleur-de-Lys, sweetly, "that gate is now called Porte d'Enfer."

Mademoiselle de Gondelaurier knew how much the captain was annoyed by her mother's antiquated modes of speech. Indeed, he was already snickering and muttering between his teeth, "Porte Gibard! Porte Gibard! No doubt to make way for Charles VI!"

"Godmother!" exclaimed Bérangère, whose constantly roving eyes were suddenly raised to the top of the towers of Notre-Dame, "who is that black man up there?"

All the young ladies looked up. A man, in fact, was leaning with his elbows on the topmost balustrade of the northern tower, which faced the Grève. It was a priest. You could clearly see both his garb and his face, which was resting on his hands. He was as motionless as a statue. And in his gaze, riveted on the square below, there was something of the immobility of a hawk that has just discovered a nest of sparrows, and is looking down upon it.

"It is Monsieur the Archdeacon of Josas," said Fleur-de-Lys.

"Your eyes are good if you can recognize him from here," observed La Gaillefontaine.

"Look how he stares at that little dancing girl!" remarked Diane de Christeuil.

"Let the gypsy beware!" said Fleur-de-Lys, "for he doesn't like Egypt."

"It's a great pity that he should watch her like that," added Amelotte de Montmichel, "for she dances so delightfully."

"Cousin Phoebus," said Fleur-de-Lys suddenly, "since you know the little gypsy girl, give her a sign to come up. She can entertain us."

"Yes, do, Phoebus!" cried all the others, clapping their hands for joy.

"But that's silly; no doubt she has forgotten me, and besides, I don't even know her name. However, as you wish it, ladies, I will try." And, leaning over the balustrade of the balcony, he called out, "Little one!"

The dancing girl was not at the moment playing her tambourine. She turned her head toward the voice, and, as her brilliant eyes fixed themselves on Phoebus, she stopped short.

"Little one!" repeated the captain, motioning for her to come up.

The young girl looked at him again, then blushed, so that her cheeks looked as though they had been touched with fire; and placing her tambourine under her arm, she made her way slowly through the gaping crowd to the door of the house to which Phoebus directed her, with the troubled look of a bird yielding to the fascination of a serpent.

A moment later, the tapestry at the entrance was raised, and the gypsy girl stood out of breath in the doorway of the room, blushing and confused, her huge eyes lowered, not daring to take one step farther.

Bérangère clapped her hands.

Meanwhile the dancing girl stood motionless and silent in the doorway. Her appearance had on this group of young ladies a singular effect. It is certain that a vague and undefined desire to please the handsome officer motivated all of them; that it was to the resplendent uniform that all their coquetry was aimed; and that, because of his being present, there was among them a certain secret rivalry, of which they were hardly aware, but which did nonetheless constantly show itself in all their gestures and remarks. Nevertheless, as they were all equally beautiful, or nearly so, they fought with equal weapons, and each could reasonably hope for victory. The arrival of the gypsy suddenly destroyed this balance of power. Her kind of beauty was so rare that the moment she appeared at the threshold of the apartment she seemed to diffuse a kind of light all her own. Within the small confines of that room, in this rich frame of somber hangings and dark paneling, she was incomparably more beautiful and radiant than in the public square. She was like a torch which has been brought from the daylight into the dark.

The noble damsels were dazzled in spite of themselves. Each felt that in some way her own beauty had been diminished. Consequently their battle line—forgive the expression—changed immediately, without a single word being uttered by any one of them. Women understand and respond to one another more quickly than do men. An enemy had arrived; all sensed it, all rallied to one another's defense. One drop of wine is enough to redden a whole glass of water. To tinge a whole company of pretty women with a certain amount of ill-humor, it is enough for just one prettier woman to arrive on the scene—especially when there is but one man present.

Thus the reception given the gypsy girl was marvelously

frigid. They eyed her up and down, looked at each other, and their looks expressed more than a thousand words—they understood each other. Meanwhile, the young girl, waiting for them to speak to her, was so embarrassed that she dared not raise her eyelids.

The captain was the first to break the silence. "Upon my word," he said with his tone of fatuous assurance, "what a charming creature! What do you think of her, cousin?"

This remark, which a more tactful admirer would have made at least in an undertone, was not calculated to allay the feminine jealousies which were arrayed against the gypsy girl.

Fleur-de-Lys answered the captain with a sugary affectation of contempt.

"Not bad."

The others whispered together.

At length, Madame Aloïse, who was no less jealous because she so admired her own daughter, addressed the dancing girl.

"Come here, little girl."

"Come here, little girl," repeated with comic dignity little Bérangère who would have reached about to the gypsy's hip.

The gypsy advanced toward the noble lady.

"My pretty child," said Phoebus, taking a few steps in her direction, "I don't know whether I have the supreme good fortune to be remembered by you . . ."

She interrupted him, with a smile and a look of infinite sweetness, "Oh, yes."

"She has a good memory," observed Fleur-de-Lys.

"So," resumed Phoebus, "you fled in great haste the other evening. Did I frighten you?"

"Oh, no," answered the gypsy girl. There was an intonation of this "Oh, no," following immediately after the "Oh, yes" that wounded Fleur-de-Lys to the quick.

"You left me in your place, my beautiful one," continued the captain, whose tongue was unloosed now that he spoke to a girl of the streets, "you left me a grim-faced fellow, a one-eyed hunchback, the bellringer of the bishop, I believe. They say he is the archdeacon's bastard and a devil by birth. He has a funny name too—Ember Week, Palm Sunday, Shrove Tuesday—something like that. At any rate some name taken from one of the holidays on which bells are rung. What the devil did that screech-owl want with you, eh?"

"I don't know," she answered.

"Imagine his impudence! A bellringer carrying off a girl like a viscount! A common fellow playing the gentleman, a rare bit of insolence! But he paid dearly for it. Master Pierrat Torterue is the roughest groom who ever curried a scoundrel, and I can assure you, if that will please you, your bellringer's hide got a tanning."

"Poor man!" said the gypsy girl, the scene at the pillory being brought back to her by these words.

The captain burst out laughing. "The devil! Your pity is about as well placed as a feather on a pig's tail. May I have a belly like a pope if—" He caught himself. "Pardon me, ladies; I forgot myself."

"Fie, sir!" said La Gaillefontaine.

"He speaks to this creature in her own language," added Fleur-de-Lys under her breath, her vexation increasing minute by minute.

This vexation was not diminished when she saw the captain, delighted with the gypsy, and above all with himself, spin round on his heel and repeat with naive and soldier-like gallantry, "Lovely girl, upon my soul!"

"Rather barbarously dressed!" said Diane de Christeuil, laughing to show her beautiful white teeth.

The remark was like a light to the others. It exposed the gypsy's assailable side. As they could find no fault with her beauty, they picked at her dress.

"That's very true," said La Montmichel. "But why do you run the streets without either neckerchief or wimple?"

"And with such a short, disgraceful petticoat," added La Gaillefontaine.

"My dear," continued Fleur-de-Lys, spitefully, "the gendarmes will arrest you for that gilt belt of yours."

"My poor girl," resumed Christeuil, with an unkind smile, "if you wore your sleeves a decent length, your arms wouldn't be so sunburned."

It was a sight worthy of a more intelligent onlooker than Phoebus, to watch these fair damsels, with their envenomed and angry tongues, squirming, gliding, and writhing around the street dancer. They were graciously cruel; they searched and pried maliciously into every part of her poor, artless, tawdry finery of spangles and tinsel. They giggled cruelly and heaped humiliation after humiliation upon her. Sarcasm, haughty condescension, and spiteful glances rained down upon the gypsy from every side. One might have thought they were young Roman ladies amusing themselves by pricking the breast of some pretty slave girl with their golden pins; or you might have imagined they were graceful greyhounds circling, with distended nostrils and flaming eyes, some poor hind of the forest which the will of their master forbade them to devour.

And what was she after all to these highborn ladies but a miserable dancing girl of the streets? They seemed to take no account of her presence, but spoke about her, in front of her, and to her, aloud, as of something pretty enough, perhaps, but at the same time, abject and unclean.

The gypsy girl was not insensitive to these pricks. From time to time a blush of shame or a flash of anger lit up her eyes or cheeks; a disdainful retort seemed to freeze on her lips, as she made that little contemptuous pout with which the reader is already familiar. She kept silent, remained motionless, but with her eyes fixed, resignedly, sadly, yet sweetly on Phoebus. In her look, there was mixed, too, both joy and tenderness. It seemed as if she restrained herself for fear of being driven away.

As for Phoebus, he laughed, and took the gypsy's part with a mixture of impertinence and pity.

"Let them prattle, my little one," he repeated, clicking his gold spurs. "Perhaps your dress is a little extravagant and unusual, but when a girl is as lovely as you, what does it matter?"

"My Lord!" exclaimed the blond Gaillefontaine, arching her swanlike neck and smiling bitterly, "I see that monsieur the king's archer is easily fired by the bright eyes of the gypsy."

"And why not?" said Phoebus.

At this reply, thrown carelessly by the captain, like a stone hurled at random without bothering to see where it falls, Colombe began to laugh, as did Amelotte, and Fleur-de-Lys, too, though tears rose at the same time in her eyes.

The gypsy girl, who had cast her eyes on the ground as Colombe de Gaillefontaine spoke, raised them, all beaming with joy and pride, and fixed them again on Phoebus. She was positively beautiful.

The old lady, who was watching all this, felt offended without exactly knowing why.

"Holy Virgin!" she suddenly screamed, "what is that rubbing against my legs? Ah, that horrid animal!"

It was the goat, who had just arrived looking for her mistress, and which, in hurrying toward her, had got her horns entangled in the folds of the noble lady's dress as they lay amassed about her feet, a usual situation whenever she was seated.

This made a welcome diversion. The gypsy, without uttering a word, disentangled her goat.

"Ah, it's the pretty goat with the golden hoofs," cried Bérangère, jumping for joy.

The gypsy squatted on her knees, and pressed her cheek caressingly against the goat's head. She seemed to be asking forgiveness for having left her behind.

Meanwhile Diane bent over and whispered in Colombe's ear. "Ah, my God! why didn't I think of it before? Why it's the gypsy girl with the goat. It's rumored she's a witch and her goat does miraculous tricks."

"Well," said Colombe, "we must have the goat amuse us and perform a miracle for us."

Diane and Colombe together eagerly addressed the gypsy. "Little girl, make the goat do a miracle for us."

"I don't know what you mean," she replied.

"A miracle, a feat of magic, or witchcraft, or something."

"I do not understand," she replied. And she began to caress the pretty goat again, repeating, "Djali! Djali!"

At that moment, Fleur-de-Lys noticed a small leather bag hanging around the goat's neck.

"What's that?" she questioned.

The gypsy raised her large eyes toward her, and said, gravely, "That's my secret."

"I should like to know her secret," thought Fleur-de-Lys.

Meanwhile the noble lady had risen. "Come now, gypsy girl," she said angrily, "if neither you nor your goat will dance for us, what are you doing here?"

The gypsy, without answering, slowly made her way to the door. But the nearer she approached, the slower became her pace. A powerful magnet seemed to hold her back. Suddenly she turned, her eyes wet with tears, toward Phoebus, and stopped.

"Please!" entreated the captain. "Don't go away like that. Come back and dance for us. By the way, my little darling, what is your name?"

"La Esmeralda," said the dancing girl, not taking her eyes off him.

At this strange name, the ladies burst into a fit of laughter.

"A frightful name, indeed, for a young lady!" said Diane.

"You see plainly enough," remarked Amelotte, "that she's a witch."

"My dear," quite solemnly cried Dame Aloïse, "your parents never got that name from a baptismal font."

Meanwhile, Bérangère, without anyone's noticing, had a few minutes before enticed the goat into a corner of the room with a marzipan. Right away they had become good friends, and the curious child had taken the little bag hung around the goat's neck, opened it, and had emptied its contents on the floor. There was an alphabet, each letter of which was inscribed separately on a small tablet of wood. Scarcely had these things fallen to the matting than the child saw, with surprise, the goat (one of whose tricks doubtless it was) draw toward her with her golden hoof certain letters, and arrange them, by pushing them gently about, in a particular order, so that they spelled a word. At this the goat was adept, so little time did she need to do it. Bérangère suddenly cried out, clasping her hands with admiration, "Godmother Fleur-de-Lys, look what the goat has just done!"

Fleur-de-Lys hurried over to look, and shuddered. The letters arranged on the floor spelled the word:

PHOEBUS

"Did the goat do that?" she asked with a faltering voice.

"Yes, godmother," answered Bérangère.

There was no doubt about it. Little Bérangère did not know how to spell.

"So that's the secret!" thought Fleur-de-Lys.

Meanwhile, at the child's cry, all hurried over to look, the mother, the ladies, the gypsy, and the captain.

The gypsy girl saw the trick the goat had just played. She turned red, then pale, and began to tremble like someone guilty of a crime, as the captain looked at her with a smile of satisfaction and astonishment.

"Phoebus!" whispered the girls in amazement. "That's the captain's name!"

"You have a wonderful memory!" said Fleur-de-Lys to the frightened gypsy, and then she burst into sobs. "Oh!" she stammered painfully, hiding her face in her beautiful white hands, "she's a sorceress!"

But a still more bitter voice whispered at the bottom of her heart, "She's a rival, too!"

"My child! My child!" cried the terrified mother. "Be gone, you, you hell's gypsy!"

Esmeralda hurriedly picked up the unlucky letters, made a sign to Djali, and left the room by one door, as they carried out Fleur-de-Lys by the other.

Captain Phoebus, left alone, hesitated a moment between the two doors; then he followed the gypsy girl.

2

A Priest and a Philosopher Are Not the Same

The priest whom the ladies had noticed on top of the northern tower, leaning toward the square, so intently watching the gypsy dancing, was indeed the archdeacon Claude Frollo.

Our readers have not forgotten his mysterious cell in this tower. (Incidentally, I do not know whether this is the same cell, the interior of which may, to this day, be seen through a small square window, on the east side, at about the height of a man who might stand upon the platform from which the towers rise. It is, today, only a small room, naked, empty, and dilapidated. Its crudely plastered walls are decorated here and there with some poorly executed yellow engravings showing the facades of cathedrals. I presume that this hole now is jointly inhabited by bats and spiders, and that consequently a double war of extermination is waged there against the flies.)

Every day, an hour before sunset, the archdeacon customarily climbed the staircase of the tower, and shut himself up in this cell, where he sometimes spent whole nights. On this particular day, just as he reached the low door of his retreat and was putting into the lock a small, deeply notched key which he always carried with him in the purse suspended at his side, the sound of a tambourine and castanets reached his ears. The music was coming from the Place du Parvis. The cell, as we have already said, had only one window overlooking the back of the church. Claude Frollo quickly withdrew the key from the lock and in another minute, he was at the top of the tower, and posed in that gloomy, pensive attitude in which the young ladies had seen him.

There, grave, motionless, and absorbed, he gazed intently, with but one thought in mind. At his feet was all Paris with her thousand spires and her circular horizon of gently rolling hills, with her river winding under her bridges, and her people milling in the streets, with her cloud of smoke drifting over her mountainous chain of rooftops, that pressed upon Notre-Dame with its double slopes of slate. Yet in all that city, the archdeacon saw but one spot on its pavement—the Place du Parvis; in all that crowd, but one figure—the gypsy girl.

It would have been difficult to explain his expression and even more difficult to understand the flame that issued from that fixed gaze, seemingly full of tumult and trouble. By the tenseness of his body, only stirred now and then by an involuntary shiver, as a tree is shaken by the wind, by the rigidity of his elbows, more marble than the balustrade on which they rested, by the cold smile solidified on his face, you might have said that no part of Claude Frollo was alive but his eyes.

The gypsy was dancing. She twirled the tambourine on the tip of her finger, and threw it into the air as she danced the saraband. She was so agile, light, and joyous, quite unaware of the threatening gaze which fell on her head.

The crowd swarmed around her. From time to time, a man wearing a yellow and red coat widened the circle, then returned to sit on his stool close by the dancer, and rested the head of her goat upon his knees. The man appeared to be the gypsy's companion. Claude Frollo, from his high vantage point, could not make out his features.

From the moment the archdeacon saw this unknown, his attention seemed to be divided between him and the dancer, and his face became more and more somber. All of a sudden the priest straightened, and a tremor ran through his whole body. "Who is that man?" he muttered to himself. "I have always seen her alone!"

Then he disappeared into the winding vault of the spiral staircase and went down. Passing before the door of the bellroom, which was partly open, he saw something that startled him. There was Quasimodo, leaning over one of those slatted eaves, which resemble enormous blinds, looking intently down into the square. He was lost in deep contemplation. His wild eye had a singular expression, full of fascination and tenderness.

"That's peculiar!" thought Claude. "Is he too watching the gypsy?"

He continued down the steps. In a few minutes the archdeacon came into the square by the door at the base of the tower.

"Where's the gypsy girl?" he said, mingling with the group of spectators which the music of the tambourine had attracted.

"I don't know," replied a bystander. "She just disappeared. I think she went to dance a fandango in that house over there. Someone called her."

Instead of the gypsy, on the same carpet, whose arabesques but a moment before seemed to vanish beneath the fantastic patterns of her dance, the archdeacon saw only the man in the yellow and red coat, who himself, in order to earn a few sous, was strutting around in a circle, his elbows on his hips, his head thrown back, his face all red, his neck stretched out, with a chair rung between his teeth. On the chair, he had tied a cat, lent to him by a woman in the crowd. The poor tabby at that moment was yowling with terror.

"Notre-Dame!" cried the archdeacon, just as the mountebank, perspiring profusely, passed in front of him with his chair and cat. "What is Master Pierre Gringoire doing here!"

The stern voice of the archdeacon so confused the poor devil that he lost his balance, and the whole edifice, chair and cat, fell pell-mell on the heads of the bystanders, to the accompaniment of inextinguishable hooting.

It is probable that Master Pierre Gringoire (for it was indeed he) would have a fine explanation to give to the owner of the cat, and to all the bruised and scratched faces around him, had he not hastily taken advantage of the uproar to find refuge in the church, whither Claude Frollo had motioned him to follow.

The cathedral was dark and empty. The transepts were in deep shadow. The altar lamps in the chapels were beginning to glitter like stars. Only the great rose-window, whose thousand colors were accentuated by the horizontal rays of the sun, gleamed in the cathedral's darkness like a cluster of diamonds and scattered its dazzling spectrum to the opposite end of the nave.

When they had gone a few steps inside, Dom Claude Frollo leaned against a pillar and stared at Gringoire. It was not a stare from which Gringoire had anything to fear; but he was ashamed at being surprised in his clownish costume by so serious and learned a personage. There was nothing in the priest's glance that indicated mockery or irony; it was serious and calm, but piercing. The archdeacon was the first to speak.

"Come here, Master Pierre! You have much to explain to me. But first of all, why have I not seen you for two months, and why, when I do meet you, do I see you in the streets, garbed in yellow and red, like a Caudebec apple? Really!"

"Messire, a strange costume indeed," said Gringoire piteously, "and you see me feeling just about as comfortable as a cat with a calabash on its head. It is, I confess, a poor trick to present under this thin coat the back of a Pythagorean philosopher to be beaten by those gentlemanly sergeants of the watch. But what can you do under the circumstances, my reverend master? The fault lies with my old doublet, which cowardly abandoned me at the beginning of the winter season under pretense that it was falling into tatters, and so had need of a rest in the ragpicker's pack. What was I to do? Civilization is not so far advanced that one can go naked, as old Diogenes would have wished. Moreover, the wind was blowing very cold, and January is not the month to introduce humanity, with any degree of success, to such a new style. So this coat offered itself; I took it, and cast aside my old black tunic, which, for a hermetic such as I am, was far from being hermetically closed. So here I am, garbed like a comedian, like Saint Genest. What would you have? It's a disguise. Apollo, you know, watched the flocks of Admetus."

"A very respectable trade you are following!" replied the priest.

"I confess, my master, that it is better to philosophize and poetize—to blow the flame in the furnace, or to receive it from heaven—than to be carrying cats in the public square. And that's why, when you addressed me, I felt as stupid as an ass before a turn spit. But what can I do, messire? We must eat every day, and the most beautiful Alexandrine verses are as nothing in the mouth compared to a piece of Brie cheese. Now, I wrote for Lady Margaret of Flanders that famous epithalamium, you know, and the town hasn't yet paid me for it, under the pretext that it wasn't excellent enough, as if, for four écus, anyone would write a Sophoclean tragedy.

"Well, I was starving to death. Fortunately, I have a rather strong jawbone, so I said to my jaw, 'Perform some marvelous feats of balancing; get your own food.' *Ale te ipsam.*[1] A band of beggars, with whom I became friends, taught me twenty different kinds of Herculean tricks. And now, by the sweat of my brow, every night I feed my teeth the bread they have earned during the day. After all, *concedo,* I concede it is but a sorry employment for a man of my intellectual faculties, and that man is not born to spend his life making music on the tambourine and biting on the rungs of chairs. But, reverend master, not only must we live, we must earn our living."

Dom Claude was listening in silence. All at once, his sunken eyes assumed such a knowing and penetrating expression that Gringoire felt that the deepest recesses of his soul were being searched.

"Very well, Master Pierre. But how is it that you are now in the company of that gypsy dancer?"

[1] "[You] nourish yourself."

"For the very good reason that she is my wife and I am her husband."

The dark eyes of the priest caught fire. "How could you do such a thing, you villain?" he cried, rudely seizing Gringoire's arm. "Have you so abandoned God as to touch that girl?"

"By heaven above me, monseigneur," answered Gringoire, trembling all over, "I swear to you, I have never touched her, if that's what so disturbs you."

"But what are you talking about then, husband and wife?" pursued the priest.

Gringoire hastened to relate to him as briefly as possible everything that the reader already knows—his adventure at the Court of Miracles, and his broken-pitcher "marriage." It seems he added that the marriage had never been consummated, as the gypsy girl had each night robbed him of his conjugal rights as on that first night.

"It is terrible," he said, concluding his story; "but that's what I get for having the ill fortune to marry a virgin."

"What do you mean?" asked the archdeacon, who was somewhat appeased by this tale.

"It's difficult to explain," answered the poet. "It's all based upon a superstition. My wife is, so an old thief, known among us as the Duke of Egypt, has told me, an orphan or a lost child, which is the same thing. She wears around her neck an amulet, which, they say, will someday be instrumental in finding her parents, but which will lose its virtue if the girl loses hers. Hence we both remain quite virtuous."

"Thus, Master Pierre," resumed Claude whose brow was now brightening more and more, "you think this creature has never known a man?"

"What can a man do, Dom Claude, in the face of a superstition? You can't get it out of her head. I deem it rare indeed that this nunnish prudery is maintained vehemently among all those gypsy girls so easily seduced. But three things protect her: the Duke of Egypt who has taken her under his safekeeping, counting, perhaps, on selling her to some loose abbot; her whole tribe, who hold her in singular veneration, like the Blessed Lady; and a certain cute little dagger, which the hussy always carries on her somewhere or other, in spite of the provost's ordinances, and which she whips out if you put your arm around her waist. She's a defiant wasp, that's all!"

The archdeacon plied Gringoire with more questions.

According to Gringoire, La Esmeralda was a harmless, charming, pretty creature—even with, or because of, a pout peculiarly hers—she was naive and passionate; ignorant, but enthusiastic about almost everything. She scarcely knew the difference between man and woman. She was wild about dancing, about noise of any kind. She loved the open air; a kind of female bee, with invisible wings for feet, and living in a constant whirl. She owed this nature to the vagabond existence which was all she knew. Gringoire had found out that, as a young child, she had traveled all through Spain, Catalonia, and even to Sicily; he even believed that the caravan of zingari, to which she belonged, had taken her into the kingdom of Algiers, a country situated in Achaia. Achaia is contiguous on one side to lesser Albania and Greece, and on the other side, to the sea around Sicily, which is the way to Constantinople. The Bohemians, said Gringoire, were vassals of the King of Algiers, in his capacity as chief of the nation of white Moors. What is certain is that La Esmeralda had come to France while yet very young, by way of Hungary. From all these countries, she had brought scraps of strange jargon, songs, and peculiar ideas, which made her speech as motley as her half-Parisian, half-African costume. Also, the people of the quarters which she frequented loved her for her gaiety, her gentleness, her lively manner, her dances, and her songs. In all of Paris, she thought she was hated only by two people, of whom she often spoke with dread, the Sachette in the Tower of Roland, that distraught recluse who bore a strange malice against gypsy women, and who cursed the poor dancer every time Esmeralda passed in front of her window; and a priest, who never met her without casting upon her looks and words that frightened her. This last remark visibly upset the archdeacon, though Gringoire scarcely noticed his agitation, so completely had the lapse of two months effaced from the thoughtless poet's memory the presence of the archdeacon on the night of the singular circumstances when he first met the gypsy girl. Except these two, then, the little dancer feared nothing; she told no fortunes, and so was secure from those prosecutions for magic that were so frequently instituted against gypsy women. Beside, Gringoire, if not a husband, was like a brother to her. After all, the philosopher bore very patiently with this kind of platonic marriage. There was always lodging and food for him. Each morning he set out from the thieves' quarters, most frequently in the company of the gypsy. He assisted her in the streets, gathering up her coins; each evening he returned with her to the same roof; he let her lock herself in her little room, and slept the sleep of the just. It was a very pleasant existence, in all, he said, and very conducive to dreaming.

And then in his mind and heart, the philosopher was not quite sure that he so desperately loved the gypsy girl. He loved her goat almost as much. It was an interesting animal, gentle, intelligent, clever, an educated goat. Nothing was more common in the Middle Ages than these clever animals, which excited much wonderment and which sometimes brought their instructors to the stake. However, the tricks of the goat with the gilded hoofs were harmless enough. Gringoire explained them to the archdeacon, who seemed keenly interested in all these details. In most cases, it was sufficient to present the tambourine to the goat in such and such a way to obtain from it the desired trick. Djali had been trained by her mistress, who had such a rare talent for this that only two months were needed to teach the goat to arrange, with movable letters, the word *Phoebus*.

"Phoebus!" said the priest. "Why Phoebus?"

"I don't know," replied Gringoire. "Perhaps it's a word that she thinks endowed with some magical and secret powers. She repeats it often to herself when she thinks she's alone."

"Are you sure," inquired Claude, with his penetrating look, "that it's only a word, and not a name?"

"The name of whom?" asked the poet.

"How do I know?" rejoined the priest.

"This is what I think, messire. These gypsies are a sort of Guebres, and worship the sun. Whence Phoebus."

"That does not seem so conclusive to me as it does to you, Master Pierre."

"Well, it makes no difference to me. Let her mumble her

Phoebus to her heart's content. All I know is that Djali loves me almost as much as she does the gypsy."

"Who's this Djali?"

"That's her goat."

The archdeacon placed his hand under his chin, and seemed lost in thought for a moment. All at once, he turned abruptly to Gringoire, saying, "And you swear that you have never touched her?"

"Who?" said Gringoire. "The goat?"

"No, that woman."

"My wife? I swear to you, no."

"And you are often alone with her?"

"Every night! For a full hour."

Dom Claude knit his brow.

"Oh! oh!" he said, *"solus cum sola non cogitabuntur orare Pater Noster."*[2]

"Upon my soul, I could recite the Our Father and the Hail Mary, and the Credo, without her paying any more attention to me than a chicken to a church."

"Swear to me by your mother's womb," repeated the archdeacon vehemently, "that you have not touched this creature with so much as your little finger!"

"I could swear, too, by the head of my father, for the two things are connected in more than one way. But, my reverend master, allow me to ask you one question."

"Speak, sir."

"Why does that concern you?"

The pale face of the archdeacon reddened like a girl's cheek. For a moment he kept silent, then ostensibly embarrassed, he said, "Listen, Master Pierre Gringoire. As far as I know, you are not yet damned. I am interested in your soul, and wish you well. But the least contact with that diabolical gypsy girl would make you Satan's vassal. You know it is always the body that damns the soul. Woe to you if you go near that woman! That's all I have to say."

"I tried once," said Gringoire, scratching his ear. "It was the first day, but I only got stung."

"And you had that effrontery, Master Pierre?"

[2] "A man and woman alone together do not think of reciting the Our Father."

Again the priest's brow darkened.

"Another time," continued the poet, with a grin, "before I went to bed, I looked through her keyhole, and saw the most delicious damsel in her chemise that has ever made a bedstead creak under her naked foot."

"To the devil with you!" cried the priest, with a terrible look; and, pushing aside the astonished Gringoire, he strode away into the darkness of the cathedral.

3

The Bells

Ever since the morning of his flogging, the people who lived in the neighborhood of Notre-Dame thought they noticed that Quasimodo's passion for bell-ringing had cooled. Before that day, the bells had been rung even for the slightest occasion: long tollings which lasted from prime to compline; peals from the great bell for high mass; rich, melodious chimes from the small bells for a wedding, or a christening, overspreading Paris like a delicate embroidery of rich sounds. The old church had vibrated and resounded with the never-ending, joyful song of her bells. Some whimsical spirit of sound had seemed always to be present in the cathedral, singing her melodies. Now, that spirit seemed to have left. The cathedral was sullen, like someone willfully guarding her silence. Feast days and funerals had their simple tolling, plain and unadorned—just what the ritual required and nothing more. Of the double music which you associate with a church, that of the organ within and the bells without, now only the organ was heard. It seemed as if the musician had quitted the steeples. Nevertheless, Quasimodo was still there. What had happened to him, therefore? Was it that the horror and despair of the pillory still festered in the bottom of his heart? Could he still feel with his imagination the lashes of the tormentor's whip? Had the brutality of such treatment extinguished all feeling in him, even his passion for the bells? Or rather, was it that Marie had a rival in the heart of the bellringer of Notre-Dame, and that she and her fourteen sisters had been abandoned for something more lovable and beautiful?

It happened that in this year of grace 1482, the feast of the Annunciation fell on Tuesday, the twenty-fifth of March. On that day the air was so fresh and clear that Quasimodo felt his affection for his bells returning. Accordingly he climbed to the northern tower, while the sexton below opened wide the doors of the church, which were at that time enormous panels of strong wood, covered with leather, bordered with gilt-headed iron nails, and adorned with carvings, "very skillfully wrought."

When he reached the high cage of the belfry, Quasimodo gazed for some minutes at his six bells; then, with a sorrowful shake of his head, he sighed to think that some other object had come between him and them. But when he had set them in motion, when he felt this cluster of bells moving under his hand, when he saw, for he did not hear, the palpitating octave ascending and descending that sonorous scale like a bird flitting from branch to branch, when the demon of music—that demon which shakes a sparkling bundle of stretti, trills, and arpeggios—had taken full possession of the poor deaf hunchback, then he became happy again; he forgot everything else, and his face radiated joy.

Clapping his hands, he ran to and fro from one rope to another, awakening his six songsters by his voice and his gestures, as a maestro leads his skilled musicians.

"Go on! Go on, Gabrielle!" he said, "pour all your music into the square. Today's a feast day. Thibauld, don't be lazy. You're slowing down! Go, go on! Are you becoming rusty, loafer? That's it. Quick! Quick! Don't let the clapper be seen. Make them all deaf like me. That's it, bravo! Thibauld! Guillaume! Guillaume! You're the biggest, but Pasquier's the smallest, and Pasquier swings better than you! Those who can hear, I'll wager you, hear him better than you! Well done! Gabrielle! louder, louder! Hey! you up there, you sparrows! I don't see you making any noise. What's the matter with those brazen beaks of yours, that seem to be yawning when they ought to be singing? Come on, work! Sing! It's the Annunciation. There's beautiful sunshine; we have to have beautiful music! Poor Guillaume! All out of breath, my big one!"

He was entirely busy goading on his bells, which were all six rearing and shaking their shiny haunches, like noisy teams of Spanish mules, guided this way and that by the cries of the driver.

All at once, as he happened to cast his eye down between the large slate tiles, which cover, up to a certain height, the perpendicular wall of the belfry, he saw in the square a young girl strangely dressed, who had stopped, and was laying down a carpet, on which a little goat came and took its position. A group of spectators was gathering around them. This scene suddenly changed the train of his thoughts. It froze his musical enthusiasm as a gust of cold air congeals a stream of flowing resin. He turned his back on the bells, and, squatting behind the slate eaves, fixed his eyes on the dancer with that dreamy, tender, gentle look which had already once astonished the archdeacon. Meanwhile all the forgotten bells slowed to silence, to the great disappointment of the lovers of carillon music, who had been listening delightedly to the pealing as they stood on the Pont-au-Change, but who now went away, confounded like a dog that has had a bone offered him only to have it snatched away.

4

'ANÁΓKH

One fine morning in this same month of March, I believe it was Saturday the 29th, the feast day of Saint Eustache, it happened that our young scholar friend Jehan du Moulin discovered while dressing that his breeches, containing his purse, gave forth no jingling sound of coin. "Poor purse!" he said taking it from his pocket. "What! not one little parisis! How cruelly have the dice, Venus, and mugs of beer disemboweled you! Just look at you, empty, wrinkled, and flabby like the bosom of a strumpet! I would ask you, now, Messer Cicero and Messer Seneca, whose dog-eared volumes I see scattered on the floor, do I not know better than any master of the mint, or than any Jew on the Pont-aux-Changeurs, that a gold crown is worth thirty-five unzains at twenty-five sous eight deniers parisis each, though I've not one wretched black liard to bet on the double-six! Oh, Consul Cicero! This is not a calamity from which one can extricate himself by periphrases—by *quemadmodum*[1] and *verum enim vero!*"[2]

Dejected, he dressed. As he was lacing his boots, he had an idea, which, at first, he discarded. But it returned, and he put on his vest wrong side out, an unmistakable sign of a violent mental struggle.

At length, he threw his cap vehemently on the ground, and exclaimed, "So be it! I don't care! I'll go to my brother! I'll get a sermon, but I'll get a crown too!"

Thus determined, he hastily put on his fur-trimmed coat, picked up his cap, and hurried out.

He followed the Rue de la Harpe toward the City. As he passed the Rue de la Huchette, the odor of those delectable roasts, which were constantly turning, tickled his olfactory organ, and he cast an amorous look toward that Cyclopean rotisserie which one day drew from the Franciscan monk Catalagirone this pathetic exclamation, *Veramente, queste rotisserie sono cosa stupenda!*[3] But Jehan did not have the wherewithal for breakfast, and with a moan, he continued on his way through the gate of the Petit-Châtelet, that enormous cluster of massive towers which guarded the entrance to the City.

He did not even take time as he passed to throw a stone, as was usual, at the miserable statue of that Perinet Leclerc, who had surrendered the Paris of Charles VI to the English, a crime which his effigy, the face all battered with stones and soiled with mud, expiated during three centuries, as in an everlasting pillory, at the corner of the streets la Harpe and de Bussy.

Having crossed the Petit-Pont and having walked down the Rue Neuve-Sainte-Geneviève, Jehan du Moulin found himself in front of Notre-Dame. Then his indecision returned, and he paced nervously for some minutes around the statue of Monsieur Legris, repeating apprehensively to himself, "The sermon is certain, but getting a crown is doubtful."

[1] "In the way that."
[2] "But in truth."
[3] "Truly these rotisseries are something stupendous."

He stopped a sexton who was coming out of the cloister. "Where's Monsieur the Archdeacon of Josas?"

"I think he's in his hideout in the tower," answered the sexton, "but I advise you not to disturb him unless you come from someone like the pope or the king."

Jehan clapped his hands. "By Jove! What a wonderful opportunity to get a look at his famous magic den."

Reinforced by this reflection, he resolutely went through the little black door, and began to ascend the winding staircase of Saint-Gilles leading to the upper stories of the tower.

"We shall see!" he said as he proceeded. "By Our Lady! It must be a curious place, that cell which my reverend brother keeps all to himself. They say he lights up hell's own kitchens there, and cooks the philosopher's stone over a big fire! Ye gads! I care about as much for the philosopher's stone as I do for a pebble! I'd rather find over his fire an omelet of Easter eggs in lard, than the biggest philosopher's stone in the world."

When he reached the gallery of the small pillars, he stopped a moment to catch his breath, cursing the interminable steps by I know not how many million cartloads of devils. He then continued his ascent through the narrow door of the northern tower, today closed to the public. A few minutes after having passed the belfry, he came to a small landing contrived in a recess on one side, and, under the vaulted roof, a low arched door, which a loophole opposite, in the circular wall of the staircase, enabled him to discern with its enormous lock and strong iron bars. If curious people could visit this door today, it would be recognized by this inscription, carved in white letters on the black wall:

I ADORE CORALIE 1829 SIGNED UGÈNE

"Whew!" puffed the scholar. "This must be it!"

The key was in the lock. The door was slightly open. He pushed it gently and stuck his head in to peek.

The reader is no doubt acquainted with the works of Rembrandt, who in some respects might be styled the Shakespeare of painting. Among his many marvelous engravings, there is one in particular, an etching representing, as is supposed, Doctor Faustus, which it is impossible to look at without astonishment. The scene is a dark cell, in the middle of which is a table heaped with all sorts of hideous objects—skulls, globes, alembics, compasses, parchments scrolled in hieroglyphics. The doctor is seated before this table, dressed in a long, loose-fitting gown, wearing a fur cap falling down to his eyebrows. Only half his body is visible. He has partly risen from his immense armchair, his clenched fists are resting on the table, and he is gazing with terrified curiosity at a luminous circle, composed of magic letters, which is shining on the wall in the background like a solar spectrum in the dark room. This cabalistic sun seems to tremble before the eye, and fills the dim cell with its mysterious radiance. It is horrible and yet beautiful.

When Jehan peered through the half-open door he saw something very similar to Faust's cell. This cell was also gloomy and dimly lighted. There was here, too, a large armchair and table, compasses, alembics, animal skeletons hanging from the ceiling, a sphere rolling on the floor, glass jars filled with shining gold-leaf, skulls reposing on sheets of vellum streaked all over with figures and characters, thick manuscripts piled up, all open, without any concern for the creased corners of the parchment—in short, all the rubbish of science, with dust and cobwebs covering everything. But there was no circle of luminous letters, no doctor in rapt attention contemplating the flaming vision as the eagle gazes at the sun.

This cell, however, was not unoccupied. A man was seated in an armchair, stooped over the table. His back was turned to Jehan, who could see only his shoulders and the back of his head; but he had no difficulty in recognizing that bald head, on which nature had bestowed an everlasting tonsure, as if to mark, by this external sign, the irrevocable vocation of the archdeacon.

Jehan accordingly recognized his brother. But the door had been opened so gently that Dom Claude was unaware of his brother's presence. Our curious little scholar took advantage of this circumstance to look over the room for a few minutes unhurriedly. A large furnace, which he had not, at first, noticed, was to the left of the armchair, under the small window. The scant light which entered by this opening passed through the circular web of a spider, which had tastefully traced its delicate *rosace* in the pointed arch of the window. In the center of the snare, the insect builder remained motionless, like the hub of this lacy wheel. On the furnace were in disorder all sorts of vessels, stone bottles, glass phials, and bundles of charcoal. Jehan observed with a sigh that there were no kitchen utensils—not even a frying pan. In fact there was no fire in the furnace, and it appeared that none had been there for a long time.

Among the alchemist's implements Jehan noticed a glass mask which doubtless had been used to protect the archdeacon's face when he was compounding some deadly substance, but which now lay in a corner, covered with dust, as if quite forgotten. Beside it lay bellows, equally dusty, the upper part of which bore this motto incrusted in letters of copper: *Spira, spera.*[4]

According to the custom of hermetic philosophers, a great number of other mottoes were written on the walls—some written with ink, others carved by some sharp-pointed metal instrument. Moreover, in Gothic, Hebrew, Greek, and Roman letters mixed together, inscriptions overflowed at random, one upon the other, the more recent effacing the more ancient, and all were entangled with each other, like the branches of a bush, or pikes in a melee. It was, indeed, a confused mingling of all philosophies, all human reveries, all human knowledge. Here and there, one stood out among all the others like a banner among the heads of lances. But for the most part, the most legible was a short Greek or Latin *dictum*, after the ingenious fashion of the Middle Ages: *Unde? inde?*[5] *Homo homini monstrum!*[6] *Astra, castra, nomen, numen;*[7] then in Greek letters, "A great book, a great evil"; and *Sapere aude.*[8] *Flat ubi vult;*[9] etc. Sometimes there was a word apparently without any connection; as the Greek word for discipline, which perhaps concealed some bitter allusion to the regime of the cloister; sometimes there was a

---

[4] "Breathe, hope."
[5] "Whence? whither?"
[6] "Man's inhumanity to man."
[7] "Stars, fortress, name, divinity."
[8] "Dare to be wise."
[9] "It blows where it wishes."

simple maxim of clerical discipline, set forth in a regular
hexameter, *Coelestem dominum, terrestrem dicit domnum.*[10]
There were also, by the way, some other Greek scrawlings,
from which Jehan, who knew little Greek, could decipher
nothing. The whole was crisscrossed about in all directions
with stars, figures of men and animals, and triangles intersecting each other, which contributed not a little to make the
wall of the cell resemble a sheet of paper over which a monkey had dragged a pen full of ink.

All in all, the little room looked neglected and dilapidated,
and the shabby condition of the instruments led you to suppose that their master had long since been diverted from
their use by pursuits of some other kind.

This master, however, hunched over a vast manuscript,
adorned with unusual paintings, appeared to be tormented by
some thought which constantly interrupted his meditations.
At least, so thought Jehan, as he heard the priest muse aloud,
as a walking dreamer, "Yes, Manou said it, and Zoroaster
taught it: the sun is born of fire, and the moon is born of the
sun. Fire is the soul of the universe. Its elementary atoms are
diffused and in constant flux throughout the world, by an infinite number of currents. At the points where these currents
meet in the heavens, they produce light; at their intersecting
points on the earth, they produce gold. Light, gold, the same
thing. From fire to its concrete state—the difference between
the visible and the palpable, the fluid and the solid in the
same substance, between vapor and ice—nothing more.
These are not figments of the imagination; it is the universal
law of nature. But how to extract from science the secret of
this general law? What! this light which bathes my hand is
gold! These same atoms, which expand according to a certain law, need only be condensed according to a certain other
law. But how? Some have thought of burying a ray of the
sun. Averroës—yes, it is Averroës—Averroës buried one
under the first pillar to the left of the sanctuary of the Koran,
in the grand mosque at Cordova; but the vault must not be
opened to see whether the experiment has succeeded for the
space of eight thousand years."

[10] "Call upon the celestial god, the earthly god."

"What the devil!" said Jehan to himself. "This is a long time to wait for a crown!"

"Others have thought," continued the archdeacon, speculating, "that it would be better to experiment on a ray of Sirius. But it is very difficult to isolate this pure ray, on account of the simultaneous presence of other stars, whose rays mingle with it. Flamel is of the opinion that it is simpler to experiment with terrestrial fire. Flamel! Fortuitous that name! *Flamma!* Yes, fire. That's everything. The diamond is in charcoal; gold in fire. But how to extract it? Magistri affirms that there are certain names of women which possess so sweet and mysterious a charm that it is sufficient merely to pronounce them during the experiment. Let us read what Manou writes about that: 'Where women are honored, the divinities are pleased; where they are despised, it is useless to pray to God. The mouth of a woman is pure; it is as running water, as a ray of sunlight. A woman's name should be pleasing, sweet, and fanciful, should end with long vowels, and resemble words of a benediction.' Yes, the wise man is right. Maria, Sophia, Esmeral . . . Damnation! Always the same thought!"

And he slammed the book shut.

He passed his hand across his forehead, as if to chase some thought that was besetting him. Then he took from the table a nail and a small hammer, the handle of which was curiously painted with cabalistic letters.

"For a long time," he said, with a bitter smile, "I have failed with all my experiments. One fixed idea possesses me and tortures my brain like a fire-iron. I have not even been able to discover the secret of Cassiodorus, whose lamp burned without wick or oil—a thing simple enough."

"Oh! Plague on him!" muttered Jehan to himself.

"So, one disturbing thought then," continued the priest, "suffices to render a man weak and mad! Oh, how Claude Pernelle would laugh at me, she who could not for a moment turn aside Nicolas Flamel from his pursuit of the great work! I hold in my hand the magic hammer of Ezekiel. At each blow, which, from the depth of his cell, the formidable rabbi struck upon this nail with this hammer, one among his enemies whom he had condemned, even were he two thousand leagues off, sank a cubit's depth into the earth, which de-

voured him. The king of France himself, for having one evening inadvertently struck against the door of this thaumatur-
gist, sank up to the knees in the pavement of Paris. This
happened three centuries ago. Well, I have the hammer and
the nail, and yet these implements are no more formidable in
my hands than a punching tool in the hands of a carpenter.
And yet it is only necessary to discover the magic word
which Ezekiel pronounced as he struck upon the nail."

"What nonsense!" thought Jehan.

"Let's see! Let's try!" resumed the archdeacon emphatically. "If I succeed, I shall see a blue spark leap from the
head of the nail. *Emen-hétan! Emen-hétan!* That's not it.
Sigéani! Sigénai! May this nail open the grave for whoso-
ever bears the name of Phoebus!... Curses! Always the
same thought."

And he angrily threw aside the hammer. He then slumped
so low in his armchair and over the table that Jehan could
not see him behind the high back of the chair. For some minutes he could see nothing but Dom Frollo's convulsed,
clenched fist resting on a book. Suddenly the priest got up,
took a compass, and silently engraved on the wall in Greek
capital letters the word:

'ΑΝΆΓΚΗ

"My brother's crazy," said Jehan to himself. "It would
have been simpler to write *fatum*. Not everybody is obliged
to know Greek."

The archdeacon sat down in his chair again, and leaned
his head on his two hands, like a sick man whose head is
heavy and burning with fever.

The scholar watched his brother in amazement. He did not
know, he whose heart was as light as air, he who observed
no law in the world but the ordinary laws of nature, he who
allowed his passions to follow what course they wanted, so
that the spring of his emotions was always dry because he
opened daily so many fresh channels—he had no idea with
what fury that flood of human passions swells and surges
when it is refused outlet, how it gathers strength, and over-
flows, how it wears away the heart, how it breaks forth in
inward sobs and stifled convulsions, until it has broken away

its dikes and burst from its bed. The austere, icy exterior of Claude Frollo, that cold surface of unassailable virtue, had always deceived Jehan. The jovial scholar had never thought of the lava, deep, boiling, furious, beneath the snowy brow of Etna.

We do not know whether such ideas suddenly crossed the young man's mind, but scatterbrained as he was, he understood that he had seen what he should not have seen, that he had surprised the soul of his elder brother in one of its most secret attitudes, and that he must not let Claude know. Then, seeing that the archdeacon had fallen again into his previous immobility, Jehan stepped back softly, and made some noise on the steps outside the door, as of someone approaching and giving notice of his arrival.

"Come in!" cried the archdeacon from within his cell. "I was expecting you. I left the key purposely in the door. Come in, Master Jacques."

The scholar entered boldly. The archdeacon, extremely embarrassed by such a visitor in such a place, jerked convulsively in his armchair.

"What! is it you, Jehan?"

"Well, a J, at any rate," said the scholar, with his ruddy, saucy, joyous face all smiles.

Dom Claude's countenance had assumed its severe expression.

"What brings you here?"

"Brother," answered the scholar, trying to assume a decent, serious, and modest demeanor, and twisting his cap in his hands with an air of innocence, "I came to ask you . . ."

"What?"

"For some moral advice which I sorely need." Jehan dared not add aloud, "And for some little money, which I more sorely need."

"Sir," said the archdeacon, coldly, "I am much displeased with you."

"Alas!" sighed the scholar.

Dom Claude turned partly around and glared at Jehan. "But I am very glad to see you."

This was an ominous exordium. Jehan prepared for the worst.

"Jehan, every day I hear bad reports about you. What was

that scuffle about in which you beat and bruised with a stick a certain little viscount, Albert de Ramonchamp? . . ."

"Oh!" said Jehan, "that was nothing! Some good-for-nothing page who amused himself by splashing the scholars by galloping his horse through the mud."

"And what do you have to say," resumed the archdeacon, "about this Mahiet Fargel, whose gown you have torn? *Tunicam dechiraverunt,* reads the charge."

"Pooh! only a wretched-looking Montaigu hood! That's all."

"The charge says gown, not hood. Don't you know your Latin?"

Jehan didn't answer.

"Yes!" continued the priest, nodding his head. "Look what study and letters are come to now! The Latin language is scarcely understood; the Syriac unknown; the Greek so odious that it is not considered ignorance among the most learned to skip a Greek word without reading it, and to say: *Graecum est, non legitur.*"[11]

The scholar raised his eyes boldly. "Brother, will it please you if I tell you, in good French, the meaning of that Greek word on the wall?"

"What word?"

"That one over there."

A slight blush spread over the pallid cheeks of the arch-deacon, like a puff of smoke announcing the internal com-motion of a volcano. The scholar hardly noticed it.

"Well, Jehan," stammered the elder brother, "what does the word mean?"

"Fate."

Dom Claude turned pale again and the scholar noncha-lantly continued, "And that word underneath it, carved by the same hand, means impurity. See, I know my Greek."

The archdeacon remained silent. This Greek lesson had set him to musing. Master Jehan, who had all the art of a spoiled child, recognized the right moment for venturing his request. So, in his most dulcet tones, he began, "My dear brother, do you hate me so, then, as to look so fiercely at me on account of a few petty thumps and brushes given in a fair fight to a

11 "It is Greek, it is not read."

pack of boys and monkeys, *quibusdam marmosetis?*[12] You see, my good brother, I know my Latin too!"

But all this suave hypocrisy had not its accustomed effect on the severe elder brother. Cerberus would not bite into the honey cake. The archdeacon's brow lost not one of its frowning wrinkles.

"What is it that you want here?" he said sharply.

"Well, to come to the point," answered Jehan, bravely, "I need some money."

At this effrontery, the archdeacon's physiognomy immediately assumed the look of a schoolmaster and an angry father.

"You know, Master Jehan, that our fief of Tirechappe brings in, including both the land rents and the rents of the twenty-one houses, only thirty-nine livres eleven sous six deniers parisis. This is half as much again as in the time of the Paclets, but it's not very much!"

"I need money," repeated Jehan, stoically.

"Do you know that the official decided that the rents from our twenty-one houses were to be paid to the bishopric, and that we could only redeem this tribute by paying to his reverence the bishop two marks silver gilt at the rate of six livres parisis? Now, I have not been able to get together these two marks. You know that."

"All I know is that I need money," repeated Jehan for the third time.

"And what do you want it for?"

At this question a ray of hope shone in Jehan's eyes. Again he wore his sweet look of innocence.

"Listen, by dear brother Claude, I do not come to you ill-intentioned. I'm not going to squander your money in the taverns nor parade the streets of Paris in a suit of gold brocade with my lackey. No, my brother, it's for a charitable work."

"What charitable work?" asked Claude, a little surprised.

"Two of my friends would like to purchase some baby clothes for a poor widow of Haudry. It's a bit of charity. It'll cost three florins and I would like to contribute my share."

"What are the names of your two friends?"

[12] "To certain marmosets."

"Pierre l'Assommeur and Baptiste Croque-Oison."

"Humph!" said the archdeacon. "They are names that go as fitly with a good work of charity as a cannon would upon a high altar."

It is certain that Jehan had chosen very poorly the names of his friends. He realized it too late.

"And then," continued the shrewd Claude, "what sort of baby clothes costs three florins, and for a child of one of the Haudry widows! Since when have those widows had brats in swaddling clothes?"

Jehan broke the ice once more.

"Well, then! I need some money tonight to go to see Isabeau la Thierrye at the Val-d'Amour."

"You wretched sinner!" exclaimed the priest.

" 'Impurity!' " said Jehan.

This quotation, which the scholar borrowed, perhaps mischievously, from the wall of the cell, had a singular effect upon the priest. He bit his lip, and his sternness was hidden under a deep blush.

"Get out of here!" he said to Jehan. "I am expecting someone."

The scholar tried once more. "Brother Claude, give me at least one little parisis, to eat."

"How far have you gone with the decretals of Gratian?" asked Dom Claude.

"I've lost my notebooks."

"Where are you in the Latin classics?"

"Somebody stole my copy of Horace."

"And where are you with Aristotle?"

"Faith, brother! What is the name of that Father of the Church who says the errors of heretics have always found shelter amid the thickets of Aristotelian metaphysics? He's not worth a straw! I don't want to mangle my religion with his metaphysics."

"Young man," retorted the archdeacon, "when last the king came to Paris, there was a gentleman named Philippe de Comines, who had embroidered on his saddle this motto, which I advise you to ponder over. *Qui non laborat non manducet.*"[13]

---

[13] "He who will not work, let him not eat."

The scholar stood silent for a moment, his finger in his ear, his eyes cast down, and his look angry. Suddenly he turned toward Claude with the quick motion of a wagtail.

"So, my good brother, you refuse me a sou parisis to buy me a crust of bread?"

"*Qui non laborat non manducet.*"

At this answer of the inflexible archdeacon, Jehan buried his head in his hands, like a woman sobbing, and exclaimed some Greek word with an expression of despair.

"What does that mean, sir?" demanded Claude, taken aback by this outburst.

"Well, what?" said the scholar, raising his impudent eyes into which he had been thrusting his fists, to make them look as if they were red from tears. "It's Greek—it's an anapest of Aeschylus' which perfectly expresses grief."

And then he burst out into a fit of laughter so violent that the archdeacon could not help smiling. After all, it was Claude's fault: why had he so spoiled this boy?

"O dear brother Claude," continued Jehan, emboldened by this smile, "look at my worn-out boots. Was there ever a more tragic pair of cotherni in the world than boots like these?"

The archdeacon quickly resumed his severe look. "I'll send you new shoes. But no money."

"Only one little parisis, brother," begged Jehan. "I'll learn Gratian by heart; I'll believe in God; I'll be a veritable Pythagoras of knowledge and virtue. But one little parisis, please! Would you have me die of hunger, which now tears at me, with its gaping jaws, blacker, more stinking, deeper than Tartarus or a monk's nose?"

Dom Claude shook his wrinkled head. "*Qui non laborat . . .*"

Jehan did not let him finish.

"Well," he cried, "to the devil with you! Fun forever! I'll go to the tavern, I'll fight, I'll go see my wenches!"

So saying, he heaved his hat against the wall and snapped his fingers like castanets.

The archdeacon looked at him gloomily.

"Jehan, you have no soul."

"In that case, according to Epicurus, I lack a certain something, made of another nameless something."

"Jehan, you must begin mending your ways."

"Oh sure!" cried the scholar, looking alternately at his brother and at the alembics on the furnace. "Everything I see here seems awry, ideas as well as bottles."

"Jehan, you are slipping down an incline. Do you know where you are going?"

"Yes, to the tavern," said Jehan.

"The tavern can only lead you to the pillory."

"It has a lantern like any other, and perhaps the one with which Diogenes would have found his man."

"The pillory leads to the gallows."

"The gallows is a scale, with a man at one end and the whole world on the other. Oh, it's great being a man!"

"The gallows leads to hell."

"That's just a big fire!"

"Jehan, Jehan! your end will be bad."

"But the beginning will have been good."

At this moment, the noise of footsteps was heard on the staircase.

"Be silent!" said the archdeacon, putting his finger to his lips. "This is Master Jacques. Listen, Jehan," he added in a whisper, "be careful never to speak of anything you have seen or heard here. Hide under this furnace, and don't breathe."

The scholar crept under the furnace, and just then, a great idea came to him.

"By the way, brother Claude, a florin for not breathing too loudly!"

"Be quiet! Yes, I promise you."

"Give it to me now!"

"Take it!" said the archdeacon, throwing him his purse angrily. Jehan crept under the furnace, and the door opened.

The Two Men Dressed in Black

The gloomy person who entered Claude Frollo's cell wore a black gown and a somber look. What first struck our friend Jehan (who, as one might suppose, so curled up in his corner as to be able to see everything and to hear everything easily) was the utter sadness both of the garment and of the face of the newly arrived visitor. However, there was a gentleness in his face, but it was the gentleness of a cat or a judge. He was nearly sixty, very gray and wrinkled. White eyebrows shaded his blinking eyes, one lip drooped; and his hands were enormous. When Jehan saw that it was only some physician or magistrate, whose nose was a great distance from his mouth, a sure sign of stupidity, he curled up in his hole, annoyed that he had to remain, he knew not how long, in such an uncomfortable position and in such dull company.

Meanwhile the archdeacon did not even rise to greet his visitor, only motioned him to be seated on the stool near the door. After a few minutes' silence, during which Dom Frollo seemed to be continuing some previous meditation, he said to his caller patronizingly, "Good day, Master Jacques."

"Good morrow, master!" answered the man in black.

There was in the two ways of intoning, on the one hand, this "Master Jacques," and on the other the obsequious "master," that difference between monseigneur and monsieur, between teacher and pupil. This was evidently a meeting between master and disciple.

"Well," began the archdeacon, after another moment's silence which Master Jacques took care not to disturb, "are you succeeding?"

"Alas! master," replied the other, smiling sadly, "I keep blowing. There are more ashes than I want. But not one spark of gold."

Dom Claude gesticulated impatiently.

"I am not talking about that, Master Jacques Charmolue, but about the charge against your magician—Marc Cenaine, isn't that his name? The butler in the Court of Accounts. Does he confess to his sorcery? Did the torture work?"

"Alas! No!" answered Master Jacques, still with a sad smile. "We have not that consolation. That man is a stone. We could boil him in the pig-market before he would say anything. However we are sparing nothing to get at the truth. Every joint in his body has been dislocated. We have put all our irons in the fire, as the old comic Plautus says,

Advorsum stimulos, laminas, crucesque, compedesque,
Nervas, catenas, carceres, numellas, pedicas, boias.[1]

"But nothing works. That man is terrible. I give up with him."

"You have found nothing new in his house?"

"Oh yes!" said Master Jacques, fumbling in his leather purse, "this parchment. There are words which we do not understand. And yet Monsieur Philippe Lheulier, the criminal lawyer, knows a little Hebrew which he learned during a trial of some Jews in Brussels."

As he spoke, Master Jacques was unrolling the parchment.

"Give it here," said the archdeacon. Scanning the scroll, "Pure magic, Master Jacques!" he cried. "*Emen-hétan*! that is the witches' formula used when they meet on their sabbath. *Per ipsum, et cum ipso, et in ipso!*[2] that's the command which sends the devil back to hell. *Hax, pax, max*! that's a medical formula to prevent the evil effects of a mad dog's bite. Master Jacques! you are the king's attorney in the ecclesiastical court! This parchment is abominable!"

"We'll torture the man again. Here's something else," added Master Jacques, rummaging again in his purse, "which we found at Marc Cenaine's."

It was a vessel like one of those in Dom Claude's furnace.

"Ah," said the archdeacon, "an alchemist's crucible!"

"I must confess," replied Master Jacques, with his timid and constrained smile, "that I have tried it over the furnace, but I have fared no better with it than with my own."

[1] "Against goads, red-hot irons, crosses and double rings,
    Bonds, chains, prisons, shackles, fetters, yokes."
[2] "Through him, and with him, and in him."

The archdeacon began to examine the crucible. "What has he engraved on it? *Och! och!* a word that drives away fleas! This Marc Cenaine is stupid. I can well believe you can't make gold with this. 'Tis good for nothing."

"Speaking about errors," said the king's attorney, "I was studying the door down below before coming up here. Is Your Reverence quite sure that it's the beginning of the book of natural philosophy that's represented there on the side toward the Hotel-Dieu, and that, among the seven nude figures at the feet of Our Lady, the one which has wings on his heels is Mercury?"

"Yes," answered the priest. "It is so written by Augustin Nypho, the Italian doctor who had a bearded demon that taught him everything. But we will go down, and I'll explain it to you from the text."

"Thank you, master," said Charmolue, bowing low. "By the way, I almost forgot. When do you wish me to have the little sorceress apprehended?"

"What sorceress?"

"That gypsy girl, you know, who comes every day to dance in the square in spite of the provost's proscriptions. She has a goat which is possessed, and has the devil's own horns; it reads and writes, and understands mathematics like Picatrix, and should be enough to hang all Bohemia. The charge is all ready and will soon be issued. Upon my soul, she's a pretty creature, that dancing girl! The most beautiful black eyes, like two Egyptian carbuncles! When shall we begin?"

The archdeacon turned instantly pale as death.

"I will let you know," he stammered, in a voice scarcely audible. Then, with some effort, he added, "Concern yourself with Marc Cenaine."

"Have no fears!" said Jacques Charmolue, smiling. "When I get back I'll have him strapped to the leather bed again. But he's a devil of a man! He even tires out Pierrat Torteruc, whose hands are larger than mine. As the good Plautus says,

Nudus vinctus, centum pondo, es quando pendes per pedes.[3]

---

[3] "Naked, bound, you weigh a hundred pounds, hung by the feet."

To the rack with him! We'll break him with that. He's in for it."

Dom Claude seemed plunged in somber distraction. He turned toward Charmolue.

"Master Pierrat . . . Master Jacques, I mean, look to Marc Cenaine."

"Oh, yes, yes, Dom Claude. Poor man! He will suffer like Mummol. But what an idea! to go to the witches' sabbath! a butler in the Court of Accounts! He should have known the text of Charlemagne's ordinance, *Stryga vel mascal!*[4] As for the little gypsy, Smeralda, as they call her, I will wait upon your orders. Ah! as we go by the door, will you explain to me what is the significance of that gardener painted on the door that you see as you enter the church? It's the Sower, is it not? Hey! Master, what are you thinking about?"

Dom Claude, lost in his own thoughts, was not listening. Charmolue, following the movement of his eyes, saw that his stare was fixed on the large spider's web which hung like a tapestry in the window. Just then, a giddy fly, looking for the March sun, flew into the net and was entangled. Its struggles aroused the huge spider which suddenly bounded from his central cell, and with one lurch caught the fly, which he bent in two with his fore-feelers, then with his hideous sucker he attacked its head. "Poor fly!" said the king's attorney of the ecclesiastical court, and he raised his hand to save it. The archdeacon, as though awakened from sleep, held back Jacques' arm with convulsive violence.

"Master Jacques," he cried, "leave the fly to fate!"

The attorney turned about quite terrified. He felt as if his arm had been seized by iron pincers. The haggard, fiery eyes of the priest remained fixed on the horrible little group, the fly and the spider.

"Oh, yes," continued the priest, in a voice that seemed to come from his very bowels, "that's the symbol of everything. She flies, she is joyous, she has just been born; she searches for the springtime, the open air, liberty; oh, yes, but she strikes the fatal network; the spider emerges, the hideous spider! Poor dancer! Poor fated fly! Master Jacques, leave it alone—it's fate! Alas, Claude, you are the spider! Claude,

---

[4] "A vampire or a masque."

you are also the fly! You flew toward knowledge, toward the light, toward the sun; you only wanted to reach the pure air, the broad light of eternal truth. But rushing toward the dazzling window which opens into another world, a world of brightness, intelligence, and knowledge—blind fly! silly doctor! You did not see the subtle spider's web, spread by destiny between the light and you; you flew into it, wretched fool, and now you struggle, with crushed head and torn wings, between the iron antennae of Fate! Master Jacques! Master Jacques! Let the spider alone!"

"I assure you," said Charmolue, who looked at him but did not understand him, "that I won't touch it. But let my arm go, please, master! Your hand is like a vise."

The archdeacon did not hear him. "O madman!" he continued, not taking his eyes from the window. "And if you had been able to break through that formidable web, with your fly-wings, do you imagine that you could have reached the light? Alas! that glass farther on, that transparent obstacle, that crystal wall harder than brass, which separates all philosophies from the truth, how could you have passed through it? O vanity of knowledge! how many wise men come from afar to dash their heads against you! How many systems come buzzing to rush pell-mell against that eternal window!"

He was silent. These last ideas, which had actually diverted his mind from himself to science, seemed to calm him. Jacques Charmolue completely brought him back to reality by asking this question: "Come, master, when will you help me make gold? I want to succeed."

The archdeacon shook his head with a bitter smile.

"Master Jacques, read Michel Psellus, *Dialogus de energia et operatione daemonum.*[5] What are we doing is not completely innocent."

"Speak lower, master. I have my doubts," said Charmolue. "But surely one may practice a little hermetic philosophy when one is only a poor king's attorney in the ecclesiastical court, at thirty crowns a year. But, let's speak low."

At that moment, the anxious Charmolue heard coming from under the furnace sounds like someone chewing.

[5] "Dialogue of energy and operation of demons."

"What's that?" he asked.

It was the scholar, who, very bored and uneasy in his hiding place, had just found a stale crust of bread and a sliver of moldy cheese, and had begun to eat both, without any ceremony, for something to do, and breakfast. As he was very hungry, he made a great noise, loudly masticating each mouthful. Thus it was that he aroused and alarmed the king's attorney.

"That's my cat," said the archdeacon quickly, "feasting down there upon some mouse perhaps."

His explanation satisfied Charmolue.

"Indeed, master," he replied, with a respectful smile, "each great philosopher has his favorite pet. You know what Servius says: *Nullus enim locus sine genio est.*"[6]

Meanwhile, Dom Claude, fearing some new prank of Jehan's, reminded his worthy disciple that they had some figures on the door to study together. Therefore both of them left the cell, to the great relief of the scholar, who was beginning to fear seriously that his knee would be indelibly marked by his chin.

6

The Effect of Swearing in Public

"*Te Deum laudamus!*"[1] exclaimed Master Jehan, as he crawled from his hole. "The two old hoot owls have gone. *Och! och! Hax! pax! max!* Fleas! Mad dogs! The devil! I've had enough of their conversation! My head is ringing like a belfry. And a morsel of moldy cheese to boot! Well, let's be gone with my big brother's purse, and convert this money into bottles!"

He peeked gently, then admiringly into the precious purse, adjusted his clothing, rubbed his shoes, dusted the ashes from his sleeves, whistled a tune, danced about, looked around the cell to see if there was anything else worth taking, picked up from the furnace a glass amulet, by way of a

---

[6] "There is no place without its [particular] genius."
[1] "We praise you, God."

trinket to give to Isabeau la Thierrye, opened the door, which his brother had left unlocked as a last indulgence, and which he in turn left open as a last bit of mischief, and started down the winding staircase, hopping step by step like a bird.

In the darkness of the winding stairs he elbowed something which moved out of the way with a growl. He supposed it was Quasimodo and this so amused him that he went down the rest of the stairs holding his sides with laughter, and was still laughing when he got out into the square.

He stamped his foot when he found himself again on the ground.

"Oh, good and honorable pavement of Paris!" he exclaimed. "Cursed stairwell, enough to wind the angels on Jacob's ladder! What was I thinking of to squeeze myself into that stone gimlet which pieces the sky, just to eat a piece of wretched cheese and to see the steeples of Paris through a little window!"

He walked a few steps, and noticed the two hoot owls— namely, Dom Claude and Master Jacques Charmolue— contemplating the sculpture in the great doorway. He approached them on tiptoe, and heard the archdeacon say in a low voice to Charmolue, "It was Guillaume of Paris who had Job engraved on that stone the color of lapis lazuli with the gilt edges. Job represents the philosopher's stone, which must be tried and tortured in order to become perfect, as Raymond Lulle says, *Sub conservatione formae specificae salva anima.*"[2]

"That doesn't mean anything to me!" said Jehan to himself. "I have the purse."

At that moment he heard a loud, deep voice behind him utter a string of abominable oaths: *Sang Dieu! Ventre Dieu! Bédieu! Corps de Dieu! Nombril de Belzébuth! Nom d'un Pape! Corne et tonnerre!*

"Upon my soul," cried Jehan, "that can be no other than my friend Captain Phoebus!"

The name Phoebus reached the archdeacon's ear just as he was explaining to the king's attorney the meaning of the dragon hiding its tail in a bath whence issue smoke and a

---

[2] "Under the conservation of the specific form, the soul is intact."

king's head. Dom Claude shuddered, stopped his explanation, to the great surprise of Charmolue, turned around, and saw his brother Jehan approaching a tall officer at the door of the Gondelaurier mansion.

It was indeed Captain Phoebus de Châteaupers. He was standing with his back against the corner of the house of his betrothed, and he was swearing like a pagan.

"By my faith, Captain Phoebus," said Jehan, seizing him by the hand, "you swear with astonishing verve."

"*Corne et tonnerre!*" replied the captain.

"*Corne et tonnerre* yourself!" rejoined the scholar. "Now, my gentle captain, whence this cascade of beautiful words?"

"My apologies, friend Jehan," cried Phoebus, shaking his hand, "a runaway horse cannot stop short. I was swearing at full gallop. I have just left those silly women, and whenever I come away from them my throat is always full of oaths; I have to spit them out, or else I would choke, *ventre et tonnerre!*"

"Come and have a drink!" said the scholar.

This proposal calmed the captain.

"A good idea, but I have no money."

"But I have."

"Bah! let's see."

With a gesture both simple and majestic, Jehan opened the purse before the captain's eyes. Meanwhile the archdeacon, who had left Charmolue still mystified, approached them, but stopping a few paces away, watched the young men without their being aware of it, so absorbed were they in the contemplation of the purse.

Phoebus cried, "A purse in your pocket, Jehan, is like the moon in a bucket of water. You see it, but it is not there. It's only a shadow. I'll bet the contents are nothing but pebbles."

"Well, here are the pebbles I line my pocket with," replied Jehan coldly.

And without saying another word, he emptied the purse on a curbstone nearby, with the air of a Roman saving his country.

"By God!" muttered Phoebus, "all that money! It's dazzling!"

Jehan remained dignified and impassive. A few liards rolled into the mud; the captain, in his enthusiasm, stooped to pick them up. But Jehan restrained him. "Fie on them, Captain Phoebus de Châteaupers!"

Phoebus counted the coins, and, turning to Jehan, solemnly said, "Do you know, Jehan, there are twenty-three sols parisis here? Whom did you rob last night in the Rue Coupe-Gueule?"

Jehan threw back his curly blond head and said, half closing his eyes as if in scorn, "I have a brother who is an archdeacon and an imbecile."

"*Corne de Dieu!*" exclaimed Phoebus, "the good man!"

"Let's go and drink," said Jehan.

"Where shall we go?" asked Phoebus, "to La Pomme d'Eve?"

"No, captain. Let's go to La Vieille Science."

"The deuce with your Vieille Science. The wine is better at La Pomme d'Eve; besides, by the door there's a vine in the sun that cheers me when I am drinking."

"Very good! to Eve and her apple," said the scholar, taking Phoebus by the arm. "By the way, my dear captain, you said a minute ago, Rue Coupe-Gueule. Very badly spoken. We're not so barbarous now. We say Coupe-Gorge."

The two friends set out for La Pomme d'Eve. Of course they first picked up the money, and naturally the archdeacon followed them.

Dom Claude's face was again gloomy and haggard. Could this be the Phoebus whose cursed name, ever since his interview with Gringoire, had haunted all his thoughts? He didn't know, but, at any rate, it was a Phoebus, and this magic name was enough to insure the archdeacon's following these two thoughtless companions at a safe distance while listening to their conversation and watching their slightest gestures with anxious attention. As a matter of fact, it was easy to hear all they said, so loudly were they talking, and so little did they care if passersby knew their secrets. They talked about duels, girls, wine, and follies of all kinds.

After a curve in the street, the sound of a tambourine could be heard from a neighboring crossway. Dom Claude heard the officer say to the scholar, "*Tonnerre!* Let's hurry on."

"Why, Phoebus?"

"I'm afraid the gypsy will see me."

"What gypsy?"

"The little one with the goat."

"La Esmeralda?"

"That's the one, Jehan. I always forget her devil of a name. Let's hurry. She'd recognize me, and I don't want her to speak to me on the street."

"Do you know her, Phoebus?"

Here the archdeacon saw Phoebus grin, and whisper something in Jehan's ear. Then Phoebus burst out laughing, and shook his head with a triumphant air.

"Indeed?" said Jehan.

"Upon my soul!" replied Phoebus.

"Tonight?"

"Tonight."

"Are you sure she will come?"

"Are you mad, Jehan? No one ever doubts these things."

The archdeacon heard this entire conversation. His teeth chattered. A shudder, visible to the eye, ran through his body. He paused for a moment, leaned against a post, like a man drunk, and then followed the route of the two merry characters.

When he overtook them, they had changed their conversation. He heard them singing at the top of their lungs an old song:

> The children of the Petits-Carreaux
> Let themselves be hung like calves.

7

The Phantom Priest

The notorious tavern, La Pomme d'Eve, was located at the corner of the Rue de la Rondelle and the Rue du Bâtonnier in the University. It was just one large room on the ground floor; the low ceiling was supported in the center by a heavy wooden pillar painted yellow. There was always a crowd of men and women at the tables; shining pewter mugs hung on the walls. A vine grew by the door, over which a rusty iron marker or sign, decorated with an apple and a woman, creaked on its iron pin at every gust of wind, like a kind of weathercock. A sizable window looked onto the street.

Night was falling; the street was dark; the tavern, full of candles, flared at a distance like a forge in the dark. Through the broken panes of the casement window sounds of mugs clanking, of feasting, swearing, quarreling. Even though the heat of the room spread a mist over the glass, a passerby could see inside a mass of confused figures, from whom burst from time to time explosions of loud laughter. People, intent on their own affairs as they passed, paid no attention to this noisy place. Only now and then some little ragamuffin would stand on tiptoe to peer in, and shout the old jeering cry with which it was then customary to taunt drunkards: *"Aux Houls, saouls, saouls, saouls!"*

One man, however, kept pacing up and down imperturbably in front of the tavern, never taking his eyes off it, not wandering any farther away from it than a sentry from his box. His cloak was muffled to his nose. This cloak he had just purchased at a shop near the tavern, undoubtedly to protect himself from these cold March evenings—but perhaps also to hide his dress. From time to time, he would stop before the clouded, lead-latticed window, listening, looking, and stamping his foot as though becoming impatient.

At length, the door of the tavern opened. For that, he seemed to have been waiting. Two drinkers came out. The ray of light that issued from the doorway cast a light for a moment on their jovial, flushed faces. The man in the cloak retreated to the shadows of a porch on the other side of the street whence he could watch unseen.

"Corne et tonnerre!" said one of the two. "It's time for my assignation. The tower is about to toll seven."

"I tell you," said the other, thickly. "I don't live in the Rue des Mauvaises Paroles—*indignus qui inter mala verba habitat*. My street is the Rue Jean-Pain-Mollet, *in vico Johannis-Pain-Mollet*, and you're more horny than a unicorn if you say anything else. Everybody knows that anyone who gets once upon a bear's back is never afraid; but you've a nose for sniffing out a dainty piece, like Saint-Jacques de l'Hôpital."

"Jehan, my friend, you're drunk," said his companion.

The friend, staggering, replied, "If you say so, Phoebus, but it's a proven fact Plato had the profile of a hounddog."

No doubt the reader has already recognized our two worthy friends, the captain and the student. It seems that the man who was watching them from the shadows had recognized them too, for he was slowly following all the zigzags into which the reeling student led the captain, who, being a more seasoned drinker, had retained all his self-possession. By listening attentively to them, the man in the cloak overheard the entire conversation which follows:

"Body O'Bacchus! Monsieur scholar, try to walk straight; you know I must leave you. It is seven o'clock, and I have a rendezvous with a girl."

"Leave then! My head is spinning and I see stars! You're like the Château de Dampmartin that is bursting with laughter."

"Oh, by my grandmother's warts, Jehan, you're talking too much nonsense! By the way, Jehan, have you any money left?"

"Monsieur the Rector, there's no fault—the little slaughterhouse—*parva boucheria!*"

"Jehan, my friend, Jehan. You know I promised to meet that little girl at the end of the Pont Saint-Michel, and that I can only take her to La Falourdel's, that old madame on the bridge, and I'll have to pay for the room. The old white-whiskered wench won't give me credit. Jehan! Please, I pray you, have we drunk all the money in the purse? Haven't you at least a parisis?"

"The realization of having well spent the other hours is a just and savory sauce on our table."

"Oh, belly-wash! An end to all this gibberish! Tell me, you devil, do you have any money left? Give it to me, *Bédieu!* or I'll search you though you be as leprous as Job and scabby as Caesar!"

"Monsieur, the Rue Galiache is a street at the one end of which is the Rue de la Verrerie and at the other Rue de la Tixeranderie."

"Yes, of course, my good friend Jehan, my poor comrade, the Rue Galiache, good, you're right. But, in heaven's name, get a hold of yourself! I need only one sol parisis—and for seven o'clock."

"Silence, all round! Listen to this refrain:

> When the rats devour the cats,
> The King of Arras shall be lord.
> When the sea, so deep and wide,
> Shall be frozen in summertime,
> Then you'll see upon the ice
> The men of Arras shall flee."

"Well, my anti-Christ scholar, be hanged with your mother!" cried Phoebus, and he roughly shoved the intoxicated scholar, who reeled against the wall and slid slowly to the pavement of Philippe-Augustus. Inspired by a remnant of that fraternal pity which never absolutely deserts the heart of a drinker, Phoebus, with his foot, rolled Jehan to one of those pillows of the poor which heaven provides at every street corner of Paris, and which the rich scornfully stigmatize by the name dung-heaps. The captain propped Jehan's head on a bundle of cabbage stalks, and immediately the scholar began to snore in a magnificent bass. But, as the captain still held a grudge against the student, he muttered, "So much the worse for you if the devil's cart picks you up as it passes." And off he went.

The man in the cloak, who had been following them, paused a moment by the sleeping scholar, as if undecided as to what he should do; then, heaving a sigh, he hurried after the captain.

Like these two, we will leave Jehan sleeping under the watchful eye of heaven, and we will trail his companion and the cloaked follower.

At the end of Rue Saint-André-des-Arcs, Captain Phoebus realized that someone was following him. He saw, as he happened to glance backward, a kind of shadow creeping along the walls. He stopped. The shadow stopped. He continued on again; so did the shadow. Still he was unconcerned. "Oh, bah!" he muttered to himself, "I don't have any money."

In front of the College d'Autun he halted. It was here he had begun what he euphemistically called his studies, and because of a certain refractory schoolboy habit, he never passed in front of that college without subjecting the statue of Cardinal Pierre Bertrand, at the right of the main door, to that sort of insult of which Priapus complains so bitterly in Horace's satire: *"Olim truncus eram ficulnus."*[1] He stopped therefore in front of the statue as was his custom. The street was absolutely deserted. Just as he was preparing to continue casually on his way, breathing deeply the night air, he saw the shadow approaching him slowly—so slowly that he had much time to observe that the shadow wore a cloak and a hat. When it had come close, it stopped, and remained almost as motionless as the statue of Cardinal Bertrand. But it stared at Phoebus with that luminous light which at night marks the eyes of a cat. The captain was brave, and he would not have worried very much about a robber with a rapier in his hand. But this walking statue, this petrified man, froze his blood. At that particular time there were rumors about a monk who nightly roamed the streets of Paris. Now these all came back to him confusedly. He was for a moment bewildered, but finally it was he who broke the silence, and said, with a forced grin, "Sir, if you be a thief, and I hope you are, you are much like a heron attacking a nutshell. I am the son, my friend, of a ruined family. You should go elsewhere. In the college chapel you'll find some wood of the true cross, set in silver."

A hand issued from the shadow's cloak and seized Phoebus' arm with the grip of an eagle's talon. At the same time the shadow spoke, "Captain Phoebus de Châteaupers!"

"What the devil!" said Phoebus. "You know my name?"

"Not only do I know your name," replied the cloaked man with a voice as from the grave, "I know you have a rendezvous tonight."

"Yes," answered Phoebus amazed.

"At seven o'clock."

"In fifteen minutes."

"At La Falourdel's."

"Exactly."

"The old madame on the Pont Saint-Michel."

"Yes, Saint Michel the Archangel, as the *Paternoster* says."

"Impious one!" muttered the phantom. "With a girl?"

[1] "I was once the trunk of a fig tree."

"*Confiteor*—I do confess it."

"Whose name is—"

"La Smeralda," finished Phoebus, gayly, all his buoyancy having returned to him.

At the mention of her name the specter's grip shook Phoebus' arm furiously.

"Captain Phoebus de Châteaupers, you lie!"

If you could have seen at that moment the angry face of the captain, his backward spring, so violent that it disengaged him from the iron grip which had seized him, the haughty look with which he laid his hand upon the hilt of his sword, and could you have seen even in the face of that anger, the sullen immobility of the man in the cloak, you would have been frightened. It was something like the combat between Don Juan and the statue.

"Christ and Satan!" cried the captain. "That's a word that seldom assails the ear of a Châteaupers. You don't dare repeat it!"

"You lie!" repeated the specter coldly.

The captain gnashed his teeth. Specter, phantom, rumors about a strolling monk, superstitions—all were forgotten in a flash. He saw only a man and heard an insult.

"Ah! very good!" he stammered in a voice choked with rage. He drew his sword, then still stammering—for rage as much as fear makes a man tremble—cried, "Here! Now! Come on! Your sword! Your sword! The blood of one of us must stain this pavement!"

But the other did not move. When he saw his adversary on guard and prepared to defend himself, he said, "Captain Phoebus, you forget your rendezvous."

In men like Phoebus transports of passion are like boiling milk, the ebullition of which a drop of cold water allays. Thus these few words lowered the sword glistening in the captain's hand.

"Captain," continued the man, "tomorrow, the day after tomorrow, in a month, in ten years, you will find me disposed to cut your throat. But first go to your rendezvous."

"Indeed," said Phoebus, as if seeking to come to terms with himself, "a sword and a girl are two charming things to meet in a rendezvous; but I see no reason why I should miss one for the sake of the other, when I can have them both."

So he sheathed his sword.

"Go to your place of assignation," repeated the unknown.

"Monsieur," answered Phoebus somewhat embarrassed, "many thanks for your courtesy. Tomorrow will be time enough to slash each other and to make buttonholes in Father Adam's doublet. I am much obliged to you for affording me the opportunity of spending delightfully yet another quarter of an hour. It was my sincere intention to lay you in the gutter and still to arrive on time for the fair damsel—especially as on such occasions it is genteel to make the ladies wait a little for one. But you seem to be a sporting fellow, so it is safest to put off our match till tomorrow. Now to my rendezvous! It is for seven, as you well know." Here Phoebus scratched his ear, "Ah! *Corne-Dieu!* I had forgotten. I don't have a sou to pay the price of the garret. The old wench will want to be paid in advance. She doesn't trust me."

"Here's the money," said the stranger.

Phoebus felt the cold hand of the stranger slip into his a large coin. He could not help taking the money, and pressing the hand.

"By God!" he exclaimed, "you are a good sort!"

"One condition," said the stranger. "Prove to me that I have been wrong and that you spoke the truth. Hide me in some corner where I may see if this girl is really she whose name you have mentioned."

"Oh," answered Phoebus, "that's all right by me. We shall take the Sainte-Martha room. You can see all you want from the closet that's on one side of it."

"Come then," said the specter.

"At your service," said the captain. "I know not if you are monsieur the devil himself. But let us be good friends tonight. Tomorrow I shall pay all my debts, of the purse and of the sword."

They walked on with quickened strides, and in a few minutes, the sound of the river served notice that they were crossing the Pont Saint-Michel, then lined with houses.

"First, I'll get you inside," said Phoebus to his unknown companion. "Then I'll go get the lady who was to wait for me near the Petit-Châtelet."

His companion made no answer. Since they had been

walking side by side, he had spoken nary a word. Phoebus stopped in front of a low door and pounded it violently. Light showed through cracks around the door. "Who's there?" cried a toothless voice. "*Corps-Dieu! Tête-Dieu! Ventre-Dieu!*" answered the captain. The door immediately opened, and before them stood a trembling old woman holding a wavering old lamp. The hag, clothed in rags, was stooped; her head, wrapped in a duster by way of a headdress, was shaking; her face, indented by two small eyes, was wrinkled all over as·were her hands, her face, and her neck. Her lips turned inward. All around her mouth, tufts of white hair gave her the whiskered appearance of a cat.

The interior of this hovel was no less drab than she. The walls had once been whitewashed; black beams crossed the ceiling; the fireplace had lots its mantel, and cobwebs festooned every corner. In the middle of the room were assembled some rickety tables and broken stools; a dirty child played in the ashes. Opposite the door, a staircase, or rather, a wooden ladder, led up to a trapdoor in the ceiling. As he entered this den, Phoebus' mysterious companion pulled his cloak up to his eyes. Meanwhile the captain, swearing like a Saracen, made haste to pay his écu, saying, "The Sainte-Marthe room."

The old woman bowed as if he were a lord, and put the coin into a drawer. When her back was turned, the little long-haired ragamuffin who was playing in the ashes went slyly to the drawer, removed the écu, and in its place put a dry leaf which he had plucked from a faggot.

The old woman beckoned to the two gentlemen, as she called them, to follow her, and stiffly ascended the ladder. On reaching the upper story she set her lamp on a chest, and Phoebus, as one accustomed to the house, opened a door that led into a dark closet.

"Go in there, my friend," he said to his companion. Without saying a word the man in the black cloak obeyed. The door shut behind him. He heard Phoebus bolt the door, and a moment later go down the ladder with the old housekeeper. The light had disappeared.

8

The Usefulness of Windows Opening Upon the River

Claude Frollo (for we presume that our reader, more intelligent than Phoebus, has seen in all this adventure no other specter than the archdeacon himself) groped about for some moments in the dark hole in which the captain had bolted him. It was one of those attics which builders sometimes contrive in the angle formed by the roof and the supporting walls of the house. The vertical section of this "dog house," as Phoebus so aptly called it, formed a triangle. It had neither window nor skylight, and the inclined plane of the roof prevented one from standing upright. Claude therefore had to squat in the dust and plaster that crunched underneath him. His head was burning. Fumbling about with his hand, he touched upon the floor a piece of broken glass, which he applied to his forehead, that its coolness might relieve a bit his burning fever.

What was transpiring at that moment in the dark cavernous soul of the archdeacon? Only he and God knew.

In what sinister order was he arranging in his thoughts La Esmeralda, Phoebus, Jacques Charmolue, his beloved younger brother, so lately abandoned by him at the dung-hill, his archdeacon's cassock, his reputation perhaps, thus dragged to La Falourdel's—all these images, all these adventures of his? It is impossible to say. But certain it is that these thoughts evoked horrible pictures.

He waited for a quarter of an hour; it seemed to him an eternity. Suddenly he heard the wooden ladder creaking. Someone was coming up. The trapdoor was lifted again, and again there was a gleam of light. In the worm-eaten door of his hiding place, there was a wide crack, to which he pressed his face, that he might see all that was going on in the room. The old woman with a cat's face first appeared, carrying a lamp; then Phoebus, curling his mustache; then a third person, the beautiful and graceful Esmeralda carrying her goat.

The priest saw her come up like a dazzling apparition. He trembled, a cloud passed over his eyes, his pulse beat violently, his ears hummed, his head was spinning. Then he no longer saw or heard anything.

When he revived, Phoebus and La Esmeralda were alone, seated upon the wooden chest beside the lamp which lighted up for the archdeacon their two youthful faces, and enabled him to see a couch at the farther end of the garret.

By the couch there was a window, with panes broken like a spider's web upon which rain has fallen, showing through its lacy splinters a small patch of sky, and the moon resting on a pillow of soft billowing clouds.

The young girl was blushing, confused, palpitating. Her long lashes shaded her flushed cheeks. The officer, to whom she dared not lift her eyes, radiated delight. Abstractedly, but with charming coyness, she was tracing on the bench, with the tip of her finger, meaningless lines, her eyes following the movement. You could not see her foot, for her little goat was lying on it.

The captain was very finely dressed. About his neck and wrists were ruffles of gold lace—a great elegance in those days.

Dom Claude could barely hear what they were saying because of the throbbing in his temples.

Conversation between lovers is dull enough—a perpetual "I love you"—a musical phrase monotonous and very insipid to all indifferent hearers when not adorned with a few *fioriture*. But Claude was no indifferent listener.

"Oh," said the young girl, without lifting her eyes, "do not despise me, Monseigneur Phoebus. I feel I am doing something very wrong."

"Despise you, my pretty one!" replied the officer with an air of condescending gallantry. "Despise you! My God, but why?"

"For having followed you."

"About that, my beautiful one, we are not in agreement. I ought not despise you, but hate you."

The young girl looked at him with alarm.

"Hate me! But what have I done?"

"For having required so much persuading."

"Alas," she said, "it is because I am breaking a vow . . .

I shall never find my parents . . . The amulet will lose its power. But it doesn't matter . . . what need now do I have of father or mother?"

And she fixed upon the captain her large black eyes, moist with joy and tenderness.

"The devil if I understand you!" cried Phoebus.

La Esmeralda remained silent for a moment. Then a tear trickled from her eye. Sighing, she said, "Oh, sir, I do love you."

There was around the young girl such an aura of chastity, such a charm of virtue, that Phoebus felt a little uneasy in her presence. However, these words emboldened him. "You love me!" he said with transport, and he threw his arm around the gypsy's waist. He had only been waiting for this opportunity.

The priest saw it all, and with his finger felt the edge of the dagger which he had concealed under his cloak.

"Phoebus," continued the gypsy, gently disengaging herself from the encircling arm of the captain, "you are good, you are generous, you are handsome. You saved me; I who am but a poor lost gypsy girl. I dreamed for a long time of an officer who would save my life. It was of you that I dreamed, before I even knew you, my Phoebus. In my dream he wore a handsome uniform like yours, and a sword; he looked distinguished. Your name is Phoebus; it is a fine name. I love your name; I love your sword. Draw your sword, Phoebus, so that I may see it."

"Child!" said the captain, smiling as he unsheathed his saber. The gypsy looked at the hilt, then felt the blade, examined with loving curiosity the monogram on the guard, and kissed the sword, saying, "You are the sword of a brave man. I love my captain."

Again Phoebus seized an opportunity. As she bent over to look at his weapon, he placed a kiss on the back of her neck. The girl suddenly straightened, her face crimson like a cherry.

In the darkness, the priest gritted his teeth.

"Phoebus," resumed the gypsy girl, "let me speak with you. But walk a little now, that I may see you standing tall and hear the sound of your spurs. How handsome you are!"

The captain rose to comply, his face brightened by a smile of satisfaction.

"Really, now, how like a child you are! By the way, my love, have you ever seen me in my state uniform?"

"Alas, no!" she answered.

"That's really striking!"

Phoebus returned and seated himself beside her again but much closer than before.

"Listen, my dear ..."

The gypsy in childish playfulness gave him several little taps on the lips with her pretty fingers, saying, "No, no, I won't listen to you. Do you love me? I want you to tell me if you love me?"

"Of course I love you, dear angel of my life!" cried the captain, on bended knee. "My body, my blood, my soul—all belong to you. I love you and have loved no one but you."

The captain had so frequently repeated his declaration of love on so many like occasions that he delivered it all in one breath without making one single blunder. At this impassioned declaration the girl raised here eyes with a look of angelic happiness toward the dirty ceiling which here took the place of heaven. "Oh," she whispered, "this should be the moment when we should die!" Phoebus found "the moment" suitable for stealing another kiss which further tortured the miserable archdeacon in his hiding place.

"Die!" cried the amorous captain. "What are you talking about, my angel? It's the time to live, or Jupiter is nothing but a scoundrel. To die at the beginning of such a sweet experience! *Corne-de-boeuf!* You jest! Oh, no! Listen, my dear, Similar ... Esmenarda ... Excuse me, but you have such a prodigiously Saracen name I can't pronounce it properly. It's like a bush in which I always get entangled."

"My lord!" said the poor girl, "and I thought it such a pretty name for its strangeness. If it displeases you, I would gladly call myself Goton."

"Ah, you mustn't cry over such a trifle, my love. It's a name to which I must get accustomed, that's all! Once I know it by heart, it will come to me easily enough. Listen, my dear Similar, I adore you passionately. I love you more than words can tell. I know a damsel who is mad with rage about it."

The jealous gypsy interrupted him. "Who is she?"
"What difference does it make to us?" said Phoebus. "Do
you love me?"
"Oh!" said she.
"Well then, that's sufficient. You shall see how I love you
too. May the great devil Neptune stick me with his pitchfork
if I don't make you the happiest creature in the world.
Somewhere we shall have a pretty little lodging. Under your
windows I'll parade my archers. They are all on horseback,
and Captain Mignon's can't compare with them. I'll take
you to the great Parisian parades at the Grange de Rully. It's
magnificent. Eighty thousand armed soldiers; thirty thousand
white harnesses, and men in shining armor; sixty-seven banners of the trades, the standards of the parliament, of the
Chamber of Accounts, of the Public Treasury—in short, the
whole devilish train. And then I'll take you to see the king's
own lions, which are wild beasts, you know. All women like
that."

For some moments the young girl, absorbed in her own
pleasant reveries, had been dreaming to the sound of his
voice, without giving much attention to his words.

"Oh! you'll be so happy!" continued the captain, at the
same time unbuckling the gypsy's belt.

"Pray, what are you doing?" she said sharply. His maneu-
vering had roused her from her reverie.

"Nothing," answered Phoebus. "I was only saying you
must cast aside all this wild common street clothing when
you are with me."

"When I am with you, my Phoebus!" said the young girl
affectionately. And again she became silent, lost in her
thoughts.

The captain, emboldened by her gentleness, threw his arm
around her waist, this time without her making any resistance, and began gently to unlace the poor child's bodice,
and, in so doing, quite disarranged her neckerchief, so that
the priest, all panting, could see beneath it the gypsy's beautiful bare shoulder, round and dusky like the moon rising
through a mist on the horizon.

The young girl let Phoebus have his way. She seemed unconscious of what he was doing. The captain's eyes sparkled.

Suddenly she turned to him with an expression of boundless love, and said, "Phoebus, instruct me in your religion."

"My religion!" cried the captain with a burst of laughter.
"Me, instruct you in my religion! *Corne et tonnerre!* And
what do you want with my religion?"

"So we can marry," she answered.

The captain's face assumed an expression of mingled surprise, disdain, unconcern, and licentious passion.

"Bah!" he said, "why should we marry?"

The gypsy turned pale, and her head dropped sorrowfully
upon her breast.

"My sweetest darling," said Phoebus tenderly, "what are
these silly notions you speak of? What is marriage! Would
we love each other more for having some Latin gabbled to
us in a priest's shop?"

As he spoke thus in his softest tones, he drew ever closer
to the gypsy girl. His caressing hands were again around her
slender and yielding waist, his eyes sparkled more and more.
Everything proclaimed that Monsieur Phoebus was obviously approaching one of those moments when Jupiter himself behaves so foolishly that good old Homer is obliged to
draw a cloud over the scene.

Meanwhile Dom Claude was watching everything. The
door was made with vertical planks, all rotted and decayed,
which left between them wide cracks for his vulture's gaze.
This dark-skinned, broad-shouldered priest, condemned hitherto to the austere chastity of the cloister, shivered and
seethed before this night-scene of love and passion. He felt
within him extraordinary sensations. The sight of this young
and beautiful girl, all disheveled in the arms of this young,
ardent lover turned the blood in his veins to molten lead. His
eye stared with lascivious jealousy at all these unfastened
clasps. Anyone who could have seen his distraught visage at
that moment, pressed against those worm-eaten bars, might
have thought they saw a tiger's face looking out from his
cage at some jackal devouring a gazelle. His eye gleamed
like a candle through the cracks of the door.

All at once, Phoebus, with a rapid gesture, tore off the
bodice of the gypsy. The poor girl, who had remained pale
and thoughtful, was startled, as if from a dream. She jerked
herself away from the importunate officer, and, noticing her

bosom and bare shoulders, she blushed, confused and mute
with shame, and crossed her beautiful arms over her bosom
to hide it. But for the flame that glowed in her cheeks, one
seeing her standing thus silent and motionless might have
taken her for a statue of Modesty. Her eyes she kept lowered.

The captain's attack had revealed the mysterious amulet
which hung about her neck.

"What's that?" he said, seizing this pretext for going
nearer to the beautiful creature whom he had just frightened.

"Don't touch it!" she said sharply. "It is my guardian. It
is this that will enable me to find my family, if I do nothing
unworthy of it. Oh, leave me, Monsieur le Capitaine. My
mother! My poor mother! My mother, where are you? Come
to my rescue! Please, Monsieur Phoebus, give me back my
bodice."

Phoebus drew back, and said coldly, "Oh, mademoiselle,
now I see you don't love me!"

"Not love you!" exclaimed the poor unfortunate girl, at
the same time clinging to the captain, making him sit down
beside her. "Not love you, Phoebus! What are you saying,
wicked man, to tear my heart? Oh, come! Take me! Take all
of me! Do what you will with me! I am yours. What matters
the amulet? What matters my mother? Since I love you, you
are my mother. Phoebus, my beloved Phoebus, do you see
me? It is I. Look at me. It is the little girl whom you will not
spurn, who comes, who comes herself to seek you. My soul,
my life, my all—all belongs to you, my captain. Well,
then—no! We will not marry, since you do not wish it. And
besides, what am I but a wretched girl from the gutter?
While you, my Phoebus, you are a gentleman. A fine thing,
indeed! A dancing girl to marry an officer! I was mad! No,
Phoebus, no. I will be your mistress, your amusement, your
pleasure, when you will, a girl who will be yours. For that
alone was I made, soiled, despised, dishonored, what care I?
If but loved, I shall be the proudest and happiest of women.
And when I am old and ugly, Phoebus, when I am no longer
fit to love you, monseigneur, you will still suffer me to be
your servant. Others will embroider scarfs for you; I, your
servant, will take care of them. I shall polish your spurs,
brush your uniforms, and clean your riding boots. Phoebus,

have pity! But now, take me. Here, Phoebus, all is yours. Only love me. We gypsies need only that—love and air."

Speaking thus, she threw her arms around the captain's neck, looking at him suppliantly and smiling through her tears. Her soft bosom brushed against the rough embroidery of his woolen doublet. Her beautiful half-naked body writhed about his knees. The captain, drunk with passion, pressed his burning lips to her beautiful African shoulders. And the young girl, her eyes cast upward to the ceiling, bent backward, all trembling and palpitating under his warm kisses.

Suddenly, above Phoebus' head, she saw another head, a face, livid, green, convulsive, with the look of hell in its eyes. Close to this face a hand was holding a dagger. It was the face and the hand of the priest. He had broken through the door, and there he was. Phoebus could not see him. The gypsy remained motionless, frozen, made dumb by this terrible apparition—like a dove that raises her head just when the hawk is looking into her nest with his round eyes.

She could not even utter a cry. She saw the dagger descend upon Phoebus, and rise again dripping.

"Curses!" exclaimed the captain, and he fell to the floor. She fainted.

At the moment when her eyes closed, before all feeling had left her, she thought she felt a touch of fire upon her lips, a kiss more burning than the executioner's branding iron.

When she came to, she was surrounded by soldiers of the watch. They were carrying away the captain bathed in his own blood. The priest had disappeared. The window at the back of the room, which opened onto the river, was wide open. They picked up a cloak from the floor which they supposed belonged to the officer. She heard the soldiers talking to one another about her: "She's a witch who has stabbed a captain."

BOOK VIII

1

The Coin Changed into a Dry Leaf

Anxiety gripped Gringoire and the whole Court of Miracles. For more than a month no one knew what had become of La Esmeralda, which sorely grieved the Duke of Egypt and his vagabond friends, nor what had become of her goat, which redoubled the grief of Gringoire. One evening, the gypsy girl had disappeared, and had left no trace. All investigation proved fruitless. Some taunting beggars told Gringoire they had seen her that evening, near the Pont Saint-Michel, with an officer; but this husband, after the fashion of Bohemia, was an incredulous philosopher, and besides he knew better than anyone else how pure his wife was. He had been able to judge how impregnable was her chastity resulting from the two combined virtues of the amulet and of the gypsy herself, and he had mathematically calculated the resistance of this chastity to the second power. So, on that point, his mind was at ease.

Still he could not explain her disappearance. So upset was he, he would have grown thinner if that had been possible. He had in consequence neglected everything, even his literary pursuits, even his great work *De figuris regularibus et irregularibus,*[1] which he intended to have printed as soon as he could get the money. (For he was crazy about printing ever since he had seen the *Didascalon* of Hugues de Saint-Victor printed with the celebrated type of Vindelin de Spires.)

One day when he was passing dejectedly before the Tournelle, a prison for criminals, he noticed a crowd of people milling about one of the doors of the Palace of Justice.

"What's going on?" he asked a young man who was coming out.

"I don't know, sir," answered the young man. "They say there's a woman on trial for murdering an officer. Because witchcraft seems to be entailed, the bishop and the official have an interest in the case, and my brother, who is the Archdeacon of Josas, spends all his time here. Now, I wanted to speak with him, but I couldn't get to him because of the crowds—and this annoys me because I need some money."

"Alas, monsieur," said Gringoire, "would that I could lend you some. But if my breeches have holes, it's not from the weight of crown pieces."

He dared not tell the young man that he knew his brother, the archdeacon, whom he had not sought out since their encounter at the church, a discourtesy which embarrassed Gringoire.

The student went his way, and Gringoire proceeded to follow the crowd which was ascending the staircase of the Grand Chamber. It was his opinion that there was nothing quite like a criminal trial to dissipate melancholy—the judges being usually so delightfully stupid. The people with whom he mingled were slowly moving ahead, elbowing each other in silence. After a tiresome shuffling through a long, gloomy corridor, which wound through the old Palace like an intestinal canal, he came to a low door that opened into an auditorium, which, because of his height, he was able to examine carefully over the heads of the swaying multitude.

The hall was vast and so gloomy that it appeared even more spacious. It was evening, consequently the high arched

[1] "On [rhetorical] figures, regular and irregular."

windows admitted but a few pale rays of light, which were extinguished before they reached the vaulted ceiling, an enormous trellis of carved woodwork, whose thousand figures seemed to be moving about confusedly in the shadows. There were already several lighted candles here and there on the tables. Their feeble light gleamed on the heads of the law clerks, bent over heaps of papers. The part of the hall nearest the door was occupied by the crowd; on the right and left were lawyers seated at tables; at the far end, on a raised platform, were a number of judges, with passive and sinister faces, the last rows of which vanished in the darkness. The walls were strewn with any number of painted fleurs-de-lis. Above the judges could faintly be seen a large figure of Christ; and on all sides were pikes and halberds, which the light of the candles seemed to tip with fire.

"Monsieur," asked Gringoire of one who was standing next to him, "who are all those people over there, ranged like prelates in council?"

"Monsieur," answered the man, "on the right, are the councilors of the grand chamber, and on the left are the councilors of inquiry, the masters in black gowns, and the messires in red ones."

"And above them," continued Gringoire, "who's that big fat red one perspiring?"

"That's Monsieur the President."

"And those sheep behind him?" pursued Gringoire, who, as we have already remarked, wasted no love on the magistracy, which was perhaps due to the grudge which he bore the Palace of Justice ever since his dramatic misadventure.

"They are the lawyers of the court of appeal of the royal palace."

"And that wild boar in front of them?"

"That's the clerk of the court of parliament."

"And on the right, that crocodile?"

"Master Philippe Lheulier, king's advocate extraordinary."

"And to the left, that big black cat?"

"Master Jacques Charmolue, king's attorney in the ecclesiastical court, with the gentlemen of the holy office."

"But, sir," said Gringoire, "pray, what are all these worthy folk doing here?"

"They are trying someone."

"Trying whom? I don't see the accused."

"It's a woman, sir. You can't see her. Her back is to us, and she's hidden by the crowd. Look, there she is, over by those halberds."

"Who is she?" asked Gringoire. "Do you know her name?"

"No, monsieur, I have just arrived. However, I suppose it has something to do with witchcraft since the official attends the trial."

"Well, well!" said the philosopher, "so we are going to see all these men of the robe eat some human flesh. Well, it's a spectacle like any other."

"Monsieur, don't you think," observed his neighbor, "that Master Jacques Charmolue looks like a mild sort?"

"Humph!" answered Gringoire, "I rather question mildness behind a pinched nose and thin lips."

Then bystanders imposed silence on the two talkers. Important testimony was being given.

"My lords," was saying an old woman in the middle of the room, whose face was so hidden by her clothing that she might have been taken for a walking bundle of rags, "my lords, this all is true as my name is La Falourdel, established for forty years on the Pont Saint-Michel, and paying regularly my rent, taxes, and dues. My door is opposite the house of Tassin Caillart, the dyer, who lives on the side looking up the river. I'm a poor old woman now, but once I was a pretty girl, my lords! Just a few days ago, someone was saying to me: 'La Falourdel, don't gallivant too much tonight; the devil likes to comb old women's flax with his horn. It is certain that the phantom monk who last year was roaming about the Cathedral is now roaming around the City. La Falourdel, be careful that he doesn't bang on your door.'

"One evening as I was spinning, someone knocked on my door. 'Who's there?' said I. Someone cursed. I opened the door. Two men came in—a man in black, and a handsome officer. You couldn't see the one in black, excepting his eyes, like two coals. All the rest was cloak and hat. So they said to me, 'Sainte Martha's room.' That's the room on the top floor, my lords, my cleanest room. They gave me an écu. I put the écu in my drawer, and I said to them, 'That will buy some tripe tomorrow at the slaughterhouse of the

Gloriette.' We went upstairs. When we got to the room, while my back was turned, the man in black disappeared. This astonished me a little. The officer, who was as handsome as could be, went downstairs with me. He left the house. In just the time it took me to spin a quarter of a skein he came back again with a beautiful young girl, a belle who would have shone like the sun if she had been properly dressed. She had with her a goat, a big goat, black or white, I can't remember. This made me think ... The girl, she didn't concern me, but the goat! I don't like those animals, with their beards and horns. They look like men. And then, too, a goat smells of witchcraft. But I didn't say anything. I had the money. That's all right, isn't it, Monsieur the Judge? I showed the girl and the captain to the room upstairs, and left them alone, that is to say, with the goat. I went downstairs again and continued spinning.

"I must tell you my house has a ground floor and one story above. In the back it looks onto the river, like the other houses on the bridge. A window on the ground floor and one upstairs open on the river.

"Well, I was spinning, as I said. I don't know why, but I was thinking about the phantom monk, which the goat put into my head—and then the pretty girl was really very strangely dressed! Suddenly I heard a scream upstairs, and something fell on the floor, and the window up there opened. I ran to my window, which is just below, and I saw a black mass falling. It dropped into the river. This was the phantom, dressed like a priest. There was moonlight, so I saw it very plainly. It swam toward the City.

"Then, I was all trembling, and I called the watch. The gentlemen of the guard came, and at first, not knowing what was the matter, as they were half drunk, they began to beat me. I explained to them. Then we went upstairs and what did we find? My poor room all bloodstained; the captain stretched out with a dagger in his neck, the girl pretending to be dead, and the goat all scared. 'Well!' said I. 'It will take me a fortnight to clean the floor; I'll have to scrape it. It'll be a terrible job.' They carried off the officer, poor young fellow! And the girl with no bodice on!

"But wait, the worst of all is that the next day, when I

went to get the écu to buy my tripe, I found a withered leaf in its place."

The old woman stopped talking. A murmur of horror ran through the audience.

"This phantom, this goat, all of it smells of witchcraft," remarked Gringoire's neighbor.

"And this dried leaf!" said another.

"No doubt," remarked a third, "it's a witch who is in cahoots with the phantom priest to rob the officers."

Gringoire himself could scarcely help thinking that there was probably truth in all this, and it frightened him.

"Madame Falourdel," said Monsieur the President with dignity, "have you anything further to say?"

"No, my lord," replied the old woman, "except that in the report my house is referred to as a broken-down, stinking hovel, which is a terrible insult. The houses on the bridge are not the best-looking houses, because there are so many people; but the butchers don't mind living in them, and they are rich men, married to pretty, very proper ladies."

The magistrate, who looked to Gringoire like a crocodile, rose. "Silence!" he said. "I beg you, gentlemen, to bear in mind that a dagger was found on the accused.

"Madame Falourdel, have you brought the withered leaf into which the écu given you by the officer was changed?"

"Yes, my lord," she answered. "I've found it. Here it is."

A clerk passed the dead leaf to the crocodile, who, with a doleful shake of the head, handed it to the president, who, in turn, passed it to the king's attorney of the ecclesiastical court, and so on it made the rounds of the room.

"It is a beech leaf," commented Master Jacques Charmolue, "an additional proof of magic."

A councilor then began: "Witness, two men went upstairs in your house: the man in black, whom you first saw, disappeared, then swam across the Seine in his priestly garb; and the officer. Which of these men gave you the écu?"

The old woman thought a moment, then replied, "It was the officer."

A murmur ran through the crowd.

"Ah!" thought Gringoire, "that changes my conviction."

Meanwhile, Master Philippe Lheulier, king's advocate extraordinary, again interposed, "May I remind you, gentle-

men, that in the statement written at his bedside, the injured
officer, while admitting that he was confused when the man
in black assailed him, thought then that it might be the phantom priest, and added that earlier the phantom had strongly
urged him to keep his rendezvous with the accused, and that,
when the said captain remarked that he had no money, the
phantom had given him the écu which the said officer paid
La Falourdel. Therefore, the écu is a coin from hell."

This concluding observation seemed to end all the doubts
of Gringoire and the other skeptics in the hall.

"Gentlemen, you have all the evidence," added the king's
advocate, seating himself. "You can consult the deposition
of Phoebus de Châteaupers."

At the mention of this name, the prisoner rose. Her head
now could be seen. Gringoire aghast recognized La Esmeralda.

She was pale; her hair, formerly so neatly braided and
stúdded with sequins, fell in disorder; her lips were blue; her
hollow eyes were terrifying. Alas!

"Phoebus!" she shrieked. "Where is he? Oh, my lords, before you kill me, for mercy's sake, tell me if he lives!"

"Woman, be silent!" replied the president. "That is not
our business!"

"Oh, pity! Tell me if he lives," she continued, clasping her
beautiful thin hands. And her chains clattered as they
brushed against her body.

"Well," said the king's advocate, "he is dying. Now are
you content?"

The distraught girl fell back on her seat, speechless, tearless, white, like a wax figure.

The president leaned over to a man seated at his feet, who
wore a gilt cap, a black gown, a chain about his neck, and
carried a wand in his hand.

"Clerk, bring in the second prisoner."

All eyes turned toward the little door, which opened, and
to the fearsome surprise of Gringoire, there was a pretty goat
with gilded feet and horns. The elegant creature stopped a
moment on the threshold, stretching out her neck as if,
perched on the point of a rock, she had before her a vast horizon. All at once she caught sight of the gypsy girl, and,
leaping over the table and the clerk's head in two bounds,

she was at La Esmeralda's knees. Then she rolled herself gracefully over her mistress' feet, begging for a word or a caress. But the prisoner remained motionless; even little Djali could not win a glance from her.

"Why, that's the nasty beast," said old Falourdel; "I recognize it and the girl perfectly."

Jacques Charmolue here interposed. "If it pleases your lordships, we shall proceed with the examination of the goat."

The goat was, indeed, the second prisoner. Nothing was more common in those times than to bring a charge of witchcraft against animals. We find, among others, in the records of the provostry for 1466, the curious details of the expenses for the proceedings against Gillet Soulart and his sow, "executed for their crimes, at Corbeil." Everything is there—the cost of the sty for the sow, the eleven days' care and feed for the same at eight deniers parisis per day, the three pints of wine and the bread, the last meal of the victim, shared in a brotherly manner by the executioner, and the five hundred bundles of wood taken from the wharf of Morsant. Sometimes trials went further even than animals. The capitularies of Charlemagne and Louis the Débonnaire impose severe penalties on fiery phantoms which had the audacity to appear in the air.

Meanwhile the king's attorney exclaimed, "If the demon that possesses this goat, and that resists all exorcisms, persists in its sorceries—if the goat astounds the court with them—we forewarn her that we shall be obliged to demand that she be sentenced to the gallows or the stake."

Gringoire was all in a cold sweat. Charmolue took from the table the gypsy's tambourine, and, presenting it in a certain manner to the goat, he asked, "What time is it?"

The goat eyed him with a wise look, lifted her gilded foot, and struck seven times. Indeed it was seven o'clock. A movement of terror ran through the crowd.

Gringoire could not contain himself.

"Djali'll be her own ruination," he shouted aloud. "You can see she does not know what she is doing!"

"Silence, you people in the back of the room!" cried the usher sharply.

Jacques Charmolue, by manipulating the tambourine in

several ways, made the goat answer several other questions—about the day of the month, the month of the year, etc., which the reader has already witnessed. Now, on account of the atmosphere which is peculiar to judicial proceedings, those same spectators who, perhaps, had more than once applauded in the public streets the innocent performances of Djali, were terrified by them under the roof of the Palace of Justice. The goat unquestionably was possessed by the devil.

The situation became more tense when, the king's attorney having emptied on the floor a certain leather bag full of movable letters, which Djali had about her neck, they saw the goat pick out with her foot from among the scattered alphabet the fatal name "Phoebus." The sorcery of which the captain had been the victim seemed irrevocably demonstrated, and in the eyes of all, this gypsy girl, this charming dancer, who had so often dazzled the passersby with her gracefulness, was no more than a frightful witch.

She on her part gave no sign of life. She was conscious neither of the graceful tricks of Djali nor of the threats of the judges nor of the stifled imprecations of the auditory. Nothing roused her.

To get her attention, a sergeant had to shake her pitilessly, and the president had to raise his voice solemnly.

"Girl, you are of the Bohemian race, given to evil deeds. In consort with this bewitched goat, implicated in the charge, you did, on the night of the twenty-ninth of March last, wound and stab, in concert with the powers of darkness, by the aid of charms and spells, a captain of the king's archers, Phoebus de Châteaupers. Do you persist in denying the charge?"

"O horrors!" cried the young girl, hiding her face with her hands. "My Phoebus! Oh! This is hell!"

"Do you persist in denying the charge?" repeated the president coldly.

"Yes, I do deny it!" she said vehemently. She rose and her eyes flashed.

The president continued sternly, "Then how do you explain the facts contained in the charge?"

She answered in a broken voice, "I have told you already.

I cannot. It was a priest—a priest whom I do not know. An infernal priest who pursues me!"

"Just so," replied the judge. "The phantom priest!"

"O my lords, have pity on me! I am only a poor girl . . ." And she sank to her seat.

"From Egypt," said the judge.

Master Jacques Charmolue then said as gently as he could, "In view of the persistent obstinacy of the accused, I demand the application of torture."

"Granted," said the president.

The poor unfortunate girl began to shudder. She rose, however, at the order of the guards, and, preceded by Charmolue and the priests of the office, walked with a surprisingly firm step, between two rows of halberds, toward a door, which suddenly opened and shut again after her, having the effect upon Gringoire of a mouth which had just devoured her.

When she disappeared, a plaintive bleating was heard. It was the little goat crying.

The court adjourned. A councilor having observed that the judges were tired, and that it would be long to wait for the conclusion of the torture, the president answered that a magistrate must sacrifice himself to his duty.

"What a troublesome, vexatious hussy!" said an old judge, "to make us apply the torture now, when we haven't yet supped!"

2

Sequel to the Coin Changed into a Dry Leaf

Having ascended and descended several flights of steps in passages so dark that they were lighted by lamps, even during the day, La Esmeralda, still surrounded by her lugubrious attendants, was pushed by the sergeants of the Palace into a sinister-looking room. This room, circular in shape, occupied the ground floor of one of those large towers which still in our day appear through the layer of recent edifices with which modern Paris has covered the ancient one. There were no windows in this dungeon, no other opening than the low entrance that was closed by an enormously heavy iron door. Yet there was some light. There was a furnace built into the thickness of the wall. A roaring fire blazed therein and filled the entire chamber with its red glare and almost obliterated the room's one miserable candle. The iron portcullis, which served as a door to the furnace, was raised at the moment, so that over its flaming mouth there were to be seen only the lower extremities of the bars, resembling a row of black, sharp, parted teeth, which made the furnace look like the mouth of one of those legendary dragons which vomited fire and smoke. By the blood-red light which glowed from it, the prisoner could see all around the chamber an assemblage of horrible instruments, the uses of which she did not understand. In the middle of the room lay a leather mattress that almost touched the ground, over which hung a leather strap with a buckle, attached to a copper ring which a grotesque monster sculptured in the keystone of the vault held between his teeth. Tongs, pincers, broad ploughshares, were heaped inside the furnace pell-mell, and were heating red-hot on the burning coals. This Tartarus was simply called *la chambre de la question,* the torture chamber.

Seated on the bed, unconcerned, was Pierrat Torterue, the official torturer. His assistants, two square-faced gnomes, with leather aprons and tarpaulin coats, were turning the irons over the coals.

In vain had the poor girl summoned all her courage; on entering this chamber she was seized with horror.

The sergeants of the bailiff of the Palace were ranged on one side, while the priests of the Office were ranged on the other. To one side near the wall was a table at which sat a clerk with pen, ink, and paper. Master Jacques Charmolue approached the gypsy girl with a patronizing smile.

"My dear child," he said, "you still persist in denying the allegations against you?"

"Yes," she replied in a voice scarcely audible.

"In that case," resumed Charmolue, "it will be our painful task to torture you more urgently than we should otherwise wish. Would you kindly sit on that bed. Master Pierrat, make room for mademoiselle, and shut the door."

Pierrat rose, growling. "If I shut the door," he muttered, "my fire will go out."

"Well, then, my friend," replied Charmolue, "leave it open."

Meanwhile, La Esmeralda remained standing. That leather bed, upon which so many wretches had twisted and squirmed, scared her. Terror froze the very marrow of her bones. She just stood there, frightened and stupefied. At the sign from Charmolue, the two assistants seized her and put her on the bed. They did not hurt her, but when these men touched her, when that leather bed touched her, she felt all her blood flow back to her heart. She looked wildly around the room. She imagined she saw moving and walking from all sides toward her, to crawl up her whole body and pinch and bite her, all those monstrously shaped implements of torture, which were, among the instruments of all kinds that she had hitherto seen, what bats, centipedes, and spiders are to birds and insects.

"Where is the physician?" asked Charmolue.

"Here," answered a black robe whom she had not observed before.

She shuddered.

"Mademoiselle," resumed the coaxing voice of the attorney of the ecclesiastical court, "for the third time, do you persist in denying the charges that have been brought against you?"

This time she could only make a sign with her head. Her voice had failed utterly.

"You persist then," said Jacques Charmolue. "Then, I am very sorry, but I must perform the duties of my office."

"Monsieur the King's Attorney," said Pierrat gruffly, "what shall we begin with?"

Charmolue hesitated a moment, with the ambiguous grimace of a poet who is looking for a rhyme.

"With the buckskin," he said at last.

The poor unfortunate creature felt herself so completely abandoned by God and man that her head dropped on her chest like a thing inert which has no power of itself.

The torturer and the physician both approached her at once. At the same time, the two assistants began stirring in their hideous arsenal.

At the clanking of those terrible irons, the wretched gypsy started like a motionless frog that one has suddenly prodded.

"Oh!" she murmured, so low that no one heard her. "O my Phoebus!"

She then sank again into her previous insensibility and stony silence. Her appearance would have wrung any heart, except her judges'. She resembled a poor sinful soul being questioned by Satan at hell's flaming gate. The miserable body on which was to fasten that frightful swarm of saws, wheels, and pulleys—the being about to be handled so roughly by those grim executioners and torturing pincers— was, then, that soft, fair, and fragile creature. A poor grain of millet which human justice was sending to be ground by the horrid millstones of torture.

Meanwhile, the callous hands of Pierrat Torterue's assistants had brutally stripped that charming leg and that little foot which had so often astonished the passersby with their grace and beauty in the streets of Paris.

"It's a shame!" growled the torturer, as his eyes scanned those graceful, delicate limbs. If the archdeacon had been there, he certainly would have recalled at that moment his symbol of the spider and the fly. Soon the unfortunate girl saw through the cloud which spread before her eyes the buskin approaching; soon she saw her foot, encased between the iron-bound boards, disappear within this terrible apparatus. Terror renewed her strength. "Take it off!" she screamed wildly, straightening up all disheveled. "Mercy!"

She darted off the bed to throw herself at the feet of the king's attorney, but her leg was caught in the heavy block of oak and ironwork, and she sank on the wooden trap more broken than a bee with a heavy weight upon its wings.

At a sign from Charmolue, they replaced her on the bed, and two big hands fastened around her small waist the leather strap that hung from the ceiling.

"For the last time, do you plead guilty to the charges?" asked Charmolue with his imperturbable benignity.

"I am innocent."

"Then, mademoiselle, how do you explain the circumstances of the charge?"

"Alas! my lord, I cannot."

"You deny them?"

"Everything!"

"Proceed," said Charmolue to Pierrat. Pierrat turned the

screw; the buskin tightened, and the wretched girl uttered one of those horrible cries which can't be written in any human language.

"Stop," said Charmolue to Pierrat.

"Do you confess?" he asked the gypsy.

"Yes, everything!" cried the wretched girl. "I confess! I confess! Mercy!"

She had overestimated her strength in braving these tortures. Poor child whose life till then had been so joyous, so pleasant, so sweet—the first experience of pain had vanquished her.

"Humanity obliges me to inform you," observed the king's attorney, "that in pleading guilty you have only the death sentence to look forward to."

"I wish for death," she said. And she fell back on the leather bed, limply hanging from the strap buckled around her waist.

"Come on! Up with you, my pretty one," said Master Pierrat, raising her. "You look like a golden sheep that hangs about the neck of Monsieur of Burgundy."

Jacques Charmolue raised his voice.

"Clerk, write it down—young gypsy girl, you confess your participation in the love feasts, sabbaths, and sorceries of hell, in company with evil spirits, witches, and ghouls? Answer."

"Yes," she said, so low that the word was lost in a whisper.

"You confess having seen the ram which Beelzebub causes to appear in the clouds to summon his children to their sabbath, and which is seen only by sorcerers?"

"Yes."

"You confess having adored the heads of Bophomet, those abominable idols of the Templars?"

"Yes."

"Having had, in the form of a common she-goat, frequent intercourse with the devil, as mentioned in the charge?"

"Yes."

"Lastly, do you confess and plead guilty to the charge that, with the assistance of the devil, and the phantom commonly called the phantom monk, you did on the night of the twenty-ninth of March last, attack and stab one captain named Phoebus de Châteaupers?"

She raised her large glassy eyes toward the magistrate, and answered, as if mechanically, without any display of emotion, "Yes." It was evident that her spirit was utterly broken.

"Write it down, clerk," said Charmolue, and addressing himself to the torturers, "Release the prisoner, and take her back to the courtroom."

When the buskin was removed, the attorney of the ecclesiastical court examined her foot, still numb with pain.

"Come," he said, "it doesn't hurt much. You cried out just in time. You could still dance, my pretty one!"

Then he turned toward his acolytes of the official saying, "Justice at last is enlightened. That's a comfort, my lords! Mademoiselle will bear witness that we all treated her with all possible leniency."

3

End of the Coin Changed into a Dry Leaf

When she re-entered the courtroom, pale and limping, she was greeted by a general murmur of pleasure. On the part of the public it was that feeling of satisfied impatience which is experienced in the theater at the conclusion of the last intermission when the curtain is raised and the denouement is about to unfold. On the part of the judges it was the hope of soon eating their supper. The little goat, too, bleated for joy. She wanted to run to her mistress but she had been tied to a bench.

Night had now fallen. The candles, whose number had not been increased, threw off so little light that the walls of the room could not be seen. Darkness enveloped every object in a sort of mist. A few apathetic judges' faces were scarcely visible. Opposite them, at the other end of the long room, they could barely see an indistinct white object against the somber background. That was the prisoner.

She had hobbled to her place. When Charmolue had magisterially installed himself in his, he sat down; then rose again and said, without showing too much of the vanity of success, "The accused has confessed everything."

"Gypsy girl," continued the president, "you have pleaded guilty to all your deeds of sorcery, prostitution, and the murder of Phoebus de Châteaupers?"

Her heart was broken. She was heard sobbing in the darkness.

"Whatever you please," she answered weakly, "but put me to death quickly."

"Monsieur the King's Attorney of the Ecclesiastical Court," said the president, "the court is ready to hear your requisitions."

Master Charmolue exhibited a forbidding scroll, and began to read with many gestures and with the exaggerated emphasis of the bar, a Latin oration in which all the evidence of the trial was constructed in Ciceronian periphrases, flanked by citations from Plautus, a comic author whom he much favored. We regret that it is impossible to reproduce for our readers this remarkable bit of eloquence. The orator delivered it with marvelous aplomb. He had not yet finished the exordium, when perspiration began to trickle down his forehead and his eyes seemed to bulge from their sockets. All at once, in the middle of a finely turned phrase, he suddenly stopped, and his face, which was usually mild enough, and indeed, stupid enough, became absolutely purple.

"Gentlemen," he cried (this time in French, for it was not written in the scroll), "Satan is so mixed up in this affair that, behold! he attends our councils now and is mocking their majesty. Look!"

And so speaking, he pointed to the little goat, which, seeing Charmolue gesticulating had thought it quite proper that she should do the same. So, she stood on her hind legs, and imitated as well as she could, with her forefeet and bearded head, in pathetic pantomime, the king's attorney in the ecclesiastical court. It was, if you remember, one of her cleverest tricks. This incident, this final proof, produced a hilarious uproar. The ushers tied the goat's feet, and the king's attorney resumed the thread of his eloquence.

It was a long thread indeed, but the peroration was exquisite. Here is the last sentence of it. We leave the reader's imagination to supply the hoarse voice and weary gestures of Master Charmolue:

"That is why, gentlemen, the witchcraft being proved, and the crime being obvious, as likewise the criminal intent, in the name of the holy church of Notre-Dame de Paris, which is possessed of the right of all manner of justice, high and low, on this inviolate island of the City, we declare by the tenor of those present that we do require, firstly, some pecuniary compensation; secondly, an honorable penance before the great door of the cathedral church of Notre-Dame; thirdly, a sentence by virtue of which this witch and her goat shall, either in the public square, commonly called the Grève, or on the island in the river Seine, adjacent to the point of the royal gardens, be executed."

He put on his cap and sat down.

"Whew!" sighed Gringoire, overwhelmed by this ecclesiastical Latin.

Another man in a black gown rose near the prisoner; it was her advocate. The starving judges began to grumble.

"Monsieur Advocate, be brief," said the president.

"Monsieur President," answered the advocate, "since the defendant has confessed to the crime, I have only one word to say to your lordships. Here is an excerpt from the Salic law: 'If a witch has eaten a man, and is convicted of it, she shall pay a fine of eight thousand deniers, which make two hundred sous of gold.' May it please the court sentence my client to pay the fine."

"The text is obsolete," said the king's advocate extraordinary.

"*Nego!*"[1] replied the defense attorney.

"Put it to a vote!" said a councillor. "The crime has been proven, and the hour is late."

The vote was taken without going out of the room. The judges voted by lifting their caps—they were in a hurry. Their capped heads were seen uncovered one after another in the shadows as the question was addressed to each in a low voice by the president. The poor prisoner seemed to be looking at them, but her distraught eye no longer saw anything.

[1] "I deny it."

Then the clerk began to write. When finished, he handed the long parchment to the president. The pitiable girl heard the crowd stirring, the pikes clashing, and an icy voice saying, "Gypsy girl, on such a day as it shall please our lord the king, at the hour of noon, you shall be dressed in a smock, and go barefooted, with a rope around your neck, to be taken in a tumbrel to the great door of Notre-Dame, and there you shall do honorable penance with a wax candle of two pounds weight in your hands; from there you shall be taken to the Place de Grève, where you shall be hanged and strangled on the town gibbet, and your goat likewise; furthermore, you shall pay the official three gold lions, in reparation for the crimes by you committed, and by you confessed, of sorcery, magic, prostitution, and murder upon the person of Sieur Phoebus de Châteaupers. May God have mercy on your soul!"

"Oh, it's a dream!" she murmured, as she felt rough hands laid upon her to take her away.

4

Lasciate Ogni Speranza[1]

In the Middle Ages, when an edifice was complete, there was almost as much of it underground as above. Unless it were constructed upon piles, like Notre-Dame, a palace, a fortress, or a church had always a double foundation. In the cathedrals it was some kind of second subterranean cathedral, low, dark, mysterious, blind, and mute under the upper nave, which always was resplendent with light and resounded with organ music and the pealing of the bells night and day. Sometimes the lower one was a sepulcher. In the palaces and the bastilles, this space was often used as a dungeon—sometimes as a sepulcher—and sometimes it served as both. These mighty buildings, the mode of whose formation and growth we have elsewhere detailed, not only had foundations, but, as it were, roots which branched out underground into chambers, galleries, and staircases, like the

[1] "Abandon all hope."

structure above it. The cellars of an edifice thus formed yet another edifice, into which you descended instead of ascended, and which had subterranean stories beneath the pile of exterior stories of the structure like those inverted forests and mountains which are seen mirrored in the waters of a lake adjacent to the forests and mountains on its shore.

At the Bastille Saint-Antoine, at the Palace of Justice, and at the Louvre, these underground structures were prisons. The stories of these prisons, the deeper into the ground they went, grew narrower and darker. They were like so many zones layered according to the different shades of horror. Dante could have found nothing better upon which to base his Inferno. These dungeon-funnels usually terminated in a low hollow, shaped like the bottom of a tub, into which Dante consigned his Satan, and in which society consigned the criminal condemned to death. Once a miserable human being was there confined, then farewell light, air, life, *ogni speranza*. That person never left it but for the gallows or the stake. Sometimes he rotted there. Human justice called that forgetting. Between mankind and himself, the condemned felt upon his head an accumulation of stones and jailers; the massive bastille was but one enormous complicated lock that barred him from the living world.

It was one of those deep pits, the *oubliettes* excavated by Saint-Louis, into the *in pace* of the Tournelle, that—for fear of her escaping, no doubt—they had put La Esmeralda, condemned to the gibbet, with the colossal Palace of Justice over her head. Poor fly! She could not have moved the smallest of its stones!

Surely, Providence and society had been equally unjust; such a heavy load of misfortune and torture was not necessary to crush so fragile a creature.

There she was, lost in darkness, buried, entombed, walled in. Anyone who could have seen her in that state, after having seen her laugh and dance in the sunshine, would have shuddered. Cold like night, cold like death, not a breath of air any longer in her hair, no longer a human voice to hear, not a ray of light to see, broken in two she was, burdened with chains, crouched near a pitcher and a morsel of bread, upon a little straw, in a pool of water that formed under her from the seeping dungeon, motionless, almost not breathing, almost beyond the pale of suffering. Phoebus, the sunshine, noonday, the open air, the streets of Paris, dancing to the applause of spectators, the whispered sweet nothings of love with the captain, and then, the old woman, the priest, the dagger, the blood, the torture, the gibbet. All this was again passing through her mind, sometimes like a gay and golden vision, sometimes like a monstrous nightmare. But now everything was no more than a horrible, vague struggle fought in the darkness, or like faraway music that was still playing above ground, but which was no longer audible in the depths into which the poor creature had fallen.

Since she had been there, she was neither awake nor asleep. In her misery in this dungeon she could no longer distinguish waking from sleeping, dream from reality, than she could day from night. All happenings were mingled, twisted, floating, confused, and scattered in her thoughts. She no longer felt, she no longer knew, she no longer thought. At most she dreamed. Never had a living creature been plunged so deeply into nothingness.

Thus numb, frozen, petrified, scarcely did she notice the noise of the trapdoor, the two or three times it opened somewhere about her, without even admitting a ray of light, but through which a hand had thrown her a crust of black bread. However, this periodic visit of the jailer was the only remaining contact she had with mankind.

One persistent sound only did she hear. That was the regular drip of water that filtered through the moldy stones of the vault above her head. She listened stupidly to the splash, splash, splash of each drop as it fell into the pool beside her feet.

This drop of water falling into the pool was the only movement of which she was conscious, the only clock which measured time, the only noise of all the noises made on earth that came to her.

Indeed, she also felt from time to time, in that filthy dark cesspool, something cold crawling here and there over her feet and arms, and she would shiver.

How long she had been there, she did not know. She vaguely remembered a death sentence pronounced somewhere upon someone, and that then they had carried her away, and that she had awakened, cold, in this darkness and silence. She had dragged herself about on her hands; but iron rings had cut her ankles and chains had clanked. She had discerned that there was a wall all around her—that beneath her were damp flagstones and a bundle of straw. But there was neither lamp nor window. She had then seated herself on the straw, and sometimes for a change in position, she would sit upon the lowest step of a stone flight which was in her dungeon. Once she had tried counting the dark minutes measured by the dropping water, but the monotony of this employment soon lulled her into a stupor again.

Finally, one day or night (for midnight and midday were the same color in this tomb), she heard above her a noise louder than was usually made by the jailer when he brought her bread and pitcher of water. She looked up and saw a reddish glow streaming through the cracks of the trapdoor in the vaulted ceiling of the dungeon. At the same time the heavy iron lock creaked, the trapdoor grated on its rusty hinges, turned back, and she saw a lantern, a hand, and the lower part of the bodies of two men, the door being too low for her to see their faces. The light so hurt her eyes that she had to close them.

When she opened them again, the door was closed, the lantern was sitting on a step on the staircase. A man, alone, stood before her. A monk's black robe fell to his feet, a hood of the same color hid his face. Nothing of his person could be seen, neither his face nor his hands. It was a long black shroud which stood straight, and under which she sensed something moved. For several minutes she fixed her eyes on this kind of specter. Meanwhile neither of them spoke. You might have thought two statues were confronting each other. Two things alone seemed to be alive in this tomb: the wick of the lantern, which hissed because of the dampness in the atmosphere, and the drop of water from the ceiling which broke the irregular hissing sound by its monotonous splash, and made the flame of the lantern flicker in concentric rings on the slimy water of the pool.

At length it was the prisoner who broke the silence.

"Who are you?"

"A priest."

The word, the tone, the sound of the voice, made her tremble.

The priest continued in a low voice, "Are you prepared?"

"For what?"

"For death."

"Oh!" she said, "will it be soon?"

"Tomorrow."

Her head, which she had raised joyfully, fell back again on her bosom.

"It is a long time till then!" she murmured. "Why not today? It would have made no difference to them."

"Are you very unhappy then?" asked the priest, after a long silence.

"I am very cold," she answered.

She held her feet between her hands, and her teeth chattered.

The priest's eyes, shaded by his hood, seemed to wander around the dungeon.

"Without light! Without fire! In water! This is horrible!"

"Yes," she answered, with that bewildered air which misery had given her. "Daylight is for everyone. Why do they give me only the night?"

"Do you know," resumed the priest, after another long silence, "why you are here?"

"I think I knew it once," she said, passing her bony fingers across her brow as if to aid her memory, "but I don't any more."

Suddenly she began to cry like a child. "I want to leave here, monsieur. I am cold and afraid. And there are insects crawling all over my body."

"Well, follow me."

With these words, the priest took her arm. The wretched girl was frozen to her bones, yet that hand felt cold to her.

"Oh!" she murmured. "It's the icy hand of death. Who are you?"

The priest raised his hood. She looked. It was that sinister face which had haunted her for so long, that demon's head that had appeared to her at La Falourdel's, above the adored head of her Phoebus, that eye which she had the last time seen flashing beside the dagger.

This apparition, always having boded ill to her, had pushed her from one misfortune to another, even to death. It now roused her from her stupor. It seemed to her as if the sort of veil which had woven itself across her memory was torn away. All the horrible details of her adventure, from the night scene at La Falourdel's to her condemnation at the Tournelle, all at once came to mind, not vague and confused as hitherto, but distinct, clearcut, palpitating, terrible. These remembrances, almost effaced by an excess of suffering, were revived at the sight of the gloomy specter before her, just as the approach of fire brings out afresh upon the white paper the invisible letters traced on it with sympathetic ink. All the wounds of her heart were reopened and bleeding again.

"Ha!" she cried, her hands over her eyes and trembling convulsively, "it's the priest!"

She then let fall her arms, limp, and remained sitting, her head down, her eyes fixed on the floor, speechless. Her trembling continued.

The priest looked at her with the eye of a hawk which has been for a long time descending in silence from the highest reaches of heaven, in circles gradually more and more contracted around a poor lark swinging on a reed, and, having suddenly pounced like winged lightning upon its prey, clutches the panting victim in its talons.

She began to murmur in a low tone, "Finish me! Finish me! The last blow!" And she settled her head between her shoulders like a sheep which awaits the butcher's fatal blow.

"Are you afraid of me?" he asked at last.

Her lips contracted as if she were smiling. "Yes," she said. "The executioner jeers at the condemned! For months he has pursued me, threatened me, terrified me. But for him, my God, how happy I was! It is he who has thrown me into this abyss! It is he who has killed. . . . It is he that killed him, my Phoebus!"

Here, bursting into sobs, and lifting her eyes toward the priest, she cried, "O wretch! who are you? What have I done to you? Do you hate me so? Alas! what do you hold against me?"

"I love you!" cried the priest.

Her tears suddenly stopped. She looked at him with a vacant look. He had knelt at her knees and fixed upon her his fiery eyes.

"Do you hear? I love you!" he cried again.

"But with what kind of love?" she shuddered.

"The love of one damned!"

Both remained silent for some minutes, crushed by the weight of their emotions; he frantic, she stupefied.

"Listen," said the priest at last, and a singular calm now possessed him. "You shall know everything. I am going to tell you what till now I have scarcely dared to tell myself, when secretly I have searched my conscience in those deep hours of the night when it has been so dark that it seemed as if God could no longer see me. Listen. Before I met you, young girl, I was happy . . ."

"And I too!" she sighed feebly.

"Don't interrupt me. Yes, I was happy. At least I thought I was. I was pure. My soul was filled with limpid light. No head was raised so high or so proudly as mine. Priests consulted me about chastity, doctors about doctrine. Yes, knowledge meant much to me. She was a sister, and a sister who filled all my needs. But now, with maturity, other thoughts torment me. More than once my blood has quickened at the passing of some female form. The power of sex and of a man's blood that, foolish youth, I had thought stifled forever has more than once shaken convulsively the chain of iron vows that bind me, miserable wretch, to the cold stones of the altar. But fasting, prayer, study, the mortifications of the cloister again made my soul mistress of my body. Besides, I avoided women. Moreover, I had only to open a book for all the impure vapors of my brain to evaporate before the splendor of science. In a few minutes all the gross things of earth fled from before me, and again I became calm, beguiled, serene in the peaceful light of everlasting truth. So long as the demon only sent me vague shadows of women to encounter; so long as women passed here and there before my eyes, in church, on the streets, in the fields, and rarely appeared in my dreams, I vanquished them easily. Alas! if victory did not stay with me, the fault was God's, who did not make man and the devil of equal strength. Listen. One day . . ."

Here the priest stopped, and the prisoner heard rise from his chest a sigh which seemed to tear and twist him.

He resumed, "One day I was leaning against the window of my cell . . . What was I reading then? Oh! all is confused now in my mind. I was reading. My window overlooked the square. I heard the music of a tambourine. Peeved at being disturbed in my reverie, I looked down on the square. What I saw, and there were others who saw it too, was not a spectacle for human eyes. There, in the middle of the pavement—it was noontime with bright sunshine—a creature was dancing—a creature so beautiful that God would have preferred her to the Virgin, and would have chosen her for His mother, would have been born of her, if she had existed when He became man! Her eyes were black and sparkling. In her raven hair, there were strands which the sunbeams caught, and they gleamed like threads of gold. Her feet flowed together, in their quick movements, like the spokes of a wheel that is spinning rapidly. Around her head, in her black tresses, there were sequins, which sparkled in the sunlight and formed about her brow a diadem of stars. Her blue dress was studded thickly with spangles, that twinkled and sparkled, like fireflies on a summer night. Her brown, graceful arms twined and untwined about her body like two silk scarves. Her figure was of rare beauty. Oh! the dazzling figure, which stood out like something luminous even in the sunlight itself! Alas! young maiden, it was you! Surprised, intoxicated, enchanted, I allowed myself to go on looking. I looked at you for so long that all at once I shivered with fright. I felt that the hand of Fate had touched me."

The priest, quite overcome, again stopped for a minute before continuing.

"Already half seduced, I tried to cling to something that would break my fall. I recalled the snares which Satan had already laid for me. The creature before my eyes was of that supernatural beauty which can come only from heaven or hell. She was no mere girl made of a little of our earth, and feebly lighted within by the flickering ray of a woman's soul. It was an angel, but of darkness—a flame, not a light. Just when I was thinking these thoughts, I saw near you a goat, a witch's beast, which looked at me and laughed. The noonday sun turned its horns to fire. Then I spotted the demon's trap, and I no more doubted that you came from hell, and that you came to destroy me. I believed so."

Here the priest looked in the face of the prisoner, and

added coldly, "I believe it still. But your charm operated slowly, your dancing whirled in my brain. I could feel the mysterious spell working within me. All that should have been alert fell asleep in my soul, and like those who die in the snow, I found pleasure in yielding to this slumber. All at once, you began to sing. What could I do, wretch that I was? Your song was more bewitching than your dance. I wanted to flee. But it was impossible. I was caught, rooted in the pavement. It seemed that I had sunk to my knees in the marble flagstones. I had to stay to the end. My feet were ice; my brain was a boiling cauldron. At length, you took pity upon me; your singing ceased and you disappeared. But the picture of the dazzling vision, the echo of the enchanting music, vanished by degrees. Then I slumped into the corner of the window, more inert and insecure than an unseated statue. The tolling of Vespers woke me. I rose. I fled, but alas! there was something in me that had fallen, never to rise again— something had come upon me from which I could not flee!"

He paused again and then continued, "Yes, from that day forward, there was within me a spirit I did not know. I had recourse to all my remedies: the cloister, the altar, work, books. Folly! Oh! how hollow does science ring when a head full of passions is dashed against it. Do you know, young girl, what I always see between the book and me? It is you. Your shadow, the picture of that luminous apparition which one day crossed the space before me, ever haunts me. But that vision no longer wears the same color. Now it is somber, funereal, dark—like the black splotches that linger before the eyes of the imprudent one who has gazed too long into the sun.

"I am unable to get rid of it. I am always hearing your song ringing in my ears, always seeing your feet dancing on my breviary; always in my dreams at night, I feel your form close in my arms. I have wanted to see you again, to know who you are, to touch you, to see if I should find you indeed equal to the ideal image that I had of you, to change perhaps my dream into reality. In any case, I had hoped that a new impression would banish the former one, because the former had become for me insupportable. I sought you. I saw you again. Alas! Having seen you twice, I wanted to see you a thousand times. I wanted to see you always! So, how to stop my slide into hell! Then I belonged no longer to myself. The other end of the thread with which the demon had attached me to his wings, he had tied to your foot. I became a vagrant like you. I waited for you under porches; I spied on you from street corners; I watched you from the top of my tower. Every night, searching the innermost depths of my soul, I found myself more charmed, more desperate, more bewitched, more lost!

"I learned who you are, a gypsy, a Bohemian, a gitane, a zingara. So how could I doubt your powers of magic? Listen. I hoped that a trial would release me from your charm. A sorceress had bewitched Bruno of Asti; he had her burned, and he was cured. I knew that, so I wanted to try the remedy. I sought first to get you banned from the Parvis of Notre-Dame, hoping that I would forget you if you came no more. But you did come again, regardless of the prohibition. Then I thought of carrying you off. One night I attempted it. There were two of us. Just as we had caught you, that wretched officer came upon us and saved you. Thus he became the beginning of your misfortunes, of mine, and of his own.

"Finally, not knowing what further to do, not knowing what was to become of me, I denounced you to the official. I thought I would be cured like Bruno of Asti. I thought, also, confusedly, that a trial would deliver you into my power, that in prison I should possess you; that there, you could not escape me. Since you had possessed me so long, I desired to possess you in my turn. When one thinks evil, one may as well consummate it. 'Tis madness to stop midway! The extremity of crime has its delirium of joy. A priest and a witch may join in ecstasy upon the straw of a dungeon floor!

"So I denounced you. It was then that I terrified you whenever I met you. The plot that I was scheming against you, the storm that I was brewing over your head, showed in my muttered threats and lightning glances. Still, however, I hesitated. My plan, if executed, was so appalling that I did pause.

"Perhaps I should have renounced my designs; perhaps the hideous idea would have left my brain without producing any result. I imagined that it would depend on me to follow up or to stop the proceedings whenever I pleased. But every evil thought is inexorable, and desires its realization; and thus, when I thought myself all-powerful, fate was more powerful than I. Alas! Alas! It is fate that seized you and delivered you to the terrible operations of the machine which I had secretly set in motion! Listen. I have almost finished.

"One day—it was another day full of sunshine—I saw a man pass before me who pronounced your name and laughed. There was lust in his eyes. Damnation! I followed him. You know the rest."

He was silent.

The young girl could find only the words, "O my Phoebus!"

"Do not utter that name!" said the priest, violently seizing her arm. "Don't mention that name. Oh, wretched creatures that we are, it is that name that has been our undoing! Or rather, fate's inexplicable ways have been the undoing of us all! You are suffering, are you not? You are cold. Darkness blinds you. This dungeon envelops you. But perhaps you have still some light shining within you. Perhaps it is only your childish love for that empty being that was trifling with your heart! While I, I bear the dungeon within me, within me is the winter, the ice, the despair. Darkness is in my soul. Do you know all that I have suffered? I attended your trial. I was seated on the official's bench. Yes, under one of those priestly hoods were the contortions of one damned. When they led you in, I was there. When they questioned you, I was there. O den of wolves! It was my crime, my gibbet that I saw being constructed over you! At each deposition, at each proof, at each pleading, I was there. I could count each one of your steps on your road of sorrow. I was there too when that wild beast . . . Oh, I had not foreseen torture! Listen. I followed you into that chamber of torment. I saw you undressed and stripped half naked by the vile hand of the torturer. I saw your foot, that foot I would have given an empire to press one kiss upon and die, that foot under which I could feel such delight in having my head crushed, that foot I saw put into the horrible buskin, that buskin which turns the limb of a living being into one bloody pulp! O miserable wretch! While I watched all this, I had a dagger under my cassock with which I was lacerating my breast. And when you screamed, I plunged it into my flesh. Had you screamed

again, I would have plunged it into my heart! Look. I believe it still bleeds."

He opened his cassock. His chest was torn as if by the
claws of a tiger, and in his side there was a large wound,
hardly healed.

Esmeralda recoiled in horror.

"Oh," said the priest, "young girl, have pity upon me!
You think yourself miserable. Alas! Alas! You do not know
what misery is. Oh, to love a woman! to be a priest! to be
hated! to love her with all the fury of one's soul! to feel that
one would give, for the least of her smiles, one's blood,
one's life, one's fame, one's salvation, immortality and eternity, this life and that which is to come; to regret not being
a king, or an emperor, or a genius, or an archangel, or God,
that one might place a greater slave under her feet; to hold
her day and night in one's dreams, in one's thoughts; and
then to see her in love with a soldier's uniform, and to have
nothing to offer her but a priest's soiled cassock, which
frightens and disgusts her! To be present, with one's jealousy and one's rage, while she lavishes on a stupid braggart
her treasures of love and beauty! To behold that form which
maddens, that voluptuous bosom, that flesh panting and
blushing under the kisses of another! O heaven! To love her
foot, her arm, her shoulder—to think of her blue veins, of
her brown skin, till one writhes for whole nights on the
pavement of one's cell, and to see all those caresses one has
dreamed of end in her torture—to have succeeded only in
laying her on the bed of leather! O these are true pincers
heated in the fires of hell! Oh blessed is he that is sawed in
two between two planks, or torn to pieces by four horses!
Do you know what torture it is when, during long nights, the
arteries boil, the heart is bursting, the head is splitting, and
one's own teeth bite one's own hands; when inexorable tor-
mentors are unceasingly turning one, as on a burning grid-
iron, because of thoughts of love, jealousy, and despair?
Young girl, mercy! I beg you, desist for a moment! Place a
few ashes on this living coal. Wipe away, please, the perspiration that streams in large drops from my brow! Child, torture me with one hand, but caress me with the other! Have
pity! Have pity on me!"

The priest rolled in the water on the floor, striking his

head against the corners of the stone steps. The young girl
listened to him, watched him. When he stopped, exhausted
and panting, she said again half in a whisper, "O my Phoebus!"

The priest crawled to her on his knees. "I implore you,"
he cried, "if you have any feeling of compassion, do not
spurn me. Oh, I love you! I am a miserable wretch! When
you say his name, it is as if you were grinding between your
teeth every fiber of my heart. Mercy! Mercy! If you come
from hell, there will I go also. I have done enough to deserve that. The hell where you will be is my paradise. The
sight of you is more to be desired than that of God! Oh,
speak, will you not have me! I should have thought that
mountains would have been moved before a woman would
have repulsed such a love. Oh, if you wished, how happy we
should be! We would run away. I would arrange for you to
escape. We would go somewhere. We would seek that spot
on the earth where the sun is brightest, the trees most luxuriant, the sky the bluest. We would love each other. Our two
souls would be as one, and each of us would have an unsat-
isfied thirst for the other, which we would quench incessantly and in common at that inexhaustible fountain of
love!"

She interrupted with a terrible and loud laugh.

"Look, father! you have blood under your nails!"

"Yes, yes," he at length replied, with unusual mildness.
"Insult me, jeer at me, scorn me! But come, come. Let us
hasten. It is tomorrow, I tell you. The gibbet of the Grève!
It is always ready. It is horrible! To see you carried off in
that tumbrel! Oh mercy! I never knew until this moment
how much I love you. Oh, follow me! You will take your
own time to love me after I have saved you. You can hate
me as long as you wish. But come now! Tomorrow! Tomorrow! the gibbet! Your death! Save yourself! Spare me!"

He took her arm, he was mad, he wanted to drag her
away.

She fixed her eyes intently upon him.

"What has become of my Phoebus?"

"Ah!" said the priest, letting go of her arm. "You are
without pity!"

"What has become of Phoebus?" she repeated coldly.

"He's dead!" cried the priest.

"Dead!" she said, still cold and motionless. "Then why do you talk to me of living?"

He was not listening to her.

"Oh yes," he said as if speaking to himself, "he must be dead. The blade entered deep. It was his heart I touched with the point. Oh, my whole life was in that dagger's point!"

The young girl rushed at him like a furious tigress. She pushed him against the steps with superhuman strength.

"Go! monster, leave! Leave, murderer! Leave me to die! May the blood of both of us be an everlasting stain upon your forehead! Be yours, priest? Never! Never! Nothing shall unite us, not even hell itself! Be gone, accursed one! Never!"

The priest stumbled on the steps. He untangled his feet from the folds of his robe, took up his lantern, and began slowly to ascend the steps leading to the door. He reopened the door and went out.

All at once the young girl saw his head reappear; its expression was terrible, and he screamed at her, hoarse with rage and despair. "I tell you, he is dead!"

She fell with her face to the floor. And no other sound was heard now in the dungeon but the drip, drip of water which stirred the surface of the pool in the darkness.

5

The Mother

I wonder if anything gives a mother more delight than the contemplation of her infant's shoe, especially if it be a holiday, a Sunday, or a baptismal shoe, a shoe embroidered to its very sole—a shoe worn before the child has taken its first step. That shoe so cute and tiny covered a foot too young to walk; it is the shoe that recalls her baby so poignantly that it seems as if the child were present. So she smiles at it; she kisses it; she talks to it; she asks herself if a foot could really have been that small. She thinks she sees her sweet, fragile creature. She does see her—whole, living, joyous, with her delicate hands, her round head, her sweet lips, her innocent eyes with their whites so blue. If it be winter, there is the baby girl creeping on the carpet, clambering up a stool; and the mother trembles when she goes near the fire. If it be summer, the child crawls around the yard, the garden, pulling up the grass from between the stones; gazes happily and fearlessly at the big dogs, and the bigger horses, or plays with shells and flowers, making the gardener scold when he finds gravel in his flower beds and dirt on his walks. All the world is bright and shining; even the warm breezes and the sunlight playfully contend among her wispy locks of hair. All these pictures, the little shoe conjures up to the mother, and her heart softens as a wax candle near a fire.

But when the child is lost, those thousands of joyful, charming, tender images which crowded around the little shoe become so many monstrous memories. The pretty embroidered shoe is now but an instrument of torture endlessly tearing the mother's heart. Here is the same sensitive heartstring that vibrated formerly to the caressing touch of an angel but which now is plucked by a demon.

One morning as the May sun was rising in one of those deep blue skies under which Garofalo loves to paint the Saviour being taken down from the cross, the recluse of Roland's Tower heard a noise of wheels, of horses, and of clanking irons in the Place de Grève. It scarcely roused her, but she knotted her hair over her ears so as not to hear it, and on her knees resumed her contemplation of the inanimate object which she had been thus adoring for fifteen years. That little shoe, as we have already said, was her universe. Her thoughts were locked up in it, and were never to leave it until death. What bitter denunciations she had hurled toward heaven, what touching lamentations, what prayers and sobs on account of this darling, pink, satin toy, only the gloomy cell in the Tower of Roland knew! More sorrow has never been expended on anything more charming and delicate.

That morning, it seemed that her despair was more violent than usual, for her lamentations in a loud and monotonous voice that wrung one's heart could be heard outside the cell.

"O my daughter!" she moaned. "My poor dear little child! I shall see you no more! Hopeless! It seems as if it all happened but yesterday. My God! my God! Thou didst take her from me so quickly. Better hadst Thou not given her to me! Surely Thy knowest that our children are flesh of our flesh, and that a mother who has lost her child can no longer believe in God. Ah, wretched am I that I went out that day! Lord! Lord! Why didst Thou take her from me so? Didst Thou never see me with her, when I warmed her, all joyous, by my fire, when she smiled at me when I suckled her, when I made her little feet creep up my bosom to my lips? Oh, if Thou hadst but watched, Thou wouldst have rejoiced in my joy. Thou wouldst not have taken from me the only love of my heart. Was I such a wretched creature, Lord, that Thou couldst not look at me before condemning me? Alas! Alas! Here is the shoe, but the foot, where is it? Where is the rest? Where is the child? My baby! my daughter! What have they done with her? Lord, give me back my daughter. For fifteen years I have flayed my knees, praying to Thee, my God. Is that not enough? Give her to me for a day, for an hour, for a minute, just for a minute, O Lord. Then cast me to the devil for all eternity! Oh, if I knew how or where to touch but the hem of Thy garment, I would clutch it with both hands, and Thou wouldst be obliged to give me back my child. Her pretty little shoe, hast Thou no pity for it, O Lord? Canst Thou condemn a poor, poor soul to fifteen years of torture? Good Virgin! Good Virgin of heaven! My own infant Jesus! They have taken her from me; they have stolen her; they have eaten her on the heath; they have drunk her blood; they have chewed her bones! Good Virgin, have pity on me! My daughter! I must have my daughter. What matters it to me if she be in heaven? I don't want your angels; I want my child! I am the lioness, I want my cub! Oh, I'll writhe on the floor; I'll dash my head against these stones; I'll damn myself; I'll curse Thee, O Lord, if Thou keepest my child from me! See how I have gnawed my arms, O Lord? Has the good God no compassion? They can give me but salt and black bread, provided I have my daughter to warm me like the sun! Alas, Lord God! I was only a vile sinner; but my child made me good. For her, I was full of religion, and I saw Thee through her smile as through an opening to heaven. Oh! let me only once, just once again, put this shoe on her pretty rosy foot, and I will die, good Virgin, singing your praises! Ah, fifteen years! She would be

grown up now! Unhappy child! What! Is it true, then, I shall
see her no more, not even in heaven? For I, I shall never go
there. Oh, what misery to have to say, 'Here is her shoe, and
that is all!' "

The distraught woman had thrown herself on this shoe,
her consolation and despair for so many years; her heart was
torn with sobs as on that first day. For to a mother who has
lost her child, it is always the first day. Her grief never
grows old; though the mourning garments become threadbare and lose their color, her heart ever remains black.

Just then, the merry, squealing voices of some children
passed before her cell. At the sight or sound of children, this
poor mother would fling herself into the darkest corner of
her tomb, with such vehemence that one would think that
she was striving to bury her head in the stone that she might
not hear them. But this time, she sat up, and listened intently. One of the little boys had just said, "They're going to
hang the gypsy today."

With the alertness with which a spider pounces on a fly at
the shaking of its web, she darted to the window, which
overlooked, as you know, the Place de Grève. Indeed, there
was a ladder leaning against the permanent gibbet, and the
hangman was busy adjusting the chains rusted by the rain.
Some people were standing around.

The laughing group of children was already in the distance. The Sachette looked for some passerby whom she
might question. She spied, close to her cell, a priest, who
feigned to be reading in the public breviary, but whose mind
was much less occupied with the lattice-guarded volume
than with the gibbet, toward which, from time to time, he
would cast a wild and gloomy look. She recognized Monsieur the Archedeacon of Josas, a holy man.

"Father," she asked, "who are they going to hang there?"

The priest looked at her without answering. She repeated
her question.

"I don't know," he replied.

"Some children passed, saying it was a gypsy," continued
the recluse.

"I think so," said the priest.

Then Pâquette-la-Chantefleurie burst into wild and hyster-
ical laughter.

"Sister," said the archdeacon, "do you hate gypsies that much?"

"Hate them!" cried the recluse. "They are witches, child stealers! They have eaten my daughter, my baby, my only child! There is no heart in my body. They have eaten me too!"

She was frightening, but the priest eyed her coldly.

"There is one especially that I hate and that I have cursed," she resumed, "a young one who's about the age my daughter would have been now if her gypsy mother had not eaten my baby. Every time that young viper passes my cell, she makes my blood boil."

"Well, sister, be joyful," said the priest, cold like a marble statue on a tomb, "for it is she whom you will see die."

He lowered his head, and walked away slowly.

The recluse wrung her hands with joy. "I told her so; I told her that she would hang there! Thank you, priest," she cried.

Then she began to pace to and fro behind her barred window, her hair disheveled, her eyes glazed, hurling her shoulder against the bars like a caged wild she-wolf that has been hungry for a long time but now senses that the hour of her meal is drawing near.

6

The Hearts of Three Men Made Differently

But Phoebus was not dead. Men like him are hard to kill. When Master Philippe Lheulier, king's advocate extraordinary, had said to poor Esmeralda, "He is dying," he was either misinformed or jesting. When the archdeacon had repeated to the condemned, "He is dead," the fact is that he knew nothing about the matter, but he believed it; he was counting on it, he had no doubt about it; he fully hoped it was so. It would have hurt him too much to give good tidings of his rival to the female whom he loved. Any man in his place would have felt the same.

Phoebus' wound was serious, but was less so than the archdeacon hoped. The master surgeon to whose residence the soldiers of the watch had immediately carried him had for a week feared for the patient's life, and had even told Phoebus so in Latin. But youth had triumphed, and, as often happens, notwithstanding prognostics and diagnostics, Nature amused herself with saving the patient in spite of the physician. It was while he was yet lying upon his sickbed at the home of the master surgeon that he was first questioned by Philippe Lheulier and by representatives of the official. This he found most tedious. So, one fine morning, feeling much better, he left his gold spurs in payment for the medicine and treatment, and made himself scarce. This, however, by no means impeded the judicial proceedings. Justice in those days was little concerned about propriety and precision in its proceedings against a criminal. Just as long as the accused was hung, that was all that was important. Furthermore, the judges had enough evidence against Esmeralda. They believed Phoebus to be dead, and that decided the matter.

Phoebus, on his part, fled no great distance. He merely went to rejoin his company, then on garrison duty at Queue-en-Brie, on the Ile-de-France, a few posting-stations from Paris.

After all, he felt no great desire to make a personal appearance at the trial. He had a vague feeling that he would cut a rather ridiculous figure. As a matter of fact, he did not know what to think of this whole affair. Irreligious and superstitious, like every soldier who is nothing but a soldier, when he reviewed the details of this adventure, he could not tell what to make of the goat, of the peculiar circumstances under which he had first met La Esmeralda, of the strange manner in which she had revealed her love, of her being a gypsy, and lastly, of the phantom monk. He supposed in all this there was much more magic than love; probably she was a sorceress, perhaps the devil. In short, the whole thing was a comedy, or to use the language of the day, a mystery, and a very disagreeable one, in which he played an extremely awkward part, the character who is beaten and laughed at. The captain was quite humiliated by this; he felt the sort of shame which La Fontaine so exquisitely defined:

As ashamed as a fox outwitted by a hen.

Besides, he hoped that the affair would not be bruited about, that in his absence, his name would scarcely be mentioned in connection with it, or, at any rate, would not be heard beyond the courtroom of the Tournelle. In this he was quite correct. At the time there were no newspapers, and as hardly a week passed in which there was not some counterfeiter boiled in oil, some witch hanged, or some heretic burned at some one of the innumerable "places of justice" of Paris, people were so accustomed to see at every crossroad the old feudal Themis, with her arms bare and her sleeves rolled up, busy with her gibbets and pillories, that they scarcely took notice of such events. In those days the aristocracy hardly knew the name of the sufferer whom they might pass at the corner of the street, and the common people at most regaled themselves with this coarse fare. An execution was an incident no more unusual to the public than the oven of a baker or the butcher's slaughterhouse. The hangman was but a kind of butcher though a bit more sinister than the other.

Phoebus therefore quickly put his mind at ease respecting the sorceress Esmeralda, or Similar, as he called her, the stab he received from the gypsy, or from the phantom monk—he did not care which—and the outcome of the trial. But no sooner did these images vacate his heart than that of Fleur-de-Lys re-entered. The heart of Captain Phoebus, like the natural philosophy of the day, abhorred a vacuum.

Besides, Queue-en-Brie was a dull place, a village of blacksmiths and milkmaids with chapped hands, and a long string of tumbledown thatched cottages bordering the main road for half a league—a tail, in short, as its name imports.

Fleur-de-Lys, a pretty girl, with an excellent dowry, was his last love but one. So, one fine morning, quite recovered from his wound, and presuming that the affair with the gypsy must, after two months, be over and forgotten, the amorous cavalier came swaggering to the door of the Gondelaurier mansion.

He paid no attention to the sizable crowd that was gathered in the Place due Parvis, in front of Notre-Dame. Remembering that it was the month of May, and supposing that there was some religious procession or holiday, he fastened his horse's bridle to the ring at the porch, and in good spirits mounted the staircase to his fair betrothed.

She was alone with her mother.

Fleur-de-Lys had mulled over and over the events of the day when the sorceress, her goat, and the accursed alphabet had been there. Also, the long absence of Phoebus still weighed heavily upon her heart. Nevertheless, when she now saw her captain enter, she thought he looked so well, wearing a new uniform and a shining baldric, and, as he hurried toward her with such an impassioned air, she blushed with pleasure. The noble damsel herself was more lovely than ever. Her heavy blond hair was becomingly braided. She was dressed in that azure blue which so well enhances a fair complexion—a bit of fashion which she had learned from Colombe—and her eyes suggested an amorous languor which added to her seductiveness.

Phoebus, who had, in the matter of beauty, lately been seeing nothing better than the wenches of Queue-en-Brie, was absolutely intoxicated by Fleur-de-Lys. Hence his manner was so gallant and attentive that his peace was instantly made.

Madame de Gondelaurier herself, maternally seated as usual in her large armchair, had not the heart to scold him. As for the reproaches of Fleur-de-Lys, they died away in tender cooings.

The young lady sat near the window, still embroidering her grotto of Neptune. The captain leaned over the back of her chair. She softly upbraided him.

"What became of you these past two months, you naughty man?"

"I swear," answered Phoebus, a little embarrassed by the question, "you are beautiful enough to make an archbishop dream."

She could not repress a smile.

"That's all very fine, monsieur. But leave my beauty aside, and answer my question. Beauty, indeed!"

"Well, my dear cousin, I was recalled for duty at the garrison."

"And where was that, prithee? And why did you not come to bid me farewell?"

"At Queue-en-Brie."

Phoebus was delighted that the first question enabled him to evade the second.

"But that is close by, sir. How is it you have not come once to see me?"

Here Phoebus was seriously embarrassed. "Why ... uh ... the duty ... and besides, my charming cousin, I have been ill."

"Ill!" she exclaimed in alarm.

"Yes ... wounded."

"Wounded!"

The poor child was quite upset.

"Oh, don't be frightened about it," said Phoebus, casually, "it's nothing. A small quarrel, a mere scratch; what is that to you, my dear?"

"What is that to me!" exclaimed Fleur-de-Lys, raising her tear-filled eyes. "Oh, you cannot mean what you are saying. What was it all about? I want to know everything."

"Well, my fair one, I had a squabble with Mahé Fédy. Do you know him, the lieutenant of Saint-Germain-en-Laye? Each of us tore a few inches of the other's skin—that's all."

The lying captain knew only too well that an affair of honor always makes a man appear advantageously in a woman's eyes. Indeed, Fleur-de-Lys did look at him with mingled feelings of fear, pleasure, and admiration. But she was not yet completely reassured.

"But, my Phoebus, you are completely cured!" she said. "I don't know your Mahé Fédy, but he must be a scoundrel. How did this quarrel begin?"

Here Phoebus, whose imagination was only mildly inventive, began to puzzle over how he might squirm out of his position of false prowess.

"Oh, I don't know ... something trifling ... a horse ... something was said! ... My beautiful cousin," he exclaimed to quickly change the conversation, "What's all that noise in the Parvis?"

He went over to the window. "My word, cousin, such a crowd in the square!"

"I don't know," said Fleur-de-Lys, "it seems that there's a witch who must do penance this morning in front of the church before she is hanged."

The captain was so sure that his affair with La Esmeralda

had been terminated that he paid little attention to these words of Fleur-de-Lys. He nevertheless posed one or two questions.

"What is the witch's name?"

"I don't know," she answered.

"And what do they say she has done?"

Again she shrugged her white shoulders and replied, "I don't know that either."

"Oh, my dear Jesus," said the mother, "there are so many witches nowadays, that they burn them without ever knowing their names. It would be better to try to know the name of every cloud in the sky. After all, we may rest easily: the Good Lord above keeps an accurate record."

Here the venerable dame rose and came to the window.

"Lord!" she cried, "you're right, Phoebus. There is a crowd of common folk. There they are, praised be God! even on the rooftops.

"Do you know, Phoebus, that reminds me of my younger days, of the entry of King Charles VII, when there were such crowds too. I don't recollect the year. When I mention that now, it sounds to you like something in the distant past, but to me it seems only yesterday. Oh, the people were livelier then than they are today. There were even throngs on the battlements of the Gate of Saint-Antoine. The king had the queen on a pillion behind him, and following their highnesses came all the ladies, mounted behind their lords. I remember there was much laughing, because, by the side of Amanyon de Garlande, who was a very short man, there was the Sire Matefelon, a knight of giant stature, who had killed hordes of English. It was indeed a fine procession of all the gentlemen of France carrying their red oriflammes, though some had pennons and some banners. Let me see, the Sire of Calan had a pennon; Jean de Châteaumorant had a banner. The Sire of Coucy had a richer one than any of the others, except the Duke of Bourbon. Alas, how sad it is to think that's the way it was, and is no longer!"

The two lovers were not listening to the reminiscences of the worthy old dowager. Phoebus had come from the window to lean again on the back of Fleur-de-Lys' chair, from which advantageous position his libertine glance could peer into all the openings of her bodice, which yawned conveniently, and so revealed to him many exquisite things, which led him to imagine many others. Phoebus, quite dazzled by that skin with its satin glow, said to himself, "How can a man love any but a fair-skinned beauty?"

Both remained silent. From time to time the girl would glance at him with soft and loving eyes, and their locks of hair were mingled in a ray of spring sunlight.

"Phoebus," Fleur-de-Lys said abruptly in a whisper, "we are to be married in three months. Swear you have never loved any other woman but me."

"I do swear it, my beautiful angel!" replied Phoebus. His adoring eyes combined with the sincere tone of his voice convinced Fleur-de-Lys. Perhaps he even believed himself at that moment.

Meanwhile the good mother, charmed to see the young couple in such excellent accord, had left the apartment to attend to some domestic chore or other.

The adventurous captain, at being left alone with Fleur-de-Lys, was so much emboldened that some very strange ideas came to his mind. Fleur-de-Lys loved him; he was betrothed to her; she was alone with him; his old love for her had been revived, not in all its freshness, but in all its ardor. After all, it is no great crime to eat a little of one's own corn right off the stalk. I know not if these precise thoughts passed through his mind, but it is certain that Fleur-de-Lys was all at once alarmed by the expression in his eyes. She looked around her and saw that her mother had gone.

"Mon Dieu!" she said, blushing and upset. "I'm very warm!"

"I do think," replied Phoebus, "that it must be near noon. The sun is stifling hot. There's nothing to do but to draw the curtains."

"No, no!" cried the poor girl. "On the contrary I need some air."

And like a doe that scents the approaching pack, she rose, scampered to the window, opened it, and stepped out onto the balcony.

Phoebus, thwarted, pursued her.

The Place du Parvis Notre-Dame, which the balcony overlooked, as you well know, presented at that moment a singular and sinister sight, which suddenly changed the nature of the timid Fleur-de-Lys' alarm.

A huge crowd, which flowed into all the adjacent streets, filled the entire square. The low wall that enclosed the Parvis would not have been enough to keep the space clear if there had not been there also a close rank of sergeants with their harquebuses and their culverins in hand. Thanks to this hedge of pikes and harquebuses the Parvis was empty. The entrance was guarded by a band of the bishop's halberdiers. The great doors of the church were closed, contrasting with the numberless windows around the square, which, being all open up to the very gables, showed a thousand heads piled one above the other like cannonballs on the artillery field.

The color of this multitude was gray, dirty, grubby. The sight which they were waiting to see was evidently one of those which calls together all that is most unclean in the population of a city. Nothing could be more hideous than the noise which swelled from that swarm of yellow caps and unkempt heads. In this crowd, there were more women than men, more laughing than crying.

From time to time some harsh, shrill voice pierced through the general din.

"Hey! Mahiet Baliffre, are they going to hang her there?"

"You imbecile! This is where she is to do penance in her shift! Some good priest is going to cough Latin in her face. That's what they are going to do here at noon. If it's the gallows you want, go to the Place de Grève."

"I'll go there later."

"Say, tell me, La Boucandry, is it true she's refused to have a confessor?"

"It seems so, La Bechaigne."

"Why, the pagan!"

"Monsieur, it's the custom. The bailiff of the Palace is bound to deliver the culprit, already sentenced, for execution: if it's a layman, to the Provost of Paris; if it's a cleric, to the official of the bishopric."

"O my God!" said Fleur-de-Lys, "the poor creature!"
With this sad thought she scanned the crowded square.

The captain, much more interested in his betrothed than in the rabble below, was putting his amorous hand about her waist.

She turned around, her face entreating and smiling. "Please, Phoebus, don't do that! If my mother came in and saw your hand!"

At that moment, the clock of Notre-Dame slowly tolled noon. A murmur of satisfaction burst from the crowd. The last vibration of the twelfth stroke hardly died away when all those heads moved like waves of the sea in a gale of wind. A loud shout rose simultaneously from the square, from the windows, and from the roofs, "There she is!"

Fleur-de-Lys covered her eyes with her hands, so as not to see.

"My darling," Phoebus said to her, "are you coming in?"

"No," she answered; and those eyes which she had just closed through fear, she opened again through curiosity.

A tumbrel, drawn by a strong Norman horse, and surrounded by horsemen in violet livery with white crosses, had just emerged from the Rue Saint-Pierre-aux-Boeufs into the square. The sergeants of the watch were furrowing a passage through the crowds by vigorously swinging their leather whips. Beside the tumbrel rode some officers of justice and of police, identifiable by their black costumes and their awkward seat in the saddle. Master Jacques Charmolue led the parade.

In the fatal cart sat a young girl, her hands tied behind her back, without a priest by her side. She wore a shift; her long black hair (for it was then the custom not to cut it until she reached the foot of the gibbet) cascaded over her neck and half-covered her shoulders.

Through this flowing hair, more shining than a raven's plumage, could be seen a twisted, heavy, gray knotted rope that dug into her fragile shoulder blades and was wrapped around her slender neck like a worm twined around a flower.

Below the rope, there gleamed a small amulet, ornamented with green glass, which undoubtedly they had allowed her to keep because nothing is refused those who are about to die. The spectators huddled in the windows could discern at the bottom of the tumbrel her naked legs which she tried to conceal under her as if by a last instinct of feminine modesty. At her feet was the little goat likewise bound. The condemned girl was holding together with her teeth her ill-tied shift. One would have said, that, despite her misery, she was still conscious of the indignity of being thus exposed half-naked before all eyes. Alas! it was not for exhibitions like this that feminine modesty was made.

"Jesus!" exclaimed Fleur-de-Lys. Then, to the captain, "Look there, cousin! It's that nasty gypsy girl with her goat."

Then she turned around to Phoebus. His eyes were fixed on the tumbrel. He looked exceedingly pale.

"What gypsy with the goat?" he stammered.

"Why," rejoined Fleur-de-Lys, "don't you remember?"

Phoebus interrupted. "I don't know what you mean."

He made as if to go inside. But Fleur-de-Lys, whose jealousy recently had raged so vehemently, found it now reawakened by that same gypsy girl. So she stared at Phoebus with eyes of mistrust. At that moment she vaguely recollected having heard mentioned a certain captain who was mixed up in the trial of this sorceress.

"Whatever is the matter with you?" she said to Phoebus. "One would think that this woman threatened you."

Phoebus forced a laugh.

"Me! not at all. Me! how silly!"

"Stay, then," she said imperiously, "and let's watch till the end."

The unlucky captain had to stay. However, it reassured him a little to see that the condemned girl did not raise her eyes from the floor of the tumbrel. It was indeed Esmeralda. In this last stage of ignominy and misfortune she was still beautiful. Her large black eyes sunk in her hollow cheeks looked even larger. Her livid profile was pure and sublime. She resembled what she had been, as a Virgin of Masaccio's resembles a Virgin of Raphael's: feebler, thinner, more attenuated.

Otherwise, she seemed to be all tossing about, as it were—everything, except as far as modesty dictated, being left to chance, so completely had her spirit been broken by stupor and despair. Her body jounced at every jolt of the tumbrel, like something dead or broken. Her expression was blank and sad. A tear hung motionless in her eye as if it had been frozen there.

Meanwhile the sorry cavalcade passed through the crowd, amid shouts of joy and stares of curiosity. Nevertheless, in order to be the faithful historian, we ought to observe that on seeing her so beautiful and so overwhelmed, many were moved to pity, even the most hard-hearted. The tumbrel entered the Parvis.

It stopped in front of the central door. The escort aligned itself on each side. The crowd became silent; and amid that silence, so solemn and anxious, the two halves of the great door opened, as if by themselves, their hinges creaking like the sound of a fife. It seemed like the mouth of a cavern opening on the square resplendent with sunshine. Now one could see the whole length of the church, gloomy, draped in black, faintly lighted by a few candles twinkling from afar upon the main altar. In the shadow of the chancel, dimly could be seen a gigantic silver cross, gleaming against a piece of black drapery which hung from the vaulted ceiling to the floor. The whole nave was vacant. The heads of some priests, however, were to be seen stirring about in the distant stalls of the choir. At the moment when the great door opened, there issued from the church a solemn chant, swelling and monotonous, hurling, as it were, in puffs, fragments of doleful psalms over the head of the condemned gypsy.

"I will not fear the thousands of people surrounding me. Arise, O Lord; save me, O my God.

"Save me, O God, for the waters are come in even unto my soul.

"I stick fast in the mire of the deep; and there is no sure standing."

At the same time, another voice, isolated from the choir, chanted from the steps of the high altar this melancholy offertory:

"He who heareth my word and believeth him that sent me hath life everlasting and cometh not into judgment, but is passed from death to life."

These chants sung by old men, lost in the darkness, over that beautiful creature full of youth and life, caressed by the warm air of spring, and bathed in sunlight, was the Mass for the dead.

The people listened reverently.

The unfortunate girl, terrified, seemed to lose her perspective in the depths of this dark church. Her pale lips moved as if she were praying, and when the hangman's assistant approached to help her down from the cart, he heard her whisper the word "Phoebus."

They untied her hands, and made her descend, accompanied by her goat, which they had also untied. Djali bleated with joy to feel herself free. They then made her walk barefoot over the pavement, to the foot of the steps of the entrance. The rope which she had about her neck dragged after her like a trailing serpent.

Then, inside the church, the chanting stopped. A large golden cross and a file of wax tapers began to move in the dark. The sound of the halberds of the Swiss guards in motley-colored uniforms was heard. A few minutes later a long procession of priests in their chasubles and deacons in dalmatics advanced slowly toward the prisoner, chanting. They came into her view and that of the crowd. But her eyes were fixed on the one who walked at their head, immediately after the crossbearer. "Oh," she said to herself shuddering. "There he is again! The priest!"

It was, indeed, the archdeacon. On his left was the sub-chanter and on his right, the chanter bearing the staff of his office. He advanced with his head thrown back, his eyes raised, chanting in a loud voice, "I cried out of my affliction to the Lord, and he heard me. I cried out of the belly of hell, and thou hast heard my voice. And thou hast cast me forth into the deep in the heart of the sea, and a flood hath encompassed me; all thy billows and thy waves have passed over me."

As he appeared in the broad daylight under the high arched doorway, wrapped in an ample silver cope marked with a black cross, he was so pale that more than one in the crowd thought that it was one of the marble bishops who kneel on the tombstones in the choir who had risen and was come to receive on the brink of the grave she who was going to die.

Esmeralda, no less pale and statuesque, was scarcely conscious that they had put into her hand a heavy, lighted candle of yellow wax. She did not hear the scratchy voice of the clerk reading the fatal form of the penance; but when they told her to answer Amen, she answered, "Amen."

It was not until she saw the priest make a sign to her guards to retire and himself advance toward her that she showed any sort of life and strength. Then did she feel the blood boiling in her head, and a last remaining spark of indignation was kindled in that soul already numb and cold.

The archdeacon walked over to her slowly. Even in her extremity she saw him survey her nakedness with an eye sparkling with jealousy and lascivious desire. Then he addressed her in a loud voice, "Young girl, have you asked God's pardon for your sins and misdeeds?" Then leaning toward her—as the spectators supposed, to hear her last confession—he whispered, "Will you have me? I can save you yet?"

She eyed him steadfastly, "Be gone, Satan! or I'll denounce you!"

He smiled a terrible smile.

"They will not believe you. You would but add a scandal to a crime. Answer me quickly, will you have me?"

"What have you done with my Phoebus?"

"He is dead!" answered the priest.

Just then the wretched archdeacon raised his head and saw at the other side of the square, on the balcony of the Gondelaurier mansion, the captain standing near Fleur-de-Lys. He staggered, and passed his hands over his eyes, looked again, murmured a curse, and all his features were violently contracted.

"Well, die then!" he said under his breath. "No one will have you!"

Then lifting his hand over the gypsy girl, he intoned in Latin, "And . . . now go, lingering soul, and may God have mercy on thee!"

This was the dreadful formula with which it was customary to conclude these gloomy rituals. It was the prearranged signal to be given by the priest to the hangman.

The people knelt.

"*Kyrie Eleison!*" said the priests who paused beneath the arched doorway.

"*Kyrie Eleison!*" chanted the crowd, with a murmur that ran over their heads like the spashing of an agitated sea.

"Amen!" said the archdeacon.

He turned his back on the prisoner, his head fell to his chest; he joined his hands and returned to his cortege of priests. A moment later he disappeared with the cross, the candles, and the copes, under the dim arches of the cathedral; his sonorous voice gradually died away in the choir, while chanting this verse of despair, "All thy billows and thy waves have passed over me."

At the same time the iron butt ends of the Swiss guards' pikes clanked on the stone floor with a chant of their own which gradually died away under the several intercolumniations of the nave, suggesting the striking of a clock that sounds the last hour of the condemned.

Meanwhile the doors of Notre-Dame remained open, showing the interior of the church, empty, desolate, in mourning, without candles, and voiceless.

The condemned girl remained motionless on the spot where they had placed her, awaiting what they were going to do with her. One of the sergeants had to notify Master Charmolue, who during all this scene had set himself to study that bas-relief on the great door which represents, according to some, Abraham's sacrifice, and according to others, the alchemical operation—the sun being represented by the angel, the fire by the fagot, and the operator by Abraham.

It was all they could do to draw him away from this contemplation. But at last he turned around, and at his signal two men dressed in yellow, the hangman's assistants, approached the gypsy girl to tie her hands again.

The unfortunate girl, just as she was again mounting the fatal cart, to set out on the last stage of her journey, was seized perhaps by some last heart's desire for life. She lifted her dry reddened eyes toward heaven, toward the sun, toward the silvery clouds, broken here and there with trapeziums and triangles of blue, and then cast them down around her on the ground, the crowd, the houses. All of a sudden, as the man in yellow was binding her elbows, she let out a piercing cry, but a cry of joy. On that balcony, over there, on the corner of the square, she had just caught sight of him, him, her friend, her lord, Phoebus, that other apparition of her life. The judge had lied! The priest had lied to her! It was he. She had no doubt. He was there, alive, handsome, clad in his sparkling uniform, with a plume in his hat, and a sword at his side.

She wanted to stretch out her arms toward him, trembling with love and delight, but they were bound.

Then she saw the captain frown. A beautiful young lady was leaning upon his arm, looking at him with disdainful lips and angry eyes. Phoebus then uttered something which she could not hear. Both hastily disappeared behind the casement on the balcony which immediately closed.

"Phoebus!" she cried all beside herself. "Do you believe it too?"

A monstrous thought had just occurred to her. She remembered that she had been condemned for the murder of Phoebus de Châteaupers.

Till now she had endured everything. But this last blow was too much. She slumped to the ground.

"Come," said Charmolue. "Carry her into the tumbrel, and let us be finished!"

No one had yet noticed, in the gallery of the royal statues sculptured immediately above the arches of the great door, a strange spectator, who until then had been watching all that had been going on with such absolute passiveness, a neck so intently stretched, a face so deformed, that, but for his clothing, half red and half purple, he might have been mistaken for one of those stone monsters through whose mouths the long gutters of the cathedral have disgorged the rains for six hundred years. This spectator had missed nothing of what had been transpiring since noon before the entrance of Notre-Dame. But before these events began, without anyone's thinking to observe him, he had securely fastened to one of the small columns of the gallery a heavy knotted rope, the end of which fell to the base of the cathedral's steps. This done, he had begun to watch quietly, only whistling from time to time when some blackbird flew by. All at once, just as the hangman's assistants were about to carry out Charmolue's phlegmatic order, he straddled the balustrade of the gallery, gripped the rope with his feet, his knees, and his hands, and slid down the facade like a raindrop rolling down a pane of glass. With the speed of a cat that has leaped from a rooftop, he darted toward the two executioners, knocked them down with two enormous fists, picked up the gypsy with one hand, as a child does a doll, and with one bound was inside the church, holding the girl above his head, and crying with a loud voice, "Sanctuary!"

This was done with such rapidity that had it been night, the whole might have been seen in the glare of a single flash of lightning.

"Sanctuary! Sanctuary!" repeated the crowd, and the clapping of ten thousand hands made Quasimodo's one eye sparkle with pride and joy.

The shock brought the prisoner to her senses. She opened her eyes, looked at Quasimodo, then suddenly closed them as if terrified by the sight of her savior.

Charmolue was stunned, as were the executioners and the entire escort. Indeed, within the walls of Notre-Dame, the prisoner was inviolable. The cathedral was a place of refuge. All human justice expired on its threshold.

Quasimodo had stopped under the great door. His large feet seemed as solidly rooted to the floor of the church as the heavy Roman pillars. His great hairy head was sunk between his shoulders like that of a lion, which too has a mane, but no neck. He held the young girl, all palpitating, suspended in his calloused hands, like a piece of white drapery; but he carried her so carefully that he seemed afraid of bruising her or breaking her. It was as if he felt that she was something delicate, exquisite, and precious, made for hands other than his. At moments he seemed as if he dared not touch her, even with his breath. Then, all at once, he would clutch her in his arms, to his angular breast, as if she were his only worldly possession, his treasure, as the mother of this child would have done. His gnomelike eye, bent over her, poured out tenderness, grief, and pity, and then was lifted up suddenly all flashing. The women laughed and wept; the crowd stamped their feet enthusiastically, for at that moment Quasimodo was really beautiful. He was handsome—this orphan, this foundling, this outcast. He felt himself august and strong. He looked directly into the face of that society from which he had been banished and over which he now exercised so much power—that human justice from which he had snatched its prey—all those tigers, now forced to gnash their empty jaws, those judges, those executioners—all that royal strength which he, the most lowly, had broken with God's strength.

And then there was something touching about the protection offered by a creature so deformed to one so unfortunate—one condemned to death saved by Quasimodo. Here were the two extremes of physical and social wretchedness meeting and assisting each other.

After a few minutes of triumph, Quasimodo had suddenly plunged with his burden into the church. The people, fond of daring deeds, followed him with their eyes through the dark nave, regretting that he had so quickly withdrawn himself from their acclamations. Suddenly he was seen again at one end of the gallery of the kings of France. He ran along it like a frenzied person, lifting his prize in his arms and shouting, "Sanctuary!" The crowd again burst forth with applause. When he had crossed the gallery, he plunged again into the interior of the church. A minute later, he reappeared on the upper platform, still carrying the gypsy in his arms, still running madly along, still crying, "Sanctuary!" And the crowd applauded again. At last he made a third appearance atop the tower of the great bell. There he seemed to show proudly to the whole city her whom he had saved, and his thundering voice, that voice which was heard so rarely, and which he never heard, repeated three times with frenzy, even to the clouds, "Sanctuary! Sanctuary! Sanctuary!"

"Noël! Noël!" screamed the crowd, and this immense acclamation was thundered to the opposite bank of the Seine to the amazement of the crowd assembled in the Place de Grève, and of the recluse, who was still waiting, with her eye fixed on the gibbet.

BOOK IX

1

Fever

Claude Frollo was no longer in Notre-Dame when his adopted son tore so abruptly and effectively the web in which the wretched archdeacon had caught the gypsy Esmeralda and in which he himself had been ensnared. Returning to the sacristy, he had roughly stripped himself of his alb, cope, and stole, thrown them all into the hands of the amazed sexton, hurried out by the private door of the cloister, ordered a ferryman of the Terrain to take him to the left bank of the Seine, and plunged into the hilly streets of the University, knowing not whither he was going, meeting at every step groups of men and women who were hurrying merrily toward the Pont Saint-Michel in the hope of "arriving on time" to see the sorceress hanged. Pale and wild, he was more distraught, more blinded, and fiercer than any owl let loose and pursued by a troop of children in broad daylight. He no longer knew where he was, what were his thoughts, or if all was a dream. He hastened on, walking, running, taking any street at random, only still driven onward by the Grève, that horrible Grève, which he vaguely sensed was behind him.

Thus he walked the whole length of the Hill of Sainte-

Geneviève, and at length left the town by the gate of Saint-Victor. So long as he could see, looking over his shoulder, the circling towers of the University and the scattered houses of the suburb, he continued his flight. But when at last a hill completely hid from view that despicable city of Paris, when he imagined he was a hundred leagues from it, in the country, in some wasteland, he stopped and it seemed to him he could breathe freely once more.

Frightening ideas then rushed to his mind. He saw clearly into the depths of his soul, and shuddered. He thought of that unhappy girl who had destroyed him and whom he had destroyed. With a haggard eye he scanned the double twisted path along which Fate had driven their two destinies, to the point of intersection, where she had pitilessly effected a collision. He thought of the folly of his perpetual vows, of the vanity of chastity, science, religion, virtue, of God's uselessness. He gleefully drank of these evil thoughts, and, the more he immersed himself in them, the more he felt a satanic laughter rising within him.

And while thus digging into his soul, when he saw how large a space nature had there prepared for the passions, he sneered more bitterly still. He stoked in the bottom of his heart all the hate, all the wickedness, he could, and he discovered, with the cold indifference of a physician examining a patient, that this hate and this wickedness were but vitiated love, that love, the source of every good in man, was turned into horrible things in the heart of a priest, and that man constituted as he was, by making himself a priest, made himself a demon. Then he laughed frightfully; and all at once he became pale again when he considered the most sinister aspect of his fatal passion—of that corrosive love, venomous, malignant, implacable, which had driven one to the gibbet, and the other to hell: her to death, him to eternal damnation.

And then he laughed again, when he mused that Phoebus was alive; that, after all, the captain was living, was gay and happy, had finer uniforms than ever, and a new mistress, whom he brought to see the old one hanged. His sneer intensified when he reflected that, of all the living creatures whose death he had wished for, the only being he did not hate, the gypsy girl, was the only one whom he had destroyed.

His thoughts passed from the captain to the crowd, and he was seized with a new kind of jealousy. He thought how the people too—all of them—had gazed upon his beloved in her shift, almost naked. He wrung his hands when he reflected how a glimpse of that figure, when seen in semidarkness by himself alone, would have been to him supreme happiness; but now she had been exhibited in broad daylight, at high noon, to the gaze of a whole multitude, clad as for a bridal night. He wept with rage when he thought that all those mysteries of love should be thus profaned, sullied, stripped, withered forever. He wept with rage as he imagined to himself how many unclean looks were satisfied by that loosely tied chemise; that this beautiful girl, this virgin lily, this cup of purity and delight, which he would not have dared to approach but with trembling lips, had just been transformed, as it were, into a public trough, while the vilest of the Parisian populace—the thieves, the beggars, the lackeys—had come to drink in common a shameless, impure, depraved pleasure.

And when he imagined the earthly happiness he might have found if she were not a gypsy, and he were not a priest, if Phoebus had never lived, and if she had never loved him; when he imagined that a life of serenity and love might have been his too, since at this very moment, there were on earth happy couples, engaged in long pleasant communion under orange blossoms, on the banks of some stream, in the presence of a setting sun or under a starry sky; and that, had it been God's will, he might have been one of those blessed couples, his heart dissolved in tenderness and despair.

Oh Esmeralda! Forever Esmeralda! It was this name that kept haunting him, that tortured him, that probed his brain, and gnawed his heart. He was not sorry; he would not repent. All that he had done, he would do again. He preferred to see her in the hands of the executioner than in the arms of the captain. But he suffered; he suffered so painfully that at times he tore out handfuls of his hair to see if it were not turning white.

There was one excruciating moment among many when it occurred to him that perhaps at that very minute the hideous rope which he had seen in the morning was tightening its knot about that neck so slender and graceful. This thought drove perspiration from his every pore.

There was another moment when, laughing diabolically at himself, he pictured at once La Esmeralda as he had seen her on that first day—vivacious, carefree, joyous, gaily dressed, dancing with winged, harmonious feet—and La Esmeralda on that last day, in her shift, a rope about her neck, mounting slowly, with her bare feet, the angular ladder of the gibbet. He imagined this double picture so vividly that a terrible shriek burst from his lips.

While this hurricane of despair was bending, overturning, breaking, uprooting everything in his soul, he gazed at the scene around him. At his feet, some chickens were scratching among the bushes and pecking at the scaly insects that were darting in the sun. Overhead piles of dappled gray clouds were fleeing across the blue skies. On the horizon the spire of Saint-Victor's Abbey with its obelisk of slate shot above the slope of the hill. And the miller of Copeaux was whistling as he watched the turning sails of his mill. All this active, organized, tranquil life displayed around him in a thousand different forms pained him. Again he began to walk rapidly.

He strode across the countryside. His flight from nature, from life, from himself, from man, from God, from everything went on throughout the day until evening. Sometimes he would throw himself to the ground and tear up with his nails the young plants of corn. Sometimes he would stop in the streets of some deserted village, and his thoughts were so unbearable that he would take his head in his hands to dash it against the pavement.

Toward sunset, he examined himself again, and found that he was almost mad. The storm which had been raging within him from the moment when he had lost all hope and desire to save the gypsy had left him without a single sane idea, a single rational thought. His reason, almost entirely destroyed, lay prostrate. Only two distinct images were fixed in his mind: La Esmeralda and the gallows. All the rest was black. But these two images together formed a frightful group. The more he concentrated on them—with what power of concentration remained to him—the more he saw them grow according to a fantastic progression—the one in grace,

in charm, in beauty, in light, the other in horror; until at last
La Esmeralda appeared to him like a star, the gibbet like an
enormous, fleshless arm.

It is strange, but during all this torture he never once
thought of killing himself. So the wretch was constituted. He
clung to life. Perhaps hell's fire gave him pause.

Meanwhile daylight ebbed. The living being which still
existed within him began to think confusedly of returning.
He thought himself far from Paris. But, by checking various
landmarks, he observed that he had only been traveling in
circles around the University. The spire of Saint-Sulpice and
the three tall needles of Saint-Germain-des-Prés rose above
the horizon to his right. He turned in that direction. When he
heard the "Qui vive!" of the abbot's guard around the crenelated walls of Saint-Germain's, he turned around, took a
path that offered itself between the abbey mill and the lepers' house of the hamlet, and in a few minutes found himself
on the edge of the Pré-aux-Clercs. This meadow notorious
for the brawls that took place there night and day was the
"hydra" to the poor monks of Saint-Germain. The archdeacon was afraid he might meet someone there; he was afraid
of every human face; he had just avoided the University and
the hamlet of Saint-Germain, and he wanted it to be as dark
as possible when he walked the streets of Paris again. He
skirted the Pré-aux-Clercs, took a deserted path which separated it from the Dieu-Neuf, and at length reached the banks
of the river. There Dom Claude found a ferryman, who for
a few deniers parisis took him up the Seine to the point of
the City, and let him off on that uninhabited tongue of land
on which the reader has already seen Gringoire musing, and
which extended beyond the king's gardens, parallel to the
isle of the Passeur-aux-Vaches.

The monotonous rocking of the boat and the lapping of
water to some extent lulled the unhappy Claude. When the
boatman departed, he remained standing in a daze on the
bank, looking straight before him. All the objects he beheld
seemed to dance before his eyes, forming a sort of phantas-
magoria. It is not uncommon for fatigue or violent grief to
produce this effect upon the mind.

The sun had slipped down behind the high Tower of
Nesle. It was now dusk. The sky was white; the surface of

the Seine was silvery. Between these, the left bank of the Seine, upon which his eyes were fixed, projected its somber mass, which gradually was diminished by the perspective, and pierced the haze on the horizon like a black arrow. It was crowded with houses, of which nothing was distinguishable but the dark silhouette that stood out from the light background of the sky and water. Here and there windows were beginning to glimmer with lights. This immense black obelisk, thus isolated between the two white expanses of the sky' and the river, which at this spot was very wide, had a singular appearance to Dom Claude, similar to that which would be experienced by a man lying on his back on the ground at the foot of the steeple of Strasbourg, and looking up at the enormous spire piercing the sky above him in the dim twilight. Only in this case Claude was standing and the obelisk was horizontal; but as the river, by reflecting the sky, deepened indefinitely the abyss beneath him, the vast promontory seemed leaping as boldly into the void as any cathedral spire, and the impression was the same. Here, indeed, the impression was in this respect stronger and more profound—that although it was indeed the steeple of Strasbourg, it was the steeple of Strasbourg two leagues high—something unexampled, gigantic, immeasurable—a structure such as no human eye had seen, except it were the Tower of Babel. The chimneys of the houses, the battlements of the walls, the carved gables of the roofs, the spire of the Augustines, the Tower of Nesle—all those projections which indented the profile of the colossal obelisk—added to the illusion by their old resemblance to the outline of a florid and fanciful sculpture. Claude, in the state of hallucination in which he found himself, thought he saw with his living eyes the very steeple of hell. The thousand lights scattered over the whole height of the fearful tower seemed to him to be so many openings of the vast internal furnace, while the voices and the noises that issued from it were so many shrieks and groanings of the damned. Then he was terror-stricken. He covered his ears with his hands that he might not hear; he turned his back so as not to see; he hurried away from this frightful vision.

But the vision was within him.

When he returned to the streets, the passersby, who jostled

each other in the light of the shopwindows, appeared to him like the everlasting going and coming of ghosts around him. Strange noises rang in his ears. Extraordinary fancies troubled his mind. He saw neither houses, nor pavements, nor carts, nor men, nor women, only a chaos of undetermined objects all melting into each other. At the corner of Rue de la Barillerie there was a grocer's shop, the front of which, according to immemorial custom, was all garnished with tin hoops, from each of which was suspended a circle of wooden candles, clattering against each other in the wind with a noise like that of castanets. He thought he heard, rattling against each other in the dark, the skeletons of Montfaucon.

"Oh," he muttered, "the night wind blows them against each other, and mingles the noise of their chains with the noise of their bones! Perhaps she is there among them!"

Beside himself, he knew not whither he was going. A few steps farther on and he was crossing the Pont Saint-Michel. There was a light in a window on the ground floor. He approached. Through the cracked windowpane he saw a dirty room, which brought back vaguely to his mind a memory. In that room, ill-lighted by a lamp, there was a young man, fair and young and joyous, throwing his arms with boisterous laughter about a scantily attired girl. And near the lamp there was an old woman spinning and singing in a quavering voice. Between the bursts of laughter only could the priest catch fragments of the old crone's song. It was unintelligible and horrible.

> Bark, Grève! Growl, Grève!
> Spin, spin, my brave one.
> Spin the hangman's cord
> That whistles in the prison yard.
> Bark, Grève! Growl, Grève!
>
> That pretty hemp rope!
> From Issy to Vanvre sow
> Hemp and not wheat.
> No thief has ever stolen
> That pretty hemp rope.
> Bark, Grève! Growl, Grève!
> To see the girl of pleasure

Dangle on the gibbet,
The windows are eyes,
Bark, Grève! Growl, Grève!

The young man was laughing and fondling the girl. The old woman was La Falourdel; the girl was a strumpet; the young man was his brother Jehan.

Claude continued to watch them. He saw Jehan go to a window at the other end of the room, open it, look out on the quay, where in the distance a thousand lighted windows glimmered. And then he heard him say as he shut the window, "Upon my soul, it's dark already! Folks are lighting their candles, and the good God his stars."

Then Jehan went over to the hussy, and smashed a bottle that was on the table, exclaiming, "Empty already, damn! And I've no more money! Isabeau, darling, I won't be satisfied with Jupiter till he's changed your two white breasts into two black bottles that I may suck Beaune wine from them day and night."

This jovial bit of pleasantry made the girl laugh, and Jehan left.

Dom Claude just had time to fall to the ground to avoid meeting his brother face to face and being recognized. Fortunately the street was dark, and the scholar was drunk. Nevertheless, he spotted the archdeacon lying on the pavement in the mud.

"Oh, ooh!" he said, "here's one who's had a good time today!"

He gave Dom Claude a shove with his foot and the archdeacon held his breath.

"Dead drunk!" muttered Jehan. "Come on! He's full. A veritable leech, right from the wine cask. He's bald," he added, stooping over him; "an old man too. *Fortunate senex!*"[1]

Then Dom Claude heard him go away, muttering, "It all amounts to the same thing. Learning's a fine thing, and my archdeacon brother is lucky to be wise and rich!"

Then the archdeacon got up, and ran all the way to Notre-

[1] "Happy old man!"

Dame, whose enormous towers he could see rising in the dark over the houses.

Just as he arrived, all out of breath, at the Place du Parvis, he drew back, and dared not lift his eyes toward the fatal edifice. "Oh," he whispered, "can it be true that such a thing happened here, today, this very morning?"

He ventured a glance at the church. The facade was dark, the sky behind it was twinkling with stars; a crescent moon that had risen on the horizon was just then poised over the summit of the right tower, and seemed to have perched upon it, like a luminous bird, on the edge of the black sculptured parapet.

The gate to the cloister was closed. But the archdeacon always carried with him the key to the tower where his laboratory was. He used this to enter the church.

Within, it was dark and silent like a tomb. By the heavy shadows which fell from all sides in broad masses, he perceived that the hangings for the morning's ceremonies had not yet been taken down. The large silver cross still gleamed through the darkness, sprinkled over with a number of glittering jewels, like the milky way of this sepulchral night. Above the black drapery the tall windows of the choir showed the upper extremity of their pointed arches, the stained glass of which, pierced by the moonlight, had but those doubtful colors of night—a sort of violet, white, and blue, tints to be found nowhere else but on the faces of the dead. The archdeacon, on observing all around the choir those pale pointed window tops, thought he saw so many miters of damned bishops. He closed his eyes, and when he opened them again, he imagined they were a circle of pale faces looking down upon him.

He fled through the church. Then it did seem to him that the church too moved, lived, breathed—that each heavy column became an enormous leg that beat the ground with its broad foot of stone, and that the gigantic cathedral had become a kind of prodigious elephant, breathing and walking along, with its pillars for legs, its two towers for tusks, and the immense black drapery for its caparison.

Thus his fever, or his madness, had arrived at such an intensity that the whole external world had become to this wretched man a sort of apocalypse, visible, palpable, frightful.

For a moment he was relieved. Plunging down the side aisle he perceived a reddish light coming from behind a group of pillars; he hastened toward it as toward a star. It was the feeble glimmer that lighted day and night the public breviary of Notre-Dame under its iron trellis-work. He cast his eye eagerly over the sacred book, hoping to find there some consolation, some encouragement. The book was open to a passage from Job, which he scanned: "And a spirit passed before my face, and I heard the voice as it were of a gentle wind, and the hair of my flesh stood up."

On reading this doleful text he felt like a blind man who is pricked by a staff he has picked up. His knees buckled, and he sank to the stone floor, thinking of her who had died that day. He felt so many monstrous vapors pass in and out of his brain that he felt as if his head had become one of the chimneys of hell.

Apparently he remained long in this position, thinking no more, but overwhelmed and passive under the power of the devil. At length, some measure of strength returned to him; he thought of taking refuge in the tower near his faithful Quasimodo. He got up, and as he was afraid, he took the lamp of the breviary to light his way. This was a sacrilege; but he was beyond such trifling considerations.

Slowly he climbed the staircase to the towers, full of secret dread, which was likely to be shared by the few persons crossing the Parvis at that hour and seeing the mysterious light ascending so late at night from loophole to loophole, to the top of the belfry.

Suddenly he felt a coolness on his face and found himself under the door of the uppermost gallery. The air was cold, the sky was streaked with clouds, whose broad white streamers drifted one upon the other like river ice breaking up after a thaw. The crescent moon, hidden in those clouds, looked like some celestial boat caught in those icebergs of the air.

He looked down, and for a moment, through the grill of slender columns that connect the towers, contemplated, through a light veil of mist and smoke, the silent multitude of the roofs of Paris, pointed, innumerable, crowded, and small, like the waves of a peaceful sea on a summer night.

At that moment the clock raised its shrill, cracked voice. It tolled midnight. The priest thought of noon. It was again twelve o'clock. "Oh," he whispered to himself, "she must be cold now!"

Suddenly a gust of wind extinguished his lamp, and almost at the same time he saw appear, at the opposite corner of the tower, a shadow, something white, a form, a woman. He shook. Next to this woman, there was a little goat which mingled its bleating with the last toll of the clock.

He found the courage to look. It was she!

She was pale; she looked sad. Her hair was falling over her shoulders as it had this morning. But there was no rope about her neck; her hands were not tied. She was free; she was dead.

She was dressed in white, and a white veil covered her head. She came toward him slowly, looking heavenward. The eerie goat followed her. Dom Frollo felt weighted with stones and could not flee. With each step she made toward him, he took one backward, and that was all. He retreated in this manner till he was beneath the dark vault of the staircase. He froze at the thought that she might enter here too. If she had, he would have died of terror.

Indeed, she did arrive at the door of the staircase, stopped there a few minutes, looked fixedly into the darkness, but without appearing to perceive the priest, she passed on. He thought she looked taller than when she was alive. He saw the moon through her white robe; now he could hear her breathing.

When she had passed, he started to descend the staircase as slowly as he had seen the specter move, thinking himself a specter too, haggard, his hair standing on end, the lamp still extinguished in his hand. As he descended the spiral stairs, he distinctly heard in his ear a voice laughing and repeating: "And a spirit passed before my face, and I heard the voice as it were of a gentle wind, and the hair of my flesh stood up."

2

Hunchbacked, One-eyed, Lame

In the Middle Ages, every town, and, till the time of Louis XII, every town in France, had its places of sanctuary. These sanctuaries, amid the deluge of penal laws and barbarous jurisdictions that inundated the city, were kinds of islands which rose above the level of human justice. Every criminal who took refuge therein was safe. There were in each district as many places of sanctuary as there were places of execution. This resulted in an abuse of the exemption from punishment by making it just as prevalent as was the overemphasis on capital punishment—two bad situations which tried to offset each other. The royal palaces, the residences of princes, and especially the churches exercised their right of sanctuary. Sometimes an entire town that needed to be repeopled was turned temporarily into a place of sanctuary. Thus Louis XI made Paris a sanctuary in 1467.

Once the criminal set his foot inside a sanctuary, his person was sacred, but he had to be careful not to leave it. One step beyond the sanctuary and he fell again into the sea. The wheel, the gibbet, the rack were ever watching the place of refuge, constantly on the lookout for their prey like sharks around a ship. Thus condemned prisoners have been known to turn gray in a cloister, on the stairs of a palace, in the garden of an abbey, or on the porch of a church. So the sanctuary was in fact a prison like any other. It sometimes happened that a solemn decree of parliament violated the right of sanctuary, and would return the condemned man to the hands of the executioner; but indeed this was infrequent. Parliaments were afraid of bishops, for, when two men in gowns collided, the robe didn't have a chance against the cassock. Occasionally, however, as in the case of the assassins of Petit-Jean, the Paris executioner, and in that of Emery Rousseau, who had murdered Jean Valleret, justice took precedence over the Church, and went on to the execution of its sentences. But except by a decree from parliament, woe

to him who by force violated a place of sanctuary. Everyone
knows what death befell Robert de Clermont, Marshal of
France, and Jean de Châlons, Marshal of Champagne, and yet
that case only concerned one Perrin Marc, a moneychanger's
lackey, and a penniless murderer; but the two marshals had
broken down the doors of Saint-Méry. That was the enormity.

Around the places of sanctuary there was such an aura of
respect that, according to tradition, it sometimes even extended to animals. Aymoin recounts that, when a stag hunted
by King Dagobert took sanctuary near the tomb of Saint-
Denis, the howling pack stopped short.

Usually, the churches reserved a cell in which to house fugitives. In 1407 Nicolas Flamel had constructed for them, in
the church of Saint-Jacques-de-la-Boucherie, a cell which
cost him four livres six sols sixteen deniers parisis.

In Notre-Dame there was a little cell, built over one of the
side aisles, under a flying buttress, which overlooked the
cloister, precisely in that spot where the wife of the present
concierge of the towers had made herself a garden, which is
to the Hanging Gardens of Babylon what a lettuce leaf is to
a palm tree, or what a lady doorkeeper is to a Semiramis.

It was in this cell, after his wild but triumphal race about
the galleries and towers, that Quasimodo had placed La Esmeralda. So long as his race lasted, the young gypsy had not
regained full consciousness; she had remained half stupefied, half awake, sensible of nothing but that she was rising
in the air, that she seemed to be floating there, then that she
was flying there, that something was lifting her above the
earth. Now and then she could hear roars of laughter, and the
raucous voice of Quasimodo yelling close to her ear. When
she half opened her eyes, below her she saw Paris, irregularly checkered with its thousands of slate and tile rooftops,
like a red and blue mosaic; and above her head was Quasimodo's frightening but joyful face. When she closed her
eyelids again, she was convinced that she was dead, that she
had been executed during her swoon, and that the deformed
spirit who had before presided over her destiny had again
seized her and was bearing her away. She dared not look at
him, but resigned herself to fate.

But when the panting and disheveled bellringer had deposited her in the cell of refuge, when she felt his huge

hands gently untie the rope that was cutting into her arms, she felt that kind of shock which jolts out of their sleep the passengers of a vessel that runs aground in the middle of a dark night. Her mind cleared also, and realities returned to her one by one. She saw that she was in Notre-Dame; she remembered having been snatched from the hands of the hangman; that Phoebus was still alive, that Phoebus did not love her any more. These two ideas, the one spreading so much bitterness over the other, presented themselves jointly to the poor prisoner. She turned to Quasimodo, who kept standing before her, frightening her, and said to him, "Why did you save me?"

He scanned her face anxiously, as if trying to decide what she had said to him. She repeated her question. Then, with a look of profound sadness, he hastened away, leaving her perplexed.

A few minutes later he returned, carrying a bundle which he laid at her feet. It was clothing which some kindly women had left for her at the door of the church. Now again she realized that she was almost naked, and she blushed. Life was returning to her.

Quasimodo seemed to sense her modest confusion. He covered his eye with his large hand and withdrew once more, but with slow steps.

Hastily she dressed. It was a white robe with a white veil, the habit of a novice of the Hôtel-Dieu.

Scarcely had she finished when she saw Quasimodo returning. He was carrying a basket under one arm and a mattress under the other. The basket held a bottle, some bread, and other provisions. He put it on the ground, and said to her, "Eat." He placed the mattress on the flagstone, and said, "Sleep." It was his own meal, his own bed that the bellringer had gone to fetch.

The gypsy girl raised her eyes to thank him, but she could say nothing. The poor devil was indeed horrible to look at. She lowered her head, shuddering from fright.

Then he said, "I frighten you. I am very ugly, aren't I? Don't look at me. Only listen to me. During the day, you stay here. At night you can walk around the church. But don't leave the church either by night or by day or you'll be caught. They would kill you, and I would die."

Moved by his words, she raised her head to answer. But he had gone. Alone she mused over the awesome words of this monstrous being, impressed by the sound of his voice, so raucous and yet so gentle.

Then she examined her cell. It was a chamber some six feet square, with a small window and a door that opened upon the gently sloping roof of flat stones. A number of rain spouts shaped like animals seemed to lean over her, and to stretch out their necks to look at her through the little window. Over the edge of the roof she caught sight of a thousand chimneys from which issued smoke from all the fires of Paris. This was a sorry landscape for a gypsy girl, a foundling, a prisoner condemned to death, an unfortunate creature, with no country, no family, no home!

Just when the thought of her loneliness in the world was weighing upon her heart most keenly, she felt a hairy, shaggy head nosing between her hands and knees. She shuddered (for everything frightened her now) and she looked down. There was Djali, who had escaped at the moment that Quasimodo had dispersed Charmolue's two guards, and had followed her. The goat had been at her feet nearly an hour lavishing caresses without obtaining so much as a single look. Now her mistress covered her with kisses.

"O Djali," she said, "how I had forgotten you! But you still think of me! Oh, you at least are not ungrateful!"

At the same time, as if some invisible hand had lifted the weight that had so long kept her tears within her, she began to weep; and as the tears flowed, she felt the sharpest and bitterest of her grief washing away with them.

When evening came the night was so beautiful, the moon so lovely and bright, that she walked around the high gallery that encircled the cathedral. Seen from that height, the earth seemed so calm to her that she experienced some relief.

3

Deaf

The following morning when she awoke, to her surprise she realized that she had slept. It had been a very long time since she had slept so peacefully. Cheery rays from the rising sun streamed through her window and shone on her face. But in the sunlight she saw at the window something that frightened her—the deformed face of Quasimodo. Involuntarily she closed her eyes again; but in vain, for she could still imagine through her rosy eyelids that gnome's face, one-eyed, with his widespread teeth.

Then, with her eyes still shut, she heard his gruff voice speaking to her very kindly, "Don't be afraid. I am your friend. I came to see you sleep. That doesn't hurt you, does it, that I come to look at you when you are sleeping? Does it matter if I am here when your eyes are closed? But I am going now. Now, I am behind the wall. You can open your eyes!"

More plaintive than the words was the tone with which they were uttered. The gypsy girl was touched by them; she opened her eyes. He was no longer at the window. She went over to it, and saw the poor hunchback crouching in a corner of the wall in an attitude of grief and resignation. She tried to overcome the repugnance which his appearance engendered.

"Come here!" she said softly.

By the movement of her lips, Quasimodo thought she was bidding him to go away. Then he rose and limped away, slowly, with his head cast down, not venturing to lift to the young girl his eye full of despair.

"Come here!" she cried.

But he continued to retreat. Then she rushed out of the cell, ran over to him, and took him by the arm. Feeling her hands upon him, Quasimodo trembled all over. He lifted his supplicating eye, and, seeing that she was drawing him to her, his whole face radiated joy and tenderness. She would have had him enter her cell, but he insisted upon remaining at the threshold.

"No, no!" he said, "the owl does not enter the nest of the lark."

Then she gracefully seated herself on her bed with her goat asleep at her feet. Both remained for a few minutes motionless, each contemplating in silence, he so much beauty, she so much ugliness. Each moment, she discovered in Quasimodo some new deformity. Her eye wandered from his bowlegs to his hunchback, from his hunchback to his only eye. She found it difficult to comprehend that such an ill-formed being could exist. And yet over his whole countenance there was diffused such melancholy and sorrow that she was beginning to be reconciled to his ugliness.

He was the first to break the silence.

"Did you tell me to come back?"

She nodded affirmatively, "Yes."

He understood the motion of her head. "Alas!" he said, as if hesitating to finish, "it's because . . . I am deaf."

"Poor man!" exclaimed the gypsy girl, an expression of pity suffusing her face.

He smiled sadly.

"You think that was all that was needed, don't you? Yes, I am deaf. That's the way I am made. It's horrible, isn't it? And you, you are so beautiful."

The tone of the poor creature conveyed such a profound feeling of his wretchedness that she had not the courage to speak. Besides, he could not have heard.

He continued, "Never till now have I been so aware of my ugliness. When I compare myself to you, I pity myself indeed, poor unhappy monster that I am. I must look like a beast to you. Tell me. You, you are a ray of sunlight, a drop of dew, the song of a bird! But I, I am something frightful, neither man nor beast, a something that's harder, more trod upon, and more unshapely than a stone."

Then he began to laugh—the most heart-rending laughter in all the world, and went on.

"Yes, I am deaf. But you will speak to me with gestures and signs. I have a master who talks with me that way. And then, I shall know your wishes by the movement of your lips and by your eyes."

"Well, then," she said smiling, "tell me why you saved me."

When she was speaking he looked at her intently.

"I understand," he replied; "you asked me why I saved you. You have forgotten a poor wretch that tried to carry you off one night—a poor wretch that you brought relief to on the very next day when he was tied to their shameful pillory. That drop of water and your pity are more than I could repay with my life. You have forgotten that wretch—but he has remembered."

She listened to him with profound emotion. A tear rolled in the bellringer's eye, but it did not fall. He seemed to make it a point of honor to hold it back.

"Listen to me," he went on, when he was again in command of his emotion, "we have very high towers here. If a man were to fall from one, he'd be dead before he reached the pavement. When you want me to fall, you won't even have to say a word—a look from you will be enough."

Then he rose. This strange being, unhappy as the gypsy girl was, still awakened some compassion in her. She made a sign for him to stay.

"No, no!" he said. "I must not stay too long. I am not at ease when you are looking at me. It is out of pity that you don't turn your eyes away. I will go somewhere where I can see you and you won't see me. That will be better."

He took from his pocket a little metal whistle. "There," he said, "when you need me, when you want me to come, when you won't be too horrified at the sight of me—whistle for me with that. I can hear that."

He laid the whistle on the ground and went away.

4

Earthenware and Crystal

The days passed.

Little by little calmness returned to Esmeralda. Excessive grief, like excessive joy, is a too violent state to last long. The heart of man is incapable of sustaining for a long time extreme emotion. The gypsy girl had suffered so much that the only emotion she now felt was astonishment.

So, in this place of sanctuary, hope returned to her. True, she was outside the pale of society, of life, but she vaguely sensed that one day she would return. It seemed as if one dead still held in reserve the key to unlock her tomb.

The terrible images which had so long haunted her began to withdraw gradually. All the hideous phantoms, Pierrat

Torterue, Jacques Charmolue, and the rest were fading from her mind, even the priest himself.

Besides, Phoebus was still alive. Of this she was sure for she had seen him. That he was alive meant everything to her. After the numerous, terrible shocks which had overturned everything in her soul, she found nothing still standing there but one feeling, her love for the captain. For love is like a tree; it grows of itself; it sends its roots deep into our being, and often continues to grow green over a heart in ruins. How inexplicable it is that the blinder this passion the more tenacious it is; the more unreasonable, the stronger!

Assuredly La Esmeralda could not think of the captain without bitterness. Assuredly it was heinous that he too should have been deceived, that he should have believed such a thing possible as that a poniard stab would have come from her who would have given a thousand lives to save him. And yet, she must not be too angry with him; for had she not confessed the crime? Had she not yielded, weak woman that she was, to the torture? It was all her fault. She ought rather to have let them tear out her nails than to have made such an avowal. After all, could she but see Phoebus once more, for a single minute, a word, a look, would suffice to reassure him, to bring him back. Of this she had no doubt. Moreover she tried to understand several singular circumstances—Phoebus' happening to be present on the day of the penance at the church door, his being with that young lady. It was his sister no doubt—an explanation very improbable, but she was satisfied with it, because she had to believe that Phoebus still loved her, and loved only her. Had he not sworn his love to her? And what stronger assurance did she need, naive and credulous as she was? Besides, in this affair, was not circumstantial evidence more against her than against him? So she waited and hoped.

We might remark also that the church, this vast edifice which enclosed her, which guarded her, which was her salvation, was itself a sovereign anodyne. The solemn lines of its architecture, the religious posture of all the objects which surrounded the young girl, the pious and serene thoughts that emanated, so to speak, from every pore of these stones, acted upon her without her knowing it. The edifice had sounds, too, of such blessedness and such majesty that they soothed her suffering soul. The monotonous chant of the monks, the responses of the people to the priests, sometimes inarticulate, sometimes thunderingly clear, the harmonious trembling of the stained-glass windows, the organ bursting out like a hundred trumpets, the three bell towers humming like the hives of enormous bees, all that orchestra, over which bounded a gigantic gamut, ascending and descending incessantly, from the voices of the crowd to those of the bells, lulled her memory, her imagination, and her grief. The bells especially soothed her. It seemed that those vast machines sent a powerful magnetic current through her in strong waves.

Furthermore, each sunrise found her less pale, breathing more freely, calmer. As her interior wounds healed, beauty and serenity bloomed again in her face. Her former character also returned—something even of her gaiety, her pretty grimace, her love for her goat, her fondness for song, and her modesty. In the morning she was careful to dress in the corner of her little cell, less some inhabitant of the neighboring garrets should see her through the window.

When Phoebus' image left her mind for a moment, the gypsy girl sometimes thought of Quasimodo. He was the only bond, the only link, the only communication she had with mankind, with the living. How wretched she was! She was more cut off from the world than Quasimodo himself. She knew not what to make of this strange friend whom chance had given to her. She would often reproach herself for not feeling grateful enough to close her eyes to his deformity, but decidedly she could not accustom herself to the poor bellringer. He was too ugly.

She had left on the floor the whistle he had given to her. However, though he was not summoned, still Quasimodo did appear from time to time during the first lonely days. She did her best to conceal her repugnance when he came with his basket of provisions or the pitcher of water, but he always noticed her least fleeting expression of that kind, and then he went sorrowfully away.

Once, he came as she was petting Djali. He stood for several moments, pensive, watching that graceful group, the goat and the gypsy.

At length, shaking his heavy, deformed head, he said,

"My misfortune is that I am still too much like a man; I wish I were a beast completely, like your goat!"

She glanced at him in astonishment.

"Oh!" he replied to that look, "well do I know why." And he went away.

Another time, he came to the door of her cell, into which he never entered, while Esmeralda was singing an old Spanish ballad, the words of which she did not understand but which she remembered, because the gypsy women had rocked her to sleep with them when she was a child. At the sight of that hideous face, the young girl stopped singing with an involuntary gesture of fright. The hapless bellringer fell to his knees on the threshold of the door, and with an imploring look, clasped his huge, shapeless hands.

"Oh!" he said, sorrowfully, "I pray you, go on, and don't send me away."

She didn't want to vex him, and so, trembling, she continued her ballad. By degrees her alarm subsided, and she abandoned herself wholly to the expression of the plaintive air that she was singing. Quasimodo remained on his knees, with his hands joined, as in prayer, attentive, hardly breathing, his look fixed upon the shining eyes of this gypsy, as if through them he understood her song.

On still another occasion, he came to her shyly and more awkwardly than usual.

"Listen," he said with much effort, "I have something to tell you."

She gave a sign that she was listening.

Then he began to sigh, half-opened his lips, seemed for a moment on the verge of speaking, then looked at her, made a negative motion with his head, and slowly went away, with his hand pressed to his forehead, leaving the gypsy mystified.

Among the grotesque figures carved on the wall, there was one for which Quasimodo had much affection, and with which he often seemed to be exchanging fraternal glances. Once the gypsy girl heard him saying to it, "Oh, why am I not made of stone like you?"

At length, one morning, La Esmeralda, having mounted to the parapet of the roof, was looking into the square, over the peaked roof of Saint-Jean-le-Rond. Quasimodo was standing behind her. He used to so place himself of his own accord, in order to spare the young girl as much as possible the disagreeable sight of him.

Suddenly the gypsy shuddered: a tear and a flash of joy shone at once in her eyes; she knelt down on the edge of the roof, and stretched out her arms in anguish toward the square, crying, "Phoebus! Come! Come! One word! only one word, in Heaven's name! Phoebus! Phoebus!"

Her voice, her face, her gestures, her whole person had the agonized expression of one shipwrecked, who is making signals of distress to a distant vessel sailing gayly along in the sunshine on the horizon.

Quasimodo leaned over to look down on the square, and saw that the object of this tender and heart-rending prayer was a young man, a captain, a handsome cavalier, his side arms and uniform all glistening, who was caracoling on the square beneath, and saluting with his plumed helmet a fine young damsel, smiling, on her balcony. The officer, however, did not hear the poor unfortunate gypsy who was calling to him. He was too far away.

But the poor deaf bellringer understood. A deep sigh heaved his breast. He turned around. His heart swelled with all his repressed tears; his hands, clenched convulsively, struck against his head, and when he drew them away there came with each of them a handful of his red hair.

The gypsy was paying no attention to him.

Gnashing his teeth, he said in a whisper, "Damnation! So that's how a man should be! He need only be handsome on the outside!"

Meanwhile, Esmeralda had remained on her knees. Now she cried out, "Oh, there he is, getting off his horse! He's going into that house! Phoebus! He doesn't hear me! Phoebus! Oh, that shameless woman, to talk to him at the same time that I do! Phoebus! Phoebus!"

The deaf man kept his eye fixed upon her. He understood this pantomime. The poor bellringer's eye filled with tears, but he suffered none of them to fall. Suddenly he tugged her gently by the sleeve. She turned around. He had regained his composure and said to her, "Would you like me to fetch him?"

"Oh, yes, go! Go! Run quickly!" she cried with joy. "That

captain! Bring him to me, and I'll love you!" She clasped his knees.

He could not help shaking his head sorrowfully. "I will bring him to you," he said weakly. Then he turned and bounded down the staircase, stifling his sobs.

When he reached the square, nothing was to be seen but the fine horse fastened to the gate post at the Gondelaurier mansion. The captain had just gone inside. Quasimodo looked up toward the roof of the church. La Esmeralda was still standing in the same place, in the same posture. He made her a sad sign with his head; then leaned with his back against one of the pillars of the porch, determined to wait until the captain came out.

It was, at the mansion Gondelaurier, one of those festive days that precede a marriage. Quasimodo saw many people enter, but nobody came out. Now and then he looked up at the roof of the church. The gypsy had not moved; nor had he. A groom came, untied the horse, and led him into the stable of the mansion.

The whole day passed in this manner, Quasimodo leaning against the pillar, La Esmeralda waiting on the roof; Phoebus, no doubt, at the feet of Fleur-de-Lys.

Finally it was night, a night without a moon, a dark night. In vain did Quasimodo fix his eye upon La Esmeralda. Soon, she was nothing but a pale speck in the dusk, then nothing. All had vanished, all was black.

Quasimodo saw the front windows of the Gondelaurier mansion lighted from top to bottom; he saw the other windows of the square light up one after the other; one after another, too, he saw the light disappear from them, till every one was dark, for he remained the whole evening at his post. The officer did not come out. When the last promenaders had returned to their homes, when all the windows of the other houses were darkened, Quasimodo remained all alone, in complete darkness. In those days the Parvis of Notre-Dame was not lighted.

However, lights shone in the windows of the Gondelaurier mansion, even after midnight. Quasimodo, motionless and attentive, saw passing behind the many-colored panes a multitude of lively dancing shadows. Had he not been deaf, as the noises of slumbering Paris died away, he would have

heard more and more distinctly from within the mansion the
sounds of festivity, laughter, and music.

About one o'clock in the morning, the guests began to
leave. Quasimodo, enveloped in darkness, watched all the
guests as they came out under the torch-lighted porch. The
captain was not among them.

His thoughts were sad. Now and then he looked up into
the air, like one tired of waiting. Large, heavy, black clouds,
torn and divided, were hanging like crepe hammocks beneath the starry arch of night. They looked like the cobwebs
of heaven's vaulted ceiling.

At one of those moments, he suddenly saw the lighted
French door on the balcony, whose stone balustrade projected above him, quietly open, and two persons emerge
onto the balcony. Then the door softly closed behind them.
They were a man and a woman. With some difficulty, Quasimodo could recognize the handsome captain and the young
lady whom he had seen in the morning welcoming the officer from the same balcony. The square was in total darkness,
and a double crimson curtain, which had fallen behind the
door at the moment it had closed, hardly allowed a gleam of
light from the apartment to reach the balcony.

The young captain and the lady, as far as our deaf spectator could judge—for he could not hear a word they were
saying—appeared to be in a very tender tête-à-tête. The
young lady seemed to permit the officer to put his arm
around her waist, yet was coyly resisting a kiss.

Quasimodo, from below, witnessed this scene, the more
attractive as it was not intended to be witnessed. However,
he contemplated that happiness, that beauty, with bitterness
and rancor. After all, nature was not mute in the poor fellow;
deformed as he was, his heart nevertheless had feeling like
any other man's. He mused on the wretched lot that Providence had meted out to him—how woman, and the joys of
love, were destined everlastingly to pass under his eye without his ever being more than a witness to the happiness of
others. But what pained him most of all about this scene,
what mingled indignation with his vexation, was to think
what the gypsy girl would suffer if she were to see this. True
it was that the night was very dark, that Esmeralda, if she
had remained at the same place, as he doubted not she had,

was very far off, and that it was all that he himself could do to distinguish the lovers on the balcony. This consoled him somewhat.

Meanwhile, the conversation became more and more animated. The young lady seemed to be entreating the officer to ask nothing more of her. All that Quasimodo could distinguish was the beautiful joined hands, the smiles mixed with tears, the uplifted eyes of the young woman, and the eyes of the captain fixed ardently upon her.

Fortunately for the young lady, whose resistance was growing weaker, the door to the balcony suddenly opened and an old lady appeared, to the confusion of the beautiful one and the chagrin of the captain, and they all went inside.

A minute later, a horse pranced under the porch, and the brilliant officer, wrapped in his night cloak, passed rapidly in front of Quasimodo.

The bellringer let him turn the corner of the street, and then he ran after him, with his monkeylike agility, shouting "Ho, there, captain!"

The captain reined in his horse. "What does that scoundrel want with me?" he said to himself, on spying in the dark that queer uncouth figure hobbling after him.

Meanwhile, Quasimodo had approached, and, boldly taking the horse's reins, said, "Follow me, captain, there's someone here who wants to speak with you."

"Damnation!" grumbled Phoebus. "Here's a villainous ragged bird that I think I've seen somewhere before. Hey there! Drop that rein!"

"Captain," answered the deaf man, "don't you want to know who it is?"

"I tell you, let go of my horse," returned Phoebus angrily. "What, rogue, do you mean, hanging from my charger's bit? Do you take him for a gallows?"

Quasimodo did not let go, but rather was preparing to make him turn around. Unable to explain to himself the captain's resistance, he hastily said to him, "Come, captain; a woman is waiting for you." Then with an effort he added, "A woman who loves you."

"The impertinent rascal!" said the captain, "who thinks me obligated to trudge after every woman that loves me, or says she does, and supposing she looks like you, an owl-faced villain! Tell her that sent you that I am going to be married, and that she can go to the devil!"

"Listen," cried Quasimodo, thinking to overcome the captain's hesitation with a word. "Come, monseigneur, it's the gypsy girl you know!"

The word, in fact, produced a great effect on Phoebus, but it was not that which the deaf man expected. It will be remembered that our gallant officer had retired from the balcony with Fleur-de-Lys a few minutes before Quasimodo delivered the penitent out of the hands of Charmolue. Since then, in all his visits to the Gondelaurier mansion, he had been careful to avoid mentioning that girl, the recollection of whom, after all, was painful to him; and Fleur-de-Lys, on her part, had not deemed it politic to tell him the gypsy girl was still alive. So Phoebus believed poor Similar, as he called her, to have been dead for a month or two. It must be noted too that the captain had been thinking for a few minutes of the darkness of the night, the supernatural ugliness and sepulchral voice of the messenger; that it was past midnight, that the street was as deserted as it had been on the evening the phantom priest had accosted him, and that his horse had snorted at the sight of Quasimodo.

"The gypsy girl!" he cried, almost terrified. "What, are you come from the other world?"

And he grasped his dagger.

"Quick, quick!" said the deaf man, trying to turn the horse around. "This way."

Phoebus gave him a violent blow in the chest with his boot.

Quasimodo's eye flashed. He made a movement to throw himself upon the captain, but quickly checked himself. "Oh, lucky for you that someone loves you!"

He emphasized the word "someone" and, dropping the horse's rein, he said, "Now go!"

Phoebus spurred his horse and galloped off, swearing. Quasimodo watched him plunge into the misty darkness of the street.

"Oh!" whispered the poor fellow, "to refuse that!"

He went back into Notre-Dame, lighted his lamp, and went up to the tower again. Just as he had thought, the gypsy girl was still in the same spot.

The moment she saw him coming, she ran to meet him. "Alone!" she cried, wringing her beautiful hands in agony.

"I could not find him," said Quasimodo, impassively.

"You should have waited for him the rest of the night," she shot back vehemently.

He saw her angry gesture and understood her reproaches.

"I'll watch for him better next time," he said, lowering his head.

"Go away!" she said.

He left her. She was dissatisifed with him. He would rather be ill-treated by her than cause her pain, so he kept all the grief to himself.

From that day forward, the gypsy girl saw him no more. He no longer came to her cell. Now and then, indeed, she caught a distant glimpse of the bellringer's face looking sadly down upon her from the top of one of the towers, but as soon as she caught sight of him, he was gone.

We must admit that she was little disturbed by Quasimodo's voluntary absence. At the bottom of her heart she was glad of it. Nor was the hunchback himself under any illusion about the matter.

She saw him no more, but she felt the presence of a good genius around her. Her provisions were brought to her by an invisible hand while she slept. One morning, she found at her window a cage of birds. Over her cell there was a piece of sculpture that frightened her. She had repeatedly said this in Quasimodo's presence. One morning (for all these things were done at night), she saw it no longer—it had been broken off. He who had climbed up to that piece of carving must have risked his life.

Sometimes in the evening, she heard the voice of some unseen person concealed under the penthouse of the steeple singing, as if to lull her to sleep, a strange, melancholy song, without rhyme, such as a deaf man might make.

> Look not at the face,
> Young maiden, look at the heart:
> The heart of a handsome man
>   is often deformed.
> There are hearts that cannot hold
>   love for long.

Young maiden, the pine tree is not handsome
Nor fair like the poplar;
But it keeps its leaves in wintertime.

Alas, why say that?
Beauty loves only beauty—
What is not fair ought not to be—
April turns her back on January.

Beauty is perfect;
Beauty can do all.
Beauty is the only thing that does not
     live by halves.
The raven flies only by day,
The owl, only by night,
The swan flies night and day.

On waking one morning she saw in her window two vases
full of flowers. One was in a bright, handsome crystal vase
but cracked; it had let all the water escape, and the flowers
it contained were faded. The other vase was of earthenware,
rude and common, but had kept all the water, so that its
flowers remained fresh and blooming. I know not whether it
was done to convey a message, but La Esmeralda took the
faded flowers and wore them all day in her bosom.

That day she did not hear the voice from the tower
singing—a circumstance that gave her very little concern.

She passed her days fondling Djali, watching the door of
the Gondelaurier mansion, talking to herself about Phoebus,
and in feeding the swallows with crumbs of bread.

Besides, she had altogether ceased to see or to hear Quasimodo. The poor bellringer seemed to have disappeared
from the cathedral. One night however, as she lay awake,
thinking of her handsome captain, she heard the sound of
someone breathing near her cell. She rose, frightened, and
saw by the light of the moon a shapeless man lying across
the front of her door. It was Quasimodo asleep on the stones.

5

The Key to the Porte-Rouge

Meanwhile, by public rumor, the archdeacon had been informed of the ingenious manner in which the gypsy girl had been saved. Hence he knew not what his feelings were. He had reconciled himself to Esmeralda's death; he had drunk the cup of misery to its bitter dregs. The human heart—Dom Claude had meditated on these matters—cannot contain more than a certain quantity of despair. When the sponge is soaked, the ocean could pass over it without its absorbing one drop more.

Now the sponge being filled by the death of Esmeralda, all was over and done for Dom Claude on this earth.

But now to know she was alive—and Phoebus too—was to begin over again the tortures, the shocks, the torments of life. And Claude was weary of all that.

When he heard the news, he locked himself in his cloister cell. He appeared neither at the Chapter conferences nor at the services in the church. His door was closed to all, even to the bishop. For several weeks, he remained walled up in this manner. They thought he was ill, and so he was indeed.

What was he doing while thus shut up? With what thoughts was this poor wretch struggling? Was he engaged in the last contest with his indomitable passion? Was he scheming another plan of death for her and of damnation for himself?

Jehan, his cherished brother, his spoiled child, came once to his door, knocked, swore, begged, called out ten times. But Claude would not open the door.

He passed whole days with his face pressed against his window. From that window, located in the cloister, he could see Esmeralda's cell. He often saw her himself, with her goat, sometimes with Quasimodo. He remarked the deaf wretch's little attentions, his obedience, his delicate and submissive manner with the gypsy girl. He remembered, for he had a good memory, and memory is the tormentor of the

377

jealous, he remembered the singular look which the bellringer had cast upon the girl dancing in the square on a certain evening. He wondered what motive could have impelled Quasimodo to save her. He witnessed a thousand little scenes between the gypsy and the bellringer, which pantomime seen from a distance and accented by his passion, he thought very tender. He mistrusted the capricious fancies of women, and presently he felt awaking within him a jealousy such as he had never anticipated—a jealousy that made him blush for shame and indignation.

"As for the captain," he thought, "that might pass, but this one!" And the idea overwhelmed him.

His nights were dreadful. Ever since he had learned that the gypsy girl was alive, the cold vision of specter and tomb which haunted him for a whole day had vanished from his mind, and the flesh began again to torment him. He writhed on his bed to know the dusky beauty was so near him.

Each night, his feverish imagination conjured up pictures of Esmeralda in all the positions most calculated to inflame his passionate blood. He beheld her stretched over the wounded captain, her eyes closed, her soft naked bosom besplattered with the blood of Phoebus, at that moment of delight when the archdeacon had imprinted on her pale lips that kiss in which the girl, half dead as she was, had sensed his burning passion. He saw her undressed by the savage hands of her torturers; he saw them expose her finely shaped leg and her white supple knee while they encased her delicate foot in the horrid iron-screw. Lastly he imagined to himself the girl in her chemise, with the rope about her neck, her shoulders bare, her feet bare, almost naked, as he had seen her on that last day. These voluptuous pictures made his fists clench and a chill run up and down his spine.

One night in particular they so cruelly inflamed his priestly virgin blood that he tore his pillow with his teeth, leaped from his bed, threw a surplice over his nightshirt, thus half-naked, wild, with fire in his eyes, carrying his lamp, he left his cell.

He knew where to find the key to the Porte-Rouge, which opened from the cloister into the church, and, as we know, he always carried about him a key to the tower staircase.

6

Sequel to the Key to the Porte-Rouge

That night La Esmeralda had fallen asleep in her little cell, forgetful of her miseries, full of pleasant thoughts and hope. She had been asleep for some time, dreaming as always of Phoebus, when she thought she heard a noise. Her sleep was ever light—the sleep of a bird. The slightest thing awakened her. She opened her eyes. The night was black. Yet, she could see, at the window, a face looking at her; there was lamplight shining on this apparition. But, when the face knew itself to be seen by Esmeralda, the light was blown out.

Nevertheless the young girl had caught a glimpse of the visage. She closed her eyes in horror.

"Oh!" she said in a feeble voice, "the priest!"

All her past misfortunes, as if shown by lightning, flashed before her mind. She fell back on her bed, frozen with horror.

A moment later, she felt something touch her that made her tremble so violently that she sat upright, wide awake and furious. The priest had tiptoed up to her and had clasped her in his arms. She wanted to cry out but could not.

"Begone, monster! Begone, murderer!" she said in a low voice, that trembled with hate and dread.

"Mercy, mercy!" murmured the priest, pressing his lips to her shoulders.

She seized the scanty hair of his head and tried to squirm away from his kisses as if he were biting her.

"Mercy!" repeated the wretched man. "If you only knew my love for you! It is fire, molten lead, it is a thousand daggers in my heart!" And he held her arms with a bestial force.

"Let me go!" she cried wildly, "or I'll spit in your face!"

He let her go.

"Vilify me, strike me, be angry with me, do what you will, but for mercy sake, love me!"

Then she struck him with all the fury of a child. She curled her fingers to tear at his face. "Begone, demon!"

379

"Love me, love me! Pity!" cried the poor priest, grappling with her and answering her blows with kisses.

All at once she felt his superhuman strength overpowering her.

"There must be an end to this," he said, gnashing his teeth.

She was vanquished, panting, broken in his arms, at his mercy. She felt a lascivious hand wander over her body. She made a last effort to cry out. "Help! help me! A vampire! A vampire!"

But no one came. Djali alone was awake and bleating with fear.

"Be quiet!" panted the priest.

Suddenly, while they struggled, rolling on the stone floor, the gypsy's hand felt something cold and metallic. It was Quasimodo's whistle. She seized it with convulsive hope, put it to her lips, and blew with all her remaining strength. The whistle sounded clear, shrill, and piercing.

"What's that?" said the priest.

Simultaneously, the priest felt himself lifted by a powerful arm. The cell was dark, he could not clearly distinguish who it was that held him thus. But he heard teeth chattering with rage. The dim light in the cell was sufficient to show Dom Claude a large cutlass blade shining just above his head.

The priest thought he could distinguish the form of Quasimodo. He supposed it could be no one else but him. He remembered having stumbled, when entering Esmeralda's cell, against a mass of something that was lying outside across the doorway. Yet as the newcomer uttered not a word, he knew not what to think. He threw himself upon the arm that held the cutlass, crying out. "Quasimodo!" forgetting in his fright that Quasimodo was deaf.

In a split second the priest was thrown to the floor, and he felt a leaden knee weighing upon his chest. By the shape of that knee he recognzied Quasimodo. But what could he do? How was he to make himself known? Night rendered the deaf hunchback also blind.

Dom Claude was done for. The young girl, with as much pity as an enraged tigress, did not intervene to save him. The cutlass was descending upon his head. The moment was crucial.

Suddenly his adversary seemed seized with hesitation. "No blood upon her!" he said, in a muffled voice.

It was in fact the voice of Quasimodo.

Then the priest felt a huge hand dragging him by the feet out of the cell. It would be there he was to die. Fortunately for him, the moon had just come up a few minutes before.

When they had crossed the threshold of the cell, its pale beams fell upon the face of the priest. Quasimodo looked at him, a tremor came over him; he let go the priest and stood back.

The gypsy girl, having come to the door of her cell, was surprised to see them suddenly change roles—for now it was the priest who was threatening, and Quasimodo who was entreating.

The priest, who was flinging gestures of anger and reproach upon the deaf man, motioned him violently to leave.

The deaf man lowered his head, then came and knelt before the gypsy's door.

"Monseigneur," he said, in a gravely resigned voice, "afterward you will do what you please—but kill me first."

As he spoke, he offered the priest his cutlass. The priest, beside himself with rage, was going to seize it. But the girl was quicker than he. She snatched the cutlass from Quasimodo's hands, and burst into wild laughter.

"Approach," she said to the priest.

She held the blade above her head. The priest hesitated. She would certainly have struck.

"You would not dare to approach, coward!" she screamed at him. Then she added, looking at him pitilessly, knowing full well that she was going to twist the dagger that constantly the priest wore in his heart, "Ah, hah! I know that Phoebus still lives!"

Then Dom Claude with a violent kick knocked Quasimodo to the floor, and plunged into the vault of the staircase.

When he had gone, Quasimodo picked up the whistle which had just saved the gypsy girl. "It was rusting," he said, returning it to her. Then he left her alone.

The young girl, upset by this violent scene, fell exhausted on her bed and began to sob aloud. Her horizon had again become overcast.

For his part, the priest groped his way back to his cell. It was done. Dom Claude was jealous of Quasimodo! Lost in thought he repeated his doleful words, "No one shall have her!"

BOOK X

1

Gringoire Has Several Wonderful Ideas in Succession in the Rue des Bernardins

When Pierre Gringoire, from his attendance at the trial in the Palace of Justice, realized that torture, penance, and hanging were in store for La Esmeralda, the principal character in this drama, he wanted no part of it. The vagabonds, or Truands, among whom he had remained, considering, as he did, that, after all, they were the best company in Paris, continued to feel anxiety for the gypsy girl. He thought that very natural in people who, like her, had nothing but Charmolue and Torterue in prospect, and who did not, like him, Gringoire, soar aloft in the regions of imagination on the wings of Pegasus. He had learned from their conversations that his bride of the broken pitcher had found refuge in Notre-Dame, for which he was most pleased. But he did not even feel tempted to go to see her there. He sometimes thought of the little goat, but that was all. In the daytime he performed feats of strength to earn his bread; and at night he was fabricating a paper against the Bishop of Paris. Gringoire remembered being drenched by His Reverence's mill wheels, and bore malice against him for it. He also was writing a commentary upon the fine work of Baudry-le-Rouge, Bishop of Noyon and Tournay, *De Cupa Petrarum,* which had given him a fervent interest in architecture. This new craze had supplanted in his breast a passion for hermetics. This is understandable because there is an intimate connection between hermetical philosophy and stonework. Gringoire had passed from the love of an idea to the love of the substance.

One day he had stopped near the church of Saint-Germain-l'Auxerrois, at the corner of a building called *Le For-l'Evêque,* which was opposite another called *Le For-le-Roi.* There was at this For-l'Evêque a charming fourteenth-century chapel, the chancel of which was on the street side. Gringoire was examining intently its external sculpture. It was one of those moments of selfish, exclusive, and supreme enjoyment, in which the artist sees nothing in the world but art, the world itself being encompassed in that art.

All at once he felt a hand placed heavily on his shoulder; he turned around. There was his old friend, his old master, the archdeacon. He was quite confounded. It was long since he had seen the archdeacon. Dom Claude was so serious and zealous that a meeting with him always disturbed and embarrassed a skeptical philosopher.

The archdeacon for some moments kept silent, during which time Gringoire leisurely observed him. He found Dom Claude much changed—pale as a winter morning. His eyes were deep-sunken, his hair almost white. The priest was the first to speak, saying in a quiet but cold tone, "How goes it with you, Master Pierre?"

"My health?" said Gringoire. "Why, one might say, so-so. But on the whole, I would say good! I don't take too much of anything. You know, master, the secret of good health, according to Hippocrates, *id est cibi, potus, somni, Venus, omnia moderate sint.*"[1]

"Then, you have no problems, Master Pierre?" rejoined the archdeacon, looking steadfastly at Gringoire.

"Faith, not I."

"And what are you doing now?"

"You see for yourself, master. I am examining the cut of these stones, and the way in which this bas-relief is chiseled."

---

[1] "That is, food, drink, sleep, Venus, all things are moderate."

The priest smiled, one of those bitter smiles which raises only one corner of the mouth.

"And that amuses you?"

"It is sheer paradise!" exclaimed Gringoire. And leaning close to the sculpture, with the dazzled look of a demonstrator of living phenomena: "Now, for example, don't you find that this metamorphosis in low relief is executed with consummate skill, grace, and patience? Look at that small column. Around what capital have you ever seen foliage more delicately and gently touched with the chisel? Note these three medallions by Jean Maillevin. They are not the finest examples by that incomparable genius. Nevertheless, the simplicity, the sweet expression on the faces, the gaiety of the postures and draperies, and that inexplicable charm which blends with all the imperfections, render the miniature figures so very light and delicate—perhaps even too much so. Don't you find this amusing and entrancing?"

"Yes, I do," said the priest.

"And if you could see the interior of the chapel!" continued the poet, with his loquacious enthusiasm. "Sculpture everywhere! Leafy like the heart of a cabbage. The styling of the chancel is just divine, and so unusual; I have never seen anything like it anywhere!"

Dom Claude interrupted him. "You are happy then?"

"Why yes, upon my honor," replied Gringoire emphatically. "First I loved women, then animals. Now I love stones. They are just as diverting as animals or women, and not so perfidious."

The priest passed his hand across his forehead. It was a gesture habitual with him. "Indeed!"

"Listen!" said Gringoire. "There is so much pleasure in all this." He took the arm of the priest, who did not resist, and led him up under the staircase turret of the For-l'Evêque.

"Now there's a staircase! Every time I behold it, I am happy. That flight of steps is the most simple and yet the most unusual in all of Paris. Every step is hollowed underneath. Its beauty and simplicity consist in the details of the steps. They are about a foot in depth, and are interlaced, morticed, jointed, interlocked, encased, set one in the other, and butting into each other, in a way that's truly both solid and architecturally beautiful."

"And you desire nothing else?"

"Nothing!"

"And you regret nothing?"

"I neither regret nor desire anything. I have ordered my whole life."

"What man orders," said Claude, "circumstances disorder."

"I am a Pyrrhonean philosopher," answered Gringoire, "and I keep everything in balance."

"And how do you earn your living? your life?"

"I still write now and then, epic poems and tragedies. But what brings me the most money is that industrious talent of mine which you are aware of—carrying pyramids of chairs in my teeth."

"A menial occupation for a philosopher."

"Again it's a question of balance," said Gringoire. "When one gets an idea in one's head, one finds the same thought in everything."

"I know it," answered the archdeacon.

After a momentary silence, the priest went on, "And yet you are just as poor as ever?"

"Poor—yes; unhappy—no."

Just then there was the sound of horses' hooves, and our two friends saw parading at the end of a street a company of the king's archers, with their lances raised, and an officer leading them. The cavalcade was brilliant; its marching resounded on the pavement.

"Why are you staring at that officer?" said Gringoire to the archdeacon.

"I think I know him."

"What's his name?"

"I believe," answer Claude, "his name is Phoebus de Châteaupers."

"Phoebus! What a curious name! There is also a Phoebus, Count of Foix. I remember having known a girl who never swore by any other name."

"Come away," said the priest. "I have something to say to you."

Since the passing of that troop, a degree of agitation

seemed to animate the reserved archdeacon. He walked on. Gringoire followed him, accustomed to obeying him, like all who had once approached that formidable being. They reached in silence the Rue des Bernardins, which was quite deserted. Dom Claude stopped.

"What have you to say to me, master?" asked Gringoire.

"Don't you think," said the archdeacon, with a look of deep reflection, "that the dress of those archers who have just passed is finer than yours or mine?"

Gringoire shook his head.

"Faith, no! I prefer my red and yellow cloak to those shells of iron and steel. A fine pleasure that, only to make a noise when marching like an iron wharf in an earthquake!"

"Then, Gringoire, you have never envied those handsome fellows in their warlike coats of mail?"

"Envied them for what, Monsieur the Archdeacon, for their strength, their armor, their discipline? Give me rather philosophy and independence in rags. I would rather be the head of a fly than the tail of a lion."

"That is most strange," mused the priest. "A handsome uniform is nevertheless handsome."

Gringoire, seeing him pensive, took leave of him to go and admire the porch of a nearby house. He returned clapping his hands.

"If you were less occupied with the fine clothes of the soldiers, Monsieur the Archdeacon, I would beg you to go and see that doorway. I have always said that the entrance to the Sieur Aubrey's house is the most superb in the world."

"Pierre Gringoire, what have you done with that little gypsy dancing girl?"

"La Esmeralda? My, how abruptly you change the conversation!"

"Was she not your wife?"

"Yes, thanks to a broken pitcher, we were married for a period of four years. By the way," added Gringoire, with a half-bantering tone and air, "you still think of her then?"

"And you, don't you think of her any more?"

"Very little—I have so many other things! . . . My God, how pretty her little goat was!"

"Didn't the gypsy girl save your life?"

"By God! that's true!"

"Well! what has become of her? What did you do with her?"

"I can't tell you. I think they hanged her."

"You think?"

"I'm not sure. When I saw someone was to be hanged, I got myself out of the affair."

"And that's all you know about her?"

"Wait a minute! Someone told me she took sanctuary in Notre-Dame, and that she was safe there—and I'm delighted—and I've not been able to find out whether the goat escaped with her—and that's all I know about her."

"Then, I am going to tell you more," cried Dom Claude, and his voice, until then low, deliberate, and hollow, became like thunder. "She has indeed taken refuge in Notre-Dame. But in three days justice will drag her again from there, and she will be hanged at the Grève. There is a decree by parliament for her execution."

"That's a pity," said Gringoire.

The priest in a moment had become cool and calm again.

"And who the devil," continued the poet, "has taken the trouble to solicit a sentence of reintegration? Couldn't they leave the parliament alone? Of what consequence can it be that a poor girl takes shelter under the buttresses of Notre-Dame among the swallows' nests?"

"There are satans in the world," answered the archdeacon.

"Well, that's a devilish bad piece of work!" observed Gringoire.

The archdeacon resumed after a short silence, "She saved your life, then?"

"Yes, among my good friends, the Truands. I was within an inch of being hanged. They would have been sorry for it today though."

"Don't you want to do something for her?"

"I ask nothing better, Dom Claude; but perhaps I may get my own neck into an ugly noose!"

"What does it matter?"

"What does it matter! You're very kind, master. But I have begun two works of colossal importance."

The priest struck his forehead. In spite of the calm which he affected, from time to time this violent gesture betrayed his inward convulsions. "How can she be saved?"

"Master," replied Gringoire, "let me tell you: *Il padelt,* which in Turkish means, 'God is our hope.' "

"But how save her," repeated Claude, assuming an attitude of thoughtfulness.

Gringoire in his turn struck his forehead.

"Listen, my master. I have some imagination. I am going to find expedients. Suppose we asked pardon from the king?"

"From Louis XI? Pardon?"

"Why not?"

"Go take a bone from a tiger!"

Gringoire began to search for other solutions.

"Wait! Listen! Shall I draw up a parchment from the matrons of the city declaring that the girl is pregnant?"

The pupils of the priest's hollow eyes sparkled.

"Pregnant! Stupid! What do you know about it?"

Gringoire was terrified at his manner and hastened to say, "Oh no! not by me! Our marriage was a regular *forismaritagium*—I was shut out. But at any rate, we could obtain a stay of execution."

"Madness! Insane! Be silent!"

"You are wrong to be angry," grumbled Gringoire. "If one gets a respite, that doesn't harm anyone, and it puts forty deniers parisis into the pockets of the matrons who are poor women."

The priest wasn't listening to him. "She must get out of there," muttered the priest. "The sentence is to be carried out in three days. Otherwise, it would not be valid—That Quasimodo! Women have depraved tastes!" He raised his voice, "Master Pierre, I have well considered the matter. There is but one way to save her."

"And how is that? For my part, I see no way."

"Listen, Master Pierre; remember you owe your life to her. I will tell you frankly my idea. The church is watched day and night, no one is allowed to come out but those who have been seen to go in. Thus you can go in. You shall come, and I will take you to her. You will change clothes with her. She will take your doublet and you will take her skirt."

"So far, so good," observed the philosopher, "and then what?"

"What then? Why she will go out wearing your clothes, and you will stay behind with hers. You may get hanged perhaps, but she will be saved."

Gringoire scratched his ear and grimaced seriously.

"Well!" he said, "that's an idea that never would have crossed my brain."

At Dom Claude's unexpected proposal the open and benign countenance of the poet had become instantly overcast, like a smiling Italian landscape when a chance gust of wind suddenly dashes a cloud across the sun.

"Well, Gringoire, what do you say to the plan?"

"I say, master, that I shall not be hanged perhaps, but that I shall be hanged indubitably."

"That does not concern us."

"The deuce it doesn't!"

"She saved your life. You are repaying a debt."

"But there are many debts that I don't pay."

"Master Pierre, you must do it!"

The archdeacon spoke imperatively.

"Listen, Dom Claude," replied the poet in consternation, "you may cling to that idea, but you are wrong. I don't see why I should get myself hanged instead of another."

"What can you have to attach you so strongly to life?"

"Ah, a thousand attachments!"

"What are they, pray tell."

"What are they? The air, the sky, the morning, the evening, the moonlight, my good friends the Truands, our romps with the good-natured damsels, the beautiful architectural works of Paris to study, three big books to write, one of them against the bishop and his mills—I know not what else. Anaxagoras used to say he had been put in the world just to admire the sun. And then, I have the happiness of passing all my days, from morning till evening, with a man of genius, who is me, and that's very pleasant."

"Oh, you rattlebrain!" grumbled the archdeacon. Then he continued, "Well, tell me, that life you make out to be so charming, who saved that life for you? To whom are you indebted for air to breathe, for the sky to see, for being still able to amuse your larklike spirit with trash and foolery? But for her, where would you be? Would you have her die, she, by whom you live? Would you have her die, that creature, so lovely, so sweet, so adorable—a creature necessary to the light of the world—more divine than divinity itself—while you, half philosopher, half fool, a mere sketch of something, a kind of vegetable which fancies it walks and thinks, would continue to live with the life you have stolen from her, as useless as a taper at noonday? Come, Gringoire, a little pity! Be of generous mind. She has set an example for you!"

The priest was vehement. Gringoire listened to him at first with an air of indecision, then became moved and concluded by pouting, which likened his wan face to that of a small baby in a seizure of colic.

"You sound very pathetic!" he said, wiping away a tear. "Well, let me think about it. It's a queer idea of yours. After all," he pursued, after a pause, "who knows? Perhaps they won't hang me; there's many a slip between the cup and the lip. When they find me in that cell, so grotesquely muffled in cap and skirt, perhaps they'll roar with laughter. And then, if they do hang me, oh well, the rope is a death like any other. Or rather, it's not a death like any other. It's a death worthy of a philosopher who has been oscillating all his life, a death which is neither fish nor fowl, like the mind of a true skeptic, a death marked with Pyrrhonism and hesitation, which holds the middle between heaven and earth, which leaves one in suspense. It's a philosopher's death, and perhaps I was predestined to it. It is fine to die as one has lived."

The priest interrupted him. "Agreed?"

"After all, what is death?" continued Gringoire still in a burst of enthusiasm. "An unpleasant moment, a toll, a passage from little to nothing. When someone asked Cercidas of Megalopolis if he would die willingly, 'Why not?' he replied, 'for after death I shall meet those great men, Pythagoras, among the philosophers, Hecataeus, among the historians, Homer, among the poets, and Olympus, among the musicians.' "

The archdeacon held out his hand. "Then, we are agreed? You will come tomorrow?"

This gesture brought Gringoire back to reality.

"Faith, no!" he said, with the tone of a man just awaking. "Be hanged! That's too absurd! I will not."

"Adieu, then!" And the archdeacon added between his teeth, "I shall find you again!"

"I don't want that devil of a man to find me again," thought Gringoire to himself, and he ran after Dom Claude.

"Hey, wait, Monsieur the Archdeacon! No harm done between old friends! You have an interest in that girl, my wife, I mean. That's good. You have thought of a stratagem for getting her safe out of Notre-Dame, but your plan is extremely unpleasant for me, Gringoire. Now, suppose I could suggest someone other than myself? A great idea just came to my mind. If I had a way of extricating her from her sorry plight without compromising my neck in the smallest degree, what would you say? Would that satisfy you? Is it absolutely necessary that I should be hanged to make you happy?"

The priest was tearing the buttons from his cassock with impatience. "You're a babbling brook of words! What is your scheme?"

"Yes," continued Gringoire, talking to himself, and touching his nose with his forefinger as a sign of deep cogitation. "That's it! The Truands are fine fellows. The Egyptian tribe love her. They will rise at the first word. Nothing easier. A sudden attack. By means of the disorder they will easily carry her off. Tomorrow evening. Nothing would please them more."

"The scheme! Speak!" said the priest, shaking him.

Gringoire turned imperiously toward him.

"Let me be! You can see I am planning."

He reflected a few minutes more, then began to clap his hands at his thought, exclaiming, "Admirable! a sure success!"

"The plan!" repeated Claude angrily.

Gringoire was beaming.

"Come over here. I must whisper this to you. It's a brilliant counterplot that will get us all out of this mess. You must confess, I'm not a dolt!"

He stopped short. "Ah, but the little goat, is it still with the girl?"

"Yes, may the devil take you!"

"They would have her too, would they not?"

"What's that to me?"

"Yes, they would have hanged her. They hanged a sow last month, sure enough. The executioner likes that. He eats the animal afterward. To think of hanging my pretty Djali! Poor little goat!"

"Curses!" cried Dom Claude. "The hangman is you! What means, imbecile, have you devised for saving her! Must you be delivered of your scheme with forceps?"

"Softly, master! You shall hear."

Gringoire leaned over and whispered in the archdeacon's ear, at the same time casting an uneasy look from one end of the street to the other, though there was no one passing. When he had finished, Dom Claude took his hand and said coldly, "It's good. Till tomorrow, adieu!"

"Till tomorrow," repeated Gringoire, and while the archdeacon withdrew one way he went off the other, saying low to himself, "This is a nice affair, Monsieur Pierre Gringoire! Never mind, it's not to be said that because one's of little account one's to be frightened at a great undertaking. Biton carried a great bull on his shoulders; wagtails, linnets, and swallows cross the ocean."

2

Turn Truand

When the archdeacon returned to his cell he found his brother, Jehan du Moulin, who had been waiting for him and who had been whiling away the time sketching in charcoal on the wall his brother's profile, caricatured by a very large nose.

Dom Claude's thoughts were so busy with other matters that he scarcely glanced at his brother. That happy-go-lucky, impish face, the brightness of which had so many times restored serenity to the gloomy physiognomy of the priest, was now incapable of dissipating the mist which each day was gathering thicker and thicker over a corrupted, mephitic, stagnant soul.

"Brother," said Jehan dryly, " I have come to see you."

The archdeacon didn't even raise his eyes.

"What do you want?"

"Brother," resumed the young hypocrite, "you are so good to me, and you give me such excellent advice, that I always come back to you."

"What now?"

"Alas, brother, you were right when you said to me, 'Jehan! Jehan! *cessat doctorum doctrina, discipulorum disciplina,* Jehan, be prudent! Jehan, be studious! Jehan, do not pass the night away from the college without just reason and the permission of your master. Do not beat the Picards, *noli, Joannes verberare Picardos.* Don't rot like an unlettered ass, *quasi asinus illitteratus,* upon the straw of the school. Jehan, submit to punishment at the discretion of the master. Jehan, go every evening to the chapel, and sing an anthem and pray to the glorious Blessed Virgin Mary!' Alas! this was very excellent advice."

"And so?"

"Brother, you see standing here a sinner, a criminal, a wretch, a libertine, a monstrous reprobate! My dear brother, Jehan has taken your gracious counsels as mere straw and dung to be trodden underfoot, and he has been well chastened for it. The good Lord is exceedingly just. So long as I had money, I squandered it in foolish, joyous living. Oh! how hideous and vile to look back upon that debauchery which seemed at the time so charming! Now I have not a single sou left; I have sold my linen, my shirt, and my towel. No more gay life for me. The burning candle has gone out, and I have only the poor wick that smokes under my nose. The girls make fun of me. I am drinking water. I am harassed by remorse and creditors."

"What else?" asked the archdeacon.

"Alas! my very dear brother, I would like to live a better life. I come to you, contrite of heart, penitent. I confess my evil ways. I beat my breast with heavy blows. You are very right to want me to become one day a licensee and submonitor of the college of Torchi. At this very moment I feel called to that office. But I have no ink left; I need to buy some; I have no pens, I must buy some; I have no paper, no book, I must buy some. To buy them I have need of a little money. And I come to you, brother, with my heart full of contrition."

"Is that all?"

THE HUNCHBACK OF NOTRE-DAME

"Yes," said the scholar. "A little money."

"I have none."

The scholar then said with an air at once grave and determined, "Well, my brother, I regret to inform you that I have received from other quarters very fine offers and propositions. You will not give me any money? No? In that case, I will become a Truand."

On pronouncing this monstrous word he assumed the stance of an Ajax expecting a thunderbolt to fall upon his head.

The archdeacon said to him coldly, "Then become a Truand."

Jehan made a low bow, and descended the cloister staircase whistling.

Just as he was passing through the court of the cloisters, under the window of his brother's cell, he heard the window open. Raising his head he saw the archdeacon's severe face looking through the opening.

"Go to the devil!" said Dom Claude. "This is the last money you will get from me."

So saying, the priest threw out a purse to Jehan, which made a large bump on his forehead. With that the youth set off, at once angry and pleased, like a dog that has been pelted with marrow-bones.

3

Hurray for the Gay Life!

The reader perhaps has not forgotten that a part of the Court of Miracles was enclosed within the ancient wall of the town, a great number of the towers of which were beginning at that time to fall into ruin. One of these towers had been converted by the Truands into an entertainment hall. There was a tavern on the lowest level, and other activities were carried on in the upper stories. This tower was the liveliest spot, and therefore the most hideous, of the whole vagabond quarter. It was a kind of monstrous hive, which buzzed night and day. At night, when all the rest of the rabble were asleep, when not a lighted window was to be seen

in the dingy fronts of the houses in the square, when not a
sound was heard to issue from its innumerable houses, from
those swarms of thieves, loose women, and stolen or bastard
children, the joyous tower could always be distinguished by
the noise which proceeded from it, by the crimson light
which, gleaming at once from the air holes, windows, and
crevices in the gaping walls, escaped, as it were, from every
pore.

The cellar was then the tavern. The descent to it was by
a low door and stairs as rugged as classic Alexandrine verse.
On the door there was by way of a sign a marvelous daub
representing new-coined sols and dead chickens, with this
pun underneath: *Aux sonneurs pour les trépassés.*

One evening, at the moment when the curfew bell was
ringing from all the steeples in Paris, the sergeants of the
watch, had they been allowed to enter the formidable Court
of Miracles, might have noticed that still greater tumult than
usual was going on in the tavern of the Truands; there was
more drinking and the swearing was louder. Outside, in the
square, were numerous groups conversing in subdued tones,
as if some important plot were brewing; and here and there
a fellow squatted down to sharpen an evil-looking blade
upon a paving stone.

In the tavern itself, wine and gaming diverted the minds
of the truandry so intently from the ideas which had occupied them that evening, that it would have been difficult to
have guessed from the conversation of the drinkers what affair so agitated them. Only they looked gayer than usual, and
between the legs of each of them was seen glittering some
weapon or other—a pruning hook, an ax, a large broad-
sword, or the crook of an old harquebus.

The room, circular in form, was vast, but the tables were
so close together and the drinkers so numerous, that the
whole contents of the tavern—men, women, benches, beer
jugs, the drinkers, the sleepers, the gamblers, the able-
bodied, the crippled—seemed thrown helter-skelter together
with about as much order and arrangement as a heap of oys-
ter shells. A few greasy candles were burning on the tables,
but the real luminary of the tavern, that which sustained in
the pothouse the character of a chandelier in an opera house,
was the fire. The cellar was so damp that the fire was never

allowed to go out even in midsummer. An immense fireplace, under a carved mantelpiece, was furnished with heavy andirons and kitchen utensils. In it, there burned one of those huge fires of wood and turf, which at night in village streets produce, by their glare on the opposite walls, the appearance of the windows of a smithy. A large dog, gravely sitting among the ashes, was turning a spit laden with meat before the fire.

In spite of the confusion, after a first inspection, there might be distinguished in this multitude three principal groups, pressing around three personages with whom the reader is already familiar. One of these, fantastically accoutered with many an Oriental ornament, as Mathias Hungadi Spicali, Duke of Egypt and Bohemia. The scoundrel was seated on a table, his legs crossed, his finger jabbing the air, as he imparted in a loud voice sundry lessons in black and white magic to many a gaping face around him. Another group had gathered around our old friend, the valiant King of Thunes, who was armed to the teeth. Clopin Trouillefou, with a very serious air and in a low voice, was superintending the pillage of an enormous cask full of arms staved wide open before him, from which tumbled in profusion axes, swords, firelocks, coats of mail, lance and pike heads, crossbows and arrows, like apples and grapes from a cornucopia. Each person was helping himself from the heap: one a helmet, another a long rapier, and another a cross-handled dagger. Even the children were arming themselves, and there were even legless cripples who, cuirassed and accoutered, passed between the legs of the drinkers like large beetles. Finally, a third group, the biggest, the noisiest, and the most jovial, crowded the benches and tables from the midst of which a flutelike voice was haranguing and swearing from inside a heavy suit of armor complete from helmet to spurs. The individual who had thus screwed himself up in full panoply was so lost under his warlike trappings that nothing could be seen of his person but a red, impudent, turned-up nose, a lock of fair hair, red lips, and a pair of daring eyes. About his waist he wore a belt loaded with daggers and poniards, a long sword hung at his right side, a rusty crossbow on his left. Before him sat a huge jug of wine, and a strapping wench, with her breasts exposed, was seated on his right. All the mouths around him were laughing, swearing, and drinking.

Add to these twenty secondary groups, the waiters, male and female, running back and forth with pitchers above their heads; the gamesters stooping over billiards; the dice; and the impassioned game of tringlet; loud arguments in one corner, kisses in another, and some idea then may be had of the whole scene, over which flickered the light of the great flaming fire, making a thousand grotesque and enormous shadows dance on the tavern walls.

As for the noise, it was like the interior of a loudly pealing bell.

The dripping pan in which a shower of grease continuously crackled filled the intervals of those thousand dialogues which crossed each other in all directions from one end of the hall to the other.

In the midst of this din and confusion, seated on a bench in the chimney corner, was a philosopher, absorbed in meditation, his feet in ashes, and his eyes fixed on the burning brands. It was Pierre Gringoire.

"Come quick! Hurry up! Get your arms! We are marching in an hour!" shouted Clopin Trouillefou to his band.

A girl was humming a tune:

> Goodnight, mother and father!
> The last douse the fire!

Two card players were arguing.

"Knave!" cried the angrier of the two, shaking his fist at the other. "I'll mark you with a club. You'll be able to take Mistigri's place in Monseigneur the King's own card party!"

"Ouf!" bawled one, whose nasal accent betrayed his Norman origin, "we are packed in here like the saints of Caillouville."

In his falsetto voice, the Duke of Egypt said to his band, "Lads, the witches of France are going to the sabbath without brooms, or anything to ride on, or ointment, bearing only a few magical words. The witches of Italy have always a he-goat that waits for them at their door. All of them are bound to go out of the house through the chimney."

The voice of the young scamp, armed from head to toe, was heard above the uproar.

"Noël! Noël!" he was shouting. "My first day in armor! A Truand! I am a Truand, by the belly of Christ! Pour me a goblet of wine! My friends, my name is Jehan Frollo du Moulin, and I am a gentleman. I'll bet if God were a gendarme, he'd be a robber. Brothers, we are going on a great expedition. We are valiant. We are to lay siege to the church; break down the doors; carry off the damsel; save her from the judges and priests; dismantle the cloister; burn the bishop in his palace—we'll do this in less time than it takes a burgomaster to eat a spoonful of soup. Our cause is just; we'll pillage Notre-Dame, and that's final. We'll hang Quasimodo. Do you know Quasimodo, my fair ladies? Have you seen him all out of breath on the big bell on Whit-Sunday? By the devil's horns! It's a sight! You would say he was the devil riding a ghoul. My friends, hear me! I am a Truand to the bottom of my heart; I'm an Argotier in my soul, I'm a born wastrel. I was very rich, but I spent it all. My mother wanted me to be an officer; my father, a subdeacon; my aunt, a counselor of inquisition; my grandmother, a king's protonotary; my great aunt, keeper of the short robe: but I, I was made to be a Truand. I told my father, and he spat curses in my face. I told my mother, and she, poor old lady, began to cry and slobber like the log upon that andiron there. Hurray for the gay life! I am a real madman! Barmaid, my darling, give me some different wine! I still have enough to pay! I don't want any more of that Suresnes wine. It irritates my throat. Why, by God, I'd rather gargle with poison!"

Meanwhile, the rowdy mob applauded with bursts of laughter; and, seeing that the tumult was swelling around him, the scholar shouted, "What wonderful noise! *Populi de bacchantis populosa debacchatio!*"[1]

Then he began to sing, his eyes drowned in ecstasy, with the tone of a monk chanting vespers. *"Quae cantica! quae organa! quae catilenae! quae melodiae hic sine fine*

---

[1] "Of the people celebrating, a populous transport."

decantantur! sonnant melliflua hymnorum organa, suavissima angelorum melodia, cantica canticorum mira! "[2]
He stopped. "Hey there, you devil's barmaid, give me something to eat."

There was a moment of almost complete silence, broken only by the shrill voice of the Duke of Egypt giving instructions to his Bohemians. "The weasel is called Aduine; the fox, Blue-Foot or the Wood-Ranger; the wolf, Gray-Foot or Gilt-Foot; the bear, the Old-Man or the Grandfather. A gnome's cap makes one invisible, and enables one to see invisible objects. Whenever a toad is to be baptized, it ought to be dressed in red or black velvet, with a bell around the neck and one tied to its feet. The godfather holds it by the head, the godmother, by the hind legs. The demon Sidragasum has the power of making girls dance all naked."

"By the holy Mass!" interrupted Jehan, "then I should like to be this demon Sidragasum!"

In the meantime, the Truands were continuing to arm themselves, whispering to one another at the other side of the tavern.

"That poor Esmeralda!" remarked one gypsy. "She is our sister. We must get her out of there."

"So, she's still in Notre-Dame, is she?" asked a Jewish peddler.

"Aye, *pardieu!*"

"Well, comrades," resumed the peddler, "to Notre-Dame! For a second reason, there in the chapel of Saints Féréol and Ferrution, there are two statues, one of Saint John the Baptist, the other of Saint Anthony, both of solid gold, weighing together seventeen gold marks and fifteen estellins; and the pedestals, of silver gilt, weigh seventeen marks five ounces. I, a goldsmith, can vouch for this."

Just then Jehan received his supper. Throwing himself on the bosom of the girl who sat by him, he shouted, "By Saint Voult-de-Lucques, called by the people Saint Goguelu, I am perfectly happy. Over there directly in front of me I see an

[2] "What songs! what instruments! what chants! what melodies are sung here without end! They resound as sweet as honey, the instruments of hymns, the sweetest melody of angels, admirable song of songs!"

imbecile that's staring at me with the patronizing air of an archdeacon. There's another, to my left, with teeth so long they hide his chin. And too I'm like the Maréchal de Gié at the siege of Pontoise—my right hand is fingering a teat. *Ventre-Mahom!* comrade! you look like a draper, and you have the gall to come sit next to me! I am a nobleman, my friend! and trade is incompatible with nobility. Get you gone! Hey, you there! don't fight. What! Baptiste Croque-Oison! are you not afraid to risk your beautiful nose to the clumsy fists of that simpleton? You dolt! *Non cuiquam datum est habere nasum.*[3] Verily, I say you are divine, Jacqueline Ronge-Oreille! It's a pity you are bald. Hey, my name is Jehan Frollo, and my brother is an archdeacon. Let the devil take him. Everything I say is the truth. By making myself a Truand, I have with gaiety thereby renounced half of a house in Paradise which my brother had guaranteed me. *Dimidiam domum in paradiso!*[4] I am citing the exact text. I've a fief, Rue Tirechappe, and all the women are in love with me. All this is as true as that Saint Eloy was an excellent goldsmith, and that the five trades of the good city of Paris are the tanners, the leather-dressers, the baldric makers, the pursemakers, and the shoemakers, and that Saint Lawrence was broiled over eggshells. I swear to you, comrades,

> That I shall drink no wine
> For a year, if I tell you lies!

"My charming one, there is a moon. Look over there, through the window! How the wind doth ruffle those clouds—just as I do your bosom. Girls! put out the children and snuff the candles. Christ and Mahomet! What am I eating now? Hey there, you old hussy! the hairs that are not on the heads of your wenches are in your omelets! Do you hear, old woman? I like my omelets bald. May the devil flatten your nose! A fine tavern of Beelzebub this is—where the wenches comb their hair with the forks!"

[3] "It is not given to just anyone to have a nose."
[4] "Half of a house in Paradise."

With this last remark he smashed his plate on the floor and began to sing at the top of his lungs:

> By God's blood,
> I have
> No faith, no law,
> No hearth, no house
> No king!
> No God!

Meanwhile, Clopin Trouillefou had finished distributing the arms. He went over to Gringoire, who seemed absorbed in profound reverie, with his feet on the andirons.

"My friend, Pierre," said the King of Thunes, "what the devil are you thinking about?"

Gringoire turned around and his smile was melancholy. "I like fireplaces, my dear seigneur. Not for any such trivial reason that fires warm our feet and cook our soup, but because they give off sparks. Sometimes I spend whole hours looking at the sparks. I see a thousand things in those stars that sprinkle the dark back of the chimney place. Those stars themselves are worlds."

"Deuce if I understand you!" said the Truand. "Do you know what time it is?"

"No, I don't," replied Gringoire.

Clopin then went up to the Duke of Egypt. "Comrade Mathias, this is not a good time. They say King Louis XI is in Paris."

"A good enough reason to get our sister out of his clutches," answered the old gypsy.

"You speak like a man, Mathias," said the King of Thunes. "Besides, we shall do the thing well enough. There's no resistance to fear in the church. Their canons are like so many hares, and we will go in full force. The men of parliament will be finely surprised tomorrow when they look for her. By the bowels of the pope! I won't have them hang that pretty girl!"

Clopin then left the tavern.

Meanwhile Jehan was shouting hoarsely, "I eat; I drink; I'm drunk; I'm Jupiter himself! Eh, Pierre l'Assommeur, if you look at me like that again, I'll belt your nose!"

Gringoire on the other hand, aroused from his meditation, had begun to contemplate the wild and noisy scene around him, muttering between his teeth, *"Luxuriose res vinum et tumultuosa ebrietas.*[5] Alas, what good reason have I to abstain from drinking, and how excellent is the saying of St. Benedict's, *Vinum apostatare facit etiam sapientes."*[6]

At that moment, Clopin returned and thundered, "Midnight!"

At this word, which had the same effect on the Truands as an order to mount has on a regiment, the entire band—men, women, children—rushed out of the tavern, with a great clatter of arms and iron implements.

The moon was overcast.

The Court of Miracles was completely dark. No light was to be seen. It was nevertheless far from being deserted. There a great crowd of men and women could be distinguished talking to each other in low voices. One could hear this human swarm buzzing.

Clopin mounted a huge stone.

"To your ranks, Egypt! To your ranks, Galilee!"

There was movement in the darkness. The multitude seemed to be forming a column.

In a few minutes, the King of Thunes again raised his voice, "Now, silence, in passing through Paris! The password is *'Petite flambe en baguenaud!'* We'll not light the torches till we reach Notre-Dame! March!"

Ten minutes later, the horsemen of the king's watch fled panic-stricken before the long black procession of silent men who were marching toward the Pont-au-Change. They filled the winding streets which ran in all directions through the widespread quarter of the Halles.

[5] "Wine and tumultuous inebriation are luxurious things."
[6] "Wine makes even wise men apostatize."

4

An Awkward Friend

That same night Quasimodo did not sleep. He had just made his usual latest rounds of the church. He had not noticed, when he was closing the doors, that the archdeacon passed near him. Consequently Quasimodo was not aware that Dom Claude had shown some ill-humor at seeing him bolt and padlock with care the enormous iron bar which gave to the heavy doors the solidity of a wall.

Dom Claude was more preoccupied than usual. Moreover, since the nocturnal adventure in Esmeralda's cell, he ill-treated Quasimodo constantly. But, in spite of this harshness and even though he sometimes struck the hunchback, nothing could shake the submission, patience, and devoted resignation of the faithful bellringer. From the archdeacon he could suffer anything, abusive language, threats, blows, without murmuring a reproach, without uttering a complaint. At most he would follow Dom Claude anxiously with his eye, as he ascended the stairs to the tower. But the archdeacon had of himself avoided seeing the gypsy girl again.

That night, then, Quasimodo, after glancing at his bells, at Marie, at Jacqueline, at Thibault, all of whom had recently been neglected, went to the top of the north tower, and there, placing his shuttered lantern on the steps, began to gaze over sleeping Paris. The night, as we have already said, was very dark. Paris, which had no street lights at this particular period, seemed then a confused heap of black masses, cut here and there by the silvery, winding Seine. Quasimodo could not see a light except one from the window of a distant building, whose dim and somber outline was sketched above the rooftops in the direction of the Porte Saint-Antoine. There, too, was someone watching.

While his only eye scanned that expanse of mist and darkness, the bellringer felt within him an inexpressible anxiety. For several days he had been aware of sinister-faced men constantly loitering near the church; they seemed to be memorizing every nook and cranny of Esmeralda's sanctuary. He wondered if some plot might be hatching against the unfortunate refugee, who, he imagined, was, like himself, thoroughly hated by the populace; he feared some dire outcome soon. So he remained in his tower, dreaming within his dream, as Rabelais says, his eye by turns cast upon her cell and upon Paris, keeping watch like a trusty dog, with a thousand suspicions in his mind.

All at once, while he was reconnoitering the great city with that eye which nature, as if by way of compensation, had made so piercing that it almost supplied the deficiency in Quasimodo's hearing, he realized that there was something unusual in the outline of the quay at the Vieille Pelleterie—that something moved there—that the top of the parapet which stood out black against the whiteness of the water was not straight and still like that of the other quays, but that it undulated as waves on the river or as the heads of a crowd moving.

This appeared strange to him. He redoubled his attention. The movement seemed to be toward the City where there was no light. This undulating mass remained some time on the quay; then flowed slowly off it, entering the interior of the island, where it stopped. The line of the quay became straight and motionless again.

Just as Quasimodo had exhausted all his conjectures, it seemed to him that this movement was reappearing in the Rue du Parvis, which runs into the City at a right angle to the front of Notre-Dame. Notwithstanding the darkness, he could see the head of a column issuing from that street, and in an instant a crowd spreading itself over the square. He could distinguish nothing further than that it was a crowd.

This spectacle terrified Quasimodo. It is probable that that strange procession, which seemed so anxious to cloak itself under this profound darkness, observed a silence no less profound. Still some sound must have escaped from it, were it only the shuffling of feet. Hence that multitude, which Quasimodo could indistinctly see and from which he could hear nothing, was nevertheless moving with purpose near him, and so produced on him the effect of an assemblage of the dead mute, impalpable, lost in fog. He sensed advancing toward him a mist peopled with men—a shade full of moving shades.

Then he was truly afraid; the idea of an attempt against the gypsy girl presented itself again to his mind. He had a vague feeling that the situation was critical. In this crisis he held counsel with himself, and his reasoning was more just and prompt than might have been expected from a brain apparently so ill-organized. Should he waken the gypsy girl and assist her to escape? Which way? The streets were beset; behind the church was the river; there was no boat, no egress! There was but one measure to be taken—to meet death on the threshold of Notre-Dame, to resist at least until some assistance came, if any were to come, and not to disturb the sleep of La Esmeralda. The unhappy girl would awaken soon enough to die. This resolution once taken, he proceeded to reconnoiter the "enemy" more calmly.

The crowd seemed to be increasing every moment in the Parvis. He concluded, however, that very little noise was being made, since the windows of the street and the square remained closed.

All at once a light shone out; and in an instant seven or eight lighted torches were waved above the crowd, shaking their tufts of flame in the deep shadow. Quasimodo then saw distinctly, milling in the Parvis, a frightful troop of men and women, partisans in rags, armed with scythes, pikes, pruning hooks, their thousand points all sparkling. Here and there, black pitchforks added horns to those hideous visages. He had a confused recollection of that populace, and thought he recognized these same heads as those which a few months before had greeted him as the Fools' Pope. A man holding a torch in one hand and a birch rod in the other mounted a boundary-stone, and appeared to be haranguing. At the same time the strange army performed some evolutions, as if taking up a station around the church.

Quasimodo took up his lantern and descended to the platform between the towers, to watch more closely, and to deliberate further on means of defense.

Clopin Trouillefou, having arrived in front of the middle door of Notre-Dame, had, in fact, placed his troops in battle array. Although he did not anticipate any resistance, yet, like a wise general, he wished to preserve such a degree of order as would, in case of need, enable him to face a sudden attack by the watch. He had accordingly drawn out his brigade in such a manner that, seen from above or at a distance, it might have been taken for the Roman triangle of the battle of Economa, the pig's head of Alexander, or the famous wedge of Gustavus Adolphus. The base of this triangle was placed along the back of the square, in order to bar the entrance to the Rue du Parvis; one of the sides looked toward the Hotel-Dieu, and the other toward the Rue Saint-Pierre-aux-Boeufs. Clopin Trouillefou had placed himself at the summit, with the Duke of Egypt, our friend Jehan, and the boldest of the beggar tribe.

An enterprise such as the Truands were now attempting against Notre-Dame was not an uncommon occurrence in the cities of the Middle Ages. What we in our day call a police force did not then exist. In densely populated towns, especially in the capital cities, there was no sole central power in command. Feudalism had constructed those great municipalities by a strange pattern. A city was an assemblage of innumerable seigneuries, which divided it into divisions or compartments of many shapes and sizes. Thence there arose a thousand contradictory establishments for city order. In Paris, for example, independent of the hundred and forty-one lords claiming censive or manorial dues, there were twenty-five claiming judicial and censive powers, beginning with the Bishop of Paris, who controlled five hundred streets, to the Prior of Notre-Dame-des-Champs, who had authority over only four. All these feudal justiciaries recognized only nominally the paramount authority of the king. All had the duty of highway maintenance; they were, in short, their own master. Louis XI was the indefatigable workman who began on a large scale the demolition of this feudal structure, which was carried on by Richelieu and Louis XIV, to the advantage of the royalty, and which was completed under Mirabeau in 1789 to the advantage of the people. Louis XI had indeed tried to break this network of seigneuries which covered Paris, by establishing to oppose it two or three ordinances for general protection. Thus in 1465 the inhabitants were ordered to light candles in their windows at night, and to shut up their dogs, under pain of the gallows. In the same year came the order to close the streets in the evening with iron chains, and to abstain from carrying daggers or other offensive weapons on the streets at night. But in a short time all these attempts for municipal protection fell into disuse. The townspeople allowed the candles in their windows to be extinguished by the wind, and their dogs to stray; the iron chains were only stretched across in case of siege; and the rule against carrying daggers resulted only in changing the name of the Rue Coupe-Gueule to Rue Coupe-Gorge, which surely was a manifest improvement. The old framework of the feudal jurisdictions remained, an immense accumulation of bailiwicks and seigneuries, crossing one another in all directions throughout the city, straitening and entangling each other, being interwoven with each other, projecting one into the other—a useless thicket of watches, underwatches, and counterwatches, through which armed bands of brigandage, rapine, and sedition were constantly passing. Thus it was not unusual, in this state of confusion, for a part of the populace to lay violent hands on a palace, a town house, or an ordinary mansion, in the most densely populated sections. In most cases, the neighbors did not interfere in such an affair unless the pillage reached them. They stopped their ears to the sound of gunfire, closed their shutters, barricaded their doors, and let the struggle exhaust itself with or without the watch; and the next day it would be casually said in Paris, "Last night Etienne Barbette had his house broken into," or "The Maréchal de Clermont was laid hold of," etc. Hence, not only the royal residences—the Louvre, the Palace, the Bastille, the Tournelles—but such as were simply seigneurial—the Petit-Bourbon, the Hotel de Sens, the Hotel d'Angoulême, etc.—had their battlemented walls and their turreted gates. The churches were protected by their sanctity. Some of them, nevertheless, but Notre-Dame was not among them, were fortified. The Abbey of Saint-Germain-des-Prés was castellated like a baronial mansion, and more weight of metal was to be found there in cannons than in bells. This fortress could still be seen in 1610, but now only the church remains.

But let's return to Notre-Dame.

When the first arrangements were completed, and we must say to the honor of the Truands' discipline that Clopin's orders were executed in silence and with admirable precision, the worthy leader of the band mounted the parapet of the Parvis and raised his hoarse and surly voice as he faced Notre-Dame, and waved his torch, whose light flickered in the wind, and, veiled at intervals by its own smoke, made a reddish light appear and disappear on the front of the church.

"To thee, Louis de Beaumont, Bishop of Paris, councillor in the court of parliament, I, Clopin Trouillefou, King of Thunes, Grand Coësre, Prince of Argot, Bishop of Fools, say, 'Our sister, falsely condemned for magic, has taken sanctuary in your church; you must give her refuge and safeguard. Now the court of parliament wants to remove her thence, and you give consent to it; so that she would be hanged tomorrow in the Grève, if God and the Truands were not here now. So, we come to you, Bishop. If your church is sacred, our sister is too; if our sister is not sacred, neither is your church. We summon you, then, to surrender the girl to us if you would save your church; or we shall take the girl and plunder the church. This would be better. In witness whereof I here plant my banner. And so, may God save you, Bishop of Paris.' "

Unfortunately, Quasimodo could not hear these words, uttered with a sort of sullen, savage majesty.

Then a Truand presented the banner to Clopin, who solemnly planted it between two of the pavement stones. It was a pitchfork from whose prongs hung a bleeding piece of carrion.

When this was done, the King of Thunes turned around and scanned his army, a ferocious multitude whose eyes gleamed almost as much as their pikes.

After a moment's pause, he shouted his order, "Onward, lads! To our task, blackguards!"

Thirty husky men, square shouldered, with the faces of smithies, bearing hammers, pincers, and crowbars on their shoulders, stepped from the ranks, advanced toward the main door of the church, went up the steps, and, crouching under the arch, worked on the door with pincers and levers. A crowd of Truands pressed against them either to help or just to watch. The eleven steps swarmed with vagabonds.

The door, however, did not yield.

"Devil!" said one, "it is tough and stubborn."

"She's old and her joints are stiff," said another.

"Courage, my friends," shouted Clopin. "I'll bet my head

against a slipper that you'll have opened the door, carried away the girl, and dismantled the main altar before there's a sexton awake. There! I think the lock is giving way."

Clopin was interrupted by a frightful crash behind him. He turned around. An enormous beam had just fallen from above, crushing a dozen of the Truands upon the church steps, and rebounded onto the pavement with the sound of a cannon. Some legs were broken. Many in the crowd, with cries of horror, scampered off in every direction. In the wink of an eye, the confined enclosure of the Parvis was empty. The men working on the door, though protected by the deep arches of the doorway, abandoned it, and Clopin himself retreated to a respectful distance from the church.

"I just narrowly escaped!" cried Jehan. "I felt the wind of it, *tête-boeuf*! But Peter the Demolisher has been demolished."

The astonishment mingled with dread which fell upon the remaining brigands with this unaccountable piece of timber is indescribable. They stood for some minutes gazing fixedly at this beam in greater consternation than they would have felt at an onslaught of twenty thousand of the king's archers.

"The devil!" growled the Duke of Egypt, "this smells of magic!"

"It's the moon that hurls this log at us," said Andry-le-Rouge.

"Why," remarked François Chanteprune, "you know, they say the moon's a friend of the Virgin's."

"Thousand popes!" shouted Clopin, "you are all a pack of fools!" But even he did not know how to explain this falling plank.

In the meantime nothing was distinguishable upon the facade of the building; the light from the torches did not reach to the top. The heavy beam lay in the middle of the Parvis, and groans were heard from the miserable wretches who had received its blow and who had been almost cut in two by the edges of the stone steps.

At last the King of Thunes, his first astonishment being over, hit upon an explanation which seemed to his comrades plausible.

"By God's gullet! Are the monks making a defense of it? Then sack! sack!"

"Sack!" echoed the mob with a loud hurrah. And they let loose a general discharge of crossbows and harquebuses against the front of the church.

These reports awoke the peaceful inhabitants of the neighboring houses. Several window shutters opened, and nightcaps and hands holding candles appeared in the casements.

"Fire at the windows!" cried Clopin.

The windows were immediately shut again, and the poor citizens, who had scarcely had time to cast a bewildered look upon that scene of glare and tumult, went back trembling to their wives, wondering whether the witches were now holding their sabbath in the Parvis of Notre-Dame, or whether they were being assaulted by the Burgundians as in the year '64. Therefore the husbands dreaded theft, the women rape, and all of them trembled.

"Sack! Sack!" repeated the Argotiers. But they dared not approach. They looked first at the church and then at the beam. The beam did not move. The edifice remained firm and aloof; but something had frozen the Truands.

"To your work, comrades!" cried Trouillefou. "Force down the door!"

No one moved.

"Beard and belly!" exclaimed Clopin. "What, men! afraid of a beam?"

One of the old men stepped forward to speak.

"Captain, it's not the beam that bothers us; it's the door that's overlaid with iron bars. The pincers are of no use."

"What do you need, then, to knock it down?" asked Clopin.

"Ah! We need a battering-ram."

The King of Thunes ran bravely up to the formidable piece of timber and put his foot on it. "Here's one, lads. The one the monks just sent us." And making a mock reverence to the church, he added, "Thank you, canons!"

This bravado had a good effect. The spell of the beam was broken. The Truands again found their courage; and soon the heavy beam, picked up like a feather by two hundred strong arms, was driven with fury against the great door which they had already attempted to break down. Seen thus, by the dim light which the few scattered torches of the Truands cast over the square, the long beam, borne along by that number of men, rushing on with its end pointed toward the church door, looked like some monstrous animal, with innumerable legs, running, head down, to attack a stone giant.

At the shock given by the beam the half-metal door resounded like an immense drum. It didn't give, but the whole cathedral shook; the innermost recesses of the edifice groaned. At the same instant a shower of huge stones began to rain down upon the assailants from the upper part of the front.

"Devil," cried Jehan, "are the towers shaking down their balustrades upon our heads?"

But the incentive had been given. The King of Thunes stuck to his explanation: definitely the bishop was putting up a defense. And so they rammed the door all the more furiously, in spite of the stones that were fracturing their skulls right and left.

It is to be noted that these stones fell one by one, but they followed each other so rapidly that the Argotiers always felt two of them at one and the same time, one against their legs, the other upon their heads. Nearly all of the rocks took effect. Already the dead and wounded were thickly strewn, bleeding and panting under the feet of the assailants, who, now, becoming more enraged, filled instantly the places of the disabled. The long beam continued to batter the door with timid strokes, the stones to rain down, the door to groan, and the interior of the cathedral to reverberate.

Undoubtedly the reader has guessed that this unexpected and exasperating resistance to the Truands' attack proceeded from Quasimodo.

Chance had unluckily favored our courageous hunchback.

When he had descended to the platform between the towers, his thoughts were all confused. He ran to and fro along the gallery for some minutes like one distraught, looking down upon that compact mass of Truands ready to rush against the church. He implored the devil or God to save the gypsy girl. He once thought of ascending the southern steeple and sounding the alarm bell; but before the loud voice of Marie could have uttered a single sound, would there not be an interval long enough for the door of the church to be forced ten times over?

It was just at this moment that the vagabonds were coming up to the door with their tools. What was to be done?

All at once he recollected that some masons had been at work the whole day, repairing the wall, the woodwork, and the roofing of the southern tower. This thought provided the spark for his subsequent action. The wall was stone; the roofing was lead, and then there was the woodwork, so heavy and so thickly set upright that it went by the name of "the forest."

Quasimodo ran to this tower. The lower chambers of it were, in fact, full of materials. There were piles of building stone, sheets of lead rolled up, bundles of lath, strong beams already cut by the saw, heaps of rubbish—in short, a complete arsenal.

Time was of the essence. Levers and hammers were at work below.

With strength multiplied tenfold by the feeling of imminent danger, the hunchback lifted an end of one of the beams, the heaviest and longest of all. He managed to push it through one of the loopholes; then laying hold of it again outside the tower, he shoved it over the outer edge of the balustrade surrounding the platform, and let it fall into the Parvis beneath. This enormous piece of wood, in its fall of a hundred and sixty feet, grazing the wall, breaking the sculptured figures, turned several times upon its center, like one of the two cross arms of a windmill that is gyrating by itself. At length it reached the ground. A horrible cry arose; and the dark piece of beam rebounded upon the pavement like a serpent rearing and striking.

Quasimodo saw the Truands scatter like ashes blown by a child. While some fixed their superstitious gaze upon the immense log fallen from the sky and others peppered the stone saints of the portal with a discharge of bolts and bullets, Quasimodo was efficiently piling up stones and rubbish, and even the masons' bags of tools, upon the edge of that balustrade from which he had already pushed the beam.

Accordingly, as soon as the vagabonds began to batter the great door, a shower of heavy stones began to fall, assuring the men that the church must be shaking itself to pieces upon their heads.

Anyone who could have seen the bellringer at that moment would have been frightened. Besides the projectiles, which he had heaped upon the balustrade, he had amassed a heap of stones upon the platform itself. As soon as the large stones which he had heaped upon the very edge were spent, he had recourse to this latter heap. As he stooped, rose, crouched, rose again, with incredible agility, he thrust his great gnome's head over the balustrade, and dropped an enormous stone—then another—then another. Now and then he followed some good big stone with his eye, and when he saw that it served well his purpose, he ejaculated a "Hum!" of satisfaction.

Meanwhile the beggars had not lost courage. More than twenty times the massive door which they were so furiously assailing had shaken under the assault of the oaken battering-ram propelled by a hundred strong men. The panels had cracked; the carvings were splintered; the hinges, at each blow, had danced on their hooks; the jambs had sprung out of place; the old wood had fallen in showers of dust as it had been bruised between the iron bands. Fortunately for Quasimodo's defense, there was more iron than wood.

Nevertheless he felt that the big door was beginning to buckle. Each blow of the battering-ram, notwithstanding that he did not hear it, awakened not only echoes within the church, but apprehension in his heart. As he looked down upon the Truands he beheld them, full of exultation and rage, shaking their fists at the dark front of the edifice; and he coveted, for the gypsy girl and himself, the wings of the terrified owls that were flocking away over his head. His shower of stones had not sufficed to repel the assailants.

It was in this moment of anguish that he noticed a little below the balustrade from which he had been hurling the rocks two long stone gutters which emptied directly over the main doorway. The upper opening of these gutters was in the floor of the platform. An idea occurred to Quasimodo. He ran to the little lodge which he occupied as bellringer and fetched a faggot. Over this he placed bundles of lath and rolls of lead—ammunition of which he had not yet made any use—and after pushing this pile into the proper position with regard to the openings of the gutters, he set fire to it with his lantern.

While he was thus engaged, the stone no longer fell; consequently the Truands ceased looking upward. The brigands, panting like a pack of hounds baying the wild boar in his lair, were pressing tumultuously round the great door, whose carvings were disfigured and shapeless from the strokes of the ram, but still erect. They waited in a sort of shuddering anxiety for the great stroke—the stroke which would stave it in. Each was striving to get nearest, in order to be the first, when it should open, to rush into that well-stored cathedral, that vast repository which had been accumulating riches for three centuries. The brigands reminded one another, with roars of exultation and greed, of the fine silver crosses, of the rich brocade copes, of the heavy silver gilt monuments, of all the magnificences of the choir, of the dazzling holiday displays—the rich Christmas decorations often illuminated with torches, and the Easter suns—of all those splendid solemnities in which shrines, candlesticks, ciboriums, tabernacles, and reliquaries embossed the altars, as it were, with coverings of gold and jewels. Certain it is that at that exciting moment every one of the Truand mob was thinking more about plundering Notre-Dame than about saving the gypsy girl. Indeed, we could even go so far as to believe that, in the minds of many, La Esmeralda was merely a pretext—if, indeed, thieves ever need a pretext.

All at once, when they were crowding about the battering-ram for a final effort, each one holding his breath and tensing his muscles, so as to give full force to the decisive stroke, a howling more terrifying yet than that which had burst forth and expired after the fall of the great beam rose from the midst of them. They who had cried out, they who were still alive, looked, and saw two jets of molten lead falling from the top of the edifice into the thickest of the crowd. The waves of that human sea parted under the boiling metal, which, at the two spots where it fell, made two black and reeking hollows in the crowd, like the effect of hot water thrown upon snow. There were dying wretches burned half to cinder and moaning in agony. Around the two principal jets drops of that horrible rain fell scatteringly on the assailants, penetrating their skulls like red-hot gimlets.

The outcry was horrible. Dropping the beam on the dead bodies, men, the boldest as well as the most timid, fled in disorder. The Parvis was empty for a second time.

From the square all eyes now looked upward to the top of the church where they beheld an extraordinary sight. On the topmost gallery, higher than the round central window, was a great flame rising between the two towers, sending up clouds of sparks—a blaze, irregular yet furious, a portion of which, by the action of the wind, was at intervals enveloped in smoke. Below that flame, which rose behind the trifoliated balustrade showing dark against its glare, the two monster-headed gutters were emitting incessantly their slow, scalding streams. The silver trickling shone against the black stones of the lower facade. The two jets of liquid lead, as they approached the ground, scattered into myriad drops, like water sprinkled from the small holes of a watering can. Above the flame the faces of the two towers, sharply outlined, one quite black, the other red, seemed huger still by all the enormity of shadow which they cast. The restless, flickering light from the unaccountable flame made the innumerable sculptured demons and dragons assume a formidable aspect—as if they were moving. Some of the gooselike heads seemed to be laughing; some of the gargoyles you might have fancied yelping; there were salamanders puffing at the fire; animal monstrosities sneezing in the smoke. Among those freaks thus awakened from their stony slumber by that unearthly flame, by that unwonted clamor, there was one walking about. He could be seen from time to time passing in front of the blazing pile like a bat before a torch.

Assuredly this strange beacon light must have awakened the faraway woodcutter on the Bicêtre hills. He must have been startled to see drifting over his coppices the gigantic shadows of the towers of Notre-Dame. .

A hush of terror now settled upon the Truands, during which nothing was heard but cries of alarm from the canons, who, shut up in their cloisters, were more uneasy than horses in a burning stable. Also, windows were opened stealthily, but quickly closed. There could be distinguished, too, stirrings in the interior of the houses and in the Hotel-Dieu. All around were the whispers of the wind blowing the flames; the last groans of the dying, and the constant crackling of the shower of boiling lead upon the pavement.

Meanwhile the Truand leaders had retreated under the porch of the Gondelaurier mansion and were there holding a council of war. The Duke of Egypt, seated upon a corner-stone, was contemplating fearfully the phantasmagoric blaze two hundred feet aloft. Clopin Trouillefou was gnawing his great fists with rage.

"Impossible to enter now!" he muttered to himself.

"An old bewitched church!" grumbled the old gypsy, Mathias Hungadi Spicali.

"By the pope's whiskers!" said a surly old gray-beard who had seen active army service, "there are two church gutters that spit molten lead at you better than the loopholes at Lectoure!"

"Do you see that devil packing back and forth in front of the fire?" screamed the Duke of Egypt.

"By God!" said Clopin, "it's the damned bellringer! It's Quasimodo!"

The gypsy shook his head. "No it isn't, I say. It's the spirit Sabnac, the great marquis, the demon of fortifications! He has the form of an armed soldier with a lion's head. Sometimes he rides a hideous horse. He turns men into stones, and builds towers of them. He commands fifty legions. It's him! I recognize him. Sometimes he's dressed in a fine golden robe, after the fashion of the Turks."

"Where's Bellevigne de l'Etoile?" asked Clopin.

"He's dead," answered a female Truand.

Here Andry-le-Rouge observed, laughing idiotically, "Notre-Dame's finding work for the Hotel-Dieu."

"Is there no way to force the door then?" cried the King of Thunes, stamping his foot.

Hereupon the Duke of Egypt with a melancholy air pointed to the two streams of boiling lead which streaked the dark front of the building, looking like two long phosphorescent distaffs.

"Churches have been known," observed he with a sigh, "to defend themselves in this manner, without man's help. Saint-Sophia's, at Constantinople, some forty years ago, threw down to the ground three times, one after another, the crescent of Mohammed just by shaking her domes, which are her heads. William of Paris, who built this cathedral, was a magician."

"Well, are we to go away then like so many cowards,"

said Clopin, "and leave our sister here for those hooded wolves to hang tomorrow?"

"And leave the sacristy, where there are cartloads of gold?" interjected a Truand whose name we are sorry to say we do not know.

"Beard of Mohammed!" exclaimed Trouillefou.

"Let's try again, just once more," rejoined the Truand.

Mathias Hungadi shook his head.

"We shall not enter by that door," he said. "We must find some other way—a hole—a false postern—a joint of some sort or other."

"Who's for it?" asked Clopin. "I'll go at it again. By the way, where's our little scholar Jehan who was clothed in armor?"

"No doubt he's dead," answered someone. "No one has heard him laugh lately."

The King of Thunes frowned.

"Too bad. There was a brave heart under all that armor. And Master Pierre Gringoire?"

"Captain Clopin," said Andry-le-Rouge, "he beat it before we got as far as the Pont-aux-Changeurs."

Clopin stamped his foot. "God's gullet!" he cried. "It was he who got us into this business, and then he leaves us here right in the thick of the mess. A talking soft-headed coward!"

"Captain Clopin," cried Andry-le-Rouge, looking up the Rue du Parvis, "here comes the little scholar!"

"Praised be Pluto!" said Clopin. "But what the devil is.he dragging after him?"

It was in fact Jehan, coming as quickly as he could, accoutered as he was like a knight, with a long ladder, which he was stoutly dragging over the pavement, more out of breath than an ant which has harnessed itself to a blade of grass twenty times its size.

"Victory! *Te Deum!*" cried the scholar. "Here's the ladder from the Saint Landry wharf."

Clopin went over to him.

"Look, child," he said, "what are you going to do with that?"

"I have it," answered Jehan panting, "I knew where it was—under the shed of the lieutenant's house. There's a girl there whom I know who thinks me quite a Cupid. It was through her I managed to get the ladder. The poor girl came down nearly naked to let me in."

"Yes, yes, go on!" said Clopin, "but what are you going to do with the ladder?"

Jehan gave him a roguish, knowing look, and snapped his fingers. At that moment he was really sublime. He wore on his head one of those overloaded helmets of the fifteenth century which frightened the enemy with their hideous peaks. The one which he wore was jagged with no less than ten peaks of steel, so that Jehan might have contended for the formidable epithet, "Armed with ten spikes," on the Homeric ship of Nestor.

"What do I want to do with it, august King of Thunes?" said he. "Do you see over the three doors that row of statues that look like nincompoops?"

"Yes. So?"

"It's the gallery of the kings of France."

"So what?" said Clopin.

"Now just wait! At the end of that gallery there's a door that's never locked. With this ladder I'll get up to it, and then I'm in the church."

"Lad, let me go up first."

"No, friend, that's my ladder. You can go second."

"May Beelzebub strangle you!" said Clopin, turning sulky. "I'll not go after anybody."

"Then, Clopin, go get a ladder."

And therewith Jehan set off again across the square, dragging along his ladder, and shouting, "Follow me, boys!"

In a jiffy the ladder was raised and leaned against the balustrade of the lower gallery, over one of the side doors. A cheering crowd of Truands pressed close to the foot of it to ascend. But Jehan maintained his right, and was the first to go up the ladder. The climb was a long one. The gallery of the French kings is, even today, about sixty feet from the ground; to which elevation was, at that period, added the height of the eleven steps from the pavement. Jehan ascended cautiously, much encumbered by his heavy armor, keeping one hand on the ladder and the other on his crossbow. When he was halfway up he cast a sad glance upon the poor dead Argotiers strewn over the steps of the grand portal.

"Alas!" he said, "here's a heap of dead worthy the fifth book of the *Iliad!*"

Then he continued upward.

The Truands followed him, one upon each step of the ladder. To see that line of mailed backs thus rise undulating in the semidarkness, one might have imagined it a serpent with steely scales, rearing itself to strike the church. And the whistling of Jehan, who formed its head, completed the illusion.

At length the scholar reached the parapet of the gallery, and climbed nimbly over it, receiving the applause of all the vagabonds. Thus master of the citadel, he gave forth with a joyful shout, but stopped short all at once, petrified. He had just espied, behind one of the royal statues, Quasimodo concealed, his eye flashing in the dark.

Before another of the besiegers had time to gain footing on the gallery, the formidable hunchback sprang to the head of the ladder, and, without saying a word, grasped the two upright ends with his powerful hands, lifted them, pushed them away from the wall, balancing for a moment, amid cries of anguish, that long and pliant ladder crowded with Truands from top to bottom, and suddenly, with superhuman strength, threw back that cluster of men into the square. There was an instant in which even the bravest faltered. The ladder, thrown backward, stood upright for a moment and seemed to hesitate, then swayed, then suddenly, describing a terrifying circular arch eighty feet in radius, it crashed to the pavement more swiftly than a drawbridge when its chains give way.

There arose one widespread imprecation, then all was still. A few mutilated wretches were seen crawling out from under the heap of dead.

Then a murmur of pain and anger replaced the recent acclamation of triumph among the besiegers.

Quasimodo, unmoved, his elbows resting on the balustrade, was quietly looking on, with the mien of some old long-haired king looking out his window.

Jehan Frollo, on the contrary, was in a desperate situation. He was alone on the gallery with the redoubtable bellringer,

separated from his companions by eighty feet of perpendicular wall. While Quasimodo was dealing with the ladder, the
scholar had run to the postern, which he expected to find unlocked. No such thing. The bellringer, as he entered the gallery, had fastened it behind him. Jehan had then hidden
himself behind one of the stone kings, not daring to breathe,
but watching the monstrous hunchback with apprehension.
He felt like the man who, once upon a time, while in love
with the wife of a zookeeper, went one evening to meet her
in their place of assignation. But he scaled the wrong wall,
and suddenly found himself face to face with a white bear.

For the first few moments, the hunchback seemed unaware of Jehan, but when he turned his head, he saw the
scholar.

Jehan prepared himself for an attack, but the hunchback
remained motionless. He only stared at the young fellow.

"Ho! ho!" said Jehan. "Why do you look at me with that
one melancholy eye of yours?"

As he was speaking, the young rogue was stealthily
readying his crossbow.

"Quasimodo," he cried, "I'm going to change your nickname. Henceforth they shall call you Blind One."

Jehan let go the feathered arrow. It whizzed, and pierced
the left arm of the hunchback. This no more disturbed Quasimodo than a scratch would have bothered King
Pharamond. He grasped the arrow, drew it out of his arm,
and quietly broke it over his big knee. Then he simply
dropped the two pieces on the gallery floor. But he did not
give Jehan time to shoot another. As soon as he had broken
the arrow, Quasimodo, breathing loudly through distended
nostrils, jumped like a grasshopper upon the scholar, flatten-
ing his armor against the wall.

Then, in the wavering half-light of the torches, was en
acted a scene of horror.

Quasimodo grasped in his left hand both the arms of
Jehan, who did not struggle, so utterly did he give himself
up for lost. With his right hand the hunchback took off, one
after another, with ominous deliberateness, the several
pieces of armor, the sword, the daggers, the helmet, the
breastplate, the arm pieces—like a monkey peeling a hickory

nut. Piece after piece of the scholar's iron shell Quasin ⟩ dropped at his feet.

When the scholar saw himself disarmed and unclothed, helpless and naked, in those powerful hands, he did not attempt to speak to his deaf enemy; but he began laughing scoffingly in Quasimodo's face, and singing, with the careless assurance of his sixteen years, a popular air of the time:

> The town of Cambrai
> Is richly clad
> But Marafin has stripped her . . .

He did not finish. Quasimodo stepped to the parapet of the gallery, and, holding the scholar by the feet with one hand only, swung him around like a sling over the abyss. There followed a noise like some box made of bone smashing against the wall. Something fell, but it stopped a third of the way down, being arrested in its descent by one of the architectural projections. It was Jehan's body, which remained suspended there, bent double, the loins broken and the skull empty.

A cry of horror arose from the Truands.

"Revenge!" cried Clopin.

"Attack!" answered the multitude. "Attack! Attack!"

Then there was an ominous howling, a babel of languages and dialects, in all tones of voice.

The poor scholar's death filled the crowd with frenzy. They were seized with shame and fury at having been so long held at bay before a church by a hunchback. Their rage found them ladders, and multiplied their torches. Soon, Quasimodo, in confusion and despair, saw a frightful swarm ascending from all sides to ravage Notre-Dame. They who had no ladders had knotted ropes, and they who had no ropes climbed up by means of the projections on the sculpture. They even clung to one another's tattered clothing. There was no way to resist this rising tide of frightful visages. Fury blazed in those ferocious faces; their dirty foreheads streamed with perspiration; their eyes were wild; all that ugliness and malice was aimed at Quasimodo. It seemed as if some other church had sent its gorgons, its dogs, its dragons, its most fantastic sculptures to assault Notre-Dame. It was like a layer of living monsters crawling over the stone monsters of the facade.

Meanwhile a thousand torches had been kindled in the square. This disorderly scene, obscured until then in semi-darkness, was now displayed by a sudden blaze of light. The Parvis was resplendent, and cast a radiance on the sky; while the pile that had been lighted on the high platform of the church still flamed and highlighted the city far around. The vast outline of the two towers, projected afar upon the roofs of Paris, threw into that light a huge shadow. The whole town seemed now to be roused from its slumber. Distant alarm bells were mournfully ringing. The Truands were howling, swearing, climbing, panting. And Quasimodo, powerless against so many enemies, trembled for the gypsy girl. Seeing all those furious faces approaching nearer and nearer to his gallery, he implored a miracle from heaven, and wrung his hands in despair.

5

The Retreat Where Monsieur Louis of France Prays

The reader has probably not forgotten that, on the night of the raid on Notre-Dame, when Quasimodo was surveying Paris from the top of his tower, he had seen but one single light which shone from a window on the topmost floor of a lofty gloomy building, in the direction of the Gate Saint-Antoine. This building was the Bastille, and the flickering light came from Louis XI's candle.

King Louis XI had, in fact, been in Paris for two days. He was to leave again on the day after the morrow for his fortress of Montilz-les-Tours. His visits to the good city of Paris were rare and always of short duration because he felt there a lack of personal security, due to an insufficient number of trapdoors, gibbets, and Scottish archers.

He had arranged to sleep that night in the Bastille. He disliked the great chamber at the Louvre, thirty feet square, with its massive chimney piece adorned with twelve great beasts and thirteen great prophets, and its huge bed, twelve feet by eleven. He, a good bourgeois king, felt lost in all that grandeur; he preferred the Bastille with its smaller room and smaller bed. And besides, the Bastille was more impregnable than the Louvre.

This chamber which the king had reserved for himself in the famous state-prison was, however, quite spacious; it occupied the uppermost floor of a turret forming part of the dungeon keep. It was a circular room; the floor was covered with shiny straw matting; gilded pewter fleurs-de-lis adorned the rafters of the ceiling, while the spaces between them were colorful, being wainscoted with rich wood, sprinkled with rosettes of white powder, and painted a fine light green made of crushed orpine.

There was only one long and pointed window, covered with brass wire and latticed with iron bars. It admitted little light because of the beautiful stained glass, portraying the arms of the king and those of the queen, each pane of which cost twenty-two sols.

There was but one entrance, a modern door, under an overhanging circular arch, furnished inside with tapestry, and outside with one of those porches of Irish wood, frail structures of curious workmanship, which still were plentiful in old French mansions a hundred and fifty years ago. "Although they disfigure and encumber the places," says Sauval disparagingly, "nevertheless our old people don't want them removed, but keep them in spite of everyone."

In this chamber there was none of the furniture of ordinary apartments, neither benches, nor trestles, nor common box stools, nor fine stools supported by pillars and counterpillars at four sols apiece. There was only one magnificent folding armchair, whose wood was painted with roses upon a red background, and whose seat was of red morocco, decorated with long silken fringe and studded with a thousand gold-headed nails. The absence of other chairs testified that one person alone had a right to be seated in this chamber. Next to the chair, and near the window, there was a table covered with a cloth embroidered with birds. On the table sat an inkstand, spotted with ink, some parchment scrolls, pens, and a chased silver goblet. A little removed from this table stood a chafing dish on a pedestal. A prie-dieu, covered with crimson velvet embossed with studs of gold, was near the bed at the far end of the room. This was a simple bed, spread with a yellow and flesh-toned damask counterpane without any decoration of any sort except a plain fringe. This bed became famous for having borne the sleep or the sleeplessness of Louis XI, and was still to be seen two hundred years ago in the house of a councillor of state, where it was seen by the aged Madame Pilou, celebrated in the great romance of "Cyrus" under the name of *Arricidie* and that of *La Morale Vivante.*

Such was the chamber referred to as, "The retreat where Monsieur Louis of France prays."

At this time in our story, as we said, it was very dark. Curfew had tolled an hour ago. In this room there was but one flickering candle on the table to illumine the five persons standing in groups.

One of these was a lord superbly attired in doublet and hose of scarlet striped with silver. His cloak, with large puffy sleeves, was made of cloth of gold with black figures. This splendid costume, as the light played upon it, glittered with every movement. This man wore upon his breast his coat of arms embroidered in brilliant colors: a chevron, with a deer passant in the base of the shield. The escutcheon was supported on the right by an olive branch, and on the left by a stag's horn. In his girdle was an expensive dagger, its silver-gilt hilt molded like a crest surmounted by a count's coronet. This gentleman carried his head high; his bearing was haughty, and his look, wicked. At first glance you read arrogance in his face, at the second, cunning.

He stood bareheaded, with a long scroll in his hand, behind the comfortable armchair, upon which was seated, with his body ungracefully bent double, his knees crossed, and his elbow resting on the table, a person very shabbily dressed. Imagine, indeed, seated on the rich Cordovan leather, a pair of crooked joints, a pair of lean thighs poorly covered by black worsted, a trunk wrapped in a loose coat of fustian the fur lining of which had much more leather left than hair; and to crown the whole, an old greasy hat of the meanest black cloth, banded by small leaden figures. This, over a dirty skullcap, beneath which hardly a single hair was visible, was all that could be distinguished of the sitting personage. He kept his head so much bent over his chest that of his face, thus thrown into shadow, nothing could be seen but the end of his long nose, upon which a ray of light fell. The thinness of his wrinkled hand evidenced that he was an old man. This was Louis XI.

Some distance from them, talking in low voices, stood two men dressed in Flemish fashion, who were not so completely in shadow but that anyone who had attended the performance of Gringoire's mystery could not recognize them as the two principal Flemish envoys, Guillaume Rym, the sagacious pensionary of Ghent, and Jacques Coppenole, the popular hosier. It will be remembered that these two men were mixed up with the secret politics of Louis XI.

Lastly, near the door, behind all the rest, there stood in the dark, motionless like a statue, a stout, brawny, thickset man in military dress, with coat emblazoned, whose square face, with its prominent eyes, its immense mouth, its ears concealed under a great mat of hair, and with scarcely any forehead, seemed a sort of mixture of dog and tiger.

All were hatless except the king.

The lord standing by His Majesty was reading to him a long official paper, to which the king seemed to listen attentively.

The two Flemings were whispering to each other.

"By the rood!" muttered Coppenole, "I'm tired of standing. Aren't there any other chairs here?"

Rym answered him negatively, with a circumspect smile.

"By the rood!" said Coppenole again, very much discomfited that he had to speak thus in a whisper, "I'm terribly tempted to sit on the floor, with my legs crossed, like the hosier that I am, as I do in my own shop."

"You had better not, Master Jacques."

"Whew! Master Guillaume, can only one stand here?"

"Or kneel," said Rym.

At that moment the king raised his voice and they stopped talking.

"Fifty sols for the gowns of our valets, and twelve livres for the mantles of the clerks of our crown! Is that right? You're spending gold by the tons! Are you mad, Olivier?"

As he spoke the old man raised his head, and you could see gleaming around his neck the golden shells of the collar of Saint-Michel. The candle shone full upon his meager and morose profile. He snatched the paper from the hands of the other.

"You are ruining us," he cried, scanning the ledger with his hollow eyes. "What is all this? Why do we need such a heavy complement of household personnel? Two chaplains at the rate of ten livres a month each, and a chapel clerk at a hundred sols. A chamber valet at ninety livres a year! Four squires of the kitchen at a hundred and twenty livres each a year! A roaster, a soup cook, a sauce cook, a head cook, a butler, and two assistants, at the rate of ten livres a month each! Two turn-spits at eight livres! A porter, a pastry cook, a baker, two carters, each sixty livres a year! And the marshal of the forges a hundred and twenty livres! And the marshal of our exchequer twelve hundred livres! And the comptroller five hundred! And I know not who else besides! Why this is preposterous! The wages of our domestics are pillaging France! All the gold in the Louvre will melt away in such a blaze of expenditures! We shall have to sell our plateware! And next year, if God and Our Lady (here he raised his cap) grant us life, we shall drink our tisanes from a pewter mug."

When he said this, he glanced at the silver goblet that was glittering on the table. He coughed, and continued, "Master Olivier, princes who reign over great seigneuries, as kings and emperors, ought not to allow extravagance to creep into their households, for 'tis a fire that will spread thence into the provinces. So, Master Olivier, let me not have to repeat this. Our expenses are increasing every year. And this much displeases us. Why, *Pasque Dieu,* till '79 it never exceeded thirty-six thousand livres; in '80, it rose to forty-three thousand six hundred and nineteen livres—I have these figures in my head—in '81 it came to sixty-six thousand six hundred and eighty; and this year, by the faith in my body, it will amount to eighty thousand livres! Doubled in four years! Monstrous!"

He stopped, out of breath, then resumed with vehemence.

"I see all around me nothing but people who are getting fat on my leanness. You are sucking money from my every pore!"

Everyone remained silent. It was one of his fits of passion which had to run its course.

He continued, "It's just like that petition in Latin from the French nobility, requesting us to re-establish what they call the great charges of the crown! Charges, indeed! Charges that would crush us! Ah, gentlemen, you say that we are not a king to reign 'without steward or cup-bearer!' But we'll show you, by God! whether we are king or not!"

Here he smiled, conscious of his power; his ill-humor was allayed by it, and he turned to the Flemings.

"Look you, Compère Guillaume, the grand master of the pantry, the grand butler, the grand chamberlain, the grand seneschal are not so useful as the meanest valet. Remember that, Compère Coppenole. They serve absolutely no purpose. Keeping themselves thus useless, around the king, they remind me of the four evangelists around the face of the great clock of the Palace, and that Philippe Brille has just now been renovating. They're gilt, yes, but they don't mark the hour, and the hand of the clock can do well without them."

He remained thoughtful for a moment and then added, shaking his aged head, "Ho, ho! by Our Lady, but I'm not Philippe Brille, and I am not going to regild the great vassals. I agree with King Edward: Save the people and kill the lords. Proceed, Olivier."

The person whom he so addressed again took the ledger in his hands, and went on reading aloud:

". . . to Adam Tenon, keeper of the seals of the provostry of Paris, for silver, making and engraving said seals, which have been made new, because the former ones, by reason of their being old and worn out, could not any longer be used, twelve livres parisis.

"To Guillaume and brother, the sum of four livres four sols parisis, for his trouble and cost in having fed and nourished the pigeons of the two pigeon houses at the Hotel des Tournelles during the months of January, February, and March of this year, for the which he has furnished seven quarters of barley.

"To a Gray Friar, for confessing a criminal, four sols parisis."

The king listened in silence. Occasionally he coughed;

then he would lift the goblet to his lips and swallow a draught, after which he would make a wry face.

"In this year have been made," continued the reader, "by judicial order, by sound of trumpet, through the streets of Pairs, fifty-six cries—costs to be determined.

"For search made in divers places, in Paris and elsewhere, after treasure said to have been concealed in said places, but nothing has been found, forty-five livrcs parisis."

"Burying an écu to dig up a sou!" said the king.

"For putting in at the Hotel des Tournelles six panes of white glass, at the place where the iron cage is, thirteen sols.

"For making and delivering, by the king's order, on the day of the musters, four escutcheons, bearing the arms of our said lord, and wreathed all around with chaplets of roses, six livres.

"For two new sleeves for the king's old doublet, twenty sols.

"For a box of grease to grease the king's boots, fifteen deniers.

"For a new sty to keep the king's black swine, thirty livres parisis.

"Divers partitions, planks, and trapdoors, for the safe-keeping of the lions at the Hotel Saint-Paul, twenty-two livres."

"They are costly beasts!" said Louis XI. "But no matter; it's a fair piece of royal magnificence. There is a great red lion which I am very fond of for his engaging ways. Have you seen him, Master Guillaume? Princes should have those remarkable animals. We kings ought to have lions for our dogs and tigers for our cats. The great beasts befit a crown. In the time of the pagans of Jupiter, when the people offered up at the holy places a hundred oxen and a hundred sheep, the emperors gave a hundred lions and a hundred eagles. That was very fierce and very noble. The kings of France have always had thosc roarings about their throne. Nevertheless, people must do me the justice to say that I spend less money in that way than my predecessors, and that I am exceedingly moderate on the score of lions, bears, elephants, and leopards. Go on, Master Olivier. We wanted to mention this to our Flemish friends."

Guillaume Rym made a low bow, while Coppenole, with

his surly countenance, looked much like one of those bears which His Majesty had been talking of. The king did not notice. He had just then put his goblet to his lips, and was spitting out what remained in his mouth of the unsavory beverage, saying, "Bah! that horrid tisane!"

The reader continued. "For the food of a rogue and a vagabond, kept for the last six months in the lock-up of the slaughterhouse, till it should be decided what is to be done with him, six livres four sols."

"What's that?" interrupted the king. "Feeding something that ought to be hanged! *Pasque Dieu*! I'll not contribute a single sol toward such feeding. Olivier, you'll arrange that matter with Monsieur d'Estouteville. And this very night you'll make preparations for uniting this gentleman in holy matrimony with the gallows. Now, go on!"

Olivier made a mark with his thumb nail at the rogue and vagabond item, and went on.

"To Henriet Cousin, master executioner of Paris, the sum of sixty sous parisis, to him adjudged by Monseigneur the Provost of Paris, for having bought, by order of the said lord the provost, a large, broad-bladed sword, to be used in beheading persons judicially condemned for their crimes, and for having it furnished with a scabbard and all other appurtenances, and also for repairing and putting in order the old sword, which had been splintered and jagged by executing justice upon Messire Louis of Luxembourg, as can be more fully made to appear—"

Here the king interrupted him. "Enough," he said. "I shall give the order for that payment with all my heart. These are expenses I don't so much as think about. I have never begrudged money so spent. Proceed."

"For making a large, new cage . . ."

"Ha!" said the king, putting a hand on each arm of the chair, "I knew I had come to this Bastille for something. Stop, Master Olivier. I want to see that cage myself. You can read the cost of it to me while I am inspecting it. Messieurs the Flemings, come see it. It is curious."

He then rose, leaned upon the arm of his interlocutor, made a sign to the sort of mute standing before the doorway to go before him, made another to the two Flemings to follow him, and went out of the chamber.

The royal train was recruited at the door by men at arms ponderous with steel, and slender pages carrying torches. It proceeded for some time through the interior of the gloomy dungeon, perforated by staircases and corridors even into the thickness of the walls. The captain of the Bastille walked ahead, and directed the opening of the successive narrow doors before the sickly, old, and stooped king, who coughed as he walked along.

At each doorway, everyone was obliged to stoop in order to pass except only the man bent with age. "Hum!" he said between his gums, for he had not teeth left, "we're quite ready for the door of the sepulcher. A low door needs a stooped person."

At length after making their way through the last door of all, so loaded with complicated locks that it took a full quarter of an hour to open it, they entered a spacious and lofty chamber, of Gothic vaulting, in the center of which was discernible by the light of the torches a great cubical mass of masonry, iron, and woodwork. The interior was hollow. It was one of those infamous cages for state prisoners which are called euphemistically *les fillettes du roi,* the king's daughters. In its walls there were two or three small windows, so thickly latticed with massive iron bars as to leave no glass visible. The door consisted of a single large flat stone, like that of a tomb—one of those doors that serve for entrance only. But in this case the tenant was alive.

The king went and paced slowly around this small edifice, examining it carefully, while Master Olivier, following him, read aloud the expenses.

"For making a great new wooden cage of heavy beams, joists, and rafters, measuring inside nine feet by eight feet, and seven feet high between the planks; mortised and bolted with great iron bolts, which cage has been fixed in a certain chamber in one of the towers of the Bastille Saint-Antoine, where, in said cage is to be kept, by command of our lord the king, a prisoner who before inhabited an old, decayed, and broken-down cage. Used in making the said new cage, ninety-six horizontal beams and fifty-two perpendicular; ten joists, each eighteen feet long. Employed, in squaring, planing, and fitting all the said woodwork in the yard of the Bastille, nine carpenters for twenty days—"

"Very fine oak too!" said the king, rapping his knuckles on the timbers.

"Used in this cage," continued the other, "two hundred and twenty great iron bolts, of eight and nine feet, the rest of medium length—together with the plates and nuts for fastening said bolts—the said irons weighing altogether three thousand seven hundred and thirty-five pounds; besides eight heavy iron clamps for fixing the said cage in its place, with the clamp irons and nails, weighing altogether two hundred and eighteen pounds—without counting the iron for the trellis work of the windows of the chamber in which the said cage has been placed, the iron bars of the door of the chamber, and other articles—"

"There's enough ironwork there to restrain the levity of any spirit," observed the king.

"The whole comes to three hundred and seventeen livres five sols seven deniers."

"*Pasque-Dieu!*" cried the king.

With this swear word, which was King Louis XI's favorite, someone stirred inside the cage. There was the rattle of chains being dragged across the floor, and a voice, so feeble that it might have come from a tomb, exclaimed, "Sire! sire! mercy!"

He who spoke could not be seen.

"Three hundred and seventeen livres five sols seven deniers!" repeated the king.

The piteous voice which had come from the cage had chilled the blood of all but one present, even that of Master Olivier. Only the king appeared not to have heard it.

Upon his order, Master Olivier continued with reading and His Majesty coolly continued his inspection of the cage.

"Besides the above, there has been paid to a mason who made the holes to receive the bars of the windows, and the bars to support the floor of the chamber where the cage is, because the floor could not have upheld such a weight, twenty-seven livres fourteen sols parisis . . ."

Again there was a moan inside the cage, followed by the same voice saying, "Mercy, sire! I swear to you it was Monsieur the Cardinal of Angers who committed the treason, not I."

"The mason's price is high," said the king. "Proceed."

Olivier continued, ". . . to the carpenter for windows, beds, closet stools, and other things, twenty livres two sols parisis . . ."

The weak voice continued too.

"Alas! Sire! Will you not hear me? I declare it was not I who wrote that thing to Monseigneur de Guyenne, but Cardinal La Balue!"

"The carpenter is expensive," observed the king. "Is that all?"

"No, sire. To the glazier for the window glass of said chamber, forty-six sols eight deniers parisis."

"Have mercy, sire! Is it not enough that all my property has been given to my judges, my plateware to Monsieur de Torcy, my library to Master Pierre Doriolle, and my tapestry to the governor of Roussillon? I am innocent. It is fourteen years that I have shivered in this iron cage. Have mercy, sire, and you will meet mercy in heaven.'

"Master Olivier," said the king, "what is the total bill?"

"Three hundred and sixty-seven livres eight sols three deniers parisis."

"Blessed Lady!" exclaimed the king. "An outrageously expensive cage!"

He snatched the ledger from the hands of Master Olivier, and began to add the figures for himself with his fingers' help, examining by turn the pages and the cage.

Meanwhile the prisoner was heard sobbing. In the dark the sound was doleful indeed; those accompanying the king looked at one another and turned pale.

"Fourteen years, sire! Since April, 1469, fourteen years! In the name of God's holy Mother, sire, hear me! You have enjoyed all this time the warmth of the sun. Shall I never again see the light of day? Mercy, sire! Be merciful! Clemency in a king is a noble virtue that turneth away wrath. Does Your Majesty believe that at the hour of death it will be a great satisfaction for a king to have left no offense unpunished? Besides, sire, it was not I who betrayed Your Majesty, it was Monsieur of Angers. But I have a very heavy chain about my feet, with a huge iron ball at the end of it, much heavier than is needed. Oh, sire! have pity on me!"

"Olivier," said the king, shaking his head, "I notice that they have put down a bushel of plaster at twenty sols, though it's worth only twelve. Will you send back this account?"

He turned his back on the cage, and began to move toward the door of the chamber. The wretched prisoner judged, by the dimming torchlight and the receding footsteps, that the king was leaving.

"Sire, sire!" he cried in despair.

But the door closed again; and he could hear nothing but faintly the hoarse voice of the turnkey, singing a popular song.

> Master Jean Balue
> Has lost sight
> Of his bishoprics;
> Mister de Verdun
> Has not one
> All are gone.

The king returned in silence to his retreat, followed by his train, who were horror-stricken by the pleas of the condemned. All at once His Majesty turned around to the governor of the Bastille.

"By the way," he said, "wasn't there someone in that cage?"

"*Pardieu,* yes, sire," replied the governor, astonished by the question.

"Who was it?"

"Monsieur the Bishop of Verdun."

The king knew this better than anybody else, but it was a way he had.

"Ah!" said he naively, as if he were thinking about it for the first time, "Guillaume de Harancourt, the friend of Monsieur the Cardinal La Balue. A good devil of a bishop!"

A few minutes later, the door of the retreat opened and then closed upon the five personages whom the reader found there at the beginning of this chapter. All resumed their places, their postures, and their whispered conversations.

During the king's absence, there had been placed on his table several dispatches, whose seals he immediately broke. He began to read them hastily one after the other. He then motioned to Master Olivier, who seemed to be acting in the capacity of a secretary, to take up a pen, and after communicating to him the content of each dispatch, began in a low voice to dictate his answers, which Olivier wrote, kneeling very uncomfortably at the table.

Guillaume Rym was watching closely.

The king dictated with such a low voice that the Flemings could catch nothing, except here and there some isolated, scarcely intelligible fragments like—"to maintain the fertile places by commerce, the sterile ones by manufacturers . . . To show the English lords our four cannons, the London, the Brabant, the Bourg-en-Bresse, and the Saint-Omer . . . It is because of the artillery that war is now more judiciously carried on . . . To our friend Monsieur de Bressuire . . . The armies cannot be maintained without taxes."

Once he raised his voice, "*Pasque-Dieu*! Monsieur the King of Sicily seals his letters with yellow wax like a king of France! Perhaps we are wrong to allow him to do so." Then, examining the seal, he continued, "My fair cousin of Burgundy authorized no arms on a red field with parallel lines. The greatness of a house is assured by maintaining the integrity of its prerogatives. Note that, Compère Olivier."

Then reading another, "Oh, oh," he said, "an audacious message! What is our brother the emperor asking of us?" On casting his eyes more carefully over the dispatch, he interrupted his perusal here and there with brief interjections. "Of course Germany is so large and so powerful that it's hardly credible! But we don't forget that old proverb, 'The finest country is Flanders; the finest duchy, Milan; the finest kingdom, France.' Is it not so, Messieurs the Flemings?"

This time Coppenole bowed as well as Guillaume Rym. The hosier's patriotism was aroused.

The last dispatch made Louis XI frown. "What's this?" he exclaimed. "Complaints and petitions against our garrisons in Picardy! Olivier, write with all speed to Monsieur the Marshal de Rouault: that discipline has relaxed; that the gendarmes of the guard, the nobles, the free archers, the Swiss archers, are doing infinite mischief to the inhabitants; that the military establishment, not content with what they find in the houses of the husbandmen, compel them, with heavy blows with stones or sticks, to go and fetch from the town wine, fish, groceries, and other luxuries; that the king knows all these things; that we intend to protect our people against annoyance, theft, and pillage; that such is our will, by Our Lady! And furthermore, that it does not please us that any musician, barber, or servant at arms should go clad like a prince, in velvet, silk, and gold rings; that such vanities are despicable to God; that we, who are gentlemen, content ourselves with a doublet made of cloth at sixteen sols parisis an ell; that messieurs the soldiers' lackeys may even come down to that price, too. Order and command. To our friend, Monsieur de Rouault. Good."

He dictated this letter aloud, in a firm tone, and in short, abrupt sentences.

When he had finished, the door opened to admit a messenger, who rushed in, frightened and out of breath, crying, "Sire, sire, there's an uprising in Paris!"

The grave countenance of Louis XI contracted, but whatever emotion he experienced left no visible sign. He contained himself, and said with a tone and a look of quiet severity, "Compère Jacques, you come storming in rather abruptly!"

"Sire, sire! there is a revolt!" Compère Jacques repeated, still panting.

The king, who had risen from his chair, seized him roughly by the arm, and, with eyes flashing angrily, yet glancing obliquely at the Flemings, whispered in his ear, so as not to be heard by anyone else, "Hold your tongue or speak low."

The newcomer understood, and, in a restrained manner, told the king a terrifying story, to which the monarch listened calmly.

Meanwhile Guillaume Rym was quietly calling Coppenole's attention to the face and dress of the courier—to his furred cap, his short cloak, his black velvet gown, which bespoke a comptroller.

No sooner had this person given the king some details than Louis XI exclaimed, with a burst of laughter, "Indeed? Speak louder, Coictier! What have you to whisper about? Our Lady knows we have nothing to hide from our good Flemish friends."

"But, sire . . ."

"Speak up!"

"Compère." Coictier remained dumbfounded.

"Come, come," insisted the king, "speak up, sir. There's a commotion among the inhabitants in our fair city of Paris?"

"Yes, sire."

"Which is directed, say you, against Monsieur the Bailiff of the Palace of Justice?"

"So it seems," stammered the compère, quite confounded at the sudden and inexplicable change in the king's manner.

Louis XI resumed, "Where did the watch encounter the mob?"

"Coming along from the great truandry toward the Pont-aux-Changeurs, sire. I met the crowd myself as I was coming here in obedience to Your Majesty's command. I heard some of them shouting: 'Down with the bailiff of the Palace!' "

"And what grievances have they against the bailiff?"

"Ah," said Compère Jacques, "that he is their seigneur."

"Really!"

"Yes, sire. They are the rabble from the Court of Miracles. They have been complaining about the bailiff whose vassals they are. They don't want him either for a justiciary or as keeper of the highways."

"So, so!" said the king, with a satisfied smile which he strove in vain to disguise.

"In all their petitions to parliament," continued Compère Jacques, "they claim that they have only two masters: Your Majesty and their God, who I think is the devil."

"Hee, hee!" chuckled the king.

He rubbed his hands, laughed with that inward mirth which lightens the countenance. He was quite unable to dissemble his joy, though he now and then strove to compose himself. None of those present could understand—not even Master Olivier. At length, His Majesty remained silent for a moment, with a thoughtful and satisfied air.

All at once he asked, "Are there great numbers of them?"

"Yes, sire, there certainly are," answered Compère Jacques.

"How many?"

"At least six thousand."

The king could not help saying, "Good!" He went on, "Are they armed?"

"Yes, sire, with scythes, pikes, hackbuts, pickaxes—all sorts of dangerous weapons."

The king seemed not at all disturbed by this detail. Compère Jacques thought proper to add, "Unless Your Majesty sends help quickly to the bailiff, he is lost."

"We shall do so," said the king, with a look of affected gravity. "Good! We certainly will. Monsieur the Bailiff is our friend. Six thousand! They are determined rascals. Their boldness is magnificent, and we are very angry about it. But we have few men with us tonight. There will be time enough tomorrow morning."

Compère Jacques' voice rose again. "Immediately, sire! They'll have time to sack the bailiff's house twenty times over, violate the seigneurie, and hang the bailiff himself. For God's sake, sire, send help before tomorrow!"

The king eyed him sternly and said, "I have told you tomorrow morning!"

It was one of those looks to which there is no reply.

After a pause, Louis XI again spoke, "My Compère Jacques, you must know what was," he corrected himself, "what is the feudal jurisdiction of the bailiff?"

"Sire, the bailiff of the Palace has the Rue de la Calandre, as far as the Rue de l'Herberie, the square Saint-Michel, and the squares commonly called Les Mureaux, situated near the church of Notre-Dame-des-Champs" (here the king lifted the brim of his hat), "which mansions amount to thirteen; besides the Court of Miracles, and the lazaretto called the Banlieu, and all the highway beginning at that lazaretto and ending at the Porte Saint-Jacques. Of those several places he is the overseer—in charge of high, middle, and low justice—a full and entire lord."

"So ho!" said the king, scratching his left ear with his right hand, "that covers a good slice of my town! So Monsieur the Bailiff *was* king of all that, eh?"

This time he did not correct himself. He continued, ruminating as if talking to himself, "Softly, Monsieur the Bailiff, you had a pretty piece of our Paris."

Suddenly he exploded.

"*Pasque-Dieu!* Who, among our people, are all these persons that pretend to be highway-keepers, justices, lords, and masters, along with us—who have their tollgate at the corner of every field, their court of justice and their executioner at every crossroad? So that, as the Greek thought he had as many gods as he saw stars, so the Frenchman reckons up as many kings as he sees gibbets. *Pardieu!* This is a terrible state of affairs and all this confusion displeases me. I should like to know now whether it be God's pleasure that there should be in Paris no highway-keeper but the king—no jus- ticiary but our parliament—no emperor but ourself in this empire! By the faith of my soul, the day must come when there will be in France but one king, one lord, one judge, one headsman, as there is but one God in heaven!"

He again lifted his cap, and continued, still ruminat- ing, and in the manner of a huntsman cheering on his pack, "Good! my people! Well done! Crush these false lords! Do your work! At them! Sack them! Hang them! Pillage! Ah, so you want to be kings, messeigneurs!"

Here he abruptly stopped himself, bit his lip, as if to recall his half-formulated thoughts, and fixed his piercing eye in turn upon each of the five persons around him. Then sud- denly taking his hat between his hands, and looking stead- fastly at it, he said, "Oh, I would burn you if you knew what I have in my head!"

Then, once more casting around him the cautious, anxious look of a fox stealing back into his hole, "No matter," he said, "we will send help to Monsieur the Bailiff. Unfortu- nately, at this time we have very few troops to oppose such a number of the populace. We must wait until tomorrow. Or- der then shall be restored in the city, and all who are taken shall be forthwith hanged."

"That reminds me, sire," said Coictier, "I forgot in my first perturbation that the watch has arrested two stragglers belonging to the band. If it be Your Majesty's pleasure to see these men, they are here."

"If it be my pleasure!" exclaimed the king. "Indeed! *Pasque-Dieu!* How could you forget such a thing? Run, quick, Olivier. Bring them here!"

Master Olivier left and returned a moment later with the two prisoners surrounded by the archers of the ordnance. The first captive had a huge, idiotic face; he was drunk and befuddled. His clothing was in rags. He walked with one knee bent and the foot dragging. The other had a pale, half-smiling face, with which the reader is already acquainted.

The king scrutinized them for a moment, saying nothing. Then abruptly he addressed the first.

"What is your name?"

"Gieffroy Pincebourde."

"Your trade?"

"A Truand."

"What were you hoping to gain by that damnable sedition?"

Swinging his arms stupidly, the Truand fixed his eyes on the king. His was one of those heads, all out of shape, in which the intellect is about as effective as a light under a water extinguisher.

"I don't know," he said. "Everybody was going, so I went."

"Were you not going to outrageously attack and plunder your lord the Bailiff of the Palace?"

"I know they were going to take something from somebody, that's all."

A soldier showed the king a pruning hook which had been seized from the Truand.

"Do you recognize this weapon?" questioned the king.

"Yes, it's my pruning hook. I work in a vineyard."

"And is this man your comrade?" asked Louis XI, pointing to the other prisoner.

"No. I don't know him at all."

"Enough," said the king; and, motioning with his finger to the silent person standing motionless by the door, whom we have already pointed out to the reader, "Compère Tristan, there's a man for you!"

Tristan the Hermit bowed. In a low voice he gave an order to the archers who led the poor Truand away.

Meanwhile the king was questioning the second prisoner, who was perspiring profusely.

"Your name?"

"Sire, Pierre Gringoire."

"Your profession?"

"A philosopher, sire."

"How comes it, knave, that you have the audacity to go

and beset our friend Monsieur the Bailiff of the Palace? And
what have you to say about this popular commotion?"

"Sire, I had nothing to do with that."

"How now, varlet! Have you not been arrested by the
watch in that bad company?"

"No, sire, there's a mistake. It was by chance. I write tragedies, sire. I beg Your Majesty to hear me. I am a poet. It's
the hard lot of men of my profession to wander about the
streets at night. By ill luck I happened to be strolling this
evening. They arrested me without cause, I am an innocent
party in this civil storm. Your Majesty saw that the Truand
did not recognize me. I entreat Your Majesty . . ."

"Silence," said the king, between two swallows of his tisane. "You talk too much."

Tristan the Hermit stepped forward, and said, pointing to
Gringoire, "Sire, shall we hang this one too?"

These were the first words he had uttered.

"Oh, why not," answered the king carelessly, "I don't see
any objections."

"But I see a lot," said Gringoire.

At this moment, our philosopher's face was greener than
an olive. He saw, by the cool and indifferent manner of the
king, that his only help lay in something dramatic; so he
threw himself at the feet of Louis XI with gestures of despair.

"Sire, will Your Majesty deign to hear me? Sire, vent not
your wrath on such a poor creature as I. God's lightning
does not strike a lettuce plant. Sire, you are an august and
all-powerful monarch. Have pity on a poor, honest man, as
incapable of fanning the flame of revolt as an icicle of striking a spark. Most gracious sire, mildness is the virtue of a
lion and of a king. Alas! severity does but exasperate the
minds of men. The fierce blasts of the north wind do not
make the traveler lay aside his cloak; but the sun's rays little
by little warm him so that at length he will gladly strip himself. I swear to you, my sovereign lord and master, that I am
not one of the Truands, a thief, or a disorderly person. Sedition and robbery belong not in the train of Apollo. I am not
a man to mingle with those clouds which burst into seditious
clamor. I am a faithful vassal of Your Majesty. The same
jealousy which the husband has for the honor of his wife—

the affection with which a son should requite his father's love—a good vassal should feel for the glory of his king. He should exhaust himself in upholding his king's house and in promoting his service. Any other passion that might possess him would be mere frenzy. Such, sire, is my political creed. Do not, then, judge me to be seditious and plundering because my garment is out at the elbows. If you show me mercy, sire, on my knees I will pray to God, night and day, for you. Alas! I am not very rich, it is true. Indeed I am rather poor, but I am not wicked because I am poverty-stricken. That isn't my fault. Everyone knows that great wealth is not acquired by letters, and that the most accomplished writers have not always a warm hearth in wintertime. The lawyers take all the wheat for themselves and leave nothing but chaff for the other learned professions. There are forty most excellent proverbs about the philosopher's threadbare cloak. Oh, sire, clemency is the only light that can enlighten the interior of a great soul. Clemency carries the torch before all the other virtues. Without her they are blind, and grope for God in the dark. Mercy, which is the same thing as clemency, produces loving subjects, who are the most powerful bodyguard of the prince. What can it matter to Your Majesty, by whom all faces are dazzled, that there be one poor man more upon earth, a poor, innocent philosopher, creeping about in the darkness of calamity, with his empty watch pocket flat upon his empty stomach? Besides, sire, I am a man of letters. Great kings add a jewel to their crown by patronizing letters. Hercules did not disdain the title of Musagète. Mathias Corvin favored Jean de Monroyal, the ornament of mathematics. Now, it would be an ill way of patronizing letters to hang the lettered! What a stain to Alexander if he had had Aristotle hanged! Such an act would not have embellished his reputation by even a small patch; but it would have been a virulent ulcer to disfigure it. Sire, I wrote a very appropriate epithalamium for Mademoiselle of Flanders and Monseigneur the most august Dauphin. That was not like a firebrand of rebellion. Your Majesty sees that I am no dunce—that I have studied excellently—and that I have much natural eloquence. Grant me mercy, sire. By so doing, you will do an

act in honor of Our Lady; and I assure you, sire, that I am
very much frightened at the idea of being hanged."

So saying, the desolate Gringoire kissed the king's slip-
pers, while Guillaume Rym whispered to Coppenole, "He
does well to crawl upon the floor. Kings are like the Jupiter
of Crete—they hear only through their feet."

But, quite inattentive to the Cretan Jupiter, the hosier, his
eyes upon Gringoire, answered with a heavy smile, "Ah,
that's good! I could fancy I heard the Chancellor Hugonet
asking me for mercy."

When at last Gringoire finished, quite out of breath, trembling, he raised his eyes toward the king, who was scratching with his fingernail a spot which he saw upon the knee of
his breeches, after which His Majesty took another swallow
from his goblet. But he uttered not a syllable—and this silence kept Gringoire in torture.

At last the king looked at him. "Here's a terrible prater,"
said he. Then, turning to Tristan the Hermit, he ordered,
"Bah! let him go!"

Gringoire fell back on his rear, quite overcome with joy.

"Let him go?" grumbled Tristan. "Will Your Majesty not
have him put in the cage for a while?"

"Compère," returned Louis XI, "do you think it is for
birds like these that we have cages made at three hundred
and sixty-seven livres eight sols three deniers apiece? Let
the knave go immediately, put him out with a beating."

"Oh," exclaimed Gringoire in ecstasy, "this is indeed a
great king!"

Then, for fear of a countermand, he rushed toward the
door, which Tristan opened for him with very ill grace. The
soldiers went out after him, belaboring him violently with
their fists, which Gringoire endured like a true stoic philosopher.

The good humor of the king, ever since the revolt against
the bailiff had been announced to him, manifested itself in
everything. This unusual clemency of his was no small sign
of it. Tristan the Hermit, in his corner, was looking as surly
as a mastiff denied his bone.

Meanwhile the king was gaily tapping with his fingers on
the arm of his chair the Pont-Audemer march. Though a dis-
sembling prince, he was much better able to conceal his sor-

row than his rejoicing. These external manifestations of joy, on the receipt of any good news, sometimes carried him great lengths; as, for instance, on the death of Charles the Bold of Burgundy, he ordered balustrades of silver added to Saint-Martin of Tours; and on his accession to the throne, he forgot to make arrangements for his father's funeral.

"Ha, sire," suddenly put in Jacques Coictier, "what have become of the sharp pains which made Your Majesty send for me?"

"Oh," said the king, "truly, my compère, I am in great pain. I hear a ringing in my ear, and red-hot rakes furrow my breast."

Coictier took the king's hand, and felt his pulse with a knowing look.

"Look, Coppenole," said Rym in a whisper, "there he is between Coictier and Tristan. That is his whole court—a physician for himself, and a hangman for the rest of his kingdom."

While taking the king's pulse, Coictier was assuming a look of greater and greater alarm. Louis XI watched him with some anxiety; while the physician's face grew more and more grave. The king's bad health was the only estate the good man had to cultivate, and accordingly he made the most of it.

"Oh! oh!" he muttered at length. "This is serious, indeed."

"Yes?" said the king uneasily.

"Pulse quick, irregular, intermittent," continued the physician.

"*Pasque-Dieu!*"

"In three days this could carry off a man."

"Notre Dame!" cried the king. "And the remedy, compère?"

"I am thinking, sire."

He made the king stick out his tongue, shook his head, made a face, and in the midst of this grimacing exclaimed, "By God, sire, I must tell you that there is a receivership of episcopal revenues vacant, and that I have a nephew ..."

"Compère Jacques, I give the receivership to your nephew," answered the king, "but get this burning sensation off my chest."

"Since Your Majesty is so kind," resumed the physician, "I am sure you will not refuse to assist me a little in the building of my house on the Rue Saint-André-des-Arcs."

"Hmm!" said the king.

"I'm at the end of my finances," said the doctor, "and it would really be a pity that the house should be left without a roof—not for the sake of the house itself, which is quite plain and homely, but for the sake of the paintings by Jehan Fourbault that adorn its wainscoting. There's a Diana flying through the air—so excellently done, so tender, so delicate, in action so artless, her head so well dressed, and crowned with a crescent, her flesh so white that she leads into temptation those who examine her too curiously. Then there's a Ceres, and she too is a very beautiful goddess. She sits upon cornhusks, and is crowned with a handsome wreath of ears of corn intertwined with goatsbeard and other flowers. Never were seen more amorous eyes, rounder legs, a nobler air, or a flowing robe more graceful. She's one of the most innocent and most exquisite beauties ever produced by brush."

"Cutthroat!" grumbled the king. "What are you after now?"

"I want a roof over these paintings, sire; and although it is but a trifle, I have no money."

"How much would it cost, your roof?"

"Why, uh, a copper roof, figured and gilded, two thousand pounds at the most."

"Wretched thief!" cried the king. "He never draws me a tooth but he makes a diamond of it!"

"May I have my roof?" said Coictier.

"Yes, and the devil take you! But cure me!"

Bowing low, Jacques Coictier said, "Sire, it is a repellent that will save you. We will apply to your loins the great deterrent concocted of cerate, Armenian bole, white of eggs, oil and vinegar. You are to continue with your tisane, and we will answer for Your Majesty's safety."

A lighted candle never attracts one gnat only. Master Olivier, seeing the king in a generous mood, and deeming the moment opportune, approached in his turn.

"Sire."

"What now?" said Louis XI.

"Sire, Your Majesty is undoubtedly aware that Master Simon Radin died.'

"So?"   .

"He was the king's comptroller."

"Well?"

"Sire, his post is vacant."

While thus speaking, Master Olivier's haughty countenance had exchanged its arrogance for a fawning expression—the only alternation that ever takes place in the aspect of a courtier.

The king looked him full in the face and said dryly, "I understand.

"Master Olivier, the Marshal de Boucicaut used to say, 'There's no gift but from a king; there's no good fishing but in the sea.' I see that you are of the marshal's opinion. Now be this understood: our memory is good; in '68, we made you groom of our chambers; in '69, castellan at the bridge of Saint-Cloud, with a salary of a hundred livres tournois, (you wanted them parisis); in November '73, by letters given at Gergeole, we appointed you keeper of the Bois de Vincennes, instead of Gilbert Acle, Esquire; in '75, warden of the forest of Rouvray-lez-Saint-Cloud, in place of Jacques le Maire; in '76, we graciously bequeathed to you, by letters-patent sealed with green wax, an annuity of ten livres parisis, to you and your wife, upon the Place-aux-Marchands, situated at the Ecole Saint-Germain; in '79, we made you warden of the forest of Senart, in place of that poor Jehan Daiz; then captain of the Château of Loches; then governor of Saint-Quentin; next captain of the bridge of Meulan, because of which you call yourself count. Moreover, out of the fine of five sols paid by every barber who shaves on a holiday you get three sols, and we get only two. Also, we were pleased to change your name of Le Mauvais, which was too much like your countenance. In '74 we granted to you, to the great displeasure of our nobility, an armorial shield of a thousand colors, that gives you a breast like a peacock's. *Pasque-Dieu*! Aren't you satisfied? Is not the net full of fishes fine and miraculous enough? Are you not afraid that a single salmon more would be sufficient to sink your boat? Pride will be your ruination, compère. Pride

is ever followed close behind by ruin and shame. Consider
all this and be silent."

These words, uttered in a tone of severity, brought back to
the momentarily chagrined physiognomy of Master Olivier
its former insolent expression. "Good," he muttered, almost
aloud. "It's plain enough that the king is ill today, for he
gives everything to his physician."

Louis XI, far from being annoyed by this remark, resumed
with some mildness, "Wait, I forgot to add that I made you
ambassador to Madame Marie at Ghent. Yes, gentlemen,"
added the king, turning to the Flemings, "this man has been
an ambassador. There, compère," he continued, addressing
himself again to Master Olivier, "let us not quarrel; we're
old friends. It's very late. We've finished our work. Shave
me!"

Our readers have undoubtedly already recognized in Master Olivier that terrible Figaro whom Providence, that greatest dramatist of all, so artfully mixed up in the long and
sanguinary play of Louis XI's reign. We shall not here un-
dertake to develop at full length that singular character. This
barber to the king had three names. At court he was called
politely Olivier le Daim; among the people, Olivier le
Diable. But his real name was Olivier le Mauvais; or the
Bad.

Olivier le Mauvais, therefore, stood motionless, looking
sulkily at the king, and enviously at Jacques Coictier.

"Yes, yes! the physician!" he muttered.

"Well, yes, the physician!" resumed Louis XI with singular good humor; "the physician has yet more influence than
you. It's all very simple. He has got our whole body in his
hands, and you do but hold us by the chin. Come, come, my
poor barber, there's nothing wrong. What would you say,
and what would become of your position, if I were a king
like King Chilpéric, whose way it was to hold his beard with
one hand? Come, compère, perform your office, and shave
me. Go get what you need."

Olivier, seeing that the king had resolved to take the matter in jest, and that there was no way even to provoke him,
went out grumbling to execute his commands.

The king rose from his chair, went to the window, and
suddenly opened it in extraordinary agitation, exclaiming,

"Oh, yes!" Then, clapping his hands, he continued, "There's a glare in the sky over the City. It's the bailiff burning; it can't be anything else. Hah! my good people, so you help me, then, at last, to do away with these seigneuries!"

Then turning to the Flemings, "Gentlemen," he said, "come and see. Is not that a fire that glares so red?"

The two Flemings came forward to look.

"A large fire," said Guillaume Rym.

"Oh," added Coppenole, whose eyes all at once sparkled, "that reminds me of the burning of the house of the Seigneur d'Hymbercourt. There must be a big revolt there."

"You think so, Master Coppenole?" interjected the king. And he looked almost as pleased as the hosier himself. "Don't you think it will be difficult to quell it?"

"By the rood! Sire, it may cost Your Majesty a good company of soldiers."

"Ha! cost me! That's different," returned the king. "If I chose . . ."

The hosier rejoined boldly. "If that revolt be what I think it is, you would choose in vain, sire."

"Compère," said Louis XI, "two companies from my ordnance and one discharge from a cannon are quite enough to rout this mob of common people."

The hosier, in spite of the signs that Guillaume Rym was making to him, seemed determined to provoke the king.

"Sire," he said, "the Swiss were common people too. Monsieur the Duke of Burgundy was a great gentleman, and made no account of the rabble. At the battle of Grandson, sire, he called out, 'Cannoneers, fire on those villains!' and he swore by Saint George. But the avenger, Scharnachtal, with his club, rushed upon the goodly duke and his people; and at the attack of the peasants, with their bull hides, the shining Burgundian army was shattered like a windowpane by a stone. Many a knight was killed there by those lowly knaves, and Monsieur de Château-Guyon, the most powerful lord in Burgundy, was found dead, with his great gray horse, in a small marshy meadow."

"Friend," returned the king, "you're talking about a battle. But this is only a riot, and I can put an end to it with a single frown when I please."

The other replied indifferently, "That may be, sire. In that case the people's hour has not yet come."

Guillaume Rym thought he must intervene.

"Master Coppenole," he said, "you are talking to a mighty king."

"I know it," answered the hosier gravely.

"Let him speak, Monsieur Rym, my friend," said the king. "I like his speaking plainly. My father, Charles VII, used to say the truth was sick. For my part I thought it was dead, and had found no confessor. But Master Coppenole shows me I was mistaken."

Then putting his hand familiarly on Coppenole's shoulder, "You were saying then, Master Jacques?. . ."

"I was saying, sire, that perhaps you are right; that, with you, the people's hour has not yet arrived."

Louis XI looked at him with his penetrating eye.

"And when will that hour come, master?"

"You will hear it strike."

"By what clock, please?"

Coppenole, his plain face calm, motioned the king to come to the window

"Listen, sire. Here is a dungeon, an alarm-bell, cannons, people, soldiers. When the bell-tower rings out, when the cannons roar, when, with a great noise, the dungeon walls crumble and fall, when the townspeople and the soldiers shout and kill each other; then the hour will have struck."

Louis' face became gloomy and pensive. For a moment, he was silent, then gently caressing with his hand the thick wall of the dungeon, as if patting the shoulder of a war horse, "Ah no!" he said, "thou wilt not so easily crumble, wilt thou, my good Bastille!"

Then, turning around abruptly to the bold Fleming, he said, "Have you ever seen a revolt, Master Jacques?"

"Sire, I caused one," answered the hosier.

"What does one do to cause one?" asked the king.

"Oh," replied Coppenole, "it's not very hard to do. There are a hundred ways. First of all, there must be unrest in the town, which often there is. And then, the character of the inhabitants is important. The people of Ghent are ever inclined to revolt. They always like the son of the prince, but never the prince himself. Well, one morning, let's suppose, somebody comes into my shop, and says, Father Coppenole, there's this or that; for example, the Lady of Flanders wants to save her ministers, the high baliff is doubling the toll on vegetables, or something else—anything you like. Me, I leave my work, go out of my shop into the street and cry: 'Revolt!' There's always a convenient barrel. I climb on it, and shout the first words that come into my head about whatever has been on my mind; for, when one is of the people, sire, one has always something on his mind. A crowd gathers. They shout. They sound the alarm. They arm themselves with weapons they have taken from the soldiers; the market people join us, and then the revolt is on. It will always be thus, as long as there are seigneurs in the seigneuries, townspeople in towns, and peasants in the country."

"And against whom do you rebel like that?" asked the king. "Against your bailiffs? Against your lords?"

"Sometimes. That depends. Against the duke, too, sometimes."

Louis XI took his seat again, and said with a smile, "Ah! but here they have gotten no further than the bailiff!"

Just then Olivier le Daim returned, followed by two pages carrying the king's toilet articles; but what surprised Louis XI was to see him also accompanied by the Provost of Paris and a knight of the watch, both of whom seemed alarmed. The face of the cantankerous barber also betrayed alarm, but satisfaction was also there. He was the first to speak.

"Sire, I ask Your Majesty's pardon for the calamitous news I bring you."

The king turned so quickly that he tore the floor matting with the legs of his heavy chair.

"What is it?"

"Sire," replied Olivier with the evil look of a man rejoicing that he is about to deal a violent blow, "it is not against the bailiff of the Palace that the mob is rebelling."

"Against whom then?"

"Against you, sire!"

The old king sprang to his feet, and stood erect like a young man.

"Explain yourself, Olivier! Explain; and beware of your head, compère, for I swear, by the cross of Saint-Lô, that if you lie to us in this matter, the sword that cut Monsieur of Luxembourg's throat is not so notched but it can saw your head too!"

The oath was formidable. Louis XI had never but twice in his life sworn by the cross of Saint-Lô.

Olivier opened his mouth to reply. "Sire ..."

"On your knees!" interrupted the king violently. "Tristan, watch this man carefully."

Olivier fell to his knees and tersely reported.

"Sire, a witch has been condemned to death by your parliament. She has taken sanctuary in Notre-Dame. The people want to take her from there by force. Monsieur the Provost and Monsieur the Knight of the Watch, who have just come from the spot, are here to correct me if I speak not the truth. The people are laying siege to Notre-Dame."

"Ah, yes?" said the king in a low voice, pale and trembling with rage. "Notre-Dame! So they are besieging Our Lady, my good mistress, in her own cathedral! Get up, Olivier. You are right. I give you Simon Radin's office. You are right. It is I whom they are attacking. The witch is safeguarded by the church. The church is under my protection. And I thought they were rioting against the bailiff. But it's against me!"

Then, as if rejuvenated by his fury, he began to stride up and down the room. He was no longer laughing. His mien was frightening. He paced back and forth. The fox had changed into a hyena. He seemed choked with rage. His lips moved but no words came. He wrung his bony hands. All at once he raised his head, his hollow eyes seemed full of light, and his voice shrilled like a clarion.

"Attack them! Tristan, attack these blackguards. Go, Tristan, my friend! Kill them! Kill them!"

When he had controlled himself, he sat again in his chair, and spoke calmly but with emphasis.

"Here, Tristan! There are right here in this Bastille fifty lances of the Viscount de Gif, and three hundred horses. Take them. There is also Monsieur de Châteauper's company of archers of our ordnance. You will take them. You are the provost marshal and have the men of your provostry. Take them. At the Hotel Saint-Pol you will find forty archers of Monsieur the Dauphin's new guard. You will take them.

With all these forces, you will go in haste to Notre-Dame. Ah, gentlemen of the mob of Paris, so you would throw yourselves against the crown of France, and at the holiness of Our Lady, and at the peace of this commonwealth! Exterminate them, Tristan! Exterminate them! And let not one escape except to be hanged at Montfaucon!"

Tristan bowed. "Very good, sire." But after a pause, he added, "What shall I do with the witch?"

The king thought.

"Ah! the witch! Monsieur d'Estouteville, what do the people want do with her?"

"Sire," answered the Provost of Paris, "I suppose that, since the people are come to drag her away from her sanctuary in Notre-Dame, it is her impunity that offends them, and that they want to hang her."

The king seemed in deep thought: then he addressed Tristan the Hermit, "Well then, compère, wipe out the people and hang the witch."

"That's a fine thing!" whispered Rym to Coppenole. "Punish the people for their intentions, and then do what they wished to do!"

"Enough, sire," answered Tristan. "If the witch is still in Notre-Dame, must we take her away in spite of the sanctuary?"

"*Pasque-Dieu*! the sanctuary!" said the king, scratching his ear. "And yet that woman must be hanged."

Here, as if seized with a sudden thought, he knelt in front of his chair, took off his hat, put it upon the seat, and looking devoutly at one of the leaden figures with which it was adorned, "Oh," he said, joining his hands,"Our Lady of Paris, my gracious patroness, pardon me. I will only do it this one time. That sorceress must be punished. I assure you, O Lady Virgin, my worthy mistress, that a witch is unworthy of your kind protection. You know, Lady, that many very pious princes have trespassed upon the privilege of the churches, for the glory of God and the necessity of the State. Saint Hugh, bishop of England, allowed King Edward to seize a magician in his church. My master, Saint Louis of France, transgressed for the same reason in the church of Saint-Paul. And Monsieur Alphonse, son of the king of Jerusalem, so profaned the Church of the Holy Sepulcher it-

self. Pardon me, then, this once, Our Lady of Paris. I will
not do it again. And I will give you a beautiful statue of silver like that which I gave last year to Our Lady of Ecouys.
Amen!"

He crossed himself, rose, put on his hat, and said to Tristan, "With all speed, compère. Take Monsieur de
Châteaupers with you. Ring the alarm. Crush the mob. Hang
the witch. I have spoken. You will defray all the costs of the
execution and bring me an account of them. Come, Olivier,
I shall not go to bed tonight. Shave me."

Tristan the Hermit bowed and left. Then the king, motioning to Rym and Coppenole to retire, said, "God keep
you, gentlemen, my good Flemish friends! Go and take
some rest. Night is far spent; we are nearer to morning than
evening."

Both retired, escorted by the captain of the Bastille.

Upon reaching their apartment, Coppenole said to
Guillaume Rym, "Humph! I've had enough of this coughing
king. I have seen Charles of Burgundy drunk, but he was not
as evil as this sick Louis XI."

"Master Jacques," replied Rym, "that is because a king
finds less cruelty in his wine than in his tisane."

6

The Password

Leaving the Bastille, Gringoire ran down the Rue Saint-
Antoine with the speed of a runaway horse. Reaching the
Porte Baudoyer, he walked right up to the stone cross which
stood in the middle of the square, as if, in the dark, he could
see the figure of a man clothed and hooded in black, sitting
upon the steps of the cross.

"Is that you, master?" said Gringoire.

The person in black rose. "Death and passion! you make
me mad, Gringoire! The man upon the tower of Saint-
Gervais has just been calling half past one in the morning."

"Oh," returned Gringoire, "it's not my fault, but that of
the watch and the king. I've just had a narrow escape. I'm
always just missing being hung. It's my predestination."

"You just miss everything," said the other. "But let's go quickly. Do you know the password?"

"Just think, master, I've seen the king! I just left him. He wears woollen breeches. It was an adventure."

"Oh, you blabbering fool! What's your adventure to me? Do you know the password of the Truands?"

"I have it. Be calm! It's *petite flambe en baguenaud.*"

"Good. Otherwise we should not be able to make our way to the church. The Truands are barring the streets. Fortunately it seems, they're meeting with some resistance. Perhaps we'll get there in time.'

"Yes, master. But how shall we get into Notre-Dame?"

"I have the key to the towers."

"And how shall we get out?"

"Behind the cloister, there's a little door which opens onto the Terrain, and so to the water side. I have the key to it; and I moored a boat there this morning."

"I just missed being hanged," repeated Gringoire.

"Quick! Come along," said the other.

Both proceeded hastily in the direction of the City.

7

Châteaupers to the Rescue!

The reader probably remembers the dire situation in which we left Quasimodo. The brave bellringer, assailed from all sides, and lost, if not all courage, at least all hope of saving, not himself—he wasn't thinking of himself—but the gypsy girl. He ran wildly along the gallery.

Notre-Dame was just about to be taken by the Truands, when all of a sudden a great galloping of horses was heard in the nearby streets, and, with a long file of torches and a full column of cavalry, lances and heads lowered, this battle array came rushing into the square like a hurricane, shouting, "France! France! Cut down the knaves! Châteaupers to the rescue! Provostry! Provostry!"

The Truands, terror-stricken, turned back.

Quasimodo, who could hear nothing, saw the drawn swords, the torches, the pike heads, the whole cavalry, at the head of which he recognized Captain Phoebus. He saw the confusion of the Truands, their terror, the indecision of the boldest among them. This unexpected help so much revived his own energies that he hurled back from the church the foremost of the assailants, who were already striding over the gallery parapet.

These were, in fact, the king's troops who had just arrived.

The Truands bore themselves bravely and defended themselves desperately. Attacked on the flank from Rue Saint-Pierre-aux-Boeufs, and in the rear from Rue du Parvis, with their backs to Notre-Dame, which they had been assailing, and which Quasimodo was defending—they, at once besieging and being besieged, were in the singular situation which subsequently, at the famous siege of Turin in 1640, was that of Count Henri d'Harcourt, between Prince Thomas of Savoy, whom he was besieging, and the Marquis of Leganez, who was blockading him—*Taurinum obsessor idem et obsessus,*[1] his epitaph read.

The melee was tremendous. "Wolves' flesh calls for dogs' teeth," as Father Mathieu phrases it. The king's cavalry, among whom Phoebus de Châteaupers bore himself valiantly, gave no quarter, and they who escaped the thrust of the lance fell by the edge of the sword. The Truands, ill-armed, foamed and bit with rage and despair. Men, women, and children threw themselves upon the bridles and breasts of the horses, and clung to them like cats with their teeth and claws; others struck the archers in the face with torches; and others again aimed their hooks at the necks of the horsemen, trying to pull them down, and mangled such as fell. One of the Truands was seen with a large glittering scythe, with which for a long time he mowed the legs of the horses. It was frightful. He went on, singing a song with a nasal intonation, taking long and sweeping strokes with his scythe. With each stroke, he described around him a great circle of severed limbs. He advanced in this manner into the thickest of the cavalry, with quiet slowness, with the regular motion of head and drawing of the breath of a reaper putting the

[1] "Besieging Turin at the same time as being besieged."

scythe into a field of corn. This was Clopin Trouillefou. Musket fire felled him.

Meanwhile the windows had opened again. The neighbors, hearing the war whoops of the king's men, began to take part in the fray, and from every story bullets were showered on the Truands. The Parvis was full of thick smoke which the musketry streaked with fire. Through this smoke was faintly discernible the facade of Notre-Dame and the tottering Hotel-Dieu, where a few pale-faced invalids looked from the dormer windows.

At last the Truands retreated. Tired, lacking good weapons, surprised by this sudden attack of musketry from the windows, and the spirited charge of the king's troops, all this quite overwhelmed them. They broke through the line of their assailants and began to flee in all directions, leaving the Parvis strewn with dead.

When Quasimodo, who had not for a moment stopped fighting, saw this rout, he fell on his knees and lifted his hands to heaven. Then, intoxicated with joy, he flew with the swiftness of a bird to the little cell, the access to which he had so bravely defended. Now, he had but one thought: to throw himself at the feet of her whom he had just saved for the second time.

When he entered the cell, he found it empty.

BOOK XI

1

The Little Shoe

When the Truands began besieging the church, La Esmeralda was sleeping.

But it was not long before she was awakened by the constantly increasing noise about the cathedral. The uneasy bleating of her goat further disturbed her. She sat up on her bed, and listened. Half dazed, she looked around; then, frightened by the light and the noise, she ran from her cell to see what was the matter. The disturbance in the square below, the hideous mob, jumping about like a mass of frogs, half seen in the darkness, the croaking of this hoarse crowd, the few red torches running around and crisscrossing each other in the darkness like so many meteors that streak over the misty surface of a marsh—all this scene seemed to her like a mysterious battle being waged between the phantoms of a witches' sabbath and the stone monsters of Notre-Dame. Imbued from infancy with the superstitions of the gypsy tribe, her first thought was that she had surprised the strange beings peculiar to the night in their unholy pranks. Then, frightened, she ran back to her cell to bury herself in her bed, to ask of it a less horrible nightmare.

Slowly, however, the first waves of fear were dispelled

from her mind. Then, by the ever-increasing noise, together with all those other signs of reality, she discovered that the cathedral was being attacked, not by specters, but by human beings. Then her fright, although not increased, changed in form. She had thought of the possibility of a popular uprising to drag her from her asylum. The idea of once again losing life, hope, Phoebus, who was still ever-present in her thoughts, the absoluteness of her weakness, all flight barred, her abandonment, her loneliness—these thoughts and a thousand others overwhelmed her. She fell on her knees, with her head on her bed, her hands joined above her head, her heart full of anxiety and apprehension. Gypsy though she was, an idolatress and a pagan, she began to sob, to ask mercy of the Christian God and to pray to Our Lady, her hostess. For, though one believes in nothing, there are moments in life when one accepts the religion of the temple nearest at hand.

She remained prostrated thus for a considerable time, trembling indeed more than she prayed, her blood running cold as the breath of that furious mob approached nearer and nearer. As she was ignorant of the nature of this popular storm—of what was its cause, its function, its intent—she could only feel a presentiment of some terrible end.

In the very midst of all this anguish she heard footsteps approaching. She raised her head and turned around. Two men, one of whom carried a lantern, had just entered her cell. She let out a feeble cry.

"Have no fear," said a voice she did not recognize. "It is I."

"Who?" she asked.

"Pierre Gringoire."

The name reassured her. She raised her eyes, and saw that it was indeed the poet. But standing near him was another figure all in black, terrifying.

"Ah!" resumed Gringoire reproachfully, "Djali recognized me before you did."

The little goat, in fact, had not waited for Gringoire to introduce himself. No sooner had he entered than she began to rub herself affectionately against his knees, covering the poet with caresses and white hair, for she was shedding her coat. Gringoire returned the caresses.

"Who is that with you?" asked the gypsy girl softly.

"Rest easy," replied Gringoire. "It's a friend of mine."

Then the philosopher, putting his lantern on the floor, squatted on the stones, and exclaimed with enthusiasm, squeezing Djali in his arms. "Oh, it's a charming animal, no doubt more remarkable for its cleanliness than for its size; but clever, cunning, and learned as a grammarian! Let's see, now, my Djali, if you have forgotten what Master Jacques Charmolue does? . . ."

The man in black didn't let him finish. He came over to Gringoire and nudged him rudely on the shoulder. Gringoire got up.

"True!" he said, "I forgot we are in a hurry. However, master, that's no reason for pushing like that. My beautiful child, your life is in danger and so is Djali's. Again they are determined to hang you. We are your friends, and we have come to save you. Follow us."

"Is that true?" she exclaimed, overcome.

"Yes, very true. Come quickly."

"I will," she stammered. "But why doesn't your friend speak?"

"Ah," said Gringoire, "because his father and mother were peculiar people and gave him a taciturn disposition."

She had to be satisfied with this explanation. Gringoire took her by the hand. His companion took up the lantern and walked first. The young girl was still fearful, but she let them lead her away. The goat trotted with them, so delighted to see Gringoire again that she caused him to trip at almost every step, by thrusting her horns against his legs.

"That's life," said the philosopher each time he was almost laid prostrate, "it's often our best friends who make us fall."

They quickly descended the staircase of the tower, crossed through the church, all dark and empty, but resounding with the uproar without, which made a frightful contrast, and went out by the Porte-Rouge into the courtyard of the cloister. The cloister was deserted, the monks having taken refuge in the bishop's house, there to offer up their prayers together; but some terrified servingmen were skulking in the darkest corners. Esmeralda, Gringoire, and the dark-cloaked man proceeded toward the small door leading from the court to the Terrain. The one in black opened it with his key. Our readers are aware that the Terrain was a strip of ground enclosed with walls on the side next to the City, and belonged to the chapter of Notre-Dame. This Terrain terminated the island eastward, behind the cathedral. They found the enclosure empty. Here, too, they found the tumult in the air appreciably diminished. The noise of the Truands' assault dimly reached their ears. The cool breeze which follows the current of the river stirred the leaves of the one tree planted at the point of the Terrain to a whisper which even now they could hear. Nevertheless, they were still very near danger. The buildings nearest to them were the bishop's palace and the church. There was evidently great confusion within the bishop's residence. Its dark mass was spotted in many places by lights hurrying from one window to another, just as after burning a piece of paper there remains a dark heap of ashes, over which bright sparks run in a thousand fantastic courses. Beside it the huge towers of Notre-Dame, seen thus from the rear, with the long nave from which they rise, showed black against the vast red light which glowed above the Parvis, looking like the gigantic andirons of some Cyclopean hearth.

What was visible of Paris seemed wavering on all sides in a sort of shadow mingled with light, resembling some of Rembrandt's backgrounds.

The man with the lantern walked straight to the projecting point of the Terrain, where, at the extreme edge of the water, were the rotten remains of a fence of stakes with laths nailed across, upon which a low vine spread out its few meager branches like the fingers of an open hand. Behind this kind of lattice work, in the shade which it cast, a small boat lay hidden. The man motioned to Gringoire and the young girl to board it; and the goat jumped in after them. The man himself got in last of all, cut the rope, pushed off from shore with a long pole, and, laying hold of a pair of oars, he seated himself in the bow, and rowed as hard as he could across the river. The Seine is very rapid at that particular spot, and he found considerable difficulty in rounding the point of the island.

Gringoire's first care on entering the boat was to place the goat upon his lap. He placed himself in the stern of the boat; and the young girl, whom the sight of the stranger filled with indescribable uneasiness, seated herself as close as possible to the poet.

When our philosopher felt the boat moving he clapped his hands, and kissed Djali on the head.

"Oh," he exclaimed, "now the four of us are safe!" He added, with the look of a profound thinker, "Sometimes we are indebted to fortune, something to cunning, for the happy issue of a great undertaking."

The boat was moving slowly toward the right bank. The young girl watched the movements of the unknown person with a secret terror. He had carefully turned down the light of his dark lantern, and he looked now like a specter, at the head of the boat. His hood, which he wore constantly pulled down, was a sort of mask over his face, and, while rowing, every time that he half opened his arms upon which he had large black hanging sleeves, they looked like a pair of enormous bat wings. But he had not yet spoken a single word. There was perfect stillness in the boat, broken only by the rhythmic splash of the oars, and the rippling of the water against the side of the boat.

"Upon my soul!" all of a sudden exclaimed Gringoire, "we are as merry as owls! Silent like Pythagoreans or fish! *Pasque-Dieu!* my friends, I'd like somebody to say something! The human voice is music to the human ear. By the way, that's not one of my sayings, but one from Didymus of Alexandria. And they are noble words too! Didymus of Alexandria is no mean philosopher. One word, my pretty girl, do just speak one word to me, I beg you. By the way, you used to have an odd little pout. Do you still make it? You must know, my darling, that the parliament has complete jurisdiction over all places of sanctuary, and that you were running great risks in that little cell of yours in Notre-Dame. Alas! the little trochilus bird builds its nest in the crocodile's mouth. Master, there's the moon again. I hope they don't see us! We're doing a commendable job saving the lady. And yet, they'd hang us in the king's name if they were to catch us. Alas! There are two sides to every human act. One man gets praised for what another gets blamed for; one man admires Caesar and reproaches Catiline. Is that not so, master? What say you to that philosophy? As for me, I follow the philosophy of instinct, of nature, *ut apes geometriam.*[1] So nobody answers me. What bad humor you're both in! I must talk to myself. That's what we call in tragedy a monologue. *Pasque-Dieu!* I'll have you know that I have now just seen King Louis XI, and it's from him I've learned this new swearword, *Pasque-Dieu.* They're still making a glorious howl in the City. He's evil, a mischievous old king. He's all wrapped about in his furs. He still owes me the money for my play; and he all but hanged me tonight, which would have been very awkward for me indeed. He's stingy with men of merit. He should read Salvien of Cologne's four books, *Adversus-avaritiam.*[2] Indeed! He's a king very paltry in his dealings with men of letters, and one who commits very barbarous cruelties. He's a sponge sucking up the money that's raised from the people. His savings are as the spleen, which grows big upon the pining of the other members. And so complaints about the hardness of the times turn to murmurs against the prince. Under this mild and pious lord of ours the gibbets are overloaded with carcasses, the blocks are stained with blood, the prisons are jammed like full bellies. This king takes with one hand and hangs with the other. He's a purveyor for Dame Tax and Monseigneur Noose. The nobles are stripped of their dignities, and the poor are everlastingly loaded with fresh burdens. He's an extravagant prince. I don't like this monarch. What say you, master?"

The man in black let the loquacious poet run on. He was still struggling against the strong current which separates the prow of the City from the stern of the Ile Notre-Dame, now called Ile Saint-Louis.

"By the way, master," Gringoire began again suddenly, "just as we reached the Parvis through the enraged Truands, did your reverence observe that poor little devil whose brains that deaf man of yours seemed in a fair way to knock out upon the balustrade of the gallery of kings? I'm nearsighted and could not make out his face. Who do you think it was?"

The unknown answered not a word. But he suddenly stopped rowing, his arms dropped as if they had been bro-

[1] "As the bees do geometry."
[2] *Against Avarice.*

ken, his head fell upon his breast, and La Esmeralda could hear him sighing convulsively. She gave a start. She had heard sounds like that before.

The boat, left to itself, followed for some moments the impulse of the stream. But at length the man in black recovered himself, seized the oars again, and again set himself to row against the current. He passed the point of the Ile Notre-Dame, and made for the landing place, the Port-au-Foin.

"Ah," said Gringoire, "over there is the Barbeau mansion. There, master, look, that group of black roofs that make such odd angles—there, under that heap of low, dirty, ragged clouds, where the moon is all crushed and spread about like the yolk of an egg when the shell has been broken. It's a fine mansion. There's a chapel with a little vaulted roof, embellished with fine sculpture. You can see the belfry above it, with its rare and delicate tracery. There is also a pleasant garden, with a pond, an aviary, a mill, a labyrinth, a wild-beast house, plenty of thick-shaded walks very agreeable to Venus, and furthermore an echo. And then there's a rogue of a tree which they call the Lovers' Tree because it once favored the pleasures of a famous princess and a certain constable of France, a man of wit and gallantry. Alas! We poor philosophers are to a constable of France as a cabbage plot or a radish bed is to the Tuileries gardens. After all, what does it signify? Human life is a mixture of good and evil for the great as well as for us. Sorrow ever attends upon joy— the spondee upon the dactyl. Master, I must tell you that story about the Barbeau mansion. It ends tragically. It was in 1319, during Philip V's reign, the longest of all the French kings'. The moral of the story is that temptations of the flesh are pernicious and evil. Let us not look too persistently at our neighbor's wife, however much our senses may be charmed by her beauty. Fornication fills a libertine's thought, adultery is prying into another man's pleasure. Eh? the noise yonder is getting louder!"

The tumult was, in fact, increasing around Notre-Dame. They listened, and could very distinctly hear shouts of victory. All at once a hundred torches glittered upon the helmets of men-at-arms, and spread themselves over the church at all elevations—on the towers, on the galleries, even under the buttresses. Those torches seemed to be looking for something. Soon the distant noises were clarified in the ears of the fugitives. "The gypsy!" they heard in the shouting. "The witch! Death for the gypsy girl!"

The head of the unfortunate girl dropped upon her hands, and the unknown began to row with greater vigor toward the bank. Meanwhile our philosopher was deep in thought. He pressed the goat in his arms, and sidled very gently away from the gypsy girl, who kept pressing closer and closer to him, as to her only remaining protection.

It is certain that Gringoire was in a state of cruel perplexity. He reflected that poor Djali too, according to the existing legislation, would be hanged if she were retaken; that would be a great pity; that the two condemned females thus clinging to him would be too much for him; and that his companion would be most happy to take charge of the gypsy girl. Yet a violent battle was going on in his mind, wherein, like Jupiter of the *Iliad*, he placed in the balance alternately the gypsy girl and the goat. As he looked first at one, then at the other, his eyes moistened, and he muttered to himself, "And yet I cannot save you both!"

A jolt of the boat told them that they had reached the shore. The fearful acclamations were still resounding through the City. The unknown oarsman rose, came to the gypsy girl, and offered to take her arm in order to help her out of the boat. She pushed him away, and grasped Gringoire's sleeve; he in turn, being fully occupied with the goat, almost repulsed her. Then she leaped ashore by herself. She was in such a state that she did not know what she was doing nor where she was going. For a few moments she remained thus, quite stupefied, watching the water as it coursed by. However she soon realized that she was alone upon the landing place with the man in black. It appears that Gringoire had taken the opportunity as they landed to make off with the goat into the mass of houses on the Rue Grenier-sur-l'Eau.

The poor gypsy girl trembled when she found herself alone with this man. She tried to speak, to cry out, to call for Gringoire. But her tongue would not move; no sound came from her lips. All at once she felt the stranger's hand in hers. It was strong and cold. Her teeth chattered. She was paler than the moon rays that shone upon her. The man did not speak, but began to walk up to the Place de Grève at a rapid pace, still holding her by the hand. Just then she realized the futility of trying to resist fate. She had no more strength. She let herself be pulled along, running while he walked. The quay at that place sloped upward before them, yet it seemed to her as if she were going down an incline.

She looked about her. No one was to be seen. The quay was absolutely deserted. She could hear no noises; she saw no one stirring, except in the glaring and tumultuous City, from which she was separated by an arm of the Seine, and from which her name reached her ear mingled with shouts of "Death!" The rest of Paris lay spread around her in great blocks of shadow.

Meanwhile the unknown was still dragging her onward in the same silence and with the same rapidity. She had no recollection of any of the places through which she was passing. Once as they went by a lighted window she made an effort, suddenly drew back, and cried out, "Help!"

A window opened. Its owner, half awake, in his nightgown with a lamp in his hand looked out on the quay, said something she couldn't understand, and closed his shutters again. So the last ray of hope was extinguished.

The man in black uttered not a word. He held her hand tightly, and walked on more quickly than before. She made no more resistance, but followed him like a creature utterly powerless.

Now and then, indeed, she gathered just enough strength to say, with a voice interrupted by the unevenness of the pavement and the rapidity of her motion which had almost taken her breath, "Who are you? Who are you?" But he made no answer.

Proceeding thus along the quay, they arrived at a large square. It was the Place de Grève. A little of the moon was showing between the clouds. A sort of black cross could be seen, standing in the middle of the square. That was the gibbet. When she saw all this, she knew where she was.

The man stopped, turned to her, and lifted his hood.

"Oh!" she stammered, almost petrified, "I knew it was he again!"

It was the priest. He looked like the ghost of himself.

Moonlight produces this effect. It seems as if by that light
one beholds only the specters of objects.

"Listen," he said; and she shuddered at the sound of that
funereal voice, which she hadn't heard for such a long time.
He continued, speaking with short broken sentences which
betrayed his deep emotional distress. "Listen! We are here.
I must talk to you. This is the Grève, the place of decision.
Fate has surrendered each of us to the other. I am going to
dispose of your life—and you, of my soul. Here is a place
and a night beyond which one sees nothing. Now listen to
me. I am going to tell you . . . First of all, don't talk to me
of your Phoebus." (So saying, he paced up and down, like a
man incapable of standing still, dragging her after him.) "Do
not talk about him. Do you understand? If you utter his
name, I don't know what I'll do, but it will be awful!"

Then, like a body which has found its center of gravity
again, he once more stood still. But his next words betrayed
no less agitation. His voice grew lower and lower.

"Do not turn your head away like that. Listen to me. This
is serious. First of all, I will tell you what has happened.
There will be no laughing about this, I assure you. What was
I saying? Remind me! Ah, it is that there's a decree of parliament, delivering you over to the executioner again. I've
just now taken you out of their hands. But they are pursuing
you. Look."

He stretched out his arm toward the City, where, indeed,
the search seemed to be eagerly continuing. The clamor
came nearer. The tower of the lieutenant's house, situated
opposite the Grève, was full of noise and lights. Soldiers
were running over the quay opposite, with torches in their
hands, shouting, "The gypsy woman! Where is the gypsy
woman? Death! Death!"

"You can see plainly enough that they are hunting you,
and that I am not lying to you. I love you. Open not your
lips. Rather, don't speak at all, if it be to tell me that
you hate me. I will not hear that again. I have just now
saved your life. Let me first finish. I can save you completely; I have arranged for everything. You have only to
will it. What you wish, I can do."

Here he violently checked himself.

"No, that is not what I must say."

And running, making her run too, for he never let go her arm, he went straight up to the gibbet and pointing to it, said coldly, "Choose between us."

She tore herself from his grasp and fell at the foot of the gibbet, and clasped that dismal support. Then she half turned her beautiful head, and stared at the priest over her shoulder. She looked like the Virgin at the foot of the cross. The priest stood motionless, like a statue, his finger still raised toward the gibbet.

At length the gypsy girl said to him, "It is less horrible to me than you are."

Then his arm slowly lowered, his eyes fell to the ground, his head hung in deep dejection.

"If these stones could speak," he muttered, "they would say, 'Yes, here indeed is an unhappy man!' "

He resumed. The young girl, kneeling before the gibbet, covered by her long flowing hair, let him continue without interrupting him. Now his tone was mild and plaintive, markedly contrasting with the haughty harshness of his features.

"I love you! It is true I do. No fire can be fiercer than the fire that consumes my heart. Alas! my little one, it is a love of the night and of the day; I tell you, it is torture! Oh, I suffer too much, my child! It is a state worthy of compassion, I assure you. You see that I am speaking gently to you. I would that you cease to detest me. After all, when a man loves a woman, it is not his fault. O my God! Can it be that you will never forgive me? Will you hate me always? Is all finished? Don't you see, that's what makes me bad, and horrible to myself. You never even look at me. You are thinking of something else, perhaps, while I talk to you as I stand shuddering on the brink of eternity for both of us! But above all do not talk to me of the officer. Bah! I would throw myself at your feet. Harken! I would kiss, not your feet—you would not allow that—but the ground under your feet! Oh! I would sob like a child; I would cast from my breast, not words, but my very heart, to tell you that I love you! And yet all would be in vain—all! Still there is nothing in your soul but what is kind and tender. You are radiant with the loveliest gentleness, completely sweet, merciful, charming! Alas! you have no hate but for me alone! What a fatality!"

He buried his face in his hands. For the first time, the girl heard him crying. Standing thus erect and shaken by his sobs, he looked even more wretched and imploring than on his knees. For a while longer he cried.

"But come," he continued, as soon as these tears were shed, "I can find no proper words, though I had well thought out what I would say to you. Now I tremble and grow faint-hearted at the decisive moment. I feel that something supreme envelops us, and my voice falters. Oh, I shall fall to the ground if you do not take pity on me, pity on yourself! Do not condemn us both! If you knew how much I love you! What a heart is my heart! Oh, what desertion of all virtue! What desperate abandonment of myself! A doctor, I mock at science; a gentleman, I tarnish my name; a priest, I make my missal a pillow of desire. I spit in the face of my God! All that for you, enchantress, to be more worthy of your hell! And yet you reject the reprobate! Oh, let me tell you all—more still—something even yet more horrible!"

As he uttered these last words his expression became utterly wild. He was silent for a minute; then resumed as if talking to himself, and in a strong voice, "Cain, what have you done with your brother?"

After another silent pause, he went on, "What have I done to him, O Lord? I have taken him to myself, nourished him, reared him, loved him, idolized him, and killed him! Yes, Lord, just now, before my eyes, have they dashed his head upon the stones of your house. And it was because of me, because of this woman, because of her!"

His eye was haggard; his voice, barely audible. He repeated several times mechanically, at spaced intervals, like the last strokes of a rundown clock, "Because of her— because of her!" Then there was no more articulation, though his lips continued to move. All at once he collapsed, like something crumbling to pieces, and remained upon the ground with his head between his knees.

The slight movement of the young girl's drawing her foot from under him roused him. He passed his hand slowly over his hollow cheeks, and looked for some moments in stupor at his wet finger.

"What!" he murmured, "have I been weeping?"

Then, turning suddenly to the gypsy girl, he cried with inexpressible anguish, "Alas! you have seen me weep unmoved! Child, do you know that those tears were lava? And is it, then, so true, that from the man we hate nothing can move us? You would see me die and would laugh. But I don't want to see you die. One word—one single forgiving word! Tell me not that you love me, tell me only that you want to love me. That would suffice, and I will save you. If not—oh, time is passing—I entreat you, by all that is sacred, do not wait until I become like a stone again, like this gibbet, which claims you too. Think that I hold both our destinies in my hand, that I am maddened—this is terrible—that I may let all go, and that here is beneath us, unhappy girl, a bottomless abyss, wherein my fall will pursue yours for all eternity. One word of kindness, say one word, but one word!"

She opened her lips to answer him. He threw himself on his knees before her, to receive with adoration the word, perhaps of relenting, which was about to fall from those lips. She said to him, "You are a murderer!"

The priest took her in his arms with violence, and laughed an abominable laugh. "Well, yes, a murderer," he said, "and I will have you. You shall not have me for your slave; I will be your master. I will have you. I have a den to which I shall drag you. You will follow me. You must follow me, or I'll deliver you to the executioner. You must die, fair one, or be mine—the priest's, the apostate's, the murderer's—this very night. Do you hear? Come, my joy! Come, kiss me, madwoman. The grave, or my bed!"

His eyes were sparkling with rage and licentiousness, and his lascivious lips were reddening the young girl's neck. She struggled in his arms, but he kept covering her with his frothy kisses.

"Don't bite, monster!" she cried. "Oh, you hateful, poisonous monk! Leave me! I'll pull out your vile gray hair and throw it by handfuls in your face!"

He turned red, then pale, then let go of her, and gazed at her sorrowfully.

She now thought she was victorious and continued, "I belong to my Phoebus. It is Phoebus whom I love. It is Phoebus who is handsome. You, priest, you are old and ugly. Go away!"

He shrieked, like some wretch under a branding iron.

"Die then!" he cried, grinding his teeth. She saw his frightful look, and wanted to fly. But he seized her again, shook her, threw her upon the ground, and walked rapidly toward the corner of the Tower of Roland, dragging her after him by her beautiful hands.

On reaching that point, he turned to her. "One last time, will you be mine?"

"No."

Then he called out in a loud voice, "Gudule, Gudule! here's the gypsy girl. Take your revenge!"

The young girl felt herself seized suddenly by the arm. She looked. It was a fleshless arm extending through a window in the wall that grasped hers with a hand of iron.

"Hold fast," said the priest. "It's the gypsy girl who escaped. Don't let her go. I'll go fetch the sergeants. You shall see her hanged."

A guttural laugh from the interior of the cell answered those deadly words, "Ha, ha, ha!"

The gypsy girl saw the priest hurry away toward the Pont Notre-Dame where trampling of horses was heard.

The girl recognized the malicious recluse. Panting with terror, she strove to disengage herself. She twisted about, made several bounds in agony and despair; but the other held her with incredible strength. The thin, bony fingers that pinched and clenched her flesh seemed as if they were riveted to her arm. It was more than a chain, more than an iron ring; it was a pair of pincers with life and understanding that issued from the wall.

Quite exhausted, she fell back against the wall; and then the fear of death came over her. She thought of life, of her childhood, of the sight of heaven's blue sky, of the aspects of nature, of love, of Phoebus, of all that was flying from her; and then of all that was approaching—of the priest who was denouncing her, of the executioner who was coming, of the gibbet that was there. Then she felt terror, even to the roots of her hair, as she heard the eerie laugh of the recluse, and her saying low, "Ha, ha! You are going to be hanged!"

She turned tragic eyes toward the window of the cell and saw the wild face of the Sachette through the bars.

"What have I done to you?" she whispered.

The recluse made no reply, but began to mutter, in a sing-song, irritated, and mocking tone.

"Daughter of Egypt! Daughter of Egypt! Daughter of Egypt!"

The unfortunate Esmeralda hid her face under her long flowing hair, understanding that this was no rational human being.

All at once the recluse exclaimed as if the gypsy's question had taken all that time to reach her consciousness, "What have you done to me, gypsy woman? Well, listen! I had a child, you see, a little child, a pretty little child, my Agnes!" She continued wildly, kissing something in the dark, "Well, you see, daughter of Egypt, your people took my child from me. They stole my child; they ate my child. That's what you did to me."

The young girl answered, like the lamb in the fable, "Alas! perhaps I was not then born."

"Oh yes," rejoined the recluse, "you must have been born. You were one of them. She would have been your age now. For fifteen years I have been here; fifteen years have I been suffering, fifteen years have I been knocking my head against these four walls. I tell you, they were gypsy women who stole my baby, do you hear that? They ate her. Have you no heart? Only think what it is to see one's child playing, nursing, sleeping. So innocent! Well, that's what they took from me, what they killed. The Good Lord knows! To-day, it's my turn. I'm going to eat some gypsy woman's flesh. Oh, how I would bite you, if these bars didn't stop me! My head's too big. Poor little child! while she was sleeping! And if they woke her while taking her away, in vain she may have cried. I was not there! Ha! you gypsy mothers, you ate my child; now come and look at yours."

Then she laughed or gnashed her teeth. How alike were the two in that frantic face!

Now the dawn was spreading over this scene an ashy tint. The gibbet loomed in the center of the square. On the other side, toward Notre-Dame, the condemned girl thought she heard the cavalry approaching.

"Madame!" she cried, clasping her hands and falling upon her knees, her hair disheveled, her eyes wild, and her mind distracted with the extremity of dread. "Madame, have pity!

They're coming! I've done nothing to you. Do you wish to
see me die in that horrible manner before your eyes? You
pity me, I am sure. This is too awful. Let me flee for my
life. Let me go! Please! I don't want to die like that."

"Give me back my child!" said the recluse.

"Mercy! Mercy!"

"Give me back my child!"

"In heaven's name, let me go!"

"Give me back my child."

And now again the young girl sank exhausted, powerless,
having already the glazed eye of one dead.

"Alas!" she stammered, "you seek your child. I seek my
parents!"

"Give me back my little Agnes!" continued Gudule.
"Know you not where she is? Then die! I'll tell you. I was
once a girl of pleasure. I had a child. They took my child
from me. It was a gypsy woman. You must die! When your
gypsy mother comes to ask for you, I shall say to her,
'Mother, look at that gibbet! But, where is *my* child?' Do
you know where she is, little girl? Here, let me show you,
here's her shoe, all that's left to me of her. Do you know
where the other one is? If you do, tell me, and even if it be
at the other end of the world, I'll go there on my hands and
knees to fetch it!"

So saying, with her other arm extended through the window, she showed the gypsy girl the little embroidered shoe.
There was now daylight enough to distinguish its shape and
color.

"Show me that shoe!" cried the gypsy trembling. "My
God, my God!"

At the same time, with her free hand she tore open the little bag adorned with green beads which she wore about her
neck.

"Oh, oh!" muttered Gudule, "fumble away in your infernal amulet!"

Then she stopped short, and trembling, she cried out in a
voice that came from her depths, "My daughter!"

The gypsy had taken from her bag a little bootee exactly
like the other. To this little shoe was attached a piece of
parchment, upon which was written this couplet:

When you find its match,
Your mother will stretch out her arms to you.

Quickly, the recluse compared the two shoes, read the writing on the parchment, and then put close to the window bars her face now all beaming with celestial joy, exclaiming, "My daughter! my daughter!"

"My mother!" answered the gypsy girl.

Here words fail us.

The wall and the iron bars were between them.

"Oh, the wall!" cried the recluse. "Oh, to see her, and not to be able to embrace her! Your hand! Your hand!"

The young girl passed her arm through one of the openings. The recluse threw herself upon that hand, pressed her lips to it, and remained there, absorbed in that kiss, giving no sign of life but a deep sob from time to time. Meanwhile she wept continuously, in the silence, in the darkness, as rain falls at night. Over that adored hand now was gushing that deep dark well of sorrow into which all the mother's grief had filtered drop by drop for fifteen years.

Suddenly she rose, threw her long gray hair back from her forehead, and without uttering a word, strove with both hands, with the fury of a lioness, to shake the bars of her cell. But the bars were not to be shaken. She then went and brought from one corner of her cell the large paving stone which she used as a pillow. She hurled it against the bars with such force that one broke, casting off innumerable sparks. A second blow drove out the old iron cross which barricaded the window. With both hands, she managed to loosen and remove the rusty stumps of bars. There are moments when the hands of a woman are possessed with superhuman strength.

The passage thus cleared, and it was all done in a minute, she took her daughter by the arms and pulled her into the cell.

"Come," she muttered, "let me drag you out of the abyss."

As soon as she had the girl in the cell, she set her gently on the ground, then took her up again, and carrying her in her arms as if she were still her little Agnes, she paced up and down, in her narrow cell, intoxicated with joy, shouting, singing, kissing her daughter, speaking to her, laughing aloud, melting into tears—all at once and all with vehemence.

"My child, my daughter!" she repeated. "I have my daughter again! Here she is! God has returned her to me. Ha! you—come all of you. Is there anybody there to see that I've got my daughter? Lord Jesus, how beautiful she is! You have made me wait fifteen years, my God, but it was that you might give her back to me beautiful. So the gypsy women did not eat her! Who said that? My little girl! My little girl! Kiss me! Those good gypsy women! I love the gypsy women! So it's really you! And this was why my heart leaped every time you passed. And I mistook it for hate! Forgive me, Agnes, forgive me! You thought I was wicked, didn't you? I love you. Do you still have that little mark on your neck? Let me see. Yes, there it is. Oh, you're so beautiful! It was I who gave you those large eyes, mademoiselle. Kiss me. I love you. What matters it to me that other mothers have children? I can laugh at them now. Let them come. I have mine. Look at her neck, her eyes, her hair, her hands. Show me something more beautiful than these? Oh, I swear she'll have plenty of lovers. I've wept for fifteen years. All my beauty has faded, but has come again in her. Kiss me."

She said a thousand other extravagant things to Esmeralda in a tone which made the words beautiful. In her ardor, she disarranged the poor girl's dress in such a way as to make her blush; she kissed her little hands, her feet, her knees, her eyelids, her forehead; she stroked the gypsy's silken hair; she was enraptured with everything. The girl was quite passive the while, only repeating at intervals, very low and with infinite sweetness, "My mother!"

"Ah, my little Agnes," resumed the recluse, constantly interrupting her words with kisses, "how I shall love you! We will fly away from here. We shall be so very happy. I have an inheritance in Rheims, in our own country. You know Rheims? Oh, no, you can't know, you were too little. If you could only know how pretty you were at four months of age! Such little feet that people came to see all the way from Epernay, which is seven leagues distant. We shall have fields and a house. You shall sleep in my bed. My God, my God, who would believe it! I have my daughter again."

"O my mother!" said the young girl, controlling her emotion enough to speak, "a gypsy woman told me these things too. Among our people there was a good gypsy woman who died last year, but she had always taken care of me like a foster mother. It was she who put this little bag about my neck.' She used to say to me, 'Little girl, take care of this trinket. It is a treasure, it will be instrumental in finding your mother again. You are wearing your mother about your neck.' She, the gypsy woman, foretold our meeting."

The recluse clasped her daughter in her arms. "Come," she said, "let me kiss you. How sweetly you speak! When we are in the country, we'll put the little shoes on the feet of an Infant Jesus in a church. We owe so much to the Good Virgin. My God, how lovely your voice is! When you were talking to me just now it was like music. Ah, my Lord God, so I have found my child! And yet who would believe the story? Surely nothing can kill one, since I have not died of joy!"

And she began clapping her hands and laughing and crying. "We shall be so happy!"

At that moment the cell resounded with the clanking of arms and the galloping of horses, which seemed to be approaching nearer and nearer from the Pont Notre-Dame. The gypsy girl threw herself in agony into the arms of her mother. "Save me, save me, my mother! They are coming!"

The recluse turned pale. "O God in heaven! What are you saying? I had forgotten. They are coming for you! Why, what have you done?"

"I don't know," answered the poor wretched girl, "but I have been condemned to death."

"To death!" exclaimed Gudule, reeling as if stricken by a thunderbolt. "To death!" she repeated slowly, looking upon her daughter with staring eyes.

"Yes, my mother," repeated the girl in wild despair. "They want to kill me. They're coming to hang me. That gallows yonder is for me. Save me, save me! They're here. Save me!"

For a few minutes the recluse remained in petrified stillness, then she shook her head doubtingly. Next, suddenly bursting into laughter, that former frightful laughter which had now returned to her, she cried, "Oh no! Oh no! It's a dream you are telling me. Indeed yes, it is a dream that I lost her, that I could then have her only a minute before they should take her from me again. It is only a dream that now she is beautiful, that she's grown up, that she talks to me, that she loves me, and that now they should come and devour her before my eyes, before the eyes of her own mother! Oh no! It can't be reality. The Good Lord would never allow anything like that."

Now the cavalcade seemed to stop, and a voice at a distance was heard saying, "This way, Messire Tristan. The priest says we shall find her at the Trou-aux-Rats."

The trampling of horses was then heard to recommence.

The recluse sprang up with a cry of despair.

"Flee! Flee! my child. It all comes back to me now. You are right. It is your death. O horror—malediction! Flee!"

She put her head through the cell window, and drew it back hastily.

"Stay!" she said portentously, in a low voice, pressing convulsively the hand of her daughter, who was already more dead than alive. "Stay, but don't breathe. Soldiers are all around. You can't leave. There's too much daylight."

Her eyes were dry and burning. For a few moments she said nothing, only paced nervously up and down in the cell, stopping now and then to pluck gray hairs in frenzy from her head.

All at once she spoke.

"They're coming nearer. I'll talk to them. Hide in that corner. They won't see you there. I'll tell them you have escaped, that I let you go!"

She carried her daughter to a corner of the cell which could not be seen from the outside. She made her crouch down, arranged everything carefully, so that neither foot nor hand should project from the corner's shadows; she unbound the black hair, and spread it over her girl's white gown to cover it; and she placed a pitcher and the paving stone in front of her, the only articles of furniture therein, imagining that they would serve as a screen for concealment. When all was finished, finding herself more calm, she knelt and prayed.

The dawn was only just breaking; there was still deep gloom in the Trou-aux-Rats.

At that instant, the voice of the priest—that infernal voice—passed very near the cell, crying, "This way, Captain Phoebus de Châteaupers!"

At that name, spoken by that voice, La Esmeralda, squatting in her corner, stirred.

"Don't move!" commanded Gudule.

As she was speaking, a tumultuous crowd of men, swords, and horses gathered around the cell. The mother, rising quickly from her knees, posted herself in front of the window, to cover it like a curtain. She saw a strong body of armed horse and foot soldiers drawn up on the Grève. Their commander dismounted and walked up to her.

"Old woman," said this man, whose face had a terrifying, evil expression, "we're looking for a witch to hang her. They told us you have her."

The poor mother, assuming as indifferent an air as she was able, replied, "I don't know what you mean."

The other resumed, "*Tête-Dieu!* Then what sort of a tale was that half-mad archdeacon telling us? Where is he?"

"Monseigneur," said a soldier, "he's disappeared."

"Come, come, you old hag. Don't lie to me. Someone gave you the witch to guard. What have you done with her?"

The recluse would not give a flat denial, for fear of arousing suspicion, but answered in a forthright but surly tone, "If you're talking about a tall young girl that was given me to hold just a little while ago, I can tell you she bit me, and I let go of her. That's all. Now let me be!"

The commander made a grimace of disappointment.

"Let's not have any lying, hag. My name is Tristan the Hermit. Do you hear me? I am the king's compère." And he added, looking around at the Place de Grève, "That's a name that is well known around these parts."

"Were you Satan the Hermit," replied Gudule, mustering hope, "I'd have nothing more to tell you."

"*Tête-Dieu!*" said Tristan. "There's a hussy for you! So the witch-girl has escaped. And which way did she go?"

Gudule answered in a tone of unconcern. "By the Rue du Mouton, I think."

Tristan turned around and motioned to his men to make ready to march again. The recluse breathed more easily.

Just then an archer said, "Monseigneur, ask the old lady how it is that the bars of her cell are so broken."

This question plunged the heart of the wretched mother into anguish again. Still she did not lose all presence of mind.

"They were always that way," she stammered.

"Bah!" returned the archer. "No longer ago than yesterday the bars formed a fine black cross that it made one devout to look at."

Tristan cast an oblique glance at the recluse. "I think the old lady is confused," he said.

The unfortunate woman felt that all depended upon keeping her self-possession; and so, though death was imminent, she began to jeer at them. Mothers rise to occasions like these.

"Bah!" she replied. "That man is drunk. It's more than a year since the back of a cart laden with stones ran against my window, and burst out the bars. I well remember how I cursed the driver."

"That's true," said another archer. "I was here when it happened."

There are always to be found, in all places, people who have seen everything. This untoward testimony of the archer's revived the spirits of the recluse, who, in undergoing this questioning, was crossing an abyss upon the edge of a knife. But she was doomed to sway alternately between hope and alarm.

"If a cart had done that," resumed the first soldier, "the stumps of the bars would have been driven inward; but you can see they've been forced outward."

"Ha! ha!" said Tristan to the soldier, "you have the nose of an inquisitor at the Châtelet. Give answer to that, old woman!"

"My God!" she exclaimed, reduced to the last extremity, and bursting into tears despite herself, "I assure you, monseigneur, that it was the cart that broke those bars. You hear—that man saw it. And besides, what has all this to do with the gypsy girl you talk of?"

"Hum!" growled Tristan.

"Devil!" continued the soldier, flattered by the provost's commendation, "the iron looks quite recently broken."

Tristan shook his head. She turned pale. "How long is it, do you say, since this cart affair?" he asked.

"A month—perhaps a fortnight, monseigneur, I can't remember."

"At first she said a year ago," observed the soldier.

"This looks suspicious," said the provost.

"Monseigneur," she cried, still standing close up to the window, and trembling lest suspicions should prompt them to put their heads through to look around. "Monseigneur, I swear to you it was a cart that broke these bars. I swear it to you by all the angels in Paradise. If it was not done by a cart, I hope to go to everlasting perdition, and I deny God!"

"You're extravagant with this oath of yours," said Tristan with his inquisitorial manner.

The poor woman felt her assurance deserting her more and more. She was already making blunders, and had a terrible consciousness that she had said what she should not have said.

Just then another soldier came up shouting, "Monseigneur, the old hag lies. The witch did not run away down the Rue du Mouton. The chain of that street has been stretched across all night, and the chainkeeper has seen nobody pass!"

Tristan, whose face was becoming every minute more sinister, again questioned the recluse.

"What have you to say to that?"

Still she tried to bear up against this new incident.

"That I don't know, monseigneur," she replied. "I may have been mistaken about the street. In fact, I think she went across the water."

"That's on the other side," said the provost. "And yet it's not very likely that she should have wanted to go back into the City, where they were looking for her. You lie, old woman!"

"And besides," added the first soldier, "there's no boat, neither on this side of the water nor on the other."

"She could swim across," suggested the recluse, defending her ground inch by inch.

"Do women swim?" asked the soldier.

"*Tête-Dieu!* old woman, you lie! You lie!" replied Tristan

angrily. "I have a good mind to leave the witch and take you. A quarter of an hour's questioning will perhaps get the truth out of your throat. Come. You're going with us."

She seized these words eagerly. "Just as you please, monseigneur. Take me, take me. The torture! Take me. Quick, quick! Let's leave right away." "In the meantime," she thought, "my daughter will escape."

"*Mort-Dieu!*" said the provost, "what an appetite for torture! This madwoman's quite past my comprehension."

An old gray-headed sergeant of the watch now stepped out of the ranks, and, addressing the provost, said, "Mad in truth, monseigneur! If she let the gypsy go, it's not her fault, for she's no liking for gypsy women. For fifteen years have I been on duty here, and every night I hear her cursing those gypsy women with execrations without end. If the one we are seeking be, as I believe she is, the little dancing girl with the goat, she hates her above all the rest."

Gudule made an effort and repeated, "Above all the rest."

The unanimous testimony of the men of the watch confirmed to the provost what the old sergeant had said. Tristan the Hermit, despairing of getting anything out of the recluse, turned his back upon her; and she, with inexpressible anxiety, watched him walk slowly back to his horse.

"Come," he muttered between his teeth. "On! we must continue our search. I will not sleep until this gypsy woman is hanged."

Still he hesitated for a minute before mounting his horse. Gudule was vacillating between life and death while she watched him throw around the square the restless look of a hound that feels himself to be near the game's hiding place and so is reluctant to leave. At last he shook his head, and leaped to his saddle.

Gudule's heart, which had been so horribly compressed, now dilated; and she said in a whisper, casting a glance upon her daughter, at whom she had not ventured to look since the arrival of her pursuers, "Saved!"

The poor girl had remained all this time in her corner, without breathing or stirring, as she stared at death's image. No particular of the scene between Gudule and Tristan had escaped her; each pang of her mother's had vibrated in her own heart. She had heard, as it were, the successive snapping of the threads which had held her suspended over the abyss. Oftentimes she thought they all must have broken; it was only now that she dared to breathe and to feel secure again. At that moment she heard a man say to the provost, "*Corboeuf!* Monsieur the Provost, I am a man-at-arms. It is not my business to hang witches. Such rabble are beneath me. I leave you to do your own work by yourself. You'll allow me to rejoin my company which is waiting for its captain."

The voice was that of Phoebus de Châteaupers.

What effect it produced on the gypsy girl is not easy to describe. So he was there, her friend, her protector, her support, her shelter, her Phoebus! She raised herself and, before her mother could stop her, she had sprung to the cell window, crying out, "Phoebus! here, my Phoebus!"

Phoebus was no longer there. He had just galloped round the corner of the Rue de la Coutellerie.

But Tristan had not yet gone away.

The recluse rushed upon her daughter with a moan of agony, and pushed her violently back, her nails cutting the flesh of the poor girl's neck. A mother tigress is not too gentle.

It was too late, however. Tristan had seen.

"Ha! ha!" he cried, with a laugh that showed all his teeth, making his face resemble the snout of a wolf, "two mice in the trap!"

"I thought so!" said the soldier.

Tristan slapped him on the shoulder, saying, "You're a good cat. Come," he added, "where is Henriet Cousin?"

A man who had neither the dress nor the mien of a soldier now stepped out of their ranks. His hair was combed flat to his head; he wore a suit half gray, half brown, with leather sleeves; he carried a bundle of ropes. This man was in constant attendance upon Tristan, as Tristan was upon Louis XI.

"Friend," said Tristan the Hermit, "I presume that this is the witch we are seeking. Hang that one for me. Do you have your ladder?"

"There's one under the shed of the Maison-aux-Piliers," answered the man. "Is it at that place of justice we're going to do the job?" he continued, pointing to the stone gibbet.

"Yes."

"Ho! ho!" responded the man, with a laugh more loud and brutal even than the provost's, "we don't have far to go."

"Hurry up," said Tristan, "and laugh later."

Meanwhile, since the moment when Tristan had seen her daughter, and all hope was lost, the recluse had not yet uttered a word. After she had thrown the poor gypsy girl, half dead, into the corner of the cell, she had resumed her post at the window, her two hands resting upon the bottom of the stone window frame, like the claws of some animal. In that attitude she kept glaring intrepidly at all the soldiers, with eyes wild and frantic. When Henriet Cousin approached the cell, she looked at him so savagely that he shrank back.

"Monseigneur," he said, turning back to the provost, "which shall I take?"

"The girl."

"So much the better, for the old one seems not so easy to handle."

"Poor little dancing girl with the goat!" said the old sergeant of the watch.

Henriet Cousin again went over to the window. The mother's eye made his drop. Very timidly he said, "Madame . . ."

She interrupted him with a low and furious voice.

"What do you want?"

"Not you," he said, "but the other one."

"What other?"

"The young one."

She began to shake her head, shouting. "There isn't anybody else! There's no one! There's no one!"

"Yes, there is! You know it as well as I do! Let me take the young girl. I don't want to do you any harm."

She answered with a strange sneer, "Ha! you don't want to do me any harm!"

"Let me have the other, madame; Monsieur the Provost has given his orders!"

"There's no one here!" she repeated with a wild look.

"I tell you there is!" replied the hangman. "We've seen that there were two of you."

"Well, take a look!" said the recluse with a sneer. "Poke your head through the window."

The hangman eyed the mother's nails, and dared not.

"Hurry up!" cried Tristan, who had just drawn up his

troops in a circle around the Trou-aux-Rats and had posted himself on his horse near the gibbet.

Henriet once more went over to the provost quite embarrassed. He had put his ropes on the ground, and was fumbling sheepishly with his hat.

"Monseigneur, how can I get in?" he asked.

"Through the door."

"There isn't any."

"Then, through the window."

"It's too narrow."

"Widen it then," said Tristan angrily. "Have you no picks with you?"

The mother, still at the window, was closely watching them. She had lost all hope. She no longer knew what she wanted, except that she did not want them to take her daughter.

Henriet Cousin went to fetch the box of tools from under the shed of the Maison-aux-Piliers. He also brought out from the same place the double ladder, which he immediately leaned against the gibbet. Five or six of the provost's men armed themselves with pickaxes and crowbars, and Tristan proceeded with them to the cell window.

"Old woman," began the provost severely, "give us that girl, quietly."

She looked at him like someone who did not understand.

"*Tête-Dieu!*" resumed Tristan, "what does it matter to you if that witch is hanged? It's the king's wish."

The wretched woman began to laugh wildly again.

"What does it matter? She's my daughter."

The tone in which she said this made even Henriet Cousin shudder.

"I am sorry," replied the provost. "But it's the king's order."

She cried, laughing her maniacal laugh with redoubled loudness, "What matters your king to me? I tell you she is my daughter!"

"Break down the wall!" ordered Tristan.

To make an opening sufficiently large, it was only necessary to pry loose one large stone below the window. When the mother heard the pickaxes and the crowbars razing her fortress, she let out a dreadful scream. Then she began to run around her cell with frightful quickness—the habit of a wild beast, which her long confinement in that cage had given her. She spoke no more, but her eyes flamed. The soldiers felt their blood run cold to their very heart.

All at once she took up her paving stone, laughed again, and with her two hands, hurled it at the workmen. The stone, badly thrown, for her hands were trembling, missed its mark completely, and rolled to the feet of Tristan's horse. She gnashed her teeth with rage.

In the meantime, although the sun had not yet risen, it was daylight, and a beautiful rose tint brightened the old decayed chimneys of the Maison-aux-Piliers. It was the hour when the earliest risers in that great city happily opened their windows. A few stragglers, a few fruit venders, going to Les Halles upon their donkeys, were beginning to cross the Grève. They stopped for a moment before this group of soldiers gathered around the Trou-aux-Rats, stared in astonishment, and passed on.

As the picks were prying out the stones, the recluse went to sit down by her daughter, covering her with her body, her eyes fixed, listening to the poor child, who no longer moved, but was murmuring low the one word: "Phoebus! Phoebus!"

As the work of the demolishers advanced, the mother shrank farther away from the opening, pressing the young girl closer and closer against the back wall, but all the while watching the workmen. She saw the stone shake, and she heard Tristan urging on his workmen.

Then, starting out of the sort of stupor into which her spirit had sunk for some minutes, she cried out. As she spoke her voice now screeched like a saw striking a knot in wood, then it faltered as if every kind of malediction had crowded to her lips to burst forth at one and the same time.

"Ho! ho! ho! this is horrible! You're robbers! Are you really going to hang my daughter? I tell you, she's my daughter. Oh, you cowards! Lackeys of the hangman! You miserable murderers! Help! Help! Fire! Are they going to take my daughter from me like that? Who is it who calls God good?"

Now frothing at the mouth and with haggard eyes, she tensed on all fours, bristling like a panther, and screamed at Tristan, "I dare you to come and take my daughter from me!

Do you understand when I tell you she's my daughter? Do you know what it is to have a child? Eh? You wolf? Have you never lain with your mate? Have you never had a cub by her? And if you have little ones, when they howl, does nothing stir within you?"

"Take down the stone," said Tristan. "It's giving way now."

The crowbars now lifted the heavy stone. It was, as we have said, the mother's last bastion. She lifted her arms to it as if she wanted to hold it up; she tried to curl her fingers around it, but the massive block, loosened by the six men, escaped her grasp and slid gently down to the ground over the iron levers.

The mother, seeing an entrance made, threw herself across the opening, barricading it with her body, twisting her arms, beating the flagstones with her head, and screaming in a voice so hoarse with exhaustion that her words were hardly articulate.

"Help! Fire! Fire!"

"Now, take the girl," said Tristan coldly.

The mother looked at the soldiers with so menacing a manner that they wanted to retreat rather than advance.

"Let's go!" resumed the provost. "You, Henriet Cousin!"

No one budged.

The provost swore, "*Tête-Dieu*! My warriors! Afraid of a woman!"

"Monseigneur," said Henriet, "do you call that a woman?"

"Her mane is like a lion's," remarked another.

"Go in!" repeated the provost. "The opening is large enough. Enter three abreast, as at the breach of Pontoise. Let's finish with it, death of Mahomet! The first one who turns back, I'll cut in two!"

Placed between the provost and the mother, and threatened by both, the soldiers hesitated a moment, then resolutely advanced toward the Trou-aux-Rats.

When the recluse saw this, she suddenly raised herself on her knees, threw back her hair from her face, and put her thin, lacerated hands upon her thighs. Big tears started from her eyes, trickling down the wrinkles in her face, like a stream along the bed which it has dug for itself. At the same time she began to speak, but in a voice so suppliant, so gentle, so submissive, so heartrending that more than one old hardened flesh-eater in Tristan's company wiped his eyes.

"Gentlemen, and messieurs the sergeants, one word! There's something I must tell you. She's my daughter, understand? My dear little girl whom I lost. Listen to my story. Look, I know very well you are sergeants. Sergeants were always good to me when little boys threw stones at me because I led a loose life. So you see, you'll leave me my child when you know everything! I am a profligate woman. The gypsy women stole my baby away from me. Look, here is her shoe which I have kept for fifteen years. Her foot was no bigger than that. In Rheims! La Chantefleurie, Rue Folle-Peine. Perhaps you knew me then. It was I. In your youth, in those days—it was a merry time. We had good times. You'll have pity on me, my lords, won't you? The gypsy women stole her from me. They hid her from me for fifteen years. I thought she was dead. Think, my good friends, I thought she was dead! I've spent fifteen years here in this cave, with no fire in the wintertime. That's hard! The poor dear little shoe! I cried so much that God finally heard my prayers. This night He has returned my daughter to me! It's one of God's miracles. She isn't dead! You won't take her from me, I'm sure. If it were myself, I wouldn't protest; but to take her, a child of sixteen! Give her time to see the sun! What has she done to you? Nothing at all. Nor I either. If you only realized that she is the only one I have, that I am old, that it's a blessing the Holy Virgin sends me! Besides, all of you are very kind gentlemen! You didn't know she was my daughter—but now you do. Oh, I love her so much! Monsieur the Grand Provost, I would rather have a hole in my bowels than a scratch on her finger! You look like a good seigneur! What I tell you now explains everything to you, doesn't it? Oh, if you have had a mother, monseigneur! You are the captain, leave me my child. Consider that I am begging you on my knees, as they pray to Christ Jesus! I ask nothing of anyone. I am from Rheims, monseigneur. I have a little field there that belonged to my uncle, Mahiet Pradon. I'm not a beggar. I want nothing, just to keep my child! I just want my child! God Almighty, Who is our master, has not given her back to me for nothing! The king you say, the

king! It can't be any great pleasure to him that they should
kill my little girl. And besides, the king is good. She's my
daughter! my daughter! mine! She's not the king's. She's not
yours! I want to go away from here! Both of us. And when
two women are going along, mother and daughter, you can
let them go quietly. Let us go! We are from Rheims. Oh,
you're good men, messieurs the sergeants. I love all of you.
You won't take my daughter from me, will you? You
couldn't do that, could you? My child! My child!"

We will not try to give an idea of her gestures, her tone,
the tears which she drank as she spoke, the clasping and
twitching of her hands, the agonized smiles, the delirious
looks, the sighs, the moans, the distraught and piercing cries,
which she mingled with those disordered, wild, and incoherent words. When she had stopped, Tristan the Hermit
frowned, but it was to conceal a tear that was rolling from
his tiger's eye.

However, he overcame his weakness, and said curtly,
"The king wills it!"

Then leaning down to Henriet Cousin, he whispered in his
ear. "Finish quickly!"

Perhaps the redoubtable provost felt even his will failing
him.

The hangman and the sergeants entered the cell. The
mother did not resist; she merely crept up to her daughter,
and threw herself madly upon her.

When the gypsy girl saw the soldiers approaching, the
horror of death roused her.

"Mother!" she cried out in a tone of indescribable distress.
"Mother! they are coming! Protect me!"

"Yes, my love, I will protect you," answered her mother
faintly, and clasping her tightly in her arms she smothered
her with kisses.

To see them both thus on the ground, mother and daughter, was indeed pitiable.

Henriet Cousin grasped the girl around the middle under
her beautiful shoulders.

When she felt the touch of his hand, she cried, "Heugh!"
and fainted.

The hangman, from whose eyes big teardrops fell on the
gypsy, wanted to carry her off in his arms. He tried to draw

away the mother, who had, as it were, fastened her hands in a knot about her daughter's waist; but her grasp was too powerful to loosen. Henriet Cousin then dragged the young girl out of the cell, and the mother with her. The eyes of the mother were closed too.

The sun was rising at that moment, and a rather sizable crowd of people had gathered in the square, looking from a distance to see what was being dragged along the ground toward the gibbet. It was Provost Tristan's habit at executions not to allow the curious to come too near.

There was nobody at the windows. Only from a distance could be seen, atop one of the towers of Notre-Dame which looks upon the Grève, two men, whose figures stood out darkly against the clear morning sky. They seemed to be looking on.

Henriet Cousin, with what he was dragging, stopped at the foot of the ladder, and scarcely breathing, so deeply was he moved to pity, he passed the rope around the young girl's lovely neck. The unfortunate girl felt the horrible touch of the hemp. She opened her eyes and saw the skeleton arm of the stone gibbet looming over her head. Then she shook herself, and cried in a loud and heartrending voice, "No! No! I don't want to die!"

The mother, whose head was buried under her daughter's garments, said not a word, Her whole body trembled as she multiplied her kisses upon her child. The executioner took advantage of the moment to unclasp, by a strong and sudden effort, the arms with which she held fast the condemned; and, whether from exhaustion or despair, they yielded.

Then he put the young girl over his shoulder, where her charming figure fell gracefully, bending over his large head. He set his foot on the ladder to ascend.

At that moment, the mother, who had collapsed upon the ground, suddenly opened her eyes. Without uttering a cry she started up with a terrible expression; then, like a beast rushing upon its prey, she threw herself upon the executioner's hand, and sank her teeth into it. It was all done in the flash of an eye. The hangman howled with pain. Men came to help him. With difficulty they freed his bleeding hand from the teeth of the mother. She was silent. They pushed her away with brutal violence, and it was remarked that her head fell back heavily upon the ground. They raised her; she fell back again. She was dead.

The hangman, who had not relaxed his hold on the young girl, began to ascend the ladder.

2

La Creatura Bella Bianco Vestita[1] (Dante)

When Quasimodo saw that the cell was empty, that the gypsy girl was not there, that while he had been defending her, someone had carried her off, he tore his hair and stamped with astonishment and rage. He ran all through the church looking for his gypsy, howling strange noises into every corner, strewing his red hair upon the pavement. It was just then that the king's archers were entering Notre-Dame, victorious, also looking for the gypsy girl. Quasimodo assisted them, without in the least suspecting their fatal intentions, as he thought that the enemies of the gypsy girl were the Truands. He himself showed Tristan the Hermit every possible hiding place, opened for him all the secret doors, the double-bottomed altars, the inner sacristies. Had the unfortunate girl still been there, it would have been he himself who would have delivered her to them. When Tristan grew tired of searching, and he wasn't easily tired, Quasimodo continued the search by himself. Twenty times, a hundred times, he made the rounds of the vast cathedral, from top to bottom, from one end to the other, ascending, descending, running, calling, shouting, peering, rummaging, ferreting, poking his head into every nook and cranny, thrusting a torch under every vault, desperate, mad. A male animal who has lost its mate could not be more bereft.

At length, when he was sure, quite sure, that she was gone, that it was all over, that they had stolen her from him, he slowly reascended the tower staircase, that staircase he had so nimbly and triumphantly mounted the day that he had saved her life. Now, with drooping head, voiceless, tearless, and scarcely able to breathe, he passed those same spots.

[1] "The beautiful creature dressed in white."

The church was deserted again and plunged again into silence. The archers had left to pursue the sorceress in the City. Quasimodo, all alone in that vast cathedral of Notre-Dame, just a while ago so besieged and tumultuous, went back to the cell where the gypsy girl had slept for so many weeks under his guardianship. As he approached, he fancied that he might find her there again. When, at the bend of the gallery which looks upon the roof of the side aisle, he perceived the narrow cell, with its little window and door, lying close under one of the large flying buttresses like a bird's nest under a branch, the poor fellow's heart failed him, and he leaned against a pillar so he wouldn't fall. He imagined that perhaps she might have come back, that some good spirit might have returned her, that this small cell was too quiet, too safe, and too charming for her not to be there— and he dared not go one step farther, for fear of dispelling the illusion.

"Yes," he said to himself, "she is sleeping, perhaps, or praying, I must not disturb her."

At last, mustering his courage, he approached on tiptoe, looked, entered. Empty! The cell was still empty! The poor unfortunate man walked around slowly, lifted her bed, looked under it, as if she could have been hiding between the mattress and the stone floor. Then he shook his head, and stood stupefied. All at once he furiously crushed out his torchlight, and, without muttering a word, or breathing a sigh, he hurled himself with all his might head first against the wall, and slumped unconscious to the floor.

When he revived, he threw himself on the bed, twisted convulsively upon it, kissing frantically the indented spot where the young maiden had slept.

For some minutes he remained motionless, as if he were going to die there, then he rose again, streaming with perspiration, panting, frenzied, and fell to beating the walls with his head, with the frightful regularity of the clapper of his bells and the resolution of a man determined to break open his skull. At length, exhausted, he slumped to the floor a second time; then, on his knees, he dragged himself outside the cell and crouched in front of the door with a look of astonishment. He remained thus for more than an hour, motionless, with his eye fixed upon the empty cell, more gloomy and more pensive than a mother seated between an empty cradle and a full coffin. He uttered not a word; only, at intervals, a violent sob racked his body, but it was sobbing without tears, like summer lightning flashes with no rumbling.

It seems that it was then, as he was trying in his doleful reverie to guess who could have been the unexpected ravisher of the gypsy girl, that he thought of the archdeacon. He remembered that Dom Claude alone had the key to the tower leading to the cell. He remembered the priest's nocturnal attempts upon La Esmeralda, the first of which he, Quasimodo, had aided; the second of which he had prevented. He recalled a thousand details, and soon in his mind there was no doubt that it was the archdeacon who had taken his gypsy maiden from him. Yet such was his reverence for the priest, his gratitude, his devotion, his love for this man, the roots of which sank so deeply in his heart, that they resisted, even now, the fangs of jealousy and despair.

He reflected that the archdeacon had done it, but the murderous resentment which he could have felt against any other individual was turned, in this instance, in the poor bellringer's breast, simply into increase of sorrow.

While he was thus thinking about the priest, while the buttresses were whitening in daybreak, he saw on the upper story of Notre-Dame, near the corner formed by the external balustrade which runs around the top of the chancel, a figure walking. It was coming toward him. He recognized it—the archdeacon. Claude was pacing along gravely and slowly. He was not looking before him as he walked toward the north tower. His face was turned toward the right bank of the Seine, and he held his head high, as if he was trying to see something over the rooftops. The owl has often that oblique attitude, flying in one direction and looking in another. The priest thus passed above Quasimodo without seeing him.

The deaf bellringer, petrified at this sight, watched him disappear behind the door of the northern tower, which, as the reader knows, gives a commanding view of the Hotel-de-Ville. Quasimodo rose and followed the archdeacon.

He ascended the tower staircase to find out why the priest was going up. But the poor ringer did not know what he himself was going to do, what he was going to say, nay, even what he wanted. He was full of rage and full of fright. The archdeacon and the gypsy girl were contending in his heart.

When he had reached the top of the tower, before issuing from the shadows of the staircase onto the open platform, he cautiously looked around to see where the priest was. The archdeacon had his back to him. An open balustrade goes around the platform of the belfry. The priest, whose eyes peered down on the town, was leaning his breast upon the side of the balustrade which looks toward the Pont Notre-Dame.

Quasimodo, with wolf's steps, stole up behind him to see what he was looking at. Dom Claude's attention was so completely absorbed that he did not hear the deaf man behind him.

Paris, seen from the towers of Notre-Dame in the cool dawn of a summer morning, is a charming and magnificent sight, especially Paris in those days. It might have been a day in July. The sky was perfectly clear. A few lingering stars were fading at different points, and away to the east, in the lightest part of the sky, there was one still brilliantly shining. The sun was just about to come over the horizon. The pure white light brought out vividly the endless varieties of outline which its buildings presented in the east, while the giant shadows of the steeples traversed building after building from one end of the great city to the other. Paris was beginning to stir. Voices and noises were to be heard from several quarters of the town. Here was the stroke of a bell, there that of a hammer, and again, the clatter of a moving wagon. All sorts of indistinct sounds floated over this half-awakened city. Already the smoke from some scattered chimneys was rising over the rooftops, as if through the fissures of some vast sulphur mine. The river that splashes against the piers of so many bridges, against the points of so many islands was shimmering in folds of silver. Around the town, beyond the ramparts, the view was dimmed by a wide circle of fleecy mists, through which the dim line of the plains and the graceful swelling of the hills were indistinctly discernible. Eastward the morning breeze chased across the sky a few light flecks plucked from the fleecy mantle of the hills.

Down in the Parvis, some housewives, with their milk pails in hand, were pointing out to one another, in astonishment, the singularly battered condition of the central door of Notre-Dame, and the two congealed streams of lead between the crevices of the front. This was all that remained of the night's tumult. The pile kindled by Quasimodo between the towers was out. Tristan had cleared the ground of the square, and had had the dead thrown into the Seine. Kings like Louis XI take care to clean up the pavements quickly after a massacre.

Outside the balustrade of the tower, precisely beneath the place where the priest had stopped, was one of those fantastically carved stone gargoyles which bristle all over Gothic buildings. In a crevice of this gargoyle two fine wall-flowers in bloom dipped in the breeze, as if they were bowing to each other. Above the towers, high in the sky, twittered the cheerful voices of early birds.

But the priest neither saw nor heard any of this. He was one of those men for whom there are no mornings, no flowers, no birds. In all that immense horizon, spreading around him so many different points of interest, his gaze was fixed only on one spot.

Quasimodo yearned to ask him what he had done with the gypsy girl. But the archdeacon seemed at that moment to be out of this world. He was evidently in one of those states when the earth itself might fall to ruin without his noticing. So, with his eyes fixed upon that spot, he remained motionless and silent; yet in that silence and immobility there was something so formidable that the simple bellringer shuddered at the sight and dared not intrude. All that he could do—and that was one way of questioning the archdeacon—was to follow the priest's line of vision, which thus guided the eye of the wretched hunchback to the Place de Grève.

He now saw what the priest was looking at.

A ladder was standing against the permanent gibbet. There were people in the square and a lot of soldiers. A man was dragging along the ground something white to which something black was clinging. The man stopped at the base of the gibbet.

There something was happening that Quasimodo could not plainly see, not because his eye had lost its long vision, but because the soldiers were in the way, and prevented his seeing everything. Moreover at that moment, the sun appeared and there was such a burst of light coming over the horizon that it seemed as if every point of Paris—spires, chimneys, and gables—was catching fire all at once.

Meanwhile the man was beginning to climb the ladder. Then Quasimodo could see him distinctly. He was carrying a female figure draped over his shoulder—a girl clad in white. There was a noose around her neck. Quasimodo recognized her. It was she.

The man reached the top of the ladder. There he arranged the noose.

Now the priest, to see better, kneeled upon the balustrade.

All at once the man at the gibbet kicked away the ladder with his heel, and Quasimodo, who for some moments had not breathed, saw swinging from the end of the rope, about two yards from the ground, the unfortunate girl, with the man crouched upon her shoulders. The rope twisted around several times, and Quasimodo saw the girl writhe with horrible contortions.

On the other hand, the priest, with outstretched neck and eyes that seemed to be popping from his head, was contemplating that frightful scene of the man and the girl—the spider and the fly.

At the most dreadful moment, a demoniacal laugh, a laugh such as can come only from one who is not human, burst from the livid face of the priest. Quasimodo didn't hear the laugh, but he saw it. The bellringer took a few steps back from the archdeacon, and then, rushing at him furiously, with his two huge hands, he struck the priest's back and pushed Dom Claude into the abyss over which he had been leaning.

"Damnation!" cried the priest as he fell.

The gargoyle beneath broke his fall. He clung desperately to it, and, just as he was about to cry out again, he saw looking over the edge of the balustrade, above his head, the ugly and avenging face of Quasimodo; and he was silent.

The abyss was beneath him, a fall of two hundred feet to the pavement. In this terrible situation the priest uttered not a word nor a groan. He only writhed on the gargoyle, making incredible efforts to climb up. But his hands could find no hold on the granite; his feet scraped against the blackened wall, without finding a toehold. Those who have climbed to the towers of Notre-Dame know that the wall swells out immediately below the balustrade. It was on this retreating slope that the wretched archdeacon exhausted himself in fruitless efforts. It was not only a wall that went straight down against which he was waging battle, but a wall that sloped away from under him.

Quasimodo had only to stretch out his hand to pull him back from the abyss, but he didn't even look at Dom Claude. He was watching the Grève. He was staring at the gibbet. He was staring at the gypsy girl. The poor deaf creature leaned his elbows on the balustrade in the very place where the archdeacon had been kneeling a moment before, and there, keeping his eye fixed upon the only object in the world which existed for him at that moment, he remained mute and motionless. A steady stream of tears flowed from that eye which till then had shed but one.

The archdeacon was panting. His bald forehead was beaded with perspiration; his nails were bleeding on the stones; his knees were scraped against the wall. He could hear his cassock, which had hooked on the gargoyle, ripping more and more with every twist of his body. To add to his misery, the gargoyle terminated in a leaden pipe which bent under his weight. The archdeacon could feel the pipe bending slowly. The wretched man was saying to himself that when his cassock tore apart, when his hands could hold no longer, when that lead pipe bent completely, he must of necessity fall. Terror froze his vitals. Sometimes he would glance wildly downward to a sort of narrow ledge formed about ten feet lower by some accident of sculpture. He implored heaven from the bottom of his distressed soul that he might be permitted to spend the remainder of his life, though it were to last a hundred years, upon that narrow space two feet square. Once he glanced below him into the square. But when he lifted his head again, his eyes were closed and his hair stood on end.

There was something frightening about the silence of these two men. While the archdeacon was agonizing in that horrible manner but a few feet from him, Quasimodo was crying bitter tears while staring at the Place de Grève.

The archdeacon, realizing that all his exertions served only to weaken the frail support that was left to him, at length resolved to remain perfectly still. There he was— holding onto the gargoyle, scarcely breathing, moving not at all—with no other motion than that convulsion in the stomach, such as is felt in a dream when we fancy we are falling. His glazed eyes were open wide with a stare of pain and astonishment. Meanwhile he felt himself slipping little by little; he sensed more and more the weakness of his arms and the bending downward of the lead pipe under the weight of his body. Beneath him was the frightful, sharp roof of the church of Saint-Jean-Le-Rond, like a small card bent in two. He observed one after the other the impassive sculptures of the tower, like him suspended over the precipice; but without terror for themselves or pity for him. All around him was stone—before his eyes, the gaping monsters; in the square below, the pavement; above him, Quasimodo, still weeping.

Down in the Parvis, there were several groups of curious people who were calmly trying to guess who could be the madman amusing himself in so strange a fashion. The priest could hear them speaking, for their voices rose to him clear and shrill, "Why, he'll break his neck!"

Quasimodo wept.

Finally, the archdeacon, fuming with rage and fright, understood that all was useless. But he gathered all the strength he could for one last effort. He drew himself up on the gargoyle, pushed against the wall with both his knees, dug his hands into a cleft of the stonework, and succeeded in climbing up perhaps a foot. But the force which he was obliged to use caused the leaden pipe that supported him to bend, and the same effort rent his cassock completely. Then feeling everything give way, having only his benumbed and powerless hands with which to cling to anything, the unfortunate man closed his eyes and let go. He fell.

Quasimodo watched him fall.

A fall from such a height is rarely straight downward. The archdeacon tumbling into space fell at first with his head downward and his arms extended; then he spun several times. The wind dashed him against the roof of one of the houses where his body crumbled. However he was not yet dead when he landed. The ringer could see him making an effort to cling to the gable with his hands, but the slope was too steep, and there was no more strength left in him. He slid rapidly down the incline, like a loosened tile, and crashed to the pavement. There he moved no more.

Quasimodo then raised his eye to look upon the gypsy girl whose body he could see, suspended on the gibbet, quivering in the distance under its white robe in the last struggles of death. He then looked down at the archdeacon, sprawled out at the bottom of the tower and no longer having a human form, and, with a sob that shook his deep chest, he cried, "Oh, all that I ever loved!"

3

Phoebus' Marriage

Toward evening of that same day, when the judiciary officers of the bishop came to remove the archdeacon's mangled body from the pavement of the Parvis, Quasimodo had disappeared from Notre-Dame.

About this affair many rumors were being bruited about. No one doubted that the day had come, when, according to their pact, Quasimodo, that is to say the devil, was to carry away Claude Frollo, that is, the sorcerer. It was presumed that he had broken the body in taking away the soul, as a monkey cracks the shell to get at the nut.

For this reason the archdeacon was not interred in consecrated ground.

Louis XI died the following year, in August, 1483.

As for Pierre Gringoire, he not only managed to save the goat, but he became somewhat a success as a dramatist. It appears that, after delving into astrology, philosophy, architecture, hermetics, and having tasted every variety of silly pursuit, he returned to tragedy, which is the silliest of all. It was what he called *coming to a tragic end*. Of his dramatic triumphs, in the records of 1483 we read, "To Jehan Marchand and Pierre Gringoire, carpenter and writer, who made and composed the mystery play presented at the Châtelet of Paris, at the entry of Monsieur the Legate, and for duly ordering the characters, with dresses and costumes meet for the said mystery; and for constructing the scaffolds which were necessary for said performance, one hundred pounds."

Phoebus de Châteaupers likewise came to a tragic end—he married.

4

Quasimodo's Marriage

We have just said that Quasimodo disappeared from Notre-Dame the day on which the gypsy and the archdeacon died. He was never seen again nor was it ever known what became of him.

On the night following the execution of La Esmeralda, the hangman's helpers took her body down from the gibbet, and carried it away, as was the custom, to the vault of Montfaucon.

Montfaucon, as Sauval says, "was the most ancient and magnificent gibbet in the kingdom." Between the suburbs of the Temple and Saint-Martin, about a thousand feet from the wall that surrounds Paris, a few bowshots from the village of La Courtille, was to be seen, on the top of an almost imperceptible rise, yet sufficiently elevated to be visible for several leagues around, an edifice of curious form, somewhat resembling a druidical cromlech, and where human sacrifices were performed.

Imagine if you will, based upon a mound of plaster, a heavy oblong mass of stonework, fifteen feet high, thirty feet wide, forty feet long, with a door, an exterior ramp, and a platform. On this platform imagine sixteen enormous pillars of unhewn stone, thirty feet high, ranged in a colonnade around three of the four sides of the huge block supporting them, and connected at their top by heavy beams from which chains were hanging at frequent intervals. From all of these chains hung skeletons. Not far away, on the plain, a stone cross and two secondary gibbets rose like shoots from the great central tree. Above all this crows flew constantly. Such was Montfaucon.

At the end of the fifteenth century, this formidable gibbet, which dated from 1328, was already much dilapidated. The beams were rotted; the chains rusted; the pillars green with mold. The blocks of hewn stone gaped apart, and grass grew upon the platform where feet walked no more. Against the sky it made a horrible profile—especially at night, when the moonlight gleamed upon the whitened skulls, or when the evening breeze brushed the chains and skeletons, making them rattle in the dark. The presence of this gibbet was enough to induce a belief that all the environs were haunted.

The mass of stonework which served as the base of this repulsive structure was hollow. An immense vault had been constructed within, the entrance of which was closed with an old battered iron grating. Into this were thrown, not only the skeletons taken down from the chains of Montfaucon, but also the remains of people who had been executed on all the other permanent gibbets of Paris. Into this deep charnelhouse, wherein so many human bodies and the memories of so many crimes putrefied together, many great men of the world, and many innocent ones, at one time or another, have come to contribute their bones—from Enguerrand de Marigni, who was the first to arrive at Montfaucon, and who was a good man, down to the Admiral de Cologni, with whom it was closed, and who also was a good man.

As for the mysterious disappearance of Quasimodo, this is all we could discover.

About a year and half or two years after the events which conclude this story, when a search was made in the vault of Montfaucon for the body of Olivier le Daim, who had been hanged two days before, and to whom Charles VIII granted the favor of being interred in the church of Saint Laurent with better company, there was found among all those hideous carcasses two skeletons, the one clasped in the arms of the other. One of these two skeletons, that of a woman, had still about it some tattered clothes, apparently of a stuff that had once been white. About its neck was a string of beads of adrezarach seeds, together with a small silken bag, ornamented with green glass, which was open and empty. These objects had been of so little value that the hangman, no doubt, had not cared to take them. The other skeleton, which held this one close in its arms, was that of a man. It was noticed that its spine was crooked, the head compressed between the shoulder blades, and that one leg was shorter than the other. Also, there was no break of the vertebra in the neck, whence it was evident that it had not been hanged. The man to whom it had belonged had therefore come there of himself and died there. When they tried to detach this skeleton from the one it embraced, it crumbled to dust.

Afterword

One day in the early summer of 1830, Victor Hugo bought a new bottle of ink and a gray woollen body stocking, locked his outdoor clothes away in the wardrobe and sat down to write a novel that was already a year overdue. The publisher had granted him a new deadline: 1 December 1830. Whatever M. Hugo chose to write, and whatever the critics said about it, the novel was bound to be a success.

At the age of 28, Hugo was the most famous living writer in France—a poet, playwright, novelist and, in his latest prose work, *The Last Day of a Condemned Man,* a campaigner against the death penalty. That February, his Romantic drama *Hernani* had caused a riot at the great cathedral of French culture, the Comédie Française. Backed by an army of long-haired Bohemians in historical costume, "the Attila of the French language" (as the Académie Française had called him) dealt a crushing blow to Classical tradition. The brash vitality of popular melodrama, with its promiscuous blend of comedy and tragedy, had entered the mainstream like a mob storming a palace.

While outraged reactionaries threatened to kill Victor Hugo, the younger generation worshipped him as a god. Fifteen years after the Napoleonic dream had vanished in the gunsmoke of Waterloo, there was a great hunger for heroes. Rumors began to spread that Victor Hugo was not entirely human. It was said that he could eat half an ox at a single sitting, work nonstop for a week, and detect the sound of moles moving underground. He walked through the city at night, unarmed but mysteri-

501

ously invulnerable. His vast brow was thought to be a sign of God-given genius.

For the everyday Hugo, who sat at his desk researching his novel, peering at Medieval texts through green eyeshades, his audience was a strange mirror: it showed him a face that was obviously his own and yet alarmingly unfamiliar. It seemed to suggest that his books were more revolutionary than the man who wrote them.

Hugo's own attitude to popular revolt had always been painfully ambiguous. His quarreling parents—a Napoleonic general and a Royalist conspirator—had stood on opposite sides of the great chasm in modern French history: the Republic and the Monarchy. Growing up among the ruins of the Ancien Régime and the Empire, in Paris and in occupied Spain, Hugo saw the cataclysms of recent French history enacted in the breakup of his parents' marriage. To declare his allegiance to one side or the other was to betray a part of his own past.

Now, in July 1830, a bloody insurrection in Paris replaced the old monarchy with a more liberal regime. While the insurgents' bullets smashed the roof tiles of his home by the Champs-Élysées, Hugo fled like a sensible bourgeois to the countryside with his young family and his unfinished novel. When he returned to the city, he found himself hailed as a hero of liberal reform.

When Hugo depicts King Louis XI in the Bastille, in Book X of *Notre-Dame de Paris,* ordering the massacre of six thousand rioters, he is attaching his Medieval tale to the present. The teeming crowds and half-human monsters of *Notre-Dame de Paris* are an image of the People's Revolution—that blind force which, in Hugo's view, brought progress and enlightenment at a terrible cost. Could barbarism, cruelty and chaos really be the progenitors of civilization? The Cour des Miracles, that magnificent "sewer" of humanity at the center of Hugo's Medieval Paris, is a nightmare of absolute equality, the unpoliced ghetto of the modern metropolis and of the Romantic imagination: "Sometimes a dog resembling a man could be seen to pass, or a man resembling a dog.

The lines dividing races and species seemed to vanish in
that city as in a pandemonium."

Hugo found a suitably capacious form for this pandemonium in the modern genre of the historical novel.
Like his contemporaries—Vigny, Balzac, Dumas and
Mérimée—he had been thrilled by the bestselling novels
of Walter Scott in which real historical figures rubbed
shoulders with fictional characters. Scott had turned the
novel into a respectable literary form. He showed that
it was possible, without sacrificing accuracy or excite-
ment, to bridge the cultural gap between the aristocratic
salons on the first floor and the servants' attics on the
sixth.

Walter Scott's version of history was a living drama
in which tiny, humdrum details could be as significant as
battles, kings and proclamations: a peculiar form of
dress, a forgotten form of language, the shadow cast by
an oil lamp. Above all, it expressed a new awareness
that societies, their institutions and beliefs, are fragile
and impermanent.

Hugo made himself at home in this new genre and
extended its domain. In *Notre-Dame de Paris,* he used
it to investigate history itself and its obscure connections
with human destiny. This was not a cosy costume drama
to while away the hours. It was a form of retrospective
science fiction that enabled the reader to experience a
poet's sense of strangeness. The Medieval past was a
door into the unfamiliar world of the imagination. If we
could mingle with the crowds of fifteenth-century Paris,
says Hugo, "we should find ourselves surrounded by
things so ancient that they would appear completely
new."

Even that massive symbol of the continuity of tradition—Notre-Dame Cathedral—is transformed into something alien and bizarre: "an enormous, double-headed
sphinx squatting in the middle of the city." Hugo's prefa-
tory note relegates Christianity to a single stratum of
human archaeology. The word he claims to have found
etched on the wall of one of the towers—'ΑΝΑΓΚΗ
(Fate)—hints at the survival of more ancient, pagan be-

liefs. Implicitly, like the tormented priest Claude Frollo, it calls salvation into question.

Notre-Dame de Paris is the first detective story of the modern mind: an obsessive narrator scours the city, looking for reasons to believe in final justice. If history could be seen from a sufficient height, like Paris from the towers of Notre-Dame, would a pattern emerge? Or is the world, like the graffiti on the walls of Frollo's cell, as chaotic as "a sheet of paper over which a monkey had dragged a pen full of ink?"

In some respects, *Notre-Dame de Paris* is more closely related to modern historical novels like Don DeLillo's *Underworld* (1997) than to Vigny's *Cinq-Mars* (1826) or Mérimée's *Chronique du Règne de Charles IX* (1829). The novel is riddled with personal allusions like clues to a lost treasure or an undetected crime. Claude Frollo's mad zigzagging through the city in Book IX takes him past most of Victor Hugo's earlier Paris addresses. The name "UGÈNE," scratched on a door in the northern tower, eerily evokes Hugo's brother Eugène, who lost his head and was locked away in a padded cell. Quasimodo has the red hair and pustular face of Hugo's former friend, the critic Sainte-Beuve.

It was during the writing of the novel that Hugo discovered that his wife was having an affair with Sainte-Beuve. Once again, the family had proved to be a flimsy refuge. It is significant that all the main characters of *Notre-Dame de Paris* are orphans. Esmeralda rediscovers her long-lost mother only to see her die a few hours later.

The cathedral itself is a model of Hugo's mind, the ruined temple of his royalism and Catholicism, "which I sometimes contemplate with respect but where I no longer go to pray." Instead of attending mass, he liked to climb the bell towers and stand on the narrow platform like a stone gargoyle, peering down over "the inextricable web of bizarrely twisted streets," hallucinating with vertigo. The dizzying, cinematic perspectives of Hugo's descriptions give the solid structure a peculiar fluidity, as if its disintegration is only momentarily arrested. Yet, as Hugo points out, the cathedral, like his own sturdy imagination, retains "the same internal framework, the same logical disposition of its parts."

Notre-Dame is the first of those gigantic self-projections, in the shape of a capital "H," that dominate Hugo's novels: the twin towers of the Cathedral, the mighty rock formation in *The Toilers of the Sea* and, in *Ninety-Three*, the guillotine.

Notre-Dame de Paris. 1482 appeared in the bookstores on 16 March 1831. It was an expensive edition and reached its audience slowly. The fact that the "eighth edition" appeared in December 1832 suggests a commercial success. But this was a common publisher's trick: in reality, the "eighth edition" was only the second. Nevertheless, the illustrated edition of 1836 had a huge print run of 11,000 copies. Within a few years, almost every literate person in Europe and America knew the story.

Hugo's characters were so beautifully exaggerated and aroused such memorable emotions that they seemed to have existed for centuries: the penniless poet Gringoire; the demonic, lecherous priest Frollo; the handsome, empty-headed guardsman Captain Phoebus; the deaf bell ringer Quasimodo; and the beautiful gypsy girl they all fall in love with—Esmeralda, whose only friend in the world is her performing goat, Djali (the name Madame Bovary gives to her lapdog twenty-six years later).

Dozens of pirated editions and unauthorized translations appeared. Most of them, to Hugo's annoyance, changed the title and ignored the fact that the cathedral itself is the central character: *Esmeralda, or The Deformed of Notre-Dame, A Drama,* by Edward Fitz-Ball; *The Hunchback of Notre-Dame,* "with a sketch of the life and writings of the author;" *Notre-Dame, or The Bell-Ringer of Paris.* Two English translations appeared in 1833 alone. One of the translators observed that while Victor Hugo might be called "a horrorist," "he can never be accused of the great vice, in modern times the most heinous of all—dullness."

The first critics were disturbed by what they saw as the godlessness of Hugo's novel. Goethe called it "the most abominable book that ever was written." Victor

Hugo "is a fine talent," he conceded, "but quite entangled in the unhappy romantic tendency of his time, by which he is seduced to represent, together with what is beautiful, also that which is most insupportable and hideous." There were complaints about Hugo's violent images: a heroine who trembled "like a galvanized frog," a boy who used his tongue as a handkerchief. Even in 1874, the delicate Robert Louis Stevenson was shocked by Hugo's graphic depictions of extreme mental states: "So unbearable were his thoughts that he took his head in both hands and tried to pull it off his shoulders in order to smash it onto the paving-stones."

Almost everyone, however, recognized the novel as a masterpiece of dramatic organization and style. Hugo had revitalized the French language by returning to the age before the Académie Française had "purified" it and banished all those "barbaric" Medieval words. Hugo wrote like a Gothic architect: the nooks and crannies of his carefully convoluted style, the higgledy-piggledy of lists and epigrams, were marshaled by insistent rhythms like architectural motifs. His vast digressions were the flying buttresses that supported and extended the structure.

Notre-Dame de Paris also had a dramatic effect on the outside world. To forward-thinking Parisians of the time, that dingy, dilapidated old church on the Île de la Cité was a relic of the barbarian past. In 1831, "Medieval" meant unsafe housing, dark doorways and festering drains. The word "Gothic" was an insult. When critics wanted to accuse Hugo of artistic vandalism, they called his writings "Hugothique."

Hugo's call to save these Medieval treasures from the hammer of progress (in the preface to the second edition) put Notre-Dame on the tourist map of Paris. Thousands of visitors came to see "Victor Hugo's Cathedral," though it was not until the urban redevelopment of the 1850s and '60s that the space around the cathedral was opened up. Some were disappointed not to find the towering monstrosity of Hugo's imagination, but there was a garrulous guide (as Hugo discovered) who would show them the little room close to the bell tower on the side nearest the Seine where M. Hugo had supposedly written his novel. Visitors were also shown the famous mystery inscription. But there were soon so many 'ANÁΓKHs on the walls of Notre-Dame that no one was sure which was the original.

In the second edition, Hugo inserted three chapters: "Unpopularity," "*Abbas Beati Martini*" and "This Will Kill That." In "This Will Kill That," he explained that he had set his story at the historical crossroads when the printed word began to dominate and annihilate that older form of record keeping—architecture.

This infects the whole work with an interesting paradox. Hugo was contributing his own "basketful of rubble" to "the second Tower of Babel of the human race"—the Babel of books—helping to destroy the civilization embodied in Notre-Dame. At the same time, he was founding a new tradition. *Notre-dame de Paris* anticipates the experiments of the twentieth-century novel in its self-consciously exotic language and its tendency to hand the narrative over to elements that, until then, had only been picturesque embellishments of the plot.

Hugo knew that his novel would in turn become a historical monument, an obscure relic of a vanished age. He knew that even literary masterpieces are not immortal and that time erases their meanings, just as it eats away at cathedrals. "Dust" is the last word of the novel.

Like the pseudo-Medieval restoration of Notre-Dame by Viollet-le-Duc, attempts to renovate literary masterpieces are often an unconscious act of aggression. By changing the plot, the Disney animation of *The Hunchback of Notre-Dame* (1996) shows how disturbing Hugo's vision has remained. The cartoon "Quasi" is a self-pitying, dorsally challenged teenager who suffers from the modern handicap of shyness. If only he could stop playing with his bells, he would find that the world outside is a warm and loving place. . . . Hugo made no such concessions to wishful thinking. *Notre-Dame de Paris* is not another "Beauty and the Beast." Quasimodo has been scarred in the womb by blind or malevolent fate. As in life, one injustice leads to another: the mon-

ster's soul has been "atrophied," his view of reality
skewed by his repulsive appearance. His rescue of Esmeralda is an act of defiance and revenge. The final
scene—two disintegrating skeletons locked in a hideous
embrace—parodies the lovers' kiss at the end of popular romances.

Hugo's religious doubts were the dark background to
his social philosophy. The gypsy and the hunchback represent "the two extremes of physical and social wretchedness"— *"les deux misères extrêmes de la nature et de
la société."* The word *"misères"* looks forward to Hugo's
next novel, which he began in 1845. In *Les Misérables,*
history is again described from the point of view of the
scapegoat. Hugo's achievement, in *Notre-Dame de Paris*
and *Les Misérables,* is to conduct a kind of moral coup
d'état: the reader is forced to think of these outcasts,
not with indignation or sentimentality, but with forgiveness and intelligence.

Compassion is always controversial. The Disney *Hunchback* belongs to a more cruel and sheltered age. Society
as it happens to exist is presumed to be good. Evil is
the exclusive property of the scapegoat. In Hugo's novel,
the mad priest is not an absolute villain. He loves his
little brother and saves the infant Quasimodo out of pity.
In the Disney version, Frollo is forced to adopt Quasimodo as penance for his evil deeds. The audience is
invited to celebrate the status quo and to crucify the
scapegoat.

Adaptations are also, of course, a mark of the novel's
success. Hugo did not write his book for professional
critics. He wrote it for the people. Throughout the Victo-
rian age, it appeared in cheap, popular series that testify
to its broad appeal: "Standard Novels," "Sixpenny Novels," "Parlour Library," "Railway Library."

This unprofessional majority leaves little trace in literary history. But there is one splendid description of the
novel's effect on an ordinary reader in the diary of the
actress Fanny Kemble:

Sunday, 29th [January 1832].—Went into my
mother's room before going to church. Henry Gre-

ville has sent her Victor Hugo's new book, *Notre-Dame de Paris,* but she appears half undetermined whether she will go on reading it or not, it is so painfully exciting. . . .

In the afternoon, I found my mother deep in her French novel, from which she read me two very striking passages—the description of Esmeralda, which was like a fine painting, and extremely beautiful, and the sketch of Quasimodo's life, ending with his riding on the great bell of the cathedral. Very powerful and very insane—a sort of mental nightmare, giving one as much the idea of disorder of intellect as such an image recurring to one in a dream would of a disordered stomach. Harmony, order, the beauty of goodness and the justice of God, are alike ignored in such works. How sad it is for the future as well as for the present!

Monday, 30th. . . . Victor Hugo has set my mother raving. She didn't sleep all night, and says the book is bad in its tendency and shocking in its details; nevertheless, she goes on reading it.

Hugo himself was often terrified by his own imagination and the monsters it created. But he had the courage to live with them and even allowed them to dictate the work.

It is a defining characteristic of Romanticism that the writer is never quite certain where the work will lead and whether it will reflect his original intentions. When the leader of the French Romantic movement received his copies of the published novel in the spring of 1831, he might well have asked, like Gringoire watching the performance of his own mystery play in the Cour des Miracles, "Whose masterpiece is this?"

—Graham Robb

SELECTED BIBLIOGRAPHY

Works by Victor Hugo

Cromwell, 1827 play
The Last Day of a Condemned Man, 1829
Hernani, 1830 play
The Hunchback of Notre-Dame, 1831 (Signet Classic 0-451-52788-7)
Les Contemplations, 1856 poetry
Les Misérables, 1862 (Signet Classic 0-451-52526-4)
William Shakespeare, 1864
The Toilers of the Sea, 1866 (Signet Classic 0-451-52772-0)
The Laughing Man, 1869
Ninety-Three, 1874
The End of Satan, 1886
God, 1891

Biography and Criticism

Brombert, Victor. *Victor Hugo and the Visionary Novel.* Cambridge, MA.: Harvard University Press, 1984.

Grant, Elliott M. *The Career of V. Hugo.* Cambridge, MA.: Harvard University Press, 1945.

Grant, Richard B. *The Perilous Quest: Image, Myth, and Prophecy in the Narratives of Victor Hugo.* Durham, NC.: Duke University Press, 1968.

Houston, John Porter. *Victor Hugo.* Boston: Twayne, 1988.

Maurois, André. *Olympio: The Life of Victor Hugo.* Trans. Gerard Hopkins. New York: Harper, 1956.

Peyre, Henri. *Victor Hugo: Philosophy and Poetry.* Trans. Roda P. Roberts. University, AL.: University of Alabama Press, 1980.

Robb, Graham. *Victor Hugo.* New York: Norton, 1998.

Fact, Fiction, and Film

William R. Pace

Of the many things you can call Victor-Marie Hugo, under-achiever is not one of them. Playwright, poet, novelist, poli-tician, important member of French literary Romanticism, beloved French icon . . . the man did it all. And while today in France he is best remembered for his vibrant poetry, the rest of the world remembers and honors him for the novels he wrote that helped spawn a literary movement.

Born in 1802 in Besançon, France, the son of an officer of Napoleon Bonaparte, he was an "army brat" who moved frequently owing to his father's various postings in France, Spain, and Italy. Finally settling in Paris, he quickly gravi-tated to the literary arts and almost immediately received recognition for his talent when the French Academy hon-ored a poem he wrote at age fifteen. By age twenty he published his first volume of work, *Odes et Poésies Diverses* (*Miscellaneous Odes and Poems*), following the tenets of Classicism. While in decline in other European countries at the time, Classicism—an aesthetic devoted to strict Greek and Roman principles of art—still held sway in France, al-though Hugo's literary idol, François-Auguste-René de Chateaubriand, had already blazed a trail that begged to be followed. By Hugo's next published book of poems, *Nouvelles Odes* (he published his first novel in between), he was on the same path, and then moved on, adding play-writing to his literary repertoire.

Even more than the other arts, French drama was partic-ularly suffering under a Neoclassicism heritage that claus-trophobically adhered to the Three Unities of time, place,

511

and action, in which a play's story could not exceed a twenty-four-hour time period; had to occur in one location; and had to contain only one plotline. No fans of Shakespeare, the Classicists also demanded the language be pristine and not feature low-life characters.

The various political revolutions occurring in the late 1700s helped fuel the rise of Romanticism; as the political order of the day was upheaved by the rejection of monarchal rule, so was Classicism's imperious rule. In France, the revolution of 1789 opened the door for Romanticism, but the First Republic's subsequent failure may have stalled Romanticism's progress. In Hugo's own lifetime, France went through three emperors, three monarchs, and two Republics; he himself vacillated greatly in his political beliefs before ultimately supporting a French Republic. But while his political beliefs were not yet finalized in 1827, his literary ones were, and he proclaimed them in the preface to his play *Cromwell*, decrying Classicism's restrictions. The preface became a rallying cry for other budding Romantics straining to break free of artificial restrictions, and he followed his own advice; his second play, *Marion de Lorme* (1829), was banned because it was about a courtesan. Hugo came back with another play in 1830, *Hernani*, which again broke the rules. Its production was literally a battle between the young Romantics and the old Classicists; opening night was the scene of a colorful confrontation between the two orders with the Romanticists succeeding, announcing the permanent arrival of Romanticism in France. (*Hernani* went on to even more success when Italian composer Giuseppe Verdi later adapted it into his opera *Ernani*, the composer being the first of many to adapt Hugo's works.)

Hugo's ties to Romanticism were the foundation upon which his early success and fame were laid. The very qualities for which he is so famous—sprawling stories, fervid imagination, verbosity, characters lower than low—are everything that rigid, restrained, and rational Classicism was not. Classicism was about reason; Romanticism was, as the English poet Wordsworth wrote, "the spontaneous overflow of powerful feelings." And Hugo's work, especially his fiction, was nothing if not an overflow of powerful feelings and images.

All of which came to an extremely successful fruition in his 1831 novel, *Notre-Dame de Paris*. Or, as it is better known in English, *The Hunchback of Notre-Dame*.

Because this was his first novel since embracing and leading the charge of Romanticism, Hugo deliberately set out to showcase what could be accomplished in this new style. One of his first dramatic choices was to make a deformed and ugly individual one of the major characters. Classical literature was obsessed with beauty and idealized form; merely by picking a hunchback to be a central character, Hugo slapped a glove across the face of Classicism. But that was not enough; other characters included a gypsy—gypsies, being considered "lowlifes," were typically expelled from civilized French society—numerous thieves and charlatans and a lascivious priest. Rather than revel in the "higher" deeds of historical leaders, nobles, and statesmen, as Classicism preferred, Hugo chose to roll around in the gutter of Paris and tell the stories of its occupants. But the character who truly dominates the book, as the original French title suggests, is Notre-Dame itself.

The cathedral that stands today is actually the *second* Notre-Dame to stand on that spot; the original—the "parish church to the kings of Europe"—was torn down in 1160 to build a grander one. Construction started in 1163 and it was nearly two hundred years before all the various phases were completed. But by Hugo's time, the cathedral had fallen into severe disrepair. The French Revolution had been particularly hard on it, as valuable items were either stolen or destroyed and it was used as a food storage facility. Hugo, a passionate lover of Gothic architecture and a medieval scholar (as a couple of *Hunchback*'s more "educational" chapters attest), seized upon the cathedral as the perfect setting for his Romantic novel. After all, what could possibly be more Gothic (a later offshoot of the Romantic movement) than a medieval cathedral? And by placing the action in 1482, he was able to depict Notre-Dame in its "prime" while using it as a vantage point to overlook a historical period that reflected some of France's recent history, as well as indulge the Romantic's fascination with the Middle Ages, a time before the Renaissance revival of Classicism had taken root.

Louis XI was in his next to last year of being king in 1482; known as the "universal spider" (an image Hugo uses in the book) because of the long reach of his devious political machinations, he worked hard to abolish the lords who controlled the feudal system (an action Hugo depicts with some amusement) and, in so doing, paved the way for the end of the Middle Ages. But there was much unrest and jockeying for power, and Louis XI had a terrible reputation for extravagant methods of imprisoning and executing those who did not do as he pleased. In the book, when Louis XI worries that Clopin's march on Notre-Dame may be meant for him and pats a wall, saying, "You will not crumble so easily, will you, my good Bastille," Hugo intended for all French readers to be reminded just how easily the old order did crumble one July day. And even as Hugo began writing *Hunchback*, political change was literally outside his window on another July day; the 1830 "July Revolution" erupted when the reinstalled absolute monarchy was overthrown and replaced with a constitutional monarchy. All these swirling elements found their way into *Hunchback*, helping fuel another striking Romantic element of the novel: the language itself.

Hugo was not afraid to be "indelicate" with such lines of dialogue as "Guts of the pope I don't want them to hang the pretty girl," and descriptions that rival those of Stephen King: "It was a dead body which remained hanging there, bent double, its loins broken, its skull empty." People were literally aghast at reading such lurid and intense writing. There are reported instances of people throwing the book down in horror . . . only to pick it back up to read on, which may account for its phenomenal instant success.

The book was so successful, that, among other things, it revived interest in Parisian Gothic architecture in general and Notre-Dame specifically, leading to a restoration of Hugo's beloved cathedral in 1845. As one of the grandest examples of religious Gothic architecture, Notre-Dame would surely be highly regarded on its own had Hugo never made it the star of his novel, but there can be no doubt its enduring fame is fueled by the book and the many adaptations that have been made of it over the generations.

Hugo, who was not yet thirty when the book was published, went on to produce many, *many* more works of fiction, poetry, and drama (including his other best-known book, *Les Misérables*). He died at the age of eighty-three, was given a national funeral reportedly attended by two million people, and was laid to rest in the Paris Pantheon, the final resting place for France's great citizens. He is still revered today for many things, but perhaps most popularly for the creation of a character who loved Notre-Dame as much as he.

While Hugo's novel is considered a classic of Romantic literature, surprisingly its best-known film version is often categorized as a horror classic. Strictly speaking, the 1923 silent film version starring Lon Chaney is not a horror film at all; it's actually more of a love story (which would surely shock Hugo). But due to the horrific and iconic images of many of Chaney's characters—he was known as the Man of a Thousand Faces because of the elaborate makeup and prosthetics he employed—his Hollywood star is firmly hitched to the horror genre, even though he actually made fewer than a handful of true horror films. The root of this enduring legacy can be traced back to his monsterish makeup and exuberant turn as the titular deaf and misshapen hunchback. And in a way, it makes perfect sense that he should rise to fame and acclaim playing a deaf character in a silent film, for in real life he was the son of two deaf parents.

Born on April 1, 1883, Lon (originally Leonidas) Chancy grew up in a household that relied on expressions and pantomime to communicate, which turned out to be perfect preparation for the coming world of silent film acting. But before he made his screen debut he was on the stage for over ten years, where he first learned his makeup skills. Chaney might have stayed in the theater forever if it hadn't been for a terrible personal tragedy. He had married young to an even younger singer, Cleva Creighton, who suffered mental illness. After years of touring together, both their marriage and her mental state deteriorated such that one night she entered the theater Chaney was working in and tried to commit suicide by drinking a bottle of poison. She failed in her attempt to kill herself, but the marriage died and the two divorced. Chaney found himself unable to book work in the theater world following the scandal of Cleva's public suicide attempt. Winning custody of his son (who would later assume the stage name Lon Chaney, Jr., and also become a horror movie icon, most notably as the Wolf Man), Chaney entered the world of movies working for the Universal Film Manufacturing Company.

Like every actor lucky enough to work in film during that period, Chaney put a significant amount of time in the cinema salt mines. From 1913 until 1919, Chaney was in over 110 films. His big break came in *The Miracle Man* (1919), in which he played the part of a con man who pretends to be crippled. That role set the stage for Chaney to begin a series of performances as characters with various deformities or disabilities that perfectly exploited his prodigious makeup talent and near-masochistic ability to physically transform his body into whatever shape the part required. A popular joke of the day was "Don't step on that spider—it could be Lon Chaney!"

Had Chaney's only gift been creating visual grotesqueries, he would most likely be remembered solely as a gimmicky craftsman and not have inspired the devoted following that continues to this day. But because of a childhood spent communicating wants and needs to parents who could not hear him, he was an actor who brought life, emotion, and empathy to characters whom "normal" society would otherwise not have understood.

However, while he was highly regarded in 1923, he was not yet a major box-office draw and was unable to get a dream project off the ground, *The Hunchback of Notre-Dame*. Legendary Producer Irving Thalberg, often known as the "Boy Wonder" because by the age of twenty he was already executive in charge of production for Hollywood's most successful studio, is often erroneously credited for coming up with the idea of making *Hunchback* with Chaney

as Quasimodo. That may be because he was such a powerful figure and exerted so much control over his productions,
but the truth is Chaney shared his idea of a *Hunchback*
film with Thalberg on an earlier film they had worked on
together. But if Thalberg didn't come up with the idea, he's
the one who decided to make not just a movie but an *event*.
To that end, the production became a monster all its own,
costing $1.25 million to make (roughly the equivalent of
well over $100 million today). An entire façade of the
Notre-Dame cathedral, plus a public square and village that
fronted it, was built on nineteen acres; over two thousand
extras were used for the crowd scenes and nearly a thousand crew people employed to build, light, and run the set.
And then there was Chaney's makeup and costume.

If Thalberg decided to make the movie a major event,
Chaney decided to do no less with his Quasimodo. Reports
of the weight of the device he wore to create Quasimodo's
famous hump vary from twenty pounds all the way up to
seventy, with most hovering around fifty. Whatever the
weight, it was only one part of a full-scale onslaught to
transform into an accurate re-creation of Hugo's best-
known character; there were also false teeth, mounds of
face putty to create accentuated cheekbones, a huge wart
covering one eye, an unruly wig, and dark hair glued onto
his face and hands to exaggerate the creature's primal nature. It took over three hours for Chaney to get into full
costume, and because he constructed the hump prosthesis
in such a way that it would painfully constrict his movements to re-create Hugo's descriptions of Quasimodo, he
could work only a few hours at a time. But the end effect
was an astounding metamorphosis; this slim five-foot-eight-
inch man became the living embodiment of Hugo's words,
"a giant who had been broken and badly put together
again." No wonder his Quasimodo is so often categorized
as one of the great creatures of horror.

But Chaney did not rely simply on the makeup and prosthesis; he threw himself wholeheartedly into the performance (to a degree that contemporary audiences, not used
to silent film acting, may find it over the top), depicting an
entity that, with all its gleeful grimacing and tongue lolling,

was not quite human . . . yet was also something more than a primitive beast: a soul capable of the finest human values of love, loyalty, and self-sacrifice.

It was a star-making turn and that's exactly what happened: Chaney entered the role as a journeyman film actor but emerged as a superstar who would dominate the silent film landscape not only for the remainder of his short life, dying as he did only seven years later in 1930 (having made just one "talkie"), but for all cinematic eternity.

But while Chaney was faithful to Hugo's hunchback, the filmmakers were less devout to the author's story line and intent. The movie starts off with a typical screen-adaptation strategy of jettisoning the book's lengthy setup and highlighting the main characters as soon as possible to get right to the main action. The Feast of Fools is in progress at Notre-Dame (as opposed to the Palace of Justice), allowing us to swiftly meet the centerpiece of the film, Quasimodo. He sneers at the crowd below and, as a title card explains, "For their jeers he gave them scorn and bitter hate."

In swift succession we meet other players. Although he doesn't appear until almost three-quarters of the way through the novel, Louis XI is introduced as "a crafty oppressor of his people," which allows the filmmakers to initiate a central dramatic theme of the movie, monarchal repression. We next meet another "king," Clopin, King of the Beggars, who, interestingly, like Louis XI, scowls at the feast celebrations. Then we meet Dom Claude Frollo, "the saintly Arch-deacon of Notre-Dame," who is . . .

What! "*Saintly* Arch-deacon"?

Yes. In a *radical* revision of Hugo's original story line, Dom Claude is presented as a paragon of virtue. Gone is the repressed religious intellectual whose years of carnal self-denial lead to him becoming an obsessed medieval stalker. But if not Dom Claude, which character sets the wheels of dark destiny into motion?

His brother, Jehan, who in the novel was a ribald university student more interested in carousing than studying. Hugo's Jehan borrowed money from his brother to indulge the pleasures of the flesh while Claude, with no sanctified outlet for his pent-up passion—and already flirting with

heresy in his pursuit of the secret to alchemy—turned fully
to the dark side. By excising the tortured guilt of a religious
figure and turning a secular character into a straight-ahead
black-hat villain, the movie softens much of Hugo's dramatic punch.

With the spate of scandals that have rocked modern
Church clergy, men of the cloth are hardly looked upon
today as moral members beyond reproach, but in Hugo's
time they certainly held that position, and for him to suggest otherwise was audacious. Only a century or more earlier he could have been declared a heretic and made to
suffer greatly. And while it was not heretical to depict a
lust-obsessed priest in 1920s America, it was certainly not
in Hollywood's best interest. Lon Chaney biographer Mi-
chael F. Blake has suggested Hollywood was particularly
motivated in the early twenties to "putting a more religious
overtone to their films" due to a series of high-profile ce-
lebrity scandals—most infamously the Fatty Arbuckle
case—involving the unholy trinity of drugs, rape, and murder. Public outcry grew as the seedier side of the film business began to make its way into the papers, and so
Thalberg and his crew chose to not fan the flames. Instead,
they encased Claude in all-white robes and introduced
Jehan—"who had forsworn a priest's robes for more
worldly garb," as a title card informs us—in nearly all
black.

Once the movie establishes who the villain is, it intro-
duces the catalyst to all that follows: the lovely, dancing
Esmeralda. To strengthen a necessary plot element of the
climax when Clopin leads a charge against Notre-Dame,
the movie codifies her relationship to Clopin by making her
a child he "raised as his own." Later, a title card will tell
us, "Clopin's fierce heart burned at the injustice of the
world; but it became tender only to his foster-child." More
important than setting up a familial connection, the filmmakers are taking the opportunity to buttress a basic theme
of their movie: the inequality between two classes of people. Time and time again, Clopin's title cards make refer-
ence to an "us versus them" mentality and when he learns
that Phoebus, the dashing captain of the guard with whom

Esmeralda is smitten, has taken her to an aristocratic party (another major deviation from the original story line, as Phoebus is actually in love with Esmeralda), Clopin storms in with his rabble and demands her back. "Keep to your own women," he warns Phoebus, and, "You nobles have lorded it over us and trampled on us—but you can't do it forever."

In essence, they have recast Hugo's plot in terms of the French Revolution, in which the peasants revolted against the monarchy. And while it is an extremely interesting slant—and certainly valid in light of Hugo's own experiences with France's continual revolts—it does flatten and simplify the complexities of Hugo's novel. However, simplifying the convoluted story lines of books is part of the job of adapting them to the medium of film, as film is often better at conveying the external rather than the internal. So the idea of reducing the overall conflict to a case of class warfare might have been a good one . . . if the movie had been consistent, which it's not.

On one hand, it wants us to feel for Clopin and his fellow thieves, who chafe under the bitter yoke of repression and classism. On the other, though, the movie wants us to root for Esmeralda to wind up with Phoebus, who is a member of the nobility and works directly for the tyrannical king. These are conflicting agendas that the film never manages to resolve, especially at the end, in the famous climactic siege of Notre-Dame. Fearing Esmeralda will be hanged if not rescued, Clopin leads his people to break in to the cathedral. Quasimodo, not understanding their purpose (and, in fact, Esmeralda frantically warns him of their arrival), sees them as the enemy who must be repelled, and he uses all at his means to do so: timber, stones, and molten lead. But once Phoebus and his guards storm into the square and disperse Clopin's motley troops, Quasimodo cheers, claps, and dances. When the most sympathetic character of the story shows us that the put-down of this revolt is a happy occasion, the audience must side with him and even Clopin's final words of "My children, I would have set you free. . . . Fight on, Fight on" won't undercut the audience's identification with Quasimodo's victory. The irony of misunderstood motives that is so clear and painful in the novel is missing here. Add to that the thematic confusion of having the dashing knight—nobility—come in at the end to sweep the beautiful young gypsy girl—peasant—off her feet and the filmmakers' attempt to establish a theme of revolution is undermined.

But that does not take away from the power the film does retain of Hugo's work: the forceful feeling of sympathy and sadness for its tortured character, the put-upon hunchback. More than anything, it is the audience's empathic connection with Quasimodo that keeps both the novel and its successful movie adaptations a constant touchstone of emotional Gothic art.

And while the Hollywood ending doesn't reflect Hugo's original downbeat climax—there's no danger of this Esmeralda swinging from the gallows—some of the original's melancholic power still shines through. A wounded Quasimodo (Jehan stabbed him before Quasimodo could fling him to his death) witnesses the beautiful couple embrace and knows that his feelings for Esmeralda will never be returned. He stumbles to the bell tower and begins ringing the big bell, the one reliable joy in his meager life. As it rings and his life ebbs from him, he seems to have a vision; he reaches out to someone and very clearly mouths the word "Esmeralda." He lingers for a moment, then collapses to the floor, dead. As the big bell slows in its arc, Dom Claude arrives and sees Quasimodo is gone. The final image is Quasimodo's bell slowly coming to a complete standstill. While maybe not on the same order of magnitude as one skeleton lovingly embracing another, as in Hugo's dénouement, it does poetically illustrate the devoted—yet unrequited—love of a soul more beautiful on the inside than on the out.

Discussion Points

1. The main action of the book occurs at Notre-Dame, a reigning symbol of Gothic architecture. What symbolic role does Notre-Dame play in the novel? What does Notre-Dame's architecture specifically represent? What role, in general, does architecture play in the novel?

2. What role does fate play in the novel? Are the characters destined to reach the end they do? What role does self-determinism play in their lives? What position does Victor Hugo take on fate versus self-determinism?

3. What elements of Romanticism are to be found in *The Hunchback of Notre-Dame*? How do these break the rules of Classicism?

4. Victor Hugo had a brother, Eugene, who was committed to a mental institution in 1822, eight years before Hugo wrote *The Hunchback of Notre-Dame*, and stayed there the rest of his life. What role do the relationships of brothers play in the novel? What role does madness play? Are the two intertwined, and, if so, how?

5. Hugo's political beliefs fluctuated throughout his life, from supporting a monarchy to supporting a French republic. Does Hugo support a political system in the novel? Which one? What evidence confirms your supposition and how?

6. Hugo was a famous playwright at the time *The Hunch-*

back of Notre-Dame was published, whose plays the Classicists had vilified. What is the role of the playwright Gringoire in the book? What is Hugo's view of Gringoire? Of his play, which opens the book? What does the Gringoire character represent in the overall scheme of the book?

7. If we define a movie protagonist as a character whose actions propel the plot forward, is the protagonist of the 1923 silent film starring Lon Chaney the title character Quasimodo? Why or why not? If not him, then who?

8. In what ways do the filmmakers use the French Revolution as an element of the characters and action? Since the French Revolution would not occur until over three hundred years after the events of the 1482 story setting, is using the Revolution a valid thematic ploy? Why or why not?

9. The movie changes the villain from Claude Frollo to his brother Jehan. How does this affect Hugo's themes of hypocrisy and the true internal value of a person versus his external appearance?

10. Phoebus returns La Esmeralda's affection and wants to marry her, but what obstacle stops them from being together? In what ways does this support Hugo's original vision? In what ways does it undermine it?

WILLIAM R. PACE attended New York University's graduate film and TV program, receiving his master's of fine arts in film production. A screenwriter and film producer, he has several independent feature-film credits, including *Charming Billy*, which he also directed, and episodes of series TV. Pace currently teaches screenwriting at the New School University in New York City, and lives in West Harlem.

Film journalist SUSANNAH GORA appears regularly on national television networks such as NBC, VH1, CNN Headline News, MTV, Court TV, E!, Fox News Channel, and CNBC. She can also be heard covering entertainment news in a weekly segment for the Associated Press's national radio network. As an editor at *Premiere* magazine, Gora interviewed hundreds of stars, such as Anthony Hopkins, Denzel Washington, and Meryl Streep. She lives in New York City, where she was born and raised.